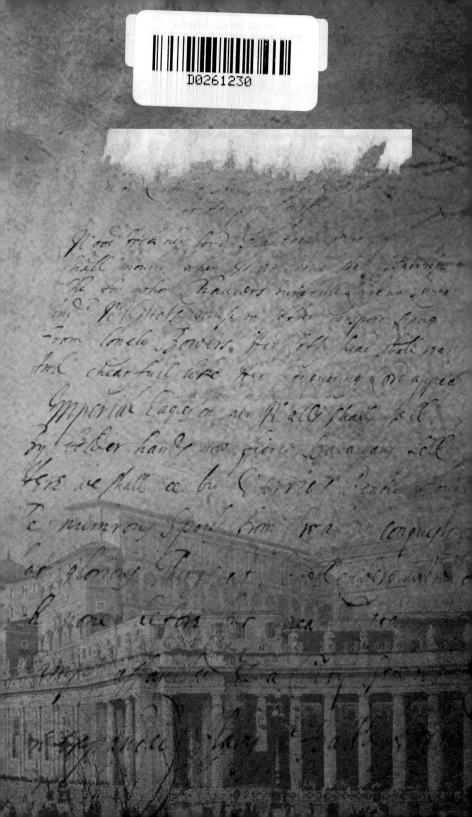

SECRETUM

Monaldi & Sorti

֍

Translated from the Italian by Peter Burnett

Polygon

First published in Italian in 2004
First published in Great Britain in 2009 by Polygon,
an imprint of Birlinn Ltd

West Newington House
10 Newington Road
Edinburgh
EH9 1QS

9 8 7 6 5 4 3 2 1

www.birlinn.co.uk

The publishers gratefully acknowledge permission from The Folio
Society for quotations from William Gillis's translation of Sebastian
Brant's *The Ship of Fools* (© copyright The Folio Society Limited 1971),
and from the University of Delaware Press for quotations from Thomas
Sheridan's translation of Battista Guarini's *The Faithful Shepherd*.

ISBN: 978 1 84697 104 4

British Library Cataloguing-in-Publication Data
A catalogue record for this book is available on request from the British Library.

Typeset by SJC

Printed and bound by Scandbook, Sweden

Everything on this earth is a masquerade, but God has determined that the comedy be played in this manner.

Erasmus of Rotterdam
In Praise of Folly

Contents

To His Excellency Msgr
Alessio Tanari
Secretary of the Congregation for the Causes of Saints
Vatican City

Dearest Alessio,

A year has passed since I last wrote to you. You never replied.

A few months ago, I was suddenly transferred (but that you perhaps already know) to Romania. I am one of a handful of priests to be found in Constantia, a small town on the Black Sea.

Here, the word "poverty" takes on that relentless, irrevocable character that it once had in our part of the world. Dreary, decrepit houses; ragged children playing in dirty, nameless streets; women with tired faces blankly staring from the windows of horrendous blocks of flats; the legacy of real socialism, bare and dilapidated: wherever one turns, greyness and wretchedness.

This is the city, this is the land to which I was sent a few months ago. I am called here to carry out my pastoral mission, nor shall I fail in my duties. The misery of this country will not distract me from them, nor will the sadness which pervades every inch of it.

As you well know, the place from which I came was very different. Until a few months ago, I was Bishop of Como, the gay lakeside city which inspired the immortal prose of Manzoni; that ancient pearl of opulent Lombardy, laden with noble memories, with its characteristic old town, its businessmen, its captains of the fashion industry, its footballers and its prosperous silk manufacturers.

I shall not, however, be deterred from my mission by this sudden, unexpected change. I have been told that I am needed here in Constantia, that my vocation can, more than any other, respond to the spiritual needs of this land, that the transfer from Italy (with only two weeks' notice) should not be taken as a demotion, let alone a punishment.

When first I was apprised of the news, I expressed no few doubts (and, let me add, no little surprise), for never in the past had I exercised my pastoral duties outside Italy, apart from a few months of training in France, in the now far-off years of my youth.

While I considered my position as Bishop of Como to be the best possible crowning of my career, and despite my advanced age, I would gladly have accepted a transfer to a new, distant, diocese: in France, in Spain (countries where the language is not unfamiliar to me) or even in Latin America.

It would still, of course, have been an anomaly, for bishops are rarely transferred to distant lands from one day to the next, unless there are grave stains on their career. This was, as you know, certainly not the case with me, and yet – precisely because of the abrupt and unprecedented character of my removal – many good Catholics in Como were understandably misled into feeling themselves entitled to suspect such a thing.

I would nevertheless have welcomed such a decision as one welcomes the will of God, unreservedly and uncomplainingly. Instead, it was decided to send me here to Romania, a land of which I know nothing, neither the language nor the traditions, neither the history nor the current needs. I find myself here straining my old limbs in vain attempts to play football with the local lads in the church precincts and to grasp some meaning from their loquacious speech.

My soul is beset – pardon the confession – by a subtle yet incessant torment. This derives, not from my destiny (which the Lord has so willed and which I gratefully and willingly accept) but from the mysterious circumstances which determined it: circumstances which I now want to clarify with you.

I last wrote to you a year ago, to bring an unusually delicate affair to your attention. At the time, the process of canonisation of the Blessed Innocent XI Odescalchi was forging ahead. Reigning from 1676 until 1689, this pontiff of glorious memory promoted and sustained the Christian armies in their battle against the Turks at Vienna in 1683, when the followers of Mahomet were at last driven from Europe. Since Pope Innocent XI came from Como, the honour fell to me of instructing the cause of canonisation, one which was close to the Holy Father's heart; the clamorous and historic defeat of Islam had in fact taken place on 12th September 1683 when, taking account of the time lag, it was still 11th September in New York. Now, some forty years after the tragic assault by Islamic terrorists on the Twin Towers in New York on 11th September 2001, the coincidence between the two dates had not escaped the attention of our well-beloved pontiff, who therefore wished to proclaim Innocent XI – the anti-Islamic pope – a saint, on a date to coincide precisely with the two anniversaries, as a gesture of reaffirmation of Christian values and of the abyss that separates Europe and the West as a whole from the ideals of the Koran.

It was, then, on completion of my assignment that I sent you that text – do you remember? It had been typed by two old friends of mine, Rita and Francesco, with whom I had lost touch years previously. It revealed a long series of circumstances which blacken the record of the Blessed Innocent. The latter had during his pontificate acted in pursuit of crass personal interests. While he had unquestionably made himself the Lord's instrument when inciting the Christian princes to take up arms against the Turk, his covetousness had on other occasions led him to commit grave offences against Christian morality and to cause irreparable damage to the Catholic religion in Europe.

At that juncture, I asked you (as you will recall) to submit the matter to His Holiness, so that he personally could decide whether to pass over the matter in silence or – as I hoped – to give the *imprimatur* and order its publication, thus making the truth available to all.

I did honestly expect at least a note of acknowledgment. I thought that, quite apart from the grave matters of which it was my duty to apprise you, you would, when all was said and done, be glad to hear from your old tutor at the seminary. I was well aware that the reply would take time, perhaps a very long time, given the gravity of the revelations which I was bringing to the attention of His Holiness. I did, however, imagine that you would, as is normal practice, at least respond with a card.

Instead, not a word. For months, I received neither a written communication nor a telephone call, despite the fact that the outcome of the process depended upon the reply which I awaited. I was mindful of His Holiness's need to reflect, to evaluate, to weigh up all the issues and perhaps, in all confidentiality, to consult expert opinion. I was resigned to waiting patiently; also because, being sworn to secrecy and to protecting the honour of the Blessed, I could reveal what I had discovered to no one but yourself and the Holy Father.

Then, one day I saw it in a Milan bookshop, among a thousand others: the book which bore the names of my two friends.

When at last I opened it, my fears were confirmed: it was that very book. How was this possible? Whoever could have arranged its publication? Soon I said to myself that publication could only have been ordered by our pontiff in person. Perhaps the *imprimatur* which I had hoped the Pope would deliver had at length been handed down, definitively and authoritatively requiring publication of Rita and Francesco's text.

Clearly, the process of Pope Innocent XI's canonisation was now blocked once and for all. Only, why had I not been informed? Why had I received no word of this, not even after publication, and in particular why had I heard nothing from you, Alessio?

I was on the point of writing to you again when one day, in the early morning, I received a communication.

I recall it all unusually clearly, as though it were today. My secretary came to find me when I was about to enter my study, bearing an envelope. Opening it in the dark corridor, I could just make out the papal keys printed in relief on the envelope; and then the card which it contained was in my hands.

I was invited for an interview. I was struck above all by the extremely short notice of the time indicated on the card: only two days later and, what is more, on a Sunday. But that was as nothing compared to the hour of the summons (six in the morning) and the identity of the person who was inviting me to confer with him: Monsignor Jaime Rubellas, the Vatican Secretary of State.

The meeting with Cardinal Rubellas could not have been more courteous. He began by inquiring after my health, about the exigencies of my diocese and the situation with regard to vocations. He then asked me discreetly how the process of canonisation of Innocent XI was progressing. Shocked, I asked him whether he was not aware of the book's publication. He did not reply, but looked at me as though I were defying him.

It was then that he told me how badly I was needed here in Constantia, and he spoke of the new frontiers of the Church today and of the shortcomings in the care of souls in Romania.

The amiability with which the Secretary of State spoke of my transfer almost caused me to lose sight, during our meeting, of why he in person should be announcing all this to me; why I had been summoned in such an unusual manner, almost as though everything had to be done far from prying eyes; and finally, of how long my absence from Italy might last.

Closing the interview, Monsignor Rubellas asked me quite unexpectedly to maintain the strictest confidentiality about our talk and its content.

All the questions which I did not ask myself that morning keep raising their heads here in Constantia, every evening when I patiently practise my Romanian, a strange language in which nouns come before articles.

Soon after my arrival, I learned that under the Roman Empire, of which it was part for a very long time, Constantia had been called Tomi. Then, glancing at a map of the region, I noticed the presence nearby of a locality by the strange name of Ovidiu.

It was then that alarm bells rang in my head. I quickly consulted my manual of Latin literature: my memory had not betrayed me. When Constantia was called Tomi, it was here that the Emperor Caesar Augustus had the famous poet Ovid exiled; officially on the grounds that he had written licentious poems, but in reality because he was suspected of having become acquainted with far too many of the secrets of the imperial household. For ten long years, Augustus turned a deaf ear to his appeals, until Ovid died. Without ever again setting eyes on Rome.

Now I know, dear Alessio, how the trust which I placed in you a year ago has been repaid. My banishment to Tomi, the place of exile for "literary crimes", has opened my eyes to that. Not only did the publication of my two friends' text not originate in the Holy See but it fell upon you all like lightning from a cloudless sky. And you all believed that I was behind this, that it was I who had arranged for this publication. That is why you had me banished here.

But you are mistaken. Like yourselves, I am completely ignorant of how that book came to be published; the Lord, *quem nullum latet secretum*, "who knows all secrets" – as they recite in the Orthodox churches in these parts – also uses for His ends those who act against Him.

If you have taken a glance at the folder annexed to this letter, you will already know what it is: yet another typescript by Rita and Francesco. This too is perhaps an historical document, perhaps a novel. You may amuse yourself trying to discover which is the case by referring to the documentary evidence I received, annexed to the text, and which I am also sending you.

Obviously, you will be wondering when I received this typescript, where it was sent from and, lastly, whether I have found my old friends once more. This time I shall not, however, be able to help you satisfy your curiosity. I am sure you will understand why.

Lastly, I am sure that you will be asking yourself why I am sending this to you. I can just imagine your confusion, and how you will be wondering whether I am naïve, or mad, or whether mine is a form of logic which you cannot follow. One of these three is the answer that you seek.

May God inspire you, once more, in the reading which you are about to undertake. And once again, may He make you an instrument of His will.

Lorenzo dell'Agio, *pulvis et cinis*

TRUE AND DISTINGUISHED
RELATION
of certain Glorious Deeds

which took place under the Pontificate of

INNOCENT XII

IN ROME IN THE YEAR OF OUR LORD 1700

Dedicated to the most Excellent
and Venerable Patron,
Abbot Atto Melani

With the Privilege of the Authorities

Printed in Rome, by Michel'Ercole

MDCCII

Most Eminent and Reverend Sir,

With ev'ry Hour that passeth, I am the more persuaded that Your Lordship will without a Doubt be most sensible of a compendious Account of those extraordinary Events which took place in Rome in July of the Year 1700, of which the most renowned and illustrious Protagonist was a faithful Subject of His Most Christian Majesty King Louis of France, concerning whose Successes one may here enjoy a great Wealth of Descriptions and Commentaries.

This is the Fruit born of the Labours of a simple Son of the Soil; and yet I dare trust that the luminous Genius of Yr Most Illustrious Lordship will not disdain the Offspring of my Savage Muse. Poor indeed is the Gift, yet rich is the Intent.

Will you pardon me, Sir, if in the Pages that follow I have not included Praises enow? The Sun, altho' ne'er praised by Others, is yet the Sun. In Recompense, I expect Nothing other than that which you have already promised me, nor shall I repeat that, mindful as I am that never could a Soul as gen'rous as Yours deviate from Itself.

May I wish Yr Excellency a Life long enough to be for me a Harbinger of lasting hope; and most humbly do I make my Reverence.

Day the First
7TH JULY, 1700

✠

Ardent and high in the heavens above Rome shone the sun on that midday of the 7th of July in the year of Our Lord 1700, on which day the Lord did grace me with much hard labour (but against discreet recompense) in the gardens of the Villa Spada.

Lifting mine eyes from the ground and scrutinising the horizon beyond the distant wrought-iron gates flung open for the occasion, I glimpsed, perhaps even before any of the lackeys who stood guard around the gate of honour, the cloud of white dust from the road which announced the head of the long serpent of the guests' carriages moving in slow succession.

Upon that sight, which I was soon sharing with the other servants of the villa, who had as ever forgathered, drawn by curiosity, the joyous fervour of the preparations became yet more fevered; presently, they all returned to bustle around in the back rooms of the *casino* – the great house – where the major-domos had for days now fussed impatiently, shouting orders at the servants, as they muddled and collided with the varletry busily heaping up the last provisions in the cellars, while the peasants unloading cases of fruit and vegetables hurried to remount their carts stationed near the tradesmen's entrance, calling back their wives whenever they tarried too long in their search for the right pair of hands into which religiously to deliver majestic strings of flowers as red and velvety as their cheeks.

Pallid embroideresses arrived, delivering damasked cloths, hangings and eburnean hemstitched tablecloths, the very sight of which was blinding under the blazing sun; carpenters finished nailing and planing scaffolding, seats and platforms, in bizarre counterpoint to the disorderly practising of the musicians, who had come to try out the acoustics of the various natural theatres; architects squinted through puckered eyes as they verified the enfilade of an avenue, kneeling, wig grasped awkwardly in one hand, panting because of the great heat, as they checked again and again on the final effect of a *mise-en-scène*.

All this commotion was not without cause. In barely two days' time, Cardinal Fabrizio Spada would be solemnising the marriage of his one-and-twenty-year-old nephew Clemente, heir to the most copious fortune, with Maria Pulcheria Rocci, likewise the niece of a most eminent member of the Holy College of Cardinals.

In order worthily to celebrate the event, Cardinal Spada would be diverting with entertainments a multitude of prelates, nobles and cavaliers at the family villa, which stands, surrounded by magnificent gardens, on the Janiculum Hill near to the source of the Acqua Paola, whence one enjoys the loveliest and most aerial prospect of the city's roofs.

Such was the summer's heat that the villa seemed preferable to the family's grandiose and celebrated palace down in the city, in the Piazza Capo di Ferro, where the guests would not have been able to taste the delights of the countryside.

In advance of the ceremonies proper, festivities were already commencing that very day when, at around midday, as expected, the carriages of the more eager guests were already to be seen on the horizon. Noble names in plenty would soon be forgathering, together with churchmen coming from far and wide, the diplomatic representatives of the great powers, the members of the Holy College and scions and elders of all the great families. The first official entertainments were to take place on the day of the nuptials, when everything would be ready to bedazzle the guests with scenic effects both natural and ephemeral, with exotic flowers set among the native plants and papier mâché challenging the onlooker to recognise it under a thousand guises, richer than the gold of Solomon, more elusive than the quicksilver of Hydria.

The cloud of dust from the carriages, which still moved seemingly without a sound because of the excessive clangour of the preparations, was drawing ever nearer and, from the high point of the great curve before the gates of the Villa Spada one could already descry the first flashes of the magnificent ornaments which adorned coaches and equipages.

The first to arrive, or so we had been told, would be the guests from outside Rome, who would thus be able to enjoy a well-deserved repose after the fatigues of the journey and to savour two evenings of gentle rustic peace. Thus they would come to the festivities refreshed, at ease and already diverted by a little merry-making; all of which would surely augment the general good humour and make for the greatest possible success of the celebrations.

The Roman guests, on the other hand, would have the choice of lodging at the Villa Spada or, if they were too occupied with official business or other matters, of arriving by carriage every day at midday and returning to their own residences in the evening.

After the wedding, there were to be several more days and evenings of the most spectacular and varied divertissements: hunting, music, theatrical performances, several parlour games and even an academy, all culminating in fireworks. Counting the wedding day, this would amount to a full week of festivities, until 15th July, when, before taking their leave, the guests would enjoy the special favour of being escorted into town to visit the resplendent and grandiose Palazzo Spada in Piazza Capo di Ferro, where the great-uncles of Cardinal Fabrizio had, together with the late Cardinal Bernardino and his brother Virgilio of precious memory, assembled half a century earlier a most imposing collection of pictures, books, antiquities and precious objects, not to mention the frescoes, the *trompe l'oeil* perspectives and all manner of architectural contrivances, on which I had never as yet set eyes but which I knew to have astounded all those who beheld them.

By now, the sight of the carriages on the horizon was accompanied by the distant clatter of their wheels on the cobbles and, looking carefully, I realised that, for the time being, only one carriage was arriving; indeed, said I to myself, gentlemen always took care to maintain a certain distance between their respective trains, so as to ensure that each should be correctly received and to avoid the risk of any involuntary discourtesy, as the latter not uncommonly degenerated into dissensions, lasting enmity and, heaven forfend, even into bloody duels.

On the present occasion, such risks were, in reality, limited by the adroitness of the Master of Ceremonies and the Major-Domo, the irreproachable Don Paschatio Melchiorri; these two would be seeing to the guests' reception, for, as was already known, Cardinal Fabrizio was much busied with his duties as Secretary of State.

As I tried to make out the coat of arms on the approaching carriage and could already distinguish the distant dust clouds from those that followed, once again I bethought myself of how sagacious a choice the

Villa Spada had been as the theatre for the celebrations: in the gardens of the Janiculum, after sunset, cool air was assured. That, I knew well, as I had frequented the Villa Spada for no little time. My modest farm was but a short distance from there, outside the San Pancrazio Gate. My spouse Cloridia and I enjoyed the good fortune of being able to sell fresh potherbs and good fruit from our little field to the household of the Villa Spada; and from time to time I would be summoned for some special task, particularly when this involved climbing to some difficult place, such as rooftops or attics, operations which my small stature greatly facilitated. I was also called upon whenever there was a shortage of staff, as was the case on the occasion of the present celebration, when the entire establishment of Palazzo Spada had been transferred to work at the villa, and the Cardinal had taken advantage of the Palazzo being empty to have some work done on the interior decoration, including frescoes for the Alcove of the Spouses.

For two months or so, I had thus been under the orders of the Master Florist, industriously hoeing, planting, pruning and caring for the flowers. There was no little to be done. Villa Spada must not fail to make the right impression on behalf of its masters. The open space before the gates had been covered with little loggias all decorated with greenery which, trained to climb in fecund spirals, snaked soft and sweet-smelling around columns, pilasters and capitals, gradually thinning out until it merged into the fine embroidery of the arcades. The main carriage-drive, which in ordinary times passed between simple rows of vines, was now flanked by two marvellous sets of flower beds. Everywhere the walls had been painted green, with false windows depicted on them; the gentle sward, mown to perfection according to the instructions of the Master Florist, cried out for the contact of bare feet.

Arriving at the casino of the villa, that is to say, the great house, one was greeted by the welcome shade and the inebriating odour of an immense pergola of wisteria, supported by temporary arcades covered with greenery.

Next to the casino, the Italian garden had been made as new again. It was a secret, walled garden. Upon the walls that concealed it were painted landscapes and mythological scenes; from all sides, deities, cupids and satyrs peeped out, while within the garden, in the cool shade, whosoever wished to withdraw in quiet and contemplation, far from prying eyes, could admire, undisturbed, elms and Capocotto poplars, wild cherry and plum trees, generous vines of sweet Zibibbo and other grapes, trees from Bologna and Naples, chestnuts, wild shrubs, quinces, plane trees, pomegranate bushes and mulberry trees, not to mention little fountains and waterspouts, *trompe l'oeil* perspectives, terraces and a thousand other attractions.

There followed the physic garden, likewise entirely and freshly replanted from end to end, wherein were grown fresh curative herbs for tisanes, cataplasms, plasters and every use known to the art of medicine. The medicinal plants were enclosed betwixt hedges of sage and rosemary pruned into strict geometrical shapes, their odours penetrating the air and entrancing the visitor's senses. Behind the building, an avenue, passing close to the bosky shade of a little grove, led to the private chapel of the Spada family, where the nuptials were to be solemnised. Thence, following the slopes that led down towards the city, three drives fanned out, one of which led to an open-air theatre (built especially for the festivities, and now almost ready), the second, to a farmhouse (fitted out as a dormitory for the guards, actors, plumbers and others) and the third, to the back entrance.

Returning however to the front of the villa, in the midst of the rustic setting of the vineyard, a long avenue (parallel to that of the main carriage-drive, but more internal) led to the rotunda of the fountain with the *nymphaeum* and continued until it came at last to a well-tended little meadow whereon had been laid, for light meals in the open air, tables and benches copiously ornate with rich carvings and marquetry, shaded by sumptuous canopies of striped linen.

The unsuspecting visitor would halt, lost in admiration, until he became aware that this display was but the frame and invitation to the most spectacular sight of the whole vineyard; his eyes would squint in sudden amazement at that plunging vista over Roman bastions and battlements, extending on the right towards the horizon, as they emerged from the depths of their invisible, somnolent, millenary foundations. Eyelids would flutter as they beheld that dramatic and unexpected prospect and the heartbeat would quicken. Among those delights, o'erflowing with perfumes and enchantment, every thing seemed born for pleasure, all was poesy.

The Villa Spada rose thus to the occasion, no longer that modest but delightful summer residence almost eclipsed by the wealth and magnificence of the sumptuous Palazzo Spada in Piazza Capo di Ferro, but the great theatre of the forthcoming celebrations.

Now the villa could without blushing contend with the most famed of the summer pavilions built two centuries previously, when Giuliano da Sangallo and Baldassare Peruzzi graced Rome with their services, the former with his commission for the Villa Chigi, the latter with the villa which he designed for Cardinal Alidosi at Magliana, while Giulio Romano created the villa of the Datary Turini on the Janiculum, and Bramante and Raphael built the Vatican Belvedere and the Villa Madama respectively, both to ingenious designs.

In reality, it had since time immemorial been the custom of great lords to have elegant residences built in the nearby countryside in which to forget the daily round of cares and sorrows, even if they stayed there only a few times a year. Without going as far back as the rich mansions which the Romans had erected (and which were celebrated by so many excellent poets, from Horace to Catullus), I was well aware from my reading and from conversations with a few erudite booksellers (but even more with old peasants, who know the vineyards and gardens better than anyone) that, in the past two hundred years in particular, the great princes of Rome had made a fashion of building themselves pleasure pavilions on the outskirts of the city. The desolate no-man's-land and damp little fields within the Aurelian Wall and in its immediate vicinity had gradually given way to the vineyard and its casino, in other words to gardens and to villas.

While the first villas had battlements and turrets (still visible at the entrance of the otherwise undefended Capponi vineyard), an obvious legacy of the turbid Middle Ages when a gentleman's abode was also his fortress, within a few decades styles grew lighter and more serene and soon every nobleman boasted a residence with vineyards, vegetable gardens, fruit trees, woods or pine groves, thus creating the gentle illusion of possessing and exercising lordship over all that the eye could see without so much as moving from one's seat.

⁊❦⁊

The flowering of scenic wonders within the villa's verdant bounds went well with the gay atmosphere reigning in the Holy City. The year of Our Lord 1700 was a Jubilee Year. Multitudes of pilgrims were converging from all the world over in hope of obtaining remission of their sins and benefit of the indulgence. No sooner did they arrive from the Via Romea at the ridge from which they could make out the cupola of Saint Peter's than the faithful (known therefore as "Romei") would intone a hymn to the most excellent of all cities, red with the purple blood of the martyrs and white with the lilies of the virgins of Christ. Hostelries, hospices, colleges and even private houses, which were subject to the law of hospitality, were full to over-flowing with pilgrims; alleyways and piazzas resounded night and day to the footsteps of the pious as they filled the air with their litanies. The night was lit up by the torches of the confraternities who cease-lessly enlivened the streets of the central quarters. 'Midst so much fervour, even the cruel spectacle of the flagellants no longer inspired horror: the crack of the scourges with which the ascetics tormented their lacerated sweat- and blood-covered backs formed a counter-point to the chaste chanting of novices in their cool cloisters.

No sooner had they arrived in the city of the Vicar of Christ than the pilgrims would converge upon Saint Peter's, and only after pray-ing at the tomb of the apostle would they allow themselves a few hours' respite. On the next day, before leaving their lodgings, they would kneel on the ground, raise their hearts heavenward, cross themselves and meditate upon the life of Christ and of the Most Holy Virgin Mary; then, telling their rosary beads, they would begin the tour of the four Jubilee basilicas, followed by the Forty-hour Ora-tion and the ascent of the Holy Ladder, whereby to obtain total and complete remission of sins.

All in all, everything seemed to be moving in perfect and joyous harmony for the twenty-fifth recurrence of those Jubilees which, since the time of Boniface VIII, had brought tens of thousands of Romei to Rome; and yet one could not truly say "everything", for an undertow of anguish and distress moved silently through the crowds of pilgrims and Romans: His Holiness was gravely ill.

Two years previously, Pope Innocent XII (whose baptismal name had been Antonio Pignatelli) had been struck down by a severe form of gout, which had gradually worsened until it prevented him from attending to affairs after the manner accustomed. In January of the Holy Year, there had been a slight improvement in his condition, and in February he had been able to hold a consistory. Owing to age and its infirmities, he was, however, in no condition to open the Holy Gate. The further the Holy Year advanced, the greater the number of pilgrims who arrived in Rome, and the Pope complained of his inabil-ity to accomplish the customary acts of devotion, in which bishops and cardinals had to substitute for him. The Cardinal Penitentiary heard the confessions of the faithful at Saint Peter's, where they arrived daily in their thousands.

In the last week of February, the Pontiff suffered a relapse. In April, he found the strength to bless the multitudes of the devout from the balcony of the Papal Palace at Monte Cavallo. In May, he even visited the four basilicas in person, and towards the end of the month he received the Grand Duke of Tuscany. By halfway through June, he seemed almost recovered; he had visited many churches as well as the fountain of San Pietro in Montorio, a stone's throw from the Villa Spada.

Nevertheless, all knew that His Holiness's health was as delicate as a snowflake in the advancing spring, and the heat of the summer months promised nothing good. Those close to the Pontiff spoke *sotto voce* of frequent crises of debility, of night-long sufferings, of sudden and most cruel bouts of colic. After all, as the cardinals murmured gravely among themselves, the Holy Father was fourscore-and-five years of age.

There was, in other words, a distinct possibility that the Jubilee of the year 1700, happily inaugurated by Our Lord Innocent XII, might be closed by another pope: his successor. This was something unheard of, so people murmured in Rome; and yet was it not unthinkable. Some predicted a conclave in November, some, even in August. The most pessimistic opined that the heat of the summer would overwhelm the Pontiff's last defences.

The humour of the Curia (and that of every Roman) was thus torn between the serene atmosphere of the Jubilee and the grave tidings concerning the Pope's health. Even I had an intense personal interest in the question; for as long as the Holy Father lived, I would have the honour, however occasionally, of serving him whom Rome feared and honoured above all others: His Eminence Cardinal Spada, whom His Holiness had appointed as his Secretary of State.

I could not of course claim true acquaintance with the most illustrious and benign Cardinal Spada, but I heard it said that he was a most upright man, as well as being astute and exceedingly sharp-witted. It was no accident that His Holiness Innocent XII desired always to have him by his side. I therefore guessed that the festivities which were about to begin would be no ordinary convivial gathering of noble spirits but an august conference of cardinals, ambassadors, bishops, princes and other persons of quality; and all would raise their eyebrows in arches of astonishment at the performances of musicians and actors, the poetical divertissements, the oratorical displays, the rich symposia 'midst verdant settings and the papier mâché theatres in the gardens of the Villa Spada, beguilements such as had not been seen in Rome since the times of the Barberini.

ॐ

Meanwhile, I had been able to identify the coat of arms on the first carriage: it was that of the Rospigliosi family, but under it there was a bright damask bearing their colours, which signified that the carriage bore some honoured guest under the protection of that great family, but not of their lineage.

The carriage was on the point of approaching the gate of honour, but I was no longer curious about the arrival of coaches at the villa, the opening of doors and all the ritual of hospitality among gentlefolk that would duly follow. When first I joined the household, I had indeed hidden behind the corners of the great house to spy on the swarm of footmen, the stools being placed for alighting from the carriages, the servant girls bearing baskets laden with fruit, the first tributes from the master of the house, the speeches by the Master of Ceremonies, invariably broken off half-way by the fatigue of the newly arrived guests, and so on and so forth.

I moved away so as not to disturb the arrival of those gentlemen with my obscure presence and once more set to work. While I was intent on hoeing the borders of lawns, pruning bushes, trimming hedges and weeding, I would from time to time look up to enjoy the view over the city of the seven hills, while the gentle summer breeze bore me the gift of graceful notes from an orchestral rehearsal. Covering my forehead with my hand to deflect the glare of the sun, I beheld to the far left the grandiose cupola of Saint Peter's, to my right the more modest but no less splendid one of Sant'Ivo alla Sapienza, just beside the subdued pagan dome of the Pantheon and, last of all, in the background, the Pontifical Palace of the Quirinale on Monte Cavallo.

After one such brief pause, I bent down and was about to trim a few bushes, when I saw a shadow lengthen beside my own.

For a long time I observed it; it did not move. My hand, however, moved of its own accord, grasping the sickle. The tip of its blade traced the shadow by my shoulders on the sand of the drive. The soutane, the abbot's periwig and hood. . . It was then that the shadow, as though condescending to inspect my hand, turned slowly towards the sun and revealed its profile; on the ground, I could clearly make out a hooked nose, a receding chin, an impertinent lip. . . My hand, which was almost caressing those features rather than merely outlining them, began now to tremble. No longer could I be in any doubt.

Atto Melani: still unable to raise my eyes from the silhouette I had discovered in the sand, a tangle of thoughts obscured my vision and my feelings. Signor Abbot Melani. . . Signor Atto, to me. Atto, Atto himself.

The shadow waited benignly.

How many years had passed? Sixteen? No, seventeen, I calculated, trying to gather the courage to turn around. And, despite the laws of time, a thousand thoughts and memories flashed across my mind within those few seconds. Almost seventeen years without the least sign of life from Abbot Melani, and now he had reappeared; his shadow was there, behind me, merging with my own, so I repeated mechanically to myself as at length I rose and very slowly turned around.

At last my pupils acknowledged the sun's affront.

He was leaning on a walking stick, a little shorter and more bent than I had left him. Seeming almost like some shade from another century, he wore an abbot's wig, hood and mauve-grey soutane, exactly as he had when first we met, little caring that this attire had long been outmoded.

Confronting my glazed and dumbstruck expression, he spoke with the most laconic and disarming naturalness: "I am going to take a rest: I have only just arrived. We shall meet later. I shall have them call for you."

Seeming almost spectral, he disappeared into the blazing midsummer light, moving in the direction of the great house.

I stood as though petrified. I do not know how long I remained thus immobile in the midst of the garden. My breast seemed like the cold white marble of Galatea, and only gradually did the breath of life return to warm it, when I was of a sudden unnerved by the bursting into my heart of that o'erflowing torrent of affection and pain which had for years seized me whenever I recalled Abbot Melani.

The letters which I had sent to Paris had been swallowed up by an abyss of black silence. Year after year, I had uselessly laid siege to the office for post from France, awaiting a reply. If only to put an end to anxiety, I would eventually have been resigned to receive some sadly final message, as I had imagined a thousand times over:

It is my sad duty to inform you of the death of Abbot Melani. . .

Instead, nothing; until now, when his unexpected reappearance had taken my breath away. I was incredulous; directly upon his arrival, the first action of the illustrious guest of the Rospigliosi, invited with all honours to the Villa Spada, had been to seek me out: me, a mere peasant bending over his mattock. The friendship and faith of Abbot Melani had overcome distances and years.

After finishing what I was doing in all haste, I hurried home on my mule. I could not wait to inform Cloridia! As I rode, I kept repeating to myself, "Why should I be surprised?", tenderly realising that this impetuous and unexpected reappearance was utterly typical of the man. Such emotions, such a tightening of the heart-strings! As in a dream, I relived the turmoil of teachings and intellectual passions which Abbot Melani had revealed to me and the dangerous pursuit into which I had been plunged when I followed him. . .

Little by little, however, emotions and gratitude came to be attended by a doubt. How had Atto managed to trace me to the Villa Spada? It would have been logical for him to seek me at the Via dell'Orso, in the house which was formerly the Locanda del Donzello, the inn where I had served and in which we had met. Instead, Atto, who had clearly been invited by Cardinal Spada to his nephew's wedding, had come straight to me upon arriving, as though he well knew where to find me.

From whom could he have learned that? Certainly not from anyone at the Villa Spada; none there knew of our erstwhile frequentation, quite apart from the fact that my person was never the object of anyone's attention. Besides, we had no common acquaintances, only the adventure we had both lived through at the Donzello seventeen long years ago. Concerning that extraordinary episode, I had at first kept a concise diary, based on which I had drawn up a detailed memoir, of which I was, moreover, inordinately proud. I had even mentioned it to Atto in the last missive which I had sent him only a few months previously, in one final attempt to obtain tidings of him.

As I trotted across the fields, I gave free rein to memories, and for a few moments I relived in a daydream those distant and remarkable events: the plague, the poisonings, the manhunts in the underground galleries, the battle of Vienna, the conspiracies of the sovereigns of Europe. . .

How brilliantly, I thought, I had succeeded in telling it all in my memoir, so much so that I had at first taken pleasure in poring over it on sleepless nights. Nor was I perturbed by having once again before my eyes all the iniquitous deeds perpetrated by Atto: his transgressions, his failings and blasphemies. I need only to go to my writings to recover my spirits, even to feel positively merry, and then I was minded of the love of my Cloridia, which still *Deo gratias* accompanied me, and of the purity of work on the land and, lastly, of my fresh connection with the Villa Spada. Ah yes, the Villa Spada. . .

As though I had been attacked by a thousand scorpions, I spurred on my mule and hastened home. Now I understood only too well.

Cloridia was not at home. I rushed to the trunks in which I kept all my books. Feverishly I emptied them, rummaging at the bottom of each one: the memoir had disappeared.

🙢🙠

"Thief, brigand, blackguard," I growled under my breath. "And I am a dolt, an imbecile, a gullible jackass."

How foolish I had been to write to Atto about my memoir! Those pages contained too many secrets, too many proofs of the infidelities and betrayals of which Abbot Melani was capable. No sooner did he know of its existence – alas, only now did I realise this – than he unleashed some ruffian of his to purloin it. It must have been child's play to enter my unguarded house and search it.

I cursed Atto, I cursed myself and whoever he had sent to steal my beautiful memoir. Anyway, what else could I expect of Abbot Melani? I had but to turn my mind to all I knew of his turbid misdeeds.

Castrato singer and French spy: that already said all that was to be said about him. His career as a singer was long since over. In his youth, he had, however, been a famous soprano and had taken advantage of his concerts to spy on half the courts of Europe. Subterfuge, lies and deceit were his daily bread; ambushes, plots and assassinations, his travelling companions. He was capable of grasping a pipe and making it pass for a pistol, of hiding the truth from you without lying, of expressing and inspiring deep feelings out of pure calculation; he knew and practised the arts of stalking and theft.

His intellect, on the other hand, was both fulminating and penetrative. His knowledge of the affairs of state I recalled as reaching into the best-hid secrets of crowned heads and royal families. What was more, his keen and lively mind was capable of dissecting the human soul like a knife cutting through lard. His sparkling eyes gained him sympathy, nor had he ever the slightest difficulty in winning over those around him.

Alas, all his best qualities were at the service of the most sordid ends. If he enlightened you with some revelation, it was only in order to win your compliance. If he said he was on a mission, he certainly did not betray his base personal interests. If, lastly, he offered his friendship, I thought bitterly, it was with a view to extorting whatever favours he needed most.

The proof of all that? His indifference to old friends. He had left me without news for seventeen years. And now, as though nothing had happened, he was calling me urgently to his service. . .

"No, Signor Atto, I am no longer the young lad I was seventeen years ago." Thus would I speak to him, looking him straight in the eyes. I'd show him that I was now a man well-versed in the business of life, no longer timid in the company of gentlemen, only deferential; capable of weighing up every occasion and discerning where my own interest lay. And if, because of my slight stature, everyone still called me a boy, I was and felt myself to be a very different person from the little prentice whom Atto had known so many years ago.

No, I could not accept Abbot Melani's conduct; and, above all, I could not tolerate the theft of my memoir.

I threw myself down on the bed, trying to rest and to part company with these and other sad cogitations and endlessly tormenting the sheets. Only then did I remember that Cloridia had told me that she would not be returning home; like every good midwife (as she had become after prolonged practice over the past few years) she would spend the last few days before the confinement at the home of the mother-to-be. With her had gone my two adored little ones, no longer so little: at ten and six years of age, already big girls, my daughters had become the full-time helpers of their mother (whom they adored) not only as pupils, to be instructed in this most important discipline, but as assistants ready to meet her every need, for instance by handing her oils and hot greases, towels, scissors and thread for cutting the umbilical cord; or in dexterously pulling forth the afterbirth and other such matters.

I dedicated a few thoughts to them: the little pair followed their mother like a shadow, their behaviour in public as sensible as it was vivacious 'twixt our four domestic walls. Their absence now made the house seem even emptier and sadder, and I was reminded of my melancholy infancy as a poor foundling.

Thus, favoured by solitude, grave thoughts had gained the upper hand. Insomnia wrapped me in its cold embrace and I knew how cold the connubial couch can be without the consolation of love.

After an hour or so, having missed my lunch for lack of appetite, I resolved to return to the Villa Spada in order to pursue my duties. Such repose as I had taken, however brief, had had the desired effect: the insistent thoughts of Abbot Melani and his sudden return, of which I knew not whether it was most welcome or opportune for me, at long last left me. Abbot Melani had, I thought, emerged like some selfish protean sea-god to perturb the quiet counterpoint of my existence. It was right that I should try now not to think of him.

He would have me called, so he had told me; until then, I could at least dedicate myself to other matters. I had much to do and so I set about one of the tasks which most pleased me: the cleaning of the aviary. The servant who habitually undertook this was more and more frequently confined to bed by an ugly wound to his foot which refused to heal. It was thus not the first time that I was discharging this duty. I went to collect the feed and set to work.

The reader should not be surprised to learn that the Villa Spada was graced by an attraction as exotic as the aviary. In the Roman villas, all forms of diversion were in great demand. At his Villa on the Pincio, Cardinal de' Medici kept bears, lions and ostriches; at the Villas Borghese and Pamphili, roe deer and fallow deer wandered freely. At the time of Pope Leo X an elephant, Annone by name, had even promenaded among the gardens of the Vatican. Apart from animals, sportive entertainments to astound and divert the guests had never been lacking, such as pall-mall (which was played at the Villa Pamphili), or *trucco*, otherwise known as billiards, which was played at the villa of the Knights of Malta and at Villa Costaguti, on a court polished with soap or a cloth-covered table, or billiards in the open air, which was to be found at the Villa Mattei, to overcome the melancholy humour of the summer evenings.

The aviary was situated in a secluded corner of the villa, between the chapel and the vegetable gardens, hidden from view by a line of trees and by a tall, thick hedge. It had been so placed as to enjoy sunlight in winter and shade in summer, in order to spare the birds the discomfort of inclement weather. Its aspect was that of a little manor built to a square plan, with a tower at each corner and the central corpus covered in metallic mesh cupolas, surmounted in their turn by splendid pinnacles crowned by iron weathercocks. The interior was painted with frescoes depicting views of the heavens and of distant landscapes, so as to give the fowls an illusion of greater space. Holm oaks and bay laurel bushes, which are evergreen, were planted there, and there were vases with brushwood for building nests as well as four large drinking bowls. The birds (of which there were a number of groups in separate cages) were numerous and most pleasing both to the eye and the ear: nightingales, lapwings, partridges, quails, francolins, pheasants, ortolans, green linnets, blackbirds, calandra larks, chaffinches, turtle-doves and hawfinches, to name but a few.

I entered the aviary timidly, immediately provoking a great flapping of wings. Birds, or so I have been told, should always be fed and cared for by the same person. My presence, instead of their usual master, had sown no little disquiet. I made my way in cautiously while a number of lapwings followed me nervously and a flock of little birds darted around me with hostile movements. I shivered when a blackbird settled boldly on my shoulder, somehow avoiding a collision with a francolin which was fluttering defiantly in my face.

"If you do not stop this at once, I shall depart, and then you shall go without lunch!" I threatened.

In response to this I received only a more aggressive and strident wave of cackling, whistling and fluttering, and further dangerous aerial incursions only a hand's breadth from my head. Intimidated, I took refuge in a corner until the squall calmed down. The government of birds and of aviaries was not, I thought, a trade for me.

When even the most impertinent volatiles had returned to order, I began to clean and refill the drinking and feed bowls with fresh water, chicory, beet, yarrow, lettuce, plantain seeds, grain, bird seed, millet and hemp seed. I then furnished the aviary with fresh supplies of asparagus grass, which is good for building nests. As I was scattering a few pieces of dry bread, a hungry young francolin jumped onto my arm, trying to snatch the tasty booty of breadcrumbs from his companions.

Once I had cleaned the feed bowls and swept the dejections from the ground, I moved at last towards the exit, happy to leave behind me the stink and chaos of the aviary. I was just closing the door when suddenly my heart leapt into my throat.

A pistol shot. A projectile whistled by very close to me. Someone was shooting at me.

I bent down with my hands clutching my head in a gesture of protection. Then I heard a hard, loud voice, clearly addressing me: "Arrest him! He's a thief."

Instinctively, I raised my hands in surrender. I turned around, and saw no one. I slapped my forehead and smiled, disappointed at the shortness of my memory. Only then did I slowly look upwards and see him there, in his usual place.

"How witty," I replied, closing the door of the aviary and trying to hide my shock.

"I said, 'Arrest him, he's a thief!' *Boooom!*"

That second pistol shot, which seemed even more real than the first one, clearly announced the strangest creature in all the Villa Spada: Caesar Augustus, parrot.

I should take this opportunity to explain the nature and conduct of that bizarre volatile, which was to play no small part in the events I am about to recount.

I knew that, because of its unique qualities, the parrot had been given such grandiose names as "Light of the Avian Realm" and "Monarch of the East Indies", and that the first exemplars had been brought to Alexander the Great from the Isle of Taprobane, since which time many other species had been discovered in the West Indies, especially in Cuba and Manacapan. Everyone knows that the parrot (of which some say there exist over a hundred varieties) possesses the most singular faculty of imitating the human voice, and not only that, but noises, sounds, and much else. Years ago in Rome, the parrot of the most excellent Cardinal Madruzzo and that of the Cavalier Cassiano Dal Pozzo were renowned for imitating the human voice poorly while perfectly mimicking dogs and cats. Then there were those which knew how to imitate the song of other birds, even of more than one species. Outside the Papal States, the parrot belonging to His

Most Serene Highness the Prince of Savoy was still remembered for its prompt and fluent eloquence. It is said that Cardinal Colonna's parrot could recite the whole Creed. Lastly, another white and yellow parrot of the same species as Caesar Augustus had just arrived on the Barberini estate, adjoining the Villa Spada, and this one too was said to be a good speaker.

Caesar Augustus was, however, on quite another level from all his fellow parrots. He mimicked human speech to perfection, even the voices of persons whom he had known for only a very short time and whose accents he had barely heard, reproducing tones, cadences and even slight defects in pronunciation. He reproduced the sounds of nature, including thunder, the rushing of torrents, the rustling of leaves and the howling of the wind, even the sound of the waves breaking on the beach. He was no less skilled an imitator of dogs, cats, cows, donkeys, horses and of course all kinds of birds, and perhaps he could also mimic other sounds which I had not yet heard him produce. He would faithfully imitate the squealing of hinges, approaching footsteps, the firing of pistols and muskets, the ringing of a doorbell, horses' hooves trotting, a door slamming hard, the cries of street vendors, an infant crying, the clash of blades in a duel, all the subtleties of laughter and lamentations, the clatter of dishes and glasses, and many more sounds.

It was as though for Caesar Augustus the whole cosmos was an immense gymnasium in which he could day after day refine his indescribable, unsurpassable talents for mimicry. Gifted with a prodigious memory, he was able to bring forth voices and whispers weeks after hearing them, thus surpassing any human faculty.

No one knew how old he was: some said fifty, others even seventy. In truth, anything was possible, given the well-known longevity of parrots, which not infrequently live for over a century and survive their masters.

His incomparable talent, which could have made of Caesar Augustus the most famous parrot of all time, did, however, have its limits. The parrot of the Villa Spada had, indeed, refused to display his gifts for as long as anyone could remember. In short, he pretended to be dumb. Fruitless were requests, flattery, orders, even the cruel fast to which he was subjected, on the orders of Cardinal Spada himself, to convince him to perform. Nothing worked; Caesar Augustus had for years and years (no one knew how many) withdrawn into the most stubborn silence.

Of course, no one knew why this had happened. Some remembered that Caesar Augustus had first belonged to Father Virgilio Spada, the uncle of Cardinal Spada, who had died some forty years previously. It had been Virgilio, a man of letters immersed in antiquities and the classical world, who had named the parrot after the most celebrated Roman emperor. It must have been a token of love; it was indeed said that Virgilio cared much for his feathered friend and there were those among the servants who murmured that the death of his master had cast Caesar Augustus into the blackest melancholy. Had it been the weight of mourning that stopped the parrot's beak? It was indeed as though he had taken a vow of silence, in the sad and insensate expectation of his late master's return to life.

I, however, knew that this was not the case. Caesar Augustus did speak, verily, and I was witness to that: the sole witness, to be exact. I myself could not tell why this should be; I suspected that he felt a particular liking for me. I was in fact the only one who treated him with courtesy; unlike the servants of the villa, I avoided teasing him with twigs or pebbles to make him talk.

I had tried to induce him to speak in the presence of others, swearing that, only minutes before, when we had been alone, he had done so without the slightest difficulty; whereupon he remained silent, looking vacantly at everyone. He made a fool of me, and after one or two more attempts, no one would believe me; the parrot speaks no more, said they, giving me a pat on the shoulder, and what is more, perhaps he never did speak.

Gradually, with the death of the older servants of the Spada household, all memory of the past deeds of Caesar Augustus came to be forgotten. By now I was perhaps the only one to know of what that big white bird with the yellow crest was capable.

On that very day, for a change, the bird had reminded me of this. The false pistol shots and the sergeant's voice (one of many that Caesar Augustus must have heard in Rome) had taken me by surprise, seeming more real than the real thing. It was impossible to know where he might have heard the original sounds. Caesar Augustus in fact enjoyed a unique privilege: he was not held in reclusion like the other birds and had his own special cage with its perch and feed bowl. Thence he would often take flight for who knows what destinations, sometimes simply exploring the villa, sometimes absenting himself for weeks on end. Wandering around the city, he would add to his repertoire of imitations with ever new examples, to which I was in the end to be the one and only stupefied witness.

"*Dona nobis hodie panem cotidianum,*" chanted Caesar Augustus, reciting the verse from the Lord's Prayer.

"I have told you a thousand times not to blaspheme," I warned him, "otherwise. . . Ah, I see what it is that you want. You are quite right."

I had indeed replenished the water and food of all the other birds, leaving the parrot until last. His pride was hurt, and not only that. Caesar Augustus had always been blessed with an excellent appetite and would eat anything: bread, ricotta, soup (especially when prepared with wine), chestnuts, walnuts, apples, pears, cherries and many other things. But his passion, worthy not of a fowl but of a gentleman, was chocolate. From time to time, some guest of the Villa Spada would push some dregs towards him and he would be permitted to dip his beak and his blackish tongue into the costly and exotic beverage. So greedy was he for it that he was capable of cajoling me for days on end (conduct most exceptional, given his bad character) until at length I procured him a spoonful of it.

I had just renewed his water and filled his little bowl with fruit and seeds when I heard hurried footsteps approaching.

"My boy, are you still here?" chided one of the major-domos. "Someone is looking for you. He is waiting for you at the foot of the back stairs."

❧

"Come, come, weep not. Well you knew that, sooner or later, we were bound to meet again. Atto Melani is as tough as old leather!" exclaimed Atto taking me by the forearms and shaking me fraternally.

"But I am not weeping, I. . ."

"Quiet, quiet, say nothing, I have just asked after you and they tell me that you have two lovely little girls. What are their names? Such emotions!" he murmured in my ear, caressing my head and rocking me with embarrassing tenderness.

A pair of young peasant girls observed the scene with astonishment.

"What a surprise, you are a father!" continued the Abbot, quite undaunted. "Yet, to see you, one would never imagine that. You seem the same as ever. . ."

Upon that observation (I could not tell whether it was meant as a compliment or an insult) I at last succeeded with great difficulty in breaking free from Atto's grasp and taking a step backwards. I was as shocked as if I had had to defend myself from an assault. I was incredulous: he seemed to have been bitten by a tarantula. I had in truth noticed how, when he saw me arriving, the Abbot's small triangular eyes observed me closely and how, when confronted with the frown which I was unable to banish from my forehead, Atto's mood had changed of a sudden and he had turned into this garrulous old man who was now covering me with kisses and embraces.

He pretended not to notice my coldness and took me by the arm, leading me through the gardens of the villa.

"So tell me, my boy, tell me how life has been treating you," said he in a low voice, and adopting a familiar manner, as with some difficulty we entered the little avenue of locust trees busy with the goings and comings of the hired gardeners making their finishing touches.

"In truth, Signor Atto, you should already be well informed. . ." I endeavoured to retort, thinking of the theft of my memoir, in which I had also recounted my recent history.

"I know, I know," he interrupted at once in paternal tones, as he stopped in admiration before the fountain of the Villa Spada which had, on the occasion of the festivities, been transformed by means of scaffolding into a splendid work of ephemeral architecture. In the place of the usual modest basin into which the water poured from a great stone pineapple finial, there now arose a magnificent and serpentine Triton who, clinging by the tail to a pyramid-shaped rock, blew vigorously into a jar, causing a capricious spurt of water to gush up from it in the shape of an umbrel, falling at last to the feet of its creator with a musical gurgle. All around, the Nymphaeum's mirror of water offered the languid spectacle of aquatic plants, ornamented by fine white flowers which floated lazily, half open.

Atto observed the Triton and its fine fountain with admiring interest.

"A splendid fountain," he commented. "The Triton is well made, and the imitation rocks too are a fine piece of work. I know that at the Villa d'Este in Tivoli there was once a water organ which was subsequently imitated in the garden of the Quirinale and in the Villa Aldrobrandini at Frascati, but also in France, on the orders of Francis I. It reproduced the sound of trumpets and even birdsong. It sufficed to blow into a few fine metal tubes placed in earthenware vases half full of water, hidden among the water-lilies."

He looked around the fountain. I did not follow him. He stopped at the far end, spying on me through the spray; then he turned to me.

"To see an old friend whom one had feared dead may cause confusion not only for the heart but for the mind," he resumed, "but you will see that, given time, we shall recover our former sentiments."

"Given time? How long do you then intend to sojourn in Rome?" I asked, obscurely anxious at the idea of becoming involved in some dubious undertaking of his.

He stopped. He looked at me through half-closed eyes which he then directed, first towards the fountain, then the horizon, as though he were skilfully distilling his reply.

It was then that for the first time I had leisure enough to observe him. Thus, I saw the soft, falling flesh of his cheeks, the wrinkled skin of his nose and forehead, the furrows that beset his lips and the corners of his mouth, the bluish veins that crossed his temples, the eyes still lively, but small and deep-set, in which the white had grown yellow, and the neck, more than anything else, marked by the cruel scalpel of time. The thick layer of ceruse on his face, instead of softening the effects of age, came close to transforming Atto into the sad simulacrum of a phantom. Last of all, the hands, only in part hidden by the froth of lace at the cuffs, were now shrivelled, blotchy and hooked.

Seventeen years ago, I had met a man mature yet vigorous. Now I faced one with autumn in his bones.

As though he had not noticed my stare, which implacably investigated his decline, he remained silent for a few instants with his regard lost in the azure, as he leaned with one hand on my shoulder. Suddenly he struck me as being terribly tired.

"How long shall I tarry in Rome?" he repeated the question to himself in absent tones. "'Tis true, my goodness, I must decide how long I shall be staying. . ."

He seemed as though touched by second childhood.

Meanwhile, we had come to the pergola of the wisterias. The fresh breeze which stirred in the shade revived us. We were already at the height of a hot month of July and the nights barely alleviated the burning heat of the day.

"Thank heavens for a little shade," sighed Atto, seating himself on a bench and dabbing at the perspiration on his forehead with the little handkerchief of lace-ornamented white silk which he held in his hand. Then he stood up, stretched towards one of the wisterias, plucked a flower and sat down once more, deeply inhaling the fine perfume. Suddenly, he gave me a little slap on the back and burst out laughing: "Remarkable, you're still asking the same questions as ever! Ah, it is wonderful to find one's friends unchanged, it is truly a great blessing. How long shall I be staying in Rome? But, my boy, the answer is quite obvious! I shall stay here at the Villa Spada for the whole week's festivities, as you may well imagine. But I shall not leave Rome until the conclave! Now, come with me, and enough of questions," said he, springing to his feet as though he were some bold young spark and taking me joyfully by the arm.

What manner of devil is this Melani, thought I, at once troubled and amused; one moment he seemed to have grown dull and aged, and now here he was slipping away like an eel. With him one could never know where the truth lay.

"Signor Atto," I resumed, raising my voice. "Never would I dare to be lacking in respect for you; but yesterday I suffered one of the worst affronts of my whole life, and so. . ."

"Oh, how very disagreeable for you. And what of it?" quoth he, once again sniffing at the flower while with his other hand he drummed lightly on the pommel of his cane.

"I suffered a theft. Do you understand? I was *robbed*," I proclaimed emphatically, inflamed by the repressed anger which was once again rising within me.

"Ah, well, you may console yourself," said he complacently. "That has happened to me too. I well remember how at the convent of the Capuchins at Monte Cavallo, it must have been thirty years ago, they robbed me of three gold rings, set with gems, a heart-shaped diamond, a book of lapis lazuli bound in gold and studded with rubies and turquoises, a coat of French camlet, gloves, fans, pastilles and Spanish wax. . ."

It was then that I exploded.

"Enough, Signor Atto. Stop feigning innocence: you took my memoir, the account of what took place seventeen years ago, when we first met! Only to you have I confided this, only you knew of its existence, and what was your sole response? To have it stolen off me!"

Atto did not lose his composure. With ostentatious delicacy, he laid the wisteria flower down on a hedge and continued drumming on the silver pommel of his cane, letting me continue with my outburst.

"Not for one minute did you spare a thought for me! I who wept warm tears for you, who wrote to you continually, forever imploring a reply! And your sole concern was that someone might read that memoir and discover that you are an intriguer, that you steal good people's secrets, that you betray your own friends, that you are capable of all manner of infamy and. . . well. . . that you are utterly shameless."

I wiped the sweat from my forehead with the palm of my hand, panting with emotion. Atto extended his little lace handkerchief to me, holding it between the tips of two fingers, and in the end I accepted it. I felt empty.

"Have you finished?" he asked at length, distantly.

"I. . . I am incensed by what you have done. I want my memoir back," I stammered, cursing myself for my inability to convey anything better than the same boyish petulance as had been mine seventeen years before, and this at a time when my age is by no means so green.

"Ah, that is out of the question. Your writings are now in a safe place. I have hidden them carefully in Paris, before anyone could give them their *imprimatur*."

"Then you admit it: you are a thief."

"Thief, thief. . ." he chanted. "You really do have too much of a taste for strong words. With the pen, on the other hand, you have some ability. I took much pleasure in reading your little tale, even if you did at times raise the tone too much and even if you wrote things which could give offence to me. And then, you have been very naïve indeed. Really. . . to have written such things about Abbot Melani, and then to have informed him of it. . ."

"True, I realise that too," I admitted.

"As I told you, I did not mind reading your efforts. At times, on the contrary, I found your writing most effective. Yours is a good pen, sometimes a trifle artless, but never tedious. Who knows whether it may not prove useful to you? 'Tis a pity that you failed to mention that you had become a father, I would have been glad to know that. . . But I can understand why: the radiant dawning of the new day, which little ones are for every genitor, surely had no place in that sombre old tale."

I maintained a hostile silence, the better to make him understand that I had no intention of speaking with him of my little ones.

"I imagine that during all these years, you will have read books, gazettes, a few rhymes. . ." said he, changing the subject, as though to move me to speak.

"In truth, Signor Atto," I confirmed, "I am much given to buying books that treat of history, politics, theology and the lives of the saints. Among poets, I enjoy Chiabrera, Achillini and Filicaia. Gazettes. . . No, those I do not read."

"Perfect. It is you that I need."

"And what for, pray?"

"Showed you this memoir to any persons?"

"No."

"There exist no other copies of it?"

"No, I never had the time to transcribe it. Why do you ask?"

"Will a thousand suffice?" he retorted dryly.

"I do not follow your meaning," said I, beginning, however, to understand.

"Very well, then. One thousand two hundred scudi in Roman coin. But not one more. And the memoirs are to become two."

It was thus that Abbot Melani purchased the lengthy memoir in which I had described our first encounter and all the adventures which had arisen thereafter. In the second place, he was, for that sum, advancing payment for another memoir, or rather, a journal: a description of his sojourn at the Villa Spada.

"At the Villa Spada?" I exclaimed incredulously, as we resumed our stroll.

"Precisely. Your master, the Secretary of State, is present and the conclave is imminent; do you imagine that the flower of the Roman nobility and of the ecclesiastical hierarchy, not to mention the ambassadors, would assemble here merely for the pleasure of the occasion? The chess game of the conclave has already begun, my boy; and at the Villa Spada, many important pawns will be moved, of that you may be sure."

"And you, I suppose, would not wish to miss a single move."

"The conclave is my trade," he replied, without so much as a hint of modesty. "Do not forget that the illustrious Rospigliosi of Pistoia, whose guest I am honoured to be, owe me the distinction of numbering a pope among their family."

I had already heard tell, seventeen years previously, of how Atto went around boasting of having favoured the election of Clement IX, of the Rospigliosi family.

"So, my son," concluded Melani, "you will pen for me a chronicle in which you will give a judicious account of all that you see and hear during the coming few days, and you will add thereto whatever I may suggest to you as being desirable and opportune. You will then deliver the manuscript to me without retaining any copy thereof or thereafter reproducing any of its contents. There, those are my terms. For the time being, that is all."

I remained perplexed.

"Are you not content? Were it not for writers, men and their fame would die together on the same day and their virtues would be entombed with them, but the mem'ry thereof which remains written in books – that can never die!" Thus spake the Abbot with courtly prose and honeyed voice, in his endeavours to flatter me.

He was not so mistaken, I reflected, while Atto continued with his homily.

"Thus spake Anaxarchus, a most wise and learned philosopher, saying that one of the most worthy things that one can possess in this life is to be known by the world as intelligent in one's own profession. Indeed, even where there are millions of men learned and expert in one and the same art, only those who take pains to make themselves known will be held worthy of praise, nor will their fame die out in eternity."

Abbot Melani wished, if I had understood him well, for a sort of biographer to celebrate his deeds during those days: a sign that he was intent upon accomplishing memorable feats, so I bethought myself, as I anxiously recalled the Abbot's enterprising audacity.

". . . Wherefore I, considering these things," continued Atto with an air at once pompous and vigorous, "took great pains, when young, to learn, and when I had come of age, to put into practice that which I had learned; and now I strive so to act that the world may know me. Thus, having through my words pleased several princes and great men, and having penned for them divers masterly reports in the art of diplomacy, many there have been who have availed themselves and who yet avail themselves of my skills."

"But not all profited thereby," thought I to myself, recalling the cavalier manner in which Atto would transfer his fidelity from one master to another.

೭∞೯

With two little lasses to bring up, all that money was an extraordinary blessing for me and Cloridia. I had therefore not hesitated to accept Atto's offer to acquire from me what he had already stolen, well aware that I would never have my memoir back. "Just one thing, Signor Atto," said I at length. "I do not believe that my pen is worthy to bear witness to your deeds."

In reality, I was terrified by the thought that multitudes of gentlemen and eminent persons might one day hold writings of mine in their hand. Atto understood.

"You fear the readers. And such is your fear that you would prefer simply to continue exercising your peasant's calling, is that not so?" he asked, stopping to pick a plum.

I replied with a look which confessed all.

"Then, in your foreword, instead of addressing the 'kind reader', you must address the 'unkind reader'."

"What do you mean?"

Melani drew breath and, in didactic prose and with a presumptuous little smile on his face, he polished the plum with his lace handkerchief while instructing me as follows: "You know, many years ago, when I first gave some of my essays to be printed, I too followed the common and vulgar custom of presenting to the gentle reader my excuses for such errors as might, through my own fault, be discovered in my opus. Now, however, experience has taught me that the gentle reader, prudently perusing the works of others, will, being replete with goodness, discover the good where'er it may be, and, where he finds it not, will accept the author's goodwill. Thus was I persuaded that it was far more opportune to dedicate the foreword to my books to malign and maledicent readers, whose ears are so tender that they will be scandalised by the minutest error."

Biting the little plum, he stopped to scrutinise my distracted expression.

"To suchlike *nasuti* (to use the Latin expression), to suchlike slanderers and detractors, to whom every book appears superfluous, every work imperfect, every concept erroneous and every endeavour vain, I do proclaim my desire that they should refrain from reading my works and turn away from them, for as little as the said works will please them, so much the more will they please others. Do you know what I reply when one of those birds of ill omen importunes me with his acid considerations?"

I responded with a questioning air.

"I reply: if Your Worships find my work long, they should read but half of it; if short, let them add thereto whate'er they will; if it seemeth too clear, let them console themselves, knowing that they will have less trouble understanding it; if too obscure, let them make comments in the margin; if too lowly the matter and the style, so be it, for it will suffer less in falling than it would have, had it fallen from a great height."

The Abbot closed his disquisition, sharply spitting out the plum stone almost as though it were a detractor's pen. I stood in admiration before his sagacity; from Atto Melani, thought I, one never ceased to learn.

"I have never read your works, Signor Atto, but I am sure," I flattered him, "that the worst one could say of them would be that they are too learned."

"Have no fear!" he replied easily, speaking with his mouth full. "That they are too learned, they will never admit; for that too is praise and such is the nature of these crows that they would not know how to give praise, even unintentionally. However, remember that most ancient oracle according to which the greatest misfortune that could befall a man is to be loved and praised by the wicked, and the greatest favour, that of being hated and blamed thereby. The truth is that the works of men are imperfect owing to the defects of our poor wits and they find detractors because of the infelicity of our times. So may it please the Lord our God to grant us the grace to acknowledge our faults, thus to emend them, and others, not to blame us for what was well meant; that the Divine Majesty be not offended either by our own errors or those of others. Do you understand?"

I nodded in affirmation.

Melani looked at me with an air of satisfaction and handed me a letter of exchange, payable by a moneylender in the ghetto. Slowly, I took it. It was done: I had sold myself to Atto for, so to say, a literary service, which nonetheless included in the price (as all too often happens when the pen is a means of gain) my placing myself completely at his disposal. Torn between love, disgust and interest, while the sweet and sour savour of the cherries lingered on in my mouth, I was already at his service.

❧

We had meanwhile turned back towards the great house, before which we found the massed carriages of the guests who had just arrived. In the end, what was most dreaded had happened: the guests from Rome had also arrived at the festivities two days early. Knowing that there would already be banqueting from that evening onwards, no one (Atto included) had had the patience and good taste to await the official opening of the celebrations.

Atto seemed to be scrutinising attentively the coats of arms borne by the carriages, doubtless guessing at who might be sharing the magnificent hospitality of the Spada family with him throughout the week's revels.

"I have overheard someone tell a servant of your master that Don Livio Odescalchi is about to arrive, accompanied by the Marchesa Serlupi. Wait. . ." said he, holding me back and looking towards the carriages, far enough removed to be able to see without himself being noticed. "That is a well-known face; it seems to me. . . Yes, indeed, it is Monsignor D'Aste," said Atto as in the distance we saw descending from his carriage a hoary and emaciated little old man who seemed almost lost in his cardinal's vestments. "He is so small, scraggy and ill-favoured that His Holiness calls him Monsignor Stracetto – little rag!" he tittered freely, showing off his familiarity with Roman gossip.

"I see a great movement of lackeys over there," he continued. "One of the Barberini or the Colonnas will be arriving and wants to give himself airs; they always think themselves to be the centre of the world. The carriage behind seems to bear the arms of the Durazzo family, it must be Cardinal Marcello. Of course, to have come from Faenza, where he is Bishop, is quite a journey; he'll need to take a good rest if he wants to enjoy himself. Ah, here is Cardinal Bichi," he commented, peering more intently. "I did not expect him to be on such good terms with Cardinal Fabrizio."

"Apropos, Signor Atto, I myself did not know you were acquainted with Cardinal Spada," said I, deliberately interrupting his show of recognising guests from a distance.

"Oh, but he was for years Nuncio in France, did you not know? At one time we frequented one another quite assiduously in Paris. He is – how can I put it? – a most accommodating person. His first concern is not to make enemies. And he does well to act thus, for in Rome that is the best way to reach high office. I'll wager that he well remembers his time in Paris, since it was then that the cardinal's hat was conferred upon him; if I am not mistaken, 'twas in 1676. He had already been Nuncio in Savoy, so he had a certain amount of experience. He has taken part in three conclaves, that of Innocent XI in 1676, that of Alexander VIII in 1689 and that of the present Pope in 1691. The coming election will be his fourth: not bad for a cardinal who is but fifty-seven years of age, what?"

The years had passed, but not Atto's habit of recording in the greatest possible detail the careers of dozens of popes and cardinals. His Most Christian Majesty could count upon an agent who was perhaps no longer athletic but certainly enjoyed a still excellent memory.

"Do you think that he could be elected pope this time?" I asked in the secret hope that I might one day be able to become part of a pontiff's army of servants.

"Absolutely not. Too young. He might reign for twenty or thirty years; the other cardinals have but to think of such things to take to their beds with a fever," laughed Atto; "Now with me, he will be somewhat distant, for he will be afraid to be taken for a vassal of the King of France if he salutes Abbot Melani. Poor things, one feels for these cardinals!" he concluded, grinning scornfully.

∽∾

In the meanwhile, we continued to loiter by the gate until there appeared from the street that passed before the villa a man ancient and hunchbacked with a tremulous air and two hairs on his head, bearing on his hump a great basket full of papers. Humbly he stopped, hat in hand, to ask something of the lackeys, who responded rudely, trying to chase him away. Indeed, whoever he might have been, he ought to have presented himself at the tradesmen's entrance, where the lowly run no risk of provoking the disdain of the villa's noble guests by their mere presence.

The Abbot drew near and gestured that I should follow him. The old man had rolled-up sleeves and his stomach was covered by a blackened apron; he was plainly an artisan, perhaps a typographer.

"You are Haver, the bookbinder from the Via dei Coronari, is that not so?" Atto asked him, coming out from the gate and standing in the middle of the road. "It was I who called you. I have work for you," and he drew forth a little bundle of papers.

"How do you want the cover?"

"In parchment."

"Any inscription or sign on the spine or the cover?"

"Nothing."

The two rapidly agreed on other matters and Atto placed a handful of coins in the old man's hands as an advance on payment.

Suddenly we heard a piercing scream coming from the greenery by the roadside to our left.

"After him, after him!" called a stentorian voice.

Out darted a swift shadow and passed between us, colliding heavily with the bookbinder and Abbot Melani and causing the latter to tumble onto the gravel with a dull cry of rage and pain.

All the papers which Atto was holding in his hand were scattered into the air in an unhappy and disorderly swirl, and the same fate befell the bookbinder's basketful of papers, while the shadow which had dashed against us rolled on the ground in a series of dramatic and indescribable somersaults.

When at last it stopped rolling, I saw that it was a dirty and emaciated young man with a torn shirt, several days' growth of beard and a dazed and lunatic expression following the wretched accident. Around his neck he bore a poor pouch of cheap material from which various filthy objects had fallen: it seemed to me a leathern bag, a pair of old stockings and a few greasy papers, perhaps the miserable fruit of a visit to some rubbish heap in search of something edible or useful for survival.

I did not, however, have time to observe any better or to offer assistance to Atto or the stranger, for the uproar which I had first heard was growing louder and more violent.

"Catch him, catch him, by all the blunderbusses!" yelled the powerful voice which I had heard before.

I heard a clamour of cries and curses coming from the building housing the catchpolls guarding the villa. The young man rose to his feet and began to run again, disappearing once more into the bushes.

Atto meanwhile was propping himself up and trying unsuccessfully to rise to his feet. I was coming to assist him and the bookbinder was starting humbly to gather up the papers in his basket, when a pair of catchpolls from the villa rushed shouting out into our midst and joined the pursuer. The latter, alas, collided again with poor Atto, who collapsed on the ground. The pursuer rolled over in his turn, by some miracle avoiding the lackeys, two nuns whom I often saw bringing small hand-made objects to offer Cardinal Spada, and a pair of dogs. What with the cries of the nuns and the barking of the dogs, the road was in utter turmoil.

I rushed to assist Abbot Melani, who lay groaning disconsolately. "Aahh, first one madman, then the other. . . My arm, damn it."

The right sleeve of Atto's jacket, which seemed to be soaked with some blackish liquid, was badly lacerated by what looked like a slash from a knife. I freed him from the garment. An ugly wound, from which the blood gushed freely, disfigured the Abbot's flaccid and diaphanous arm.

A pair of pious old maids, who dwelled in the great house, where they worked in the linen-room, had seen all that had happened and gave us some pieces of gauze with a little medicinal unguent which, they assured us, would soothe and bring sure healing to Atto's wound.

"My poor arm, it seems to be my destiny," complained Atto as they bandaged his wound with gauze. "Eleven years ago I fell into a ditch and injured my arm and shoulder badly; indeed, I came close to dying. Among other things, that accident prevented me from coming to Rome for the conclave after the death of Innocent XI."

"One might almost say that conclaves are bad for your health," I commented spontaneously, earning an ugly look from the Abbot.

Meanwhile, a little crowd of curious onlookers, children and peasants from the neighbourhood, had gathered around us.

"Good heavens – those two!" muttered Melani. "The first was too fast, the second, too heavy!"

"Zounds!" exclaimed the stentorian voice. "How say you, heavy? I had almost caught him, the *cerretano*."

The circle of people opened up suddenly, growing fearful upon hearing those rough and grave words.

The speaker was a colossus, three times my height, twice my girth and weighing perhaps four times more than I. I turned and stared at him fixedly. Fair he was, and of virile appearance, but an old wound, which had split one of his eyebrows, conferred upon him a melancholy expression, with which his rough and youthful manners contrasted sharply.

"In any case, and that I swear upon the points of all the halberds in Silesia, I had no intention of causing you any offence." Thus spake the uncouth giant, stepping forward.

Without so much as a by-your-leave, he lifted Atto from the ground and effortlessly set him on his feet, as though he were a mere pine-needle. The huddle of bystanders pressed around us, greedy to know more, but was at once dispersed by the lackeys and valets from the villa, who had meanwhile arrived in large numbers. The bookbinder was busy carefully recovering all of Atto's papers, scattered here and there on either side of the gateway.

"You are a sergeant," observed Atto, tidying himself and dusting down his jacket, "but whom were you following?"

"A *cerretano*, as I said: a canter, a ragamuffin, a slubberdegullion, a money-sucking mountebank or whatever the deuce you want to call such rogues. Dammit, Sirrah, perhaps he meant to rob you."

"Ah, a beggar," said I, translating.

"What is your name?" asked Atto.

"Sfasciamonti."

Despite his pain, Atto looked him up and down from head to toe.

"One who smashes mountains. . . Why, that's a fine name, and eminently well suited to you. Where do you work?" he inquired, not having seen whence Sfasciamonti came.

"Usually, near the Via del Panico, but since yesterday, here," said he, indicating the Villa Spada.

He then explained that he was one of the sergeants paid by Cardinal Spada to ensure that the festivities should take place undisturbed. The bookbinder drew near, as one with pressing tidings.

"Excellency, I have found the arm which injured you," said he, handing Atto a sort of shiny dagger with a squared-off handle.

Sfasciamonti, however, promptly seized the blade and pocketed it.

"One moment, Sir," protested Atto. "That is the knife that struck me."

"Precisely. It is therefore *corpus delicti* and to be placed at the disposal of the Governor and the Bargello. I am here to supervise the security of the villa and I am only doing my duty."

"Master Catchpoll, have you seen what happened to me? Thank heavens that wretch's dagger caressed my arm and not my back. If your colleagues catch him, I want him to pay for this too."

"That I do promise and swear unto you, by Wallenstein's powder-flask!" roared Sfasciamonti, raising a timorous murmur among the bystanders.

The wound was no light one, and the bleeding still by no means staunched. Two maidservants rushed up with more gauze and bandaged the arm so as to stop the flow. I had occasion to admire how stoically Abbot Melani bore pain: a quality of which I was as yet unaware. He even stayed behind in order to settle arrangements with the bookbinder, who had in the meantime gathered up all Atto's papers, upon which he was to confer the form and dignity of a volume. They rapidly agreed on the price and set an appointment for the morrow.

We moved towards the great house, where Atto intended to summon a physician or chirurgeon to examine the ugly wound.

"For the time being, it is not too painful; let us hope that it will not get worse. Heaven help me and my idea of giving an appointment to that bookbinder, but I cared too much about my little book."

"Apropos, what was it that you had bound?"

"Oh, nothing of importance," he replied, raising his eyebrows and pursing his lips.

恢怹

We had returned to the house without exchanging another word. The affected carelessness with which Abbot Melani had replied (or rather, failed to reply) to my question, had left me in some perplexity. Those one thousand two hundred scudi compelled me to share the fate of the Abbot for a period of several days, in order to keep a record of his sojourn at the Villa Spada. Yet it still was not given to me to know what precisely awaited me.

I requested the Abbot's permission to take my leave, on the pretext of a number of most urgent duties which had accumulated since his arrival. In actual fact, I did not have much to do on that day. I was not a regular servant of the household and, moreover, preparations for the festivities were almost complete. I did, however, desire a little solitude in which to reflect upon the latest occurrences. Instead, the Abbot begged me to attend him until the arrival of the chirurgeon.

"Please tighten the bandages on my arm even more: those women's dressings are causing me to lose blood," he requested with a hint of impatience.

So I waited on him and added yet more bandages which the *valet de chambre* had taken care to provide.

"A French book, Signor Atto?" I resolved at length to ask him, referring to his previous allusion.

"Yes and no," he replied laconically.

"Ah, perhaps it circulates in France but was printed in Amsterdam, as often happens. . ." I hazarded, in the hope of extracting something more from him.

"No, no," he cut me short with a sigh of fatigue, "really, it is not even a book."

"An anonymous text, then. . ." I butted in yet again, scarcely dissimulating my growing curiosity.

I was interrupted by the arrival of the chirurgeon. While the latter was feeling around Atto's arm, giving orders to the *valet de chambre*, I had a moment in which to reflect.

It was plainly no accident that Atto Melani should have reappeared after seventeen years, asking me, as though it were a mere bagatelle, to be his chronicler; and even less surprising that he should have been among the guests at the nuptials of Cardinal Fabrizio Spada's nephew. The Cardinal was Secretary of State to Pope Innocent XII, who hailed from the Kingdom of Naples, and was consequently of the Spanish party. Pope Innocent was about to die and for months all Rome had been preparing for the conclave. Melani was a French agent: in other words, a wolf in the sheepfold.

I knew the Abbot well and by now I needed few clues to make my mind up about him. One had but to follow one single elementary rule: to think the worst. It always worked. Having learned from my memoir that I worked for the Cardinal Secretary of State, Atto must deliberately have arranged to have himself invited to the Spada celebrations, perhaps taking advantage of his old acquaintance with the Cardinal, to which he had alluded. And now he intended to make use of me, well pleased with the fortuitous circumstance which had placed me where I could serve him. Perhaps he wanted something of me other than a mere chronicle of his feats and deeds with a view to the forthcoming conclave. But whatever could he have in mind this time? That was less easy for me to guess at. One thing was quite clear in my mind: never would I, insofar as my limited means permitted, allow Abbot Melani's plotting in any way to harm my master, Cardinal Spada. In this respect, at least, it was a good thing that Atto had assigned me that task: it enabled me to keep watch over him.

The chirurgeon had meanwhile completed his work, not without extracting from Atto a few hoarse protests at the pain and a fine heap of coin which had to be paid by the wounded man in the temporary absence of the Major-Domo.

"What kind of hospitality is that?" Atto commented acidly. "They stab the guests and then leave them to pay for their cure."

The Secretary for Protocol of the Villa Spada then arrived at Abbot Melani's bedside, in the absence of Don Paschatio, the Major-Domo, and ordered that he should at once be served luncheon, that two valets should stay to assist him with his meal, so as to give respite to the injured arm, and that his every desire should be satisfied forthwith; he apologised profusely, cursing in the most urbane language the delinquency and mendacity which with every Jubilee invariably reduced the Holy City to little better than a lazaret and assured him that he would be reimbursed immediately, with the necessary interest, and would indeed most certainly be liberally compensated for the grave affront which he had suffered, and said it was as well that they had hired a sergeant to watch over security at the villa during the festivities, but now the Major-Domo would call the catchpoll to account. He continued in this vein for a good quarter of an hour, without realising that Atto was falling asleep. I took advantage of this to leave.

The strange circumstances of the attack on Atto had left in me a turmoil of dismay, mixed with curiosity, and on the pretext of trimming some hedges by the entrance, I grasped the shears which I had in my apron and marched back to the gate.

"Was today's incident not enough for you, boy?"

I turned, or rather, I raised my eyes heavenward.

"The woods around here must be full of *cerretani*. Do you want to get into trouble yet again?"

It was Sfasciamonti, who was mounting guard.

"Oh, are you keeping watch?"

"Keeping watch, yes, keeping watch. These *cerretani* are a curse. May God save us from them, by all the stars of morning," quoth he, looking all around us with a worried air.

Cerretani: his insistence on that sinister-sounding term, the exact meaning of which escaped me, seemed almost an invitation to ask for some explanation.

"What is a *cerretano*?

"Shhh! Do you want to be overheard by everybody?" hissed Sfasciamonti, seizing my arm violently and dragging me away from the hedge, as though a *cerretano* might lie concealed under the greenery. He pushed me against the wall of the estate, looking to the right then to the left with an exaggeratedly alarmed demeanour, as though he feared an ambush.

"They are... How can I put it? They are starvelings, beggars, vagrants, men of the mobility... Nomads and vagabonds, in other words."

Far away, in the park, the notes of the orchestral players hired for the wedding mingled with the last hammer blows nailing together scaffolding ephemeral and theatrical.

"Do you mean to say that they are beggars, like the Egyptians?"

"Well, yes. I mean, no!" he shook himself, almost indignantly. "But what are you making me say? They are far more, I mean less... The *cerretani* have a pact with the Devil," he whispered, making the sign of the cross.

"With the Devil?" I exclaimed incredulously. "Are they perhaps wanted by the Holy Office?"

Sfasciamonti shook his head and raised his eyes dejectedly to the heavens, as though to emphasise the gravity of the matter.

"If you knew, my boy, if you only knew!"

"But what exactly do they get up to?"

"They ask for charity."

"Is that all?" I retorted, disappointed. "Begging is no crime. If they are poor, what fault is it of theirs?"

"Who told you they were poor?"

"Did you not tell me just now that they are mendicants?"

"Yes, but there are those who beg by choice, not only necessity."

"By choice?" I repeated, laughing, beginning to suspect that within that mountain of muscle called Sfasciamonti there might be no more than half an ounce of brain.

"Or better: for lucre. Begging is one of the best-paying trades in the world, whether you believe that or not. In three hours, they earn more than you can in a month."

I was speechless.

"Are they many?"

"Certainly. They are everywhere."

For a moment, I was struck by the certainty with which he replied to my last question. I saw him look about himself and scrutinise the avenue full of carriages and bustling with servants, as though he were afraid of having spoken too freely.

"I have already raised the matter with the Governor of Rome, Monsignor Pallavicini," he resumed, "but no one wants to know about this. They say, Sfasciamonti, calm down. Sfasciamonti, go take a drink. But I know it: Rome is full of *cerretani* and no one sees them. Whenever something ugly happens, it is always their doing."

"Do you mean that, even before, when you were following that young man and Abbot Melani was wounded. . ."

"Ah yes, the *cerretano* wounded him."

"How do you know that he was a *cerretano*?"

"I was at the San Pancrazio Gate when I recognised him. The police have been on his heels for some time, but one can never catch these *cerretani*. I knew at once that he was up to some mischief, that he had some mission to accomplish. I did not like the fact that he was so close to the Villa Spada, so I followed him."

"A mission? And what makes you so sure of that?" I asked with a hint of scepticism.

"A *cerretano* never goes down the street without looking to the right and to the left, in search of people's purses and many other such knavish and swindling things. They are arrant rogues, forever robbing, loitering and engaging in acts of poltroonery or luxuriousness. I know them well, that I do: those eyes that are too sly, that rotten look, they are all like that. A *cerretano* who walks looking in front of him, like ordinary people, is certainly on the point of committing some major outrage. I cried out until the other sergeants of the villa heard me. A pity he escaped, or we'd have known more."

I thought of how Abbot Melani would behave in my place.

"I'll wager that you'll manage to obtain information," I hazarded, "and so to discover what became of that *cerretano*. Abbot Melani, who is lodging here at the Villa Spada, will certainly be most grateful to you," said I, hoping to arouse the catchpoll's cupidity.

"Of course, I can obtain information. Sfasciamonti always knows whom to ask," he replied, and I saw shining in his eyes, not so much the hope of gain as professional pride.

છે‍જ

Sfasciamonti had resumed his rounds and I was still watching his massive figure merge into the distant curve of the outer wall when I noticed a bizarre young man, as curved and gangling as a crane, coming towards me.

"Excuse me," he asked in a friendly tone, "I am secretary to Abbot Melani, I arrived with him this morning. I had to return to the city for a few hours and now I can no longer find my way. How the deuce does one get into the villa? Was there not a door with windows in it here in front?"

I explained to him that there was indeed a door with a window, but that was behind the great house.

"Did you not say that you are secretary to Abbot Melani, if I heard you correctly?" I asked in astonishment, for Atto had said nothing to me about his not being alone.

"Yes, do you know him?"

❧❦

"About time! Where were you hiding?" snapped Abbot Melani, when I brought his secretary to his apartment.

While escorting him to Atto, I was able to observe him better. He had a great aquiline nose planted between two blue eyes which sheltered behind a pair of spectacles with unusually thick and dirty lenses and were crowned by two fair and bushy eyebrows. On his head, a forelock strove in vain to distract attention from his long, scrawny neck, on which sat an insolently pointed Adam's apple.

"I. . . went to pay my respects to Cardinal Casanate," said he by way of an excuse, "and I tarried awhile too long."

"Let me guess," quoth Atto, half in amusement, half in irritation. "You will have spent plenty of time in the antechamber, they'll have asked you three thousand times who you were and who was sending you. In the end, after yet another half an hour's wait, they will have told you that Casanate was dead."

"Well, just so. . ." stammered the other.

"How many times must I insist that you are always to tell me where you are going, when you absent yourself? Cardinal Casanate has been dead these six months now: I knew that and I could have spared you the loss of face. My boy," said Atto, turning to me, "this is Buvat, Jean Buvat. He works as a scribe at the Royal Library in Paris and he is a good man. He is somewhat absent-minded and rather too fond of his wine; but he has the honour to serve sometimes in my retinue, and this is one such occasion."

I did indeed recall that he was a collaborator of Atto's, as the Abbot had told me at the time of our first encounter, and that he was a copyist of extraordinary talent. We saluted one another with an embarrassed nod. His shirt ill tucked into his breeches and ballooning out, and the laces of his sleeves tightened into a knot with no bow were further signs of the young man's distracted nature.

"You speak our language very well," said I, addressing him in affable tones, in an attempt to make amends for the Abbot's brutality.

"Ah, spoken tongues are not his only talent," interjected Atto. "Buvat is at his best with a pen in his hand, but not like you: you create, he copies. And he does that like no other. But of this we shall speak another time. Go and change your clothes, Buvat, you are not presentable."

Buvat retired without a word into the small adjoining room, where his couch had been arranged among the trunks and portmanteaux.

Since I was there, I spoke to Atto of my conversation with Sfasciamonti.

ﻬ

"*Cerretani*, you tell me: canters, secret sects. So, according to your catchpoll, that tatterdemalion came accidentally with dagger drawn to try out his blade on my arm. How interesting."

"Have you another hypothesis?" I asked, seeing his scepticism.

"Oh, no, indeed not. That was just a manner of speaking," said he, laconically. "After all, in France too something of the kind exists among mendicants; even if people know of these things only by hearsay and never anything more precise."

The Abbot had received me with his windows open onto the gardens, wearing a dressing gown as he sat in a fine red velvet armchair beside a table bearing on the remains of a sumptuous luncheon: the bones of a large black umber, still smelling of wild fennel. I was reminded that I had not yet eaten that morning and felt a subtle languor in my stomach.

"I do know of a number of ancient traditions," continued Atto, massaging his wounded arm, "but these are things that have now been somewhat lost. Once in Paris, there was the Great Caesar, or King of Thulé, the sovereign of those ragamuffins and vagabonds. He would cross the city on a wretched dog-cart, as though mimicking a real sovereign. They say that he had his court, his pages and his vassals in every province. He would even summon the Estates-General."

"Do you mean an assembly of the people?"

"Exactly, but instead of nobles, priests and ladies, he would summon thousands of the halt, the lame and the blind, thieves, beggars, mountebanks, whores and dwarves. . . Yes, I mean all manner of beings," he broke off, hastening to correct himself, "but please do remove that apron with all those tools, it must be so heavy," said he, trying to change the subject.

I did not take offence at Abbot Melani's unfortunate expression; well I knew that many of my less fortunate fellows populated the dark lairs of the criminal fraternity, and I was aware that I for my part had been kissed by good fortune.

Buvat had returned, washed, combed and wearing clean clothes, but the sateen of his dark green shoes was visibly threadbare, if not torn; one of the oaken heels was shattered and the buckles dangled, almost completely ripped away from their moorings.

"I left my new shoes behind at the Palazzo Rospigliosi," he at last summoned up the courage to admit, "but I promise you that I shall go and retrieve them before evening."

"Take care not to forget your head, then," said the Abbot with a sigh of resignation that betrayed contempt, "and do not waste time loafing around as usual."

"How is your arm?" I asked.

"Magnificent, I simply adore being sliced up with a sharp blade," he replied, remembering at last to open the letter which had been delivered to him.

As he read it, a rapid succession of contrasting expressions crossed his features: first he frowned, then his face opened for a few instants in a fleshy and heart-warming smile that caused the dimple on his chin to tremble. At length, he looked pensively out of the window, his gaze lost in the sky. He had grown pale.

"Some bad tidings?" I asked timidly, exchanging a questioning glance with his secretary.

We understood from the vacant look on the Abbot's face that he had heard nothing.

"Maria. . ." I seemed to hear him murmur, before slipping the badly crumpled letter into the pocket of his dressing gown. Suddenly, Atto Melani looked old and tired again.

"Now go away. You too, please, Buvat. Leave me alone."

"But. . . are you sure that you need nothing else?" I asked hesitantly.

"Not now. Kindly return tomorrow evening at nightfall."

We had left the Abbot's apartments and descended the service stairs, and within moments my forehead and that of Buvat felt again the scorching breath of the afternoon heat.

I was dumbstruck: why had Atto fallen into such grave prostration? Who was the mysterious Maria whose name had so softly touched his lips? Was she a woman of flesh and blood or had he perhaps invoked the Blessed Virgin?

In any case, I thought, as I walked vigorously beside Buvat, it all seemed inexplicable. Atto's faith was certainly not fervent: never – not even at moments of the greatest danger – did I once recall him invoking the assistance of heaven. And yet it would be even stranger if this Maria were a woman of this world. The sigh with which Atto had murmured that name and the pallor which came into his face suggested a promise not kept, an old and unrequited passion, a torment of the heart: in short, a love entanglement.

Love for a woman: the one test, I thought, to which Atto the castrato would never be equal.

"You will have a long ride under the sun to Palazzo Rospigliosi, if you want to recover your shoes," said I, turning to Buvat, as I looked in the direction of the stables, seeking the groom.

"Alas," he replied with a grimace of discontent, "and I have not even had lunch."

I seized the opportunity without an instant's hesitation.

"If you so desire, I shall arrange for something to be prepared for you quickly in the kitchens. That is, of course, if you do not mind. . ."

Abbot Melani's secretary did not need to be asked twice. We turned swiftly on our heels and, after leaving the great house through the back door we were soon in the chaos of the Villa Spada's kitchens.

There, amidst the to-ing and fro-ing of the scullions who were cleaning and the assistant cooks who were getting ready to prepare the evening meal, I gathered together a few leftovers: three spiny needlefish cleansed of their salt, two unleavened ring-cakes and a fine white and azure chinoiserie in the form of a goblet, full of green olives with onions. I also obtained a small carafe of Muscatel wine. For myself, by now almost dying of hunger, I broke off a pair of rough hunks from a large cheese with herbs and honey and laid them on lettuce leaves which I retrieved still fresh from the remains of the luncheon's garnishings. It was certainly not enough to sate my appetite after a day's work, but it would at least enable me to survive until suppertime came.

In the febrile activity of the kitchens, it was not easy to find a corner in which to consume our late meal. What was more, I was looking for a discreet recess in which to further my acquaintance with that strange being who was acting as secretary to Atto Melani. Thus I might perhaps be able to clarify my ideas somewhat about this Maria and the singular behaviour of the Abbot, as well as the plans which the latter was hatching for his own future and, *a fortiori*, for mine.

I therefore proposed to Buvat, who needed no persuading, that we should sit on the grass in the park, in the shade of a medlar or peach tree, where we should also enjoy the advantage of being able to pluck a tasty fruit for our dessert directly from the tree. Without so much as a by-your-leave, we seized a basket and a double piece of jute and walked along the gravel scorched by the midday sun in the direction of the chapel of the Villa Spada. The dense grove of delights which stood behind it was the ideal place for our improvised picnic. Once within the perfumed shade of the undergrowth, the soft freshness of the ground gave instant relief to the soles of our feet. We would have settled on the edge of the wood near the chapel if a subdued and regular snoring had not revealed to us the presence of the chaplain, Don Tibaldutio Lucidi, curled up in the arms of Morpheus, evidently having thought the time ripe to enjoy a brief respite from the fatigues of divine service. After, therefore, placing a certain distance between the chaplain and ourselves, we at length chose as our roof the welcoming umbrella of a fine plum tree replete with ripe fruit, ringed by little wild strawberry bushes.

"So you are a scribe at the Royal Library in Paris," said I to open our conversation, as we stretched out the ample piece of sacking on the sward.

"Scribe to His Majesty and writer on my own behalf," he replied, half seriously and half facetiously as he fumbled greedily in the basket of provisions. "What Abbot Melani said of me today is not exact. I do not only copy, I also create."

Buvat had resented Atto's judgement, yet there was a hint of self-deprecating irony in his voice, the fruit of that resigned disposition which – in elevated minds destined to fill subaltern roles – results from the impossibility of being taken seriously, even by themselves.

"What do you write?"

"Above all, philology, although anonymously. On the occasion of a pilgrimage I made to Our Lady of Loreto, in the Marches of Ancona, I arranged for the printing of an edition of certain ancient Latin inscriptions which I had discovered many years previously."

"In the Marches of Ancona, did you say?"

"Yes," he replied bitterly, allowing himself to fall to the ground as he plunged his fingers into the goblet of olives. "*Nemo propheta in patria*, saith the Evangelist. In Paris I have never published a thing: I must even struggle to obtain any pay. 'Tis as well that Abbot Melani is there to commission some small piece of work from time to time, otherwise that envious old skinflint of a librarian. . . But do tell me about yourself. It seems that you too write, or so the Abbot tells me."

"Er. . . not exactly, I have never had anything printed. I should have liked to do so, but did not have the means," I replied, embarrassedly turning away my gaze and pretending to fuss over serving him some slices of needlefish with butter. I said nothing to him about my one and only opus, the voluminous memoir of the events which had befallen the Abbot and myself at the Donzello inn many years before, and which Atto had now stolen from me.

"I understand. But now, if I am not mistaken, the Abbot has commissioned you to keep a record of these days," he replied, grasping an unleavened *focaccia* and greedily hollowing it out to make room for the stuffing.

"Yes, although it is still far from clear to me what I am supposed to. . ."

"He mentioned his intention to me, saying that you do not write at all badly. You are fortunate. Melani pays handsomely," he continued, slipping a pair of fish slices into the *focaccia*.

"Ah yes," I concurred, glad that the conversation was at last turning towards Atto, "and, by the way, what kind of work were you telling me that Abbot Melani commissions you to carry out?"

Buvat seemed not to have heard. He paused, as though reflecting, taking his time and spraying the stuffed *focaccia* with lemon, whereupon he asked me: "Why not show me what you have written? Perhaps I could help you to find a printer. . ."

"Mmm, it would not be worth the trouble, Signor Buvat. It is but a diary, and it is written in the vulgar tongue. . ." said I, fumbling for pretexts with my nose buried in my lumps of cheese with herbs, yet deploring the weakness of my excuse.

"And what does that signify?" retorted Buvat, brandishing his bread in protest. "We are no longer in the sixteenth century! Besides, were you or were you not born free? Therefore, you can work in your own way. And just as you would not be compelled to justify yourself to anyone for having written in German or in Hebrew, so you need not justify yourself for having written in the vernacular."

He broke off to take a bite of his meal, while with his other hand he gestured to me to pass him the wine.

"And is the majesty of the vulgar tongue not such that it may offer a worthy place to every subject, e'en to matters most exquisite?" he declaimed with his mouth full. "The Reverend Monsignor Panigirola expressed therein the deepest mysteries of theology, as did before him those two most singular minds, Monsignor Cornelio Muso and Signor Fiamma. The most excellent Signor Alessandro Piccolomini found a place in it for almost all philosophy; Mattiolo adapted thereto almost all simple medicine and Valve, all anatomy. Can you not find room in it for the mere bagatelle of a journal? Where the Queen, namely Theology, may commodiously dwell, there too may enter the Maiden Philosophy, and with yet greater ease the Housewife Medicine; how then could there be no place for a mere serving wench like a diary?"

"But my vernacular is not even Tuscan but the Roman tongue," I countered, chewing the while.

"'Ah, so you have not written in Tuscan!' Thus would the master Aristarchus pass sentence. Yet, I tell you that you wrote not in Tuscan as you wrote not in German, for you are a Roman and whosoever would take pleasure in things Tuscan, let him then read Boccaccio and Bembo. That will soon tire him of his Tuscan tastes." Such was the abrupt riposte of my companion, striking up bizarre poses and speaking with the hoarsest of voices before concluding with a great gulp of Muscatel.

A fine, sharp intellect, this Buvat, thought I, as I tore off a good piece of lettuce. Despite the sweet freshness of the salad, I felt a slight twinge of envy burning my stomach: if only I too possessed his same quick wit. What was more, being French, he was not even expressing himself in his mother tongue. Ah, the lucky man!

"I must say, nevertheless," he was at pains to make clear, as he went for the onions with a will, "that you Italians are beset by the most evil custom: as a people, you are veritable dealers in envy. But what kind of barbarous practice is this? What manner of inhuman trade is it to be the mortal enemy of another's praise! No sooner does a good mind make his way forward among you with growing renown and reputation, than he becomes a prey to great locusts which infest him and tear him to pieces, and spread invective and calumny in his path until his worth often falls back into the dust."

He was surely right, I reflected, with the ease in reaching agreement of one who has just allayed the pangs of hunger, yet I was by no means persuaded that such a vice was exclusively Italian. Had he not himself complained of the vexations which he had been compelled to suffer at the hands of his own envious chief librarian who would let him die of hunger rather than part with a penny? And had he not only moments earlier confessed to me that in Paris they would not let him publish so much as a single line, while in Italy he had found a literary refuge? I did not, however, point this out to him. A weakness common to all peoples, apart from the Italians, is national pride. And I had no interest in wounding that of Jean Buvat; on the contrary.

Our collation was now drawing to a close. I had succeeded in drawing nothing from Jean Buvat about Abbot Melani, indeed, the conversation had been diverted perilously close to my memoir; not that the Abbot did not deserve that I should denounce his theft to his scribe, only that this would surely have unleashed a whole series of questions about Atto from Buvat, nor did it seem in the least judicious to betray the misdeeds of his patron. I therefore changed the subject, pointing out to Buvat – who, as I spoke, continued tirelessly poking around with his hand in the basket of provisions – that we had just eaten all the food we had brought with us and it remained for us only to pick some good fruit from the boughs of the plum tree whose shade we were enjoying. It was, for obvious reasons, Buvat who took upon himself the task of harvesting the fruit, whilst I looked to polishing the ripe plums with the jute and arranging them in our empty basket. The conversation having died away of its own accord, we swallowed a good basketful in religious silence, interrupted only by the parabolic curves described by the plum stones, laid bare by the labours of our jaws.

Perhaps it was the rhythmical patter of plum stones on the fresh grass under the trees, or perhaps the gentle rustling of the fronds caressed by the zephyrs of early summer, or yet the wild strawberries which – our bodies by now stretched out on the damp maternal bosom of the earth – we picked directly with our lips, or mayhap all these things together; anyway, I know not how it came to pass, but we fell asleep. And, almost in unison, hearing Buvat's snores and telling myself that I must shake him, for he had to go into town to recover his shoes, otherwise he would not return in time before evening, I heard another loud noise grow yet louder, drowning his snoring, and this noise was far nearer and more familiar: I too had dozed off and was blissfully snoring.

Evening the First
7ᵀᴴ JULY, 1700

✠

The sun was setting when sounds awoke us. The park of the Villa Spada was now becoming animated by the strolling and conversations of the guests who wandered about admiring the scenic constructions which would, two days hence, provide a worthy setting for the Rocci-Spada wedding, and the echo of voices reached even into our little thicket.

"Eminence, permit me to kiss your hands."

"My dearest Monsignor, what a pleasure to encounter you!" came the reply.

"And what pleasure is mine, Eminence!" said a third voice.

"You too, here?" resumed the second speaker. "My dearest, most esteemed Marchese, I am almost speechless for joy. But wait, you have not given me time to salute the Marchesa!"

"Eminence, I too would kiss your hands," echoed a feminine voice.

As I would later be able to tell without a moment's hesitation (having seen them time and time again during those festive days), those who were thus exchanging compliments were the Cardinal Durazzo, Bishop of Faenza, whence he had just arrived, Monsignor Grimaldi, President of the Victualling Board, and the Marchese and Marchesa Serlupi.

"How went your journey, Eminence?"

"Eh, eh, 'twas somewhat fatiguing, what with the heat. I leave you to imagine. But as God willed it, we did arrive. I came only out of the love I bear the Secretary of State, let that be clear. I am no longer of an age for such entertainments. Too hot for an old man like me."

"Indeed yes, it is so hot," assented the Monsignor condescendingly.

"One seems almost to be in Spain, where they tell me 'tis so very torrid that it feels almost like fire," said the Marchese Serlupi.

"Oh no, in Spain one is very well indeed, I retain the most excellent memory of that land. A splendid memory, of that I can assure you. Oh! Excuse me, I have just seen an old friend. Marchesa, my compliments!"

I saw Cardinal Durazzo, followed by a servant, break off somewhat brusquely the conversation which he had only just begun and move immediately away from the trio to approach another eminence whom I was later to recognise as Cardinal Barberini.

"Now really, that allusion. . ." I heard Marchesa Serlupi upbraiding her husband.

"What allusion? I didn't mean to say anything. . ."

"You see, Marchese," said Monsignor Grimaldi, "if Your Benevolence will permit me to explain, Cardinal Durazzo, before receiving his cardinal's hat, was Nuncio to Spain."

"And so?"

"Well, it seems – but this is of course only gossip – that His Eminence was not at all appreciated by the King of Spain and, what is more, and this however is certain truth, the kinsfolk whom he brought in his train were assaulted by persons unknown, and one of them died of his wounds. So, you can imagine, with the times in which we are living. . ."

"What do you mean?"

Monsignor Grimaldi glanced indulgently at the Marchesa.

"It means, dearest husband of mine," she broke in impatiently, "that since His Eminence is among the *papabili*, the likely candidates at the forthcoming conclave, he takes umbrage at even the slightest reference to the Spaniards, for that could put an end to his election. We spoke of these things at our home only two days ago, if I am not mistaken."

"I really cannot be expected to remember everything," grumbled the Marchese Serlupi, feeling bewildered as he realised the *faux pas* he had just made before a possible future pontiff, while his wife took her leave of Monsignor Grimaldi with a smile of benevolent forbearance and the latter greeted another guest.

That was the first occasion on which I became fully aware of the true character of the festivities which were about to begin. Abbot Melani was right. Though all in the villa seemed designed for revelry and to divert the mind away from serious matters, yet the hearts and minds of the participants were focused on the affairs of the day: above all, on the imminent conclave. Every discourse, every phrase, every single syllable was capable of causing the eminences and princes present to jump in their seats as though prodded with a spike. They had come pretending to seek distractions, while in reality they were present at the villa of the Secretary of State only in order to seek their own advancement, or that of the powers which they served.

At that very moment, I realised that the personage whom Monsignor Grimaldi had gone to greet was none other than Cardinal Spada himself, who, after duly saluting Grimaldi, continued on a tour of inspection accompanied by his Major-Domo, Don Paschatio Melchiorri. Despite his purple cardinal's cape, I had almost failed to recognise Fabrizio Spada, so furious was his countenance; he seemed nervous and distracted.

"And the theatre? Why is the theatre not yet ready?" fumed the Secretary of State, panting at the heat as he walked from the little grove towards the great house.

"We have almost attained the optimum, Your Eminence, that is to say, we have made great progress and we have practically resolved, almost resolved the problem of the. . ."

"Signor Major-Domo, I do not want progress, I want results. Do you or do you not realise that the guests are already arriving?"

"Your Eminence, yes, of course, nevertheless. . ."

"I cannot see to everything, Don Paschatio! I have other matters on *my* mind!" snapped the Cardinal, at once exasperated and disconsolate.

The Major-Domo nodded and bowed agitatedly without succeeding in getting in a single word.

"And the cushions? Have the cushions been sewn?"

"Almost, almost completely, Your Eminence, only a very few. . ."

"I see, they are not ready. Am I to seat the aged members of the Holy College on the bare ground?"

With these words, Cardinal Spada, followed by a throng of servants and retainers, turned his heel on poor Don Paschatio, who remained immobile in the middle of the avenue, unaware that he was being observed by me as he dusted down his shoes which were bedaubed with mire.

"Heavens, my shoes!" muttered Buvat, rising with a start at the sight of Don Paschatio's gesture. "I was meant to go and fetch them."

It was, however, by then too late to fetch his shoes at Palazzo Rospigliosi and so, jumping lightly to my feet, I suggested that we should, taking unfrequented byways, make our way discreetly to the attic of the great house, where we could be sure of finding a servant willing to lend him a pair in better condition than his own.

"A lackey's footwear!" mumbled Buvat with a hint of shame, while we hurriedly piled the remains of our picnic into the basket, "but they will surely be better than my own."

With the rolled-up piece of jute under my arm, we turned furtively away from where we could hear voices. We took care to keep to the edge of the park, far from the festive lights, moving along the rim of the dark slope that led down to the vineyard of the villa. Aided and abetted by twilight, we had no difficulty in reaching the service entrance of the house.

Once Buvat was, for a modest consideration, shod with a fine pair of livery shoes in black patent leather with bows, we hurried to our appointment with Abbot Melani. We had no need even to knock at his door: the Abbot, bewigged, powdered and resplendent with ribbons and ruffles, wearing embroidered satin ceremonial dress, his cheeks shining with carmine red and dotted with black beauty spots after the French fashion (and not at all small, but large, ridiculous ones) awaited us on the threshold, nervously ill-treating his walking-cane. I noticed that he was wearing white stockings instead of his usual red abbot's hose.

"Where the deuce have you been hiding, Buvat? I have been waiting for you for over an hour. You would not wish me to come down unaccompanied like a plebeian, would you? All the other guests are already in the garden: explain to me why I came here. Was it to look down from the window at the Marchese Serlupi chattering blissfully away with Cardinal Durazzo, while I rot here in my chamber?"

The Abbot's gaze was drawn suddenly to the shine which the lackey's shoes worn by his secretary gave off in the candle-light.

"Say nothing. I do not wish to know," he warned, raising his eyes heavenward, when Buvat most unwillingly resigned himself to explaining what had happened.

Thus they set off, without Melani paying the slightest attention to my presence. As Buvat nodded to me in sorrowful commiseration, Atto turned to me without stopping and gestured that I was to follow him.

"Keep your eyes open, my boy. Cardinal Spada is Secretary of State, and if anything important is unfolding, I am sure that you will know how to catch the scent of it. We are certainly not interested in his arguments with his Major-Domo."

"In truth, I never promised to spy on your behalf."

"You will have to spy on nothing whatever. In any case, you would not be capable of it. You have only to make good use of your eyes, ears and brain. That's all you need to know the world. Now, get on with it. That is all. Tomorrow at dawn, here in my chambers."

How eager the Abbot was, I noted, to join in the conversations with the other illustrious guests of the Spada family, and certainly not from any desire for distraction. Yet it was clear that he had, from his window, overheard Cardinal Fabrizio rebuking Don Paschatio and he would thus have noted the singular apprehensiveness of the Secretary of State. Perhaps that was why he had made me that last recommendation: to keep my eyes well trained on the master of the house.

That night, I thought, it would be better to stay at the great house, seeing that I had an appointment with Atto at a very early hour on the morrow, but above all, because my Cloridia was not at home. To sleep in our empty bed was for me the worst of torments. Better then that I should sleep on the improvised couch that awaited me in the servants' hall under the eaves.

I was on my way down to offer my last services to the Major-Domo when I remembered that I had left my gardener's apron and tools behind in Atto's lodgings. The Abbot would not, I thought, mind if I entered briefly to retrieve it. I obtained permission from one of the *valets de chambre* to take the keys to Melani's apartment. I had worked long enough among the villa's servants for them to trust me blindly.

Having entered and taken my apron, I was about to leave again when my attention was caught by what lay on Atto's bureau: a neat pile of absorbent powder and, nearby, two broken goose plumes. The Abbot must have written much, and in a great state of excitation, during our absence that afternoon. Only a fevered hand could have twice broken a pen. Might this have something to do with the letter which he had received and which had so perturbed him?

I glanced out of the window. Abbot Melani and Buvat were moving down one of the walks in the garden. They were on the point of disappearing from view when I remembered that a short while before I had, without being certain of recognising it, glimpsed a device in Atto's lodgings. I looked around me. Where could he have hidden it? On the dining chair, that was it. I was not mistaken. It was a telescope. Although I had never held one in my hands, I knew what these things looked like and how they functioned, for in Rome the celebrated Vanvitelli used similar devices to paint his famous and wonderful views of the city.

So I took the telescope and brought it to my eye, pointing it at the figures of Atto and his secretary now receding in the distance. I was surprised and delighted by the miraculous power of that machine, capable of rendering distant things near and minute things large. Thus, like wit, to cite Father Tesauro, it is able to render interesting that which is tedious, and gay, that which is sad. Flushing with emotion, with my eyelids still recoiling from the hard metal of the device, I aimed in error at the indigo of the sky and then at the green of the vegetation, at last succeeding in pointing its powerful regard in the right direction.

I saw Atto stop and bow deeply to a pair of cardinals, then to a noblewoman accompanied by two young ladies. Buvat, with a glass of his beloved wine already in one hand, tripped over a piece of wood and came close to falling against the noble lady. Melani went to great lengths to present his excuses to the three ladies, then upbraided Buvat discreetly but bitterly, while the latter, after setting down his glass, brushed the soil clumsily from his black stockings. It was not, however, easy to move along the drives; all around were the usual comings and goings of lackeys, servants and labourers, while the walks still had not been cleared of materials and refuse from the works for the construction of the theatre, the ephemeral architectural effects, the open-air tables, not to mention the gardening and irrigation works.

No sooner had I seen Atto and Buvat meet and talk to another pair of gentlemen than I decided. This was the opportune moment. If the French wolf had found his way into the sheepfold of the little Spanish lambkins, that gave me the chance now to spy out the wolf's lair.

To tell the truth, I was rather ashamed of my idea. The Abbot had taken me into his service, paying me handsomely. I was therefore beset by some hesitation. Yet, said I to myself at length, I may perhaps be more useful if I know better the requirements of my temporary master: including those which, for whatever reason, he had not yet revealed to me.

I therefore began to explore the apartment with some circumspection in search of the letters, or more probably *one single letter* which the Abbot had penned with such passion during our absence. I was certain that he had not yet had it sent; Buvat who, as the Abbot had already told me also copied his letters, had returned too late to produce a copy for Atto's archives, in accordance with the common practice among gentlemen. This was evident from the fact that I found no traces of sealing wax on the bureau, and the table candle (on which Atto would have had to heat the wax to seal his letter) was still uncut.

I searched fruitlessly. In Atto's trunk and among the things in the two wardrobes with which his apartment was furnished there was, on the face of it, no trace of the missives. Next to a geographical map and the manuscript of a number of cantatas, I came upon a little folder of commentaries on items of news. It was a set of notices and flyers from gazettes, heavily marked and annotated by the Abbot. They dealt for the most part with matters pertaining to the Holy College of Cardinals, and a number of Atto's notes referred to events far back in time. It was, in substance, a collection of gossip on the relations between the various eminences, on their rivalries, the tricks played on each other during conclaves, and so on and so forth. I found no little amusement in perusing them, however rapidly.

Spurred on by the scant time at my disposal, I soon took my search further. I opened a little medicine chest which, however, revealed only creams and ointments, a perfume for wigs and a bottle of the Queen of Hungary's Water; then, a second chest with a little mirror, a brooch, metal-tipped cords, a belt and two watch dials. I found nothing, nothing. My heart leapt suddenly when, lifting a woollen cloth, I discovered a pistol. Seventeen years earlier, he had got the better of our adversaries by disguising a pipe as a pistol, succeeding perfectly in deceiving the enemy. Now, however, he must truly fear for his own safety, said I to myself, if he has decided to travel armed.

After looking through shoes and purses, I began unwillingly to rummage through clothing; as usual, the Abbot had brought with him enough to last ten years. I diligently perused the long series of greatcoats, collars, short coats, hussar-style cloaks and cloaks in the

Brandenburg style, capes and capouches, sashes and jabots in pleated Venetian lace, breeches, cuffs, mantles of pleated silk and long stockings. My rough hands smoothed the precious silks, the shining satins, the twills, the chamois leathers, the suedes, the damasks, the silk taffeta, the grograms, the striped and flowered linens, the ermines, with silks patterned or damasked, or in the Florentine style, the ferrandine silk and wool blends, the doublets, the brocaded cloth of gold and silver, the satins, shiny or quilted, the Milanese *salia* and the Genoese sateen. My eyes scanned the most *recherché* hues, from mouse-grey, pearl, fire, musk rose, dried roses, to speckled colours, scarlets, black cherry, dove-grey, jujube-red, *berrettino* grey, nacre, tawny, milky white, moiré and *gris castor*, and the silver and gold foil and thread of fringes and braiding.

Among all that rich attire, the mauve-grey soutane in which Abbot Melani had appeared to me on that day, after so many years' silence, seemed distinctly out of place. With surprise, I saw that there were in fact no other outmoded items of apparel in that sumptuous wardrobe; on the contrary. I quickly realised that Atto had worn it deliberately for my sake, so that the sudden change in his manner of dress should not add to the gradual erosion which time effects upon faces and to ensure that his appearance today should correspond as far as possible to my memory. In other words, he knew how much I had missed him and wished to make a strong impression.

Still uncertain whether I should be grateful to him or resentful (it depended from which viewpoint one chose to consider the matter), I examined the soutane, which, I confess, was for me not without precious and distant memories of my youth. On its breast I felt something which I took initially for a jewel of some sort, but it turned out to be sewn onto the inside. Examining the lining of the soutane, I discovered not without extreme surprise a small scapular of the Madonna of the Carmel, the miraculous little scapular which the Most Holy Virgin had promised would, if worn on one's person, free the wearer from the torments of purgatory on the first Saturday after their death. What had, however, captured my attention were three little protuberances: in a tiny bag sewn onto the scapular, exactly at the level of the heart, were three little pearls.

I recognised them at once: they were the three *margaritae*, the Venetian pearls which had played so important a part in the last stormy discussion between Atto and myself seventeen years earlier at the Inn of the Donzello, before we lost sight of one another. Only now did I learn that Atto had lovingly gathered them up from the floor where I had thrown them down in a rage, and kept them; and, for all these years, he had worn them close to his heart, perhaps in a mute prayer to the Holy Virgin. . .

The thought crossed my mind that Atto must not have worn the scapular with my little pearls every single day, since he had now left them hanging inside the soutane in the wardrobe. It was, however, also true that he had found me again, so perhaps he now considered his vow to have come to an end. Ah, rascal of an abbot, I protested inwardly, while yielding to emotion at discovering myself to be so dear to him; for all my old bitterness, I too still loved him from the depths of my soul, there was no use in denying that now. And if my feelings – with which I had lived uneasily for almost two decades – had not been extinguished by his most recent misdeeds, very well, I must then perhaps resign myself to that love.

I reproved myself severely for having wanted to spy on him, yet, when I was on the point of leaving shamefully, I stopped on the threshold, hesitating; I was no longer a child, the movements of my heart no longer obscured the light of the intellect. And the intellect was now whispering in my ear that, in any case, one could place but little trust in Atto.

It was thus that my state of mind altered yet again. Were it only for myself, I began to reason, never would I have dared violate the Abbot's privacy. Yet Atto's deep affection for me, as mine for him, must not make me forget the task I had assumed, namely to keep a diary of his words and deeds during those days, which might in all probability (of this I was certain) involve all manner of risks and pitfalls. What if someone were to accuse him of being in Rome in order to spy and to disrupt the proceedings of the forthcoming conclave? Such a danger was not that remote, given that he himself had made no mystery of his desire to protect the interests of the Most Christian King of France at the election of the next pontiff. This might also affect Cardinal Spada, my master and his unsuspecting host. It was therefore not only my right, I concluded, but my bounden duty, also toward my beloved family, to know both the nature and extent of the risks to which I was likely to be exposed.

With my scruples thus silenced, I therefore resumed my search. One last inspection under and behind the bed, on top of the wardrobes, under the cushions of the armchairs and the little brocatelle sofa ornamented with golden plumes proved fruitless. Behind the pictures, nothing; nor was there any sign of anyone having opened them to conceal anything between the canvas and the frame. Further investigations into the remaining anfractuosities of the apartment likewise yielded nothing. Buvat's few personal effects in the modest adjoining chamber concealed even less.

Yet I knew for a fact that Atto travelled, as I well recalled from our first encounter, with a fair quantity of paper. The times had changed, and I with them. Atto, however, had not; at least, not in the habits arising from his natural bent for intrigue and adventure. In order to act, he must know. In order to know, he must remember, and for that purpose he needed the letters, memoirs and notes which he carried with him, the living archive of a lifetime of spying.

It was then that, breaking off the pointless exercise of eyes and muscles, intent upon the search for the hidden papers, I had a flash of inspiration: specifically, a reminiscence from seventeen years before, a distant yet still vivid memory of how Atto and I had, by night, retraced the key to the mystery which had wound us in its coils. This had consisted of papers, and these we had found in a place to which instinct and logic (as well as good taste) had hitherto failed to lead us: within a pair of soiled drawers.

"You have underestimated me, Abbot Melani," I murmured to myself as, for the second time, I opened the basket of dirty clothes and groped, no longer among but inside them. "How very imprudent of you, Signor Atto, said I with a self-satisfied grin when, feeling inside a pair of Holland drawers, I felt crumpling beneath my fingers a bundle of papers. I grasped the drawers; the lining was not sewn but attached to the main body of the item of apparel by a series of minuscule hooklets. Once I had unfastened the latter, I could reach into the space between the two layers of stuff. This I did, and found my fingertips touching a wide, flat object. I extracted it. It was a parchment envelope, tied with a ribbon. It was well designed, in such a way as to contain a number of papers, and only those; in other words, it was as flat as a pancake. In silent triumph, I turned it over in my hands.

Not much time remained to me. Atto was certainly keen to explore the villa and to meet the other guests who, like him, had arrived early for the wedding. It would, however, take only some necessity on his part to return to his apartment for the Abbot to surprise me. I was spying upon a spy: I must move swiftly.

๛

I undid the bow. Before opening it I noted on the cover, written near the bottom in a minuscule hand, an inscription so tiny that it seemed destined only to be to be found by an eye already aware of its existence:

Spanish succession – Maria

I opened the envelope. A set of letters, all addressed to Melani, but all unsigned. The agitated, irregular calligraphy which appeared before my eyes seemed incapable of repressing any emotion. The lines were not, so to speak, confined by the margins of the page; the additions which the writer's hand had inserted into a number of sentences curled their way into the following lines. Moreover, this writing belonged without any possible doubt to a feminine hand. It seemed clearly to be that of the mysterious Maria: the name which I had overheard Atto sighing.

What the Spanish succession might be, I was soon to learn in great detail from those letters. The first letter, which seemed to be deliberately imprecise, so as to betray neither the identity of the writer nor morsels of news that might be too pleasing to unfriendly eyes, began, as I recall, as follows:

> *My dearest Friend,*
> *Here I am, already in the environs of Rome. Things are moving fast. I learned during a halt something of which you will already be apprised: a few days ago the Spanish Ambassador, the Duke of Uzeda, obtained a double audience with the Pope. On the day after he had attended the Holy Father in order to thank him for conferring a Cardinal's hat on his compatriot Monsignor Borgia, Uzeda received by special courier an urgent dispatch from Madrid, which induced the Duke to request yet another audience with His Holiness. He delivered a letter from the King of Spain, containing an entreaty: El Rey requests a mediation by Innocent XII on the question of the Succession!*
> *On the same day, our mutual friend the Secretary of State Cardinal Fabrizio Spada was seen to visit the Duke of Uzeda at the Spanish Embassy in Piazza di Spagna. The affair must have reached a turning point.*

Since I was not in the habit of reading gazettes, the question of the Spanish succession was not at all familiar to me. The mysterious correspondent, however, seemed very well informed.

I imagine that all Rome must be chattering about it. Our young Catholic King of Spain, Carlos II, is dying without heirs. El Rey is departing, my friend, ever more evanescent are the traces of his brief and dolorous sojourn on this earth; but no one knows to whom his immense kingdom will pass.

I remembered that Spain included Castile, Aragon, the overseas possessions and colonies, as well as Naples and Sicily: a multitude of territories.

Shall we, ev'ry one of us, be equal to the onerous task that awaits us? O, Silvio, Silvio! who in thine early years hast found the fates propitious, I tell thee, too early wit has ignorance for fruit.

I was utterly astonished. Why in the letter was Atto called by the name of Silvio? And whatever could those expressions signify which seemed to accuse Abbot Melani of ignorance and immaturity of mind?

The letter then came to an end on a no less cryptic note:

Tell Lidio that with respect to that whereon he questions me, I have no answer to give. He knows why.

I continued reading. Attached to the letter was a precise summary in the form of an appendix:

A CONSPECTUS OF THE PRESENT STATE OF AFFAIRS

It contained a mixture of information and, in sum, detailed the troubled progress of the Spanish succession in recent times.

Spain is in decline and no one thinks of the Catholic King with the same just terror as when the mind turns to the Most Christian King of France, Louis the Fourteenth, First-born Son of the Church. Yet the Sovereign of Spain by the Grace of God is King of Castile, of Aragon, of Toledo, Galicia, Seville, Granada, Córdoba, Nursia, Jaen, of the Algharbs of Algeciras, Gibraltar, the Canary Isles, the Indies, and of the Islands and Terra Firma of the Mare Oceanum, of the North, of the South, of the Philippines and of whatsoever other islands or Lands have been or may yet be discover'd. And, through the Crown of Aragon, the Heir will succeed to the Throne of Valencia, Catalonia, Naples, Sicily, Majorca, Minorca and Sardinia; without counting the State of Milan, the Duchies of Brabant, of Limburg, Luxembourg, Guilderland, Flanders and all the other Territories which in the Nether Lands belong or may belong to El Rey. He who sits on the Throne of Spain will truly be the Master of the World.

The King of Spain, or El Rey, as he was called by the mysterious epistler, was dying without direct heirs and this was what rendered so difficult the problem of determining who was to inherit all those enormous possessions scattered across the whole world, which made of the Spanish crown the globe's greatest kingdom. Until not long ago, as I learned from the remainder of the letter, there had in fact been an heir designated for the succession to the Spanish throne: this was the young Prince Elector of Bavaria, Joseph Ferdinand, who was in terms of blood relationships without a doubt best entitled to succeed to the throne of Spain. Yet, little over a year before, Joseph Ferdinand had suddenly died: a death so unexpected and so weighed down with consequences that a suspicion of poisoning at once spread through the courts of Europe.

There now remained two possibilities: the dying Sovereign of Spain, Charles II, could name as his heir a nephew of the French Sovereign, Louis XIV, or a subject of the Emperor of Austria, Leopold I. Both solutions, however, were beset with risks and uncertainties. In the first case, France, which was the most feared military power in Europe, would also become the greatest monarchy in Europe and in the world, uniting *de facto* with its own overseas possessions those of the crown of Spain. In the second case, if Charles were to nominate a subject of Vienna, this would signify the rebirth of that empire which only the glorious Charles V had been able to unite under his sway: from Vienna to Madrid, from Milan to Sicily, from Naples to the distant Americas.

This second hypothesis was the more probable of the two, for Charles II was a Habsburg like Leopold of Austria.

Hitherto, the letter went on to explain, France had succeeded in maintaining equilibrium with its enemies (meaning, all the other states of Europe). The peace with Spain was indeed long-standing; and with England and Holland a pact had been agreed for the future partition of the enormous Spanish possessions, seeing that it had long been realised that Charles II was in no condition to have children. When, however, the partition pact had been made public, about a month previously, the Spaniards became furious: the King of Spain could not accept that the other states should be preparing to divide his kingdom among themselves as the centurions divided the raiment of Our Lord on the cross.

The report therefore concluded:

> *If El Rey dies now, there is a risk that the situation may become explo-*
> *sive. The pact of partition has become too difficult to implement. On the*

other hand, France cannot accept encirclement by the Empire. Nor can the others, from the Emperor Leopold I to the King of England and the Dutch heretic William of Orange, allow her to swallow Spain in a mouthful.

The next letter was written in another hand; it was Atto's reply, for which I had searched so hard. As I expected, it was not yet sealed, pending Buvat's preparation of a copy for the Abbot's archives:

Most Clement Madame,

As you well know, in these months, the Ambassadors of all the Powers and their Sovereign Lords are losing their heads utterly because of the Spanish Succession. All ears and all eyes are constantly on the lookout, hungry for news and for secrets to seize from the other Powers. All gravitates around the Ambassadors of Spain, France and the Empire; or Penelope and her two Suitors. All three Kingdoms await the opinion of the Pope concerning the Succession: France or the Empire? What will be the advice of His Holiness to the Catholic King? Will he choose the Duke of Anjou or the Archduke Charles?

All was now clear to me: in Rome would be decided the fate of the Spanish Empire. Evidently, all three powers were prepared to accept the judgement of the Holy Father. The noblewoman's letter had, in fact, spoken of mediation by the Pontiff, not of an opinion.

Here in Rome, the air is pregnant with a thousand turmoils. All this is further complicated by the fact that, as you know, all three Ambassadors of the great Powers, namely Spain, France and the Empire, are new to these parts. Count Leopold Joseph von Lamberg, Ambassador of His Caesarean Majesty Leopold I of Habsburg, Holy Roman Emperor, arrived here some six months ago.

The Duke of Uzeda, a sharp-witted Spaniard, has been in post for about a year.

The same is true of the French diplomatic representative, Louis Grimaldi, Duke of Valentinois and Prince of Monaco, a great polemicist, who does more harm than good and has already argued with half Rome over stupid questions of etiquette. So much so that His Majesty has been obliged to pull his ears and remind him above all to cultivate fruitful relations with the nation whose guest he is.

That one can do little for France. Fortunately, the Most Christian King need not count only on him.

But let us change the subject to ourselves. I hope that you are now in perfect health and will ever continue so to be. Alas, I cannot say the same of myself. Today, upon my arrival at the Villa Spada, a bizarre incident befell me: I was stabbed in the right arm by a stranger.

And here the Abbot, in truth exaggerating a little, dwelt at some length upon the blood which had stained his white shirt and the operations of the chirurgeon which he had borne heroically, and so on and so forth, rising to a paroxystic crescendo. . .

> *Ah, cruel stilet which pierced my tender side. . . Alas I'm tired! This painful wound makes me so weak I can't support me longer. The wound still stabs at me, and that most grievously.*

Did Atto wish to impress this Maria? The tone of the letter seemed to conceal a seductive intent.

Abbot Melani went on to write that, despite the fact that the sergeant of the villa was certain that it had been only a beggar, he, Atto, feared that he had not been a mere accidental victim but rather the target of an attempt on his life organised by the opposing faction; for which reason he intended to request a private audience with Ambassador Lamberg as soon as he – who was also among the guests at the wedding of Cardinal Fabrizio's nephew – arrived at Villa Spada.

> *However, dear Friend, let us cure the wound and not the offence, for vengeance ne'er did heal a wound.*

These revelations surprised me. I had noticed Atto's scepticism when I spoke to him of my conversation with Sfasciamonti; now, however, I discovered that Atto had very specific suspicions. Why had he not mentioned this to me? He could not fail to trust Buvat; he entrusted him with copying all his letters. Perhaps he did not trust me? This last supposition was however no less improbable: had he not paid me to be his chronicler? Nevertheless, I bethought myself, with Abbot Melani one could never be sure of anything. . .

The letter ended in honeyed tones, which I could scarce have imagined on the lips or pen of Atto Melani:

> *You cannot know how bitter was the Dolour inflicted on me by the Knowledge that you will tarry e'en longer at the Gates of Rome.*
>
> *Ah, cruel one! If thou hast shot at me, 'twas thine own Mark, and proper for thine Arrow. The Letter, which gave the deadly Wound, obeyed the sure direction of your lovely Eye.*
>
> *My Arm has once more begun to bleed and 'twill bleed on until it has the Joy and Honour to support Yours. Haste you then to the Villa Spada and to me, my most beloved Friend, or you will have me on your Conscience.*

After the intolerably cloying sirop of those lines, I read a postil:

> *Even now, then, is Lidio's Felicity Nothing to you?*

Here, once again, was that Lidio. I did not even ask myself who
this stranger with the curious name might be. I was most unlikely to
learn that unless I could first discover the identity of Abbot Melani's
mysterious correspondent.

So, I summed up, this Maria was also expected at the Villa Spada.
And she was late; that explained the frown on the face of Abbot Melani
when he read her letter. I reflected that she must be a noblewoman of
a certain age, given that Atto spoke to her as to an old friend. In the
two letters, moreover, he made no mention of her family; it seemed
indeed that she was travelling alone. She must truly be a personage
of great importance, as well as of high rank, thought I, if they had
dared invite her to the wedding unaccompanied: ancient and single noblewomen, whether or not they be widowed, generally enclose
themselves in the isolation of prayer, when not indeed in cloister.
They withdraw from society and no one dares disturb them save for
pious works. This lady seemed, what is more, to be of a truly singular
temperament to have accepted the invitation!

I felt deeply curious to know her or at least to know who she
might be. I glanced rapidly at the other letters in the bundle; they
were hers, and they spoke of events in Spain. She must be Spanish;
or perhaps an Italian (for she wrote my language so beautifully) who
dwelt there or at any rate possessed great interests in that country. In
all the epistles, the secret of the writer's identity was, alas, well preserved. I must therefore resign myself to awaiting her arrival at the
villa, who knows when; either that, or discreetly interrogate Buvat.

I put off reading these letters to another day; I had profited unduly
from the Abbot and his secretary's absence. I durst not risk discovery
one moment longer.

৵৽৹

As I had intended to do before my incursion into the Abbot's apartment, I returned downstairs in order to obtain something for supper
and then to present myself to the Major-Domo.

I returned the keys to the Abbot's chambers to their proper place
and was about to enter the kitchens when I saw the coachman who
served Cardinal Fabrizio at the Apostolic Palace emerging all breathless
and red in the face. I asked a Venetian milkmaid who frequented the
villa and was on the point of leaving whether by any chance something
had happened.

"No, 'tis nothing. 'Tis only Cardinal Spada who is always in a furious rush these days, for it seems there's much afoot at the Apostolic Palace. And it must be something really important to give him such a headache, that it must. His Eminency is always in such ill humour and the coachman is almost going out of his mind, what with carting the master back an' forth from a cardinal to an ambassador and then back again for some business about a papal bull or I know not what, and having to put up with his state of nerves."

I was dumbstruck. The power of women! This modest milkmaid had needed only the few minutes of her regular visit to the villa's kitchens to understand what it would have taken me a whole day, and much good fortune, to get wind of. I had come to realise this when my Cloridia became one of the most respected and sought-after midwives for Rome's noble matrons (and their maids): with all the news that she brought back home every day I could easily have filled a gazette.

"Ah, and please give my regards to the Signora your wife and a kiss to the little ones," added the milkmaid, as though she had been reading my thoughts. "You know, my sister's confinement has been going perfectly since la Cloridia brought that old goat of a brother-in-law of mine to reason. She's a really fine woman, your wife, you know."

Of course I knew that Cloridia was now not just a midwife but a veritable godmother: an authoritative and willing counsellor to whom women, both those of the people and society ladies, went for advice and assistance in the most intimate and delicate matters. From the education of the husband during his wife's pregnancy to the weaning of the infant: for every circumstance, my wife had a smile and the right words. Such was her ability that she was sometimes called upon by the famous *medicus* and chirurgeon Baiocco to assist him with confinements that took place within the ancient walls of the Fatebenefratelli Hospital on the island of San Bartolomeo on the Tiber.

Affable, gay, gracious, bantering, courageous, Cloridia always enheartened women with child, assuring them that they would give birth without much pain. She could tell that from many signs which, she swore, she had observed in others; the which, although untruths, were recommended even by Plato in *The Republic* for consoling the sick.

All in all, after fifteen years exercising the office of midwife, Cloridia was accorded by her women, and not only them, the respect due to a judge presiding over a family court.

Once I had quit the milkmaid, I found myself a place at a corner of the table where the servants were devouring their supper. While eating my meal in silence, I meditated upon Atto's words: to know the world, all you need is to make good use of your eyes, ears and brain. Was that not exactly what my Cloridia did too? I, however, was unable to do that, and I was perfectly aware of the fact; in this respect I had not progressed one iota since the days when I was a young and innocent apprentice at the Locanda del Donzello. In those days, inexperience played its part, but now I was, on the contrary, held back by an excess of accumulated experience which had prompted me to withdraw in disgust from the mean quotidian round of worldly affairs.

Perhaps my wife was right to reprove me for being a new Cincinnatus. It was true. Leaning upon my hoe and on Sundays over my books, I neither saw, heard nor ever asked myself questions. Even with the neighbours, I had been at pains never to form bonds of friendship, scarcely even of acquaintance. So much so that, whenever I happened to learn some news and to mention it to Cloridia in the evening, I would invariably receive the same reply: "Well, are you surprised? That's old hat. By now, everybody knows."

Mine was disdain for the world but also – yes, I must confess – fear of it, fear of the evil I had seen there.

Now, however, something had changed. The sudden reappearance of Abbot Melani had brought about an earthquake in my life. Cloridia would – I knew – mock me to scorn for allowing myself once more to be caught in Melani's gins. But what did that matter? I loved her so, even when she lashed me derisively with knowing words, as though I were a mere schoolboy. Besides, she'd not laugh so much at the twelve hundred scudi which my memoir had earned for us. . .

Yes, something had changed; although I remained a dwarf in body as in spirit, yet it was time now to disinter and put to good use those few talents which Divine Providence had given me. Of course, with Atto one knew where one was starting from but not where one would end up. On the other hand, as I had been able to discover from his scapular, old age had markedly increased the Abbot's fear of God.

How much did I really owe Abbot Melani? I owed him not only the disillusionment which had engendered so much mistrust in me, but also such good things as had happened in my poor life: Cloridia, above all. If the Abbot had not come seventeen years earlier to upset the rhythm of my days and those of the other lodgers at the Locanda del Donzello, never would I have approached my beloved wife, and she herself would have remained caught up forever in the turbid profession in which I had found her. Neither would I ever have been able to acquire the science of men's thought nor indeed knowledge of the affairs of the world, wherewith I was now measuring that world. It was, without a doubt, a most bitter science, but one which had from a tremulous lad forged a man.

After supper, I set such thoughts aside and, as I rose from the table, I began once again to reflect upon the latest news. Going by the information I had received from the milkmaid, I must acknowledge that Abbot Melani was right. On the upper storeys of the Apostolic Palace of Monte Cavallo, important manoeuvres were taking place.

Barely had I had time to take my cordial leave of the chief cook and set foot outside the kitchen than a voice recalled me to my duties: "Signor Master of the Fowls!"

He who was now calling me by a title which in reality I did not deserve was just the man I sought: Don Paschatio Melchiorri, the Major-Domo.

Don Paschatio was above all things respectful of the prerogatives of those whose labour he, with the most pompous and dignified ceremoniousness, lovingly directed; and since in Don Paschatio's eyes the first attribute to be respected was the title, he had liberally endowed each of his subordinates with a title in keeping with the magnificence of the Spada household, which we all humbly and faithfully served. So it was that I, who more and more frequently supplied the aviary with feed and water, had become the Master of the Fowls. A peasant from the neighbourhood who, from time to time performed the duties of hoeing, weeding and manuring the flower beds was no longer to be called Giuseppe (his real name) in Don Paschatio's presence, but Master of the Hoe. The husbandman of the vineyard, Lorenzo, who provided the Villa Spada with golden clusters of grapes and white wine, was graced with the title of Master Viticulturist. With the passing of time, similar names had been granted by Don Paschatio to all the servants of the villa, down to the last and humblest day-labourers like myself. When Don Paschatio was doing his rounds, 'twas midst a veritable flowering of sonorous titles, like "Master of the Horse, good day to you, Sir!", "Master Deputy Bursar, good evening!", "Master Assistant Steward, good day to you, show me the luncheon table!", while those whom he addressed were merely a groom, a clerk assisting with kitchen supplies and one of the cook's assistants. And this he did, not out of love for rhetoric, but from the highest regard for the service of his lord. One could have asked Don Paschatio quite unceremoniously whether one could cut off a finger, yet he'd reflect before refusing. No one, however, could ever have asked him to deprive himself of the pleasure and the honour of devotedly and faithfully serving the distinguished and noble Spada family.

It so happened that Don Paschatio had overheard me that evening taking my leave of the Steward with the words "Farewell till tomorrow, chief!", which he found undignified and over-familiar: "You see, Signor Master of the Fowls," quoth he, upbraiding me with courteous gravity, as though to put me on guard against some danger, "the Steward commands the cook, the carver, the scullions and the kitchen barons as well, of course, as the bursars."

"Don Paschatio, I know, I. . ."

"Let me tell you, let me tell you, Signor Master of the Fowls. The good Steward must prepare the list of purchases for the bursar, and make sure that what is bought corresponds thereto, and that from the pantry it passes directly into the hands of the cook. The disposition of the provisions, which must. . ."

"Believe me, truly, I meant only to. . ." I interrupted in vain.

". . . of the provisions, as I was saying, which must appear magnificent, both on the ordinary table and on the banqueting table, all of which depends upon the worthiness and good judgement of the Steward who, being excellent at his profession, makes little appear much and with sparse purchases can produce as fine a display of victuals as another less expert might manage, spending twice as much. For a steward who cannot perfectly order and administer will be cheated, which will be prejudicial to his own honour and to that of his master. Do you follow me, Signor Master of the Fowls?"

"Yes, Don Paschatio," I nodded resignedly.

"The Steward must so arrange matters that the viands are well kept, in order of time, so that they are served up at table in small quantities and promptly, so that they do not grow cold, and meet the master's desires; he must ensure that no strangers enter the pantry or the secret kitchen, where he commands, and sometimes not even members of the household. He must take great care in controlling that the comestibles which reach his lord's mouth are of the best quality and pass through as few hands as possible, so as to avoid any possibility of the dishes being spoiled or indeed even poisoned. The Steward, in sum, hold's his master's life in his hands."

"I understand your meaning, but I only permitted myself to salute. . ."

"Signor Master of the Fowls, having due regard to what I have just brought to your attention, I beg you to make your salutations in the manner prescribed by the rules of the Spada household and to address the Signor Steward with all due deference," said he in heartfelt tones, as though I had gravely offended the interested party who, at that moment, had very different matters on his mind.

"Very well, that I promise you, Signor Major-Domo," I replied, carried away by the abuse of appellations, even forgetting that I myself was wont always to address Don Paschatio by his name.

Don Paschatio's natural tendency was obviously accentuated in those days by the great preparations for the nuptials.

"Signor Master of the Fowls," said he at length, "a foreign gentleman, or so I am informed, one whom we have the honour of numbering among the guests of His Eminence Cardinal Spada, has of late requested your services. I know that he is a person of note and do not intend to interfere in the matter; nevertheless, I trust that you will be so good as to fulfil your duties, where these do not conflict with the requirements of the gentleman in question, with unaltered alacrity."

"Pardon me, but how did you know?" I asked in surprise.

"I have been notified, simply and. . . well, yes, I hope that I meet with your complaisant and responsible understanding," replied Don Paschatio.

It was clear that Atto, in order to be able to enjoy my services undisturbed during those days at the Villa Spada must have paid some sizeable gratuity, perhaps to the Major-Domo himself, thus acquiring for himself the reputation of a gentleman who can, if he so desires, be quite generous. I therefore informed Don Paschatio that I was at that moment at his service, if he so desired.

"But of course, Master of the Fowls," he replied with ill-concealed satisfaction, "there are indeed a number of tasks which you could fulfil, seeing that certain persons have, how shall I put it, betrayed their trust."

He explained to me that a number of servants had that afternoon inexplicably absented themselves, failing to nail the steps of the theatre's stairways, so that the work could not be completed on time, as Cardinal Spada had peremptorily ordered a few weeks previously. I knew the reason (perfectly trivial, in truth) for that desertion: they had met a group of country girls and had carried them off to gallivant amongst the vines outside the San Pancrazio Gate behind the Corsini's House of the Four Winds; a circumstance which I kept to myself, not so much in order to avoid being a tell-tale as not to aggravate the mood of Don Paschatio. The Master of the Household was already furious; yet again, he had been abandoned by his subordinates and the dressing-down which he had received from Cardinal Spada had left its mark on him.

"I have proposed to Cardinal Spada a list of subjects to be punished," said he, lying, not knowing that I had overheard his conversation with our master. "We are, however, in difficulties and we urgently need more hands. It would be most helpful if you, Master of the Fowls, could, drawing upon your versatility in serving this august Spada household, put on appropriate apparel – livery, to be exact – and take part in serving viands and beverages at table, as the guests of His Excellency may require. They are all now on the meadow near the fountain, and are just beginning to dine. I shall be near at hand. Go, then, I beg you."

ક—૭

I gave a start when the time came to don the livery: I was handed a white turban, a scimitar, a pair of oriental slippers, baggy pantaloons, a tunic and a great arabesque cummerbund to wear around my chest. The costume was, of course, three sizes too large for me.

Ah, but I had forgotten: it had been decided that the *mise en scène* for these dinners was to be in exotically oriental style, as, accordingly must be the liveries. The long gay plume that stood on my headdress showed beyond a doubt that this was the costume of a janissary, a member of the most powerful and terrible guards of the Grand Turk. And this was as nothing when compared to what I was to see later.

After donning this Turkish uniform, I was handed two great silver chargers for serving the first cold course: fresh figs, served on leaves and adorned with their flowers, all set in snow; and, on another dish, tunny-fish served in well garnished roundels. Others bore pies of fish roe, Genoa cakes, pistachios on sticks with slices of citron, fat capons served up in roundels, sole in tricolour garnish, royal salads and iced white cakes.

Passing under the great pergola, I took the drive which led from the great house to the fountain, and thence to the place where the tables were set. As I made my way there, I was enthralled by the perfume drifting over from the flower beds lining the parallel entrance driveway, the smell of the Indian narcissi, the belladonna lilies, the autumn crocuses which had just opened, and by the fresh exhalations from the soft, damp earth of the vineyard. The heat of the day was at last giving way to the gentle embrace of evening's shadows.

Upon reaching my destination, I was astounded by the quality and the generous opulence of the décor. Under the dome of the starlit night, on the soft grassy carpet, the illusion had been created of a veritable oriental palace with Turkish pavilions, made in truth of delicate and brilliantly coloured Armenian gauze, mounted upon light wooden frames and crowned, at the top of each pavilion, by a golden half-moon. All around, the nocturnal braziers had been lit, from which rose, in great spirals, perfumes to mellow one's thoughts and please the senses. A little way off, but concealed by an artificial hedge, stood the far more modest table for the secretaries (among whom Buvat was intently helping himself to glass upon glass of wine) attendants and other members of the retinue of the eminences and princes. Many of these personages were indeed aged or suffering from gout and thus always in need of a helper at hand.

While we waiters served at the high table, which stood upon camelhair-coloured carpets, other janissaries, perspiring yet impassive, upheld great torches which generously illuminated the table.

Thus it was in the midst of such splendour that the dinner began, opening with the very dishes which I myself, amongst others, was serving. Well-nigh stunned by such luxury and pomp, I drew near to that great theatre of pleasure and prepared to serve the guests in accordance with the orders of the Chief Steward, who had appropriately placed himself behind a torch to be able, like one conducting an orchestra, to direct the peaceful militia of the waiters. The wine had just been served to the last guest, and so I moved towards the table. I realised that I was about to serve someone important, for Don Paschatio's eyes and those of the Steward followed me, blazing with anxiety.

". . . And so I asked him once again: Holiness, how do you think you can resolve the problem? The Holy Father had just finished eating and was at that very moment washing his hands. And he answered me: 'Really, Monsignor, can you not see? Like Pontius Pilate!'"

All those at table burst out laughing. I was so nervous about my delicate and unexpected task that this sudden outburst of hilarity, which I would never have expected from that assembly of high prelates and persons of noble lineage, that I was left well-nigh paralysed. He who had aroused the good humour of the company was none other than Cardinal Durazzo, recounting with malicious wit the words of one of the many pontiffs he had known during the course of his long career. Glancing at the far end of the table I noticed that, curiously, only one face remained impassive and almost glacial; later, I was to learn the explanation for this.

"And yet he was a holy pontiff, one of the most virtuous of all time," added Durazzo when some of the guests had quietened down and were wiping away the few tears brought on by excessive laughter.

"Holy, truly holy," echoed another eminence, rapidly dabbing with a napkin at a few drops of wine that had run down his chin.

"Throughout all Europe, they want to beatify him," one added from the far end of the table.

I raised my eyes and saw that the Steward and Don Paschatio were striving desperately to attract my attention, gesticulating wildly and pointing at something under my nose. I looked: Cardinal Durazzo was looking at me fixedly and waiting. Half stunned by the general outburst of laughter a few moments before, I had forgotten to serve him.

"Well, well, my boy, rather than Pontius Pilate, do you want me to be like Our Lord in the wilderness?" said he, causing yet another storm of laughter.

Hurriedly, I served the figs to the Cardinal and his neighbours, overcome by a deplorable state of mental confusion. I knew that I had committed an unpardonable gaffe and caused Cardinal Spada to lose face and, if only for a few moments, I had become the laughing stock of the company. My cheeks were on fire and I cursed the moment when I had offered my services to Don Paschatio. I dared not even raise my eyes; I knew that I would find those of the Major-Domo fixed on me, full of anxiety, and those of the Steward, full of fiery wrath. Fortunately that evening was not yet the official feast.

Cardinal Spada himself was absent and would be coming only two days later, at the start of the formal festivities.

"... But yes, he's right to think that he will soon be better. Or so we hope, at least," said someone speaking in sad tones as I continued serving.

"So we hope, ah yes," echoed Cardinal Aldrovandi, whose name in truth I did not yet know. "In Bologna, whence I arrived today, they keep asking me insistently for news of his health, every day and at all hours. They are all very worried."

I understood that they were speaking of the Pope's health and every one of them had his word to put in.

"We hope, we hope, and we pray; prayer can resolve everything," said another prelate in a sorrowful and in truth rather insincere voice, ending up by crossing himself.

"How much good he has done for Rome!"

"The Hospice of San Michele a Ripa Grande along with a hundred and forty thousand scudi every year for the poor. . ."

"A pity that he did not succeed in draining the Pontine Marshes. . ." said the Princess Farnese.

"Your Highness will permit me to remind her that the miserable state of the Pontine Fields and the unhealthy effluvia that issue therefrom to oppress Rome are not the fruit of nature, but of the imprudent deforestation practised by past popes, above all Julius II and Leo X," retorted Monsignor Aldrovandi, striving to stifle at once the least allusion to any lack of success on the part of the reigning Pope, "and, if I am not mistaken, Pope Paul III too."

This last barb was a polite reminder of the fact that the Princess was herself a descendant of Paul III, Alessandro Farnese.

"The Baccano Woods," she retorted, "were cut down because they were a refuge for assassins and thieves."

"As is happening today with the forests of Sermoneta and Cisterna!" came the heated rejoinder of one whom I was later to recognise as the Prince Caetani. "We should cut them all down and leave it at that. For the sake of public order, I mean," he added, embarrassed by the coolness of his audience.

The Princes Caetani, and this I had myself learned some time previously, asked every new pope for permission to cut down those woodlands, which belonged to them, so that they could make money from the operation.

"His Holiness Innocent XII has for years issued decrees for the defence of heaths and woodland," replied Monsignor Aldrovandi imperturbably.

A murmur of approval flowed down the table, at least among those who were not engaged in close, gossipy conversation with the person seated next to them.

"A pity that he had the Tor di Nona Theatre demolished," said the same gentleman who had not laughed at Cardinal Durazzo's joke.

Monsignor Aldrovandi, who had not realised that all his praise of the Pope resembled an obituary, had succeeded in silencing the first, veiled criticism of the Pontiff, but this second one (referring to the unpopular decision to destroy one of Rome's most splendid theatres) he pretended not to hear, turning to his neighbour and showing his back to the person who had addressed him.

While serving him, I was fortunate enough to hear two ladies whisper: "But have you seen Cardinal Spinola di Santa Cecilia?"

"Oh, have I seen him!" giggled the other. "With the approach of the conclave he's been trying to put it about that he no longer suffers from gout. In order not to be left out of the charmed circle, he goes around behaving like a young lad. And then this evening, here, eating, drinking and laughing, at his age. . ."

"He's Spada's bosom friend, even if both of them try to hide it."

"I know, I know. . ."

"Has Cardinal Albani not arrived?"

"He will be coming in two days, for the wedding. They say that he is working on a very urgent papal breve."

The dining table was shaped like a horseshoe. Having almost reached the end of the second branch of the table, I was serving a guest with familiar features, and whom I was shortly to recognise, when I felt a sharp but powerful blow to the arm which was holding the charger. It was a disaster. The figs, catapulted to the left together with the leaves, flowers and snow, landed on the face and clothing of the aged nobleman whom I had just served. The dish crashed to the ground with a clangour like that of a breaking bell. A murmur halfway between amusement and disapproval spread among the nearby guests. While the unfortunate nobleman removed the figs with dignity, I looked all around in panic. How could I make Don Paschatio and the Steward understand that what had just occurred was not my fault and that it had been the guest whom I was just serving who had sent my dish flying? I looked at him, full of mute resentment, knowing well that I could do nothing against him, for the servant is always in the wrong. And then I recognised him. It was Atto.

Punishment was swift and discreet. Within five minutes, I was no longer holding a charger in my hand, but one of those enormous, immensely heavy, incandescent torches which illuminated the dinner as though it were almost daylight. I was bursting with rage at Abbot Melani and tormented myself with wondering why he should so cruelly have tricked me, getting me punished and imperilling my present and future employment at the Villa Spada. While the dinner continued, I sought his eyes in vain, for he was seated with his back to me and I could see only the nape of his neck.

Transformed into some new Pier delle Vigne, I must needs bear up: dinner was only beginning and I had better arm myself with patience. The first half of the first hot course had only just been served: fresh eggs drowned in milk with soup under that, butter, slices of lemon, sugar and cinnamon; and boiled head of sturgeon, with its bland savour, served with flowers, herbs, lemon juice, pepper and almonds (one slice for each guest).

The heat from the torch was unbearable, and under the Turkish turban I sweated buckets. The servants who had gone off a-courting with the peasant girls had done well, said I to myself. Yet I knew all too well that I would never have had the heart to betray Don Paschatio and abandon him at so critical a time. The only relief from the heat and the torment of immobility was to know that I was in the company of seven others like myself, each bearing his torch and, what is more, to be able to be a spectator at this meeting of all those eminences and as many noblemen. The place to which I was assigned near the table was, moreover, singular, as I shall soon have occasion to explain.

Hardly had I resigned myself to my punishment when, all of a sudden, Atto turned to me.

"Come, my boy, where I am sitting, 'tis so dark that I feel as though I were in a cave, will you or will you not be so kind as to come closer with that torch of yours?" he called out to me in a loud voice, making an ugly grimace as though I were an anonymous servant quite unknown to him.

I could but obey. I stood right behind him, lighting up his part of the table, which was in any case already perfectly well lit, as well as

I could. What the deuce could Atto have in his head? Why had he ill-treated me and why was he now tormenting me?

In the meanwhile, the conversation between the guests, which was conducted quite freely, had turned to frivolous subjects. Unfortunately, I was not always able to understand who was speaking, since from my viewpoint I could see a good many of the guests, but not all of them. Moreover, on that evening, most of the faces and voices were still unknown to me (while in the following days I was to learn to recognise almost all of them).

". . . Pardon me, Monsignor, but only a kennel-man is permitted to bear an arquebus."

"Yes, Your Excellency, but let me tell you, if you will permit me, that he may have it carried by a groom."

"Very well. And so?"

"As I was saying, if the boar is cowardly and dares not fight in the open, it is killed with the arquebus, as was the custom on the Caetani estates, which are the best hunting grounds."

"No, no, how then are we to speak of those of Prince Perretti?"

"Pardon me, all of you, and please do not take offence, but all these are nothing compared to the lands of the Duke of Bracciano," corrected the Princess Orsini, widow of the said Duke.

"Your Highness must mean those of the Prince Odescalchi," said a thin, icy voice. I looked at the speaker. It was the nobleman who had not joined into the laughter at Cardinal Durazzo's witticism about the pope who compared himself with Pontius Pilate.

For a moment, the table talk froze. The Princess Orsini, in her passion to defend the memory of the family possessions, had all too easily forgotten that, in order to avoid bankruptcy, the Orsini had sold land and more land to Prince Livio Odescalchi and that those estates and the feudal rights that went with them had changed their names as well as changing hands.

"You are quite right, cousin," said she condescendingly, addressing the gentleman as do nobles when speaking to persons with whom they have bonds of kinship or amity. "And 'tis indeed most fortunate that they should now bear the name of your household."

The person who had contradicted the Princess was, then, Don Livio Odescalchi, nephew of the late Pope Innocent XI. It followed that this must have been the pontiff concerning whom Cardinal Durazzo had told an amusing anecdote only moments earlier, which had however not amused Prince Odescalchi, to whom his late uncle had left his immense fortune. At last I was seeing in person the nephew of that pope about whom I had, seventeen years previously at the Locanda del Donzello, learned things to make one's hair stand on end. I hurriedly dismissed those memories of episodes which had caused such suffering for my wife and my late father-in-law.

I learned that evening that Don Livio had also owned a box at the Tor di Nona theatre, which he would no longer be able to enjoy, since the present Pope had had the theatre demolished. This explained why Monsignor Aldovrandi had insisted on that topic.

"By the smithy of Hephaestus, boy, you are roasting my neck. Would you kindly move that way?"

Atto had yet again turned around rudely to upbraid me, almost shoving me to a new post, further away from him. By means of these two moves he had shifted me almost five yards from my original position, almost to the far end of that branch of the table.

Dinner was proceeding with singular freedom of manners and speech, a point which even I who was utterly unfamiliar with that most elevated milieu remarked at once. Only from time to time, irrepressibly, did the quarrelsome haughtiness of the great families and the subtle but venomous pride of those at the summit of the ecclesiastical hierarchy show its face. Yet the rigid protocol which those eminences and princes would have had to observe when meeting one another individually had been magically dissolved, perhaps by the amenity and delightful qualities of the place chosen for banqueting.

"Pray, pardon me, all of you, a moment's silence! I should like to raise my glass to the health of Cardinal Spada, who is, as Your Excellencies well know, absent on account of pressing affairs of state," said Monsignor Pallavicini, Governor of Rome, at a certain point. "He has recommended me to be, if not a father, at least an uncle to his guests tonight."

A gentle ripple of approving laughter ran through the assembly.

"As soon as I see him," continued Monsignor Pallavicini, "I shall express to him my gratitude for his political gifts, and in particular for not providing us with a table laid in the Spanish or in the French style, but surrounded instead by Ottomans."

Another amused murmur arose.

"And this last reminds us of our shared destiny as Christians," added Pallavicini amiably, while throwing a swift glance at Cardinal d'Estrées, Ambassador Extraordinary *a latere* of the Most Christian King, always too much in cahoots with the Ottoman Sublime Porte.

"And as the enemies of heresy," came the prompt reply of d'Estrées, whose call to order alluded to the fact that, although a Catholic, the Austrian Emperor was allied with Dutch and English heretics.

"Let us not speak too much to him of the Sublime Porte or D'Estrées will take umbrage and be off," I heard someone whisper rather too loudly.

"Gently, gently with all this talk," quoth Cardinal Durazzo, who had missed nothing. "First a janissary would not deign to serve me figs and now that he hears all this murmuring about heretics, he'll get it into his head to set his torch to me and burn me."

The company burst once more into hearty roars of laughter as soon as they caught the allusion to my initial misadventure with Cardinal Durazzo, while I must needs stay sadly impassive and keep holding my torch quite straight.

It was precisely in view of such political skirmishing that Cardinal Spada, that most prudent of men, had, as I had learned from Don Paschatio, taken a series of counter-measures. So as to avoid, for example, the possibility that someone might peel fruit after the French fashion or, on the contrary, according to that of Spain, fruit was served already peeled.

Of course, for some years now there had no longer been any risk of seeing some gentlemen apparelled in the Spanish fashion and others, *à la française*, for thanks to the splendours of Versailles, it was now the great mode for all to dress after the manner of the Most Christian King. Yet, for that very reason, it was all the rage to show to which party one belonged by means of a whole series of little details: from the handkerchief in one's cloak (those of the Spanish party wearing it on the right, while the Francophiles wore it on the left), or the stockings (white for the French party, red for the Hispanophiles), so that it was no accident if Abbot Melani had that evening chosen to wear white in the place of his usual red Abbot's hose.

Nor could the ladies be prevented from getting themselves up with a bunch of flowers on their right bosom if they were Guelphs (that is, of the Hispanic persuasion) or on the left if they were Ghibellines (on the French side). However, in order to avoid the table at which all were to eat being set too much in accordance with the traditions of the one side or the other, in particular as to the placing of the crockery which is, as is well known, the decisive factor for determining the political affiliation of the guests, it had been decided to abandon established etiquette and to do something new: knives, forks and spoons had been placed vertically in the glasses, which had caused no little astonishment among the guests, while avoiding pointless polemics.

"But with hounds, it is quite a different matter," insisted another cardinal, who was wearing a striking French wig.

"I beg your pardon?"

"I am only saying that once Prince Perretti had sixty hounds. When the season was over, he'd send them elsewhere for the summer, as hounds suffer from the heat, and thus he economised too."

It was Cardinal Santa Croce who, overshadowed by his own bulky periwig, sang the praises of hunting to hounds.

"There was no need to remind everyone that he has money problems," I heard a young canon, not far from me, whisper to his neighbour, taking advantage of the fact that the conversation had broken up in disorder into many little groups.

"Ah, Santa Croce is all at cross purposes with himself," the other responded with a snigger. "He's so hungry that his tongue hangs out and the very words that he ought to keep in his mouth come tumbling down onto the floor."

The speaker was another cardinal, whose name I did not yet know; I noticed that he seemed unwell, and yet he ate and drank enthusiastically, as though his humour were sanguine.

Fate (or rather, another factor, of which I shall speak later) came to my rescue, for at that moment, a servant approached this cardinal with a note.

"Eminence, I have a note for His Eminence Cardinal Spinola. . ."

"For Spinola di Santa Cecilia or for my nephew Spinola di San Cesareo, who is sitting on the other side of the table? Or for Spinola, the Chairman of Ripetta? This evening, all three of us are here."

The servant was speechless for a moment.

"The Major-Domo told me only that it was for His Excellency Cardinal Spinola," he ventured timidly, his voice almost inaudible amidst the gay clamour of the banquet.

"Then it could be me. Hand it over."

He opened the note and closed it at once.

"Go and give it at once to Cardinal Spinola di San Cesareo who is seated on the far side. Do you see him? Right over there."

His neighbour at table had, meanwhile, tactfully turned his attention to his plate and begun again to eat. Spinola di Santa Cecilia (for now it was clear that it was he) turned back to him at once.

"Now, can you believe it? That fool of a Major-Domo made me receive a note from Spada for my nephew, Spinola di San Cesareo."

"Ah yes?" replied the other, his physiognomy lit up by lively curiosity.

"It said: 'All three on board tomorrow at dawn. I shall tell A.'"

"A? And who would that be?"

"How would I know? Seeing that he wants to go out in a boat, let us only hope that he doesn't drown," concluded Spinola with a snigger.

The guests took their leave at a rather late hour. I was exhausted. The flame of the torch which I had held aloft for hours had roasted half my face and bathed my whole body in perspiration. We torchbearers had to wait humbly until the last guest had left the table. Thus, despite my burning desire to ask him for explanations, I was quite unable to approach Atto. I saw him move away, accompanied by Buvat, while the servants were already snuffing out the table candlesticks. He had not deigned to accord me so much as a glance.

❧

Up in the attic, in the big servants' hall, I was so weary that I could barely think. In the dark, amidst the rumble of my companions' snoring, I was a prey to anguish; the Abbot had treated me horribly, as had never before happened between us. Nothing made sense. I was confused, nay, desperate.

I began to fear that I had committed an unpardonable error by agreeing to get involved again with Melani. I had allowed myself to be swept along by events when I ought only to have given myself time to reflect. And perhaps even – why not? – to put the Abbot to the test. Instead, within the space of a single day, Atto had been able to plummet down into my life again as though his coming were the most natural thing in the world. Ah, but the temptation of lucre had been irresistible. . .

I undressed, and, curling up on one of the pallets that had remained free, I soon slipped into a heavy, dreamless sleep.

". . . They dressed him for the undertakers."

"Where did it happen?"

"In Via dei Coronari. Four or five of them held him up and robbed him of all that he had."

Conspiratorial whispering, not far from me, had torn me from my slumbers. Two servants were clearly commenting on some dreadful assault.

"But what was his trade?"

"Bookbinder."

჻

The breathless rush that followed these tidings did not prove as useful as I had expected.

When, after a breakneck descent of the back stairs, I came and knocked at Abbot Melani's door, I found him already up and on a war footing. Far from being still in bed as I had expected, there he was with ink-stained hands, bending over a pile of papers. He must just have finished writing a letter. He greeted me with a countenance heavy and fraught with dark thoughts.

"I have come to inform you of a matter of extreme gravity."

"I know. Haver, the bookbinder, is dead."

"How did you learn of it?" I asked, dumbfounded.

"And you, how do you know?"

"I just heard tell of it now, upstairs, from two valets."

"Then I have sources better than yours. That catchpoll Sfasciamonti has just been here. 'Twas he who told me."

"At this hour?" I cried out in astonishment.

"I was on the point of sending Buvat to fetch you," retorted the Abbot, ignoring my question. "We have an appointment with the catchpoll down below in the coach-house."

"Are you afraid that this may be connected with the attack upon yourself today?"

"'Tis the same thing as you're thinking of; or else you'd not have come rushing here in the middle of the night."

Without exchanging a word, all three of us went down to the coach-house, where Sfasciamonti was waiting in an old service calash, with a coachman and a team of two horses ready to go.

"A thousand bombs blast 'em!" cried the visibly overexcited catchpoll, while the coachman led the horses out and closed the door behind us. "It seems that things went like this. Poor Haver slept in the mezzanine above the shop. Three or four men entered the shop during the night, some say there were even more of them. We have no idea how they got in. The door was not forced. They tied up the poor wretch and gagged him by stuffing a piece of wool in his mouth, then they searched the place from top to bottom. They took all the money he had and left. After who knows how long, the bookbinder managed to remove the gag and to cry out. He was found in a state of deep shock. He was utterly terrified. While he was telling the tale to all the neighbours, he felt unwell. When the doctor arrived, he found him dead."

"Was he wounded?" I asked.

"I have not seen the body, other sergeants arrived before I could. Now my men are seeking information on the case."

"Are we going to this place?" I asked.

"Almost," replied the Abbot. "We shall be going very near there."

We stopped at Piazza Fiammetta, a short distance from the beginning of the Via dei Coronari. The night was barely lit by a sliver of moon. The air was fresh and pleasant. Sfasciamonti got down and told us to wait there. We looked all around us but saw not a soul. Then a market gardener hove in sight on his cart. Not long after that, a piercing whistle made us jump. It was Sfasciamonti, half concealed in a doorway, from which his rounded belly could, however, just be seen peeping out. He was gesturing to us to join him. We drew near.

"Hey, go easy," we both protested when he dragged us both by brute force into the dank, dark porch.

"Hush!" hissed the catchpoll, flattening himself against the front door behind one of the pilasters framing it.

"Two *cerretani*, they were stalking you. When they saw me, they hid. Perhaps they've gone now. I must go and see."

"Were they shadowing us?" Atto asked worriedly.

We held our breath. Prudently craning our necks, we caught sight of two ragged and emaciated old tramps, crossing the road.

"You are a dunderhead, Sfasciamonti," whispered Atto, uttering a sigh of relief. "Do you really think those two half-dead wretches could spy on anyone?"

"The *cerretani* watch over you without giving themselves away. They are secretive," answered the catchpoll without so much as batting an eyelid.

"Very well," cut in Abbot Melani, "have you spoken with the person I told you to find?"

"All in order, by the recoil of a thousand howitzers!" came the catchpoll's immediate reassurance, accompanied by his curious imprecations.

The place was in a side-road giving onto the Via dei Coronari, scarcely a block away from the bookbinder's shop. We arrived there by the most tortuous route, as Atto and Sfasciamonti wanted at all costs to avoid passing in front of the scene of the crime, where there was a risk of encountering the sergeants assigned to the case. Fortunately, darkness was our ally.

"Why are we hiding, Signor Atto? We have nothing to do with the death of the bookbinder," said I.

Melani did not answer me.

"The criminal judge has assigned new officers to the case. I do not know them," announced Sfasciamonti as we left Piazza Fiammetta behind us, setting off towards Piazza San Salvatore in Lauro.

We defiled through the alleyways of the quarter, where Buvat stumbled upon a sleeping congregation of ragged friars, barely managing to avoid falling against a pile of boxes and baskets belonging to street vendors who lay dozing as they awaited dawn and their first customers. Under the cloths and blankets delicious odours betrayed the presence of French lettuces, sweet lupin seeds, fresh waffles and cheese.

The rendezvous was far removed from prying eyes, in the shop of a *coronaro*, that is, a maker of rosaries. We were welcomed by the artisan, an old man with a face covered in wrinkles who greeted Melani with great deference, as though he were long acquainted with him, and led us towards the back of the shop. We made our way through that cool little den replete with great rosaries made of wood and of bone, of every form and colour, finely interwoven and hanging on the walls or laid on little tables. The *coronaro* opened a drawer.

"Here you are, Sir," said he respectfully as he handed the Abbot a packet enveloped in blue velvet, which seemed to me to be in the form of a little picture.

After saying this, the *coronaro* disappeared with Sfasciamonti into the back room. Atto gestured to Buvat that we were to follow them.

I could not understand. Why ever should the death of the bookbinder have led us into that shop of devotional objects to take delivery of what I imagined to be the picture of some saint, presumably to be hung on the wall? I was unable to make a connection between the two things.

Atto guessed my thoughts and, taking me by the arm, deemed the time right for providing me with some initial explanations.

"I had arranged this morning with the bookbinder that he should leave the little book here, with this good man."

So it was not some small picture that the *coronaro* had brought Melani, but the mysterious little book of which the Abbot was so unwilling to speak.

"I know this *coronaro* well, he helps me out whenever I need it and I know that I can trust him," he added, without, however, adding what services he might need of a *coronaro* or giving me the slightest clue as to the nature of the book.

"Since the bookbinder was often absent from his shop, I thought that it would be more convenient to collect it here," continued the Abbot. "After all, I had already paid for the new binding. And I did well so to arrange matters, for otherwise, if I wanted to collect my little opuscule, I'd have found myself in a quarrel with some sergeant asking too many questions: whether I knew the bookbinder, how long I'd been acquainted with him, what relations I had with him. . . Try explaining to him how, at the very moment when I was talking with poor Haver, I was stabbed in the arm by a stranger. They'd never have believed me. I can just imagine the questions: how is it that it happened just then, there must surely be a connection, what were you doing here in Rome, and so on and so forth. In other words, my boy, it does not bear thinking about."

Then Atto beckoned me to follow him. He did not move towards the door but took me into the back room, into which Sfasciamonti had disappeared a few minutes before with the *coronaro* and Buvat. In the back of the shop, we were awaited by a little woman of about fifty, seated at a worn old table, modest and somewhat poorly dressed. She was talking with Sfasciamonti and the *coronaro* while Buvat listened as though stunned. When Atto entered, the woman stood up at once out of respect, having realised that here was a gentleman.

"Have you finished?" asked Melani.

The catchpoll and Buvat nodded.

"That woman is a neighbour of poor Haver," Sfasciamonti began to explain to us as we walked away from the shop, leaving Piazza San

Salvatore in Lauro behind us. "She saw everything from a window. She heard someone lamenting and knocking at the binder's door. The latter, who seems to have been a very pious man, opened up straight away but had no time to close the door before two other figures slipped in. They went away half an hour later, carrying off a great pile of paper with them as well as a number of books that had already been bound."

"Poor Haver. And poor fool, too," commented Atto.

"But why they took away papers, we know not," said I, looking at Atto.

"Where the *cerretani* are involved, one can never understand a thing," interrupted Sfasciamonti, his visage growing dark.

"But how can you be so sure that this was the work of your mendicants?" asked Atto, growing somewhat impatient.

"Experience. When one springs up – and here I speak of the one who was running away and who wounded you – he is invariably followed by others," said the catchpoll gravely.

Atto stopped suddenly, thus bringing all three of us to a stop.

"Come on now, what are you talking about? Sfasciamonti, we cannot go on like this with your half-baked explanations. Kindly tell me once and for all what it is that these mendicants do, these. . . Cerrisani, as you call them."

"*Cerretani*," Sfasciamonti humbly corrected.

I was sure of it. He would never have admitted it, but even then Atto Melani felt the serpent of fear slide up from his ankles into his guts.

He knew all too well that he had had a physical encounter with one of the strange individuals of whom Sfasciamonti was speaking, and from that encounter he had received a stab wound which was still hurting and hindering him, following which the bookbinder in whose presence all that had taken place had been assaulted that very night in his own shop, and had died. And he had had his own little book bound by that same unfortunate man; coincidences which could have brought pleasure to no one.

"Above all, I want to know," the Abbot added brusquely, his impatient mind struggling with the fatigue of his old limbs, "are they acting on their own behalf or for hire?"

"Do you really think it is so easy to find that out? With the *cerretani* strange things are always happening. Indeed, *only* strange things happen."

The catchpoll then began to describe what, as far as he had learned, was the origin of the *cerretani*, and the real nature of that mysterious confraternity.

"The *cerretani*. A rabble. They come from Cerreto in Umbria, where they took refuge after fleeing Rome. They were priests, and the higher priests chased them away."

In Cerreto, the account continued, the *cerretani* chose from among their number a new Upright Man or head priest who divided them up according to their talents, into groups, cells and sects: Rufflers, Clapperdogeons or Fermerdy Beggars, Pailliards, Strollers, Buskers, Bourdons or False Pilgrims, Fraters or Jarkmen, Money Droppers, Rooks, Cunning-men and Cunny-shavers, Counterfeit Cranks, Dommerers, Sky Farmers and Gaggers, Duffers, Sharks or Sharpers, Faulkners, Fators, Saint Peter's Sons, Files, Bulkers, Nippers and Foysters, Hedge Priests or Patricoes, Swigmen, Abram Men, Amusers, Anglers (or Hookers), Chop-churches, Collectors, Pinchers, Swaddlers, Ark Ruffians, Wiper Drawers, Badgers, Bawdy Baskets, Sneaks, Snudges, Cleymers, Cloak Twitchers, Crockers, Flying Porters, Rum Dubbers, Lully Triggers, Leggers, Lumpers, Heavers, Hostelers, Jinglers, Whipjacks, Kid Lays, Queer Plungers, Reliquaries, and so on and so forth.

"How do you manage to remember all those names?"

"With the job I do. . ."

He went on to explain that the Fraters, who are also known as Jarkmen, counterfeit the seals of pontiffs or prelates – which they call jarks in their gibberish – and show them off, pretending that they have permits to issue indulgences, saving sinners from purgatory and hell and to absolve all sins, in exchange for which they exact payment in gold from the credulous.

"The Cunning-men are so-called because they are false, they pretend to be soothsayers and hoodwink simple villagers, claiming in exchange for money to foresee the future and to be full of the Holy Spirit. The Hedge Priests are false friars or false priests who have never taken either minor or major orders. They go from village to village and say mass, after which they make off with the takings from the collection; as penitence, they impose yet more charity, all of which ends up in their pockets. The Bourdons are false pilgrims who beg for alms on the pretext that they must travel to the Holy Land or to Santiago de Compostela or to Our Lady of Loreto. The Dommerers claim to have relatives or brothers in the hands of the Turks and beg for alms to ransom them, but it is not true. The Swigmen, on the other hand. . ."

"One moment: if the *cerretani* do all these things, then how come no one stops them?" Atto objected.

"Because they are secretive. They are divided into sects, no one knows how many there are nor where they are."

"But are they sects, as you claim, or just groups of rogues?"

"Both. They are above all rogues, but they have secret rituals which they use to swear fidelity to the group and to tighten the bonds of brotherhood. Thus, if one of them is taken, the others can be sure that he will never talk. Otherwise he could fall victim to a curse. That, at least, is what they believe."

"What rites do they practise?"

"Ah, if only one could know. Black masses, sacrifices, blood pacts and other such things, probably. But no one has ever seen them. They go into the countryside to do such things in isolated places: deconsecrated chapels, abandoned villas. . ."

"Are they numerous, here in Rome?"

"They are *especially* to be found in Rome."

"And why is that?"

"Because the Pope is here. And where there are popes, there's money. What's more, there are the pilgrims to be gulled. And now, there's the Jubilee: more money and more pilgrims."

"Has no pontiff ever issued an ecclesiastical ban against these sects?" interrupted Atto.

"If a sect – or a group of criminals – is to be prohibited, it must be clearly known," replied Sfasciamonti. "Specific actions must be attributed to it and its members must have names and identities. How can one ban a vague grouping consisting of wretched homeless and nameless vagabonds?"

Atto nodded in silence, thoughtfully scratching the dimple on his chin.

When we returned to the calash, dawn was about to break. Sfasciamonti took leave of us.

"I shall be coming later to the Villa Spada. First I must go home. My mother is expecting me. It is today that I must deliver her provisions, and if I do not come on time, she worries."

☙◦❧

"Together?" I exclaimed in astonishment, as I and Buvat looked at one another in unison.

We had barely taken our leave of Sfasciamonti. Abbot Melani had already taken his place in the calash to return to the Villa Spada when, instead of making room for us, he closed the door behind him.

"You, stay here for the time being," said he laconically.

He then held out a letter to me, already closed and sealed. I recognised it at once: it was *that* letter, the reply to his mysterious Maria.

"But Signor Atto," came Buvat's and my own weak protests, for in truth we both longed for a little rest before facing the new working day.

"Later. Now, be on your way. Buvat will deliver the message. Alone, however, for you," and here, he turned to me, "are not appropriately dressed. I shall have to make you a present of a new suit sooner or later. I shall explain to you where you must go: with Buvat, I'd be wasting my breath."

"Permit me to insist," I retorted.

I quickly read the addressee's name:

Madama la Connestabilessa Colonna

My thoughts criss-crossed in my head and I knew not to which I should give precedence. I could not wait to return home and rest (also, to meditate upon the latest disquieting occurrences), but at the same time, I found myself suddenly faced with the revelation of the identity of the mysterious Maria who corresponded with Atto in secret and whose arrival was awaited at the Villa Spada. The Connestabilessa Colonna: I knew that name. Indeed, who in Rome had not heard of the Grand Constable and Roman Prince Lorenzo Onofrio Colonna, scion of one of the most ancient and noble families in Europe? He had died some ten years previously and she must be the widow. . .

"Come, then, let us hear," Atto burst in, interrupting the flow of my thoughts. "What do you want?"

At that instant, I saw the Abbot's face shift from an attitude of impatience to an expression of stupefaction, as though he had been struck by a lightning-like idea or a sudden memory.

"How silly of me! Come, sit down with me, my boy," he exclaimed, opening the door for me and offering me a seat. "Of course, we must talk. Come now, tell me all. I suppose that during the night you have had the good taste to set aside a few moments from your well-deserved rest in which to compile for me a detailed account of all that you overheard," said he with the most natural air in the world, without so much as sparing a thought for the fact that we had just spent the night gallivanting across Rome.

"Heard? Where?"

"But is it not obvious? At last night's dinner, when I used the pretext of the torch to make you dance that minuet all around the table just in order to place you behind Cardinal Spinola. Come, tell me, what did they say?"

I was dumbfounded. Atto was admitting to having pretended to mistreat me when he ordered me to draw close to him because, so he said, there was not enough light; and then he had sent me brusquely to the other end of the table on the pretext that the torch was burning his neck. Not only that; the Abbot had arranged the whole thing in order to induce me to listen to the diners' conversations!

"Really, Signor Atto, I cannot see how any of those conversations could be of interest to anyone. I mean, they spoke of frivolous and unimportant matters. . ."

"Unimportant? In every utterance of a cardinal of the Holy Roman Church, there is not a single syllable, my boy, that is not imbued with some significance. You may even say that they are all old goats, and I in my turn might even decline to contradict you, but whatever issues from their mouths is always interesting."

"It may well be as you say, but I. . . Well, there was just one thing that seemed somewhat curious to me."

I told him of the misunderstanding that had taken place between the two Cardinals Spinola and how Cardinal Spada's message addressed to the one had been delivered to the other, as well as its content.

"It said: 'All three on board tomorrow at dawn. I shall tell A.'"

Atto remained silent and pensive. Then he declared: "That would be interesting; truly interesting, if. . ." said he to himself, staring meditatively at Buvat sitting hunched up by the side of the road.

"What do you mean?"

He stayed silent a moment longer, looking me straight in the eyes, but in reality mentally following the rushing chariot of future events.

"What a genius I am!" he exclaimed at length, giving me a great slap on the shoulder. "That Abbot Melani is really a genius to have sent you off on the pretext of that torch to stand close to those persons who laugh out of turn and talk too freely."

I looked at him in astonishment. He had collated past deeds unknown to me and future events which he already saw vividly unfolding before him, while for me they were all thick fog.

"Well, soon we too shall have to go on board," said he, rubbing and massaging his hands, almost as though to prepare them for the decisive moment.

"Aboard a boat?" I asked.

"Meanwhile, go and deliver the letter," Melani commanded impatiently, again opening the carriage door and making me descend with scant ceremony. "All in good time."

Day the Second
8ᵗʰ JULY, 1700

✠

A few minutes later, Buvat and I were in the street while Atto's calash disappeared into the byways. Thoughts were racing through my head. Was Maria, the Connestabilessa Colonna (for that must indeed be the identity of the mysterious noblewoman with whom Atto had for some time been in secret contact), already in Rome? The Abbot had told me to deliver the letter to the monastery of Santa Maria in Campo Marzio. And yet, had not this same Maria written in her last missive that she had stopped near Rome and would not be arriving until the next day?

The sky was implacably clear. Soon, however, all gave way to the overpowering midsummer heat. Walking was, however, made more difficult not by the closeness but by Buvat's uncertain, absent-minded gait. He advanced with his nose in the air; from time to time he would stop, observing with delight a cupola, a campanile, a plain brick wall.

In the end I decided to break the silence.

"Do you know into whose hands we are to deliver this letter?"

"Oh, not of course those of the Princess. We must pass it to a little nun who is very devoted to her. You know, the Princess herself spent some time here when she was young, for the abbess was her aunt."

"Certainly, the Princess will know Abbot Melani."

"Know him?" said Buvat, laughing, as though the question were one that invited irony.

I kept quiet for a few moments.

"You mean that he knows her well," said I.

"Do you know who the Princess Colonna is?"

"Well, if I remember. . . if I am not mistaken, she was the wife of the Connestabile Colonna, who died some ten years ago."

"The Princess Colonna," Buvat corrected me, "was, in the first place, the niece of Cardinal Mazarin, that great statesman and most refined of politicians, glory of France and of Italy."

"Yes, indeed," I mumbled, embarrassed at my inability to recall to memory what, years before, I had known perfectly well. "And now," I added, trying to extract myself from this discomfiting situation, "on behalf of Abbot Melani, we are about to deliver this letter in all confidence."

"But of course," said Buvat, "Maria Mancini is in Rome incognito!"

"Maria Mancini?"

"That is her maiden name. She cannot bear so much as to hear it pronounced, because the pedigree was not of the highest. The Abbot will be very excited. It is quite some time since he and the Princess last saw one another."

"Quite some time? How long?"

"Thirty years."

This, then, was the mysterious Maria, whose name Atto's lips had murmured in such heart-rending tones. It was she who, years before, had married Prince Lorenzo Onofrio Colonna and, by the excessive freedom of her conduct, had earned herself a reputation as a stubborn and inconstant woman, which still persisted decades later. All this I knew only by hearsay, since the events which gave rise to it had taken place when I was still a little boy.

How was it possible that Atto should not have explained to me precisely to whom the letter confided to Buvat and myself was destined? What was the nature of their relationship? From the letters on which I had spied, I had learned scarcely anything in that regard, while I had learned much about the question of the Spanish succession, a matter evidently close to both their hearts. I must, however, set aside these questionings until later, however fascinating they might be; for now we had reached our goal.

We stood before the Convent of Santa Maria in Campo Marzio. After knocking at the main entrance, Buvat told the sister who received us that he had a letter to deliver to Sister Caterina in person, which letter he showed her. In compliance with Atto's instructions, I stood aside. After we had waited for a few minutes, another nun came to the door.

"Sister Maria has not yet arrived," said she hurriedly, before snatching the letter from Buvat's hands and swiftly closing the heavy wooden door.

Buvat and I exchanged perplexed glances.

So the mystery was resolved: so secret was the contact between Abbot Melani and the Connestabilessa that letters passed through the convent even though Maria had not yet arrived (and, what was more, she was due to arrive, not at the convent but at the Villa Spada). Delivery was confided to the iron discretion of the nuns.

We then proceeded to the Palazzo Rospigliosi at Monte Cavallo, where Buvat briefly left me waiting in the street while he went to collect his shoes which, the day before, he had forgotten to bring with him to the Villa Spada. I was thus able to admire that imposing and immense building which cut a fine figure on the Quirinal Hill, concerning which I had read that it overflowed with beautiful things and had gardens with stupendous curved terraces and marvellous pleasure pavilions.

On the way back, Melani's secretary kept stopping to look at the surrounding landscape, constraining me to make many detours. What was more, every time he meant to return to the road on which we had been travelling, he invariably and confidently set off in the opposite direction.

"But is this not the way?" he would ask in surprise time and again, unaware of his own distraction and of my efforts to keep him on the right road.

I then recalled that Atto, when introducing me to his secretary, had hinted at one last defect of his. Here was perhaps the moment to take advantage of that. I decided that it would not be difficult to lead Buvat in the wrong direction, since that was where his natural tendency took him.

We crossed a narrow little street in which were trading some of the many poor wretches drawn to Rome by the Jubilee. Within instants, we were surrounded by that motley humanity which a hundred times, a thousand times, one might encounter in the streets, always different yet ever the same: vendors of powders to cure intestinal wind, alum of wine dregs which makes the flame of tapers everlasting, oil of badgers to cure colds, lime paste for killing rats, spectacles with which one can see in the dark. And then there were prodigious characters who fearlessly held in their hands tarantulas, crocodiles, Indian lizards and basilisks; others who danced on a tight rope performing mortal leaps or ran swiftly on their hands, lifted weights with their hair, washed their face with molten lead, had their nose sliced off with a knife or drew from their mouths cords ten yards long.

Suddenly there arrived in the street a little group of decently attired gallants accompanied by as many women, likewise fashionably dressed, and they announced that they wished to perform a play.

The troupe of actors was immediately surrounded by a multitude of small children, women, curious bystanders, minders of other people's business, wastrels, passers-by joking loudly and old men malevolently mumbling yet never leaving off from staring at the scene. The actors produced a few trestles from who knows where and with incredible speed erected a little stage. The most attractive woman in the group which had just arrived stepped forward and began to sing, accompanied on the guitar by one of the actors. They began with a medley of songs and popular jokes and the people, drawn by the free entertainment, came crowding in, most numerous. When the first set of songs had come to an end, and while the people were awaiting the start of the play, there came on stage instead the oldest member of the troupe and, drawing from his pocket a little jar full of dark powder, announced that this was a wondrous medicine, whereupon he began to extol its great and incomparable qualities. Part of the public began to murmur, having realised that the actors were really charlatans and the speaker was the arch-charlatan. However, most of the people remained most attentive to the explication: the powder was none other than a magical quinte essence, capable of instantly rendering its possessor wealthy. On the other hand, when mixed with good oil, it became a miraculous ointment against the scrofula; and when mixed with cat's excrement, it was perfect for preparing plasters and poultices.

While the arch-charlatan was selling the first little jars of powder, enthusiastically acquired by some passing peasants who had listened open-mouthed to the talk, we moved away from the tight, malodorous throng which now packed the side-street and returned to the main road. On arriving in front of a tavern, I made my proposal as though it were some mere passing thought.

"I am sure that, instead of a well-earned rest, you would not be displeased to raise your spirits in another way," said I, tarrying a little.

"Ah. . . Yes, I do indeed think so," said he, hesitantly, his nose tilting upwards towards a campanile.

Then, catching sight of the tavern's sign, but above hearing the clinking of glasses and the clamour of the drinkers issuing forth from within, his tone changed.

"No, by the powers of darkness, of course not!"

While I dipped the ring cake which I had ordered for breakfast in a glass of good red wine, Buvat resolved to satisfy my curiosity and began at last to reveal to me something of the life of the Connestabilessa.

"In the decade before he died, the last years of his rule in France, Cardinal Mazarin called from Rome to Paris a multitude of kinsmen: two sisters and seven young nieces. And every one of the latter was marriageable."

The nieces of the Cardinal's first sister, Anna Maria and Laura Martinozzi, married the Prince of Conti and the Duke of Modena. Two better matches could not have been hoped for. However, there remained on the Cardinal's hands those nieces for whom it would be harder to find suitable husbands: the daughters of the other sister, the five Mancini sisters: Ortensia, Marianna, Laura, Olimpia and Maria.

They were capricious and astute, cunning and most attractive, and their arrival had set off throughout the court twin passions that mirrored one another: the women's hatred and the men's love. Someone called them mockingly "the Mazarinettes". But they, the Mazarinettes, knew how to mix in the cup of seduction the opposing nectars of innocence and malice, prudence and boldness. Whoever drank from that cup found himself ruled by them according to the exact and implacable science of the passions.

Despite this (perhaps, indeed, because of their ambitious aims) His Eminence succeeded in time in finding the right husbands for them. Laura was taken soon enough by the Duc de Mercoeur. Marianna wed the Duc de Bouillon. Ortensia fell to the Marquis de la Meilleraye and Olimpia to the Comte de Soissons. A series of marriages that no one could ever have hoped for. Before coming to Paris, these Roman girls were nothing. Now, they were countesses and duchesses, married to princes of the blood royal, to grand masters of the artillery, to descendants of Richelieu and of Henri IV, and what was more, immensely wealthy. Their mothers, Mazarin's sisters, belonged to the Roman nobility, but to its most minor ranks.

"Of course, the Mancini family is of the most ancient nobility," the secretary insisted. "It stretches back to before the year one thousand, but the family has never enjoyed the affluence befitting the flower of the aristocracy. Their names betray this: Martinozzi, Mancini. . ." he chanted, stressing the *ozzi* and the *ini*. "Anyone can see that these are not high-sounding names."

Despite the girls' temperament, all the marriages of the Mazarinettes were, when all is said and done, arranged and celebrated without excessive difficulties. Only one niece brought Mazarin a veritable mountain of difficulties: Maria.

She had arrived in Paris at the age of fourteen, when the young Louis was one year older. She took up lodgings in the palace of her uncle, almost stunned by the pomp and luxury which, during the years of the Fronde, had excited the people's enmity against the Cardinal. At first, the Queen Mother, Anne of Austria, treated her benevolently, as indeed she did Mazarin's other nieces, almost as though they were of the same blood.

"One day, the mother of the Mancini girls fell gravely ill and His Majesty went with a certain regularity to visit the sick woman. Here, every time, he found Maria. Of course, in the beginning, everything was rather formal: 'I am so pained at your noble mother's ill health,' *et cetera, et cetera*; 'Oh, Your Majesty, despite the sad occasion, I am most honoured by your words, and so on,'" said Buvat, miming first royal concern, then womanish modesty.

In the end, Maria's mother died and, on the day of the funeral, some persons noted that the freedom with which the young girl spoke with the Sovereign was considerably greater than when her mother had enjoyed good health.

On the very evening of Maria's mother's funeral, a ballet with a prophetic title was performed at court, *L'Amour Malade*. Louis, as was his wont when young, was among the dancers. In the great hall of the Louvre, before the entire court, Louis' royal pirouettes opened the first of ten *entrées*, each of which represented a remedy to cure the languishing deity.

No few courtiers noticed that Louis's steps were livelier than usual, his breath longer, his leaps more ample, his look firmer and more expressive, as though an invisible force sustained him, whispering to him the secret remedy whereby love is first cured and at last triumphant.

At court, no one, among all the King's noble companions of the same age, was able to treat with him on a basis of true friendship. He was too irascible and proud, too serious even when he smiled, and too smiling when he commanded. Whenever they spoke with him, young women, in the grip of awe and embarrassment, hid behind the heavy mantle of curtsies and formalities.

Only Maria was not afraid of Louis. When, in the King's presence, all others trembled with fear (and the desire to be chosen by him), the young Italian girl played the game of love with the same tranquil malice as she might have employed with any good-looking young man.

In public, he was icy and distant; only she distracted and, often without even realising it, melted the mask of indifference, transforming it into that of desire. He was dying to grant her every confidence, as etiquette forbade him to, and even found himself stammering, blushing and comically at a loss for words.

"His Majesty was observed," swore Buvat, "at night, before going to sleep, tormented by the memory of minute yet insufferable embarrassments, and he bit his pillow when he remembered how some witty sally of Maria's had caused him first to laugh, then to stutter painfully, losing both his royal composure and the right moment in which to say: 'I love you'."

Events again took the upper hand because of an illness. At the end of 1658 in Calais, after a series of exceedingly fatiguing voyages and inspections, and perhaps because of the bad air which troubles the humours, Louis became seriously ill. The fever was most violent and persistent, and for a fortnight all Paris feared for the Sovereign's life. Thanks to the skill of a provincial physician, Louis recovered in the end. Upon his return to Paris, the gossip on all court tongues soon came to his ears: in all the city, the eyes which had wept the most, the mouth that had most invoked his name and the hands most joined in prayer for his recovery had been Maria's.

Instead of an open declaration (which none could dare utter to a Sovereign) Maria had thus sent Louis an involuntary and far more potent message, and the whole court, through its whispering, was suggesting to the King: she loves you, and you know it.

In the months that followed, the court sojourned at Fontainebleau, where Mazarin, who still held the reins of government, kept the young Sovereign entertained each day with new diversions: excursions by carriage, plays and trips on the water followed one another without a break, and, whether in his carriage, on the park's drives or on its lawns, Louis' path kept crossing that of Maria. They sought one another constantly and were forever finding one another.

"Permit me to ask you a question," I interrupted him. "How come you know all these details so well? These events took place over forty years ago."

"Abbot Melani knows these things better than anyone else," was his sole reply.

"Ah, I see. So he has also told you all about that period, as he told me," said I, deliberately exaggerating, "about the secret missions he carried out for Mazarin, concerning Fouquet. . ."

I had purposely mentioned two well-hidden secrets from Melani's past: his friendship (which he himself had revealed to me seventeen years previously) with Superintendent Fouquet, France's Minister of Finance, who was persecuted by the Most Christian King, and the fact (learned from others) that Atto had been a secret agent in the service of Mazarin.

I seemed to detect a sudden flash of surprise in Buvat's expression. He probably thought that Abbot Melani had confided the most precious secrets to me and I must therefore be worthy of his trust.

"He will then have also told you," he added, "that he himself was deeply in love with Maria, obviously without anything taking place between the two of them, and that when reasons of state constrained the King to marry the Infanta of Spain, she left Paris and came to Rome, where she married the Constable Colonna. In Rome, she and the Abbot continued to frequent one another, seeing as he had arrived there shortly afterwards. And they still correspond. The Abbot has never forgotten her."

I brought the glass to my lips and drank deeply, seeking to cover my face as much as possible so that my surprise should not be visible. I had succeeded in making Buvat believe that I knew enough about what had taken place behind the scenes in Atto's life, so that he could talk freely with me. I must not let him see that I was learning all this from him for the first time.

So Atto had been in love with Maria, and at the very time when she was courting the young King of France. Now that explained his sighs, thought I to myself, when at the Villa Spada he received that letter from the Connestabilessa!

I recalled then, while ordering another ring cake, a far-off conversation from seventeen years before, at the time when I had made Atto's acquaintance: a conversation between the guests at the inn where I was working. And I remembered how it had then been mentioned that Atto had been the confidant of a niece of Mazarin, with whom the King was madly in love, so much so that he wanted to marry her. Now I knew *who* that niece of Mazarin's was.

Suddenly, we were interrupted by a scene all too common in establishments like that in which we sat. A quartet of mendicants had entered in order to beg, provoking the wrath of mine host and mute discontent among the other customers. One of the intruders began to exchange insults with a pair of young men seated near us and, within moments, a brawl broke out, so that we were forced to move in order to avoid getting involved. What with the vagabonds, the tavern's customers, the host and his apprentice, there must have been some ten persons involved in the struggle. In the confusion, they fell against our table and nearly knocked over the jug of wine.

Fortunately, once the row had died down and the mendicants had gone on their way, we saw that our jug was still there and we could once more sit down. I heard the master of the house muttering for a long time after that against the flood of beggars unleashed on Rome during Jubilees.

"Ah yes, I too knew that Abbot Melani was very much in love with Maria Mancini," I lied, in the hope of getting something more out of Buvat.

"So much in love that, the moment she had gone, he went every day to visit her sister Ortensia," continued Buvat, pouring wine into our glasses. "So much so that he incurred the wrath of her husband, the Duc de La Meilleraye, a bigoted and violent fellow, who sent ruffians to hunt him down and give him a beating, thus causing him to leave France."

"Ah yes, the Duc de La Meilleraye," I repeated while drinking, again remembering what I had heard years ago from the guests at my inn.

"The Abbot who, it seems, could not do without contact with one of the Mazarinettes, took advantage of the situation to go to Rome and find Maria, with the King's blessing – and a fat payment. But now I think it is time we were on our way," said Buvat, seeing that we had by now emptied the whole jug of wine. "Several hours have passed now and the Signor Abbot will be wondering what has become of me," said he, asking the host for the bill.

❧

Having hired two nags, we rode to the Villa Spada without exchanging another word. I was beset by great somnolence, while Buvat was suffering from fits of giddiness caused, said he, by the unseemly hour at which the Abbot had got him out of bed. I too realised with surprise that I was exhausted: the events of the day – and the night – before were perhaps beginning to be too much for me. I was no longer the fresh young prentice I had once been. I had barely the strength to take my leave of Buvat with a nod in lieu of salutation, after which I mounted my mule and let myself be borne back to my little house. I already knew that I would still not find Cloridia there. That blessed delivery was still keeping everyone waiting. As I let myself fall back on the bed and slip into drowsiness, I rejoiced at the thought that we would be meeting again that very evening at the Villa Spada, where the arrival was expected of the Princess of Forano in an advanced state of pregnancy. For safety's sake, Cloridia's presence would certainly have been requested. Then I gave in to sleep.

❧

I was awoken in a most disagreeable and, to say the least, unexpected manner. Heavy and hostile forces were shaking me, accompanied by a thunderous, peremptory and insistent voice. Any attempt to return to the immaterial world of dreams and to resist these unwanted calls from the world would have been quite in vain.

"Wake up, wake up, I beg you!"

I opened my eyes, which were at once painfully hurt by the light of the sun. My head was hurting as it had never done in my whole life. My shoulder was being shaken by a servant of the Villa Spada, whom I recognised with difficulty because of the great pain in my head and my difficulty in keeping my eyes open.

"What are you doing here and. . . how did you get in? "I asked weakly.

"I came to deliver a note from Abbot Melani and when I got here I found the door open. Are you all right?"

"So so. . . the door was open?"

"As far as I was concerned, I meant only to knock, believe me," he replied with the deference which he believed to be my due in my capacity as the addressee of a message from a guest of such distinction as Abbot Melani, "but then I dared enter in order to make sure that nothing had happened to you. I think that you have been the victim of robbers."

I looked around me. The room in which I had been sleeping was in the most utter chaos. Clothes, blankets, furniture, shoes, the bedpan, the night pot, Cloridia's obstetrical instruments, even the crucifix which normally hung above the conjugal bed, were scattered all over the place, on the bed, on the floor. A glass lay shattered near the threshold.

"Did you notice nothing on your return home?"

"No, I. . . I think that all was in order. . ."

"Then it happened while you were sleeping. But your sleep must have been very heavy. . . Would you like me to help you tidy up?"

"No, it does not matter. Where is the message?"

As soon as the servant had gone on his way, I tried to overcome the shock by putting a little order in the house. Instead, I only increased my surprise and disquiet. The other rooms too, the kitchen, the pantry, even the cellar, had been violently turned upside down. Someone had entered the house while I was sleeping and had looked everywhere in search of something hidden. All the worse for them, I thought: the only objects of value were buried under a tree and only I and my wife knew where that was. After a good half hour spent putting things back in order, I realised that in fact nothing of any importance was missing. I sat down on the bed, still tormented by my aching head and by fatigue.

Someone had entered my house in broad daylight, I repeated to myself. Had I noticed anything on my return? I could remember nothing. It was then, still half befuddled, that I realised I had not yet read the message sent me by Atto. I opened it and remained all agape:

> *Buvat drugged and robbed.*
> *Join me at once.*

❧

"But it is obvious, you have both been slipped some narcotic," said Abbot Melani, nervously pacing up and down his apartment at the Villa Spada.

Buvat was seated in a corner with two huge bags under his eyes, apparently incapable even of yawning.

"It is not possible that you should not have heard the thieves when they were turning your whole house upside down," continued Abbot Melani, turning to me, "nor is it possible that Buvat should not have been aware of someone lifting his mattress, throwing him to the ground, rummaging through the blankets and finally stripping him of everything, including his money and leaving him half naked. No, all that is not possible without the help of a powerful sleeping draught."

Buvat nodded timidly, without managing to conceal his feelings of guilt and shame at what had happened. So Buvat, too, on his return from our mission in town, had fallen into a leaden sleep. The Abbot was right: we had been drugged.

"But how did they manage it?" trilled Melani, looking at us.

Buvat and I looked at one another with vacant, tired eyes: we had not the slightest idea how.

"And did they make no attempt to enter your chamber?" I asked Atto.

"No. Perhaps because I, instead of going to pothouses," said he emphatically, casting a meaningful look at us, "stayed wide awake and worked."

"But did you hear nothing?"

"Nothing whatever. And that is the strangest thing. Of course, I had bolted the door communicating with Buvat's little room. Whoever did it must have been a real magician."

"Perhaps Sfasciamonti will not yet have returned, but the other catchpolls of the villa will surely have seen. . ." said I.

"The catchpolls, the catchpolls. . ." he chanted excitedly. "They know only how to drink and to enrich the brothels. They'll have let in some strumpet who, after taking care of the guards, helped the thieves. We know how these things are done."

"How very strange," I observed; "and all this only a few hours after the horrible assault on the bookbinder. Could the two things be connected?"

"Good heavens, I really do hope not!" exclaimed Buvat with a start, for he had no wish to be, however indirectly, the cause of someone's death.

"Of course, they were looking for something which could be in the hands of one or other of you," replied Atto. "The proof is that, among all the apartments in the great house, they wormed their way in only here. I put a few discreet questions to the servants, but it all meant nothing to them. No one had disturbed them."

"We must advise Don Paschatio Melchiorri at once," I exclaimed.

"Never," Atto cut me off. "At least, not until we have clearer ideas about this affair."

"But someone has got into the great house! We could all be in danger! And it is my duty to inform Cardinal Spada, my master. . ."

"Yes. . . And thus you'd cause a general alarm, the guests would protest at the villa's lack of protection and they would all leave. So, adieu to the nuptial celebrations. Is that what you want?"

Abbot Melani was so accustomed to having a dirty conscience that in murky cases like this it mattered not that he himself was the victim; he feared nevertheless that he might have something to hide and invariably opted for secrecy. I was, however, bound to admit that his objections were far from unfounded: I dared not so much as to consider that I might have risked ruining the nuptials of Cardinal Fabrizio's nephew. So I resigned myself to seconding the Abbot.

"But what were they looking for?" said I, changing the subject.

"If you do not know, I too have no idea. The thieves' objective concerns me, obviously, as I am the only one who knows both of you. Now, however. . ."

"Yes?"

"I must think, and think deeply. Let us take things in order. There are other knots to be untied first, and who knows if, once that has done, we may not find our way to this? You, my boy, will now accompany me."

"Where?"

"On board, as I promised you."

After a quick visit to the kitchens to pick up something on which to lunch, we left the Villa Spada in the greatest secrecy; we cut across the vineyard while avoiding the main avenue and surreptitiously gained the entrance gate. While we were taking that irregular route and dirtying our shoes with the soil of the vineyard, Atto must have sensed on the back of his neck the warm breath of my curiosity.

"Very well, this is what we are about," he exclaimed, going straight to the point. "Your master must board something in the company of Spinola di San Cesareo and a certain A."

"I remember perfectly."

"So the first problem, contrary to what you might imagine, is not the place of the meeting, but who will be taking part in it."

"You mean, who A is."

"Exactly. Because only once we know the state and the prerogatives of the participants to a secret meeting shall we be able to discover the place where it is to be held. If it is a prince meeting with two ordinary burghers, it will take place on the prince's estates, for he certainly will not discommode himself for the sake of two inferiors; if it is between two thieves and an honest man, it will surely be in a place chosen by the thieves, who are used to plotting at secret meetings, and so on."

"Fine, I understand what you are telling me," said I with a hint of impatience, while we made our way painfully through the mud.

"Right. We have two cardinals. One warns the other and tells him that he will personally contact a third party. The latter will certainly be one of their peers, otherwise your master would have used other terms in his message, for instance: 'Let us meet on board tomorrow. A too will be present,' to stress the fact that this third person is not of their rank. However, what he did say was: 'I shall advise A.' Is that not so?"

"Yes, that is so," I confirmed as we crept out from the gate of the villa.

"How can I put it? This time, I shall advise him, don't you worry about it. In other words, that message makes me think that all three are involved and there may be frequent, familiar and customary relations between them."

"Agreed. So?"

"So, it is a third cardinal."

"Are you sure of that?"

"By no means; but it is the only clue we have to work on. Now, look at this."

Fortunately, we were far enough from the gates of the villa not to be descried by its inhabitants. With a rapid gesture, he drew from a pocket a half-crumpled sheet of paper, folded down the middle. I opened it.

Acciaioli
Albani
Altieri
Archinto
Bichi
Boncompagni
Borgia
Cantelmi
Carpegna
Cenci
Colloredo
Cornaro
Costaguti

. . .

"Well, I ask you, how many cardinals' names begin with the letter 'A'?"

"Signor Atto, what are you showing me?" I asked, troubled by that strange document. Was Atto perhaps involving me in some sort of espionage?"

"Just read. These are the cardinals who will elect the next pontiff. Which ones begin with 'A'?"

"Acciaoli, Albani, Altieri, Archinto and Astalli," I read from the first lines.

He folded the paper at once and at once replaced it in the pocket from which it has come, while we continued on our way.

We were now right in front of the San Pancrazio Gate from which one leaves the city to the east, by the Via Aurelia. I watched Atto for an instant darting glances all around us, for he too did not desire to arouse too much attention. To be surprised while in possession of such a document might give rise to accusations of espionage, with dreadful consequences.

"Let us see then," said he with a great easy smile, as though we were speaking of any trivial matter. I realised that he was relaxing the muscles of his face for our imminent meeting with the guards at the San Pancrazio Gate, through which we were about to continue his chosen itinerary, the destination of which he had not as yet revealed.

"Astalli is Papal Legate to Ferrara, he is not in Rome at this moment and he will come, if he does come, only for the conclave.

Archinto is in Milan, too far off to come to your master's festivities. Acciaioli, the first on the list, is not as far as I know a good friend of the Spada family."

"So there remain only Altieri and Albani."

"Exactly. Altieri fits in very well with our hypothesis, for, like Spada, he is one of the cardinals created by Pope Clement X of blessed memory. But Albani fits even better for reasons of political equilibrium."

"What do you mean?"

"Simple: a secret meeting between three cardinals only makes sense if it is a meeting of the representatives of as many different factions. Well, Spinola is regarded as the favourite of the Empire. Spada, however, being Secretary of State to a Neapolitan Pope, thus belongs to a Spanish fief, and may therefore be regarded as close to Spain. Albani, on the other hand, is regarded by many as being a friend of France. So we have here a little synod meeting in preparation for the conclave. That is why your master is so uneasy at this time: that lecture to the Major-Domo, that nervous, worried air. . ."

"A milkmaid mentioned that Cardinal Spada is forever moving back and forth between an ambassador and a cardinal, about matters relating to a papal breve," I recalled, surprised that I too possessed interesting information which I had not yet, however, been able to exploit.

"Excellent. Unless I am mistaken, Albani is Secretary for Breves, is he not?" concluded Melani, sounding most satisfied.

He was not mistaken; I had heard this mentioned by two ladies during last night's meal.

At that juncture, we broke off, having come within sight of the guards of the San Pancrazio Gate who obviously knew me well because, living outside the walls, I passed through the gate in one direction or the other every single day. To be in a gentleman's company was an added advantage. We were allowed through without any problem.

"You have still not told me where we are going," said I, although a certain idea was already forming in the ramblings of my imagination.

"Well, our three cardinals are to hold their little meeting on board a vessel. On the Tiber, perhaps?"

"That does not seem very likely."

"To tell the truth, it might well be so, if they really wanted to keep out of sight of prying eyes. The fact is, however, that they have a far more convenient place on dry land, and just here, a stone's throw from the Villa Spada. We are almost there. Perhaps you have heard tell of this; it is called the Vessel."

༚ঙ্গ

After all Atto's deductions, that was the name I was expecting.

"Of course I have heard of it," I replied. "I walk by it every day on my way from home to the Villa Spada, but I realised that it might be a meeting place for the three cardinals only after you had set forth your considerations," I admitted, "and then I knew that the expression 'on board' was just a play on words. . ."

Atto began to walk faster, registering my diplomatic declaration of inferiority with a mute smile.

"You will see," he resumed, "it is a truly singular place. It is a site, as perhaps you may know, which is fairly closely bound up with France, and that makes the encounter between Spinola and your master Spada even more interesting: a Hispanophile cardinal and a friend of the Empire attending a clandestine meeting in a French house."

"In sum, it is a meeting to choose the next pope. If the third party proves to be Albani, the Francophile, one might say that France is running the affair."

"Now we shall go and take a look," said he without answering me. "The meeting will certainly have taken place at dawn, the hour for occult machinations, and it will be all over by now. But we might still be able to trace some interesting information. And yet. . ."

"And yet?"

"A coincidence. Very strange. Something rather bizarre is kept in the Vessel. Objects which. . . well, it is an old story which I shall tell you sooner or later."

Just as Atto was pronouncing these last syllables, we reached our destination and I had to postpone any request for an elucidation.

The place we were about to enter was not far distant from my rural habitation, and was to play a great part in the events which I shall be recounting; it was known to many but truly known by few. Officially, it bore the name of Villa Benedetti from the name of a certain Benedetti, of whom I knew only that he had, decades before, had the edifice built with great luxury and pomp. Because of its singular form, which made it resemble a sailing ship, the structure was also known to the local people as the Villa of the Vessel, or simply, the Vessel.

I have already said that it was known to everyone, and not just to the people of the neighbourhood; for in fact the villa enjoyed a strange notoriety. All the inhabitants of the neighbourhood knew that, after the death of its builder, some ten years ago, the palazzo and its garden had passed as a legacy to a kinsman of Cardinal Mazarin; yet the Cardinal's relative had never set foot there, so that the villa had become a forgotten place. Yet it had not been abandoned: at nightfall, lights could be seen there, and during the day, the shadows of people. From the street, one could hear music wafting through the air, the footsteps of people, gentle laughter. Perpetual was the soft plashing of a fountain, with the occasional counterpoint of a lackey's rapid paces on the gravel of the courtyard.

No visitor, however, was ever seen to enter or to leave. Never did a carriage halt before the villa to set down guests of note, nor was any servant ever seen to go out in order to fetch provisions for the kitchens or firewood for winter. Everyone knew that there must be someone within, yet he was never seen.

It was as though the Vessel was animated by a secret life, independent of any contact with the outside world. It seemed to shelter within its bounds mysterious faceless gentlemen, like the gods of some minor Olympus, caring nothing for men's society and content with their mysterious privacy. Around it, an arcane aura discouraged the curious and inspired a certain unease even in those who, like myself, passed by the villa at least once a day.

The location of the Vessel, on the other hand, could not have been finer or more desirable, overlooking the Via Aurelia from the sweet heights of the Janiculum Hill. Situated right on the boundary between city and countryside, the building enjoyed perfect air and the most agreeable and varied views, without the eye having to go begging for them. Although it rose among the gentle, modest heights of the hill, yet the Vessel had a proud and unblemished appearance: more than a villa, it seemed truly a castle. At first sight, one might say, a seagoing castle. The prow (as I was soon to see) was the double stairway of the façade, set in the green of the garden, which, with a double symmetrical and converging curve, led to a little terrace, the faithful image of an upper deck. The poop, at the opposite end, was represented by a low semicircular façade, within which a covered loggia with spacious arched windows gave onto the Via di Porta San Pancrazio behind. The ship itself consisted of the four habitable storeys, graceful and airy in design, overlooked by four turrets, in turn made perfect by as many banners, almost like pennants raised on the masts of a ship under sail.

The Vessel rose thus proudly, well above the ridge and the tops of the surrounding trees, so that it could be seen even from afar; and it mattered not that the garden was not so big, as, moreover, a Latin motto placed above the entrance proclaimed, which time and again I had had occasion to read in passing:

Agri tantum quo fruamur
Non quo oneremur.

In other words, its creator recommended the possession of just so much land as sufficed for the enjoyment thereof, rather than wasting money on the acquisition of great estates. This motto, which smacked of ancient rural wisdom, was merely the prelude to much, so much else, which we were to find within.

Atto halted, scrutinising the distant bifurcation in the Via di Porta San Pancrazio, opening the view onto the Casino Corsini.

"I know that the Vessel was built by a certain Benedetti," I resumed as we discreetly explored the road, "but who was he?"

"One of Mazarin's trusted men. He acted as his agent here in Rome. He purchased pictures, books and precious objects in his name. In time, he became something of a connoisseur. He maintained contacts with Bernini, Algardi and Poussin. . . I do not know whether those names mean anything to you."

"Of course they do, Signor Atto. These are great artists."

Benedetti had a flair for architecture, Atto continued, although not himself an architect. Sometimes he would undertake projects that were large for him. For example, he had proposed building a grand stairway up the hill between the Piazza di Spagna and Trinità dei Monti, but this led to nothing. Occasionally, however, he found ways of realising his ideas. It was, for example, his design which was adopted for the catafalque for the Cardinal's funeral held here in Rome. It was rather heavy and excessively pompous, but not ugly. Benedetti was a fine amateur.

"Perhaps he had a hand in the design of the Vessel, too," said I, wondering out loud.

"Indeed, it is said that the villa is his own work, far more than that of the architects whom he hired. And that is the truth."

"Did you know him well?"

"I helped him when he came to France, a little over thirty years ago, precisely because of the Vessel. When he died, he bequeathed me a few little things out of gratitude. A couple of nice little pictures."

We now stood before the wall surrounding the villa. He looked westward, screwing up his eyes a little against the afternoon glare.

"He had come to visit Vaux-le-Vicomte, the château of my friend Nicolas Fouquet. I accompanied him, and he revealed to me that he intended to draw on it as an inspiration for his own villa. But enough chatter now, we have arrived. You will be able to see with your own eyes, and to judge for yourself, if you so desire."

We approached the entrance gate, which was of admirable and unusual design. There rose up before us the poop of the Vessel: a great covered loggia rounded in shape, with luminous arcades, looking onto the road in which we stood. From the loggia came the gentle plashing of a little fountain. The poop was supported by the outer wall, which in turn was skilfully sculpted in the form of a reef, with windows and doors sunk into it like marine grottoes and inlets. The Vessel, afloat on imaginary waves, seemed thus to be anchored beside a cliff. In the midst of pines, oleanders, clover and daisies, on the Janiculum Hill, one beheld that delicious and absurd vision of a ship at its moorings.

No one seemed to be keeping watch over the gate to the villa. Nor, as it proved, was there anyone present. Hardly had we passed through the door than we found ourselves in a vestibule which in turn opened onto a garden.

Atto and I advanced cautiously, sure that from one moment to the next someone would come to meet us. From within the villa, voices could be heard, rendered diffuse by the distance; then the echo of a woman's laugh. No one came.

We found ourselves in an ample courtyard with, to our right, the majestically projecting hull of the Vessel. In the centre, a graceful fountain, animated by fine *jeux d'eau*, politely recited its effervescent logorrhoea, quietly plashing.

We stopped and glanced around us to find our bearings. In front of us and to the left stretched the park, which we began cautiously to explore. There were long, long hedges and vases containing citrus and other precious fruit trees set out in rows alongside; a staircase with nine separate sets of steps; espaliered roses and lines of trees trained across a few pergolas arranged in checkerboard pattern; various fruit trees, likewise espaliered; and then a little grove. The jets of a second fountain, placed on a terrace in the centre of the first floor of the building, provided an elegant and ever new counterpoint.

"Should we not announce our presence?"

"Not yet. We are trespassing on private property, I know, but there was no one guarding it. We shall, if asked, justify our presence by our desire to pay a tribute to the owner of this fine villa. In other words, we shall play dumb in order to avoid having to pay the entry fee, as the saying goes."

"For how long?" I asked, worried about the possibility of getting myself into trouble so close to my own home and to the Villa Spada.

"Until we discover something interesting about the meeting of the three cardinals. And now stop asking questions."

Before us stretched a drive covered by a great pergola of various exquisite grapes.

"The grape, a Christian symbol of rebirth: thus Benedetti welcomed his visitors," observed Melani.

The pergola ended, as we had occasion to observe, before a fine fresco of Rome Triumphant.

To approach the building would have exposed us too much; someone would have arrived sooner or later to interrupt our unauthorised inspection of the premises. Walking among the shady drives of the park, we gradually came on the contrary to feel protected and lulled by the afternoon calm, by the scent of the citrus fruit and the quiet burbling of the fountains.

Wandering around the gardens, we found a clearing with two little pyramids. On the sides of each was inscribed a dedication. On the first, one could read:

GENII AMOENITATI
Qui procul a curis ille laetus.
Si vis esse talis,
Esto ruralis.

"Well, my boy, here's something for you," came Atto's friendly challenge.

"I'd say: 'To the amenity of Genius. Blessed he who is free from cares; if you too desire this, live in the country.'"

The other pyramid bore a similar epigraph:

AMICITIAE FELICITATI
In secunda, et in adverse fortuna,
Nil solidius amico:
Hunc facilius in rure
Quam in aula invenies.

"'To the joys of Friendship. In good times and in bad, nothing is more reliable than a friend: but you'll find one more easily in the country than at Court'," I translated.

For a few seconds, we stayed silent before the two pyramids, each – or so I thought – secretly curious about the thoughts of the other. Whatever cogitations could those maxims suggest to Atto? Genius and friendship. . . If I had had to say which genius was dominant in him, I'd have thought at once of his two true passions: politics and intrigue. And friendship? Abbot Melani was fond of me, of that I had become certain when I discovered my little pearls secretly concealed close to his heart, sewn like an *ex voto* into the scapular of Our Lady of the Carmel. But, apart from that, had Atto ever, even for one moment, been my friend, a true, disinterested friend, as he liked to show so ostentatiously whenever it suited him?

Suddenly, a sinuous melody was heard in the distance: a strange song, like that of a grave siren, which seemed to come, now from a flute, now from a viola da gamba, sometimes even from a woman's voice.

"They are making music in the villa," I observed.

Atto listened attentively.

"No, it is not coming from the villa, but from somewhere around here."

We searched the park with our eyes in vain. The wind rose suddenly, with a rustling whisper raising from the drives and bushes a colourless mantle of dead leaves, premature victims of the heat.

Now the melody seemed again to be issuing from the house.

"There, it is coming from there," Atto corrected himself.

He pointed at a window to the side of the entrance courtyard, facing west, which we could see through the foliage of the trees. We turned to face it.

Thus, for the first time, we came within a few paces of the building, just under the windows, from which anyone could not only see but hear us; yet we continued to wander around undisturbed. I was incredulous that no one should have intercepted us and, little by little, I came to feel myself boldly at ease with that place which had hitherto been unknown and mysterious to me.

Our whole attention was focused on what was taking place above us, on that window (in fact, the only open one) from which the music seemed to be coming. Once again, however, the invisible cloak of silence seemed to descend on the park and on us.

"It seems that they are amusing themselves by staying hidden," joked Atto.

Thus we were able the better to admire the architecture of the Vessel. The façade under which we stood was divided into three orders; the surface was broken by a recess which at ground level was filled by a fine portico, framed by arches and columns, above which, at first-floor level, there was a terrace. We reached the portico.

"Signor Atto, look here."

I pointed out to Atto that, above each of the lunettes of the portico, there was a Latin inscription. There were four of these in all:

AERIS SALUBRITAS
LOCI SUBLIMITAS
URBIS VICINITAS
DOMUS COMMODITAS

"'Here, the air is healthy, the place is sublime, the city's nearby, the house is commodious,'" Atto translated. "A veritable hymn by Elpidio Benedetti to his villa."

There were two other similar inscriptions above the two doors in the façade:

Agricola semper in proximum annum dives est
Laudato ingentia Rura, exiguum colito

"'The farmer is always rich. . . next year. Let great fields be praised, and small ones, cultivated.' Amusing. Look, here too there are inscriptions everywhere."

Atto invited me to enter the portico. There, running my eyes over the façades, I found other proverbs, rather faded but most numerous, almost like a creeper that had invaded the walls, grouped three by three on each pilaster.

I drew near to the first inscription and read:

Discretion is the mother of virtue.
Not all men of letters are learned.
Better a good friend than a hundred kinsmen.

One enemy is too many, and a hundred friends are not enough.
A wise man and a madman know more than a wise man alone.
It matters more to know how to live than to know how to speak.

One thing is born of another, and the World governs it.
With scant brains is the World governed.
The World is governed by opinions.

At either side of the loggia stood two half-pilasters, each with its corresponding proverb:

At court, no one enjoys himself more than the jesters.
In his villa, the wise man best finds contemplation, and pleasure.

"I knew of the inscriptions at the Vessel," said Atto then, as he discovered them alongside me, "but I could never have imagined that there could be so many of them, and painted everywhere. A truly remarkable piece of work. Bravo Benedetti! Even if they're not all flour from his own sack," he concluded with a malicious smile.

"What do you mean?"

"'The World is governed by opinions,'" Atto once more recited in an insidious, strident voice, pulling down his clothes as though to mimic a surplice, his eyebrows arched in a severe expression and two fingers under his nose as though to ape a pair of moustaches.

"His Eminence Cardinal Mazarin?" I guessed.

"One of his favourite phrases. He never wrote it down, as he did with so many others."

"And which other maxims do you recognise here?"

"Let's see. . . 'Discretion is the mother of virtue': that was by my late lamented friend Pope Clement IX. Then. . . 'Better one good friend than a hundred kinsmen.' Her Majesty Anne of Austria, the late mother of the Most Christian King, would often repeat that. . . Did you say something?"

"No, Signor Atto."

"Are you sure? I could have sworn I heard something like. . . a whisper. . . Yes, that's it."

We looked all around us for a moment, vaguely perturbed. Seeing nothing, we could but continue the visit while, quietly, almost inaudibly, the melody we had heard before began again.

"A *folia*," commented the Abbot.

"Yes, it is all rather weird in here," I concurred.

"But what do you think I meant? I am speaking of the melody

we're listening to: these are variations on the theme of the *folia*. Or at least that is what it sounds like, from the little one can hear of it."

I said nothing, not knowing what the theme of the *folia* might be, in music.

"It is a popular tune of Portuguese origin, originally a dance," said Atto, answering my tacit query, "and it is quite well known. It is all based on what one might call a musical canvas, a very simple musical warp and weave, on which musicians improvise a great number of variations and the most virtuosic counterpoints."

We stayed a while again listening to the melody, which gradually unfolded as a deep, severe motif gave way to a warm, brilliant one, then to melancholy. This music was always fickle, forever on the move.

"It is very beautiful," I murmured breathlessly, while the enchantment of the music began to make my head spin.

"It is the *basso ostinato*, it, too, varied, which accompanies the counterpoint. This always captivates dreamy natures like yours," sniggered Atto. "However, in this case, you are perfectly right. Until now, I had always believed there were no better variations on the *folia* than those of maestro Marais at Versailles; however, these ones in the Italian manner are enchanting. The composer is really excellent, whoever he may be."

"But who first composed the *folia*?" I asked, beset by curiosity, while the music vanished into thin air.

"Everyone and no one. As I told you, it is a popular melody, a very ancient dance. Its origins are lost in the mists of time. Even the name "folly" is mysterious. But let me read now, here there's something by Lorenzo de' Medici," Atto continued, preparing to peruse a few verses, then breaking off suddenly.

"Did you hear that?" he hissed.

I had indeed heard it. Two voices. One masculine, the other feminine. Quite close to us. Then, footsteps on the gravel.

We looked all around us. There was no one.

"Well, after all, we are here on a friendly visit," said he, releasing the breath we had both been holding back. "There's no reason to be afraid."

Once again we resumed our exploration. I had been impressed by those verses on the walls of the vessel which enjoined one to withdraw from the world's vanities and to seek truth and wisdom in the safe harbour of nature and friendship. How curious, I thought, to find in this very place, when we were on the trail of the secret meeting of three cardinals, thoughts and words which exhorted us to accord no value to the cares of politics and business. I had withdrawn far from worldly things; I had renounced my ambition to become a gazetteer and had enclosed myself in my little field with Cloridia. Seventeen years later, Atto was still attached to these things, quite intensely! Only now (but this might be an illusion) had these verses, with their suave insistence on the vanity of sublunary things, seemed to awaken in his countenance a shadow of doubt, of reflection and regret.

"These verses. . . You know them, you reread them for the hundredth time, and yet they still seem to have something to tell you," he murmured, almost as though speaking to himself.

We read, between the arches, fine verses on the seasons by Marino, Tasso and Alemanni, and distiches by Ovid. Our attention was then caught by a series of wise maxims on the wall between the windows:

He who loses faith has nothing else to lose
He who has no friends will have no great luck
He who promises in a hurry spends a long time regretting
He who always laughs often misleads
He who seeks to mislead is often misled
Whoever wants to speak ill of others should think first of himself
Whosoever well conjectures guesses well
He who acquires a reputation acquires stuff
He who wants enough friends finds few
He who nothing ventures nothing gains
He who thinks he knows most understands least

"Curses!" Atto hissed all of a sudden.

"What's wrong?"

"How could you not have heard? A sharp noise, here, right in front of me."

"In truth. . . Yes, I heard it too, like a branch breaking."

"A branch breaking on its own? Now, that would be really interesting," he remarked ironically, looking around himself with a hint of annoyance.

I was unwilling to admit it, but our exploration seemed to be taking place along two parallel tracks: the inscriptions which we deciphered and the mysterious noises which beleaguered us, as though those two heterogeneous realities, the written word and the murmurings of the unknown, were in truth but calling out to one another.

Yet again, we summoned up our courage and moved on. The list of maxims continued in the second embrasure:

He who wants everything dies of rage
He who is unused to lying thinks that everyone tells the truth
He who is inured to doing evil thinks of nothing else
He who pays debts builds up capital
He who wants enough should not ask for too little
He who looks at every feather will never make a bed
He who has no discretion deserves no respect
He who esteems not is not esteemed
He who buys in time buys cheaply
He who fears not is in danger
He who sows virtue harvests fame

And in the third space:

BEWARE
Of a poor Alchemist
Of a sick Physician
Of sudden wrath
Of a Madman provoked
Of the hatred of Lords
Of the company of Traitors
Of the Dog that barks
Of the Man who speaks not
Of dealings with Thieves
Of a new hostelry
Of an old Whore
Of problems by night
Of Judges' opinions
Of Physicians' doubts
Of Spice Vendors' recipes
Of Notaries' et ceteras
Of Women's diseases
Of Strumpets' tears
Of Merchants' lies
Of Thieves within the household
Of a Maidservant corrupted
Of the fury of the Populace

"One must beware of old strumpets and judges' opinions, why, that's for sure," Atto assented with a little smile.

Finally, in the fourth embrasure, another set of wise maxims was inscribed:

THREE KINDS OF PERSONS ARE ODIOUS
The proud Pauper
The Rich and Avaricious
The mad Dotard

THREE KINDS OF MEN TO FLEE FROM
Singers
Old Men
The Lovelorn

THREE THINGS DIRTY THE HOUSE
Chickens
Dogs
Women

THREE THINGS MAKE A MAN SHREWD
The transports of love
A question
A quarrel

THREE THINGS ARE DESIRABLE
Health
A good reputation
Wealth

THREE THINGS ARE VERY FIRM
Suspicion which, once it has entered, will never depart
The wind, which will not enter where it sees no exit
Loyalty which, once it has gone, never returns

THREE THINGS TO DIE OF
Waiting, when no one comes
Being in bed, and not sleeping
Serving, without enjoyment

THREE THINGS ARE SATISFIED
The Miller's Cock
The Butcher's Cat
The Host's Prentice

"Bah, these are not on the same level as the rest," muttered Atto, who probably had not appreciated the saying that singers and old men, categories to which he belonged, were best avoided.

"But," I asked, with my mind cluttered up by so many sayings, "in your opinion, what are all these inscriptions here for?"

He did not reply. Obviously, he was asking himself the same question and did not want to admit to being in the same ignorance as I, whom he regarded as inexpert in the things of this world.

The wind, which had already been rising for some time, suddenly grew stronger; then, after a few moments, almost violent. Capricious eddies rose gaily, stirring bushes, earth, insects. A cloud of dust buffeted my face, blinding me. I leaned against the trunk of a tree, rubbing my eyes. Only long moments later did I recover my vision. When I could see again, the scene had changed sharply. Atto too was wiping his eyelids with a handkerchief to remove the dirt which had likewise deprived him of his sight. My head was spinning; for a few instants, the world, and with it the villa, had been taken away from us by that tremendous gust, the like of which I had never in all these years come across on the Janiculum.

I raised my eyes. The clouds, which had hitherto been lazily trailing behind one another in a sky furrowed with the orange, rose and lilac of the approaching sunset had now become the powerful, livid masters of the heavenly vault. The horizon, grown opaque and milky, shone limpid and strangely formless. The music seemed now to be coming from the great open space at the entrance to the park.

Then all became clean and clear again. As suddenly as it had vanished, the diurnal luminary reappeared, projecting a fine, golden ray onto the façade of the Vessel. For a few instants, a light breeze wafted the notes of the *folia* across to us.

"Curious," said Atto, dusting down his badly soiled shoes. "This music comes and goes, comes and goes. 'Tis as though it were nowhere and everywhere. In the palaces of great lords there sometimes exist rooms constructed using stonemasons' artifices deliberately conceived so as to multiply the points at which music can be heard, thus creating the illusion that the musicians are somewhere other than the place where they really are. But I have never heard of a garden endowed with the same qualities."

"You are right," I assented, "it is as though the melody were simply, how can one put it. . . in the air."

Suddenly, we heard two voices and silvery feminine laughter. These must have been the same voices as we had already heard, which had strangely been accompanied by no human presence.

The view was blocked by a tall hedge. Atto arranged the pleats of his justaucorps, making himself presentable and ready to answer to any question. At one point, the hedge was thinner and through it we at last discovered, two almost transparent figures, and with them, two faces.

The first was a gentleman no longer in the first flower of youth, yet vigorous, and – although the apparition was fleeting – I was struck by his open expression, his gentle lineaments, and his decisive yet courteous manners. He was conversing amiably with a young girl, to whom he seemed to be proffering reassurance. Was hers the woman's laugh we had heard when we made our entry to the Vessel?

". . . I shall be grateful to you for the rest of my life. You are my truest friend," said she.

They were dressed in the French manner, and yet (I would not have known how to explain exactly why) there was something singular about them. They remained so unaware of our presence that it seemed as though, protected by the barrier, we were spying on them.

They turned slightly, and then I could see the girl's face well. Her complexion was smoother than a crystal; her skin was not in truth extremely white, but combining candour with sanguine vivacity, blending fair and brown, it made her seem a new Venus (because, as the proverb says, brown does not diminish beauty but rather augments it). The oval of her face was not elongated, but possessed rather a roundness that equalled all the beauty of the celestial spheres. Her hair, almost disdaining the gold so common in this world, was of lustrous raven black with deepest blue reflections, and not a hint of coarseness to it; if anything, it seemed black only to presage the obsequies of whosoever should be caught up in its inexorable snares. The forehead was high and large, well in proportion with her other charms; her eyebrows were dark, but while in others this might have rendered the regard over-haughty, when her iris was revealed, it was like clouds giving way to the sun after a shower.

I looked at her, stealing the view from the accidental gap between the leaves, and those great eyes, round rather than slit, incomparable in their vivacity, capable of ferocity but not of rancour, seemed to me the sweetest and most cruel of instruments: fatal comets, casting pitiless amorous rays capable of blinding even the most lynx-like; yet, for all that, not harsh, because accompanied by myriad marks of innocent tenderness. Her lips were of animated coral, such that cinnabar could not be lovelier in colour, and vivacious. Her nose was perfectly proportioned and the whole aspect of her head was of incomparable majesty, supported by the marvellous pedestal of her neck beneath which rose two hills of Iblis, if not two apples of Paris, which would have sufficed for her to be declared instantly the Goddess of Beauty. Her arms were so lusciously rounded that it would have been impossible to pinch them; her hand (of a sudden, she raised it to her chin) was an admirable accomplishment of nature, the fingers being perfectly proportioned and with a whiteness comparable only to that of milk.

So many and admirable were the maiden's movements and actions that if only to be able to make this crude and imperfect description I have considered them one by one, so delightful and attractive were they: her laughter so moving and yet without the slightest affectation, her voice so insinuating, her gestures so harmonious with what she was saying (or seemed to be saying) that even hearing her without seeing her, anyone would have found something that went straight to his heart.

It was then, and only then that, after having grasped nothing more of the conversation between the twain than those thanks – "I shall be grateful to you for the rest of my life. You are my truest friend. . ." – which could imply everything or nothing whatever, that Atto, tugging at my arm, caught my attention.

I turned. He was as pale as if he had suffered an indisposition. He gestured that I was to go along the hedge with him and appear before the two strangers. He set out nervously before me, compelling me to follow him at a trot. Arriving at the end of the drive, he stopped.

"Look and tell me if they are still there."

I obeyed.

"No, Signor Atto, I no longer can see them. They must have moved."

"Look for them."

He sat down on a wall and seemed suddenly to have grown old and tired.

I offered no resistance to his command, since the magnificent vision of the maiden had been enough to spur my courage and curiosity. If someone had surprised me, well, I would have improvised, saying that I was in the service of a gentleman, a subject of His Most Christian Majesty King Louis the Fourteenth of France, who had permitted himself to traverse the confines of the villa solely out of a desire to render a tribute to the owner, whoever he might be. And, besides, had not the Vessel always been a French establishment in Rome?

After exploring in vain the drive in which the gentleman and the maiden had appeared, I made my way into a side-path, then another and yet another, each time emerging in the end in the great central courtyard. To no avail: the two seemed to have vanished into nothingness. Perhaps they had entered the villa, I thought; indeed, they must have done so.

When I rejoined Abbot Melani, he seemed to have recovered some colour.

"Do you feel better?" I asked.

"Yes, yes, of course. It is nothing, simply. . . a passing impression."

Nevertheless he seemed still to be in a state of shock. It was almost as though someone had just apprised him of grave and unexpected tidings. While remaining comfortably seated, he leaned on his stick.

"If you feel better, perhaps we can go," I ventured to suggest.

"No, no, we are fine here, really. And besides, we are in no hurry. How thirsty I am. I really am so very thirsty."

We approached one of the two fountains, where he quenched his thirst, while I helped him not to lose his balance. We then returned to the drives, casting an eye back from time to time on the Vessel, which had fallen silent. Atto had taken me by the arm, leaning discreetly on it.

"As I told you, the villa belonged to Elpidio Benedetti, who bequeathed it to a relative of Mazarin," he reminded me. "But you do not know who this person was. I shall tell you. Filippo Giuliano Mancini, Duke of Nevers, brother to one of the most famous women in France: Maria Mancini, the Connestabilessa Colonna."

I raised my eyes. No longer would I need to think up subterfuges to extract half-truths from Buvat: the Abbot was at last about to raise the veil on the mysterious Maria.

I seemed for an instant to hear the distant melody of the *folia* coming from the villa. It was not the same *folia* as before. This time it was more inward and learned, distant and detached; a viola da gamba, perhaps, or even a *voix humaine*, a voice both elegiac and crepuscular.

But Atto did not seem to hear it. Briefly, he fell silent, almost as though to draw within himself the bowstring of feelings, and to shoot skilfully the arrow of narration.

"Remember, my boy, a heart yearns for another heart once in a lifetime, and that is all."

I knew to what he was referring. Buvat had mentioned it to me: the first love of the Most Christian King had also been his greatest. And the woman in question was none other than Maria Mancini, Cardinal Mazarin's niece. But reasons of state had brought that story to an abrupt end.

"Louis played his card with Maria and lost," he continued, without even realising that he had begun to refer to his king with such familiarity. It was a grand passion, and it was repressed, crushed, trodden under foot, in defiance of all the laws of nature and of love. Although this was all well circumscribed in place and in time, and between two spirits only, the reaction of the forces that had been unnaturally repressed was beyond measure. That strangled love, my boy, was to bring the avenging angels down on the world: war, famine, hunger and death. The destiny of individuals and entire peoples, the history of France and of Europe: all has been trampled by the revenging wrath of the furies which emerged from the ashes of that love."

This was the revenge of history for that destiny denied, for that wrong undergone; small, when measured by the yardstick of reason. Immense, however, if calculated by that of the heart. Indeed, with no one else, not even with the Queen Mother Anne, had the young king ever enjoyed an understanding comparable to that which he experienced with Maria.

"Usually, the gift of reciprocal and lasting understanding between hearts is granted to gentle spirits," declaimed Abbot Melani. "In other words, to those who allow their passions to grow only in humble and orderly gardens. To those men and women whose hearts are like unto the magnificent exuberance of the forest it is given to know only passions as absolute as they are fleeting, straw fires capable of lighting up a moonless night, yet which last but the space of that night."

Well, continued Atto, this did not apply to Louis and Maria. Their passion burned fiercely but tenaciously. And it was from that passion that there sprung an ineffable, secret complicity of hearts which united them after a manner that would never be seen in other places or at other times.

Because of this, the world hated them. Alas, they were then still too green: their skin, and especially that of the young King, was too thin to withstand the cunning, the venom and the subtle ferocity of the court.

Not that the Sovereign was so young: when he fell in love with Maria, he was already twenty. Yet, at that no longer so tender age the King was not yet married, nor even betrothed.

"A most unusual thing, contrary to all custom!" exclaimed Abbot Melani. "Usually one does not wait so long to marry a young king. All the more so, given that the royal family of France had not many heirs to the throne: after Philippe, the King's brother, and his uncle Gaston of Orleans, who was old and sick, the first Prince of the Blood was the Grand Condé, the serpent in the family's bosom, the rebel of the Fronde, defeated and now in the service of the Spanish foe. . ."

But Anne and Mazarin were biding their time, taking care to keep Louis's head under a canopy of blissful ignorance so that they could reign undisturbed. The young Sovereign was aware of nothing; he loved entertainments, ballets and music, and he let Mazarin govern. Louis seemed never to turn his thoughts to the future and the inevitable, tremendous responsibilities of government. He seemed to be as slack and apathetic as his father, that Louis XIII whom he had scarcely known. Even the three years of exile during the Fronde, at the tender age of ten, when he had already lost his father, did not seem to have caused him more than a momentary, infantile homesickness.

"Excuse me," I interrupted him, "but how is it possible that from so meek and unwarlike a being there should have emerged the Most Christian King?"

"That is a mystery and no one can explain it except by the facts which I am about to recount to you. It has always been said that he changed because of the Fronde and that it was the revolt of the people and the nobles that dictated the reaction of the years that followed. Stuff and nonsense! Ten years passed between the Fronde and the sharp change in the King's soul. So that was not what caused it. His Majesty remained a timid, dreamy youth until 1660, almost until he married. Within the space of a single year he had already become the inflexible Sovereign of whom you too have heard so much. And do you know what took place in that year?"

"The forced separation from Mistress Mancini?" I asked rhetorically, while Atto nodded in confirmation.

"What hatred was turned against those two poor young people: the hatred of the Queen Mother, that of Mazarin. . ."

"But how was that possible? The Cardinal her uncle should have been well pleased."

"Ah, there's much that could be said on that subject. . . For the time being, it will suffice that you should know this: despite the fact that the Cardinal showed great skill in convincing everyone at court that he was placing every obstacle in the way of that love, out of his supposed sense of family honour, duty to the monarchy and so on and so forth, I never swallowed any of that. I knew Mazarin perfectly well, his forebears were Sicilian and from the Abruzzi; for him, the only thing that counted was personal profit and the rank of his family. That is all."

Atto made a gesture as though to say that he knew all about it. Then he continued his narration.

"As I was telling you, they all bitterly detested that love, but as they dared not blame the King, they nurtured a singular hatred for poor Maria, who was, moreover, already disliked both at court and within her own family."

"Why ever was that?"

"She was hated at court because she was Italian: they had had more than enough, what with all the Italians whom Mazarin had brought over to Paris," said Atto, who had himself been one of those Italians. "And in her family, she had been abhorred since her first cry; when she was born, her father compiled her horoscope and saw with horror that she was destined to be the cause of rebellions and calamities, even a war. Being obsessed with astrology – a passion which was to become one of Maria's – even on his deathbed, he recommended her mother to be on her guard against her."

Maria's mother needed no persuading: she tormented her throughout her childhood. She never failed to remind her of her defects, even physical ones ("Invisible details," Atto insisted.) She did not even want her to accompany her to Paris with her other children, and yielded only to Maria's repeated and heartfelt pleas. The maiden was then aged fourteen. Once at court, her mother isolated her as much as possible, confining her to her chamber, while her younger sisters were allowed to approach the Queen. On her deathbed, she emulated her husband: after recommending her other children to her brother the Cardinal, she begged him to place Maria, her third child, in a convent, reminding him of her father's astrological prediction.

Her mother's animosity wounded her to the quick, Abbot Melani gravely commented, and, together with that unmistakably masculine air which Maria was wont at times adopt with her intimates – her laughter sometimes a trifle too ribald, her gait perhaps too heavy and martial, those scathing jibes of hers that always found their mark but which would perhaps have been more at home in the mouth of a soldier of fortune than on the docile lips of a young maiden – all these things betrayed how little faith in her own feminine nature Maria had gained from her mother's instruction.

"Yet she was so very feminine!" exclaimed Atto.

He looked around him, as though seeking a special corner of the park, a magical place in which a presence, some entity, might lend substance to his words and from the word make flesh. He turned to look at me.

"I shall tell you more: she was beautiful, indeed perfect, a creature from another world. And that is not my judgement, but the truth. If, however, you were to refer to anyone who knew her – with the possible exception of her husband Lorenzo Onofrio, may God keep him in glory – you may be quite sure that they would be shocked to hear that and would dissent. And do you know why? Because her movements in no way accorded with her womanly qualities. In other words, she did not *behave* like a beautiful woman."

Not that she was lacking in grace, far from it. But from the moment that she sensed a man's attention focus on her, she felt almost ill. If she was walking, she would begin to limp; if she was seated at table, she would become hunched up; if she was speaking, she would fall silent, not like any timid maiden of her age, no, hers was too prompt and lively a wit. Indeed, one could be certain that, after holding her breath for a moment, she would sally forth with some infelicitous joke accompanied by raucous laughter. These things all chilled the French in her company, for none could guess that this was the expression of her inner lack of ease and thus of her great purity of heart; on the contrary, everyone was ready to despise her as though she were some country wench.

That is why her sinuous swan's neck was disdained as being too thin, her flaming eyes were seen as hard, her thick dark curls as dry and crinkled, and the pallor of her cheeks (induced by the grim, hostile looks of courtiers) was attributed to a naturally wan complexion.

"In truth, Maria's cheeks could not have been further from wan: how many times have I seen them catch fire from the élan and fervour of her young spirit! And the same could be said of her mouth, which was red and large, with perfectly spaced teeth, and yet no painter ever dared depict her as she was, so much did her mouth differ from the thin lips then in fashion, which from close up reminded one of nothing so much as a pigeon's crupper. . ."

"It is painful to know that so great a beauty should have remained hidden from itself," said I to second Melani's heartfelt eloquence.

"Of course, she did not stay that way all her life. It was maternity that transformed her. When next I saw her in Rome, a young mother, although her broken heart had remained in Paris, her entire being had attained the plenitude of femininity. By becoming a mother herself, she had at last exorcised the icy phantasm of her own mother."

"Your understanding of Maria's true nature was quite immediate," I said.

"I was not alone in this. His Majesty, too, saw it, since he fell in love with her. Even then, despite his limited experience of the fair sex, he was certainly not likely to become besotted with a displeasing face or one that was merely colourless or just acceptable! But, as I have told you, Maria was convinced, because of her mother's cruel judgements, that she was inadequate, sour, unwomanly. In other words: ugly. Oh, if only there had existed a painter magician who could, unseen, have immortalised the image of Maria in a portrait, as she was at that time! I'd have paid with my blood to commission such a picture, for when Maria was truly herself, forgetting her fears, she was magnificent. To immortalise her in an instant, when she was living according to her true nature: that would have been the necessary miracle. And not the portraits which were made at court, which express nothing but the embarrassment with which she posed before the painter, with a drawn smile and an unnatural pose: as she thought herself to be and not as she was."

At the time of her amours with Louis, Maria still felt herself to be, not the nightingale she truly was, but a screech owl croaking on a branch. But that was by no means a bad thing. It was indeed because of this that, as soon as she arrived in France, she plunged into her studies, convinced that she must make up for her lack of grace by dint of knowledge. From barely a year and a half of education at the Convent of the Visitation, she drew far greater profit than her sisters and cousins who were enclosed there with her. Her impeccable French, with the exotic charm of Italian inflections, a show of culture in all fields (which was really in Maria's case far more than a mere show), a visceral love for the literature of chivalry and for poetry – which she loved to recite aloud – and lastly a passion for ancient history, all these things placed her immeasurably above the vainglorious ladies of the court who permitted themselves to judge her so spitefully.

And thus, when she made her debut at court, Maria revealed an intellect and wit far beyond her years. Her temperament, which could not conceive of love without a challenge, soon enough found in the Sovereign much raw material which cried out only to be worked on.

"As is the case with so many young men, the intellect was ripe, and yet he was still a little child; matter still inert, yet ready to be modelled, primordial essence which invokes the enlightened wisdom of a feminine spirit, at once elevated and strong," added Atto, raising his finger to heaven in a gesture of teaching, as though in comprehension of feminine essence rather than of women themselves.

"The maker and the work of art, Hephaistos and the shield of Achilles: that was how Maria and Louis were for one another. Like that Achaean shield, he was already exquisitely fashioned; she could have given him that divine spark of strength, goodness and justice which issue only from a happy and gratified heart."

That evocation seemed to lacerate Atto's heart and soul, but not because he, who had once been enamoured of Maria, had harnessed himself to telling of her love for an unbeatable rival. His real torment, I seemed to see, was different. The elevation of the masculine material by feminine spirit about which he was now instructing me, he, Atto the eunuch, had had to accomplish in solitude, on himself.

"That boiling and formless lava had to be forged into wisdom," he continued, "into insight and purity of soul, into discernment, even into trust in one's fellow man, so that he should be as pure as a dove and as prudent as a serpent, to use the words of the Evangelist. None more than the Most Christian King was suited for such an inclination of spirit and intellect," he chanted melodiously.

This was then the royal road marked out for the fiery young King by Maria's lively vision. Maria was the first serious thing that Louis desired. She was refused him.

He clamoured for her with all the breath in his body, but did not upset the constituted order. Still unaware of his own power, Louis had remained immersed in the romantic vapours of adolescence: a protracted lethargy in which his mother Anne and the Cardinal had taken care to keep him, for their own convenience.

"And you, then, think that the Most Christian King suffered so much from this that his soul is still scarred by it?"

"Worse than that. To suffer, one must have a heart, and he renounced his own. He was left – how can one put it – a stranger to himself. Only thus was he able to emerge from the abyss of despair into which that curtailed passion had cast him. But one cannot with impunity renounce one's own heart. Saint Augustine reminds us that the absence of the good generates evil."

Thus, it was not long before coldness and cruelty took the place of suffering in the King's young heart. In a cruel volte-face, while love could have brought forth the best qualities from his nature, love denied brought forth the worst in him.

"His reign became, and remains to this day, the reign of tyranny, of suspicion, of the arbitrary, of futility raised to the rank of virtue," he whispered in a barely audible voice, aware that the words which he had just pronounced could, if they reached hostile ears, be the cause of his downfall.

He took his handkerchief and wiped his forehead and his lips with it, wearily dabbing the drops of perspiration from his face.

"All the women he had after that were despised by him," he then said with renewed passion, "as happened to his wife Maria Teresa; or venerated, but then set aside, like his mother. Or merely lusted after, like his many mistresses."

In every one of them, Louis sought Maria. But no longer having a heart to respond to, precisely because of that old loss, in reality he never sought after the soul of any of them, even when it would have been worth doing so, as with poor Mademoiselle de la Vallière. And, almost without realising it, he allowed no woman to take the place of that old love; indeed, he ended up by becoming openly misogynistic. He forbade his wife Maria Teresa to attend the Royal Council, which according to tradition was her due, and immediately after his marriage he even removed his mother Anne of Austria from it. Even if he paid her a compliment when, shortly after her death, he said that she had been "a good King", an indication of how insulting the feminine appellation seemed to him. All in all, he treated every one of his mistresses with extreme cruelty.

"In 1664, he said to his ministers: 'I order you all, if you should ever see a woman, whoever she may be, gain influence over me and govern me, to put me on my guard: I shall be rid of her within twenty-four hours.' And he had been married for three years."

"Excuse the question," I interrupted, "but how could Louis think of marrying Maria, who was not of royal blood?"

"A legitimate, but unfounded doubt. And here I shall grant you a little revelation: were you aware that His Most Christian Majesty is no longer a widower, but has taken wife again?"

"It is true that I no longer read the gazettes, but I am sure that if there were a new Queen of France, I'd have learned it just walking down the street!" I exclaimed in astonishment.

"There is in fact no Queen. This is a secret marriage, even if it is an open secret. It took place one night seventeen years ago, not long after you and I left one another and I returned to Paris. And I can assure you the august spouse is, to put it kindly, not presentable in society. A small example: when she was little, she even asked for charity."

The King, with Madame de Maintenon (for that was the name of the chosen one) had wished to accomplish what twenty-four years before had been refused him – or rather, what he had not had the courage to do: a marriage desired only by him, against the wishes of all others.

"But this gesture of his was by then only an empty shell," groaned Atto sadly. "La Maintenon is no Mancini. Her hair does not 'smell of heather' as the young King was wont to repeat, in ecstasy before the exuberant locks of my Maria. And this belated marriage," concluded Atto with conviction, "was nothing but a silent and distant homage to the first and only love of his life, while the 'secret' spouse (everyone knows this but no one dares breathe a word of it) gained from the marriage more than anything else the rages and bilious humour of the King who made it clear to her that he could be rid of her whenever the fancy took him. So now, la Maintenon, unlike Maria, cannot take the liberty of proffering the least word of advice to the King without being bitterly upbraided for all her pains. It remained to her only to boast of that, as though she had been confined to the shadows of her own volition," added the Abbot with obvious scorn.

The Most Christian King, secretly married! And what was more, or so it seemed, to a woman of lowly origins. How had that been possible? A thousand questions were on the tip of my tongue, but Atto was already continuing his tale.

"All this, in short, to tell you that in my opinion the King of France would have been prepared to marry Maria. But you must remember above all," Atto insisted, "that Louis was at that time King in name only. In fact it was Cardinal Mazarin and the Queen Mother who reigned. Nothing, but nothing, in the absolute deference which Louis showed for His Eminence and his mother gave any hint that things might change. Louis might perfectly well have spent his whole life like his father Louis XIII, leaving the affairs of state in the hands of his minister."

Atto was sure that not even Louis thought matters might sooner or later change. At twenty-one years of age, he was still taking shelter under his mama's skirts in the Cardinal's shadow, like a callow youth. Yet the King had reached his majority five years earlier! His mother's Regency had long since ended.

Louis never opposed the matrimonial plans which Mazarin prepared for him, first with Marguerite of Savoy and then with the Infanta of Spain, having already seen how fleeting such political promises could be. What was more, in twenty years of life, he had never once rebelled against his tutors, not even so much as raising a single "if" or "but".

But above all, the Abbot declaimed, what did he care for political wrangling or for the web of matrimonial manoeuvres which Mazarin was weaving around him? Louis did not live in everyday reality: it was too vulgar and squalid for him, or so he thought.

When they became friends, Maria read Plutarch's *Lives of Illustrious Men* to the young King; she too, born with a warrior's heart, dreamed of one day becoming an "illustrious man". As for Louis, anxious to escape from the political wilderness to which Mazarin had exiled him, he plunged headlong into those tales and at last felt himself to be a hero.

From that moment on his thoughts took on a different colouring, one both bloodier and truer, encompassing the distant events of the Fronde, the humiliations endured by his family at the hands of the populace in revolt, those tragic days which had, without his even realising it, robbed him of childhood's carefree joys.

Maria loved poetry and recited it well, with style and sensitivity. She recommended that Louis read romances and verse: from the historians of the ancient world like Herodotus to poems chivalrous and bucolic. He filled his pockets with them, enjoyed them, and showed powers of discernment which astonished the court, where no one was aware that he possessed such qualities.

He was transformed, gay, conversing with everyone; he emerged from the gilded apathy that had hitherto held him in subjugation and took a lively part in discussions about this or that book. Superimposing their own faces and names on the protagonists of their reading, Louis and Maria projected themselves into a universe of romance in which they felt themselves to be the heroes.

On a fine sunny morning, Louis commanded that a picnic should be held at a remote and rocky place called Franchard, and with him he brought a whole orchestra. Upon arriving, Louis descended from his carriage, filled his lungs with the fine air of the hills and, without thinking twice, set off to climb to the top of the hill. He seemed somewhat excited; everyone looked at him with a mixture of anxiety and disapproval. Maria followed him, while he held her arm chivalrously during the climb up those steep and rugged rocks. As soon as he reached the summit, Louis ordered the orchestra and the court to join him there; a desire which was fulfilled at the cost of no little effort and risk. As they grazed their knees on the stones, the courtiers cast disconcerted and impatient glances at one another. No King of France had ever set out to climb mountains like a goat, least of all with an orchestra and the whole court. Nor would Louis have done it, they thought, if it had not been for that woman, that Italian.

On another day, at Bois-le-Vicomte, Maria and Louis were walking along a tree-lined avenue. At a certain point, perhaps to help her, he held out his arm to her. Maria stretched out her hand, which lightly struck the pommel of the King's sword. Louis then drew the sword which had dared stand in the way of Maria's hand and cast it as far as he was able, in order to punish it. An act of puerile chivalry, which soon did the rounds at court.

Louis, with the ingenuousness of his passion, was making a fool of himself, even if no one had the courage to tell him so, and it was the common opinion that no adult sentiment could possibly underlie such childish behaviour.

"But the courtiers were wrong," I cried out.

"They were both wrong and right," Atto corrected me. "That love, as neither the King nor Maria dared yet call the enthusiasm which drew them to one another, did at times take on the infantile and pathetic tones of a juvenile infatuation; that I cannot deny. But this was only because Louis, too long and too closely guarded by his mother and the Cardinal, was at the age of twenty living for the first time, and suddenly, in chaotic and disorderly confusion, what his heart should already have experienced at the age of sixteen."

At the age of sixteen, however, Louis XIV had experienced only the most pallid initiation to venery. The Queen had opposed this, while his godfather had been a party to it: an old chambermaid, a few docile and willing servant girls, even a maid of honour, and a superficial friendship with a sister of Maria's. But nothing – Mazarin took good care – nothing that might touch the King's heart. Only his meeting with Maria had opened the gates of love, and Louis was no longer willing to go back on that.

All the anxieties, the intemperance, the blushes, the theatrical gestures: all the torments of burgeoning pubescence the young King suffered with Maria, at an age when a monarch has usually put such things behind him and his heart has already experienced the roughness and hardness of the art of reigning.

Likewise, Atto continued, the inexpert and imprudent youth consumes his ardour like a blaze devouring straw; he suffers from furious infatuations, for a real damsel or for the heroine of some fairy tale, and for both he feels prepared to slice the globe in two with a sword. Only, the volubility of his young heart soon tears him away from these things and he then drinks of Lethe's waters of oblivion. Next, it all begins anew: new dreams, new attachments, new passions, new senseless words, in the divine madness of those brief years of passage when the future has not the slightest importance.

But all things are destined to dissolve, one after the other, in the oblivion of a new present. Approaching the age of twenty, there remains only a confused reminiscence, a vague sensation of pleasure mixed with danger: the new man will keep a safe distance from those impetuous currents, and turning his mind to the future, will place on his heart the leash of good sense; with that good sense, choosing the mother of his children, and loving her with a heart filled with conjugal devotion.

"The heart knows no commands, Signor Atto," was my only comment.

"A King's heart is different."

When Louis, thanks to Maria, awoke from his overlong lethargy, he had the misfortune to meet the woman of his life too early and too late; he was too inexpert to know how to gain her for himself, too adult to forget her. His heart was in turmoil for her, his mind was subjugated by her. Reasons of state were still no more than a thought in the background, both remote and obscure.

I knew very well what Atto was thinking of when he expressed himself in those terms: not only of the youth of the Most Christian King but of his own; those years of glory as a castrato singer touring Europe, caught between music, espionage, the faithful service of great lords, with danger breathing down his neck and a secret amorous passion which set his senses ablaze.

It was then, as I penetrated his fervour with that oblique intuition, that, puffing up his chest, he sang a plaintive melody.

> *Se dardo pungente*
> *d'un guardo lucente*
> *il sen mi ferì,*
> *se in pena d'amore*
> *si strugge 'l mio core*
> *la notte ed il dì. . .*

Whose that lucent look was that had wounded the breast of Abbot Melani was all too clear to me. It was almost as though he, by the power of thought, had taken on Louis's flesh, as a warrior dons a coat of armour, to taste the joys and sufferings of that amorous passion which was denied him.

Atto sang in a feeble, breathless voice. Seventeen years had gone by since I had last heard him. At that time, his voice, once so famous because well tempered and powerful, was already reduced to perhaps half of its former vigour, if not less. Yet the airs which he sang, those of his master Luigi Rossi (Le Seigneur Luigi, as he called him) had lost nothing of their enchantment.

That thread of a voice was still celestial, swift, superfine, capable of speaking to the heart a thousand times better than an entire school of sages could speak to the intellect. Gone were the body and power of his song, yet there remained, vulnerable but intact, only its intimate and ineffable beauty.

Now Atto was repeating those verses, as though their words held for him some hidden, painful meaning:

> *Se un volto divino*
> *quest'alma rubò,*
> *se amar è destino*
> *resista chi può!*

---

* If a sting-heavy dart / Of a glance brightly sharp / Has made my heart fail, / If in love's travail / My breast pines away / By night and by day. . .

† If features divine / Stole this soul away, / If Fate Love entwines, / Resist then who may!

The Abbot was still tormented by the memory of Maria. He felt that he had looked upon her through Louis's eyes, he had brushed her with his palms, kissed her with his lips and even experienced with the King's heart the desperate distress of separation. Sensations which for Atto, year after year, had become more true, more real than if he had known them in his own flesh. He, the eunuch, being unable to attain Maria, had in the end possessed her through the King.

Thus was consumed and renewed that bizarre love among three, between two souls separated forever and a third, the jealous custodian of their past. To me was granted the unique and secret honour of being witness to this.

Melani suddenly broke off singing and, with a quick jump, showing that he had recovered his vigour, leapt down from the little wall which had afforded him rest and support.

"And now, let us go into the villa. There must be someone in there who will at last have us arrested," said he laughing.

I found it hard to break the enchantment which the image of Maria, evoked by the Abbot in words and in song, had wrought in my spirit.

"Was that an air by your master, Le Seigneur Luigi?"

"I see that you have not forgotten," he replied. "No, this is by Francesco Cavalli, from his *Giàsone*. I think that was the opera most played in the past half-century."

Saying this, Atto left me and walked ahead of me; he was unwilling to say more.

Jason, or jealousy. I had never heard that famous opera, but I knew very well the celebrated Greek myth of the jealousy of Medea, queen of Colchis, for Jason, the leader of the Argonauts, and his love for Hypsipyle, queen of Lemnos. Another love triangle.

We moved towards the north side of the villa, opposite that overlooking the road. A distich was inscribed above the entrance gate:

Si te, ut saepe solet, species haec decipit alta;
Nec me, nec Caros decipit arcta Domus.

Once again, I had the curious, inexpressible sensation that the words painted or carved on the walls of the villa referred to, or even mirrored, some unknown reality.

We tried the door. It was open. At the moment of grasping the door handle, I seemed to hear a hurried sound of footsteps and movement, as though someone inside had risen suddenly from a chair. I looked at Atto; if he too had heard something, he showed no sign of it.

We crossed the threshold. Within, no one.

"No vestige of the three eminences, as far as one can see," I commented.

"I certainly was not expecting to find any still here. Yet, some trace of the meeting might have been left behind: a message, who knows, perhaps some notes. . . I would need only to know in which room they met. Such details are always very, very useful. The villa is large. . . let's see. It seems as though no one has any intention of keeping an eye on it. So much the better for us."

We found a large oblong room illuminated by the light from windows on either side. At the opposite end, a closed door. This large hall was apparently intended for summer luncheons. Through an open window blew the sweet and melancholy west wind. In an adjoining room, one could see a table for playing *trucco*, or billiards, if you prefer.

Cautiously, we moved a few paces forward, keeping an eye on the door opposite, from which we imagined that someone might issue sooner or later.

In the middle of the room, a great round table was very much in evidence on which was enthroned a large tray in fine inlaid silver poplar wood. We approached. Atto cautiously pushed the tray, which rotated.

"A brilliant idea," he commented. "The servings can pass from one guest to another, without troubling one's neighbour or needing to pay a carver. Benedetti appreciated the comforts of life, I'd say. Someone must have left the room a short while before us," he added after a pause.

"How can you be so sure of that?"

"There are footprints here on the floor. His shoes were dirty with earth."

We split up, while I explored the part of the room where we had entered, while Atto saw to the rest.

I observed that in two places where the walls protruded into the room, cupboards were built in, painted in the same colours as those walls, thus discreetly concealing articles for the table and the wine cellar. I opened the drawers. They were full of fine silver, with cutlery of all forms and dimensions for every purpose, including devices for scaling fish and long, well-sharpened knives for serving meat and game. Copious and variegated were the services of goblets, chalices, beakers, drinking bowls, large glasses, wooden cups, wine carafes and decanters, large and small, punchbowls for refreshments, jugs for water, cups for broths and hot beverages, all in glass decorated, gilded and painted with delightful figures of animals, cherubs or floral motifs. The master of the villa must have loved the pleasures of the eye no less than those of the table, all to be enjoyed in the salubrious air of the Janiculum Hill and among the verdure of vineyards and gardens. The Vessel, despite its strange isolation, was truly a villa built for great pleasures.

Against a wall, near one of the cupboards, I noticed a vertical brass tube which began at a man's height with a flaring opening like that of a trumpet and which ran up until it disappeared into the ceiling. Atto noticed my questioning look.

"That tube is another of the conveniences of the villa," he explained. "It is used to communicate with the servants on the other floors, without having to take the trouble to go and look for them. One need only talk into them and one's voice issues from the openings on other floors."

I moved a few paces. On every one of the shutters of the windows were painted medallions portraying illustrious Roman women: Pompea, Caesar's third wife; Servilia, Octavian's first wife; Drusilla, the sister of Caligula; Messalina, Claudius' fifth wife; and many others including Cossutia and Cornelia, Martia, Aurelia and Calpurnia (I counted thirty-two in all), each celebrated with solemn Latin inscriptions setting out their name, family and spouse.

We realised that above the arches and in the embrasures were other sayings, all alluding to the female sex, and they were most numerous, so many that these pages would not suffice to set out a tenth part of them:

Of women the quinte element is a natural raving
It is easier to find pleasure in absence than silence in women's midst
Woman laughs when she can, and cries when she will
Women and hens annoy the neighbours
Man and woman in a tight place are like straw near the fire
Interest usually, rather than love, rules women's hearts

"Everything here is dedicated to feminine qualities and to the pleasures of the table. This is the great hall of women and the palate," said Atto, while I examined a medallion with the profile of Plautia Hercanulilla.

Until that moment, so intent had we been on finding traces of the presence of the three august members of the Sacred College of Cardinals (and we had indeed discovered footprints) that we had not deigned to accord our attention to what was most interesting in this hall: the rich collection of paintings hung on the walls. Atto stood by my side as I focused on the paintings, realising that the only subject of the collection was, as might have been expected, a set of graceful women's faces.

Abbot Melani began to pass rapidly from one picture to the next without even needing to read the names on the frames, which showed the identity of the ladies in question. He knew each face to perfection (and meant to show that off), having seen them either in the flesh or in so many other portraits, and he told me their names.

"Her Majesty Anne of Austria, the late, lamented mother of the Most Christian King," he recited, almost as though he were presenting her to me in flesh and blood, showing me the sweet, haughty face of the deceased sovereign, that rather penetrating look, the forehead not excessively high, the round but noble neck embraced with loving respect by the low-cut organza collar of her sumptuous black taffeta gown, enriched by a bodice of pleated brocade on which the diaphanous royal hands were limply abandoned.

"As I had occasion to tell you when we met, the Queen Mother loved my singing, I could say, in no ordinary way," he added with a touch of vanity, adjusting his wig with a rapid and discreet gesture. "Above all, sad arias, sung in the evening."

He then passed on to the portraits of the Princess Palatine, Countess Marescotti, and the late lamented Henrietta, sister-in-law of the Most Christian King, all so nobly and realistically depicted that it seemed as though they might just have lunched at the great table nearby.

It was then that we came to the last portrait, a little in the shade by comparison with the others, yet still visible.

Since our regard is subject to desire, while the word is ruled by the intellect, my eyes were swifter to embrace that feminine visage and to recognise it among my memories than was Abbot Melani to announce her name.

That was why, when he said: "Madama Maria Mancini," I had

already recognised her. It was without a doubt the young maiden we had glimpsed through the hedge, in the park.

೧೯೮

"Of course, all this was the play of your imagination," said Atto, after listening to my explanation, as we left the great hall, taking a door to the left. "You were unduly influenced by an agreeable and unexpected encounter. That can happen, and I can assure you that when I was your age it happened often."

When proffering those words, he turned his head away from me.

"Still, I do not understand where the maiden and her companion can have disappeared to," I objected.

Atto did not reply. On the walls of the chamber there were various prints in the form of pictures which, using a skilful optical illusion, represented ancient bas-reliefs with singular grace and lightness. What was more, here too was a series of portraits, this time, of men.

Here also, the openings in the wall were ornamented with sayings concerning life at court.

THE GOOD COURTIER
To acquire merit:
Serve with punctuality and modesty
Always speak well of your Lord and ill of no one
Praise without excess
Practise with the best
Listen more than you speak
Love good men
Win over the bad
Speak gently
Operate promptly
Neither trust someone nor mistrust everyone
Neither reveal your own secret nor listen willingly to those of others
Do not interrupt others' speeches and be not prolix in your own
Believe those who are more learned than yourself
Do not undertake things greater than you
Do not believe easily or answer without thinking
Suffer, and dissimulate

THE COURT
In Courts, there are always some wolves in sheep's clothing
Against treachery in Courts there is no better remedy than withdrawal and distance
The Court often takes light from the streets

The Court and satisfaction are two excessively great extremes
In the air of the Court the wind of ambition must of necessity blow
The affairs of Courts do not always move at the speed desired by the most
    zealous
In Courts, even the most sincere friendships are not exempt from the poison
    of false suspicions
Most courtiers are monsters with two tongues and two hearts.

"Yet, to me she does seem to be the same young maiden!" I decided to insist, while Atto was pointing his nose in the air to read the maxims. "Are you sure that today Maria Mancini is nearly sixty years of age? The maiden we saw. . . well, I tell you, she is identical to the woman in the picture, but seems rather young."

He stopped reading brusquely and looked me straight in the eye. "Do you think I could be mistaken?"

He turned his eyes away from mine and turned to the pictures, to explain them for me. The subjects of the pictures were this time illustrious names from France and from Italy: pontiffs, poets, men of science, sovereigns and their consorts, ministers of state.

"His Holiness the late Pope Alexander VII; His Holiness the late Pope Clement IX, the Cavalier Bernini, the Cavaliere Cassiano del Pozzo; the Cavalier Marino; His Majesty the late King Louis XIII; His Reigning Majesty Louis XIV. . ."

While he reviewed the list of names, passing hurriedly from one picture to the next, it seemed to me that Atto was still annoyed by my question about the age of Maria Mancini. In reality, he must be right: I could not have seen Maria in the park, not only because she had not yet reached Rome, but because, being the same age as the Most Christian King, she must, like the Sovereign, be sixty years of age or more.

"His Eminence the late Cardinal Richelieu; His Eminence the late Cardinal Mazarin; the deceased Minister Colbert; the deceased Superintendent Fouquet. . ."

He stopped.

"'Suffer, and dissimulate'. . ." said he to himself, repeating one of the maxims he had just read on the walls of the room.

"I beg your pardon?"

"'Most courtiers are monsters with two tongues and two hearts'!" he smiled, quoting another of the maxims theatrically, as though he wished to mask some unwelcome thought with a joke.

അക

"It is getting late," the Abbot commented as soon as we had left the Vessel, scrutinising the violet of the sky.

The search of the premises had not led to much. Apart from a few footprints, we had found no trace of the three cardinals and in any case there was not enough time to explore the whole villa.

"Now, go back and work in the gardens at Spada. Keep your mouth closed and behave as though nothing had happened."

"To tell the truth, I must repair the damage done by the thief before Cloridia returns. . ."

"For that I shall reimburse you at double its value, so your little wife will soon be consoled. You must be present this evening, after Vespers. Now, be on your way!" he exhorted me rather brusquely.

Atto was nervous, very nervous.

Evening the Second
8ᵀᴴ July, 1700

✠

While I was making my way towards the garden shed in order to collect my tools, I reflected that Atto had not once asked me about Cloridia: how she was, when he would be seeing her again, what she was doing now, and so on. Never a word, and not even now that he had mentioned her did he take the trouble to ask me anything, however circumstantial, about her. And this despite the fact that he had read in the memoir which he had stolen from me the whole incredible story of Cloridia. A story which, many years before, at the time of the Locanda del Donzello, he could never have imagined. Not that they frequented one another at the time. On the contrary, as far as I could recall, they had not exchanged a single word, deliberately ignoring one another. I had never heard Atto pronounce her name, save scornfully. The castrato and the courtesan: I could surely not expect a friendship to be born. . .

"You are dismissed! Your work is disgusting."

For a moment, my heart almost failed me when that strident voice caught me unawares.

I turned around and saw him a few paces from me, seated on a branch while he stroked his beak with his hooked talons.

"Dismissed, disss-*missed*!" Caesar Augustus repeated, amusing himself as he was wont to do whenever, between one task and another, I allowed myself a short break. He had probably learned that disagreeable phrase in some shop during his peregrinations across the city.

"What are you doing up there?" I asked him in my turn, irritated by the surprise. "Why do you not get back into your cage?"

He held his peace, as though there was no need to reply and rocked his head rhythmically to show his displeasure. It was one of those days, frequent during changes in the seasons, when Caesar Augustus was melancholy and irritable. Days on which, to vent his anxieties, he would always end up by doing something awful.

Giving immediate and troublesome substance to his malaise, Caesar Augustus went into action. He took flight, sped past brushing my face, turned, plummeted down, landed next to me and, with his beak, boldly seized the small sickle which I had left on the ground.

"No, for goodness sake, give that back to me at once!"

"Dismiss him, dismiss him!" he repeated again with a malign glint in his little round eyes. The small sickle, grasped firmly in his beak, in no way prevented him from imitating the human voice to perfection, the sound issuing, not from the throat, like ours, but from some unimaginable guttural cavity. He spread his great white wings, beating them clumsily in the still summer air, and took off.

In a few instants I lost sight of him; but not only because he had rapidly disappeared over the horizon. While watching Caesar Augustus's departure, I had in fact been distracted by a small detail. Out of the corner of my eye, I seemed for a few fleeting moments to catch a glimpse of a shadow observing me from behind a hedge. But it was very hot, perhaps I was mistaken.

"Move aside, boy."

I was at once roused from such ephemeral impressions by that firm and impatient voice ordering me to stand aside. Making their way between the hedges of the little drive were two valets escorting a third person: in lay apparel His Eminence Cardinal Spada was advancing, his expression even more livid than the day before.

I bowed respectfully while the trio passed me and proceeded towards the gates of the villa. When I rose and dusted down my breeches, I seemed again to hear rustling and once more had the indefinable impression that I was being watched by malign and inquiring eyes. I looked all around me, but without catching sight even vaguely of the dark silhouette which I could have sworn I had seen only moments before, moving behind the surrounding hedges. While at the end of the drive Cardinal Spada disappeared from sight with his two escorts, above their heads I saw instead Caesar Augustus fluttering silently.

Once I had finished my work trimming the hedge and accomplished my duties at the aviary, I realised that no little time remained to me before my appointment with Abbot Melani after Vespers.

I decided to make a quick visit home. There, alas, I found the same painful chaos to which, only a few hours before, I had awoken.

For a few moments I fell a prey to anguish as I saw with what rabid fury those faceless strangers had with impunity disrupted the fine order of Cloridia's and my alcove.

When I had rearranged everything properly, I returned to the Villa Spada. There, in the garden, the heat was rather oppressive. I took off my shirt and curled up in the shade of a tall beech, in a little secret place on the heights, under the outer wall, where I and Cloridia were wont to meet during brief pauses in our work, away from curious glances. From that point, one looked out over the drive below, but, concealed by the leaves, it was almost impossible to be seen. The act of putting our possessions back in order after the devastation wrought by the vandals had made the absence of my sweet wife all the more bitter. And as I sighed and moaned with nostalgia and impatience at the thought of her, I found myself thinking of the amours of the Sun King with Maria Mancini, and of the strange passion which seemed to unite Maria and Atto who, after thirty years in voluminous and secret epistolary correspondence, had still never again seen one another.

In truth everything surrounding Atto was bizarre, unusual, arcane. What could one say of the strange phenomena at the Vessel? And was there a connection between the death of the bookbinder, Atto's wounding and the strange circumstances in which this had taken place? On top of all that, there was the extremely troubling fact of the double raid on Buvat and myself, after we had both been safely drugged.

Again, I felt confusion, even desperation clutching at my breast. The languor of love for my Cloridia had given way to fear. What was really happening? Were we perhaps the victims, as Melani had written to the Connestabilessa, of some pro-imperial plot? Or was this to do with the *cerretani*, as Sfasciamonti maintained? Or both things at once?

I began once more to reprove myself for having let myself get caught up again in the Abbot's webs. This time, in truth, even he seemed to be groping in the dark. What was more, I had seen him confused and upset during our strange visit to the Vessel. My thoughts then returned confusedly to Maria, and I recalled that she now seemed to be residing in Madrid. In Spain, the very place where, as I had learned from the letters between the two, the fate of the world was now being played out. . .

Suddenly, a sensation of warm silk enveloped my naked back and drew me softly from the grey torpor into which I had slipped unawares. A murmur soothed my ears:

"Is there room for me?"

I opened my eyes: my Cloridia had returned.

లోపం

When we were sated with silent kisses and by our embrace in the warm light of sunset, Cloridia began.

"You haven't asked me how it went. If you only knew what an adventure it has been!"

For days and days, my wife who, as I have said, had for years been exercising the profession of midwife, had stayed far from me and from our conjugal bed in order to assist an expectant mother. Now she had returned and I could not wait to tell her everything and to receive comfort and counsel from her. She, however, seemed as impatient as I to tell me her latest news. So I considered that it would be better to let her speak first. Once the natural womanly loquacity of my Cloridia had been placated, I would have all the time I needed to tell her of the sudden reappearance of Abbot Melani and of my torments.

"The little ones?" I asked before all else, for our two daughters had gone with their mother to assist her.

"Have no fear, they're down below snoring happily with the other servant girls."

"Then," I said with feigned enthusiasm, "tell me all!"

"The factor of the Barberini farm is now the father of a fine, plump and well-formed infant. Healthy and with everything in the right place just as God ordered!" she murmured proudly. "Only. . ."

"Yes," said I, hoping that she would not prolong her account.

"Er, he was born after five months."

"What, that's not possible!" I exclaimed in a strangulated voice, pretending surprise, although I knew full well what she was leading up to.

"Those were the very words which the factor cried out when his poor wife was in the travails of childbirth. And yet, it is possible, my love. I spent hours and hours calming down that great ignorant beast and convincing him that, while it is true that the time assigned for a human birth is normally nine months, there are, however, cases of births in the fifth month, just as, on the other hand, there are births that take place only in the twelfth month. . ."

I freed myself from my wife's embrace and looked her in the eyes.

". . . Pliny bore witness before a tribunal in defence of a woman," Cloridia continued candidly, "whose consort had returned from the wars only five months previously, and swore that it was possible to give birth after only five months. It is, moreover, true that, according to Massurius, under the Praetorship of Lucius Papirius, a sentence was pronounced against someone in a certain controversy concerning heredity, because his mother attested that she had been pregnant for thirteen months; but it is also incontrovertible that the great Avicenna saved a mother from stoning by giving testimony before a judge that it is also possible to give birth after fourteen months."

I was trembling from my anxiety to speak to her.

"Cloridia, listen, I have so many things to tell you. . ."

But she was not listening. The air was still warm and my beautiful spouse, after all those days of absence, seemed no less so.

"I was good, was I not?" she interrupted me as though she had not heard me, pressing her cool bosom against my chest. "I explained to that madman that, among all animals, man is the only one to have an indeterminate period before coming into this world. Beasts all have a fixed time: the elephant always gives birth in the second year, the cow in the first, the horse and the donkey in the eleventh month and the pig and the dog in the fourth, the cat in the third, while the hen always hatches her chicks after twenty days' brooding, and finally, the sheep and the goat drop their young in the fifth month. . ."

Indeed, their husbands – I commented to myself – Master Ram and Master Billygoat, both have a fine pair of horns on their heads.

My Cloridia was utterly incorrigible. I had lost all count of the number of cases of dubious paternity resolved by the midwife's skills of my consort. In her love for children (whoever their father might be) and their mothers (whatever the fidelity of which they were capable), Cloridia did everything possible, swearing and forswearing, in order to convince suspicious husbands. She would stop at nothing. With a ready tongue, a smile on her lips and the most open expression in the world, she would furnish clarifications and examples in abundance for all husbands: from the freshly discharged soldier to the shepherd who had been absent for the transhumance, to the travelling vendor, even the grim mother-in-law or the meddlesome sister-in-law. And she was invariably believed, in despite of the sage's law that one should not believe all that is said by someone who talks much, for in many arguments one can almost always find lies.

Not only that: fearing that the infant, when he grew, might show too much of a resemblance to a neighbour or some other person above suspicion, Cloridia, even before the confinement, and immediately afterwards, would with tireless loquacity instruct the new father and the wary relatives, explaining that a woman's imagination could render her newborn child similar to a thing seen or imagined during coitus. She was always delighted, upon her return after a confinement, to tell me how, when and before what audience she had prepared her favourite story. In all those years, she had repeated it to me perhaps a thousand times, at every confinement spicing it with new or invented details, each time attributing to herself new ideas and discoveries. She loved that I admired her and took pride in her deeds, and the way in which I laughed when she wanted me to laugh and pretended to be surprised when she expected that. My desire was to see her gay and satisfied, and I played along for her.

Nevertheless, that afternoon, I simply could not do it. I had so much, indeed, too much, to tell her and I desperately needed her advice.

"I told the factor: 'Do you perhaps not know the story told by Heliodorus which shows how the imagination can produce creatures similar to the thing imagined? It is known the world over! Listen here,' I told him: 'Heliodorus tells, in the book of his Aethiop histories, how a beautiful white-skinned girl was born of a black mother and father, namely Idaspe, King of Aethiopia, and his Queen Persina. And this was a consequence only of the thought, or rather, the imagination of the mother, with whom the King conjoined in a chamber in which were depicted many actions of white men and women, and in particular the amours of Andromeda and Perseus; the Queen took such delight in the sight of Andromeda in the act of venery. . .'"

Obviously, I knew the rest of the tale inside out, and while, docilely but distractedly, I accepted Cloridia's sweet pressures on my body, I repeated mentally after her: the Queen took such delight in the sight of Andromeda in the act of venery that she became pregnant with a maiden similar to her; this explanation was given by the Gymnosophists who were the most learned men in that land. And Aristotle confirms. . .

I could console myself, I thought as I impatiently awaited the end of the tale: if the great Hippocrates, and Pliny and Avicenna too, had had the impudence to perjure themselves before a judge, coolly inventing such tall stories in order to save the lives of a mother and her child, my spouse was in good company.

"Alciatus, and before him Quintilian," continued Cloridia while she disarranged my clothing and gave ampler freedom to her appetites, "freed another woman from the same accusation who had given birth to a black daughter, her husband being white, because there was in her chamber the painted figure of an Aethiopian."

"And then? Did you tell him the tale of Jacob's sheep?" I asked her in order to please her, as I was beginning to fear the outcome of her manoeuvres.

"Obviously," she replied, without allowing herself to be distracted from her intentions.

"And your theory that even mere food could influence the appearance of the newborn child?" I asked, caressing the palms of her hands with my lips, so as to keep her under control and to distract her from the inspection which she was obstinately intent upon carrying out.

"Mmm, no," she replied with a hint of embarrassment. "Do you remember, when I attended the confinement of the wife of that Swiss coffee-house owner? Well, when I tried to assuage the suspicions of the husband, explaining to him that in animals one finds more resemblance than in men, because they eat always the same food, while men eat different foods, he replied with an ugly expression that in his part of the world Alpine men and women ate nothing but chestnuts and watered-down goat's milk, despite which they were born with the same differences as ourselves."

"And what did you say to that?"

"I still managed, using the story of feminine imagination. I swore that it was universally known to be true, indeed most certain, that a strong imagination and the fixed thought of a woman could mark the body of her child with the semblance and image of the thing desired. Do we not see every day infants who are born marked with pig's skin, or wine, or grapes, or other similar stains? A strong imagination can then mark in a woman's womb a body already fully formed, so much as to imprint the most varied forms on its skin, for these represent the woman's thoughts. So in the end I told him: 'You who exploit your poor wife night and day serving coffee at table now have your

just deserts: the poor thing, by dint of spending so much time looking at coffee, has produced for you a son of the same colour!'"

Alack and alas. As we can read in the works of Cesare Baronio, the
great Tertullian, a man of great fame, let himself be persuaded by a
vile woman of no account that the souls of the just were coloured.
Then just imagine my sharp-witted and erudite Cloridia allowing
herself to be caught out by some cuckold coffee-house proprietor
and, what's worse, with the thick skull of a Switzer. With this mute
consideration, I accepted with resignation the account of my lady's
prowess, while she in the meanwhile had resumed her effusions.

"Is a man's imagination worth nothing?" I asked, feigning astonishment and surprise in order to free myself a little of her over-active
embrace.

"Here, there arises a considerable doubt. According to Aristotle,
yes. According to Empedocles and Hippocrates, whose view I praise,
a man's imagination will succumb to a woman's, which is most vehe-
ment," said she, while she acted most vehemently. "Save in a single
case. That of the wise father with a foolish son. Why should a foolish son sometimes be born of a wise father? It is not possible that
the mother should desire this. And yet, yes, that is the case. Most
studious husbands are of ever-melancholy humour, and melancholy
is sister in the flesh to madness: both especially hated by women
when it comes to lovemaking. It may then be that during the carnal
act their imagination may run to desiring a happy fool rather than a
melancholy sage. Quite apart from the fact that distracted husbands
do not pay sufficient attention to that task. . ."

I winced for shame. Cloridia was right. I had not responded to
her ardour and had remained melancholy and absent. Not even when
she had put all her womanly arts into play, from the most subtle to
the most manifest, had she succeeded in calling my anxious member
to his sweet and sacrosanct conjugal duties. And to think that only
a little earlier I had so longed for her! The Devil take those damned
thoughts of the Abbot, the bookbinder and the thieves and all those
things which had so horribly cast me down into that pit of anguish.

"Would you then prefer a silly but happy consort, dear wife?" I
asked her.

"Well, a happy and foolish man is always a good thing for the quality of the offspring, for he greatly pleases the woman in their encounter and will make her desire wisdom to be united to so much gaiety,

so that, through the power of the imagination, she will succeed in generating a son who is both joyful and wise in spirit."

I smiled, embarrassed. She sat up and laced her bodice.

"Come, what's so perturbing you?"

Thus, I was at last able to tell her: of Atto's arrival, the theft of my memoir, the task of serving as the Abbot's biographer during this time and, at last, of my suspicions and lacerating doubts, without forgetting Atto's wounding, the strange death of the bookbinder, as well as the double raid on our home and against Buvat. But above all I told her of the mysterious Maria, who had then turned out to be Madama the Connestabilessa Colonna, with whom Atto was secretly in correspondence, and of the disquieting visit to the Vessel. Lastly, the news of how the incursion had turned our nest upside down caused her a shudder.

"And only now are you telling me?" was Cloridia's sole response as she looked at me wide-eyed, as though she had suddenly discovered that she had married an idiot.

My prickly consort had already forgotten how long I had had inanely to await the end of her chatter. She calmed down quickly enough: learning of the tidy little sum which the Abbot had already paid us put her in a good mood at once.

"And so Abbot Melani is again in these parts, doing damage," commented Cloridia.

My wife had never had much sympathy for the Abbot. Through me, she knew of all the base deeds of which the castrato had been capable, and thus was not in the least impressed either by the diplomat's eloquence or by my experience of countless adventures by his side.

"He sends you his greetings," I lied.

"You may reciprocate," she replied with a hint of scepticism. "And so your castrato abbot has been pining for a woman these thirty years," she added, in a tone halfway between sarcasm and satisfaction. "And what a woman!"

Cloridia, being a good tattler, had already heard tell of Maria Mancini and knew from high authority of her Roman vicissitudes as the wife of the Constable Colonna.

On the visit to the Vessel and the enigmatic apparition which I had witnessed, she made no comment. I should very much have liked her to enlighten me with her wise opinion, for she had once been so expert in the occult arts such as reading the palm, the science of numbers and guidance by the ardent rod, but my wife passed directly to the next phase: she would ask around, among her women, in order to help us with our inquiries. She would set in motion the powerful and secret network of feminine word of mouth; a thousand eyes would keep vigil – observing, following, memorising for us, shooting astute glances – unseen, behind the deceptive appearance of an expectant mother's calm contemplation or the languid eyelashes of a spouse.

We talked for a long time and as usual she was prodigal with politic advice, wise recommendations and exaggerated praise of my virtues. She knew me well and knew how much encouragement I would be needing.

I had no more doubts. Now that I had told her all and had put my trust in her, my fears had dissolved, and with them the weight which drained my senses of all strength and tumescence.

We lay together and at last we loved each other. In the shade of the great beech, like some new Titirus, I sweetly modulated my flute in honour of my woodland muse.

࿐

We had by now been overtaken by nightfall. Freeing myself from my Cloridia's embrace, I discreetly rearranged her apparel and walked slowly towards the great house and my meeting with Abbot Melani.

It was then that, my soul being touched by the grace of conjugal love, I first beheld the gardens of the villa in the gay fullness of their splendour. Cardinal Spada had spared no expense to bestow upon the festivities every imaginable perfection. Villa Spada was smaller and more modest than other noble dwellings, but its master desired that it should for the occasion be among the foremost in the display of magnificence. He had not failed to enhance that which, more than all else, makes Roman villas so very special and different from those in all the rest of the world, namely their unique situation; for, wherever their site may be, there is perforce a most delightful conjunction with the vestiges of ancient Rome.

The statues, marbles, inscriptions and all the other things which ignorant workmen had brought to light in the gardens of Villa Spada were, by order of Cardinal Fabrizio, raised from oblivion in the cellars or under the invasive maidenhair ferns and so arranged as to punctuate the modern gardens with majestic whiteness.

The beautiful concentric flower beds with shrubs along their borders, divided up by radiating drives arranged for the occasion by Tranquillo Romaùli, the Master Florist, had been adorned with columns, sarcophagi and steles, while along the outer wall, fragments of capitals alternated with espaliered citrus trees; even at the main gates, above the stairway of a ruin, rose a pergola supported by trellises, as though time, waving the green banner of nature, wished to signify the overthrow and vanity of human endeavours.

But Villa Spada was but a small example: Rome's villas often enclose temples which remain almost intact, or even entire sections of aqueduct. In the Villa Colonna at Monte Cavallo there was for a long time preserved (and then, alas, thoughtlessly demolished) a fine piece of the gigantic Templum Solis. In the Villa Medici on the Pincio, the Templum Fortunae was to be found. In the Villa Giustiniani on the Lateran Hill, the boundary was marked by the aqueduct of Claudius, flanked by other enormous, anonymous ruins. Even the interior of the Mausoleum of Augustus, a glorious and solemn vestige of the greatest of emperors, was transformed into a garden when it was the property of Monsignor Soderini. On the Palatine Hill and on the Celio, villas and ruins, edifices new and old stretched in a single inextricable web. And likewise, the little Gentili Palace backed onto the ancient Aurelian Walls, of which it had even incorporated a tower; while the Orti Farnesiani (the inestimable work of Vignola, Rainaldi and Del Duca) fused harmoniously with the vestiges of the imperial palaces on the Palatine. Even Cardinal Sacchetti, when in his villa in the Pigneto he wished to offer a sepulchre to his favourite ass Grillo, used ancient Roman remains which had come into his hands there, on his own lands, where one had only to sink a spade into the ground to strike marble from the centuries of Cicero and Seneca.

In the Villa Ludovisi a pavilion had been erected for the sole purpose of housing the statues, while at Villa Borghese, Cardinal Scipione had devoted most of the space to his collection of busts and figures.

However, antiquities were not the only items employed for the embellishment of the vineyards and casino of the Villa Spada. The avenues which led to fountains and nymphaeums, as well as the little wood, had been adorned with obelisks, as at the Del Bufalo Garden at Villa Ludovisi; or then there was the obelisk in the Medici Garden, of which I had admired splendid engravings in the books of my late father-in-law. However those at the Villa Spada were ephemeral, made of papier mâché in imitation of the admirable architectural designs of the Cavalier Bernini erected in the Piazza Navona or the Piazza di Spagna to celebrate the birth of princes or other worthy events, wonders destined to last only for the duration of a few nights' festivities.

Every Roman villa was a place conceived for repose and pleasure, as in the days of Horace (and so I believe it will still be in the centuries to come), and thus also a venue for games, extravagances and all manner of delightful distractions. And Villa Spada seemed to be rising to the present nuptial occasion as a veritable compendium of all these things.

I would have liked to stop and admire one by one the thousand delights and marvels which the villa offered, but the evening was advancing. Taking leave of my reflections, I hastened on my way to my appointment with Abbot Melani; and with the Connestabilessa who, according to what I had read in her letter to the Abbot, was expected after Vespers.

☙❧

"Good heavens, dear boy, whatever have you been doing to yourself? I seem to be receiving a delegation of Arcadian shepherds."

I lowered my head in response to Atto's remark and took an embarrassed look at my clothing, crumpled by amorous activity and stained by the grass on which I had lain with my wife.

"Buvat, put some order in these rooms," he ordered his secretary suddenly, as though he were addressing some slovenly manservant. "Wipe the floor with some cloths, and if you can find none, use the sleeves of your jacket, as you never change it. Pile up my papers, and go and get something to eat. And do it quickly, for heaven's sake, I am expecting guests."

Although unaccustomed to performing servants' duties, and wondering why Atto did not instead employ an ordinary *valet de chambre*, yet Buvat dared not rebel, seeing his master's extreme nervousness. So he began at random to tidy up the Abbot's documents, the ornaments, the remnants of luncheon still strewn on the divan and the numerous piles of books encumbering the floor here and there. Such was Buvat's inexperience that, despite the fact that I gave him a hand, instead of diminishing, the chaos only increased.

I saw that the Abbot was rubbing his injured arm.

"Signor Atto, how is your wound?" I asked.

"It is getting better, but I shall have no peace until I know who reduced me to this state. The strangest things have been happening in the past few days: first, my arm is wounded in the bookbinder's presence, then the poor man's death and, to cap it all, the attempt to rob you two. . ."

At that moment, someone knocked at the door. Buvat went to open it. I saw him take delivery of a letter from a messenger which, after closing the door, he hastened to hand to Abbot Melani.

Atto broke the seal and read swiftly. Then he stuffed the letter into his pocket and, speaking in a low voice, told us reluctantly of its contents.

"She will no longer be coming. She has had to stop, owing to a light attack of fever. She begs to be excused for her inability to advise me earlier, *et cetera, et cetera.*"

A few minutes later, Abbot Melani showed us the door. The reason, as had also been the case the day before, lay in the letter from the Connestabilessa, which Atto wished to read properly, far from our curious looks.

Once I had closed the door behind us and taken my leave of Buvat, who was going to take a look at the library of the great house, I began to feel ill at ease. What had the Abbot summoned me for if he was now dismissing me without having commanded, asked or said a single thing? Bad news of the Connestabilessa's unexpected delay had indeed arrived; besides which, my task of keeping a chronicle had only just begun the day before. Yet, when I came to think of it, Atto had used me more as an informer (as at dinner the evening before) than as a biographer. Not only that: about the nature of that little book which seemed to lie at the heart of a singular series of misadventures, the Abbot had been distinctly sparing with information. Yet, hardly had he learned of the death of the bookbinder than Atto had rushed in furious haste to recover it.

☙◦❧

Buvat had rejoined Melani, who was conversing with other guests in the gardens of Villa Spada when, an hour later, keeping the Abbot under frequent observation with his own spyglass, I set to work looking for the little bound book. When the binder had delivered it to him, it had been wrapped in a blue velvet cloth, and that now made it impossible to identify the appearance and colour of the binding.

I searched the apartment from top to bottom and examined all Abbot Melani's volumes one by one, but alas, not a trace did I find of a newly bound book: all the tomes showed signs of wear and frequent consultation. It was quite clear that Atto had brought with him to the Villa Spada only those books he most needed. Consequently, a brand new binding would certainly have caught my eye. For a few moments, I stopped again to peruse a few pages containing piquant episodes concerning cardinals: these had already proved very useful to me when it came to following the allusions and jokes which the eminences exchanged at dinner. Then I searched everywhere once more, but of that little volume there was no trace. Perhaps the Abbot had lent it to some other guest? If that were the case, the matters dealt with in the book could not be so very confidential.

Atto, as I already knew, feared that he might have been the victim of an anti-French plot, perhaps at the hands of the imperial party. Of this he was, however, not at all convinced. Sfasciamonti's talk of the *cerretani*, of whom he had never previously heard tell, had made him uncertain. To the Connestabilessa he had written that he wished to request an audience with the Imperial Ambassador, Count von Lamberg, but the latter, who was expected at the Villa Spada, had not yet arrived. He would surely be present on the morrow, at the wedding. Until then, the Abbot – and I – must needs wait.

Otherwise, I found myself thinking once more, what had I learned from Abbot Melani? A conclave was in sight, that he had indeed told me, and had even shown me a list of cardinals written in his own hand; but, apart from that? Where now was the didactic passion of the veteran agent who had imparted so many and such dense teachings to me at the time when I was working as an apprentice at the Locanda del Donzello? And Atto must indeed know plenty about conclaves: he had even boasted of getting a pope elected.

Abbot Melani had really aged, I concluded rather sadly. Now, rather than by word of mouth, I was obtaining clues and news mainly from his personal effects, which I had surreptitiously examined, from his clothing (among which I had discovered my little pearls) and, above all, from the secret correspondence with the Connestabilessa.

Madama la Connestabilessa, the Princess Maria Mancini Colonna: on her account Atto had spoken with passionate prolixity during our excursion to the Vessel a few hours earlier. But that tale dated back to many, many years ago, and had nothing to do with the forthcoming conclave. Indeed, Atto had been at great pains to keep the "current" state of his relations with the Connestabilessa strictly to himself; he had not yet, for example, breathed a word to me of their common interest in the matter of the Spanish succession. Nor of whatever the Connestabilessa, born in Rome and brought up in Paris, might have to do with the Kingdom of Spain.

At length I gave up my search for the little book bound by the late lamented Haver, plunged my hands again into the Abbot's dirty linen and took out the folder of secret correspondence between him and the Connestabilessa. As on the first occasion, I found the letter from Maria Mancini together with the reply, as yet unsealed, by the Abbot. I scanned rapidly through both: I wanted also to have time to take a glance at the previous missives, which I had set on one side the day before.

The Connestabilessa's letter opened with a reference to the assault suffered by Abbot Melani:

What pain you have caused my heart, my friend! How are you? How is your arm? Is there really any reason to suspect the hand of the cruel Empire behind all this? I pray ardently that you should at least be spared by the hand of the Imperial assassins; for many, far too many, dead men bear a banner marked with the two-headed eagle of Vienna.

Take care, keep looking all around you. I tremble at the idea of your requesting an audience with Count von Lamberg. Do not eat at his table, drink not from the chalice filled by his hand, accept nothing from him, not even a pinch of snuff. Where the dagger failed, poison, the Imperial agents' weapon of choice, might succeed.

Do you always keep on your person the Bezoar stone which I sent you a few years ago? It will preserve you from all things toxic, never forget that!

I turned my mind again to the question: had I not found a pistol among Atto's personal effects? Clearly, he had not taken his own security lightly. The letter continued:

Never forget the horrible death of the Duke of Osuna who, no sooner had he been appointed general in charge of coastal defences in the Mediterranean, began to work for a truce with the French; but alas, after taking a pinch of snuff he was struck down by paresis of the spine and suffocation, and died at three o'clock in the morning, without having been able to utter a word. And what should we say of the sudden and mysterious death of the Secretary of State, Manuel de Lira, who strove so hard for peace with France? Finally, permit me to remind you, despite the pain which the very thought causes me for reasons well known to you, of the most atrocious crime of all: the late Queen of Spain, our most beloved Marie-Louise of Orleans, the first wife of King Charles II, who never lost an opportunity to convince her consort of the need not to join the league against the Most Christian King, his uncle, and was hated by many in Spain, amongst them, Count Mansfeld, the Ambassador of the Empire.

Do you not recall? The poor Queen was afraid; she had even written to the King of France, begging him for an antidote for poison. But when this reached Madrid, Marie-Louise was already dead.

The evening before – I read in the Connestabilessa's letter – the Sovereign wanted milk, but little was available in the capital. It was said that, at the last moment, the Countess of S, a friend and protégée of the Imperial Ambassador, as well as an exile from France following the Affair of the Poisons, the first victim of which, some thirty years earlier, had been Madame, Marie-Louise's mother, arranged for her to have a little. When the Queen of Spain died in dreadful agony, some swore that the fresh and delicious milk which she had drunk before feeling ill had been prepared at the house of Ambassador Mansfeld. And it was perhaps no coincidence if the Countess of S left suddenly on the morning after the crime, so arranging matters that all trace of her was lost.

I noticed that here Maria Mancini had been at pains to conceal the name of the presumed poisoner, of French origin, yet a member of the imperial party. I would also have liked to know what the reasons "well known" to Atto might have been, which made the memory of the deed so painful for the Connestabilessa, but the letter continued with a heartfelt address to that Silvio, which pseudonym I presumed must, by means of a set of screens behind screens, conceal the person of Abbot Melani himself:

Silvio, Silvio, vain boy, if you imagine this mishap by chance befell, you widely are deceived. These accidents so monstrous and so strange befall us mortals by divine permission. Don't you reflect the Gods by you were slighted, by this your haughty pride and high disdain of love and ev'rything the world deems human? They cannot abhor, although it be in virtue. Now you are mute, who were but now so haughty!

I wondered yet again at the vehemence with which the Connestabilessa hurled indecipherable accusations against Abbot Melani.

As though that were not enough, after a few lines of excuses for her own delay (brought about by some slight fever), came the usual note about that so-called Lidio:

You charge me with according scant value to Lidio's presumed felicity. Yet I reply to you that in every matter it behoves us to mark well the end: for oftentimes God gives men a gleam of happiness, and then plunges them into ruin. And to him I repeat: with respect to that whereon you question me, Lidio, I have no answer to give, until I hear that you have closed your life happily.

Who then could this mysterious Lidio be, whom the Connestabilessa addressed through Atto's mediation, employing such impenetrable expressions? And what was the obscure mirror game which, from time to time, caused her to address the Abbot by the name of Silvio?

Nor did I learn much from Atto's reply; I was soon bogged down in a larding of unctuous flattery and affectation:

O that delightful rock on which so oft whole floods of tears and gales of sighs have struck in vain! Must I believe you live and feel some tender strokes of pity for my suff'rings? Is that a human breast, or is it marble?

Your sweetness moves me, my friend, and I tremble with anger at myself for having so improvidently caused you such agitation. Was the fever perhaps my fault too?

My ink tipp'd pen, and you curst arrows (which have pierced her side, so well by me belov'd), ye native brethren, or else for cruelty so called, I'll break you all. No longer darts or arrows shall you remain, but rods with useless wings, headed with steel in vain, lopped of your points and feathers!

And here the Abbot's letter was stained with ink; Atto had actually broken his goose quill, guilty of having written things that had worried the Connestabilessa and perhaps even made her ill. After a moment of sheer astonishment at such vehemence, I resumed my reading. (Melani had obviously found a new pen.)

Wound me then likewise with your plume, I beg of you. Indeed I demand it!

Ah, do not wound, but spare these eyes, these hands, which were the guilty ministers because by an unguilty will they were directed. Here, strike my breast, that enemy to love, foe to all tenderness, this cruel heart which was so harsh to thee. My breast is open.

After that, the tone, relinquishing passion, returned to the realms of common sense. Atto was concerned above all to show courage and boldness in his dealings with Lamberg, and not to betray the anxiety which must, however, be tormenting him.

As for me and my life, fear not, my good friend. Of course, I have with me your beautiful oriental stone. How could I ever forget the Bezoar? In France, too, it is esteemed as a protection against malignant fevers and poison.

When I am received by the Ambassador, I shall keep it jealously in my pocket, ready to help me in the event of my feeling in any way unwell.

However, when young, I knew Count von Lamberg's father well: he was Imperial Ambassador to Madrid just when I was with Cardinal Mazarin at the Isle of Pheasants for the peace treaty between France and Spain. We snatched the hand of the Infanta Maria Teresa, for whom the Emperor Leopold so longed, from under his nose. Indeed, King Philip IV ended up by granting her to Louis XIV after much arm-twisting, so as to be able to gain less humiliating peace terms. And that was most fortunate: but for this, today the Most Christian King would not be able to lay claim to rights to the Spanish Crown for his nephew the Duke of Anjou. Philip IV did, it is true, make Maria Teresa sign a document renouncing any claim to the Spanish throne (just as Anne of Austria before her had done when she married Louis XIII of France); but since then plenty of jurists have demonstrated that such renunciations are invalid.

All in all, my dear, Lamberg senior rendered Austria the worst of services, just as we rendered France the very best. If the son's abilities are equal to his father's, it is certain that neither I nor French interests in the Spanish succession will be in any danger. However, I shall soon know how matters stand: the arrival of the Imperial Ambassador is expected at any moment. And you? When will you be here?

Silvio was proud, 'tis true, but he venerates the gods, and was one day vanquished by your Cupid. Since then he has ever bowed down before you, calling you his.

Altho' his you were not.

Emotion caused me to raise my eyes after reading those last lines. Poor Abbot Melani: in reminding the Connestabilessa of the love he had borne her for forty years, in the end he was reminding her only of his immutable castrato's condition; Maria had never been his, nor could she ever have been.

As a post scriptum to the letter, a fleeting reference to that Lidio:

I come now to our Lidio. 'Tis enough to speak of him: You have won, for the time being. But what you will receive when we meet will convince you. Then you will change your opinion. You know what value he sets upon your judgement and your satisfaction.

I closed the envelope and began to reflect. Judging by his epistolary exchange with the Connestabilessa, it seemed that Atto's diplomatic interest was concerned solely with the Spanish succession and the risks (including physical ones) connected therewith. Not a word about the forthcoming conclave, for which he had told me that he had come to Rome. Not only that, but, according to the letter, Atto feared that he might be a target for an imperial stiletto (or poison) because of the Spanish succession, while he said absolutely nothing about the conclave, where he would, after all, be defending French rights at the expense of those of Austria. I might even have said that Atto cared nothing for the conclave.

For a moment, I suspended my cogitations: that impression, I told myself, seemed unreasonable, indeed unfounded. I really could not believe that Atto did not care about the conclave that seemed to be approaching.

It seemed absurd. But had I not learned from the Abbot in person, so many years before, to reason on the basis of suppositions and not to back down before truths that seemed utterly improbable? The conclave and the succession. . . or perhaps the succession and the conclave? Indeed, it seemed as though the success of the conclave depended upon that of the Spanish succession.

I skimmed rapidly through the rest of the correspondence, in the hope of casting some light on the identity of the mysterious Countess of S. The envelopes were all as bulky: confidential and extremely detailed reports on the kingdom of Spain and King Charles II. They were all numbered, with almost invisible figures written in a corner. I opened the first of them. It must have dated from some time previously; the Connestabilessa was writing from the Spanish capital.

OBSERVATIONS
WHICH MAY BE OF USE IN RELATION TO
SPANISH AFFAIRS

Here in Madrid, everyone wonders what will become of the Kingdom after the death of the Sovereign. Any hope of an heir has long since disappeared; el Rey is ill and they all say that his seed is already dead. With the Sovereign's poor body devoured by illness, all is moving towards the setting of the sun in this Kingdom on which the sun never sets: the power of Spain, the splendour of the Court, even the glorious past is obscured by the miseries of the present time. . .

I read with surprise those disconsolate, bitter, definitive lines. Who then was Charles II of Spain, *el Rey*, as the Connestabilessa called him in her letters to Atto? I realised that I knew nothing, absolutely nothing, about that dying sovereign and that limitless kingdom. I therefore plunged into the gloomy reading of that report, engulfing myself in the sense of disaster hanging over those lines which, like a skilfully distilled poison, infused my entire spirit during my furtive reading.

Let the curtains be drawn and the shutters closed on ample windows, let the sun be banished from the throne room, let a moonless night descend mercifully upon the Escorial: the body of el Rey is falling horribly apart, my friend, and with it his entire lineage. Let the wind rise and sweep away the foul stench of regal death; we are all drinking from the waters of Lethe, lest proud Spain recall the insult of so repugnant an end.

The Connestabilessa's groan of pain touched me profoundly. I read on: those were not mere metaphors that the letter evoked. Life in the royal palace really was being lived away from the light of day, by the glimmer of the occasional candle: thus they tried to attenuate for courtiers and visiting ambassadors the dreadful spectacle of the King's body and face.

His nose is swollen and cankered, his enormous forehead disfigured by threatening carbuncles, his cheeks livid, his breath stinks of rotten innards. His eyelids the colour of flayed flesh hood the deep black and bubonic bags of the eyes which now move with difficulty and are half blind. Even his tongue no longer obeys him. His speech is uncertain, reduced for all those who have not frequented him for all his life to a babbling, an incomprehensible mutter.

Exhausted, limp, wheezing – the Connestabilessa recounted in her report – *el Rey* was subject to continual fainting fits. He would swoon, throwing the court into a panic, then he would recover, suddenly rising to his feet before collapsing on the throne like a marionette without strings. He would switch from somnolence to sudden, exceedingly violent fits of epilepsy. He walked, dragging himself along with great difficulty and could stay standing only if he leaned against a wall, a table, or someone's shoulder. It was an effort for him even to bring his hand to his mouth. Both organs and limbs were worn out. His feet and his knees were ever more swollen. He was becoming dropsical. They tried to cure him with a diet based on cocks and capons fed on serpents; to drink, fresh cow's urine. For several months now, *el Rey* had been dragging himself from his bed to an armchair and from that back to bed. His body was already in a state of decomposition. And he was only thirty-nine.

I left off reading for a moment: so the King of Spain was barely two years older than me! What horrendous illness could have reduced him to such a state?

I scanned rapidly through those pages in search of a reply.

Attacks of the falling sickness, my friend, are devastating el Rey's flesh more and more with each passing day. At Court, we have by now learned to

recognise the warning signs: His Majesty's lower lip first becomes as pale as
that of a cadaver, then becomes blotched with red, blue and green. Soon his
legs are seized with tremors and then his whole body is shaken by the most
painful squirming and spasms: once, twice, ten times.

Charles II of Spain vomited several times a day. The Catholic King's
horrible lantern jaw, inherited from his Habsburg ancestors, is not just
ugly: when the monarch closes his mouth, his lower set of teeth, which
protrude too much, do not meet the upper row. One could easily place
a finger between them. King Charles cannot chew. Unfortunately, from
his forebears, particularly the Emperor Charles V, he also inherited the
appetite of a lion. Thus, he ends up eating everything whole. He gulps
down goose livers as though he were quaffing water, while the court
stands by, gloomy and powerless. Then, a little while after rising from
table, he throws up the entire meal. Vomiting is accompanied by fevers
and violent headaches which confine him to his bed for days on end.
He struggles to follow his counsellors' reasoning, and never smiles. Not
even the buffoons, the court dwarves or the marionettes, which once
made him laugh so much, can amuse him any more.

Not that his spirit, memory and ready wit have completely abandoned him; but for most of the time he remains taciturn and melancholy, torpid and listless, his days marked by the sad rhythms of
asthma.

His subjects have, with time, grown accustomed to having for a
sovereign a man reduced to this state. The ambassadors of foreign
kingdoms, however, cannot believe their eyes; as soon as they take
up their posts and are received at court for the first time, they find
themselves facing a man at the point of death, his gaze empty and
his speech fading. In his presence, one can find relief only by turning
away one's eyes, and one's nose.

I completed my reading with my heart swollen with anxiety and sorrow. All that I had just learned from my clandestine perusal of Atto's
papers threw much light on Maria Mancini's letter and the reply from
Atto which I had read the day before. The great diplomatic agitation
around the Spanish succession was not just so much febrile preparation for future confrontations between the great powers but a war already begun. It was clear that a sovereign in that state might die from
one moment to the next. Of the mysterious Countess of S., however,

I found no more trace. I would have to take my search further: there was still much correspondence to be read.

I looked up. Outside the window, Atto and Buvat had for some time disappeared over the horizon. I noticed walking down the avenue a lady who showed every sign of advanced pregnancy. This must be the Princess of Forano, that Teresa Strozzi whose health Cloridia had been called to watch over that evening. I dedicated a sweet and rapid thought to my spouse, whom I would soon be seeing again.

It was not prudent to remain any longer in Atto's lodgings; I might have been found out by him, and in any case my prolonged absence from work would sooner or later be noticed. It was better that I should be seen by Don Paschatio, who had, alas, ordered me to be a torchbearer at dinner that evening too. Fortunately, I was exempted from serving at table.

While I carefully returned the letters to their place, a mass of thoughts accumulated in my poor tired head. As ever, I feared that head was too small for great questions of state and too big for the minutiae of diplomacy.

It was clear from her letters that the Connestabilessa habitually resided at the Spanish court; but what could ever have brought her there? The report by Madama the Connestabilessa (who obviously had the most confidential sources at that court) presented a cruel and apocalyptic picture which contrasted singularly with the tender, and in truth somewhat daring words which Atto dedicated to her at the end of the letter. The correspondence was a bizarre chimera, a cross between love and politics, gallantry and diplomacy. Knowing Abbot Melani, at least two of those ways – sentiment and conspiracy – must, however, be leading up to a practical goal. The way of the heart led to the imminent encounter, after thirty years' separation, between Atto and Maria. The way of politics, however, led to a still unknown objective.

If one were to judge by his words, Melani was interested only in the forthcoming conclave; from what I read in those letters, however, the succession to the Spanish throne was a far more burning question. Atto must have some secret project, said I to myself; secret enough, at least, not to wish to reveal it to me.

Yet I too had eyes and ears; I too knew how to snatch precious details, revealing gossip, murmuring and betrayals from the eminences and princes who were then visiting the Villa Spada. Of course, Atto knew how to interpret these with a skill a thousand times greater than my own. Inured to all the dastardy and cunning intrigues of state, a true artist in behind-the-scenes activity, a handful of pebbles was enough to enable him to compose an entire coloured mosaic. I, however, had relative youth on my side. Was it not I who had snatched from the lips of Cardinal Spinola di Santa Cecilia the words which had put us on the trail of the secret meeting between Spada, Albani and the other Spinola?

My overarching intention, however, was to favour Cardinal Spada my master, even if that meant at the same time helping the reckless Abbot Melani. He, a French subject, was acting on behalf of the King of France. I, in the service of a magnanimous cardinal of the Holy Roman Church, would spy in the name of fidelity and gratitude.

Imprudently, I failed to take into account the fact that he had received a mandate from his lord, while I had not.

While exercised by these cogitations, I had by now rejoined the servant who was distributing the Turkish costumes. Now it was time to transform myself into a human candelabrum to illuminate the table of all those gentlemen and eminences and to satisfy my thirst for knowledge of the highest society, drinking at the freshest of fountains: the court of Rome, that school excelling in all forms of dissimulation and guile. I hoped only that to such intellectual refinement there should not, as on the evening before, be added Melani's expediencies, which could cost me dear. Fortunately, that evening's dinner had been announced by the Steward as being a trifle more modest than the inaugural one the evening before: the nuptials were due on the next day and stomachs were until then to be sheltered from any risks of indigestion that might affect participation in and enjoyment of the magnificent nuptial banquet.

While I was getting dressed, I caught sight of my Cloridia moving briskly towards the pergola, resplendent in the fine festive gown which she had been given for her evening in the gardens, keeping vigilant watch over the Princess of Forano. Knowing her to be near at hand gave me a feeling of great peace and serenity. She too saw me and approached briefly to tell me that the Princess did not feel like attending the dinner and was resting under the pergola.

"The little ones?" I asked, since in the event of lying in, Cloridia would need the assistance of our two daughters.

"They are at home. I do not want them wandering about in these parts, at least, not during the festivities. In case of need, I shall send for them."

I mentioned that the Connestabilessa would yet again not be arriving, as well as reporting the contents of the letter which I had just read.

"I already have some .information for you," said she, "but now there's no time. Let us meet here this evening."

She kissed my forehead and rushed off, leaving me a prey to curiosity about the news which she had in so short a time already gleaned from her women, as well as full of that admiration which her estimable promptness of spirit always aroused in me.

❧

". . . And 'tis most curious, if we come to think of it, that the Jubilee should for the first time have been opened by one pope, yet may, God forbid, be closed by another," slurred Cardinal Moriggia with his mouth full of pike cooked in apple juice, "which is what would happen if the Holy Father were to pass to a better life and a successor be elected before the end of the year."

"Most sad, you must mean, Eminence, most sad," retorted Monsignor d'Aste, Apostolic Commissioner for Arms, choking on his poached turkey *alla Svizzera*. "This turkey is really excellent; how was it cooked?"

"Larded with tripe, Your Excellency, pricked with cloves and cinnamon, cooked in wine and water, garnished with peaches in syrup, carved and interspersed with slices of lemon and covered with toasted eggs and sugar," the Steward hastened to explain to d'Aste, murmuring the recipe in his ear.

"This evening our greedy little Straccetto is making so bold as to correct those higher than he," whispered Prince Borghese ironically, using the nickname expressly chosen by the Pope who, as Atto had told me, had called D'Aste Monsignor Straccetto (or "little rag") because of his minuscule and unattractive form.

"Most sad, goodness knows, indeed *most sad*: that is, I think, just what I said," Moriggia defended himself, blushing as he gargled with a fine glass of red wine to clear his throat and free himself of his verbal embarrassment.

"Boor," someone commented without revealing himself, having evidently drunk too much.

Moriggia turned sharply but could not manage to find out who was so rudely insulting him.

"The fried crab is excellent," said D'Aste, trying to change the subject.

"Oh, exquisite," agreed Moriggia.

"Boor," came the insult once again, without anyone being able to identify who had spoken this time either.

"How did the Holy Father's visit to the hospice for poor orphans at San Michele go?" asked Cardinal Moriggia with skilfully simulated interest, in an attempt at distracting attention.

"Oh, magnificently, there was a great crowd and many pious persons who wished to kiss his feet," replied Durazzo.

"Incidentally, the expeditors of the Datary's office have been granted an indult to obtain remission of their sins by visiting the four basilicas once on the same day during the Jubilee."

"Quite right too! Even the prisoners and the infirm enjoy special prerogatives," someone commented from the end of the table.

"A holy and enlightened decision: poor expeditors of the Datary, their condition deserves to be taken into account too," approved Moriggia in turn.

"Boor."

This time, two or three guests turned around to see who dared aim such epithets at a member of the Sacred College. But the flow of conversation continued.

"'Tis a truly extraordinary Jubilee. Never has there been in Rome an atmosphere of such Christian fervour. And never, I'd say, have so many pilgrims been seen; not even on the glorious Jubilee of Pope Clement X. Is it not true, Your Eminence?" said Durazzo, turning to Cardinal Carpegna, who had personally taken part in the prodigious Jubilee celebrations a quarter of a century earlier.

The Carpegna family was among other things related to the Spada, which on that evening conferred even greater attention upon his every word.

"Oh, that was an extraordinary Jubilee, yes, indeed it was," muttered the venerable Cardinal Carpegna, rather bent over his dish and with his mouth full, somewhat befuddled by his great age.

"Tell us, tell us about it, Your Eminence, tell us of some memory that is particularly dear to you," some guests encouraged him.

"Well, well, I remember, for example. . . Yes, I recall how in the church of Gesù a great machine was erected by Mariani for the adoration of the Most Holy Sacrament, and this drew great multitudes of the people. The apparatus, which was, believe me, most beautiful, represented the triumph of the Eucharistic Lamb among the symbols of the New Testament and the Apocalypse, with a vision of the Evangelist John when he was in reclusion on the isle of Patmos. Under the watchful eyes of the Eternal Father, enveloped in a thousand clouds full of celestial spirits and splendours, seven angels were to be seen with seven trumpets; then one saw a divine Lamb holding a book which represented the vision of the Apocalypse, which was moreover sent to John, and to us, by God's love for mankind. . ."

"True!" approved Durazzo.

"Such holy words!" echoed Monsignor D'Aste.

"Praise be to our Lord Jesus Christ," said they all (except those whose mouths were too full of the fried trout that had just been served), crossing themselves (except those whose hands were too involved with glasses of wine, knives and tridents for eating fish).

"There were visions of angelic choirs," continued Carpegna with a somewhat vacant expression, "effigies of the figures symbolising the Four Evangelists, namely the Lion, the Eagle, the Ox and the Man. I remember that the breast of the Lamb was all bloodstained and 'midst silver and golden rays of light his heart opened to display the Holy Eucharist which indeed issues only from God's love for mankind."

"Good, bravo!" approved his neighbours at table.

"But this year's Jubilee too will stand as an example for the centuries to come," said Negroni pompously.

"Oh yes, indubitably: pilgrims keep arriving from all parts of Europe. 'Tis so true that the pure, disinterested work of Holy Mother Church is more powerful than any force on earth."

"Apropos, how is this Jubilee going?" Baron Scarlatti asked Prince Borghese almost inaudibly.

"It could hardly be worse," whispered the other. "There has been a tremendous fall in the number of pilgrims. The Pope is most concerned. Not a penny is reaching the coffers."

Dinner was drawing to a close. Between one yawn and the next, eminences, princes, barons and monsignors were taking leave of one another, moving slowly towards the avenue leading to the main gate and their carriages. In a humbler procession, their secretaries, attendants, retainers, servants and other members of their retinue also moved away from the nearby table set aside for them, and from their more modest fare, in order to escort their illustrious patrons. As the table emptied, we torchbearers were able at last to relax our back and abdominal muscles, which had been so tense all evening long.

No one knew it, but when at long last I removed the ridiculous Ottoman turban and placed my smoking torch on the ground, it was I who was most breathless, not from fatigue but shock.

I had seen him at once and had realised what he was about to get up to. When he had gone on to call Cardinal Moriggia a boor three times over, I was quite sure that he would be most cruelly punished. Instead, his foolishness had been equalled only by his good fortune, and in the dim light of the dinner party, no one had caught sight of him. I moved away from the other servants, towards the outer wall of the villa. Then I heard him call me, with his usual courtesy.

"Boor!"

"As far as I am concerned, 'tis you who are the boor," I replied, speaking in the direction of the part of the garden from which the voice seemed to be coming.

"*Dona nobis panem cotidianum,*" came Caesar Augustus's response from the dark.

He had been flying around throughout dinner above the canopy that covered the table. He surely hoped to get his talons into some fine piece of the delicacies being served, but he must then have realised that it would be impossible to do so without being seen. I had broken into a cold sweat every time that, for the pure pleasure of giving offence, he had insulted Cardinal Moriggia. Yet no one could have imagined that mocking little voice belonged to Caesar Augustus, for the simple reason that, as I have already mentioned, the parrot spoke to no one except myself and everyone regarded him as being dumb.

I advanced a little further onto the meadow, hoping that no one would come seeking me for some last-minute chore.

"Your little play could hardly have been in worse taste," I reproved him, chattering into the darkness. "Next time, they'll wring your neck and make a roast of you. Did you see the dish of quails they served up with the third course? Well, that's what you'll be reduced to."

I heard his wings beating in the dark and then a fluttering of feathers grazed my ear. He landed on a bush a few inches from me.

Now at last I could see him, a white feathered phantom with a yellow plume proudly rising from his forehead, almost like some mad flag fluttering the papal colours.

I sat down on the fresh, damp grass, still somewhat over-excited and worn out by those hours spent as a torchbearer. Caesar Augustus stared at me with the usual very obvious expression of one imploring a little food, for pity's sake.

"*Et remitte nobis debita nostra,*" he insisted, again reciting the Lord's Prayer, which he would drag into service in the most woeful tones every time that he was hungry.

"You have eaten perfectly well today, this is sheer greed," said I, cutting him short.

"Clink-clonk, tink," said the diabolical creature, imitating with singular precision the clatter of cutlery on plates, and the joyful clinking of glasses. That was only the latest of his provocations.

"I have had enough of you, now I am going to bed, and I recommend that you do. . ."

"To whom are you talking, my boy?"

Atto Melani had joined me.

I needed plenty of persuasion to explain to the Abbot the bizarre nature of the animal with whom he had surprised me in conversation. All the more so, as Caesar Augustus had fled into the shadows the moment that he caught sight of Abbot Melani and there was no way in which he could be persuaded to make an appearance.

It was no easy task to persuade Atto that I was not mad, nor was I talking to myself, but that there was a parrot hidden in the dark with which it was possible to communicate, although in the contorted and anomalous manner which was his preference. At the end of my conversation, however, Caesar Augustus, who must have been immobile all this time, watching Atto from the shadows with that mixture of mistrust and curiosity which I knew so well in him whenever he caught sight of a stranger, remained as mute as a fish.

"It must be as you say, my boy, but it seems to me that the creature has no intention of opening its mouth. Eh Caesar Augustus, are you there? What a pompous name! *Cra-cra-cra!* Come, come on out. Did you really call Moriggia a boor?"

Silence.

"Eh, you old crow, 'tis you I'm addressing. Out with you! Have you nothing to say for yourself?"

The fowl's beak remained sealed, nor were we vouchsafed the honour of seeing him appear.

"Well, when he deigns to show himself and puts on all those fantastic shows of which you have told me, give me a whistle and I'll fly straight to you, ha," sniggered Atto. "But now, let us get down to serious business. I have a couple of things to tell you for tomorrow, before sleep gets the better of. . ."

"*Puella.*"

Atto looked at me in shock.

"Did you say something?" he asked.

I pointed into the darkness, in the direction of Caesar Augustus, without daring to confess openly that it was he who had offended Atto, calling him by the most insulting name possible for a castrato: *puella*, or, in Latin, little girl. I remained speechless: it was the first time that the parrot had uttered a word in the presence of others. Despite the insult proffered, I'd have said that Melani was honoured.

"'Tis absurd. I have seen and heard other parrots, all of them excellent. But this one sounded just. . ."

". . . Like talking to a person of flesh and blood, as I've already told you. This time he spoke with the timbre of an old man. But if only you knew how he can imitate women's voices, children crying – not to mention sneezes and coughing."

"Signor Abbot!"

This time, it was a real human voice that was calling for our attention.

"Signor Abbot, are you there? I have been looking for you for over half an hour!"

It was Buvat who, gasping and panting, was searching for his master in the semi-darkness of the garden.

"Signor Abbot, you must come up at once. Your apartment. . . I think that someone has entered without your permission, while you were dining, and has. . . We have had thieves!"

❧◦❦

"Does anyone else know of this?" asked Atto as we opened the door of his apartment, immersed in darkness.

"No one but yourselves; what's more, your orders. . ."

"Very well, very well," assented Atto. He had arranged that in the event of an emergency, Buvat was to mention nothing to anyone before speaking to him. I was soon to understand why.

Atto lowered the handle, pushed on the door and entered, lighting his way with a candle.

"But the door has not been forced," I observed in astonishment.

"No, indeed it has not, as I'd have told you if you'd given me time," replied Buvat who, during the wild rush that had followed his announcement had barely had a chance to open his mouth.

I advanced too and entered the apartment. A second and then a third candle were lit, revealing the unmistakeable traces of an incursion. Everything – every object, every ornament – was cast into a general disorder. A chair was turned upside down. Books, gazettes and loose papers of every kind were scattered on the floor. Atto's clothes too had been roughly thrown to the ground or heaped up on the furniture, and it was quite clear that they, too, had been thoroughly searched. A window was open.

"Strange, truly strange," I commented. "Despite all the guards keeping watch over Villa Spada in recent days, the thieves have had no difficulty in getting right here into the great house. . ."

"You are right. Yet it must have been a swift job," observed Atto after taking a rapid look around. It looks to me as though they have removed only the spyglass. 'Tis a tempting enough object. Apart from that, I think that nothing is missing."

"How do you know?" I asked, given that Atto's survey had lasted only a few seconds.

"Simple: after the attack on you two, I entrusted all my precious things to a servant of the villa. Papers of a certain importance. . . well, they are not here," said he with a sly expression which I pretended not to notice, since I too knew the hiding place: the dirty linen where I myself had found Maria's letters.

The Abbot then hastened to put his apparel back in order.

"Look at this," he groaned, "how they've crumpled them. One moment. . ."

Atto was prodding his mauve-grey soutane, within which I knew that he secretly kept the scapular of the Our Lady of the Carmel, the *ex voto* into which he had sewn my three little pearls.

"'Tis not there any more," he exclaimed. "Oh heavens, I left it in here!"

"What?" I asked, feigning ignorance.

"Er, a. . . relic. A most precious relic which I was keeping inside here, in a scapular of the Madonna of the Carmel. They have robbed me of it."

My poor little pearls, I lamented inwardly, they seemed fated to be stolen. In any case, this showed that the thieves had been through Abbot Melani's apartment with a fine-tooth comb.

We now stood in the light of the large candelabrum which I had lit, the better to be able to carry out our own thorough check. Abbot Melani, who had suddenly sunk to his knees, shifted the day-bed and raised part of the herringbone parquet underneath it, near the window. He removed one block, then another just next to it, then a third one.

"No. . . By all the saints!" I heard him swearing in a low voice. "The accursed rogues!"

Buvat and I stayed silent, looking questioningly at one another. Atto stood up, dusted down his elbows and collapsed into an armchair. He stared fixedly before him.

"Dear me, what a disaster. But how is it possible? What sense does it make? Whoever could. . . I do not understand," he was raving away to himself, shaking his head with one hand clasped to his brow, quite indifferent to our amazed looks.

"This is a grave misfortune," said he, once he had recovered his aplomb, "a serious matter. I have been robbed of some most important papers. At first, I did not even take the trouble to check, so sure was I that no one could get at them. I had replaced the slats of parquet with the greatest of care and skill. I know not how they managed to find them, but that is what they have just done."

"Were they under the parquet?" I asked.

"Exactly. Not even Buvat knew that they were there," said Melani, dismissing forthwith any suspicion of a betrayal.

In the brief moment of silence that followed, Atto must have become aware of the question running through Buvat's head and my own. Since we would have to help him recover the stolen papers, he must needs furnish us with a description, however summary, of their contents.

"It is a confidential report which I have written for His Most Christian Majesty," said he at length.

"And what is it about?" I dared ask.

"The next conclave. And the next pope."

The problems, explained Atto, were two-fold. In the first place, he had promised His Majesty the King of France to deliver the report as soon as possible. The report in Abbot Melani's possession was, however, the only copy in existence and even if he were to labour for months (making superhuman efforts of memory) that would still not suffice to rewrite it. Thus, Atto ran the risk of making a fool of himself in the King's eyes; but that was the least of things.

The report revealed secret circumstances concerning the election of the last pontiffs and prognostications concerning the forthcoming conclave, and it was signed by Atto. Even if it had not been signed, it would in any case be easy to ascribe it to him, thanks to certain circumstances reported in the text.

The document was at that moment in the hands of strangers, and probably hostile ones at that. Atto thus ran the risk of being charged with espionage on behalf of France. It would not be impossible that the charge might be made even graver by accusing him of intending to disseminate the report, so that he would find himself on trial for criminal libel.

". . . A crime which, as you know, is punished most severely in Rome," he concluded.

"What are we to do?" asked Buvat, no less concerned than his master.

"Since we cannot report the theft to the Bargello, we shall have to make do with the help of Sfasciamonti. Once you have put things back in some order, you, Buvat, will go and call him. Indeed no, go at once."

Once we were alone, Atto and I spent some time crawling on the floor picking up the scattered pages. Atto uttered not a word. Meanwhile, a suspicion arose in my mind concerning the object of the theft. I decided to take the plunge and ask him.

"Signor Atto, the hiding place which you chose was excellent. How can the thieves have discovered it? And what's more, the door was not forced. Someone must have had a copy of the key. How is that possible?"

"I really do not know. Curses, 'tis a mystery. Now we shall have to place ourselves in the hands of that catchpoll who will torment me with his tales of *cerretani* or whatever the deuce they call those mendicants, if they really do exist."

"How will you describe your manuscript? Not even to Sfasciamonti can you say exactly what it is about, seeing that one can trust no one."

He remained silent, and fixed his eyes on mine. He guessed what I suspected and realised that he could no longer put off giving me an explanation. He made a grimace of vexation and sighed: he was on the point of imparting, unwillingly, something which I did not know.

In the corridor, Buvat's footsteps were already ringing out, accompanied by Sfasciamonti's more resounding ones. I know not whether by chance or by choice, but Atto spoke at just the moment when the catchpoll opened the door, meaning, at the very last free moment after which I would no longer be able to talk with him freely or to trouble him with questions to which he did not wish to reply.

"The manuscript was freshly bound. It was the little book made by Haver."

❧

Although he still seemed somewhat somnolent, Sfasciamonti listened attentively to the account of what had taken place. He inspected the hiding place under the slats in the floor, made a quick inspection of Atto's lodgings, then asked discreetly the nature of the document that had been stolen, contenting himself with the summary explanation provided by Atto.

"It is a political text. It is of extreme importance and usefulness to me."

"I understand. The book you had bound by Haver, I suppose."

The Abbot could not deny that.

"It is a coincidence," he replied.

"Of course," Sfasciamonti agreed, impassively.

After that, the catchpoll asked whether Melani intended to report the theft to the Bargello or to the Governor of Rome. Since the victim of the theft was a person of note, an edict could be posted all over the city offering a reward for the return of the loot or the capture of the thieves.

"Come now," Atto responded at once, "rewards are worthless. When I was robbed of gold rings and a heart-shaped diamond in the Capuchin monastery at Monte Cavallo, the governor placed an enormous reward on the head of the thieves. Result: nothing whatever."

"I cannot say that you're wrong, Signor Abbot," agreed Sfasciamonti. If I have understood you well, apart from this document, you were robbed only of a spyglass and the scapular of the Carmel."

"Quite."

"You have not yet told me, however, what sort of sacred relic you kept in the scapular. A thorn from the crown of Our Lord Jesus Christ? A piece of wood from the cross? There are plenty of those around, but they are still popular; you know, now that it's the Jubilee. . ."

"No," Melani replied laconically, having no desire to confess that he had jealously kept my little pearls close to his heart for all those years.

"A piece of clothing, then, or a tooth?"

"Three pearls," Atto admitted at last, glancing at me, "of the Venetian margarita variety."

"A singular relic," observed Sfasciamonti.

"They come from the luminous vestment which Our Lady wore on the day of her apparition on Mount Carmel," explained Atto with the most natural air in the world, while the stupefied sergeant remained utterly unaware of the Abbot's irony. "Will that be enough for you now?"

"Of course," replied Sfasciamonti, recovering his composure after the surprise; "I'd say. . . Yes. Let us begin by looking for the spyglass."

"The spyglass? But that's of no importance whatever to me!" protested Atto.

"To you, no. But someone else might find it an interesting object, to be resold for a good price. Quite apart from the fact that it is not the kind of thing that passes unobserved. On the other hand, the relic and your political document will be difficult to identify. For anyone who does not know its contents, that little treatise will seem like any other old bundle of papers. It might be in the hands of someone who. . . well, someone not like yourself."

"In what sense?" asked Buvat.

"In what language was your document written?"

"In French," replied Atto, after a slight hesitation.

"It might have been stolen by someone who does not know how to read Italian, let alone French. And who therefore will not have the least idea of what he has laid his hands on."

"If that were the case, he would not have gone to the trouble of looking for it down there," commented Atto, pointing to the place where the slats in the parquet had been removed.

"Not necessarily. He may have come upon that hiding place by pure chance and been curious about the care with which your document was stowed away. 'Tis useless to speculate, first we must find that stuff."

"So, what are we to do?"

"Do you know what a good lawyer does when a gang of criminals are arrested?" asked Sfasciamonti.

"What does he do?"

"He lets one of his assistants defend the leader, and he himself takes on one of the ordinary bandits. Thus, the criminal judge cannot determine who the big fish is. We shall do likewise: we shall pretend we are looking for the spyglass, but at the same time we shall be looking for your political document."

"And how shall we look for it?"

"Our first port of call will be one of those persons who resells stolen goods. I know two good ones. If your things have passed through their hands, perhaps they'll help me out. But one can be sure of nothing. We shall have to negotiate."

"Negotiate? If it is a matter of spending some money, so be it, I can surely pay for the favour. But, for heaven's sake, I cannot be seen in the company of persons of ill repute. There are cardinals here, I have connections with. . ."

"As you wish," Sfasciamonti cut him short politely but firmly. "I can deal with that. You, my boy, could accompany me. Those who steal do not willingly hang onto their loot, it burns their hands. Anything valuable disappears like lightning. We shall have to move fast."

"When, then?"

"Now."

It was thus that I began to become acquainted with Sfasciamonti's truly singular double, nay triple, nature. The imprecations which he was wont to utter, invoking arms and all manner of warlike devices, made him seem like some common braggart, swaggering and blustering, as his very name suggested. Yet, when he spoke of *cerretani*, his bravado vanished, turning into febrile apprehension, and that great mountain of a man would cower at the first old gaffer passing him by, as had happened when we stopped at the Piazza Fiammetta. Lastly, when confronted, not with the indefinite menace of the *cerretani*, but with a hard and fast case of crime, he proved to be an excellent sergeant: laconic, consistent and phlegmatic. This he had shown in the investigation of the assault on Haver; and likewise his comportment on the scene of the theft of Atto's papers had been both balanced and attentive. He had abstained from asking particulars of the stolen document and above all he had agreed with Atto about an utterly incredible circumstance: that there was no connection between the death of Haver and the theft in Atto's apartment. It was clear that this could not be the case, yet the catchpoll (whom the responsibility vested in him by Cardinal Spada had transformed almost into a private gendarme) had let it be understood that he was not interested in how matters stood but in how he could turn them to the advantage of the person hiring him.

For the time being, it was impossible to tell which of the three natures (blustering, fearful or penetrating) best corresponded to Sfasciamonti's true character. I imagined, however, that sooner or later time would tell.

For the time being, he was offering Atto his discretion and his assistance; and, what was more, during the hours of night. Atto knew that all that, like the silence which he had bought from me, had its price.

❧

So Sfasciamonti and I set out with all due speed, almost without taking our leave of Atto and his secretary. I would not be able to keep my appointment with Cloridia; I therefore asked Buvat to warn her of this. I prayed silently that she would not be too worried and unwillingly postponed the time when I would learn from her the news gathered from her women.

We left the villa stealthily under the starry mantle of night which, given the late hour and the gloom weighing down on my soul after so many grim events (killings, thefts), seemed no longer protecting but a menace hanging over our helpless heads.

The catchpoll had arranged for one of his grooms to saddle us two horses, and he helped me to mount the smaller of the two. (I have never been a great equestrian.) We straightaway took the road for the city centre. Thus I followed him towards an unknown destination; the speed of Sfasciamonti's mount, weighed down by its corpulent rider, was in truth little greater than my own.

We descended the slope towards the San Pancrazio Gate, leaving to our left the grandiose panorama over the Holy City. Thanks to the dim light of the moon, we could just descry the silhouettes of rooftops, campaniles and cupolas, and, by the faint glimmer from windows, eaves and penthouses, the space where darkness had engulfed a certain basilica or the abyss into which a palace had vanished. It was a sort of capricious game of hide-and-seek played between my sight and the vision which memory retained of that great view by day.

We veered left, towards the Piazza delle Fornaci, then, leaving the Settignano Gate to our right, we moved directly to the Sisto Bridge. Here, the view, hitherto obstructed by the walls of houses and rented apartment buildings, opened up again onto the bed of the Tiber, showing its tarnished course near the riverbanks, while the middle depths remained inky and abundant in piscatorial booty.

At last, we slowed down. After passing Piazza Trinità dei Pellegrini, we found ourselves within a stone's throw of the Piazza San Carlo quarter. Darkness and silence reigned, broken only by sparks from the horseshoes on the flagstones and the echo of pounding hooves. Only from the occasional window did the indistinct glimmer of candles penetrate the motionless air, lighting perhaps a young mother's last labour of the day (mending, nursing, consoling. . .)

Behind one such window, modestly set into the wall at street level, was our objective.

"Here we are," said Sfasciamonti, dismounting and pointing to a door. "But, please remember, you've never been here. Our man is incognito. No one knows that he sleeps in this house. Even the parish priest, when he does his Easter rounds, feigns ignorance. He accepts a gift of a couple of scudi, in exchange for which the parish records remain clean."

"Whom are we going to visit?" I asked, letting myself fall to the ground from my nag.

"Well, visit isn't the right word. Visits are announced and awaited. This, however, is a surprise, by all the mortars in Asia! Heh," he guffawed.

He stood before the door, pushing his thumbs under his belt and sticking his belly out strangely, breathing out rhythmically as though he were preparing to break the door down with his guts. He knocked. A few instants passed. Then we heard a bolt being shot. The hinges moved.

"Who is it?" asked a voice heavy with suspicion, of which I could not have said whether it was a man's or a woman's.

"Open up, this is Sfasciamonti."

Instead of one of the tender mothers about whom I had been fantasising only moments before, there appeared before us a hunchbacked and ill-formed old woman who, as the catchpoll was later to explain to me, was landlady to our man. The woman did not even attempt to protest at the late hour; she seemed to be acquainted with my companion and knew that it was useless to talk back. She began to complain weakly only when she saw us mounting the stairs to the next floor.

"But he is sleeping. . ."

"Exactly," replied Sfasciamonti, grabbing the candle from her hand to light our way and thus leaving the poor woman in the dark.

After climbing two flights of stairs, we found ourselves on a landing which gave in turn onto a closed door. The candle, which the catchpoll had handed to me, cast a sinister light on our faces from underneath.

We knocked. No answer.

"He's not sleeping. Otherwise he'd have replied. He always keeps one eye open," murmured my companion. "This is Sfasciamonti, open up!"

We waited a few moments. A key turned in the lock. The door opened up a mere crack.

"What is it?"

The catchpoll was right. The occupant of the room stood fully dressed with his nose protruding from the crack in the door. Faint candlelight glimmered from within. Weak though the light was, I could distinguish the man's features at once: an enormous rat's nose, long and swollen, with a pair of little black eyes surmounted by long, thick crow-black eyebrows; below these, an ugly, drooling and contorted mouth clumsily framing an undisciplined row of yellowing rabbit-like teeth.

"Let us in, Maltese."

The little man who answered to that curious name (which in truth derived from the fact that he came from the island of Malta) sat down on a chair, without inviting us to take a seat, which we nevertheless did, for want of better, on his bed. He lit a third candle, the light from which gave the place a less cavernous appearance. I took a quick look around. The chamber was in reality a disorderly hovel, the furniture consisting of the bed on which we were sitting, our host's chair, a little table, a chest, a few old wooden cases and a heap of old papers half abandoned in a corner.

The Maltese seemed very nervous. He stayed seated, hunched up, his eyes avoiding contact, playing with a button of his shirt, plainly scared by the visit and anxious that we should be off as soon as possible. From the conversation, I understood that the two had shared a long acquaintance, in which they had always played the same parts: the man with the big stick and the man on the wrong end of the stick.

"We are assisting a person of note, a French abbot. They have taken some things of his to which he is very attached. He is a guest at the Villa Spada. Do you know anything?"

"Villa Spada at Porta San Pancrazio, of course. The Spadas' place."

"Stop pretending you're a fool. I asked you if you know anything about the theft."

The Maltese took one glance at me, then another, questioning one at my companion.

"He's a friend, Sfasciamonti reassured him. Behave as though he were not here."

The Maltese fell silent. Then he shook his head.

"I know nothing."

"They've robbed him of an object he absolutely wants to have back: a spyglass."

"I know nothing and I've seen no one. Today I've been here all the time."

"The injured party, the French abbot, is prepared to pay to recover what belongs to him. As I said, it matters greatly to him."

"I am sorry, if I knew something, I'd tell you. I really have heard nothing."

We were disappointed, but we did not insist. From our man's timorous, rat-like frown, there did seem to emanate something like sincerity. We rose.

"Then it will be better to go and ask Monsignor Pallavicini," added Sfasciamonti carelessly. "I shall request an audience with him. Moreover, he has just dined at the Villa Spada."

The name of the Governor of Rome had the desired effect. We were about to leave when the Maltese's question stopped us on the threshold.

"Sfasciamonti, what is a spyglass?"

As our host did not know what a telescope was, we had to explain to him that it was a tubular optical apparatus, equipped with lenses,

with which one could see distant objects close, and so on. Sfasciamonti's description was pretty crude and even somewhat uncertain,
and I had to help him with it. In the end, the Maltese had given his
reply: there was someone who might know something.

"'Tis someone who buys only strange objects that are difficult to
resell: antiquities, various instruments. And he seems to have a great
passion for relics. Now, with the Jubilee, he has become very rich:
I've heard tell that he has done excellent business. He has cronies
who trade on his behalf, but no one ever sees him. I don't know why,
perhaps he does not live in town. I have never had dealings with him.
They call him the German."

The grimace which Sfasciamonti could not suppress betrayed his
disquiet.

"I know that a short while ago he bought something similar to the
spyglass which you are looking for," continued the Maltese, "a device
with lenses that can move, for seeing things bigger – or smaller – I
know not which."

Sfasciamonti assented: we were on the right track.

"I don't even recall who told me," concluded the other, "but I
think I know who bought it for him. They call him Chiavarino."

"I know him," said Sfasciamonti.

Five minutes later, we were in the street, setting out in search
of the mysterious personages named by the receiver. Sfasciamonti
murmured curses against his informer.

"'I know nothing, I know nothing.' That's that, nothing! When
he heard the Governor's name, he got cold feet and asked what a
spyglass was."

"But did he really not know?"

"People like the Maltese are scum. They buy the loot from others' thefts for a couple of lire and pass them on to others. They don't
know how to do anything else. They're animals; their only merit
lies in shouldering the risk of being the first to buy after the crime.
That's why they often pass for the authors of the theft, which they
are not. Those who buy from him, however, are better acquainted
with the value of goods. The Chiavarino's in another class, he's very
well known in the criminal fraternity. He's a murderer and thief many
times over."

I had been struck by the catchpoll's expression the moment he
heard the name of the Chiavarino's principal.

"And the German? Have you ever heard of him?"

"Of course, they've been talking of him for ages," replied Sfascia-monti. "Now, with the Jubilee. . ."

"And what do they say?"

"They don't even know whether he exists. They say he's in cahoots with the *cerretani*. Others say that the German's an invention of us catchpolls and that when we can't manage to find who's guilty of the theft of some valuables or the defrauding of some pilgrims, we blame it on him."

"And is that true?"

"Come, come!" he snapped, taking offence, "I believe that the German exists, just as I believe that the *cerretani* exist. Only, no one's really interested in finding him."

"And why is that?"

"Perhaps he has done some favour to someone important. That's how Rome works. It must not be too clean, or too dirty. The ser-geants and the Governor must be able to boast of keeping the town clean, otherwise what are they there for? But we also need the dirt to be there, fine dirt and plenty of it. Otherwise what are we there for?" quoth he, guffawing. "And then, have you seen how the Maltese gets away with it? If something's stolen off someone influential, he's there to give us a hand. In exchange, the Governor leaves him in peace, even though he knows perfectly well where he lives and could have him arrested at any time."

To the considerations already expressed concerning Sfasciamonti, another was to be added. He did not mince his words (and I was to have other demonstrations of that) when describing the misconduct and unsavoury doings of his colleagues and even the Governor. Some might have taken him for a bad defender of public order, incapable of fidelity and attachment to the secular institutions of Holy Mother Church. I, for my part, did not see it that way. If he was capable of seeing evil wherever it was, and admitting as much, even to myself, that was a sign that his character tended naturally to plain speak-ing and simplicity. The roughness of soul necessary for the operation which we were conducting was, moreover, not lacking. He had in-deed revealed to me from the outset that he wanted in the end to undertake investigations on the *cerretani*, but the Governor and his fellow-sergeants would not let him. That he should be in some way in cahoots with proven criminals like the Maltese, or perhaps the

Chiavarino, whom we were going to meet, well, I considered that to be a necessary part of his work. The main thing was that he should, at the bottom of his heart, be honest. I was to discover only far later that such thinking was not far removed from the truth, yet at the same time utterly mistaken.

As we were walking, I noticed that Sfasciamonti, who had just gone so boldly into the receiver's den, had begun to look around and behind himself with a certain frequency. We reached Piazza Montanara, then turned right into an alleyway.

"'Tis here."

It was a little two-storey house whose occupants seemed to be sunk in nocturnal repose. We stopped at the front door and then followed the instructions of the Maltese: we knocked three times loudly, three times gently and then again, loudly.

It seemed almost as though no one had come to the door, when behind it we heard a muffled voice.

"Yes?"

"We're looking for Chiavarino."

They made us wait outside, without telling us whether the person we sought would be coming or not, and not even whether our request would be honoured.

"Who's looking for him at this time of night?" we heard at last from another voice.

"Friends."

"Speak, then."

Our man must have been there behind the door, but did not seem to want to open up.

"This evening at the Villa Spada on the Janiculum, a spyglass was stolen. The owner is someone dear to us, and he's willing to pay well to have it back."

"What is a spyglass?"

We repeated in a few words the explanation given to the Maltese: the lenses that make you see little or enlarged, the metal device, and so on and so forth. This was followed by a few moments' silence.

"How much is the owner willing to pay?" asked the voice.

"Whatever's necessary."

"I shall have to ask a friend. Come back tomorrow after Vespers."

"Very well," replied the catchpoll, after a moment's hesitation, "we shall return tomorrow."

We moved off a few yards, whereupon Sfasciamonti pointed to the first side-road and there we stood guard keeping a close watch on the Chiavarino's house.

"He is not willing to conclude the deal. He told me to return tomorrow. Does he take me for a fool? By then the stolen goods will be a thousand miles from here."

"Are we waiting for him to come out?" I asked with no little trepidation, thinking of the homicides which Chiavarino had to his name.

"Exactly. Let us see where he goes. He'll suspect that the goods are too hot to handle and that he'd be wise to be rid of them as soon as possible. If I were him, I'd not move from my house. But, like the Maltese, he's a fugitive, and he'll be pretty nervous."

The prognosis proved correct. Within ten minutes, a hesitant figure peeped out from the Chiavarino's doorway, looked all around and ventured into the street. The moonlight was really too weak to be able to tell with any certainty, but he did seem to have something, a sort of package, under his arm.

We followed him from a fairly prudent distance, religiously attentive to making not the least noise. We both knew that our quarry must be carrying a knife. Better to lose him than our lives, I thought.

First, he took the road to Campo di Fiore, so that we thought he was going to the Maltese, whose secret dwelling lay more or less in that direction. Then, however, he continued through the Piazza de' Pollaioli and, after that, Piazza Pasquino.

Chiavarino, who was fortunate enough not to encounter any rounds of the watch, at length entered the Piazza Navona. Just at that instant, what remained of the moon was covered by an untimely cloud. Although the light was almost non-existent, we took the precaution of stopping behind the corner of Palazzo Pamphili, at the entrance to the piazza. Thence, we scanned the great esplanade divided into three by the great central fountain of the Cavalier Bernini and two other fountains at the opposite ends. The piazza seemed empty. We looked more carefully, but in vain. We had lost him.

"A curse on all lazy sentries," grunted Sfasciamonti.

Just then, we heard a rapid pattering of footsteps in front of us. Someone was running to our right at great speed. Chiavarino must have become aware of our presence and was in full flight.

"The fountain, he was behind the fountain!" exclaimed Sfascia-monti, alluding to the nearer of the two great complexes of aquatic statues which stand at either end of Piazza Navona.

Even now, I could not say what hidden virtue of the soul (or rather, what weakness and false audacity) caused me to emulate Sfascia-monti, who was already following the fugitive to the right.

For quite a while, I managed to keep up with the perspiring mass of the catchpoll who, despite the fact that he was giving his all, was losing ground.

"To the left, he's gone to the left!" yelled Sfasciamonti, his voice broken by his efforts.

Hardly had I turned to the left than, to my great surprise, I saw that the pursuit was about to come to an end. The fugitive, who had hitherto kept up and even increased his lead, had fallen.

Sfasciamonti was almost on top of his prey when the man re-covered his senses: skilfully dodging, he rolled to one side so that Sfasciamonti went flying into the void and fell in his turn. Although exhausted, the fugitive ran once more in the direction of the Thea-tre of Pompey; at that moment, I too had almost reached him. I was, however, distracted by an unexpected event: our man had left a par-cel on the ground, so that when I arrived, I found myself at an equal distance between the object and the man who had got rid of it. Out of the corner of my eye, I saw that only then was Sfasciamonti rising to his feet with something of a limp.

"You, go ahead!" he exhorted me, breaking once more into a run.

It was pure folly on my part unhesitatingly to follow that order in circumstances in which, given the extreme excitement that reigned, no one could possibly discern the consequences of his acts. So I did not leave off from running even when I saw the individual hesitate between right and left, then, quite unexpectedly, rush into a doorway which he perhaps already knew to be open. I crossed myself mentally and, hastening through the door in my turn, heard his footsteps on the stairs and rushed headlong after him.

The mad upward pursuit, amongst the inky shadows of the stairway, as I tripped clumsily on the steps in an effort to keep my balance, running with hands outstretched before me into clammy landing walls, all seems to me today the height of idiocy which could have resulted in something far worse than what in fact happened. It was scant consolation to hear Sfasciamonti's approaching footsteps, still far below.

I do not know, and perhaps I never shall, whether the man we were following already knew where the steps of that building led. Nevertheless, it came as no small surprise to me to see, in the last stretch of the staircase, the steps becoming, first bluish, then grey, and in the end whitish. Thus it was that, suddenly, almost forgetting what I was doing there and what awaited me, Dawn's rosy fingers gently parted my eyes and showed me, free at last of dependence on candles and torches, the precious spectacle of a new day being born.

I had opened a door at the top of the stairs. At first, it was only half open, then I was on a terrace. Above and all around I was engulfed by the harsh clarity of morn: first light had already appeared when I caught up with Sfasciamonti at Campo de Fiore but, so immersed was I in action that I was almost unaware of it.

What happened next took place in a flash. I was completely out of breath. Rather than fall to the ground, I bent over, with my hands on my knees. Then I heard Sfasciamonti's voice, which seemed to come from the floor below.

"Forget it boy, 'tis no spyglass. . ."

I turned around and saw him. He had hidden behind me; now he faced me. He collared me and thrust me against the penthouse wall, gripping me tightly. His knife was pointed at my belly. It was pointless to move; if I struggled he would stab me.

He was ill-dressed and he stank. He had pitch black eyes and a pockmarked skin. He might have been thirty years old – thirty badly lived years; thirty years of prison, hunger and nights spent sleeping in the open. He looked at me through one eye only. The other squinted like that of a stray cat.

Thanks, perhaps, to faculties unnaturally intensified by closeness to death, I read in his expression. . . indecision: should he kill at once and face the other, or run yet again? But if so, where? The terrace was in fact a mere corridor running around the penthouse at the top of the staircase. In a lightning flash of intuition, I understood how stupid I had been: I had followed him until he felt forced to kill me.

"'Tis an accursed, what do you call the things?. . ." Sfasciamonti's voice thundered, still coming from the stairs, but now very near us.

The corner of the eye that stared at me had sought an escape route. I could see that it had found none.

Two, perhaps three seconds, and I would know the feeling of a cold blade in my liver. I had an idea.

"The German will kill you," I managed to say, despite having my neck half crushed in his grip.

He hesitated. I felt his hand tremble.

Then it happened. Under Sfasciamonti's elephantine weight the door swung open with unbelievable violence, like armour-plated lighthouse doors smashed by the force of the raging sea. It struck my assailant's shoulder, and he tottered from the blow. Turning over and over in the air, the knife shot up between our two faces and fell to the ground with a clatter.

"A mackeroscopp!" exclaimed Sfasciamonti triumphantly, bursting onto the terrace and shaking at arm's length a half-broken metal device, while my adversary, shocked by the blow he'd received, prepared to make a break towards the left.

Sfasciamonti saw his face and yelled, with an undertone of indignation: "But you're not Chiavarino!"

We threw ourselves onto the stranger, but it was precisely in so doing that I tripped over a large brick. I rolled over on the ground and all my strength was not enough to stop my body's slide to the edge of the terrace. I fell into the abyss of the courtyard, thus suffering just punishment for all that night's demented conduct.

I fell backwards. Before being hurled to my death thirty or forty feet below, I had time to behold the dumb stupor stamped on Sfasciamonti's face: in a timeless moment, I thought absurdly that such was perhaps the sentiment (and not pain or desperation) that seizes us at the instant when we witness the imminent death of another man. Poor Sfasciamonti, I thought, just after saving me from being stabbed he again lost me.

Despite the singularity of that instant, my memory retained a detail which the catchpoll failed to notice. While I was falling to my death, just before disappearing into the abyss, the fugitive replied to the threat I had uttered moments before.

"Teeyooteelie."

Then with the sky, framed by the four walls of the courtyard, swallowing me up ever faster, faster, I offered a heartfelt prayer to the Almighty for the forgiveness of my sins, and, with heart and spirit turning to my Cloridia, I awaited the end.

Day the Third
9ᵀᴴ JULY, 1700

✠

It was the purest and lightest of chants, nor could I have said whence it came; it was, if anything, nowhere and yet all around me.

It had an air of innocence about it, of timid red-cheeked novices, of remote and solitary hermits. It was a tender psalmody and it delighted my ears as I became aware of my new condition.

At last, I realised: it was the chant of a confraternity of pilgrims in Rome for the Jubilee. It was men and women who made up the sublime blend of voices, sweet and robust, silvery and stentorian, manly and womanly; they had risen with the sun, and now they raised a song of thanksgiving to the Lord as they set out on the visit to the four basilicas to seek the remission of their sins.

The rectangle of now azure sky from which I had fallen was still there above, crystalline and immobile.

I was dead and, at the same time, alive. My eyes were full of that rectangle's blue, but I could no longer see. The sky flowed from my eyes like angels' tears. Only the music, only that pilgrims' choir drew me to itself, almost as though it alone could keep me alive.

The last sensory impressions (the precipitous fall, the walls of the courtyard swallowing me up, the air pressing against my back) had been swept away by that holy melody.

Other indistinct voices wove into each other and unwove in occult counterpoint.

It was only then, after becoming aware of the existence of other beings around me, that I broke the frail shell of my torpor.

Like a new Lucifer cast down from paradise, I felt a sinister, warm smoke envelop my limbs and engulf me ever more in the viscous belly of the Inferno.

"Let's get him out of there," said one of the voices.

I tried to move an arm or a leg, if I still had any. It worked; I raised

186

a foot. This new and promising development, came, however, mixed with an unexpected sensation.

"What a stink!" said a voice.

"Let's both work together."

"He owes his life to the shit, ha ha!"

I was not dead, nor had I smashed into the hard paving stones of the courtyard, even less been engulfed in hell: I was being lifted out of a cartful of warm, smoking manure.

As Sfasciamonti was to explain to me afterwards, while freeing my back of a few lumps of manure, I had ended my fall in a colossal mountain of fresh dung parked there during the night by a yokel who intended to sell it in the morning, for use as compost, to the superintendent of Villa Perretti.

Thus, by a pure miracle, I had not broken my neck. But when I had fallen onto the horrid heap of excrement, I had remained in a swoon, showing no signs of life. The onlookers who had meanwhile gathered were worried; someone made the sign of the cross. Suddenly, however, when the pilgrim confraternity passed by, I had moved my head and blinked. "'Tis the Lord's doing," exclaimed a little old man. "The confraternity's prayers have resuscitated him."

Up above, Sfasciamonti, distracted by my fall and anxious about my fate, had allowed our man to get away when, rather than face the catchpoll's wrath, he had let himself drop to a lower rooftop, continuing his flight on the surrounding terraces. My ally who, with his weight, would have run the risk of falling through some skylight, was compelled to abandon the chase. Once down the stairs, he had dragged me out from the manure cart with the help of a market gardener, there to sell his produce on the nearby market of Campo de Fiore, which was just about to open.

"'Tis an accursed mess," said Sfasciamonti, as he led me to a nearby vendor of old clothes to fit me out with clean apparel. "The Chiavarino had this in his hands – anything but a spyglass."

From a dirty grey cloth he pulled out the device which I had seen him brandishing victoriously when he burst out from the stairs onto the terrace, at the unforgettable moment when I had a knife pressing against my guts.

The apparatus, which had emerged badly from the night's adventures, was reduced to a mass of twisted metal, in which one could with some difficulty discern what had once been a microscope. The only parts remaining in one piece were the base, a vertical cylinder and a pivot joining this with the rest (now lost) of the optical instrument. The cloth contained a collection of glass fragments (presumably, what remained of the lenses), three or four screws, a cog wheel and a half-crushed metal plaque.

"It must have gone like this," said Sfasciamonti reconstructing the events of the night, as we entered the old clothes shop. "This was stolen not long ago. I shall check today on whether any other sergeant knows anything of this. Chiavarino must have done the job himself, or perhaps he bought it off someone else. When he heard us at the door, he misunderstood our explanation, confusing the spyglass with this mackeroscopp."

"Microscope," I corrected him.

"Well, anyway, whatever it is. Then he left the house and went to the Piazza Navona. He must have been looking for some *cerretano*," said he while, nodding to the old clothes merchant, he led me to the inner courtyard where there was a little fountain, so that I could clean myself up.

"But why?"

"Did you not hear what the Maltese said? Chiavarino works for the German. And the German, as I told you, works with the *cerretani*," said he gesturing with his head in the direction of the terrace on Campo de Fiore. "The mackeroscopp was supposed to go to the German. Many real beggars spend the night at the Piazza Navona, but there are plenty of *cerretani* there too. Chiavarino went to one of these."

"You mean the one who was on the point of killing me!" I exclaimed, remembering Sfasciamonti's scream when he saw that it was not Chiavarino.

"Of course. They met behind the fountain. Then the *cerretano* heard us and fled. We ran after him thinking it was Chiavarino, whom I know perfectly well and who looks quite different: tall and fair with a broken nose. And he's not cross-eyed, as the little monster whom we followed seemed to be."

So I had risked my life for nothing, I thought, while I took off my filthy clothes and washed quickly, for who could say where Atto's telescope might be, let alone his papers? My bones were all still aching from the fall into the manure, although it had been fresh and soft because of a generous admixture of straw.

Then there was a suspicion which gnawed at me. The Maltese did not know what a spyglass was, and probably did not know what a microscope, a far more unusual object, might be. Nor did Chiavarino know what the two devices were or what they were called, so much so that he confused the one with the other.

"How did you know that this was a microscope?" I asked the catchpoll, pointing to the little packet in which he had placed the fragments of the machine.

"What a question: 'tis written on it."

He opened the little bundle and showed me the wooden base of the apparatus, on which there was a gracefully framed little metal plaque.

MACROSCOPIUM HOC
JOHANNES VANDEHARIUS
FECIT
AMSTELODAMI MDCLXXXIII

"Microscope made in Amsterdam in 1683 by Jan Vandehaar," I translated.

He was right, it was written there. And those few simple Latin words even Sfasciamonti had been able to understand, however approximately.

"Someone will have to explain to me how you shoot with a thing like this mackeroscopp with its barrel full of glass," he muttered to himself, incapable of resigning himself to the fact that the device was not an arm.

Still confused by the breakneck piling up of events, not to mention the physical trials I had had to undergo, only then, while I was drying myself with a piece of cloth and dressing, did I remember to tell my companion of the provocation with which I had tried to confuse the *cerretano*, warning him that he would die at the hands of the German, and of the man's strange reply which I had by some miracle heard when I was falling from the terrace.

"'The German will kill you. . .' But you are insane!"

"Why? I was only trying to save my life."

"That's true, damn it, but you went and told an accomplice of the German that his principal would have him killed. . . The German's dangerous. 'Tis as well that it was, as you said, to save your life."

"Well, that's precisely why I'd like to know what the *cerretano* said. Perhaps he threatened that they'd come after me."

"What exactly did he say to you?"

"I couldn't understand, 'twas a phrase that made no sense."

"You see, it really was a *cerretano*. He spoke to you in cant."

"In what?"

"Cant. Gibberish."

"What's that, their jargon?"

"Oh, far more than that. 'Tis a real language. Only the *cerretani* know it, 'tis their own invention. They use it to talk in front of strangers without being understood. But thieves and vagrants of all kinds use it too."

"Then I understand what you're talking about. I know that criminals, when a sergeant is coming, say 'Madam's coming' or ''Tis raining'."

"Yes, but those are things that everyone knows, like that *martino* means a knife, or a *piotta* is a hundred Giulio coin. Even many of the words of the Jews are well known; if I tell you that two people are *agazim*, you'll understand perfectly that I am talking of a couple of friends. But then there's a more difficult level. For instance, what does it mean if I say to you: 'The hunchback isn't corn of the first of May?'"

"Not a thing."

"Well, that's because you don't know cant, or slang. 'The hunchback' means 'I', 'corn' means 'afraid' and 'the first of May' is God."

"So 'I'm not afraid of God'," said I, astonished by the obscurity of that short sentence which seemed so well suited to a *cerretano*.

"And that's only an example. I know it only because we sergeants do manage to pick up something. But never enough. The *cerretano* said something to you which you couldn't understand, is that not so?

"If I remember, it was something like. . . teevooteedie, teeyootiffie, no, teeyooteelie or something like that."

"That must be another kind of cant. I really don't know how it works, I've never even heard it spoken. I only know that sometimes the vagabonds use normal words but mix them all up, twist them about and complicate them using a secret method which few people know," said he, twisting, untwisting, tapping and squeezing his fingers one against the other, the better to illustrate the concept, "and you can't understand a word of it."

"So how the deuce are we to know what the *cerretano* said? We do not even have any way of continuing our investigations and finding Abbot Melani's papers," said I with ill-concealed disappointment.

"We must be patient, and besides, matters are not exactly as you say. We do at least know now that someone is collecting these strange instruments with which one can see large or small, mackeroscopps, spyglasses *et cetera*, and that he has a passion for relics. We can look for Chiavarino, but he'll already have moved to another house. He's a dangerous fellow, 'tis best to keep well away from him. The track to follow is that of the *cerretani*."

"It seems no less dangerous."

"That's true. But it does lead directly to the German."

"Do you think it was he who stole Abbot Melani's papers?"

"I believe in facts. And this is the only trail we have to follow."

"Do you have any idea of how we proceed from here?"

"Of course. But we shall have to wait until tomorrow night. Some things cannot be done by day."

కింగ

Meanwhile, we had returned to our horses. We separated: this time too Sfasciamonti had some chores to do on behalf of his mother. Since I was still in shock following my dreadful adventure, the catchpoll thought it would be better if I returned to Villa Spada on foot; he would see to the return of both our mounts.

So it was that, still stinking and rotten but at least not shameful to behold, I made my way towards the San Pancrazio Gate. At that early hour, the city was overflowing with pilgrims, pedlars, prentices, maidservants, swindlers, strollers and tradesmen. Every little alleyway was animated by washerwomen's songs, children's cries, the barking of stray dogs, street vendors' calls, as well as the curses of coachmen whenever some wobbling cart delivering dairy products cut across the path of their carriage. In the markets of each quarter, those great theatres in which the city of St Peter renews its rites each day, the festive chaos of the morning was turning into a spectacle: the fluttering black of an apostolic pronotary's gown set off the green of lettuces, a cleric's dark cloak strove to upstage the orange of fresh carrots, the perplexed eyes of dead fish scrutinised the eternal human comedy from fishmongers' counters.

I was near Via Giulia, immersed in this disorderly stream of humanity, goods and vehicles, when I came upon an even denser assembly.

I made my way as well as I could, more concerned to get through than to look at what was going on. In the end, however, I found my progress blocked and tiptoed to see what this was all about. At the centre of the crowd stood a sinister figure, his long hair gathered into a ponytail, and, on his bare breast, a large bluish sign in the form of a viper. But it was around his neck that there squirmed, slimy and treacherous, a real serpent. The public observed its contortions, at once fascinated and frightened. The young man began to whine a sort of dirge; the coluber twisted rhythmically, following the intonation and rhythm of the chant and arousing the audience's amazement. Now and again, the mummer would stop and in a low voice utter some arcane formula which had the power to halt the reptile's contortions; the animal would freeze suddenly, tense and rigid, and would come back to life only when the chant began again. Suddenly, the young man seized the creature's head and thrust a finger into its jaws, which closed on it at once. He withstood the pain a few moments then withdrew his finger. He then began to distribute a few little jars filled with a reddish ointment, explaining that this was serpent's earth, the most perfect of antidotes which, if one is bitten by a snake, counteracts the venom so that one suffers no pain whatever. The nearby onlookers threw small coins in large quantities into the straw hat at the fellow's feet.

I looked questioningly at my neighbour, a lad who was grasping a large bread-making mould.

"He's a *sanpaolaro*," said he.

"And what does that mean?"

"Saint Paul one day bestowed grace on a certain family, promising them that none of their members and descendants would ever need fear a serpent's venom. In order to be distinguished from others, the descendants of that family are all born with the sign of a serpent on their body and are known as *sanpaolari*."

Behind our backs, an old man interrupted.

"All balderdash! They catch the snakes in winter when they've little strength and almost no venom. Then they purge them and keep them on a starvation diet, so that they become soft and obedient."

In the group pressing around the *sanpaolaro* the old man's words had been clearly overheard; some heads turned.

"I know all these tricks," the old man continued. "The sign of the serpent is made by pricking oneself in several places with a very fine needle, then rubbing on one's skin a paste made of soot and the juice of herbs."

Other heads, distracted from the spectacle, turned towards the old man. But just at that moment, a cry went up.

"My purse! I have it no more! They've cut it!"

A little woman who until that moment had been staring at the spectacle of the *sanpaolaro* almost as though she had been hypnotised, was expostulating desperately. Someone had cut the string which she wore around her neck and had made off with her purse and all her money for the day. The group of spectators turned into an uncontrollable magma, in which everyone twisted around to make sure that nothing was missing (purses, necklaces, brooches).

"There, I knew it," said the old man, guffawing, "the *sanpaolaro's* friend found what he wanted."

I turned towards the man who until that moment had been drawing all our attention. Taking advantage of the general confusion, the *sanpaolaro* (if he merited the name) had vanished.

"With his accomplice, of course," added the old man.

Resuming my walk, my humour had darkened. I too had not realised that the serpent was only a means of attracting a few unsuspecting victims while an accomplice of the *sanpaolaro* looked after the business of relieving them of their money. Two real virtuosi of the art of theft, thought I: as soon as things became uncomfortable, they had vanished like snow in the sunshine. And what if they too were *cerretani*? Sfasciamonti had said that every *cerretano* was a beggar and that begging was the most profitable trade in the world. Did he perhaps also mean that every beggar, rogue or vagrant was also a *cerretano*? If that were the case, the prospect would be terrifying: without realising it I had been offering alms to an army of criminals who held the city under their control.

I abandoned these notions, which seemed too fanciful, and my thoughts returned to my fall and the horrible death which I had just faced. What had saved my life? The prayer of the pilgrims in procession or the cart full of manure? The dung had undoubtedly been the immediate cause of my salvation. Was I then indebted to good fortune? And yet, I had opened my eyes to the passing of the pious procession of pilgrims, to whose chants I had miraculously reawakened. Had I thus been touched by grace through the merit of the innocent vows of love and charity of that cortège of the faithful come from afar?

But how effective were those vows? In the pilgrims' intentions these were certainly innocent and full of ardour, I thought. But, I murmured to myself as I passed a squalid and most costly lodging house for pilgrims which I knew to be the property of a cardinal – there was also something else beyond those prayers that was perhaps less innocent and pure: the very organisation of the Jubilee.

Of course, I well knew (and it was universally known) that Pope Boniface VIII had, in the year 1300, inaugurated the solemn recurrence of the Holy Year with the best of intentions. Drawing inspiration from the noble custom of the pontiffs of ancient times, who every hundred years granted the faithful full and complete remission of their sins, provided that they visited the Basilica of St Peter in the Vatican, Pope Boniface VIII had officially instituted the Jubilee Year in the full and proper sense, adding to past practice only the obligation to visit the Basilica of St Paul, and setting aside certain days for the visits of the faithful.

The news had spread like lightning throughout Christendom and had touched the hearts of the faithful everywhere, as though the very trumpeting angels of paradise had been at work. Its success had been immense. Swarms of Romei, or pilgrims, had in that year 1300 come to the Holy City from all the world over, descending from the valleys of the Apennines, crossing valleys and ravines, crags and gullies, peaks and high plateaux, towns and villages, rivers, seas and far-away coasts, bringing with them, both for the purposes of the journey and those of the sojourn in Rome, purses well filled with money: and this the popes, and with them all the Romans, found most welcome.

To make the great journey, the Romei had often sacrificed their most precious goods: peasants had abandoned their fields, merchants had neglected their business, shepherds had sold their flocks, and fishermen, their boats. This was not, however, to pay for the journey (which was made entirely on foot, like every good pilgrimage springing from a lively and uncontaminated faith) but rather to be able to procure for oneself a place to lay one's head in Rome, where such things cost a veritable fortune. There was no thought of sleeping in the open: if one did not fall a prey to cutpurses and cutthroats, the Pontifical Guards did what they could to dissuade the less fortunate pilgrims. Indeed, why sleep in the streets when the popes themselves had organised an immense number of lodgings for the pilgrims? Confraternities and pious hospices did their very best; but beds were always scarce. At the Jubilee of 1650, it was said that even the Pope's sister-in-law, the powerful and notorious Donna Olimpia, had purchased lodgings and inns to take advantage of the arrival of the pilgrims. But in truth all the Romans enjoyed the benefits of the holy event. Aware of their responsibilities as hosts, they had turned innkeeper overnight, knowing full well that the regular inns and the religious hostels would never suffice to accommodate the influx of pilgrims. When the poor travellers, exhausted by the fatigues of the journey, came to the door of the inhabitants of the Holy City (as Buccio di Ranallo tells it so well) they were then greeted with angelic smiles, kindness and mercy without end. Once, however, they had entered their chambers, the music changed and those angels turned into ravening dogs: the guests were piled up ten to a room (which sufficed for three or four at most), the sheets were filthy, the pillows stank, manners were rough and the food, although most costly, was rubbish. One could never be rid of the suspicion that the sudden rise in the prices of foodstuffs had been caused by clever frauds, keeping supplies of commodities far from the city. The poor quality of the food was usually blamed on bad meat and cheeses which, some said (but this was never proven) were cleverly mixed with the fresh produce.

Some Romei, believing that to sleep on the hard ground was a badge of merit to be taken into account when the time came for the remission of sins, would humbly lay themselves down in the streets of Rome. In the middle of the night, they would be, however, rudely awoken by the sergeants, who first of all would give them all a sound hiding for having violated the city's decorum and the regulations for public order. Then they would say to them, "Are you pilgrims? But how did you think to sleep like vagabonds? There's a hostel for people like you just a stone's throw from here." And thus the unfortunates would be compelled to rent a room for an unbelievable price in one of the boarding houses owned by relatives of the pontiff or high prelates.

Then there were the most embarrassing episodes, such as those when pilgrims, arriving exhausted at the gates of Rome, were seized by bands of slave-traders who, after beating all the stuffing out of them, forced them to work in the fields and released them, humiliated and extenuated by hard labour, only after many months.

Yet the Faith, indifferent to such passing inconveniences, had for centuries continued to draw glorious hosts of believers to the Holy

City, and with them, huge sums of money: I knew that, among the most ancient examples, there had at the Jubilee of 1350 been one million two hundred thousand pilgrims during Lent and at Easter, and eight hundred thousand at Whitsuntide; in 1450, the Apostolic Chamber had taken one hundred thousand florins (and celebrated by converting no fewer than forty Jews and a rabbi). Finally, in 1650, only half a century before the Jubilee now being celebrated, there had been no fewer than seven hundred thousand pilgrims. Great feasting and booty was had by all: the cobblers who resoled the Romei's boots, the innkeepers who fed them, the water-sellers who sated their thirst; and by the traders who had something to offer them: rosaries, holy images, stools to sit on, medicinal herbs, wine, prayer books, bread, clothing, hats, the authentic relics of saints, pens and paper, gazettes, guides to Rome and whatever could be bought and sold.

According to the wish of Boniface VIII, one hundred years should pass between one Jubilee and the next. Such an interval of one century was a warning to all sinners that one could not and should not abuse the patience of the Most High. However, seeing the success of the initiative, and its not unwelcome economic effects, the solemn interval of one hundred years was at once reduced to a half-century by Pope Clement VI who in fact announced the next recurrence in 1350 (without himself celebrating it in person, since he was then in Avignon, which was at that time the seat of the papacy, while Rome was soiled with bloodshed in internecine warfare between noble families, exhausted by the plague and perturbed by the dark misdeeds of the lawless plebeian Cola di Rienzo).

Boniface IX later shortened the interval to forty years and proclaimed a new Jubilee in 1390, and then another barely ten years later in 1400. Martin V celebrated one in 1423, while Nicholas V even went so far as to proclaim two consecutive ones in 1450 and 1451.

The next popes were more orderly, increasing the interval between one Jubilee and the next to 25 years: Sixtus IV held one in 1475, Alexander VI in 1500 and Clement VII in 1525. There then followed yet another intense acceleration: both Paul III and Julius III celebrated three Jubilees in four years.

The pace grew more and more breathless: Pius IV celebrated no fewer than four Holy Years during his pontificate (including two in the same year) while Clement VIII proclaimed three. Paul V marked up six, at an inexorable rate: 1605, 1608, 1609, 1610, 1617 and 1619.

All of which was as nothing compared with the performance of Urban VIII who, in twenty years decreed no fewer than twelve of them.

Seeing their signal success, the popes who followed did not feel like changing course: Innocent X fitted five Jubilees into ten years, Alexander VII another five into nine years, while Clement IX even managed to compress four Holy Years into two years.

Coming to more recent popes, while it is true that Alexander VIII and Innocent XI proclaimed only two and one Holy Years respectively, Clement X had three, in quick succession (in 1670, 1672 and 1675) and even the present Holy Father, Innocent XII, could not restrain himself from celebrating four in eight years.

It is quite true that these extraordinary celebrations did not always draw great masses of pilgrims to Rome. It is also true, moreover, that the intervals, initially subject to the severe hundred-year cycle, had in the course of time become subject to steadily more and more contingent motivations, which often ran the risk of perplexing posterity, and sometimes even contemporaries.

Some extraordinary Jubilees came to be granted on a limited basis to certain nations or groups (Peru, Armenia, India, the Maronites of Lebanon, the Christians of the Aethiopic Empire) who, in the community of the faithful, especially the Italians and Europeans, did not perhaps always evoke sentiments of immediate, universal, overwhelming fraternity.

The Council of Trent, the struggle against heresy, the ransoming of prisoners in the hands of Mahometans, the peace between France and Spain, or else, fairly frequently, the enthronement of a new pope, provided other occasions (obviously called pretexts by the malign), which did not always have a character of absolute urgency and gravity.

It was striking that no fewer than nine times the proclamation of a Holy Year had been determined by the needs of the Church, or rather of its coffers, and for that very reason, Urban VIII (subsequently accused of gravely dissipating the money of the Apostolic Chamber) had proclaimed four Holy Years in 1628, 1629, 1631 and 1634.

And if many Holy Years had been granted to the faithful against the Mahometan menace, which was ever lively in the Orient, it was more difficult to understand what stringent necessity had in 1560 induced Pope Pius IV to choose as the reason for opening the Extraordinary Holy Year, the raids of a certain pirate named Dragut.

Be that as it may, in exactly four centuries, from the first Jubilee in 1300 until that opened by His Holiness Pope Innocent XII in 1700, there should, according to the original plans of Pope Boniface VIII, have been five Jubilees. The total had, however, reached thirty-nine.

So I wondered with anguish and doubt, coming to the end of my reflections, whether such a cavalier attitude did not risk weakening in the sight of the Most High, or even rendering vain, the power of the supplicants' prayers. This doubt was reinforced by the consideration that the Jubilee attracted dishonest persons and gave occasion for so many sad occurrences (theft, cheating, rapine) like that which I had just witnessed.

But such pressing questionings had at last to make way for sleep. I had reached home. I promised myself that I would later ask for the guidance of Don Tibaldutio Lucidi, the chaplain of Villa Spada.

Cloridia, as I expected, was not there. She had certainly stayed behind at the Villa Spada to watch over the confinement of the Princess of Forano. Just as well: I'd have died rather than let her see me in that horrible stinking state. The first thing I did was to fill the bathtub and to immerse myself entirely in it, in an endeavour to rid myself of the pestilential odour of which I had become the carrier. While I rinsed my head with bucketful upon bucketful of water, I shivered more from the memory of the perils which I had faced than the icy and unpleasant ablution. By the time I had dried myself, it was already full daylight. The diurnal luminary shone splendid and implacable, awakening the senses and inviting mortals to action.

Indifferent to that radiant call, I dragged myself to my bed, worn out, and already halfway between waking and sleep I prayed to thank the Blessed Virgin for having saved my life.

My hands were still joined when I saw the note. The handwriting was somewhat tremulous, but determined. It was easy to guess the author:

All night up waiting. I expect your report.

I dedicated one last irate thought to Abbot Melani. Because of him I had almost lost my life – and for nothing. Did he want my news? He would have it in good time, no sooner.

I slept for over two hours: not enough to recover all my strength, but sufficient at least to be able to walk, think and talk.

I was almost thinking of staying at home waiting for someone to come and summon me, caring not for the wrath of Don Paschatio or that of Abbot Melani. Suddenly, like a blow from a whip on my naked back, a memory caused me to wake up with a jump: it was the great day, the wedding day of Cardinal Spada's nephew!

On my arrival at the villa, I found the air dense with euphoric frenzy. Not only workmen, porters, lackeys and scullions were moving busily along the drives, through the kitchen gardens and among the rooms of the great house. Today, there was also a gay and colourful troop of artists who would be bringing joy to the hours following the nuptial banquet: the musicians of the orchestra.

I at once requested tidings of Cloridia. I interrogated more than one servant, but was told that she was still confined to the apartments of the Princess of Forano, nor had she ever left there during the night. Well, I thought, if she was so busy, she would have had no time to worry about the author of these notes.

I then made my way to the little wood and continued to the chapel in which that afternoon the august nuptials were to be celebrated between Clemente Spada, nephew of His Eminence Cardinal Fabrizio, and Maria Pulcheria, niece of Cardinal Bernardino Rocci.

Among the servants of Villa Spada, all were exceedingly curious to see the bride. Of her, we knew only that she was no great beauty. Surely, the preparations were worthy to provide a setting for the nuptials of Venus. The sacristy and the little wall running around the chapel had been exquisitely ornamented with arrangements of the freshest flowers in terracotta vases and wicker cornucopias, set about with garlands of fresh cut blooms and baskets garnished with lemons, apples, golden apples of the New World (or *tomates*, which nature has created beautiful but unpleasant to the taste), ears of corn and generously displayed fruit. Commodious armchairs in the first row and chairs of gilded intaglio wood in the successive ones had been arranged harmoniously in a semicircle, so that no guest's vision should be disturbed by the person in the row in front.

In a corner, standing against the wall and delicately covered with a damasked cloth, were the bundles of decorated sticks, bound together with coloured ribbons and culminating in crowns of flowers, which we servants, apparelled in festive dress for the occasion, were to wave with festive exultation at the end of the ceremony. The little arena with armchairs and seats was crowned with marvellous open vaulting, all built in wood and papier mâché and composed of pairs of quadrangular columns surmounted by gracefully ornate capitals, among which lovely rounded arches leaned out, garlanded with flowers, heather and mad bunches of wild herbs.

In like manner, the other nuptial decorations (hangings of blood-red velvet, draperies of golden silk, curtains with the family arms of both the spouses) had been completed and skilfully arranged. Two maids were about to finish placing the soft plush cushions on the chairs; from the chapel I heard the paternal voice of Don Tibaldutio giving the little servers their final instructions. I took heart: at least for the nuptial rite all arrangements were on time.

I felt the need to kneel before the altar and recite yet another prayer of thanksgiving for having my life saved. Within the chapel, there was a statue of the Madonna of the Carmel, the same to which Abbot Melani had for all those years confided my little pearls as an *ex voto*; this had evoked even more in me the desire to turn to that apparation of the Holy Virgin and Mother and to confide the fate of us all during the coming days to her safekeeping. I entered, sought a discreet corner, and knelt.

A short while later, Don Tibaldutio emerged from the sacristy and saw me. He set to work making final touches and putting the liturgical instruments in order, all the while keeping an eye on me. I knew why. Don Tibaldutio was a good-humoured and rubicund Carmelite who lived in a little room behind the sacristy which had been designated as the presbytery. Isolated thus from the rest of the villa, he often felt lonely and so would take advantage of my presence (when I went to the chapel to pray or was in the immediate vicinity, busied with some gardening chores, or with the aviary) to chat with me. His living as chaplain to the Spada family was no mean distinction and many of his fellow priests would have gone on hands and knees to have such a post. He, however, rather than take advantage of his position to receive petitions and forward them to his master, restricted his role to the care of souls, and nothing else. And his flock consisted not so much of the Spada family (who were often absent on business) as of the humble servants' household, a community living at the great house all the year round and changing little from one year to the next.

Now, celebrating the nuptials of Cardinal Fabrizio's nephew and heir was indeed a great honour for Don Tibaldutio, but one which he would gladly have done without.

When, after my prayers at the foot of Our Lady of the Carmel, I rose once more, Don Tibaldutio came to me with the usual open and consoling smile. He placed a hand paternally on my head, as he always did, and asked after my Cloridia.

"You do well to entrust yourself to Our Lady. Have you the special prayers for the Jubilee? If not, I can lend you a little book. If you wish, I can go and fetch it at once: I have just completed my duties in preparation for this afternoon's happy event, so I have a little time to myself."

"Don Tibaldutio," said I, at once seizing my opportunity to calm the doubts which had arisen in my mind about the validity of the Jubilee indulgence, "'twas precisely on that account that I was thinking of coming to you for enlightenment and counsel. . ."

So it was that I told him briefly of the laceration of the soul which had been mine a few hours before. I did, however, employ expressions more prudent and less direct than those of my solitary cogitations; had I bluntly apprised him of how deeply I was repelled by the unworthy manner in which the Holy Years were conducted, I would have spoken the truth, but then I might perhaps have risked scandalising that honest and temperate churchman. I therefore used various expressions and turns of speech which danced around and touched lightly upon the kernel of my doubts, without ever mentioning such concepts as "cupidity", "corruption" or "simony".

"I see," interrupted Don Tibaldutio and, raising his hand sagely and lowering his eyelids with a seraphic smile, he invited me to take a seat beside him on one of the pews at the side of the chapel.

"You too, like so many, wonder what difference there might be from plenary indulgences, and whether the Holy Jubilee indulgence might not in some way be a pretext, as it may seem to profane eyes."

"Really, Don Tibaldutio, that is not what I meant. . . The fact is that I doubted the efficacy of cases in which. . ."

"Efficacy, efficacy. But that depends upon us believers," he replied, expressing the obvious. "In order to gain the indulgence it is sufficient to carry out each of the works enjoined on us, which, as you well know, are alms, visits to and prayers at the four basilicas, all in a single day, plus visits to and prayers at thirty churches for Romans and fifteen for outsiders, who have the disadvantage of the journey. But take care not to try to cheat Jesus! Our Lord Innocent XII has laid down that, for the purposes of this Jubilee, the ecclesiastical day is to be counted from Vespers to Vespers. It is therefore within that period of time that the basilicas are to be visited in a single day; in case of need, one can also do it from midnight to midnight, as used to be the case, but never from midday to midday, as too many Romans do, out of concern for their own comfort! Nor may one go to church too early or too late; 'tis not good enough to practise one's adoration through a closed door and, on that pretext, to spare oneself from giving alms to the priest!"

He began once more to scrutinise me, while I, with my eyes fixed on the ground, waited for a suitable moment to take my leave and return disconsolately to work with the same doubts as when I had entered the chapel.

"Why, my son," he added unexpectedly in a murmur, suddenly laying aside his didactic manner, "if the Apostolic Chamber enriches itself with the Holy Years beyond the power of words to describe, do not imagine that there remains one single scudo for poor parish priests."

I raised my eyes and my regard, crossing that of Don Tibaldutio, asked at last what my tongue could not express in plain language: what, in the eyes of the Most High, was the value of believers' prayers raised to heaven as a result of Jubilees which had, alas, been organised for shady lucrative ends?

"Very well," he replied, satisfied with that mute request.

I understood. Hitherto, Don Tibaldutio had answered me in the same terms as my questions, that is, without the virtue of clarity. He gestured that I was to follow him into the sacristy.

"God is merciful, my son," he began, even as we were making our way there. "He is certainly not that severe and vindictive deity of whom we read in the Old Testament and with whom the Jews still remain involved. Consider this little precept: if one is not in a state of mortal but only venial sin, Confession is not even a necessary prerequisite for obtaining the Jubilee indulgence; it is enough to make an act of contrition within one's own heart – the so-called Confession *in Voto* which I mentioned to you a few moments ago. Not only that: even in a state of mortal sin, it suffices to accomplish the required acts in order to obtain the Jubilee indulgence, so long as the final action was accomplished in a state of grace, or after repentance and Confession. Would all that make any sense if the Lord were not infinitely merciful?"

Indeed, I thought, 'tis as in the gospel parable of the husbandmen in the vineyard: those who come last receive full wages, as though they had worked the whole day. Does that not perhaps mean that God greatly recompenses our little deeds, our nothings with wholeness?

"The actions of visiting churches are morally good: even he who does this in a state of mortal sin moves towards reconciliation with God. And that is what counts," continued the chaplain.

We had meanwhile entered the sacristy, where Don Tibaldutio offered me a seat, taking care to close the door behind us. I imagined that he was on the point of revealing to me who knows what great and secret truth.

"The God of the Christians, my son, sacrificed his only-begotten son for the redemption of our sins," he said at last, speaking plainly. "The Holy Virgin and Mother bestowed upon Saint Dominic the sacred gift of the rosary to recite for the salvation of our souls; likewise with her own hands she made the scapular of the Carmel, of which I myself am a votary, and when we wear this, we can be certain that Our Lady Queen of the World will come with her crown of stars to fetch us from purgatory on the first Saturday after our death. Do you believe that we poor mortals deserve all that? Of course not, my boy, 'tis only the infinite grace and mercy of God that so decree, and certainly not the merits we gain from reciting a few *Ave Marias* or wearing an extra piece of material, gestures which in themselves are quite worthless; least of all are they worthy of obtaining eternal life. The Lord knows how petty and slothful we are, and that is why He offers us paradise on a golden platter, in exchange for vile copper coin. In His infinite love for us His children, He is satisfied by our little act of faith and goodwill: we make a small, wavering step towards Him and lo, the Merciful Father runs to us and gathers us up in His arms."

I waited for Don Tibaldutio to continue his discourse and to come to the long-awaited revelations; but he had said all that he had to say. He opened the door of the sacristy and again accompanied me to the foot of the statue of Our Lady of the Carmel, where he had first spoken to me. After bestowing a silent benison on my forehead, he left me there, moving away serenely and without a word.

Only then did the full import of the chaplain's teaching become clear to me. It was for me to draw my conclusion on my own: Divine mercy granted the Jubilee indulgence even to those in a state of mortal sin; all the more so would it lend an ear to the prayers of innocent pilgrims, even if they had been drawn to the Holy City by others' lust for lucre.

The truth which Don Tibaldutio had revealed to me was indeed great, as I had expected, but not secret; and yet, so humble and plain that it might have troubled certain august ears. It was therefore wiser to deliver it in the subtlest of whispers behind well closed doors.

∂∞∾

I left the chapel calm and reconciled. I was about to continue on my way towards the theatre when I heard an echo of hurried martial footsteps coming towards me.

"Here Maestro, please come this way."

It was Don Paschatio, all out of breath, who was showing the way to a tall, thin individual, all dressed in black, with a forelock of pepper-and-salt hair adorning his forehead rather artistically, under which darted two flashing eyes set in a grave and irascible visage. The pair was followed by a musician (whom I recognised as such because he was attired like all the other members of the orchestra) who was carrying two violin cases and, under his arm, a capacious valise which one could imagine to be full of all manner of musical scores.

I followed them for a while until we reached the theatre. Here, the musicians had already taken their places and it was then that I had a surprise: it was no orchestra, it was a veritable tide of humanity. All in all, I estimated, they must have been over a hundred strong. They were busy tuning their instruments but they fell silent when Don Paschatio and the two individuals who were unknown to me arrived at the great amphitheatre. The man dressed in black evoked around his person an impalpable sense of devout reverence, perhaps even awe.

I observed with pleasure that the stage for the players and the benches for the public, of fine polished wood, had all been completed on time. There were only two carpenters hammering a loose floorboard; they vanished in response to a severe nod from Don Paschatio, as soon as the taller of the two strangers mounted the platform in the middle of the orchestra.

It was then I realised that this was the celebrated Arcangelo Corelli, composer and violinist of great renown, whose participation at the festivities I had heard bruited abroad during the preceding days. He was to conduct music which he himself had composed.

Nothing had I heard of him until the year before, isolated as I was from the world by my daily coming and going from the Villa Spada to my little field and thence to the conjugal home. It had been a cantor at the Sistine Chapel who had come to buy grapes who had first spoken to me of "the great Corelli". And now I had been told by Don Paschatio that he was not just a great musician but the Orpheus of our times, whose glory now spread over half Europe and would one day make him immortal.

Like a military formation, the orchestral players grasped their bows in the same gesture and pointed them in identical fashion, as though 'twere an image reflected by a thousand mirrors, each at the same angle, with the same inclination and pose, at the strings of their instruments: the violins all alike, thus too the viols. For a few moments absolute silence reigned.

"Not only does he want them to play as one man but to look like one; even today, when they are but rehearsing," whispered Don Paschatio, sitting down by my side.

From his voice, I detected the triple sentiment of excited curiosity about Maestro Corelli's performance, contentment at serving as his Amphitryon, and weariness at the size of his task.

"He truly has a dreadful temper," continued Don Paschatio. "He never talks, he looks straight in front of him and thinks only of music. He deals with clients through the musician whom you saw arriving with us. He is his favourite pupil and it is said that he is also his. . . Well, Maestro Corelli is seen only in his company and never with a woman."

At that moment, the music closed our mouths. As though moved by an invisible, ethereal force, and not only Corelli's gesture setting the music in motion, the musicians attacked in perfect, divine unison a concerto composed by their maestro. To my great astonishment, I soon recognised a *folia*.

Once again, that simple, almost elementary motif surprised me, showing me its agile, insinuating and subtle second nature. It was like a beautiful and opulent peasant girl, ignorant of the world but well versed in the human soul, who arouses the desire of a rich gentleman far more than his consort, with all her money and her pretences. Such was the nature of the *folia*: at once simple and capable of anything. Eight clear, robust measures, from D to F (or so I was to learn only later) and then again back to D; a seemingly innocent little motif, yet one capable of unleashing the most unheard of and lascivious fantasies.

At the outset, each *folia*, being a daughter of the people, seems to be all too simple: from D to F, from F to D. Corelli's was like this too: within the brief span of that eight-beat double modulation, the melody at first took the form of simple chords. The accompanying chords then uncoupled. In the second variation, they dissolved into triads, with a French-style rhythm. In the third, they broke down into arpeggios, in the fourth, they transformed into scales, in the fifth, into tremolos, progressively complicating the game with amusing embellishments, proud staccatos, lamenting legatos, a thousand artifices of adornment which ended up by casting the listener into a state of vertigo. Every now and then, a slow variation, in which the motif was reprised languidly, indolently, at last afforded both audience and players a chance to catch their breath.

After variation upon variation, the indistinct mist of the initial theme had by now dispersed. A whole landscape, once concealed amidst the few notes of the original motif, now emerged for the listener. It was as though the sense of the theme itself had at last become clear, the very meaning of the *folia*: a voyage from one tonality to another, not from D to F and back but from one world to another. And what worlds were these if not the world of sanity and of folly? One must needs journey from the one to the other because both, mutually illuminating one another, were imbued with meaning. From D to F, from F to D: no melody could so conquer the heart and the mind without that perennial fluctuation from one tonality to the other. And for no one can there ever be wisdom, or so that music seemed to suggest, without that sacred pilgrimage towards folly.

Maestro Corelli played the part of first violin; to guide the whole symphonic ensemble he needed only sharp and brief movements of the head, as an experienced horseman needs only a tap of the heels or ankles to steer his well-beloved mount. It was as though he were saying: "Now, stop and listen, you'll not leave empty-handed, for I know what you're looking for."

Shining through that music, almost as if the notes wanted to comment on my thoughts (while in nature, 'tis the contrary that's common) I sensed all the bittersweet flavour of times past, of things that had happened and things yearned for, yet which had never come to pass, of the seventeen years which had separated me from Atto, of the lessons on diplomacy and government which I had received from him; teachings which, like the work of that magician of a painter whom he had invoked for me on our visit to the Vessel to immortalise the features of the Connestabilessa when young had been imprinted in me forever. . .

Perhaps himself enraptured by the power of his creation, Corelli had ceased to conduct. He was playing almost in meditation upon his violin, with the bow caressing the third string, then the first with a suaveness that seemed almost careless, playing for his own ears only. But this was no self-love. The orchestra was following him with eyes closed, casting sudden oblique glances at its conductor, minuscule pulls on the oars keeping the barque of the *folia* in exquisite and perfect balance in its passage from a calm episode to a somewhat more lively intermezzo, then once again to another slow movement. The musicians really were playing as one man, I thought. They and Corelli formed one thing, and that thing was Corelli.

And then I remembered: the first adventure I had lived through with Atto, his lessons of (theoretical) morality, the great but forgotten music of Seigneur Luigi Rossi, which he had shown me. . .

While the notes to which I was listening spread over my head and shoulders the warm blanket of memories, while the silvery shadows of the past rained down on me, it seemed that from Euterpe's merciful hands there slipped into my lap the ultimate and true sense of my being in that place at that hour, my face barely touched by the perfume of the nasturtiums in a nearby flower bed, and I glimpsed the end to which that sublime caravel of sound was tending: after seventeen years, a man and no longer a boy, fate was calling me to Atto's side in a new test of courage, a renewed merging of heart and intellect, a most bitter and most sweet voyage at the end of which virtue and knowledge once again awaited me. This was something which only later was I to recognise to be at once true and false, because induced by that philosophy without words and without ideas which speaks through the mouths of flutes and cymbals, mocking us all.

The notes were dying out in the sweet embrace of the final chord when a voice swept away the delusive voices to which I had been giving a home in my heart.

"For heaven's sake, where you been?"

My Cloridia had found me. She read on my face the signs of the adventurous night and questioned me with a silent, worried look.

I gestured to her that we should move away from the amphitheatre and drew her towards the cane-brake which delimited the green part of the garden to the north, just before the boundary wall. This was a useful stratagem, as by now the whole of the Villa Spada was more than ever gripped by extreme agitation, and not even our beech tree would be safe from inquisitive ears. I told her briefly all that had happened between nightfall and dawn.

"You are all insane: you, Sfasciamonti and Melani," said she in a voice halfway between tears, reproof and relief at having found me safe and sound.

She embraced me and we remained for a few minutes holding each other tight. I smelled the perfume of her skin mixing with the wild odours of the cane-brake and hoped with all my heart that I no longer smelled of manure.

"I have little time. The Princess of Forano wants me constantly by her side. She keeps on swooning, feeling unwell, being overcome by little bouts of fever. In other words, she's afraid of giving birth, despite the fact that this is the fourth child she's producing."

"But how come the husband allowed her to accompany him to the Villa Spada, knowing that she's so close to her confinement?"

"In fact, he does not know that, he thinks she's only in her sixth month. . ." Cloridia winked, with a vague, sly expression on her face that spoke volumes. "She, however, absolutely insists on being present at the wedding: the bride is a good friend of hers. I've been quite unable to convince her to return home. Let's stay here and listen to me carefully, I must be quick."

As promised, Cloridia had succeeded in obtaining some interesting information. A few weeks earlier she had assisted at the difficult confinement of a chambermaid at the Spanish Embassy. The young woman was very grateful to her for, thanks to her assistance, the little one, a fine little girl called Natalia who had tried to leave her mother's womb feet first, had been most skilfully extracted by Cloridia: slipping her fine fingers into the birth canal, she had succeeded in performing Siegemundin's celebrated "double-hold" at which she was so adept, and turning the baby in her mother's womb, whereupon she had pulled her out by the head without the slightest danger.

The young mother who had previously twice miscarried had, out of gratitude, become Cloridia's friend.

"I mentioned to her what had befallen Abbot Melani and the bookbinder. In order to convince her to speak, I told her that this was perhaps of importance to the Spaniards and she should therefore tell me every curious thing that she had seen or heard. She said to me: "Jesu, Mother Cloridia, you must pray fervently for your husband and for your master, Cardinal Spada."

"And why is that?"

Cloridia had needed only gentle insistence to extract a confession from the young woman. Overhearing partly by accident (but also on purpose) the conversations of the Ambassador, the Duke of Uzeda, the little chambermaid had learned that political manoeuvres were taking place in Rome which would be decisive for the future of Spain and the world.

"Just as I read in the letters of the Connestabilessa Colonna," said I.

"You did well to spy out those letters. I am proud of you. In any case, Abbot Melani deserves no better. After all, he steals letters, that's how he gets by; even if they end up by costing him plenty," laughed Cloridia, alluding to the memoirs which Melani had arranged to be stolen from me and which he had then proceeded to buy at a high price.

Cloridia never spoke fondly of Atto. She did not trust him (and how could she be blamed for that?); indeed, of him she could hardly have thought worse. The Abbot, while perfectly aware that she was within calling distance of him, had never once thought to ask after her or to involve her in our business, were it only for the sake of appearances or to request a smattering of information; nor could Cloridia abide the idea that anyone could dare ignore her precious admonitions without running to certain doom.

Since his return she had never so much as been to present her respects or to offer her services and I was sure that if she had merely glimpsed Atto's silhouette in the park of Villa Spada, she would have changed direction so as not to meet him. The same was true of him, of that I was certain. In other words, the twain, my wife and Abbot Melani, repaid one another in the same coin.

"What else did you learn?" I continued.

"My little chambermaid mentioned to me, too, in truth very briefly, that the Catholic King is very ill and might soon die, but he has no heirs and it was said that the Pope had therefore been asked to help. Everyone at the Embassy at that time was terrified of being suspected of espionage. She, however, told me that she had heard this rumour which was current among the Spaniards in Rome from her other compatriots."

"What rumour?"

"That the Tetràchion will soon be arriving in Spain."

"Tetràchion? And what is that?"

"She does not know that either. She says only that he is the legitimate heir to the Spanish throne."

"The legitimate heir?"

"That is what she said. She asked me if I know anything of this. But it was from her that I heard tell of it for the first time. How about you?"

"Never heard of it. Not even the Connestabilessa had anything to say about that. But what's the connection between the Tetràchion, Abbot Melani's stab wound and the death of the bookbinder?"

"I have no idea. As I said, in order to soften up my little chambermaid, I told her that this business concerned the Spaniards. So she told me that, according to the rumours, the coming of the Tetràchion would bring misfortune: what happened to Melani and to the bookbinder were, in her eyes, among the early signs of that trouble."

"Do you think that she will have anything else to tell you later on?"

"Surely not, seeing how scared she was. You know how word of mouth spreads among the servants' class. Once in motion, it takes on its own life. I do not exclude the possibility that I may soon receive further information about this Tetràchion quite spontaneously. Meanwhile, take care, I beg of you. You cannot always be as fortunate as you were last night."

"You know that I am doing this for both of us," said I gravely, alluding to the bountiful compensation which Atto had paid me for writing up the chronicle of his Roman sojourn.

"Then be so good as to arrange matters so that, at the end of this story, you and I are still together. Being a widow is no pleasant business. And do not deceive yourself: he paid you to write a memoir, not to go around searching for his stolen papers."

"Do not forget that they drugged me and broke into our house. I must prevent that from happening again," I retorted in my defence.

"It will happen surely enough if you persist in keeping company with Melani. Remember Article Five: 'He who holds the purse strings is the winner.'"

She was right. With that mocking proverb Cloridia had said all that need be said. I did not have to follow Atto in all his convolutions. I had already been paid; it was therefore up to him to seek my services. Last night, however, I had not only followed him, I had gone around in his stead, and risked my life in so doing.

What would become of my family if I were to die? Cloridia could not bring up the little girls on her own. No, not even my intention of keeping watch over Atto on behalf of my master Cardinal Spada merited my running such risks.

༂

"You have made me worry, my boy, believe me."

Abbot Melani was somewhat clumsily playing the part of the good *paterfamilias*. He sat in an armchair, massaging his arm. Hardly had I finished my conversation with Cloridia than he had succeeded in getting Buvat to trace me and bring me to him. The apartment was again in good order.

"I have spoken with Sfasciamonti," he went on. "He told me everything. You have been magnificent."

I remained silent for a few seconds. Then I exploded:

"Is that all?" I asked in a loud voice.

"I beg your pardon?"

"I said: is that all you have to tell me? After risking my life for your trafficking. 'You've been magnificent!' And there's an end to the story, is that how you see it?" I added, almost screaming.

He jumped up and tried to place a hand over my mouth.

"What the Devil has got into you? You could be overheard. . ."

"Then kindly stop treating me like an idiot. I am a family man now. I have no intention of risking my life for a handful of coin!"

Atto was circling me anxiously. My voice continued to resound through the chamber and it could be heard outside.

"A handful of coin? What ingratitude! I thought you were satisfied with our arrangement."

"That arrangement made no provision for my death!" I replied, yet again at the top of my voice.

"Very well, very well, but now do speak quietly, I beg of you," said he in tones that suggested capitulation. "To all problems there is a solution."

He sat down and waved me to a chair in front of his one, almost as though acknowledging my status as that of a belligerent of equal strength, at last invited to the negotiating table.

So it was that, having entered Atto's lodgings with the firm intention of freeing myself from his service, I left after bringing about the opposite. As was his wont when discussing pecuniary matters, especially when it was he who must disburse, he was curt, exact and to the point, with just a trace of restrained bitterness in his voice. The terms of the new agreement were as follows: in carrying out Atto's instructions, or in favouring his interests, or finally in carrying out all the operations necessary for the purpose of completing the memoir for which he had paid me in advance, I was to do everything possible, without however at any time exposing myself to danger, whether mortal or of particular gravity. The term of this undertaking was obviously to coincide with Atto's departure from the Villa Spada or otherwise at some previous time, to be fixed according to his imprescriptible decision.

This ambiguous and complicated form of words meant, when all was said and done, that I was to place myself with even greater alacrity at the service of Abbot Melani, if necessary, even in difficult or dangerous situations: if possible, without paying with my life. The term "if possible" weighed down on my shoulders like a millstone.

The other part of the deal was no small matter, and Atto was all too well aware of that.

"Not just money, houses. Property. Lands. Farms. I shall make over your daughters' dowry. A rich dowry. And, when I say rich, I am not exaggerating. In a few years they will be of an age to marry. I do not want them to find themselves in difficulties," said he, affecting a generosity which I had, however, extorted from him. "I have a number of properties in the Grand Duchy of Tuscany: all valuable estates yielding excellent returns. At the end of the festivities of your master Cardinal Spada we shall go together to a notary and there we shall make over the deeds to a number of properties, or perhaps the income from them – we shall see what is most convenient. You will need to do nothing: your two little girls will become the assignees of the dowry and I hope that this will suffice to find a good husband for them. Even in these matters, you know, what counts most is help from the Lord."

He made me stand up and embraced me vigorously, as though to seal who knows what fraternal sentiment.

I let him. I was too concerned with weighing up in my mind the implications of that agreement: I could guarantee my daughters, the offspring of a humble labourer and a midwife, a sure and dignified future, even a life of ease. I had accepted in a hurry, out of unpreparedness and, above all, for fear of losing a unique opportunity. A thousand unknowns flocked on the cord joining heart and intellect, croaking their doubts: what if something (illness, death, sudden departure) were to prevent Atto from honouring his undertaking? And, above all, what if he had deceived me? I did not, however, accord much credence to this last possibility. If he had wanted to trick me, he would surely not have paid in advance for the writing of the memoir, as he had, however, done; and in cash.

In any case, I asked him: "Excuse me, Signor Atto, but. . . would it not be better to put something in writing?"

He let his wrists fall from the arms of his chair, as though exhausted by a titanic effort.

"Poor boy, you are still so ingenuous. Do you think that if someone intended to cheat you, a contract of this kind would be of any help to you in a court of law or that it might perhaps even help you to obtain your funds?"

"I really. . ." I hesitated, ignorant as I was about matters of law.

"Come, come, my boy!" Melani rebuked me. "Learn to live and think as a man of the world! And learn to look better into the eyes of those with whom you are dealing, because 'tis from your intuition about the person that your success or failure will come. Otherwise, every deal will be an enigma to you and every contract a confused mess."

He fell meaningfully silent, scandalised by my proposal of a written contract yet pitying my scant knowledge of worldly affairs.

"However," he added, "I understand you."

He took pen and paper and put all that he had just promised in writing.

He handed it to me. Melani undertook to constitute on behalf of each of my daughters a marital dowry with rents and property to be drawn up before a notary of the Capitol, but which, he now promised, would be substantial.

"Will that do?" he asked coldly.

"Yes, indeed, I think, yes; Signor Atto, I must thank you. . ."

"Please, please. . ." he gestured as though to brush off my words and at once changed the subject. "What was I saying to you? Ah yes, Sfasciamonti described all yesterday's events to me in detail. Just one question: what exactly did the *cerretano* say to you on that terrace?"

"Something like 'tiyootootay'. . . No, now I remember. He said, 'Teeyooteelie'," I replied, with a great effort of memory.

"You have really been splendid."

"Thank you, Signor Atto. A pity that all that 'splendour' – to use your words – has got us nowhere."

"What do you mean?"

"We have nothing but the remains of a microscope. No telescope, no relic, no papers."

"Nothing, you say? Now we know about the German."

"Well, about him we really do not know a thing, not even whether he really exists," I objected.

"Oh, you have not laboured in vain. I agree with Sfasciamonti that we are following up an important clue. There is someone here in Rome, this German, who collects optical instruments and relics. Not only that: this character has links with the *cerretani*. Now we know who to look for. As for the question of the secret language of the *cerretani*, that really does not trouble me at all. If we cannot manage to decipher it, we shall find ways of making them speak our language! Heh!"

It was unusual to see Atto so blindly trusting. I had the suspicion that all that optimism served mainly to appease me and not to lose my services.

"Sfasciamonti says that no one knows where he is to be found," I objected.

"These persons of the criminal underworld can always be traced. Perhaps one need only know the right name. The German, however, is but a nickname," he replied.

That observation brought to mind the strange name which Cloridia had mentioned to me and which, she thought, might also be useful to Atto.

"Signor Atto, have you ever heard tell of the Tetràchion?"

At that moment, there came a knock on the door. It was Sfascia-monti who entered quickly and without even waiting for an answer. His face too bore the marks of that horrible sleepless and over-event-ful night.

"I have news. I have been to the Governor's palace," he began. "No one knows anything about the telescope. I do, however, have news about the mackeroskopp."

Sfasciamonti had shown the remains of the optical instrument to a number of colleagues who had quickly retraced it to a burglary com-mitted a few days previously. The apparatus belonged to a learned Dutchman who had been robbed of all the effects he had left in his chamber at an inn near the Piazza di Spagna.

"There too, they opened the door with a key. No breaking and entering. No idea as to who did it."

"Interesting," observed Atto. "This is our thief's favourite method."

"Today there's the wedding," the catchpoll continued, "so I shall not be able to get away. We must wait until evening. I'd like to put some questions to a couple of wretches. Let us then meet tonight after the nuptial banquet. You, my boy, will come with me."

I looked at Atto, hesitating.

"No," he said, guessing that I had some hesitation about running yet more risks, "the matter concerns me personally. . . therefore I too shall come."

I had been caught out: in point of fact, Cloridia would have wished me to stop going out at night on behalf of Melani. Atto had offered to come, but in my company! And if an old man like him took this upon himself, I bethought myself with some embarrassment, why could not I do likewise?

The catchpoll explained the objective to us.

"Interesting. . . Most interesting," commented Atto at the end.

જ∾જ

"Who told you? Speak! From whom did you learn this?"

The attack came the moment we were alone. He grabbed me by the collar and hurled me against the wall. His was the modest strength of an old man, yet surprise, the respect which I nevertheless felt for him, and which caused me to hesitate, as well as fatigue from the night before, all prevented me from facing up to him as I ought.

"Tell me!" he screamed in my face one last time.

Then he looked behind him out of the corner of his eyes, towards the door of the chamber, fearing that he might have been overheard. He relaxed his grip, while I myself, whose sole reaction had been to grasp those almost skeletal wrists to prevent him from strangling me, broke free.

"But what has got into you?" I protested.

"You must tell me who spoke to you of the Tetràchion," said he in a firm, icy voice, as though he were reclaiming possession of something that belonged to him.

I therefore told him that a chambermaid at the Spanish Embassy had made some obscure connection between the incident which had befallen Atto and the death of the bookbinder and the coming of the Tetràchion, who was said to be no less than the legitimate heir to the Spanish throne. When I referred to the illness of the Catholic King, and to the fact that he was on the point of dying childless, I had to make a considerable effort to avoid betraying the fact that I had learned all this from Maria's letters.

"Well, well, I see that you know the main things about the Spanish succession. Obviously, you have taken up reading gazettes once more," he commented.

"Er, yes, Signor Atto. My wife does, however, hope to have further details in the next few days," I concluded, hoping that he had calmed down.

"Of that, I have no doubt. Don't imagine that you are going to get away with this so lightly," he said acidly.

I was incredulous. After all the services which I had rendered him, Atto was treating me like the most sordid of traitors.

"Anyway," I burst out at last, "who or what the deuce is this Tetràchion?"

"That is not the problem."

"Then, what is?"

"The problem is: where is he?"

He opened the door and went out, beckoning me to follow him.

❧

"Things could not go on like that forever," he began.

We were approaching the gate of the Villa Spada, in the midst of a chaotic and excited multitude of workmen, seamstresses, porters and lackeys.

He had decided to respond to my questions with facts, and was heading for an unknown destination; but with words too, taking up again the thread of the narration which he had interrupted the day before.

Gradually, as the King reached manhood, Atto narrated, Mazarin's position was becoming more delicate with every passing day. He knew that he would not be able to keep his sovereign forever in a state of blissful, nebulous ignorance of matters of state and the facts of life. After being the absolute master, what place would the Cardinal occupy under a young, vigorous monarch in full possession of his powers? Mazarin thought anxiously of this again and again during long journeys by carriage, while distractedly receiving postulants, in every single free moment that work left him and last of all, in bed, as he awaited sleep and his most pressing thoughts performed their last furious dance. Meanwhile, despite the Queen Mother's complaints about Maria, he raised not a finger to separate the young King from his niece. . .

"The King saw this and took it in, interpreting this silence as consent. And of one thing you may be certain: the Cardinal absolutely did not want to see his niece in the humiliating role of royal mistress when Louis took himself a wife!"

"In other words, Louis had the illusion that the Cardinal would let him marry her," I conjectured.

"'Twas more than an illusion. Once the King even went so far as to call Maria 'my Queen' in the presence of others. The whole court, led by the Queen Mother, cried scandal. Louis's sole response, however, was to acquire from the Queen of England a splendid necklace of huge pearls which was, moreover, one of the English crown jewels: it was to be his betrothal gift to Maria. Was it not, moreover, true that, a year previously, the hand of Maria's younger sister Ortensia had been requested by the English King Charles II? The negotiations failed later, but only because the British sovereign wanted, in addition to a dowry in money, the fief of Dunkirk, which Mazarin did not feel able to yield. So Louis's hopes were not by any means groundless."

At court, meanwhile, the couple's every sigh was spied upon and reported to Anne of Austria. A mordant comment by Maria, a word out of turn or her all-too-spontaneous laughter, all were at once transformed by courtiers' gossip into a caprice or insolence inviting loud censure. A passing glance by the young King at some damsel was enough to make the courtiers exult against Maria Mancini.

Very soon, an expedition was organised: everyone was off to Lyons, for the presentation to the King of a young maiden, Margaret of Savoy, a possible candidate for Louis's hand. He obeyed, but he took Maria with him and carefully avoided any contact with the Queen Mother. Every evening during the journey, instead of having dinner, the King performed in a ballet, having partaken of an abundant afternoon meal, so as to avoid dining with his mother. Then he would play at cards with Maria.

We had, I saw, left the Villa Spada and we were making our way towards the San Pancrazio Gate.

At the meeting with Margaret of Savoy, Atto continued, Louis was as cold as a mannequin. He had eyes and ears only for Maria. They were inseparable. During stages on the journey, he at first followed her carriage on horseback then acted as her coachman; in the end, he fell into the habit of joining her as a passenger. On moonlit nights, Louis would walk up and down until late under the windows of Mazarin's niece. When he attended some play, he would want her by his side, on a specially made platform. Those who accompanied them on their walks were by now accustomed to staying behind and leaving the lovelorn pair alone, a few yards ahead of them, so as not to disturb them. By now, they spoke of nothing else at court. The Cardinal and the Queen Mother, however, said nothing and let it be.

The whole court was stupefied by the disrespectful behaviour of the young King. The negotiations soon broke down and poor Margaret wept at the disgrace. Then came the surprise: a secret envoy arrived from Madrid. The Spanish King offered Louis the hand of his daughter Maria Teresa, Infanta of Spain.

"It seems almost as though you kept a diary of those days," I ventured, dissimulating my curiosity, for I was aware of Atto's aptitude for gathering information which he would then put to various quite unforeseeable uses.

"A diary, a diary!" he replied with some annoyance, "I was on an official diplomatic mission, in the retinue of Cardinal Mazarin, the purpose of which was to conclude with Spain the Peace of the Pyrenees; I registered every single detail with my eyes and ears, that's all there is to it. This was part of my duties."

Once the court had returned to Paris from Lyons, in February 1659, Louis's first thought was to celebrate the failure of the meeting with Margaret of Savoy.

"At the gathering, you could see festive costumes *échancrés* after the fashion of the peasants of Bressannes, a small town through which the royal progress had passed on its way to Lyons, with *manchettes* and *collerettes en toile écrue, à la vérité un peu plus fine,*" said Atto, showing off with a delighted and malicious little smile, in a mixture of French and Italian. "Mademoiselle and Monsieur were attired *en toile d'argent* with pink *passepoils, tabliers et pièces de corsage* in black velvet and gold and silver *dentelles*; while their black velvet hats bore pink, white and fire-coloured plumes and Mademoiselle's neck was covered with rows of pearls too numerous to be counted, and bestrewn with diamonds.

"And there was Mademoiselle de Villeroy, *parée de diamants*, and Mademoiselle de Gourdon, all covered in emeralds, accompanied by the Duc de Roquelaure, the Comte de Guise, the Marquis de Villeroy and the sparkling Puyguilhem (later to become the notorious Comte de Lauzun), they too costumed and coiffed *avec les houlettes de vernis*, like the peasants of Bressannes, and this was yet another silent seal which the great architect, Love, placed, 'midst scornful celebrations, upon the failure of Louis's planned nuptials with Margaret of Savoy.

"And the offer in marriage of the Infanta of Spain?" I objected.

"The negotiations had not yet begun. Between the Spaniards and Mazarin, secret contacts were taking place, but only gradually did they become public. All still remained to be decided. What was more," added Atto pensively, as we went through the San Pancrazio Gate under the watchful eyes of the guards. "What was more, I have always had the impression that the Cardinal had very different plans from these matrimonial arrangements for bringing Spain to heel and imposing peace on terms entirely favourable to himself. At least, until. . ."

"Until?"

"In March 1659, something unforeseen took place. Don John of Austria, the King of Spain's bastard son, arrived in Paris. He was coming from Flanders, of which he was the Governor, on his way to Spain. I recall those days very well, because Don John arrived incognito, at Vespers, and at court excitement was at its height. Queen Anne received him in her chambers, and I too was able to be present."

He was a small man, slight in build, well made, with a fine head and black hair – just a little rotund. Noble was the aspect of his face

and agreeable to behold. The Queen treated him with great familiarity and in his presence spoke almost entirely in Spanish. She also
presented to him the young King Louis. Don John, however, the son
of King Philip of Spain but born of an actress, ever over-proud of
his birth, behaved with excessive haughtiness, disappointing and
arousing the indignation of the entire court which was playing host
to him.

"The same embarrassing situation was repeated the day after,"
Atto recounted, "after he had had the honour of sleeping in Mazarin's
apartments. Don John came at length to the Louvre, where Anne and
the Cardinal received him with a friendliness which was not recipro-
cated. Monsieur, the King's brother, lent him his own guard without
receiving the least thanks in return. Everyone was astounded and
shocked by the Bastard's effrontery. Yet that was as nothing when
compared with what was to happen later."

"Was there a diplomatic incident?"

Atto drew breath and raised his eyes, almost as though to force
the riotous flock of memories into the sheepfold of logical discourse.

"An incident?. . . Not really. Something else. What I am about to
disclose to you is a tale known to very few."

"Do not worry," I reassured him, "I shall tell no one."

"Good. You do well to behave thus – in your own interest, too."

"What do you mean?"

"Like all scalding hot information, you can never quite tell what
awkward potentialities lie concealed in it."

Meanwhile, we had covered a good distance along the Via San
Pancrazio. I had guessed where we were going. This was confirmed
when Atto came to a halt. We were before the entrance.

"It is here. Or at least, it should be," said Atto, inviting me to
cross the threshold of the Vessel.

৵৹

We stood yet again in the fine courtyard, made gay by the ever renewed gurgling of the fountain. This time, no sign of any human
presence came from within the villa; neither music nor even the
slightest vague rustling that might stimulate one's imagination.

We advanced towards the tree-lined drives which we had explored on our first visit, near the espaliered citrus trees. After the
amiable hubbub at Villa Spada, the silence here seemed designed to

dispose Atto even more towards narration. Only a timid breath of wind caressed the foliage on the treetops, the sole witnesses to our presence. As we walked in the park of the Vessel, Abbot Melani spun out the thread of the tale.

Don John, or the Bastard, as many called him, had in his retinue a curious being, a woman who was known to all as Capitor.

"A mangled name, for in reality they called her *la pitora* or something of the sort – a word which, I believe, means in Spanish 'the cretin'."

Capitor was mad. Hers, however, was no ordinary madness. It was rumoured that she came from a family of clairvoyant lunatics who, among the folds of a distorted vision, mysteriously captured gleams of occult truth. The Bastard had made of her a sort of domestic animal, an entertainment for the cruel, rough amusement of his soldiery and, sometimes, the gentry.

"Her fame as a clairvoyant, but also as an outlandish, entertaining madwoman, had preceded her to Paris," said Atto. "So much so that, soon after his arrival, the Bastard was asked whether he had brought her with him."

Thus it was that Capitor was presented at the Louvre. She was dressed in men's clothing, with short hair, a plumed hat and a sword. One eye swore at the other: she was, in other words, cross-eyed. Her skin was yellow and full of pock-marks, framed by a mousy mane, with a hooked nose and a dark window in the middle of her front teeth, all of which made her quite phenomenally ugly. Hers was an ungainly, pear-shaped figure, with minuscule withered shoulders, while her hips spread into enormous parentheses, all of which combined to render her disastrous appearance the more droll and ridiculous.

She was always accompanied by a flock of birds of all kinds, which took shelter on her shoulders and in the ample fold of her hat: goldfinches, parrots, canaries, and so on.

"But what was so special about her?"

"She was all day long at the Louvre," replied Atto, "where the Queen Mother, the King and his brother had a wonderful time joking and teasing her. She would often respond with strange strings of words, meaningless riddles, queer rhymes and incantations. Often she'd burst out laughing without rhyme or reason, in the midst of a banquet or a speech by a member of the court, just as one would expect from a lunatic. But if someone reproved her, she would at once become as sad as a funeral and, pointing her index finger at her opponent, she would whisper incomprehensible, menacing anathemas. After which she'd again roar with laughter, mocking with odd and truly funny witticisms the poor unfortunate who had thought to punish her. Often, she would play the castanets and dance after the manner of the Spanish gypsies. She would dance in the most curious fashion, without any accompanying music; but she did it with such passion that, more than a dance, it seemed to be an arcane rite. At the end, after the last pirouette, sweating and panting, she would let herself fall to the ground, ending with a raucous cry of victory. Everyone would applaud, bewitched and perturbed by the madwoman's magnetism."

There was a strange atmosphere in those days, since that indefinable being had arrived at court. While in the beginning everyone thought they could play games with her, it was by now the contrary that had become the norm.

With her bizarre behaviour and her caprices, Capitor amused everyone; with only two exceptions.

"The madwoman had no favourite topics of conversation. Indeed, she had none at all. If she was sad, she stayed in a corner, all dejected, and there was no way of conversing with her. Otherwise, she would wait for someone to ask her something, for example: 'What is the time?' She would reply, if she was on form and she liked the questioner, with some absurd pronouncement, such as: 'Time doesn't wait for time, for otherwise it would have to wait for those who no longer have any time, or to let them die in their non-time. I shall not die, because I am already in Capitor's non-time. You, on the other hand, are in today's time, and that seems fine to you because you have the illusion that you can see it, whereas what you are really seeing is the nothingness of your own non-time. Have you ever thought about that?'"

"But that doesn't mean a thing!"

"Indeed it is not supposed to. But, believe me, when that bedevilled madwoman gushed forth her incantations, you'd be taken in like some silly child and suspect there was some sense to it, even some revelation of which only she was capable. And that suspicion was not mistaken."

"What do you mean?"

"The madwoman, Capitor, had. . . how can I describe it? Let us say, she had some special faculties. I shall explain. More than once, she was asked where some lost object was to be found, which the owner had for a long time been seeking in vain. In a trice, she'd find it."

"But how?"

"She'd think of it a moment, then she would move directly behind a wardrobe, or rummage in some drawer, and there was the thing they were looking for."

"Good heavens, and how did she manage to. . ."

"She could do even better. She could guess at the contents of sealed envelopes or the names of people who were being introduced to her for the first time. She had premonitory dreams which were extraordinarily detailed and genuine. She invariably won at cards because, as she said, she could read the cards on her adversary's face."

"This seems to be almost a case of witchcraft."

"What you say makes sense. But no one ever pronounced that word. It would have caused a scandal; besides which, everyone took Capitor for what she was: a rather strange toy with which to amuse the Bastard's soldiery and, for a few days, the royal family. At the Louvre, they were many who enjoyed the entertainment during Don John's stay. When she left, the Queen, the King's brother and Madame de Montpensier bestowed on her their portraits painted on enamel and decorated with diamonds. Madame La Bazinière, who had even invited her into her home, gave her silverware and boxes full of ribbons, fans and gloves. They all, as I said, enjoyed themselves immensely, except for two persons."

"And who were they?"

Capitor, replied Atto, pampered unguardedly by the King and the Queen Mother, had without question behaved bizarrely during those days in Paris, but never insolently. Except once. Whenever Maria Mancini was in her presence, she would always speak of the same thing: the Spanish Infanta; in other words, the woman whose hand had been offered to Louis.

"She would repeat unceasingly how beautiful the Infanta was, what a great Queen she would be one day, how she was far more beautiful than any other woman, and so on," trilled Atto.

No one knew why the madwoman provoked Mazarin's niece, whose life at court was already difficult enough, with such irritating persistence. Some held that she had been inspired to do so by the

Spaniards, who feared that the influence of the young Italian woman might prevent the marriage with the Infanta. Others thought, more simply, that Maria was not borne well by her rival, with whom she shared an instinctive, sanguine nature which, as is well known, gives rise to much discord where temperaments are equal and adverse.

Maria refused to play that game. She already had quarrels enough to pick with the court and lacked the sangfroid to put up with these provocations. She would react angrily, calling Capitor a cretin, insulting and scorning her. The madwoman responded by mocking Maria in turn with humorous, coarse verses and puns bordering on the obscene.

"And who was the other person that was not content with Capitor's presence in Paris?"

"To answer you, I must now recount for you a curious fact, which is precisely what I was intending to tell you, and which obliged me to provide this lengthy preamble."

This took place on an afternoon when it was raining heavily, during one of those sudden, violent storms which can for a few hours prevent any business from being carried on and which remind human beings of the superiority of the forces of nature.

While the driving rain was making puddles boil and flowing in muddy rivulets through the streets of Paris, a strange gathering was taking place in a room at the Louvre.

The Bastard had at last deigned to reciprocate the myriad attentions with which he had been honoured in Paris and offered the royal family a little entertainment. Capitor was to hand over a number of gifts to Cardinal Mazarin, after which the reigning family was to be entertained with a little song recital.

"And who was to sing?" I asked, growing curious, aware as I was of Atto's musical past.

"You have been well aware since the first night we met, seventeen years ago, that in my greener years I enjoyed no little public appreciation for my musical virtues, and that sovereigns and Princes of the Blood deigned to be my audience; and that, among the latter, Queen Anne enjoyed my singing more than ordinarily," said Abbot Melani, reminding me somewhat summarily of the fact that he had, when young, been one of the most acclaimed castrati in the theatres and courts of all Europe.

"Yes, I remember very well, Signor Atto," I replied briefly, mindful of the fact that Abbot Melani did not care to bring out too much from his past that seemed out of place in his current career as political counsellor to the King and secret diplomatic courier.

"Well, it fell to me to sing. And that was no easy matter. It was indeed one of the most singular performances of my entire life."

Everyone was looking forward to attending one of the madwoman's shows, explained Atto: two or three laughs and it would all be over. The company was most select: Queen Anne, Mazarin, the young King, Monsieur, his brother and, lastly, Maria whom, fearing some insolence on the part of Capitor at her expense, Louis had wanted at all costs to seat on a stool by his side. In a deep armchair near the group, but a little apart, sat Don John, accompanied by a retainer.

Upon a signal from the Bastard, three Spanish pages were ushered into the room bearing as many voluminous objects, each of them covered with a blood-red velvet cloth; whereupon I made my entry with the Capitor surrounded by her usual court of birds. The madwoman was all smiles, delighted to be the provider of the royal entertainment.

The presents, thus veiled, were placed on as many tables, arranged in a semicircle, in the middle of which the madwoman took up position, embracing a guitar.

"Courage, Capitor, show the Cardinal our gratitude," the Bastard amiably exhorted her. Capitor, after bowing submissively, turned to the Cardinal: "These presents are for His Eminence,' said she graciously, 'that he may extract the occult and presumed meaning therefrom, but also the clear and resplendent sense which instils knowledge in the soul."

She unveiled the first gift. It was a great wooden globe, containing a representation of all the known earth, the lands and the rivers that furrow them, and the seas that surround them, mounted on a monumental and imposing pedestal of solid gold. The Bastard, full of pride, explained at that juncture that the terrestrial globe was the counterpart to a celestial one; he had had the pair made in Antwerp and had kept for himself the one which represented the regions of the sky, while this one he was offering to Mazarin.

Capitor turned the globe and, caressing it with her pointing finger as she looked straight into the Cardinal's eyes, she then recited a sonnet.

Friend, look well upon this figure,
Et in arcano mentis reponatur,
Ut magnus inde fructus extrahatur,
Inquiring well into its nature.

Friend, of venture here's the wheel,
Quae in eodem statu non firmatur,
Sed in casibus diversis variatur,
And some it casteth down; to others, worldly weal.

Behold, one to the heights hath risen
Et alter est expositus ruinae;
The third is stripp'd of all, deep down, to waste is driven.

Quartus ascendet iam, nec quisquam sine
By labouring he gained his benison,
Secundum legis ordinem divinae.

"For heaven's sake, how did you manage to remember that sonnet? This all took place forty years ago!"

"What of it? You should know, my boy, that I still retain the whole of Luigi Rossi's *Orfeo*, which I had the honour to sing before the King in Paris when he was barely nine years old, in 1647; in other words, half a century ago. Be that as it may, Capitor distributed a copy of that sonnet, no doubt to be sure that the message would not be lost. If you had read it and reread it, as we all did in the days that followed, you too would still remember it today without the slightest difficulty..."

"The interpretation does not seem that difficult to me: 'venture's wheel' obviously refers to the turning globe."

"You will understand that the Cardinal hesitated when faced with that rhyming dedication which was both unexpected and somewhat insolent."

"Why insolent?"

"If you listened carefully, you will have noticed that the sonnet is rather curious."

"In the first place, it contains verses in Latin."

"Not only that."

"Well, it says something like the proverb that the world's a ladder: some go down and some, up; one day, you're in luck, the next, the wind may change."

"Quite. And Mazarin, who was at the height of his power, did not care to be reminded that, *secundum legis ordinem divinae*, in other words, according to the order of God's law, he must sooner or later resign himself to relinquishing his command."

Someone at court hastened at once to whisper in his ear that the sphere which imitates the world (giving the illusion of being able with a glance and with the sense of touch to embrace the entire terrestrial orb) subtly suggests the notion of possession of lands, cities, entire nations: in other words, the prerogative of monarchs. This was a manner of saying that Capitor, and Don John, and in the final analysis, all Spain, recognised him as the real Sovereign of France. All the more so in that the Bastard had taken pains to make it clear that he was donating the terrestrial sphere to the Cardinal, while keeping only the globe of the constellations for himself. This interpretation ended up by flattering His Eminence, so that he regained his good humour.

Capitor then unveiled the second gift. It was a great and marvellous golden charger in the Flemish style with subjects in silver in relief, representing the god of the sea, Neptune, trident in hand in lieu of a sceptre, together with his spouse, the nereid Amphitrite. They were seated rather closely side by side on a rich chariot drawn by a pair of Tritons at the gallop, gloriously parting the waves and leaving a vast land behind them.

"One of the finest Flemish chargers that I have ever seen. It must have been worth a fortune," commented Atto. "Curiously, Capitor called it by a strange name, which imprinted itself in my mind because it was neither French nor Spanish, nor of any language of our times, and this I shall tell you later."

On the dish a number of pastilles of incense had been placed, which Capitor burned, releasing their potent and noble perfume. When the smoke began to thin, the madwoman turned to the Cardinal with a lopsided smile and, pointing with menacing mien, first at the two marine deities, then at the trident, proclaimed: "Two in One!"

Mazarin, continued Abbot Melani, was rather flattered. Like many of those present, he had seen in the two deities himself and Queen Anne, and in Neptune's sceptre, the French crown, held firmly in his hand. Others, however, saw in the marine allegory of the chariot ploughing the immense sea and leaving the land behind it, and above all in the trident in Neptune's grasp, not the crown of France but that of Spain, mistress of the oceans and of two continents, exhausted by wars and thus falling into Mazarin's hands. And that sent Mazarin into raptures.

"He who deprives the crown of Spain of its sons, the crown of Spain will deprive of his sons," Capitor added even more enigmatically, instantly silencing the murmuring of the audience.

"Here too, there was a wealth of possible interpretations. Everyone understood that the warning was aimed at Philip IV of Spain, all of whose male heirs had died at a tender age. According to others, it was because his sister Anne of Austria had been made to sign a deed renouncing the Spanish throne, thus depriving the Spanish crown of its descendants in the female line; while there were those who interpreted it in terms of Philip's obstinate refusal to appoint Don John the Bastard as his heir, despite the fact that many wanted him for their future King."

Capitor moved to the third gift. Yet again, she raised the red cloth with a sharp tug, casting it away. This time, it was a splendid goblet, yet again of silver and gold, with a long stem in the form of a centaur holding up the calyx.

"An object of the finest workmanship," commented Melani, "but above all, symbolic, like the other two presents."

The goblet was in fact full of a dense and oily matter, almost like plaster. Capitor explained that this was myrrh.

"The madwoman then invited me to step forward, and handed me the music. I already knew what she had asked me to sing, and there was no need to rehearse it even once. The accompaniment on the guitar was elementary and even the lunatic's modest musical ability was quite sufficient."

"What did you sing?"

"A little song by an anonymous poet that was quite well known at the time: the '*Passacalli della vita*' or 'Passacaglia of Life'."

"And was it well liked?"

Atto made a face which betrayed all the bitterness of that memory with the icy fear induced by a bad presentiment.

"Not one bit, alas. Indeed, it was from this that all the trouble began."

"What trouble?"

In lieu of a reply, Atto chanted to me with a sure but discreet voice the passacaglia which, accompanied by a visionary madwoman, he had intoned some forty years before in the presence of the King of Spain's bastard son:

Oh, how wrong you are to think
That the years will never end –
We must die.

And our life is just a dream
And as good as it may seem
It will very soon have passed
Die we must.

Just forget the medicine
You'll have no use for quinine
All those cures are just a lie –
We must die.

Oh, when singing you can die
Or when playing lute and fife
Leave your love and lose your life –
We must die.

And when dancing you may die,
Drinking ale or eating pie,
Dust can but return to dust,
Die we must.

Maidens, youths and little babes,
All men move towards their graves –
We must die.
Sick or sound, brave or poltroon,
Death will have us late or soon –
We must die.

If this you will not contemplate,
It already is too late
All your senses you have lost,
And you've given up the ghost –
Die we must.

Then he wiped a veil of perspiration from his brow. He seemed to be living a second time the remote, chilling moments in which he realised that he had been made the instrument of some oblique warning to Mazarin.

At the end of the song, Atto cast a furtive glance at His Eminence. The Cardinal was as white as a sheet. He had in no wise lost control of his emotions, nor had he betrayed any annoyance, yet the castrato, who knew every wrinkle in his face, had clearly discerned his unexpressed fear.

"You see," Abbot Melani instructed me, "if you would truly know great statesmen, you must needs have spent no little time in their close retinue. That is because whoever governs a state needs to be a master of dissimulation, so that no one can fathom his nature. However, through the position which I had occupied, I was able to observe His Eminence from close quarters for quite some time. The Cardinal, who was by nature rather fearless and determined, feared only one thing: death."

"But how can that be?" I asked, astonished; "I thought that cardinals, princes and ministers, who are so close to the secrets and machinations of states, were. . . how can I put it?. . ."

"Somewhat more distanced from these things because distracted by the high demands of affairs of state, is that not what you thought? Absolutely false. You must know that the power which such eminent personages exercise in no way saves them from the same phantasms as beset the humble. That is because human beings are always and quite invariably made of the same substance, and indeed the fact of rising among the learned and influential exposes one to the risk of imagining oneself to be godlike, so that it becomes hard to resign oneself to the fact that Our Lady Death will sooner or later come and make us equal to the least of her subjects."

Thus, Cardinal Mazarin had for some time been engaged in a vain struggle with the spectre of death, against which every effort must in the end prove in vain. The macabre song which Capitor had made Atto sing seemed chosen to perturb the Cardinal's already unquiet conscience.

"Myrrh was one of the Three Magi's gifts to Our Lord," I observed.

"Precisely. It is a symbol of mortality, since it is scattered on corpses," remarked Melani.

The second present too concealed a recondite message. The incense which it contained, whose penetrating odour Capitor had spread through the air, is indeed used in holy places and the Three Magi gave it to the Christ Child in acknowledgement of his divinity.

Many, then, were the aspects of His Eminence evoked and honoured by those gifts: his charge as a Cardinal and ecclesiastic, represented by incense, and his nature as a mortal man, of which the emblem was myrrh.

"Lastly, the pedestal of the globe, which was in solid gold, was a sign of regal power: a homage to that of Mazarin, the Queen's lover and the absolute master of France, the most magnificent and powerful state in Europe and in the whole world," Melani commented gravely, "like unto Our Lord, who is called King of Kings."

The three objects, in sum, symbolised the three gifts which Our Lord received from the three Magi: gold, incense and myrrh; or the symbols of royal power, divinity and mortality.

"Capitor, His Eminence is grateful to you," said Queen Anne, dismissing her with benevolent ease, seeking to change the subject and to save everyone from embarrassment. "Now, let us invite the orchestra in," she concluded, gesturing that the doors should be opened.

Outside the room, a small crowd of musicians had indeed gathered, whose services Monsieur had commanded, together with a little table so laden as to relieve the guests' stomachs, once their ears had been catered for.

The doors were duly opened and the crowd of players began politely to take their places in the room, filling it with a growing hubbub. At the same time, groups of valets, panting at the effort, were bringing in tables already laid to satisfy the royal appetite. A little further off, there followed the obsequious multitude of courtiers, pressing forward keenly as they waited to be allowed to enter and partake of the remainder of the entertainment.

Louis, Mazarin and the Queen Mother were already distracted by this coming and going when Capitor, who was on the point of making way for the concert and the banquet, fixed her gaze one last time on the Cardinal.

"A virgin who weds the crown brings death," she declaimed, smiling, in a loud and clear voice, "which will be accomplished when the moons join the suns at the wedding."

Then she bowed and disappeared with her faithful retinue of birds into the human clouds of musicians and servants now bursting into the room in joyous disorder.

"Only then did Don John set aside his haughtiness," said Atto. "He turned to the Cardinal and the Queen begging their pardon on behalf of the madwoman. He admitted that her performances were supposed to be an entertainment, yet sometimes they were practically incomprehensible and, even when she seemed to overstep the limits of decency, she did not do so out of discourtesy but drawn by her bizarre and inconstant nature, *et cetera, et cetera*."

A madwoman could be forgiven for some madness, Abbot Melani reasoned, but Capitor's eccentricities that evening seemed all too much like threats; and Don John did not want to be thought of as having commissioned those hostile words.

The mad clairvoyant had made Atto sing a song that spoke of death and its ineluctability. Before that, she had offered the Cardinal three costly objects, which alluded to his being a Cardinal – which was true – to his being a King, which was almost true, but inopportune, Mazarin being the Queen's secret lover; and lastly that he was destined to die: undeniably true, but no one likes to be reminded of that twice in the same evening.

The sonnet even contained oblique references – to the inconstancy of fortune, the weight of failures – which no one would have dared to mention in the presence of the First Minister of the most powerful kingdom in Europe.

In the end, taking advantage of the arrival of the orchestra and of the valets bearing in the banquet, Capitor had escaped, leaving His Eminence a last menacingly allusive message.

None could have any doubts as to the meaning of those parting words. The *crown* was quite obviously young Louis. And who could the *virgin* be if not Maria Mancini?

"The allusion to the virgin, in particular, seemed to refer clearly to Maria, whom the King never knew: carnally, I mean."

"Really?" I exclaimed in surprise.

"No one believed that, except for myself, obviously, well aware as I was of the extreme innocence of their love, and the Cardinal who was kept informed of every minute of the young King's life. When Maria arrived in Rome and married the Constable Colonna, the latter confided in me not long after their wedding that he had found her to be a virgin and, being aware of what had passed between her and the King of France, had been frankly amazed by that."

If the marriage between the *virgin* and the *crown* were to be concluded, according to Capitor's warning, someone would pay with his life. And, seeing that the prophecy was aimed at Cardinal Mazarin, Maria's tutor and Louis's godfather, and thus arbiter of the destiny of the twain, it was easy to imagine that it was precisely his end that was being predicted, indeed even augured.

Proffered by anyone else, Capitor's words might have seemed mere harmless ravings. In the mouth of that being with her arcane faculties of divination, they sounded all too like the voice of the Black Lady with the ineluctable scythe.

"It is not easy to explain here and now, forty years later," said the Abbot. "When that ugly being opened her mouth, it set one a-shivering. Yet everyone laughed: the foolish because they were amused, the others, out of nervousness."

Atto, too, during Capitor's mad liturgy, had felt the touch of fear. He, too, had taken part, albeit passively and marginally, in the staging of the show for Mazarin.

Meanwhile, the wind had risen and the sky, which had hitherto been immaculate, seemed to have grown slightly darker.

"You yourself, Signor Atto, told me that Capitor was suspected of speaking as if she had been inspired to by the Spaniards who wanted a marriage between Louis and the Infanta and were consequently hostile to Maria Mancini. If that were the case, Capitor's message would have been, how can one put it?. . ."

"A perfectly normal threat for political ends? 'Tis true, there were those who saw it in those terms; but I believe that His Eminence was by no means so sure of it. The fact is that, from that moment on, Mazarin's attitude to Maria and the King changed sharply: no sooner had Don John the Bastard departed with his madwoman than the Cardinal became the most bitter enemy of the love between the two young people. There was, however, something else: Capitor called the dish by a Greek name: a word which you too now know."

"Do you mean?. . ."

"Tetràchion."

I was so caught up in the narration that I had almost failed to notice the curious phenomenon which had been taking place for the past few minutes: a sudden, bizarre change in climate, which had also occurred the day before in the very same place.

The wind, which was at first moderate, had found new vigour. The cirrus clouds which had quite unexpectedly begun to darken the vault of heaven swiftly gathered, by now forming a bank, then a cumulus. A powerful gust raised dead leaves and dust from the ground, forcing us to protect our eyes for fear of being blinded. As on the day before, we had to lean against a tree if we were not to lose our balance.

It lasted no more than a few instants. Hardly had the singular little squall blown over than the daylight seemed more joyful and free.

With our hands we brushed down our dusty clothes as best we could. I raised my eyes to the sun and was more dazzled than I expected: there was hardly any difference between the light now and when we had left Villa Spada. "What curious weather there sometimes is here," commented Atto.

"Now I understand," I said. "The first time that you mentioned the Vessel to me you said that there were *objects* here."

"Good. Your memory is correct."

"Capitor's gifts," I added.

He did not reply. He was moving towards the front door.

"'Tis open," he commented.

Someone had entered the Vessel. Or, said I to myself, had gone out from there.

శoctin

As we were crossing the hall on the ground floor, we heard the notes of the music which had greeted us on our first visit, the *folia*. I, meanwhile, had inevitably been besieging Atto with further questions.

"Pardon me, but why do you think that Capitor's gifts are here?"

"That is partly a matter of concrete fact, partly deduction, but there are no two ways about it."

Capitor's obscure prediction, Atto explained, circulated at lightning speed through court. No one had the courage to record it in writing, for it was said that the Cardinal had been terrified by it. Even the most meticulous of memorialists preferred to pass over the matter in silence, for their memoirs were made to be circulated and read at court, not to remain clandestine.

Yet, silence was not enough. Mazarin was already obsessed by the problem of how to retain power at the expense of the young King Louis who was bound, sooner or later, to cause him problems, and this he knew full well. After Capitor's dark prophecy, the Cardinal was beset nightly by new, black phantasms.

"As I have already told you," Atto stressed, not without irony, "the Cardinal had always been sure that his life would be long, very long."

Desperately attached to worldly glories, like a mollusc to its rock, he had ended up by confusing that rock with life itself, while it was life that gave him the strength to close up his shell.

"Remember, my boy, great statesmen are like mussels attached to a reef. They look upon the fishes darting here and there and think:

poor wretches, they're both lost and aimless, without a fine rock to bite into. But if the thought should once come to them that they may have one day to become detached from the rock, they are terrified. And they are utterly unaware that they are prisoners of their rock."

Obviously, those words did not express the thoughts of a faithful servant of Mazarin, as Atto had been forty years before. Nor did they fit in with that natural tendency of his to hunger and thirst after glory, a tendency with which I was so very familiar. These were other cogitations, those of one who has come to the last stage in life and who is measuring himself up against the same problem as that which beset Mazarin until his last hour: whether the bivalve's shell must open up and let go of the rock.

"Was that you?" said he.

"Signor Atto, what do you mean?"

"No, you are right, it came from outside," said he, moving towards one of the windows giving onto the entry courtyard.

I followed him and looked out too: there was nothing to be seen.

"It was like. . . someone running and kicking up gravel, or dirt," said Atto.

Then, almost merging into the notes of the *folia*, I heard it too. It was just like footsteps running down an avenue, the avenue whence we had come. They came and went. Then they ceased.

"Shall we go out?" I proposed.

"No. I do not know how long we can remain in here. Before leaving, I must be sure of one thing."

We took the winding spiral staircase that led to the first floor.

Meanwhile, Atto continued his tale. Mazarin could not bear that miserable state for long. He had lost the omnipotent confidence which had guided and sustained him ever since he had defeated the Fronde revolt. He feared the future: an unfamiliar and ungovernable feeling. In his hands, he held those objects, Capitor's gifts, and everyone knew that. Almost as though these were stolen goods, getting rid of them would be far from simple. In order not to have them always before his eyes, he had them stowed away in a chest.

Of that tale, he had spoken with no one. He did not want to think of it; yet, he thought of it unceasingly. He had never paid much attention to the evil eye, despite his Sicilian ancestry, but if anything was under a curse, he thought, those three trinkets were.

At length he came to a decision. If they could not change owners, the three presents must at least disappear, be sent as far away as possible.

"He entrusted them to Benedetti. He instructed him to keep them here in Rome, where Mazarin never went. Moreover, His Eminence was adamant that he did not want these gifts to remain on any property of his."

"Would it not have been simpler to destroy them?"

"Of course, but in such cases, you never know how matters will end up. And what if one day he might wish to employ a necromancer to disperse the magic power of the three objects? If he were to destroy them there could be no going back. The story was absurd from beginning to end, but Mazarin did not care for risks, not even the most insignificant ones. The gifts must remain accessible.

"So Benedetti kept them here," I deduced.

"In reality, when the Cardinal gave him his instructions, the Vessel did not yet exist, as I've explained to you. But now I am coming to the point."

The Cardinal was so beset by the memory of that visionary madwoman, Capitor, and by that absurd business of the three presents, that to the bitter end he remained undecided as to whether to keep them or send them away. After deciding to entrust them to Benedetti, his anxiety was still too great. So the Cardinal took a second decision which would, in other circumstances, have been unthinkable for a worldly-wise man like himself, who dealt with things hard and fast and cared nothing for superstition or charms to ward off the evil eye.

"Not knowing whether he had taken the right decision or not, he had their portrait painted."

"How could that be? Did he have a picture of them made?"

"He wanted at least to keep the image of them. It may sound stupid to you, but that was how it was."

"And who painted the. . . portrait of the three presents?"

"There was at that time a Fleming in Paris, a painter. He made fine things. As you may know, the Flemings are very good at painting still lives, tables laden with food, flower compositions and suchlike. The Cardinal arranged for him to paint a quick portrait of the gifts. I personally have not seen it. But I have seen the presents themselves, including the Tetràchion," he concluded, implicitly confirming that we were visiting the Vessel in order to find it.

"The idea would never have come into my head to have a portrait painted of three inanimate things and, what is more, how can I put it. . ."

"With a spell on them? Of course not. But the Cardinal had learned from the Bastard that he too had done the same thing. In Antwerp, before leaving for Paris, he had for his pleasure had a picture made of the gifts, but with the celestial globe instead of the terrestrial one, which was still in the goldsmith's workshop waiting to be attached to the solid gold pedestal."

Thus, having entered that villa for the first time on the traces of three cardinals and their secret meetings in preparation for the next conclave, I now discovered it also to be the depository of another triad: Capitor's gifts.

The great change in Atto's words at that crucial juncture could not and did not escape me. He had returned to Rome, declaring that his intention was to remain there until the next conclave, in order to watch over its proceedings on behalf of the King of France. At the same time, he had (and this was truly singular) passed over in silence the other great event of the moment: the political and dynastic struggle for the succession to the Spanish throne. This, however, was exercising him in no uncertain manner, as I had learned from reading his correspondence with the Connestabilessa. Now, at last, the Abbot was also beginning to betray his secret interest in his speech. It was no accident that, no sooner had I mentioned the mysterious Tetràchion in connection with the Spanish succession than he had reacted like a wounded animal, since when he had had no other thought than to drag me to the Vessel in search of traces of the missing object. Always assuming that it was indeed an object, as I myself observed.

"Pardon me, Signor Atto, but there is something that is not clear to me. The chambermaid at the Spanish Embassy spoke to me of the Tetràchion as the heir to the Spanish throne, thus of a person. In your view, however, it is an object."

"I know no more than you," he cut me short.

That answer did not satisfy me, and I was about to query it when it was I who started at a noise. I had heard it distinctly, quite separately from the faint sound of the music.

"Was it you?"

"No, you know perfectly well it was not."

The time had come to look around us and to find out what was going on in our neighbourhood.

From the central window in the salon, one could see them rather well. They were down below, in the garden. He was young, not very tall, and rather gauche; far from ugly, but with little eyes that seemed still unsure of where they were meant to be in the oval of his face; his lineaments were elastic, his nose too large and swollen. He was of that unripe age when the body, held hostage by disorderly springtime forces, is expanding from within and almost bursting the tender cocoon of childhood.

His nervous, uncertain gait betrayed an artificial attempt at gallantry and, at the same time, a well brought up sixteen-year-old's overwhelming desire to be able at last to act freely.

Then there was the maiden. From that angle (with our noses pressed against the window panes, but a little too far to the left) we could see her only obliquely; but I knew her all too well from the encounter the day before.

At first he took her arm, then suddenly let go of it, stood facing her and walked backwards, accompanying some pleasantry with animated gesticulation. He placed his hand in jest on the hilt of his sword, miming acts of heroism or evoking duels.

She laughed and let him play on; she was walking lightly, almost like a ballerina dancing on her toes, turning a little pink lace parasol, a magic calyx in which she captured his words. Her hair was in slight disarray, betraying the many kisses just given, or the burning desire to receive them soon, at once, behind the next corner.

Of the conversation, there reached us only a few fragments.

"I would like. . . if only you knew. . ." I managed to overhear him say, amidst the rustling of the foliage.

"Majesty, when do you. . . can happen. . ." was all I heard of her reply.

I turned to Atto.

He had stepped back and distanced himself from the window. He stood there like a stone idol, looking on with his eyes glazed, his jaws clenched, his lips tightly closed.

When I turned to observe the pair, they were disappearing behind the nearest hedge.

We remained a few moments longer, with our gaze fixed on the place where the couple had vanished from our sight.

"The maiden was. . . very like the portrait of the Connestabilessa when young," said I, hesitantly. "But the young man's face was familiar, too."

Atto remained silent. In the meantime, the melody of the *folia* became audible once more.

"Perhaps I have seen him portrayed in a statue. . . Is that possible?" I added, not daring to utter my impression more openly.

"He does indeed resemble a bust on the external façade of the Vessel, out there in one of the niches. But above all, he resembles one of the portraits you have seen here in the house."

"Which one?"

At first, he did not answer. Then he drew in breath and released the inner burden which had been weighing him down until that moment.

"There are things in this accursed place which are beyond my understanding. Perhaps the subsoil gives off unhealthy vapours; I know that does occur in some places."

"Do you mean to say that we could be the victims of hallucinations?"

"Perhaps. Whatever the case may be, we are here for a specific purpose and we shall allow no one to stand in our way. *Is that clear?*" he exclaimed, suddenly raising his voice, as though someone within those walls were listening.

Silence fell once again. He leaned against the wall, muttering some obscure imprecation.

I waited until he was calm, then I put the question to him.

"It really did look like him, did it not?"

"Let us go upstairs," said he, tacitly assenting.

Despite the many tales of phantoms, apparitions and manifestations of spirits which we all learn of from our most tender childhood and which, thanks to the power of suggestion predispose us to encounter such phenomena sooner or later, I had never witnessed so odd an occurrence.

As we climbed the spiral staircase to the first floor, I was turning over in my mind the absurdity of those visions: first, Maria Mancini, in other words, the Connestabilessa when still young, or whoever it may have been; now in gallant converse (and this was ridiculous, quite unimaginable) with the same royal lover whom Atto had attributed to her in his narration. I had first seen him in marble effigy, then in portraits (there was more than one in the Vessel) and now in flesh and blood: if the shy and absent-minded youth I thought I had seen in the garden really was made of flesh and blood.

I should have liked blindly to believe Atto's hypothesis that these were mere hallucinations due to the unhealthy air around the villa. Instead, I felt the solid marble of the stairs under my feet and, at the same time, the evanescent and perilous atmosphere of those visions. Willingly would I have escaped into dreams; instead, I found myself stuck fast in some shape-shifting marsh in which the past seemed blessedly to stagnate and, for a few instants, to weave before my confused eyes, in what seemed almost a play of light – an *ignis fatuus* – the broken threads of history.

There was, however, no time in which to find the answers, given that we were at that moment on the traces of a very different spectre: the phantom of Mazarin's terrors.

The staircase which led to the first floor was in the great hall, at the opposite end from the entrance and on the side facing east. At the top of it, we met with a surprise.

We had entered an enormous gallery, which I estimated to be no less than thirty yards long and four and a half yards wide. The floor was all paved with fine majolica tiles in three colours, each of which looked like a dice showing its sides in relief. The walls were covered in stucco work, all richly painted and gilded and, through the subtle interplay of volutes, naturally drew one's gaze upwards. Here, on the immense vault, we saw a marvellous fresco representing Aurora. Atto himself could not contain his stupefied amazement.

"The *Aurora* of Pietro da Cortona. . ." said he with his face turned upwards, briefly oblivious of the purpose of our search and the disquieting figures whom we had encountered.

"Do you know this painting?"

"When it was completed, over forty years ago, all Rome knew that a marvel had been born," said he with restrained emotion.

After the *Aurora*, in the next portion of the ceiling there followed a representation of Midday, and then an image of Night. The three frescoes thus followed suggestively the progress of daylight, from the first rays of dawn to the penumbra of sunset. The niches and smaller panels of the frieze were decorated with chiaroscuros, seascapes and many delightfully executed little landscapes.

In the spaces between the windows, one could on the long sides admire an impressive armoury: twelve great trophies of various arms both ancient and modern made of stucco modelled in bas-relief with metal enriched with gold, with a moral attached to each one of them, each referring to the value of defending body and spirit. In these admirable warlike cornucopias, there were swords and cannon, visors and cuisses, gorgets and scimitars, as well as spears, iron breastplates, mortars, slings, iron maces, pikes, arque-buses with ratchets, riding whips, standards, arrows, quivers, morions, battering rams, kettledrums, torches, military togas and much more still.

"Sfasciamonti would love all this ironmongery," observed Abbot Melani.

Every single object was decorated and completed with a Latin dictum: "'*Abrumpitur si nimis tendas*'." "'If you draw it too far it will break'," translated Atto, reading with a little smile the inscription carved into a crossbow.

"'*Validiori omnia cedunt*'." "'All yield to the strongest'," I echoed him with the saying carved on a cannon.

"'Tis incredible," he commented. "There's not a corner, not a capital, not a window in the Vessel without a proverb carved on it."

The Abbot moved off without waiting for me, shaking his head, a prey to who knows what cogitations. I followed him.

"And the most absurd thing of all is that between these walls covered in wise maxims, what music do we hear?" he called out in a loud voice, "the *folia*. . . folly!"

He was right. The melody of the *folia*, played, so it seemed to me, on a string instrument, was following us ever more closely, almost as though it were accompanying our reading of the inscriptions.

The sudden revelation of that paradox set in motion in my head a disorderly whirl of questions and thoughts of which I myself could not yet glimpse the meaning.

"So you are no longer of the view that we imagined all this?" I asked.

"Far from it," he hastened to correct himself. "Even if in all prob-ability that music is coming to us from some nearby villa where some-one is perhaps improvising on the theme of the *folia*."

After speaking thus, Melani moved on. On each of the long sides of the gallery there were seven windows. From the central ones, one could go out onto two balconies facing the opposite sides of the garden, east and west.

We turned instead to the opposite end of the gallery, facing south, in the direction of the road. The gallery ended in a semicircular loggia whose external façade was articulated by great arched windows. Moving even further, on a projecting platform which rested on the outer wall giving onto the street, there was a fountain. It took the form of two sirens lifting a sphere from which spurted a high jet of water. While enjoying that vision, the eye turned back and there, painted *al fresco* on the arch of the loggia, was a representation of Happiness, surrounded by its retinue of all the Blessings. The humble plashing of the fountain, careless of its own solitude, dispensed its sweet whisperings to the whole of the first floor. In the side façades of that first floor, on the wall of the balconies, there were two other artificial springs (one of which I had already heard from the front courtyard below) which, together with the larger and more beautiful one under the loggia formed a lovely magic triangle of murmuring waters, filling the whole gallery with their music.

"Look!" I suddenly exclaimed.

On the panels of the door leading to one of the two loggias with fountains was the whole of Capitor's sonnet on fortune:

> *FORTVNE*
> *Friend, look well upon this figure,*
> Et in arcano mentis reponatur,
> Ut magnus inde fructus extrahatur,
> *Inquiring well into its nature. . .*

"Here is the first clue!" exclaimed the Abbot triumphantly.

"Perhaps Capitor's three gifts which we seek are not far from here," I ventured.

We kept looking all around us. We saw that the semicircular loggia too, as well as the window openings and shutters, were covered in proverbs and sayings. One caught my eye.

"'From the private hatreds of the great spring the miseries of the people'," I read aloud.

Atto looked at me in some surprise. Was that not just what he was teaching me with his tale of the Sun King's misfortune in love, which had ended up by turning into a force of destruction?

"Look," said he suddenly, in a voice stifled by surprise.

Fascinated until that moment by the frescoes, the proverbs, the displays of arms and by the round loggia with its fountain, we at last turned our gaze to the other end of the gallery, facing north.

Despite all the time that has passed since then and the seemingly endless series of unusual experiences, I still recall the vertigo that overcame me.

The gallery was endless. Its two converging sides stretched out to infinity, it was almost as though my eyeballs had been torn from their sockets and projected helplessly into that abyss. Overcome by the unbearable dazzle of the light from outside, I saw the walls of the gallery melt into the displays of arms, the frescoes of the ceiling and, lastly, into the potent, solemn, fearful image outlined against the horizon, framed by the glass window as in a hunter's gun-sights: the Vatican Hill.

"Bravo, bravo Benedetti," commented Atto.

It took us a few minutes to realise what had happened. The northern end of the gallery consisted of a wall in which was set a window which gave onto a quadrangular loggia. The wall around the glass had been hung with mirrors which replicated and prolonged the gallery, making it appear endless. But that happened if the observation point was far enough away and equally distant from the two long sides: then and only then. In the middle of the wall, and thus at the point where the perspective of that architectural tunnel converged, the vista of the Vatican palaces was right at the centre of the frame; it was enough to approach that great window to include in the panorama the cupola of St Peter's Basilica.

So the prow of that ship-shaped villa pointed directly towards the seat of the papacy. It was not clear whether the coincidence was a sign of virtuosity or, rather, a threat.

"I do not understand. It seems to be aiming the barrel of a cannon, almost as though we could fire at the Vatican palaces," I commented. "You knew Benedetti. In your opinion, was it or was it not a matter of chance that the Vessel was thus oriented?"

"I'd say that. . ."

He broke off. Suddenly, the sound of footsteps could be heard in the garden. Atto did not wish to give the impression that he was alarmed, yet, forgetting what he was about to say, he began to pace up and down nervously.

We explored the rooms giving onto the gallery, which were four in all. First, there was a little chapel, then a bath chamber. Above the entrance of the first was written "*Hic anima*" and above the second, "*Hic corpus*".

"'Here is for the soul' and 'here is for the body'," translated Atto. "What a witty fellow!"

The bath chamber was most richly furnished and decorated with stuccoes and majolica tiles. It contained two baths. In each, the water was dispensed by two taps, above one of which was written "*calida*" while above the other was inscribed "*frigida*".

"Hot and cold water, on demand," Atto commented. "Incredible. Not even the King enjoys such conveniences."

We again heard a pronounced crunching of gravel outside. The footsteps sounded more hurried than before.

"Do you really not wish to go out and see whether the two. . . Well. . . whether there's someone outside."

"Of course I want to," he replied. "First, however, I intend to finish exploring this floor. If we find nothing interesting here, we shall move on to the floor above."

As was easily foreseeable, the chapel too was decorated with dozens and dozens of holy maxims, from the walls to the shutters of the windows. Atto read one at random.

"'*Ieunium arma contra diabolum*', 'Fasting is a weapon against the Devil'. We should remind all those eminences stuffing themselves at the home of Cardinal Spada of that one."

The two remaining rooms were dedicated to the papacy and to France respectively: a little chamber with portraits of all the pontiffs and another with effigies of the kings of France and of Queen Christina of Sweden. Above the two doorways, two inscriptions: "*LITERA*" for the popes, "*ET ARMA*" for the kings.

"To popes the care of the spirit, to kings the defence of the state," explained Atto; "Benedetti was certainly no friend of the temporal power of the Church," he guffawed.

In the little chamber dedicated to France, two splendid tapestries of bucolic scenes hung on the walls, which captured Abbot Melani's attention no less. The first depicted a shepherdess, with a satyr in the background attempting to abduct another one, dragging her by the hair, but failing because the maiden wore hair which was not her own. In the second tapestry, a young man with bow and arrow leaned over a nymph wounded in her side and attired in a wolf's skin, the whole enclosed in a floral frame punctuated with scrolls and medallions in relief.

"There are Corisca and Amarillis, and here is Dorinda wounded: these are two scenes from *The Faithful Shepherd*, the celebrated pastoral tragicomedy by the Cavaliere Guarini which for over a century has enjoyed such success in all the courts of Christendom," he recited with satisfaction. "Admire, my boy, these are without question two of the finest tapestries from the French manufactories. They come from the Faubourg Saint-Germain, admirably woven by the skilled hands of Van der Plancken – or de la Planche, if you prefer," he specified, speaking with all the mannerisms of an expert. "I persuaded Elpidio Benedetti to purchase these when I came from France some thirty years ago."

"They are truly beautiful," I assented.

"Originally, these were part of a set of four but, at my suggestion, Benedetti brought two of them to the Palazzo Colonna as a gift for Maria Mancini, who was then in Rome. Only I knew *how much* she would appreciate them. When I returned to Rome, I found that she had hung them in her bedchamber, just in front of her writing desk. She always loved risk: she kept them for years under her husband's nose and he never noticed a thing!" said he, sniggering.

"The husband did not notice that the tapestries had been hung?" I asked, not having understood.

"No, no, I do not mean that he never discovered them. . . Come, forget it," replied Atto, becoming suddenly evasive.

"I imagine that this *Faithful Shepherd* was one of the favourite readings of la Mancini and the King at the time of their amours," I guessed, trying to understand what Atto had meant to say.

"More or less," he mumbled, drawing suddenly away from the tapestries and pretending to take an interest in a picture of a wooded landscape. "I mean, it was the favourite reading of many at the time. It is a very famous play, as I said to you."

The Abbot seemed reticent, and then aware that I had noticed this.

"I detest gossiping about the love secrets of Maria and His Majesty," he declared in familiar tones, "above all, those they shared when they were alone."

"Alone? Yet you are informed of them," I commented dubiously.

"Yes, I and no one else."

❧

I found it distinctly curious that Melani should be seized now by qualms of conscience: he seemed never to have had any whenever he had complacently revealed to me whole series of secret and intimate episodes in the life of the Most Christian King. On the contrary. . .

I was on the point of replying when I heard the same footsteps yet again. They were drawing near at an alarming pace. They were coming up the stairs. We both turned to the spiral staircase which we had climbed at the far end of the hall.

As stiff as stockfish, both frozen by a fear which neither was willing to admit to the other, we waited with bated breath for the strange presence to manifest itself. The echoes created in the gallery by the footsteps on the marble stairs were so scattered that, without knowing where the staircase was, it would have been impossible to tell which way to turn. The footsteps drew nearer, then very near, so near that one would have sworn that they had reached the level of the gallery. Then they ceased. We both had our gaze fixed on the far end of the gallery. There was no one there.

Then he came. The shadow came between us, enormous, inconceivable. We had been deceived. The being was behind us, almost upon us, on the threshold of the loggia from which one could see the Vatican.

At that instant my mind struggled to understand how he had managed to materialise there behind us in complete silence. Simultaneously, I felt my left shoulder in his grip and knew that I was defenceless.

Transfixed by terror, I turned my head and saw the phantom. It was a small, aquiline, ill-dressed figure. His eyes were sunken, his skin, drawn. It was not necessary for me to lower my gaze to know the rest. The smell was enough: from his neck to his lower belly, his shirt was soaked in blood.

"Buvat!" cried Atto, what are you doing here?"

He did not reply.

"Your. . . your wife," stammered the pale spectre, turning to me. "You must run. . . at once."

He leaned against the wall. Then he slid to the ground and fainted.

Evening the Third
9ᵀᴴ July, 1700

✠

I ran until my chest was bursting. Helped by the now late afternoon and the first evening breezes, I covered the short yet by no means negligible distance between the Vessel and the Villa Spada at a speed which not even the fear of my own death could have given me. "Cloridia, Cloridia," I kept repeating to myself in anguish, "and the little ones? Where can they be?" The whole of the ground to be covered was quite clear in my mind, carved into it by the scalpel of anxiety: I must take the main entrance of the villa, run up the avenue, enter the great house, take a couple of short cuts inside the house, climb to the first floor, run to the apartments of the Princess of Forano. . .

Yet, the moment that I came in sight of the walls of the Villa Spada, I saw that it was going to be very difficult.

In front of the villa, absolute chaos reigned. At that moment, on the esplanade before the main gates, for hours already packed with carriages, retainers, hangers-on and servants, the party of one of the principal guests was making its entry: this was Louis Grimaldi, Prince of Monaco and Ambassador of the Most Christian King of France.

I tried to make my way through to the entrance of the villa, but in vain. From the neighbourhood there had gathered a multitude of peasants and plebeians, hungering for the sight of influential personages. All wanted to gain at least a glance at the eminences, princes and ambassadors invited to the nuptials. The crush had been worsened by the flow of persons entering and leaving the villa, under the eyes of two armed guards. Immediately outside the gates, the crowd was indescribable, the hubbub insufferable; one could see nothing for the dust raised by the horses' hooves; the human tide oozed and swelled, repelled in vain by those (coachmen, footmen, members of the escort) struggling to manoeuvre or to make their way into the villa.

"Make way, make way! I am a servant of the Villa Spada, let me through!" I cried out like a madman, struggling to traverse the heaving mass; but no one heard me.

Just then, a carriage moved backwards. Two women managed somehow to dodge it, screaming in terror. One of them fell on top of me. I fell to the ground and, in my attempt to cling on to something, pulled down another unfortunate with me. He in turn pulled down his neighbour, so that I found myself embedded in a bizarre heap of legs and arms; hardly had I regained my feet than I saw the harmless incident had degenerated into a brawl. Two footmen were flailing wildly in all directions with their staffs. Another two coachmen were pushing one another, one drew a knife; a voice rang out calling for the sergeants. The Prince of Monaco's procession ground to a halt, lurching and creaking like one immense carriage.

Ignoring the altercation, I ran again towards my Cloridia with my heart in my mouth; but the carriages barred my way and there was no way of getting through. I put my head down and plunged into the mêlée, trying to force my way through a forest of legs, boots and clogs. This gained me, first, an elbow in the chest, then a shove from a small boy. Like a ram, I hurled myself headlong, preparing to fight my way through. The boy's great blue eyes stared at me, helpless and shocked. I attacked.

Instead of encountering a soft belly, my forehead met with a surface that enveloped it firmly. It was a hand, enormous and invincible, which grabbed me by the hair and hauled my head up by brute force.

"By all the culverins! What are you doing here, boy? Your wife needs you urgently."

Still holding me by the hair, Sfasciamonti was looking at me in amusement and surprise.

"What has happened to Cloridia?" I screamed.

"To her, nothing. But something good has happened to the Princess of Forano. Now, come."

He raised me up, placing me on his massive shoulders and led me to the gate of the villa. From the height of that mount, I, like some new Hannibal on the back of an elephant, could enjoy a panoramic view of the situation.

The crowd was again becoming noisy and agitated: from his carriage, the Prince of Monaco was throwing money to the people. With

a broad theatrical gesture he would hurl dozens of coins from a little purse, showering the heads of the public with shiny *denari*. His
face betrayed all his pleasure at seeing the plebeians at each others'
throats, fighting over what, for him, was nothing.

"The Prince of Monaco is truly a blustering jackass," murmured
Sfasciamonti as we passed the armed guards at the gates of the villa
and entered the grounds at last. "One may throw money to the populace from the balcony of one's own palace, not in front of someone
else's villa."

"So," I began, at last a trifle calmer, as I dismounted from Sfasciamonti's shoulders, "is Cloridia well? And how are my little daughters?"

"They are all very well. But did not Buvat tell you? The Princess
of Forano has given birth to a fine little boy. While she was assisting
the birth, your wife needed help. She called for the little girls and
in the meantime asked for you. No one knew where you were, then
Cloridia said to look for Abbot Melani. He too was nowhere to be
found, so Buvat offered to help. The first thing that they asked him
to do was to carry out the bloodstained sheets with which he made
his shirt all filthy. Then he became very pale, saying that the sight of
blood made him ill, and off he went to fetch you. By the way, where
the deuce were you?"

ঔৎ৶

At that very moment our eyebrows arched in amazement, when into
the piazza came the procession of the bride, Maria Pulcheria Rocci.
The retinue comprised no fewer than eleven carriages and innumerable others sent by cardinals, ambassadors, princes and the principal
cavaliers of the court of Rome.

The equestrian procession was led by a team of six which, as everyone knows, is called the Vanguard; there followed the first three teams,
that is, carriages, pulling ornamental floats, all of which merit a faithful description (but of which I, owing to my small stature, had only a
partial and limited view).

In the first carriage, immediately applauded, sat the bride. The
body of the carriage was all gilded, with nude figures representing
Autumn and Winter in front and Summer and Spring behind. In the
middle sat the Sun enthroned in majesty, the clear bringer of the said
seasons, at the foot of which two rivers were depicted whose courses

were united in the end, the whole surrounded and embellished by various frolicking cupids.

There followed, as is the custom with noble nuptials, a plain, empty black carriage.

The third carriage, finally, simply upholstered in crimson within and without any retinue, announced with deliberate self-effacement he whose triumph this celebration truly was, the Secretary of State, Cardinal Fabrizio.

From the richness and brave embellishment of the coaches, the Cardinal's generosity was visible for all to see in his gift to his nephew's spouse of so memorable a display of magnificence; but this one could appreciate all the better if one reflected upon the incredible sum which – so the people murmured that evening – that splendid gesture had cost him.

"They speak of twenty thousand scudi," stammered a young lackey, taking advantage of the anonymity to be found in the humble crowd of plebeians, crushed one against the other.

The procession moved into the long avenue leading to the great house, acclaimed by the dense multitude of onlookers lining the route. Arriving at the space before the gracious façade of the great house, it wheeled to the right, passed the orange trees and at last disappeared from my sight behind the plum orchard, wending its way towards the chapel. I made haste. I wanted to embrace my wife again as soon as possible. I raised my eyes to the first-floor window, where I knew that the Princess of Forano had her lodgings, but could descry nothing. I resolved to go up to the noble lady's door: I could surely not dare to knock but perhaps I might be able somehow to approach Cloridia. I imagined her to be rather busy, what with the infant, the care of the mother and the various recommendations that must needs be made. I found the corridor deserted: everyone had gone down to watch the arrival of the bride. I heard my wife's silvery voice through the half-open door.

"Cleophanes, the unworthy son of the excellent Themistocles did not receive his mother's milk and, for the same reason, Xantippos, the son of Pericles; Caligula, son of Germanicus; Commodus, son of Marcus Aurelius; Domitian, son of Vespasian; and Absalom, son of David, whom I ought to have mentioned first, all degenerated. Is it a wonder if Aegisthus was an adulterer? He was suckled by a goat! A wolf gave suck to Romulus, whence came the cruel instinct to inveigh against his brother Remus and to ravish the Sabine women as though they were just so many ewes."

I understood at once. I knew my Cloridia's child-rearing repertoire by heart. Her passion, in the hours that followed every successful confinement, was to wax eloquent concerning the extreme importance of feeding the newborn infant at its mother's breast.

"You will agree with me, Princess, that the bond of filial love arises from having been engendered, but is increased by nursing the child with one's own milk," she explained in gentle, persuasive tones.

La Strozzi uttered not a word.

"Examples of this include Graccus, the valorous Roman," continued Cloridia, "whom they arranged to be met first at the gates of Rome on his return from the wars in Asia, by his mother and his nurse at the same time. Thereupon, he brought forth two gifts which he had taken care to procure during the campaign: a silver ring for his mother and a golden girdle for his nurse. To the mother, who was pained to find herself placed behind the nurse, Graccus replied: "You, mother, made me after bearing me nine months in your womb. But, once born, you banished me from your bosom and from your bed. This nurse received me, fondled me and served me, not for nine months but for three full years."

The Princess remained silent.

"This discourse by a pagan should make us blush," insisted Cloridia, "for being born Christians, we make the most perfect profession of faith, founded upon our belief and acts of charity; and if we are taught to love even our enemies, how much more does our faith teach us to love our children?"

"My dear," responded a tired but determined voice, which I imagined to be that of the Princess, "I have already suffered enough for this little one, and for his three brothers, without exhausting myself even further by giving him my milk."

"Oh, listen to me, I beg of you," insisted my indomitable consort, "if only you were to consider the pleasure of which you are depriving your child in banishing him from his mother's bosom, I do not believe for one moment that you would do this. For little ones, there is no pastime as sweet in the whole wide world; no comedy comparable to those tears of impatience and those sudden movements upon touching the breast, and at last, that joyful laugh when the infant opens its mouth and sinks its nose and its whole face into its mother's warm bosom."

The tender images evoked by my beautiful midwife of a spouse did not, however, seem to move the noblewoman.

"Why should I make such a sacrifice," she replied with a hint of impatience in her voice, "only to receive kicks as soon as he's able to make his first footsteps and later ingratitude and presumption when he has grown to manhood?"

"But this is precisely why children nowadays have so little love for their parents," Cloridia dared hotly to venture. "God so decrees that the lack of love at their beginnings reaps scant love once they have grown up."

"My husband has already hired a wet-nurse a long time ago. He has sent for her and she will soon be here. Now, leave me, I wish to rest," said the Princess, brusquely dismissing her.

When Cloridia emerged, red in the face and with clenched fists, she almost failed to notice me. She went rapidly down the back stairs; I followed her. Once we reached the kitchen, she exploded.

"Ah, the politics of modern childbearing!" she thundered, causing several scullery-maids to turn sharply towards us.

"Cloridia, what has happened?" they asked curiously.

"Oh, nothing! It is just that the ineradicably fertile fashion has sprung up," she moved, accompanying her words with great gestures and grimaces, "that mothers who are not of the common herd squeamishly disdain to give their breast to their own offspring, who've so long annoyed them by weighing down their wombs."

Once they had grasped the argument, the scullery-maids began to laugh heartily. One of them, whom I knew to have a two-year-old daughter, drew one breast out from her blouse and squeezed the milk from it, which sprayed forth, showing that she was still nursing her little one at the breast.

"Does that seem vulgar to you?" she exclaimed, laughing broadly.

"Adieu, little ones, adieu!" raged on Cloridia, seeming almost a prophetess and waving her arms as she paced the kitchen, striving to release her suppressed fury at the Princess of Forano. "Those who bore you can no longer bear you, for you made yourselves too odious with that all-too-tiresome pregnancy; too painful did you prove in that pressing child-bearing. The European infant is thus constrained to begin his life's journey on an unknown poop, when 'tis not a bestial one, and to wander on his peregrinations under a degenerate star, depending upon an alien nutriment. Maternal nature, thus disappointed, not to say abjured, is cast aside and milk flees the paps for fear of some deformity or the tedium of discomfort. Here we find the origin of the discrepancies between offspring and parents. The nobility of filial sentiments degenerates even from the cradle when the feeding's wrong. The spirit's genius is weakened when the body's abandoned to bovine rusticity. With milk, we drink down inclinations, and these will be sordid when their origin is a cowshed!"

It was not the first time that I had witnessed such a scene. The tale was forever repeating itself: whenever Cloridia assisted at the confinement of a noblewoman, the joy of the birth always gave way to her anxiety to use every means to convince the new mother to give the infant her own milk, without having recourse to wet-nurses, or worse, to goats or cows. All to no avail: what for a woman of the people was the most natural thing in the world (among other things, for economic reasons) became an unthinkable and outrageous chore in the eyes of a countess. And my Cloridia, who had herself given suck to our two daughters for the first three years of their lives, suffered from seeing this more than she could say and was ill-resigned to it.

After at last relinquishing her indignation with a sigh of resignation, she turned to me and, with a beautiful smile, embraced me.

"Where had you got to? Hardly had the Princess lost her waters than I sent for the little ones, but I urgently needed help and that poor lad, that Buvat, almost died of fear on seeing blood."

"I know, forgive me, but I have an excellent piece of news," said I, wishing to inform her of the agreement I had reached with Atto concerning the dowry for our little girls.

"Forget it, you will tell me later. Now let us put on our costumes, I would not miss seeing the bride for anything in the world."

We retainers and servants of the Villa Spada had indeed been permitted by the Major-Domo, Don Paschatio Melchiorri, to attend the wedding, but attired in peasants' fine festive costumes specially made up for us. Thus, we would provide a rustic setting for the celebration of the nuptials, in perfect harmony with our rural setting.

I arrived first. Cloridia stayed behind to wait for our two little lasses whom she had allowed to join us for the occasion so that they too would get a brief glimpse of the spouses.

When I arrived at the little chapel, the wedding ceremony had already been underway for quite some time. Don Tibaldutio was about to launch into the homily. They were all gathered together in the sacristy, where the wedding proper traditionally took place, the men behind the bridegroom, the women behind the bride. Don Tibaldutio began:

"We are gathered here, most illustrious and excellent signories, to celebrate a union. And union is the greatest treasure of human life. That, I shall shortly demonstrate to you. Four are the things which preserve the states of the world above all else. The first of these is religion. And, as we can readily observe, where there is no religion, there is no fear of God, and no justice. And where there is no justice, there is no peace. And where there's no peace, there is no union. And where there is no union, there can be no true state. Surely from this we can see how important is religion and a proper fear of Almighty God, upon whom all our actions depend. For such is His divine goodness that He gives us being and wellbeing in this world and, in the next, eternal rest. The second thing in order of importance is justice, whereby the wicked and villainous are punished and the good rewarded. And, by means of justice, the peace is preserved: something most necessary for the preservation of states. The third thing is peace itself, without which states could not endure: for where there is no peace, there is no union. The fourth and last thing, and the most important of all, is therefore union itself, without which religion would be weak, justice perturbed and peace unenforceable. Wherefore, if there's no union in the state, religion will be little practised, justice will sleep and the peace will fall apart."

While the sermon continued, I observed the spouses. From where I stood, I could, however, see very little of the bride's wedding gown and headdress. From time to time, I would cast a glance in the direction of the maidservants among whom I was expecting to see my Cloridia; and very soon she did indeed appear, bringing our two little ones with her. My spouse was lovelier than ever in her hymeneal white, red and gold peasant's costume. Nor were my daughters less lovely: they were both perfectly attired in costumes specially sewn for them by their mother: the elder in a reversible yellow gown with sleeves of pink damask embroidered with false gold thread, and the little one with a flesh-coloured *mocaiale* garnished with dark blue trimmings. In their hands they held little twigs covered in white flowers which were to be joyfully waved at the end of the ceremony by them and the other female servants of the Villa Spada in the retinue of the bride.

"Where there is no union," declared the chaplain, fervently, "there reigns enmity, the cause of all ruination in the world, as I shall now prove with the authority of ancient history. The first enmity that ever was took place in heaven between the Greatest Good and Lucifer; the second, between Adam and the serpent; the third, between Cain and Abel; the fourth, between Joseph and his brothers; the fifth, between Pompey and Caesar; the sixth between Alexander and Darius; the seventh, between Mark Antony and Caesar Augustus: all of which examples of enmity were the cause of the most dreadful ruin. Union is therefore the greatest fortress and treasure of human life, and preserves all the world's states. But, how is this union to be attained? The philosopher opined that husband and wife must correspond to one another in body, in other words that they must experience a mutual physical attraction; and that produces infinite and most beautiful effects. It is also, however, true that there must be correspondence between souls, whereupon the most excellent fruits will be produced."

I noticed of a sudden that Cloridia and her friends were chattering most intensely among themselves and, with their hands before their mouths, struggling hard to restrain their laughter. I was able to understand the cause of this a little later, when the bride turned briefly in my direction and I was able momentarily to catch sight of her features: Maria Pulcheria Rocci was, despite her name, hardly a model of pulchritude; to be more precise, she was indeed rather ugly.

"It was not by chance that the ancients were accustomed to light five lamps when celebrating nuptials," continued the chaplain, "as they held it for certain that the figure three, an uneven number, symbolised the spiritual form, and even numbers, like two, the material. Matrimony must, in short, involve a congruous connubial blending of form and matter, in which man, a being spiritual and active, and woman, who is passive and material, can be recognised. Indeed, the ancients, when conducting ceremonies matrimonial, would traditionally make the man touch fire and the woman, water, signifying that fire illumines and water receives the light; but also that fire by its nature purges and water cleanses, so that from this custom we may also infer something more, namely that matrimony must be clear, pure, chaste and celebrated between similar beings."

Olive pockmarked skin, lips so fine as to seem non-existent, cheeks swollen and pallid, a low forehead, small lustreless eyes: all these things gave Maria Pulcheria Rocci the profile and colouring of a turbot.

Don Tibaldutio's reference to mutual physical attraction could hardly have been less opportune, I thought with some mirth; but the laughter died in my throat when an inner voice reminded me that I, with my stature, could hardly be accounted an Adonis. . .

My vague gaze wandered towards Cloridia. For a long time I dwelt on her lovely image: skin with the sweetness of violets; sacred, gently smiling spouse and mother. Yet, she had chosen me, and had chosen freely. The same could hardly be said of the bridegroom, Clemente Spada: the reasons which had led him at last to wed the unlovely Rocci maiden must have been founded upon considerations far more prosaic than those which had first so adventurously and tenderly united Cloridia and myself.

"Matrimony must be approached with love," Don Tibaldutio warned at last, becoming aware of some yawning among the illustrious congregation, "nor must the laws and customs ordered by our Holy Mother the Catholic Christian Church in any way be contravened. Marriage must be held indissoluble and conserved with faith, as a sacrament. Above all, the use of matrimony must be to procreate and to avoid the sin of incontinence. Whosoever has any other view thereof does not deserve to be accounted a Christian."

After the long sermon with which the chaplain greeted the spouses, the nuptial rite was at last celebrated.

"The ring on the finger, the necklace on the bosom, the crown on the head," Don Tibaldutio recited solemnly, while some maids of honour placed the three objects on the spouses' bench for the blessing. "The ring denotes the purity of the act, just as giving one's hand bears witness to the limpidity of the spouse's faith. The necklace manifests sincerity of heart; and the crown, clarity of mind, for in the head dwells the perspicacity of the intellect."

It was then, during Don Tibaldutio's blessing that I saw him: resplendent and coruscating among the two-headed eagles of the imperial banners, attired rigorously in the Spanish style as a mark of his fidelity to the House of Habsburg, the Count von Lamberg, Imperial Ambassador to the pontifical court, was following the ceremony with severe faith and the profile of a sphinx. I sought Atto with my eyes and at once I found him: his forehead showing pearls of perspiration, a face covered with an over-generous coating of ceruse and cheeks shining with carmine red, beribboned *ad absurdum* with tassels and fringes of yellow and red (his favourite colours). Abbot Melani's tense, inquisitive gaze did not leave von Lamberg for one moment. The Ambassador, meanwhile, far more severely adorned in lead-coloured brocade with rigid silver lace trimmings, showed no sign of being aware of the spasmodic attention focused upon his person and stared indifferently in the direction of the chaplain. My mind moved to those mysterious deaths at the Spanish court and the suspicion of poisoning that hung over his party and to Maria Mancini's fears for Atto's life. The Abbot had written of his intention to confront the Ambassador face to face. Would von Lamberg grant him an audience?

❧

Dismissed with the swarm of other retainers at the end of the nuptial ceremony, I saw my consort coming towards me with our two little girls skipping around her, like Diana surrounded by her nymphs. With their flowering branches they had been part of the festive procession that accompanied the bride towards her new married life and they were still overexcited by the honour bestowed upon them. The orchestra accompanied the exodus of guests with a sublime melodic paean by Maestro Corelli, a most sweet counterpart to Don Tibaldutio's homily.

Cloridia, who had to go and take a look at the Princess of Forano's infant, left me the task of feeding our two little ones in the villa's kitchens, after which I was to accompany them home and put them to bed. I snatched a few moments of her time to show her Melani's written promise. Her eyes opened wide.

"If I did not see it here, in black and white, I could never believe it," she exclaimed, whereupon she jumped for joy, embracing and kissing me.

But time was short. Before rushing off, Cloridia passed me a snippet of information, overheard during the celebrations by her usual faithful informers among the maidservants.

"This evening, Cardinal Albani too will be coming to dinner, if that interests you," said she with a wink as she ran on her way.

Albani. Atto and I had searched for him in vain at the Vessel; and now he was coming to us.

❧

"'Tis said that Cardinal Bonvisi is not in the best of health," chimed in old Cardinal Colloredo who, in his capacity as Grand Penitentiary, or Confessor to the Cardinals, was always well informed about everything.

The nuptial banquet was already at its height when, after evening's shadows had fallen, I was called by Don Paschatio, the Major-Domo, once more to hold one of the torches lighting the table, in the place of one of the lackeys who was feeling unwell. After donning my janissary's costume, I arrived at the sumptuous dinner grasping the torch. The spouses with their respective families and Cardinal Spada, the tutelary deity of the festivities, were prudently seated at a separate table. For the master of the house, this measure, which was, moreover, traditional, fulfilled two purposes: to honour the bride's family and to avoid becoming embroiled in political conversations that might give rise to dissension; although unavoidable at a gathering which brought together no fewer than eighteen cardinals, such talk would have been out of place coming from the mouth of the Pontifical Secretary of State.

All around us, on serving tables lit up by yet more great three- and four-branched candelabra, were set shining silver goblets for beverages, crystal carafes, bowls for washing hands, salt cellars, trenchers, jugs, chalices and salvers, great beakers, chargers heaped up with prune jelly, chunks of black umber, huge mullet with raspberries cut into roundels, all sparkling and reflecting silver and golden light. Then came a table loaded with fish, another with all manner of fowls of the air, yet another with good fresh green vegetables, and a last one with fruit and candies which were all a pleasure for the eyes, that being, indeed, their sole purpose, for I knew that the dishes destined to be eaten were different and even more succulent than that rich display of God's bounty.

Upon hearing the bad news of Cardinal Bonvisi's indisposition, all shook their heads, affecting to be afflicted thereby.

"Yes, 'tis true, he is not very well. He himself wrote telling me that last week," Abbot Melani broke in, thus declaring his friendship for Bonvisi, who went so far as to confide his personal news to him.

"But I am counting upon his swift recovery, so that. . . because I care for his health," said Colloredo, for an instant betraying the hope that Bonvisi would be well enough to take part in the conclave which all knew to be approaching.

Colloredo was not to know that Bonvisi would die within a few weeks, on 25th August, and that he himself would not survive more than two years. In a flash of clairvoyance, he added with absorbed thoughtful expression: "On 13th June, Cardinal Maidalchini left us, and on 3rd March, Casanate."

An icy breeze ran down the backs of many cardinals present, no few of whom were advanced in years.

In the meantime, the second part of the fourth course had been served. In an effort to restore the palate and prepare it for further exercises in gluttony, a sherbet of blackcurrants and redcurrants had been served, together with slices of lemon. Then came the fried trout accompanied by sweetmeats from Parona and filled with sour cherries in syrup and citrus juice; pastries stuffed with sturgeon and *foie gras*; asparagus tips, capers, prunes, sour grapes, boiled egg yolks, lemon juice, flour and butter, borne to table under a perforated silver dome and sprinkled with sugar; turtles in pottage, cooked in their shells after their heads had been cut off (boiled thus, very little spices are needed), with toasted almonds, more *foie gras*, sweet-smelling herbs, muscatel wine and crumbled spiced cake, decorated with serpent-shaped tortiglioni sweetmeats from Orvieto, all served under a cover with a generous sprinkling of sugar and many stuffed half-eggs.

"Your Excellency should not turn his thoughts to such sad things on an occasion as gay as this magnificent wedding," said Cardinal Moriggia, whom Caesar Augustus had on the first evening called a boor. "It suffices, moreover, to remember the virtues of those who have passed away; there is no need to learn by heart the dates when they died."

"I would not have done so," replied Colloredo, "but, you know, when the question of the 19th arose. . ."

No one dared open their mouth at that juncture; everyone knew what he was talking about, even I, having read it in the court notices among Atto's papers. It had happened the year before that three cardinals had passed away at an exact interval of one month after one another: Giovanni Delfino, Patriarch of Aquileia, on 19th July; Cardinal Aguirre on 19th August and Cardinal Fernández de Córdoba, Grand Inquisitor of Spain, on 19th September. Obviously, until the 19th October, every cardinal in Europe lived in terror of a possible prolongation of the series, this time affecting him. Fortunately, however, no

such thing had transpired and the next to depart had been Cardinal
Pallavicino who had broken that unlucky sequence by departing this
life on the 11th February. The Sacred College had given a great sigh
of relief.

"Dear Delfino, as far as I knew him as a man and as a cardinal,
would have made an excellent pontiff," said Atto, pronouncing the
name which was in all minds and thus revealing another of his intimate
acquaintances among the wearers of the purple. "'Tis a pity that,
through someone's excess of zeal, matters should have gone otherwise."

The atmosphere became heavy.

"There exist certain o-ver-zeal-ous individuals, ever ready to give
counsel, even to complete strangers, so long as they can cast mud at
respectable persons," he added carelessly.

From heavy, the air became leaden. The word "zealous" which Atto
had so heavily emphasised, was a reference to the party of Cardinal
Zelanti, called the "Zealots" because they preached the independence
of the Sacred College from the influence of foreign powers. To this
party, both Colloredo and Negroni belonged.

As I knew from my instructive reading of Abbot Melani's court
notices, at the previous conclave, nine years before, Cardinal Delfino,
Atto's friend and the candidate favoured by all the crowns, was on the
point of being elected pope. The Zealots then, being unable to stomach the foreign powers making their own pope, had resorted to the
worst possible stratagems in order to destroy that candidacy. As Atto
had allusively mentioned, Colloredo had written to the Sun King's
confessor, Père Lachaise (to whom the Cardinal had never written
before) in order to canvass for the candidature of Cardinal Barbarigo,
another Zealot.

Negroni had then spread the rumour that Delfino had in his youth
even killed a man with a poker; which he had indeed done, but only
to defend himself from a thief who had broken into his house and
was attacking him with a dagger. In the end, malign tongues had
prevailed, and, in the place of Cardinal Delfino, the election went
to Cardinal Pignatelli, the Pope whose imminent death was now expected.

"The fact, however, remains that our present Pontiff Innocent
XII is a saintly, good and wise pope," said Cardinal Negroni, meaning, for those who were familiar with what had taken place behind

the scenes, that the sabotage at Delfino's expense had not done any great harm; Atto said nothing.

"This is, moreover, proven by the *Romanum decet Pontificem*," added Negroni, referring to the constitution whereby Innocent XII had, soon after his election, forbidden the relatives of popes from enriching themselves at the expense of the Church. "And I know not how many would have had the courage to do what he did."

This was yet another allusion to Delfino: in order to prevent his election, the Zealots had it cried out on the rooftops that he had a mass of nephews and intended to enrich them all from the coffers of the Vatican.

The wedding table had fallen silent. Nothing could be heard except the sound of jaws patiently chewing the "English" pie of grilled mullet in *salsa bastarda*, with little sweetmeats and prune jelly, garnished with lemon slices and candied cinnamon sticks. Decidedly, the Curia's disputes had gained the better of the wedding.

The tensions created by that skirmish, however subtly it had been conducted, had been almost contagiously transmitted to us torch-bearers too; now I was perspiring even more copiously. None dared interrupt the venomous verbal duel between Atto and Negroni.

"Oh, what you say is ungenerous towards the previous pontiff," replied Atto with a little smirk. "If Prince Odescalchi were here to-night, I know not what he would have to say about your words. He, the nephew of Pope Innocent XI, who reigned before the present pontiff and Alexander VIII, was never made a cardinal, because his uncle did not wish to be accused of favouring his kinsmen."

"And what of it?" asked Negroni.

"How can one put it, Excellency? So many things are bruited abroad – clearly all malicious gossip. It is said that Prince Odescalchi lends money to the Emperor who loses incredible sums gaming, as though it were a mere trifle, and that he offered eight million florins to the Poles to be elected king, as though that were a title to be sold to the highest bidder; and, moreover, that he paid some four hundred and forty thousand Roman scudi to purchase the fiefs of the Orsini. . . He, the nephew of a pope who fought against nepotism. . ."

"I repeat: what of it?"

"All this goes to show that, at least in the eyes of the public, it was precisely when an end was put to nepotism that popes' nephews really began to make their fortunes."

The hum of disapproval grew louder; Atto was casting aspersions on Prince Odescalchi, whom some ailment had kept to his house (he was said to be a hypochondriac), but to whom all these words would surely be reported, together with the disrespect for the present Pope who had even officially done away with nepotism: a policy that in fact pleased no one (for all hope one day to be able to take advantage of the world's injustices), although for the sake of appearances they all feigned blind approval.

"It is not my intention to offend His Holiness, heaven forbid!" continued Abbot Melani. "I am thus debating only in order to amuse the august intellects amongst whom I have the quite undeserved honour to find myself this evening. Well, Cardinal Aldobrandini, who was the nephew of Clement VIII, or Cardinal Francesco Barberini, who was the nephew of Urban VIII, and so many other examples one could cite, never lingered among the delights of Rome when it came to going forth to defend the interests of the Church, even volunteering to fight alongside armies in distant lands. Well, I ask myself: can we really say the same thing of. . .

"Enough, now, Abbot Melani, this is too much."

The speaker was Cardinal Albani. The company was not only amazed by the peremptory tone with which he had silenced Atto. As I had read in the Abbot's piquant court notices, it was Albani who had materially drafted the bull *Romanum decet pontificem* against nepotism, which had just been mentioned by Cardinal Negroni and, acting together with the master of the house, Cardinal Spada, he was also one of the cardinals who maintained contacts at the highest level between the Holy See and France. What was more, he was regarded as one of the most influential members of the entire Sacred College. He had studied, outshining the best, with the Jesuits of the Collegium Romanum, where the celebrated Hellenist and Hebrew scholar Pierre Poussines had soon noted his gifts for the study of Latin and Greek. While still a young student he had taken on the Latin translation of a homily by Saint Sophronius, Patriarch of Jerusalem, astounding all by his precocity. At the same time, he had discovered in a monastery the manuscript of the second part of the Byzantine Greek *Menologion* of Basil Porphyrogenitus, the loss of which had long been lamented. Continuing the same display of erudition, he had translated the eulogy of Saint Mark the Evangelist by Deacon Procopius which was inscribed by the Bollandist Fathers in the *Acta Santorum.*

In other words, since his earliest youth Albani had shown himself to be the possessor of a most refined and erudite mind, perhaps already presaging future, glorious achievements.

After obtaining his degree in Jurisprudence at Urbino, a lightning career had seen him become, first, governor of Rieti and Viterbo, then, under the two last popes, Secretary for Breves (or confidential correspondence): a most delicate task, reserved for the most penetrating intellects. Among the most important matters entrusted to him were a considerable proportion of relations with France; and this had soon caused him to be accused of being a Francophile. Not without cause: the year before, in 1699, many had clamoured for a bull condemning the French Abbé Fénelon, who was suspected of heresy. Albani had responded by bringing about the breve *Cum Alias*, in which twenty-three propositions contained in Fénelon's book were condemned, but the word "heresy" was never mentioned. Not only that, but he had hastened to write a letter to Fénelon to instruct him about the ways and means of arranging an appropriate submission, which was so swiftly done as even to obtain the Pope's written praises.

Even if he was far too young to be made pope (he was at the time of the facts I am narrating only just fifty-one years old), Cardinal Albani had been one of the most important collaborators of the three last pontiffs, an influential mediator with France and the actual author of some of the most important doctrinal and policy measures. One peculiarity should be noted: although a cardinal, he was not a priest. He had in fact never yet received the major orders. Such a omission was, however, not unusual among the wearers of the purple, who often arranged for the necessary formalities when a conclave was imminent, so as not to lose (one never knows!) the possibility of being elected to the papal throne. Atto had, in other words, caused a very important personage to lose patience with him, and, what was more, one with the closest links to Cardinal Spada, his host.

"Eminence, I bow down to whatever you may say," said Melani complacently.

"Come now," retorted Albani with a grimace of annoyance, "I am not asking you to bow down. I simply wonder whether you are aware of what you are saying."

"Eminence, from now on I shall in truth say nothing more."

"You cited names and facts. Now, I ask you, have you ever stopped to consider that you are the guest of a Cardinal Secretary of State?"

"In truth, I am honoured."

"Good. And have you ever considered that instead of a Secretary of State, the popes before Innocent XI had a Cardinal-Nephew, who performed the same duties and whom they appointed acting on their personal prerogative, only because he was a kinsman?"

"Really, that has even been done since, at least by Alexander VIII, I'd say."

"Yes, agreed; I meant only to say," Albani admitted somewhat reluctantly, realising that he had made a mistake, "that Pope Innocent XI of happy memory, by whom I had the honour to be appointed Referendary for the Two Signatures, undertook this just reform whereby under the present Pope we may say that not only is there no Cardinal-Nephew but not even a nephew made cardinal."

Moriggia, Durazzo, Negroni and the others laughed, thus backing Albani and forcing Atto into a corner. Indeed His Holiness Innocent XII, the present Pope, had not made any of his nephews a cardinal.

"That will have been destiny; indeed, predestination," replied Atto, biting into a mouthful of sour grape pie with a scattering of Savoy biscuits and candied sugar.

There was a moment's silence, then Albani exploded.

"Do you know what I cannot bear, Abbot Melani? That persons like you, out of Francophile partisanship, should spoil the pleasures of the table, which is something far more noble, for all these eminences and all these princes and gentlemen. To accuse Holy Mother Church of not seeing and not understanding is as absurd as to claim that the King of France is all-seeing and all-powerful!"

Albani may have been regarded as a Francophile, said I to myself, perplexed; but the way in which the Cardinal had rammed Atto's discourse back down his throat seemed utterly at odds with that view.

Atto listened calmly, without losing his composure, patiently slicing the pie in his plate with his fork. I, however, was struggling to prevent my eyes from squinting and thus losing the immobile and pigeon-chested pose required of a torchbearer. The Steward was speechless. Never could he have imagined that, faced with all the delicacies with which he had laden the table, the eminences, instead of dedicating themselves to gluttony, body and soul, should have ended up by arguing. Don Paschatio, half-hidden behind one of the little columns supporting the canopy, was simply terrified. It was the first time in his life that he had had the honour of receiving so many cardinals at table, but all the pleasure had been destroyed by Albani's sudden outburst: a display so unusual among the wearers of the purple as to make the Major-Domo fear he might soon leave, overturning his chair and cursing Villa Spada and all who in it dwelled.

"Come, come, Excellency. . ." murmured Count Vidaschi, trying to calm him.

"Indeed, these French. . ." I heard the Prince Borghese murmur.

"Ah, they're too used to making popes from Paris," replied Baron Scarlatti.

Atto's sally had been somewhat daring. When he spoke of "predestination", he had been referring to a little tome published four years previously, entitled *Nodus praedestinationis*, the author of which was the late Cardinal Sfondrati and for which Albani had written the preface. Now, Albani was quite erudite, but not in all matters doctrinal, and he had not realised that this book touched on a number of somewhat delicate theological questions, in ways that were not always orthodox. Augustinian and Jansenist circles had called for the book's immediate condemnation by the Holy Office. Then the matter had blown over, but both Pope Innocent XII and Albani had emerged from the affair with no little embarrassment. This was the one and only serious stain on the otherwise immaculate career of Cardinal Albani.

Atto's malign barb drew my attention even more to his strange behaviour that evening. At the previous dinner, he had said practically nothing. How come that he had now yielded to the temptation not only to join in the conversation but to annoy the guests? How dared he permit himself to provoke so impudently a friend and close collaborator of the master of the house? What was more, had not Atto overplayed his French background quite outrageously? Everyone knew, of course, that he was an agent in the service of the Most Christian King; but to make such a display of his partisanship (thus calling down upon himself an open denunciation by Albani) had really been most unwise. At this rate, no one would ever be able to approach him without attracting unwelcome attention. Anyone who talked openly with Melani risked being taken for an open seconder of the French King's ambitions.

Albani had at last calmed down. Not content with the effect he had produced, Atto began speaking yet again.

"Your Excellency is too subtle of understanding not to pardon me if I commit some errors, and too great-hearted not to be indulgent if I briefly recall how Pope Alexander VIII, as I was on the point of saying a few moments ago, had two nephews who were both Secretaries of State: Cardinal Rubini, who formally held the post, and Cardinal Ottoboni, who exercised it de facto. And yet it was he who pronounced those famous words: 'Take heed, for the eleventh hour has sounded.' By this he meant that matters could not go on like this much longer. And he was pope just before the present one! So, you see that. . ."

"Come, Abbot Melani, do you really want to make these excellencies angry?" Don Giovanni Battista Pamphili interrupted him; having plenty of famous cases of nepotism in his own family and being of a gay and amiable disposition, he easily succeeded in changing the tone and the direction of the conversation. "'Tis true we're in a Jubilee Year, and so must recognise our sins, but our own, not those of others!"

Laughter from those nearby at table thus succeeded in undoing the frowns of a few Zealot cardinals and silencing Atto's unwelcome incitement.

"The Prince of Monaco, the new Ambassador of the Most Christian King of France, made a most dignified entry to the Quirinale a few days ago to salute the Holy Father with a sumptuous, noble and rich equipage, served by an infinite number of prelates and the nobility," broke in Monsignor D'Aste, in an attempt to take part in Pamphili's diversion.

Someone must, however, have counselled him with a kick under the table to avoid at all costs mentioning the word "France", for a brief grimace of pain crossed his face and he fell silent at once without waiting for any answer from his neighbours.

"Monsignor Straccetto will never understand *what* and *when*," commented Prince Borghese *sottovoce* in the ear of Baron Scarlatti.

The Steward, all agitated and bathed in perspiration, ordered that other wines were to be served at once, to create a little movement and distract the table.

"On Tuesday, the Reverend Father of the Dominicans went in procession to visit the new Padre General of the Franciscans," said Durazzo.

"Yes, that I heard," replied Negroni. "He climbed right to the top of the Ara Coeli Steps with the cross on his shoulders. Heaven knows how fatiguing that must have been. And, speaking of news, I have heard that His Holiness's Privy Chamberlain has left bearing the Most Eminent Monsignor de Noailles his new cardinal's hat, which he is taking all the way to. . ."

". . . Yes, of course, and now they're choosing who is to bring it to the new Cardinals Lamberg and Borgia," said Durazzo, just succeeding in preventing Negroni from mentioning Paris, where the new Cardinal de Noailles was indeed awaiting his hat.

At that juncture, as the end of the nuptial banquet approached, all eyes turned towards the spouses' table: Cardinal Spada had risen, glass in hand, to salute the providential chairborne arrival of the Princess of Forano, the *deus ex machina* who thus brought the whole embarrassing dispute to a close.

La Strozzi remained seated in her conveyance; although visibly put to the test by her confinement, she had not been willing to forgo the opportunity to embrace the bride who, as Cloridia had mentioned to me, was a good friend of hers.

The child was not there. Needless to say, the Princess had already dumped him upon the wet-nurse. He would soon be arriving with his father. Cardinal Fabrizio greeted the Princess with a toast and a speech.

"Aristotle was mistaken when he said that woman is weak," he began in a facetious tone. "While 'tis true that the females of rapacious animals such as leopards, panthers, bears, lions and the like, are stronger and more robust than the males, I would make another point: namely that women's ways are idle and delightful, and that each of these things is enough to unnerve a Hercules or an Atlas."

Everyone laughed at the sharpness and piquancy of the Secretary of State's observation.

"Nor do I agree with Aristotle when he calls woman 'a monster' or 'an accidental animal'. Here, the great man was raving, perhaps because he was angry with his own good wife."

The renewed outburst of laughter had the effect of clearing the air and cheering souls; the tension caused by Abbot Melani had now completely vanished.

"But above all," continued the master of the house in flattering tones, "a woman like the Princess here present may certainly be said to be strong and not weak, and worthy to stand beside Lasthenia of Mantinea and Axiothea of Phlius, Plato's disciples. And while the examples of Panthasilea and Camilla are reputed favourable, those of Zenobia and Fulvia, Antony's wife, to whom Cassius Dio refers in his account of the reign of Augustus, are most true and historical. Likewise most certain is the history of the Amazons' valour and of their empire. And he who knows not of the Sibyls knows nothing. I can surely place these women beside our newly delivered Princess, so that all together, after the Most Holy Madonna, they may be upheld as models of virtue and wisdom for the bride who now sits here before us."

These words were greeted with a round of applause and a toast to wish Maria Pulcheria Rocci every good fortune: as a bride and not a mother, she was in fact less important than the new mother; besides which, the poor thing, with her seaweed-coloured turbot's countenance, was certainly not one to inspire high-flown epithalamia.

"And what should be said of Aspasia, who taught Pericles and Socrates?" the speech continued, "or of the most learned Areta, remembered by Boccaccio? Was she not simultaneously both mother and philosopher? So well did she raise her offspring that she wrote a most useful book on how to instil manners in children, and another, for the use of the children themselves, on the vanity of youth; at the same time, for thirty-five years she taught natural philosophy, having a hundred philosophers for disciples, as well as composing the most erudite works: on the wars of Athens, on the power of tyrants, on Socrates' Republic, on the unhappiness of women, on the vanity of funerary rites, on bees and on the prudence of ants."

Meanwhile, the fifth course was served, usually consisting entirely of fruit. Although I had already eaten, I could not remain indifferent to the dishes of *tartufali tartufolati* – truffles in a truffle sauce served on crusts of toasted bread with half-lemons, or to the dishes making up an imperial feast of ravioli with butter, cauliflowers, *tartuffolo* sea urchins, egg yolks, with juice of lemon and cinnamon. Nor were the other poor torchbearers unmoved by such delicacies, yet they must like Tantalus stand by and listen powerlessly to the motions of the great lords and ladies' jaws and palates. Then came the fried Ascoli olives, the Florentine *marzolino* cheeses and the Spanish olives.

"But was this not to be the fruit course?" Baron Scarlatti discreetly asked the Prince Borghese.

"The fruit is there," replied the other. "Namely, the truffles on toast and in the imperial feast, the citrus cubes inside the fried olives and the orange flowers garnishing the fresh olives."

"Ah, I see," replied Scarlatti laconically, yet remaining unconvinced that subterranean truffles could be described as fresh fruit.

Then, to refresh the palate, bowls of iced pistachios were brought to the table, together with ground pistachios, pistachios in their shells, pistachio cakes, peach pies *alla Senese*, candied lettuce stalks and, in honour of Cardinal Durazzo, who came of a noble Genoese family, bowls of candied Genoese pears, together with prunes and candied Adam's apples, citrons and medlars, all from Genoa.

At that moment the Princess of Forano's newborn babe arrived, well swaddled in his father's arms.

"*Minor mundus*," said Cardinal Spada, greeting him with the name "world in miniature" accorded to man by the ancients for the perfection of his composition. Spada blessed the child and prayed that this might be a sign most auspicious.

"May you augur a prolific future for our beloved bride and groom today!" he concluded.

There was yet another toast; the various members of the couple's families then stood up one after another and, turning to the happy pair, they eulogised, magnified, augured, remembered and exhorted as is the custom at such banquets.

࿇

The ever-generous mantle of darkness had already fallen some two hours earlier when Sfasciamonti arrived with three saddled horses. All the guests, having been regaled with the utmost sumptuousness, had by now all retired to their beds.

As agreed, Atto and I waited in a sheltered corner not far from the Villa Spada. Buvat, who had tippled somewhat too freely at the nuptial banquet, had likewise abandoned himself to the arms of Morpheus and was snoring in his little room.

"Where are we going?" I asked, while the catchpoll helped, first Atto, then me, to mount.

"Near to the Rotonda," he replied.

Sfasciamonti, as he himself had explained that morning, had received information that should enable us to find two *cerretani*. These were small fry, but it was already a great deal to lay hands on a sure pair like these. As for their names, they were known as Il Roscio and Il Marcio: Red and Rotten. Such were the colourful nicknames by which the pair whom we were stalking were known in the Roman underworld.

We moved swiftly and silently towards the Tiber and thence to the city centre. As on the night before, we crossed the river by passing through the island of San Bartolomeo.

As intended, we dismounted a short distance from the Piazza della Rotonda. We found waiting for us there a little man who was kind enough to hold the reins of our horses as we clambered down from them. He was a friend of Sfasciamonti's and would look after our mounts for as long as was necessary.

We moved to a dark corner of the piazza where a number of carts for the transport of goods were stationed, secured to one another with a heavy iron chain. These probably belonged to the poor pedlars working at the market held by day at the Rotonda. It was a *cul de sac* in which darkness, the fetid odour of rats and damp mildew were omnipresent. Atto and I exchanged a worried look: this looked like the ideal place for an ambush. Sfasciamonti, however, surprised us, moving directly into action.

He handed me the lamp which we had been carrying with us, which somewhat faintly lit the scene. He looked under the carts and shook his head in disappointment. Then he stopped next to one of the carts and leaned on it with both hands. Swinging one leg back, he then launched a great kick into the darkness beneath the cart.

We heard a raucous howl in which anger and surprise were mixed in equal measure.

"Ah, here we are," said the catchpoll with the absent-minded ease of someone looking for a pen in a drawer.

"In the name of the Governor of Rome, Monsignor Ranuzio Pallavicini, come out from there, you miserable dog," he enjoined.

As nothing was happening, he leaned under the cart, reached out with one hand and tugged hard. A hoarse growl of protest was heard, which ended when Sfasciamonti hauled out a human figure without so much as a by-your-leave. It was an emaciated old man dressed in rags with a long yellowish beard under his chin and hair as thin and stubbly as a bunch of spinach. Other details I was for the time being unable to descry owing to the semi-darkness, which could not however conceal one detail: the stench of putrefying filth that arose from the poor old man after years of living in extreme want.

"I have done nothing, nothing!" he protested, struggling not to let go of an old blanket which he had dragged with him and under which he had probably been sleeping until our arrival.

"What a stink," was Sfasciamonti's only comment as he stood the wretch on his feet like an unfortunate marionette, trembling with somnolence and fear.

The catchpoll grasped the old man's right arm and brought his hand up to his chest. He opened it and passed his fingers over it a few times as though to feel the skin. After this bizarre examination, he announced: "All right, you're clean."

Then, without even giving him the time to complain, he seated him on the cart, this time less roughly, but holding tightly onto his arm.

"Do you see these gentlemen?" said he, pointing to us. "They are persons who have no time to waste. Sometimes, two *cerretani* sleep here – here, just next to you. I am sure that you know something about them."

The old man said nothing.

"The gentlemen would like to speak with someone from among the *cerretani*."

The old man lowered his eyes and remained silent.

"I am a sergeant. If I want, I can break your arm, lock you in a cell and throw away the key," warned Sfasciamonti.

The old man still kept silent. Then he scratched his head, as though he had just been thinking.

"Il Roscio and Il Marcio?" he asked at last.

"And who else?"

"They come here only from time to time, when they have business to see to. But I don't know what they get up to, no, I know nothing of what they do."

"But you have only to tell me where they are tonight," insisted Sfasciamonti, gripping the other's arm more tightly.

"I do not know. They keep changing."

"I'll break your arm."

"Try at Termine."

❧

Sfasciamonti let go at last of the poor man's arm and the fellow hastened to lay his foul blanket under the cart and return to his wretched sleeping place.

As we moved on horseback to our new goal, the catchpoll explained a few details.

"In summer, many sleep out in that place which we have just left. If their hands are calloused, they are mendicants: people who have worked and fallen on hard times. If there are no calluses, then they're *cerretani* and have never earned a penny from work."

"So that's why you felt the old man's palm," I deduced.

"Of course, the *cerretani* like to live a life of ease, by cheating and robbing. Now let us go to Termine and see whether we have better luck there. I have known the names of the pair we seek for quite a while now and I simply cannot wait to get my hands on them."

As he said these words, I saw him try to contain his excitement by rolling up his sleeves. He was preparing for the challenge of encountering the two scoundrels and, even more, that of facing up to his secret fear of the *cerretani* which was, with every passing day, growing more corrosive and insistent.

Finding Il Marcio and Il Roscio called for an improbable degree of luck. The indication provided by the old man could not have been vaguer: Termine, the enormous space where the agricultural produce from the Agro Romano – the plain surrounding the city – was delivered and stored, and which lay just behind the Baths of Diocletian, was by night as deserted as it was vast. We left the Piazza della Rotonda behind us, moving towards Piazza Colonna, whence we proceeded to the Trevi Fountain and Monte Cavallo. From there, we came to the Four Fountains and crossed the Via Felice, entering Via di Porta Pia which brought us right next to Termine.

Our ride was uneventful, apart from a couple of encounters with the night watch in the vicinity of the papal palace of Monte Cavallo. Sfasciamonti presented his credentials and we were duly permitted to go on our way.

The silence was broken only once, when we drew level with the church of San Carlino, by a question from Atto:

"'Teeyooteelai': was that not what the *cerretano* said to you?"

"Yes, Signor Atto, why?"

"Oh, nothing, nothing."

On reaching our destination, as expected, the panorama of Termine gave no cause for optimism.

When we turned to the right from Via di Porta Pia, there before us loomed the enormous pile of the Apostolic Chamber's granaries, the great building in which the grain destined for bread production was stored. The warehouses on which the survival of the Roman population depended were in the form of a great S which, for almost half its length, adjoined the colossal bulk of the Baths of Diocletian. The ruins of the baths, eroded both by the elements and by human greed, dominated all of the second half of the Piazza di Termine. Within the ancient thermal complex, removing from their pagan origins what had once been refreshing pools and steam baths, there now stood the church of Santa Maria degli Angeli. Behind this church, whose rustic and irregular façade had, in the most unusual manner, been built from the outer wall of the baths, stretched the bulky mass of the Roman ruins. To the right, one could just descry in the dark the outer wall of the Villa Peretti Montalto, the immense estate, consisting of vineyards, gardens and manors built with such splendour by the late Pope Sixtus V and, a few years ago, on the passing away of his family, bequeathed to the Princes Savelli. Finally, behind those looking towards the granaries, stood a wall behind which was situated the vegetable garden of the monks of Saint Bernard.

No presence, whether human or otherwise, accompanied our arrival. Apart from the colossal shadows of the baths and granaries and the chirping of the cicadas: nothing. The summer night's air was enlivened by the sweet, pungent odour of wheat.

"What now?" I asked, marvelling at the desolation stretching before my eyes.

Atto said nothing. He seemed to be thinking of something else.

"I have a place in mind," said Sfasciamonti, "and I think it is the right one."

We advanced towards the granaries, the walls returning the rhythmic echo of our horses' hooves. Passing close to a great block of ruins, we found ourselves facing a high, irregularly shaped wall, with a tall unguarded doorway set into it.

"When it is not raining, many come here," said Sfasciamonti in a low voice.

We found a hidden tree to which to which we tethered our horses and at last prepared to enter the ruins.

"I warn you," insisted Sfasciamonti as we dismounted, "the people we are about to meet must not be rubbed up the wrong way. If we encounter anyone, let me do all the talking."

Thick though the silence was, with my senses no doubt deceived by the sinister nature of the place, I was, however, practically certain that I had seen an ironic little smile cross Abbot Melani's face, barely illumined by the crescent moon.

We drew near then to the doorway (now, in truth, nothing but a great gaping gap without any doors) leading inside the ruins. As we entered, in a flash of the imagination, I pictured the grandiose gatherings that must have taken place centuries ago in that place: swarms of sweating patricians, but also plebeians, enjoying the steam baths, the inhalations and ablutions, all under the protective wing of those lofty vapour-filled vaults. . .

Of vaults: there were none; the roof had collapsed. Hardly had I crossed the threshold of the great portal leading to the ruins than my eyes were drawn upwards by the moonlight, and were amazed to find themselves still under the just, indifferent gaze of the stars.

We were in a sort of great arena open to the sky, bounded on four sides by the massive walls of the ancient baths. Time and neglect had robbed them forever of the covering placed sixteen centuries ago by the zealous efforts of architects and masons.

Thanks to the moonlight, we could make our way cautiously through that alien space without constantly tripping over. Here and there, pearly white in the white sidereal glow, lay huge, indolent blocks of stone, columns painfully cast to the ground, voluble capitals and vainglorious pilasters.

In the gaps between one piece of wreckage and the next, and between these and the undulations in the terrain, sprawling on heaps of rags and quilts, one could make out the silhouettes of sleeping bodies.

"*Cerretani* and vagrants: they are scattered all over the place," murmured Sfasciamonti.

"How are we to find those two," I replied in a similarly light whisper, "what were their names. . . Il Roscio and Il Marcio?"

Instead of answering, the catchpoll broke away from Atto and me and moved towards a mound, behind which one could see a sort of architrave, so gently sunken into the ground that it seemed to have gone to sleep there after centuries of vainly awaiting the return of imperial glories.

For a while, he looked around, searching for some objective, until he found his next victim: a wretched vagabond who lay sleeping at his feet. The latter, however, inured to scenting danger, was not unaware of the catchpoll's threatening presence. He turned once or twice in his sleep and then gave a violent start. Just before the vagabond could change position, I almost stopped breathing for surprise.

Sfasciamonti had sat on the unfortunate fellow. We drew near, looking over our shoulders in fear of some reprisal on the part of the vagabond's companions. Nothing happened; Sfasciamonti had conducted his assault so discreetly that no one, among all those sleeping in the great arena, seemed to have realised a thing.

With one knee, the catchpoll had immobilised his victim's arm. Then he had sat down, planting his massive posterior on the adversary's belly, while with both hands he kept his mouth and eyes closed, thus preventing him from uttering the faintest whimper and from seeing who it was that had overwhelmed him. From the ease with which he had accomplished all this, it was plain that he must have made use of the same technique on previous occasions.

"Il Roscio and Il Marcio – two *cerretani* – do you know where they are?" he ordered, whispering in the man's ear.

Slowly he raised his hand from a corner of the poor wretch's mouth, allowing him to whisper something.

"Ask that one, under the striped blanket," said he, pointing to someone sleeping not far off.

Sfasciamonti passed rapidly to the other, on whom he practised the same interrogation technique.

"I've not seen them for days," rasped this man, of whose youthful face I caught a glimpse when the catchpoll raised his huge hands. "I don't know whether they're sleeping here tonight. Look over there, beyond the ditch."

He had pointed at a sort of ditch from which a strong stench of urine arose. That was probably where the vagabonds relieved themselves by night. Sfasciamonti loosened his grip, not without warning the young man with a last threatening look. He then moved off towards the ditch. He took one step, two, three. He was already some way off when we heard the scream.

"Roscio, the saffrons! Buy the violets!"

It was the young man whom Sfasciamonti had just interrogated. After crying out, he fled in the direction we had come from, towards the great expanse of Termine.

"Get him!" Sfasciamonti yelled at me, who, having remained a little behind, was closer to the young man.

Meanwhile, other bodies all around me, wrapped in rags and wretched greatcoats, awoke and returned to life. I felt the blood pumping hard in my veins while the air thickened in my throat. That barren space barely lit by the moon teemed with poor beggars, but also with cutthroats. Hunter and prey could exchange their roles at any moment; I began to follow the young man more from the desire to get away than that of catching him.

Sfasciamonti and I had just launched ourselves on the heels of the fugitive, and Atto in turn had got moving, when another shadow rushed forth from the darkness. He was running with some difficulty across the rough terrain towards the main door.

Thanks to the advantage gained by surprise, the pair had soon put no mean distance between us and themselves; once out in the vast space of Termine, I was already making my way towards our horses when I heard Sfasciamonti's voice.

"No, not the horses – on foot!"

He was right. The young man had run immediately to the left, towards the wall behind which, to the east, stretched the immense and grandiose Villa Peretti Montalto.

In a trice, he had already reached the corner between the wall of the villa, Piazza di Termine and the road descending towards Via Felice, and was climbing the boundary wall. Sfasciamonti and I reached the spot a few moments after the youth had jumped down the other side.

"Here, here, there are breaches that they've made!" gasped the catchpoll, pointing out a whole series of holes to me, apparently distributed at random along the surface of the wall, which made it possible to find footholds and thus to scale it rapidly.

So we imitated the fugitive's clever stratagem and in a few moments we were straddling the top of the wall. We looked down: if we were to go any further we should have to jump down no less than twelve feet, in other words, nearly twice Sfasciamonti's height. Meanwhile, in the distance, we could hear the *cerretano*'s footsteps receding fast down the neighbouring avenue.

With our feet dangling down the wall, like two anglers happily waiting for a pull on the line, we looked impotently at one another. We had lost.

"Curse it," rasped Sfasciamonti, prodding the wall in vain in search of more footholds. "He knows by heart where the breaches are to get down the other side. He had no need to jump."

Once we had got back, we took a look at the great roofless space in which we had carried out our nocturnal ambush on the sleeping beggars. All was quiet; the place was deserted.

"We shall find no one here for months," announced Sfasciamonti.

"Where is Abbot Melani?" I asked.

"He must have followed the other one. But if we had no luck, you can just imagine how he got on. . ."

"Teehereteeamteeaye!" we then heard chanted by a mellifluous and satisfied-sounding voice.

It was Atto, and he was on horseback. In one hand he held his pistol, in the other, the reins and a tether, which ended around the neck of the person whom we had seen escaping at the moment when the young man had cried out. Sfasciamonti's jaw fell. He had returned empty-handed, while Atto had succeeded.

"Il Roscio," exclaimed the catchpoll, pointing incredulously at the prisoner.

"Gentlemen, may I present you Pompeo di Trevi, alias Il Roscio. He is a *cerretano* and he is now at our disposal."

"By all the bolted visors, you may say that again!" exclaimed Sfasciamonti approvingly. "We shall now make our way to the prison of Ponte Sisto, where we shall get him to talk. Just one question: what the Devil did you say just now, when you greeted us?"

"That strange word? That's a long story. Now take this wretch and let us tie him up better, then be on our way."

Atto had chosen, as was his wont, to go against the rules and against the dictates of good sense. Instead of following the *cerretano* on foot, as Sfasciamonti wanted, he had mounted a horse, with difficulty and without any help. Before mounting, however, he had taken care to see which route the fugitive had taken: to the left of the other; in other words, moving north, in the direction of the clear, sweet-smelling countryside of the Castro Pretorio. Spurring on his modest mount, Atto had then set out on the traces of the *cerretano*. At length he had caught sight of him, by now exhausted by his exertions, in the process of scaling a wall towards citrus groves and vineyards in which he would find easy refuge.

"Another moment and I'd have lost him. I was too far off to threaten him with the pistol. So I thought I'd yell something at him."

"What?"

"What he was not expecting. Something in his own language."

"His own language? D'you mean the jargon?" Sfasciamonti and I asked in unison.

"Slang, lingo, cant. . . All stuff and nonsense. No, all teestufftee-andteenonteesense," he replied, laughing, while I and the catchpoll looked dumbly at one another .

On the way out, during our ride from Villa Spada to Termine, Atto had turned over again and again in his mind the mysterious words which the *cerretano* had uttered when I fell into the courtyard at Campo di Fiore. Suddenly, a flash of inspiration had come to him: to look, not for what made sense but for what made none.

"The jargon used by these ragamuffins is sometimes as stupid and elementary as they themselves are. There's only one principle involved: you stick a foreign element between syllables, as is sometimes done in cipher, to create confusion."

While Atto was explaining this to us, our strange caravan was wending its way across the Piazza dei Pollaioli towards the Ponte Sisto; at its head, Sfasciamonti, to whose horse the *cerretano* was firmly tethered, with his hands tied behind his back and his legs hobbled in such a way that he could not run; then came Atto's horse and then mine.

"What do you mean?" I asked.

"'Tis so simple that I'm almost ashamed of saying it. They place the syllable "tee" between the others."

"*Teeyooteelai*. . . So the cerretano said to me 'you lie'!"

"What had you said to him just before that?"

"For heaven's sake, how am I to remember?. . . Wait. . . Ah yes: I told him that the German would kill him."

"And you were indeed lying, you were trying to buy time. And that is what I was trying to do, albeit somewhat differently. When I greeted you a while ago, I said. . ."

"*Tee-here-tee-am-tee-I*. In other words, 'Here am I.'"

"Precisely. So I said something to Il Roscio in Teeese, which is what I've decided to call their stupid language full of *tees*."

That was the last thing Il Roscio had expected. Hearing the sound of Atto's voice mixed with the threatening clatter of hooves drawing near, his hands froze and he lost his grip, falling heavily to the ground.

"Pardon the question, but what did you say to the *cerretano*?"

"I acted like you and said the first thing that came into my mind."

"And what was that?"

"*Teepateeter teenosteeter*. The first two words of the *Pater noster*."

"But that meant nothing!"

"I know; but he for a moment thought that I was one of his people and was shocked. He fell like a sack of potatoes. Indeed, he hurt himself. At first, he couldn't even get up, so I had time to tie him up. 'Tis just as well that the grooms who equip these horses know what they're doing and provided a good long rope. I trussed him up thoroughly, then tied the end of the rope to the saddle and, just to remind him not to do anything silly, I pointed my pistol at him."

Melani then reconstructed what had taken place at the Baths of Diocletian. The vagabond whom Sfasciamonti had interrogated, sitting on his belly, had given us away.

"That wretch," said the Abbot, turning to the catchpoll with an ironic smile, "Il Marcio pointed out to you when he told you to ask him, but without revealing that he himself was one of the pair you were looking for. And you fell for it."

Sfasciamonti did not reply.

"So it was Il Marcio who screamed out those strange words to Il Roscio?" I asked.

"Precisely. He called out that 'the Saffrons' were there and that, I think, meant us: the catchpolls."

"He added, 'buy the violets', so that meant 'run for it' or perhaps 'take up arms'," I conjectured.

"I tend to think it meant 'run', seeing how matters developed. This isn't Teeese but some other rather more impenetrable jargon, because one needs some experience of it. But everything's possible."

With the exception of my few questions, Atto's self-satisfied account of how he had captured the *cerretano* had met with silence, punctuated only by the clip-clop of the horses' hooves on the flag-stones.

Sfasciamonti kept quiet, but I could imagine what he was feeling. Proud as he was of his crude catchpoll's abilities, he had seen the tiller of action suddenly snatched from him. Where he had failed, using force and intimidation, Atto had succeeded through intellectual sagacity, plus a pinch of well-deserved luck. It could not have been easy for the representative of the law, already scoffed at by his colleagues in the matter of the *cerretani*, to see another snatch from before his eyes one of those mysterious scoundrels who drew him as a hound is drawn to the prey when the beat is on, yet inspired in him an all-too-human fear. That, however, was what had just happened:

thanks to a mispronounced *Pater noster* we now had in our hands a member of the mysterious sect.

This was the very reason for another silence: my own. How strange, said I to myself, that in so little time we had arrested a *cerretano*, while all the catchpolls in Rome, and the Governor, Monsignor Pallavicini himself, denied their very existence. I had it in mind to raise this with Sfasciamonti, but once again events prevented me from so doing. At that very moment it was decided that I was to leave them and make my way to Villa Spada and wake up Buvat (always supposing that he had got over the effects of his tippling) and return with him. Abbot Melani's secretary would, we all three thought, be able to provide us with precious assistance (although, as I shall later recount, the nature of this assistance was to be somewhat unorthodox).

We were all to meet up at our final destination: the prison of Ponte Sisto, giving onto the Tiber just under the Janiculum Hill, not far from the Villa Spada. Here, the interrogation of the *cerretano* was to take place.

❧

The room was in a wretched basement, covered in lichen, sordid and windowless. Only a grate, high on the wall to the left, provided a little air and, in daytime, light.

The *cerretano* was still bound and in pain, his features blanching for fear of ending up before the hangman. He did not know that his presence in that stinking dungeon was thoroughly illegal. Sfasciamonti had arranged through one of his many friends to usher our entire group discreetly into the prison through a side door. Il Roscio's arrest was against all the rules: the *cerretano* had committed no crimes, nor was he suspected of any. That did not matter: the time had come for certain dirty games of which, as I shall have cause to tell later, the catchpolls had long been inordinately fond.

Sfasciamonti had procured a long coat and a periwig for Buvat, who was to play the part of a criminal notary and to draw up the charges. The sergeant himself would conduct the interrogation. Atto and I, dressed up to look like officers of the court or deputies, or goodness knows what, would be assisting, feeling safe owing to the secrecy of the ceremony and the prisoner's total ignorance of the law.

There was a table in the basement room, lit by a large candle, and here sat Buvat, solemnly busying himself with paper, pen and inkhorn. In order to lend greater verisimilitude to the scene, Sfasciamonti had taken care of every detail. Next to the candle were placed severe legal tomes such as the *Commentaria tertiae partis in secundum librum Decretalium* of Abbas Panormitanus, Damhouder's *Praxis rerum criminalium* and lastly and most threateningly, *De maleficiis* by Alberto da Gandino. Although all the titles were unintelligible, the volumes had all been placed upright and with their spines facing the prisoner, so that these obscure inscriptions would, supposing that he could read, all imbue his soul with the idea that he was in the hands of a hostile and impenetrable power.

Before the table, next to Il Roscio, stood Sfasciamonti, holding the accused tightly by one end of the rope, while gripping his arm painfully behind his back. The prisoner was a pudgy, stockily built youngster, whose little blue eyes, under a rectangular forehead beset by deep horizontal furrows, a sure sign of a dissolute life lived with impunity, were set above two rotund and florid cheeks, which bespoke a coarse, ingenuous nature. Observing him at close quarters, one could understand the origin of his nickname, the Red; for his head was crowned by a thick, bristling plumage of carrot-coloured hair.

Buvat adjusted his oversized wig and, still slightly unsteady from the effects of sleep and wine, cleared his throat a couple of times. Then, he began to write, at the same time chanting aloud the formal clauses which he was consigning to paper:

"*Die et cetera et cetera anno et cetera et cetera. Roma. Examinatus fuit in carceribus Pontis Sixtis. . .* What is it?"

Sfasciamonti had interrupted Buvat's recording to whisper a recommendation in his ear.

"But of course, yes, yes," replied the latter; only later did I learn that, as suggested by the catchpoll, the date of the interrogation was to be left blank, so that the whole report could be filed later under whatever date suited one's purpose.

"Very well, let us begin again," said Buvat, resuming his writing with a stiffly dignified expression. "*Examinatus in carceribus Pontis Sixtis, coram et per me Notarium infrascriptum. . .* Your name, young man?"

"Pompeo di Trevi."

"Where exactly is Trevi?" Buvat asked carelessly, thus revealing his limited knowledge of the Papal State, which might have sown suspicion in the mind of the prisoner, if only the latter had not been utterly confused by fear.

"Near to Spoleto," he replied, speaking barely louder than a whisper.

"So we write: *Pompeius de Trivio, Spoletanae diocesis, aetatis annorum.* . . How old are you?"

"Sixteen, I think."

"*Sexdicem incirca,*" Buvat continued, "*et cui delato iuramento de veritate dicenda et interrogatus de nomine, patria, exercitio et causa suae carcerationis, respondit.*"

Sfasciamonti shook the young man and translated the notary's words: "Swear that you will tell the truth and then repeat your name, age and the city in which you were born."

"I swear that I shall tell the truth. Have I not already given my name?"

"Repeat it. This is for the official record. Procedure so demands, we must needs be accurate," pronounced the catchpoll to make the proceedings seem more realistic.

The young man looked around himself, looking somewhat stunned.

"My name is Pompeo, I was born at Trevi, near Spoleto, I may be about sixteen years of age, I have no trade and. . ."

"That is enough," Sfasciamonti interrupted him, again moving to Buvat's side and whispering something in his ear.

"Ah, very well, very well," answered Buvat.

At that point in the record, the grounds for the arrest were to be entered, but there were no such grounds. On the catchpoll's recommendation, Buvat was therefore to enter a false deposition, namely that the *cerretano* had been arrested for begging alms during mass.

"Come on now," said the false notary, adjusting his spectacles on his aquiline nose. "*Interrogatus an sciat et cognoscat alios pauperes mendicantes in Urbe, et an omnes sint sub una tantum secta an vero sub diversis sectis, et recenseat omnes precise, respondit. . .*"

"I shall go and get the whip," said Sfasciamonti.

"The whip, what for?" said the *cerretano* with a slight tremor in his voice.

"You are not answering the question."

"I did not understand it," answered the other, who obviously did not know a word of Latin.

"He asked you whether you know other sects in Rome besides that to which you belong," intervened Atto. "He wants to know whether they are all united under a single leadership, and to complete matters, he expects you to provide him with a complete list of all of them."

"But you, however, have no intention of answering," added the catchpoll, taking a pair of keys from a bag, presumably to open up some dungeon equipped with devices to encourage reticent criminals, "and so your back is in need of a good flogging."

Suddenly, the boy threw himself to the ground on his knees, causing Sfasciamonti himself, who was holding him on a tight cord, to sway.

"Gentlemen, please listen," said he in imploring tones, turning first to Buvat, then to the catchpoll. "Among us poor mendicants there are various companies, and this is because they carry out different functions and wear different clothes. I shall tell you everything that I can remember."

There followed a moment's silence. The boy was weeping. Abbot Melani and I were utterly amazed; the first of the mysterious *cerretani* ever to fall into the hands of the law was not only willing to be interrogated by a criminal notary but refused the ordeal of the scourge and was promising to tell all.

Sfasciamonti made him stand up, his expression momentarily betraying something between surprise and disappointment. Once again, his crude catchpoll's skills would not be needed here.

"Let us give him a seat," said he with forced benevolence, clumsily putting one of his enormous arms around the shoulders of the young miscreant, who was trembling and shaking with tears and terror.

I gave him a stool and the confession began.

"The first is called the Company of the Chop-Churches. They beg for alms in crowded churches, cut purses and bags and steal all they find in them."

I called to mind the episode with the *sanpaolaro* and the little woman whose purse-strings had been cut. Was that one of these Chop-Churches?

Il Roscio stopped and looked at us one by one, studying on our faces the effect of these revelations which must, for him, amount to scarcely less than the desecration of a deity.

"The second is called the Company of Swooners," he continued. "They pretend that they're dying; they lie on the ground, screaming and groaning and begging for alms, but in reality, they're perfectly well. The third is called the Company of Clapperdogeons. They too are healthy, but slothful; they don't like to work so they pound it."

"'Slothful', I understand, but 'pound it'?"

"They go begging," answered Il Roscio; then he asked for and obtained a glass of water.

"Go on," said Sfasciamonti.

Beggars and wastrels: was not the morning crowd whom I had for years been meeting with in the streets of Rome composed mainly of suchlike? Perhaps I had in my short life unknowingly come across far more *cerretani* than I realised.

"The fourth is called the Company of Brothers of the Buskin, or strolling players," continued our hostage; "They lie curled up on the ground, shivering as though they were dying of cold, or scabby with ring-worm, and beg. The fifth is called the Company of Blockheads: they pretend to be idiotic and brainless, they always answer beside the point and go out begging. The sixth is the Company of Abram Coves. They strip naked or half-naked and show their uncovered flesh as and when suits them, and they beg. The seventh is called the Company of the Hedge Priests. . ."

"One moment, one moment," said Buvat; the pseudo-notary, equipped with too large a pen and unaccustomed to writing fast, was struggling to keep up with the full flow of the confession. He had initially been prepared to draw up a false statement for the record; now, however, he found himself having to write a real one, and a particularly precious one at that. Sfasciamonti kept gesturing to him that he was not to miss a single word. I now knew why: the catchpoll wanted at last to have hard and fast evidence of the existence of the *cerretani* to show sooner or later to his colleagues or even the Governor.

"Let us do as follows," proposed Atto. "First, tell us the names of the companies, so that we can have an idea of them. Then explain to us what they do."

The young *cerretano* obeyed and began to rattle off a list, including the companies already mentioned:

Chop-churches
Swooners
Clapperdogeons

Brothers of the Buskin
Tawneymen
Abram Coves
Hedge Priests
Dommerers
Swaddlers
Basket Ants
Watchdogs
Puppets
Bayardeers
Kinchins
Autem morts
Doxies

"Enough, that will do. Which company do you belong to?" asked Atto.

"To the Swooners."

Then Il Roscio spelt out all the infamous deeds of which the *cerretano* companies were capable but which he had not yet specified. He spoke of the Hedge Priests who disguise themselves as Austin Friars; of the Tawneymen, who pretend to be lunatics, frenzied madmen or possessed by devils, frothing at the mouth and rolling on the ground after eating a soapy mixture. He revealed the tricks of the Dommerers, who bear heavy iron chains around their necks and pretend to speak Turkish, forever repeating "Bran-bran-bran" or "Bre-bre-bre" and claiming to have been prisoners of the infidels. The Swaddlers always go about two by two, pretending to be soldiers, and when they meet some poor defenceless person in the street, they rob him. The Basket Ants are bandits who have fallen on hard times, while the Watchdogs are constables who have likewise been ruined; the Puppets pretend their bodies are shaken by tremendous convulsions, like puppets, because, so they claim, they descend from sinners who were unwilling to kneel before the Most Holy Sacrament, and that is why they are being punished. The Bayardeers rob farm bailiffs when they are delivering bread in the countryside (their name comes from a cant word for a horse, after the famous Bayard). The Kinchins are little boys who live in the streets and sing songs like "O Maria Stella!" while shamelessly begging. Lastly, the Autem Morts and Doxies are women who beg with infants in their arms, with their faces covered: the Autem Morts are married, while the Doxies are single.

"Heavens, what chaos," Atto Melani commented in the end.

"But these *cerretani* are all beggars after all," I observed.

"And did I not tell you that from the start?" replied Sfasciamonti. "Only, they use mendicancy as a cover for other nefarious activities, such as violence, cheating and robbery. . ."

"Excuse me, we have an interrogation to complete," said Buvat, calling us to order with the inflexible dignity of a true notary, as he began to transcribe the customary formula.

"*Interrogatus an pecuniae acquistae sint ipsius quaerentis an vero quilibet teneatur illas consignare suo superiori secundum cuiusque sectam illorum, respondit.* . . So, young man, I repeat: do you keep the money which you earn through mendicancy or other criminal activities for yourself or do you hand it over to your superiors in every company?"

"Sir, whoever earns money, at least among us Swooners, keeps it for himself. Our chief is Gioseppe da Camerino, and he on the contrary gives money to everyone. I have heard it said that the Hedgers and Puppets hold things in common and often meet up at inns or in other places, and that they elect their principals and officers. My companion, who fled in order not to be taken, told me that last week he was in the company of four Brothers of the Buskin, two Hedgers and two Puppets. They all met at a tavern in the Ponte quarter to have a good time together. They had all manner of good things brought to them by mine host, excellent wines and many things to eat. In other words, a meal fit for the nobility. And after the feasting, the host presented the bill and said that the whole meal came to twelve scudi, which the elder of the Hedge Priests paid in coin without uttering a word. And they enjoyed themselves together because they are never short of money, least of all the heads of the companies."

"Where do the members of your company meet?"

"At Piazza Navona, Ponte, Campo di Fiore and in the Piazza della Rotonda."

"Now, tell me whether you go to Confession, take Communion or attend mass?"

"Sir, among us there are few who do so, because, to tell the truth, most are worse than the Lutherans. Apart from that, I swear I know nothing."

"Do you gentlemen have any further questions?" said Buvat, turning to us.

Once again, Sfasciamonti drew near to Buvat in order to whisper in his ear that the next question was not to be placed on the record.

"Ah, yes, yes," the pseudo-notary reassured him. "Very well, my boy, within your company, have you heard of the theft of certain documents, a relic and a telescope from the Villa Spada?"

"Yes, Sir."

We all four looked at one another and this time even Buvat was unable to conceal a look of surprise.

"Go on, go on, for goodness' sake," said Atto with his eyes almost bursting out of his head.

"Sir, I know only that this thing was done by the German. Why, I know not. Since the Jubilee began he has been doing excellent business, mining money in all the streets of Rome."

"And where the Devil are we to find this German?" asked Atto.

The *cerretano* explained everything.

"I think that is quite clear," commented Sfasciamonti in the end.

ॐঔ৾

All that Il Roscio had spilled out concerning the German related to the search for Atto's personal effects and was therefore omitted from the record, together with many other things said by the young canter that evening.

"If anyone should find this statement on me, I shall be in real trouble," said Sfasciamonti out of the prisoner's hearing. "I shall, for safety's sake, put a fictitious date on it, say, 4th February 1595. Then I shall place it in the Governor's archives. Only I shall know where to find it, because no one now looks at the documents of the past century. I shall produce it if and when I want to: what's more, with that date, it will prove that the *cerretani* have existed for a long time, and I shall at last be able to wave this under the noses of all those who've been mocking me."

The next decision was the most difficult, but there was no choice in the matter. The *cerretano* could not be kept in prison without an arrest summons, or at least a permit from the Bargello; Sfasciamonti had in fact mentioned such a possibility to one of the gaolers, a good friend of his, who had been unwilling so much as to discuss the possibility. There are, said he, so many innocent people in gaol, and so many guilty ones at liberty; but matters such as these must be handled in the right way. Usually, they are organised by the judges, or by those in power, whose orders the former carry out, unbeknownst to the people.

It was, moreover, impossible to hold the criminal (if such he could be called) elsewhere: Villa Spada, which did of course have plenty of space in its cellars, could obviously not be used for this purpose. Nor, it was plain enough, could our private residences.

In order to make the decision seem less improvised, we made Il Roscio wait in a little side-room and pretended to confer together for a while. Then we brought him back, taking care to show long, disappointed faces.

"The notary has spoken with His Excellency the Governor," lied Sfasciamonti, "who has been so good as to reward your willingness to collaborate."

The *cerretano* cast confused glances in all directions, not understanding what was about to happen.

"Now you will be accompanied to the door. You are free."

Day the Fourth

10ᵗʰ July, 1700

✠

"Give me alms, boy."

The old man was naked. His sole covering, a great iron chain which he had borne around his neck since who knows how long and which crushed his right shoulder, biting into and infecting the poor decrepit flesh. Bent and skeletal, he held out his filthy hooked hand imploringly. Not only could his every rib be counted, but every single tendon. If he had held a scourge in his hand he would have made the perfect image of a flagellant. He leaned against a wall, and he stank. His pudenda were covered only by the immensely long grey beard reaching down almost to his feet.

I looked at him without saying a word, nor did I offer him even an obole. I was overcome by the crudity of that image of misery, unhappiness and dispossession.

"For pity's sake, my boy," the wretch repeated, first bending, then sitting on the ground, exhausted.

"Forgive me, but I have not. . ." I stammered while the old beggar stretched out, then turned onto one side.

"Teeyouteelie," he hissed, and I seemed to sense in his voice a subtle and melancholy note of reproof.

He turned again to one side, then to the other, and in the end he began to rock rhythmically ever more rapidly. He was having convulsions. I had decided to help him rise, when he was shaken by a most violent spasm, recovered briefly, then was seized by unstoppable trembling. His mouth tightly closed, the muscles of his neck so tense it seemed they might snap, he appeared to be on the point of suffocating. Without warning, he sat up and opened wide his jaws from which flowed a thick yellowish froth which horribly fouled his chest and belly; I drew back in shock and disgust. His pupils rolled back in his eye sockets, as though to turn his gaze towards some parallel universe of desperation and solitude which only he truly understood. He again held out his trembling and wrinkled hand. I felt in my pocket: there was nothing but a one scudo piece in it: a disproportionately large sum for almsgiving. I was about to tell him that I had nothing to give him when, as though he had read my thoughts, he again growled:

"Teeyouteelie."

It was then that the unthinkable happened. On the wall behind the old man I saw a rapid, rapacious shadow suddenly lengthen. A flying creature (a vampire or perhaps a demon come to punish my avarice?) was above our heads and on the point of attacking. I had no time to turn around and already I felt the air turbulent above me, the tips of the creature's wings brushing my ears, its claws sinking painfully into the soft flesh of my shoulders. I turned, but this was an ill-judged move: the flying beast was firmly ensconced on my shoulder and any attempt to distance myself from it would have been as useless as to try to bite my own ear. I struggled to drive it off with my hands but it left my shoulder and this time sank its talons into my face. I had by now forgotten the old man with his tortured body and his mouth vomiting forth its foul froth. I tried to scream, but the sharp claws of the flying beast were clamped over my lips. Yet, I could hear a voice, a strangled sound:

"Arrest him! ARREST HIM!"

It was only at that point in the dream (or rather nightmare) that I came to my senses. I brushed my face with my forearm and thought it had not been such a good idea to sleep with the window open. I felt his body, halfway between a chicken's and a little owl's, beat a hasty retreat, seeking to perch elsewhere. It was day; sunlight filled the room, flooding it with its beneficent rays.

He had found a perch on the back of a chair. I stared angrily at him. Not only had he entered without permission but while I was sleeping he had walked, first on my shoulder, then on my face, thus invading not only my bedchamber but my dream, disagreeable as it already was. He gazed obliquely at me, with his usual mixture of effrontery and doubt.

"My dream was true. You really are a monstrous being. How could you wake me up like this?"

Caesar Augustus did not answer.

Our return from the Ponte Sisto prison the night before had been swift and had passed without a word of comment; all three of us – Atto, the catchpoll and I – were too tired to utter another word.

What was more, we knew that we would not be able to resume our investigations before the following evening, so that our taste for action was distinctly cooled by the inevitable wait.

Fatigued as I was, I did not need to wait long to fall asleep. The all-too-brief repose I gained was soon spoiled by the dream vision of that decrepit beggar, obviously suggested by Il Roscio's confession. Ah yes, said I to myself, that old man reminded me of the Tawneymen who, to obtain alms, feign lunacy, frenzy and possession by devils; and roll on the ground after eating a mixture containing soap; but also the Dommerers who wear heavy iron chains around their necks. . .

"*De minimis non curat Papa*," screeched the parrot, interrupting my reminiscences.

"I know that the Pope does not deal with trifles. . . Ha, ha, and thanks for comparing me to His Holiness. I know, I know, I must provide feed for the aviary, nor do I regard that as a trifle," I retorted while rising and seeking my clothes. "If you'll only give me time to get ready."

Caesar Augustus glided lazily towards the still open window. I noticed that in his right talon he held a little bundle of twigs, something which I had often noticed in recent times. Obviously, it was not given to me to know what he was up to.

He stood a few more minutes on the windowsill, then flew off towards the villa's vineyards. While I was closing the shutters before leaving the room, I noticed another sign of Caesar Augustus's unusual behaviour: a half-liquid ochre-coloured mess in the middle of which were fragments of grain and apple pips. He was by no means in the habit of defecating in such an unsuitable place, on the window-sill. Caesar Augustus must really be very nervous.

After attending to my regular duty in the aviary, I decided to take advantage of the state of semi-liberty which the service of Atto Melani accorded me and took a short break. Atto and Buvat had not yet come to look for me, and Sfasciamonti was probably busy at his usual work as guardian of the Villa Spada's security. I sought Cloridia but learned that she was in the apartments of the Princess of Forano; the Princess was dressing and it was not for the time being possible to free my consort from her duties. Somewhat frustrated by this impediment, I filched an apple from the kitchens, chewing which I moved surreptitiously away from the Villa Spada.

As I was entering the avenue leading to the front gate, I heard a familiar voice in the distance.

"The Master of the Fowls, find me the Master of the Fowls! Is no one working here today?"

Don Paschatio, doubtless let down once more by some of his workmen, was seeking me to fill in for them.

This was, I decided, not the right day on which to make myself available. Last night's sounds and images still echoed in my head; Sfasciamonti's assault on the old beggar in the Piazza della Rotonda; the imprudent inspection of the beggars' dormitory at Termine; lastly, the chase after the *cerretano* and the interrogation of his accomplice, Il Roscio, at the prison of Ponte Sisto; all of which events, quite apart from giving rise to the nightmare visions which had met me at dawn, had left marks of anxiety even during my first waking hours. To forget all those misadventures, said I to myself, there could be no better remedy than a calm promenade in town.

I did not, however, wish to go too far and so I first walked downhill towards the Via della Scala, turning right there and then left, wandering between Piazza de' Rienzi and Santa Maria in Trastevere.

A company of pilgrims, preceded by the standard of their city and attired in long black cloaks, was advancing towards the Basilica of St Paul chanting a hymn of praise to the Virgin. The little procession wended its way through narrow streets and damp alleyways where small shops overflowing with every kind of merchandise and taverns reeking of cheap wine and roast meat opened wide their inviting doors, as though almost tugging at the arm of the passer-by. The façades of the surrounding houses hid their shame and wretchedness behind long rows of white cloths, hanging from window to window and dripping icy water onto the heads of pedestrians, while Trastevere's sleepy thoroughfares were trampled by cartwheels, the feet of children at play and the hooves of donkeys resignedly heaving their burdens.

On entering Piazza San Callisto, I heard what I can only describe as some miaowing music gradually draw nearer, while a great multitude of people came towards me. At the head of the crowd were two middle-aged men, dirty and badly dressed, who advanced painfully, leaning on walking sticks. I noticed with a certain disquiet that both had their eyeballs turned inwards, like the old man of whom I'd dreamed at dawn. Between the pair and holding each by the arm was a companion no less filthy and unpresentable, also using a stick and displaying a very obvious limp. Immediately behind, there followed a fiddler, filling the street with the insinuating melancholy of a chaconne. There followed other ragged tramps, almost all blind or crippled. Beggars, always beggars. For years I had lived in Rome in their company, without ever paying much attention to them. Now, since the return of Atto Melani, they had suddenly become not only important, but very important to me! I therefore stood aside, the better to observe the procession. The two blind men at the head of the group held a snuff box and a bowl respectively, both made of silver, and chanted in lamentable counterpoint with the sound of the fiddle.

"Charity for Saint Elizabeth, make an offering to Saint Elizabeth!"

Every now and then a benefactor would break away from the indistinct mass of passers-by, to throw some coin into the bowl. The other blind man would then offer him a pinch of snuff, which the kind person offering charity would take from the snuff box with a sort of tiny glass measure.

The rest of the procession, as I was able to observe when they turned to the right into the Vicolo de' Pazzi, was one long line of people, all muffled up and miserable-looking, every single unfortunate among them apparently eyeless, legless or armless. The cortège was surrounded by a collection of poor children begging for charity, rather like seagulls following a ship in the hope of some refuse from the vessel's stores.

A young cleric approached the head of the procession. He threw a *grosso* coin into the bowl and took a small pinch of tobacco, which caused him to cough and sneeze. When he had moved away from the cortege, I followed and accosted him.

"Excuse me, Father, what procession is this?"

"It is the Company of Saint Elizabeth. Normally they come out on Sundays, while today is Saturday. But in Jubilee time an exception or two is allowed them too."

"The Company of Saint Elizabeth?" I asked, recalling that I had in the past heard tell of it. "That group consisting entirely of the halt and the blind?"

"Yes, poor things. Fortunately, Pope Paul V gave them a permit to beg. If only there were no catchpolls. . ."

"What do you mean?"

"Oh, nothing. Just that the company has to pay many taxes for religious ceremonies, so that in the end, little remains to them. But you must excuse me now, I have to go to San Pietro in Montorio and I am already late."

I was unable to detain the young cleric any longer or to obtain from him any other particulars concerning the Company of Saint Elizabeth. After leaving the priest, I spent an infinitesimal proportion of the money received for my literary services to Abbot Melani on the acquisition from a street vendor of a carton of little fish, just fried and deliciously crisp to the teeth.

I turned towards Piazza Santa Maria in Trastevere; contemplating the noble and ancient façade of the church, I ate, leaning on the steps of the fountain in the middle of the square. I was thinking. I remembered that I had heard tell of the Company of St Elizabeth, because on the saint's day they hold a procession with a great military escort and visit the four holy basilicas. I was not, however, aware that they had a papal authorisation to beg; furthermore, I found the cleric's remark concerning the catchpolls distinctly curious. What could Sfasciamonti's colleagues have to do with the company's contribution to religious festivities? I turned and saw the dusty and sinuous serpent of the procession turning into a side-road. Behind it there remained a breath of air smelling of unwashed bodies, rotting clothes and kitchen odours.

"And I, what do I pay taxes for?" exclaimed the owner of a tavern with four tables outside, waylaying me loudly and polemically. A middle-aged man with a feline expression and a swollen pot-belly, his accent was from the Abruzzi and he seemed to be one of those people who complains about everything but does nothing about anything. After the company had gone on its way, he had begun to sweep lazily but irately in front of his door.

"But the Company of St Elizabeth never entered your inn," said I, amazed by the man's anger with those crippled, wretched outcasts.

"My boy, I don't know how long you've lived in this city, but I can assure you that I am far older than you," said he, leaning his broom against the wall, "and I have seen and heard more than you could ever imagine. For example, whoever owns a shop, market stall, warehouse, store, inn, hostelry, wine-shop, bakery or other place where goods are sold, both foodstuffs and other goods, must, in order to exercise any trade pay in advance ten baiocchi a month to have the street cleaned and washed. Hired carriages, the pozzolana quarries, the docks on the Tiber, even ordinary town carriages, all pay taxes. And even those who don't pay them must slave away to comply with the health regulations against pollution of the air: buffalo herdsmen, butchers and coachmen must cleanse their stables, coach houses and enclosures of all dung and refuse. Market gardeners and the owners of vineyards may not keep manure in the streets of Rome, either within the walls or without. Fruiterers, greengrocers, fishmongers and straw merchants must always remove all the refuse they have produced during the day, down to the last straw, leaf or wood shaving, otherwise they get a fine of five scudi. What else? Ah yes, dyers and tanners cannot throw the waste water from their work into the street and have to pour it into drains specially built for that purpose. And now I tell you: the wastrels of Saint Elizabeth's Company, when they come here, stink and befoul the streets worse than the Nubians of ancient Rome, they take up the whole roadway and make my customers go away. And they, what do they pay?"

"I have just been told that they pay a tax to the catchpolls," I replied, making immediate use of my conversation with the young cleric.

"To the catchpolls? Ha ha!" guffawed the innkeeper, grasping his broom and beginning again to sweep the pavement. "And you call that a tax? But that's the catchpolls' fee."

"The catchpolls' fee?"

He stopped and looked all around him, as though to make sure that no one was listening.

"For heaven's sake, young man, where do you live? Everyone knows that the catchpolls take money under the counter from the Company of Saint Elizabeth, in exchange for which they can beg as much as they wish, even in places where it is forbidden by orders and edicts. The money is given on the pretext of paying for religious festivities. But everyone knows that is not what it is all about."

He resumed sweeping vigorously, as though he wanted to work off an impotent, sulking rage by the activity of cleaning.

"Forgive me," I resumed, "but if you are telling me. . ."

"He talks like he eats, and what he says, even I can see."

The voice that had come between us was that of a shoe vendor, who was carrying on his shoulders two strings of footwear of every kind and size (boots and clogs, street shoes and slippers) secured to a wooden yoke by long leather thongs. He was a thin, emaciated old man with a pitilessly lined face, wearing only a grey shirt knotted at his belly, breeches that were too short and a half stoved-in straw hat.

"If people help these ragamuffins, there will only be more and more of them. Look at me, boy. I go out and earn my bread. As for those like the Company of Saint Elizabeth, they have protectors and grow fat."

"Come on now, they're blind and crippled," I insisted.

"Oh really? Then how do you explain that there are more and more beggars, vagabonds and wastrels? How do you explain that one Roman out of two begs for charity? And yet, the alms keep rolling in, indeed they do!"

"Perhaps it's because there's not enough bread for everyone."

"Not enough bread!" said the shoe-seller scornfully. "Poor fool. . ."

"The truth," the innkeeper went on, "is that the poor are not poor. A beggar who's found a good place, say in front of San Sisto's, can earn far more money than me."

"But what are you saying?"

"Let fools give alms," said the pedlar acidly.

"In Rome, poverty is the best school for theft, impurity, blasphemy and every kind of abomination," insisted the innkeeper without giving me the time to think or to respond.

The squabble which I have so crudely described in fact went on for quite some time, so that I was able to learn, if not hard facts, at least the opinions of my two contradictors, which I was in time to discover corresponded to a viewpoint widely held.

While Rome had for centuries been a universal haven for the poor, in recent times there had arisen an ever more solid wall of disgust and mistrust for them.

Until a few decades ago, pious souls among the poor were counted by the thousand. It was no accident that Robert Bellarmine in his *De arte bene moriendi* (but this I was to learn later from other sources), referring to wise philosophers and excellent doctors of the Church like Aristotle, Saint Basil, Saint John Chrisostom and above all the celebrated *De amore pauperum* of Gregory of Nazianzius, preached that in every city two cities existed side by side, that of the poor and that of the rich, united by the bond of piety and generosity. God could in fact have created everyone strong and learned, but did not so intend: with wondrous providence, he was pleased to make the one rich, the other poor, the one learned, the other ignorant; the one robust, the other weak, the one healthy, the other sick. Charity was, however, always to be directed towards the poor (among other things because, as Father Daniello Bartoli put it, he who gives charity does not lose but gains). The lax held it sufficient to give them what is superfluous. Other, more rigorous persons thought that one must always give something, because in truth there exist very few among the faithful, even among kings, who are prepared to admit that they have more than they need.

With time, however, the problem had become more serious: no longer was the question how much should be given to the poor, but whether the latter really were poor. On the streets of the Holy City (as Father Guevarre wrote, but this the two with whom I had been conversing were not to know) there abounded above all shameless individuals who made use of sackcloth and ashes, healthy limbs swathed in bandages, mimed madness and artificial tremors to extract money from the purses of the ingenuous and to find comfortable places in dormitories. Public and private subsidies, the hospices opened by the popes (like that of San Michele, inaugurated by Pope Innocent XII) and the charitable gifts of the nobility (Cardinal Farnese gave up to a fifth of his considerable income) thus ended up not in the hands of the truly wretched, but in the purses of wastrels and scoundrels, happy to live and die on the street so long as they did not have to work. They preferred a thousand times to lead a rogue's existence, so long as it was a life of ease. The beggars breathed the air of Rome; and such are the Romans that, since air is worth nothing, why, they thought, work for it?

"But they are surely not all *cerretani*, Tawneymen or Dommerers. . ." said I casually, hoping that the names of the sects would loosen the tongues of the twain even more, so that I might pick up some interesting morsel.

"*Cerretani?*" exclaimed the innkeeper in surprise.

"Those who steal," the other translated.

"No, they're all the same: *cerretani*, beggars, Romei, pilgrims and vagabonds! If you want to work you look for it and you'll surely find some honest occupation. Those who don't want work – let them rot!"

"I had hoped that the lively conversation between the two would yield some useful information, some indiscretion, and that this might prove to be one of those not infrequent occasions on which *vox populi* reveals the best hidden secrets. As it turned out, the publican had only the most approximate idea of who the *cerretani* were and the same was true of his friend. I could glean nothing from them that might be of any use for the purposes of Atto's investigations. Only one thing was news to me: the fact that a good many Romans nurtured feelings of disgust and resentment for the poor, not pious pity. I had originally believed the indigent to be all good. Then, upon learning of the sordid secret world of the *cerretani*, I had supposed them to be divided into the poor but worthy and the bad eggs. Now, however, the opinion of the man in the street was teaching me to mistrust the supposedly worthy no less than their rascally companions and to suspect that the prime cause of their condition might be not indigence, but indolence.

Who, I wondered, could ever find salvation in a world in which even the humblest and most outcast were sinners?

Yet these thoughts had no time to take wing. No sooner had I taken my leave of the publican and the shoe-vendor than I realised it was becoming late; I must hasten back to the Villa Spada and report for work. The festivities would be resuming straight away after luncheon. I cast aside the oily yellow carton from which I had eaten the fried fish and headed back.

When I reached the villa, it was almost time for the latest festive entertainments to begin. As I have said, it was agreed that the guests would return to the Villa Spada only in the early afternoon. Those who had chosen to sojourn at the villa would enjoy a leisurely lunch, a sort of picnic, for the heat was such as to rein in even the heartiest appetites. With this in mind, great pieces of coarse canvas had been spread out in the shade of the trees, covered with fine sheets of damasked stuff, on which baskets of fruit and flowers had been agreeably arranged, together with others brimming over with fresh bread, jars containing tender junket or tasty Provolone cheeses, others filled with hams of pork, venison, rabbit and bear, piles of olives stuffed with almonds, dishes of dried fruit most attractively presented, bowls of sweetmeats hot from the oven and a thousand other delicacies, both fresh and simple, such that even under the burning rays of Sirius, the guests should be disposed to eat their fill out in the open, discreetly caressed by the breezes of the Janiculum Hill, enjoying with bucolic torpor the view over the Holy City and the soft couch of the lawn.

The coaches of the guests were already crowding the square in front of the entrance; among them, I thought I recognised those of Duke Federico Sforza Cesarini, Marchese Bongiovanni and Prince Camillo Cybo; soon I would behold those great gentlemen themselves, together with others no less illustrious, honouring the nuptials between Maria Pulcheria Rocci and the young Clemente Spada by engaging their precious intellect in that most noble of pastimes: an academic discussion.

Academies, or cenacles of august intellects coming together for discussion and contemplation, had existed in Rome as far back as the fifteenth century. They had emerged joyously, out in the open, amidst the city's gardens and the perfume of freesias, under the stripy shade of wisterias and pergolas; so it was that they were graced with such names as the Academy of Husbandmen of the Vine, or the Academy of the Farnese Gardens. In the middle of the century, there had arisen the most learned Academy of the Vatican Nights and that of Civil and Canon Law, the which engaged in discussions concerning the most elevated topics of theology, logic, philosophy and gnosiology.

It was, however, in the final years of the last century that they had attained their full flowering. There was not a palace, a salon, a court-yard, a garden or a terrace unfrequented by eloquent confraternities of men of learning and genius, intent upon measuring up against one another in a noble jousting of intellects. For days on end, orations, disputes, controversies and debates followed one another, keeping minds busy late into the night.

These cenacles were, of course, not open to all comers. Every candidate had to pass a rigorous examination, upon passing which he would be baptised with some unusual name like Indomitable Starry One or Dewy Academic of the Night, or else some name forged from the models of antiquity, like Honorius Amaltheus, Elpomenides Maturitius, Anastasius Epistheno or Tenorius Autorficus.

The elevated topics forming the battlefield on which wits clashed were often drawn from the names of the cenacles concerned: the Ecclesiastical Academy, or the Academy of Divine Love, and those of Theology, the Councils, and Dogmas, all plainly engaged in discussions pertaining to the faith. On the other hand, the mathematicians

and astronomers of the Academy of Natural Philosophy were concerned with science, as were the Academy of the Lynxes (so called
because each thing was to be observed with the sharp eyes of the
lynx). The Academicians of the New Poesy met to talk of rhymes,
as did those of the famous Arcadia, a name taken from the Arcadian
shepherds who populate the bucolic visions of so many excellent
poets. Last but not least, the members of the Academy of Saint
Cecilia, the patroness of music and singers, met to celebrate the
cult of music.

Less plain, however, was the *raison d'être* of academies with obscure
names which sometimes dedicated their studies to the most curious matters. Such was the Academy of the Oracle, whose members
met in the Roman countryside. One of its members, of robust build,
would sit upon a rock, enveloping himself completely in his cloak
and pretending to be an oracle. Two others stood on either side of
him, to act as interpreters of his prophecies. Then another member
of the congregation would approach the oracle, playing the part of
a stranger, and would consult him about some future event, for instance whether such and such a marriage would or would not take
place. The oracle would respond with apparently meaningless words
like "pyramid!" or "button!" and the two interpreters would have to
explain the meaning of the reply, illustrating the angles, the figure
or the purpose of the pyramid, or the nature, form and use of the
button. Two exceedingly severe censors would check the explanation with rigid discipline, marking down even the most insignificant
errors of language, accent and pronunciation of the two interpreters.
Mistakes were punished by a fine, to be paid in cash, which, once
collected, served to acquire victuals wherewith to feed and joyously
restore the entire company.

While some doubts might be permitted as to the usefulness of
such congregations, it was not even possible to guess at the activities of certain others. One could readily suppose that the Academy
of Husbandmen of the Vine concerned itself with matters of art and
the spirit, preferably under the foliage of a vineyard. It was suspected
that the Symposiacs met from time to time to raise their elbows, as
we say, and the symposium was indeed nothing but a topers' reunion.
Likewise, the Humorists were inclined to joke. What, however, the
Academy of the Precipitate, that of the Snowy or the Academy of
the Flour-faced might get up to, who the deuce can know? What was

the real vocation of the Abbreviators or the Neglected? How did the Equivocals manage to agree matters among themselves? And did the meetings of the Suffocated take place only in writing?

The mystery grew thicker when one realised that academies did not arise one by one but in groups; like contagions and diseases. Thus, within the space of a few years, there had arisen the Imperfects, the Inexperts, the Impetuous, the Incautious, the Incongruous, the Incompetents, the Ineffectuals, the Inflammables and the Informals.

Fashions changed and it soon became the turn of academies inspired by sadness (the Debilitated, the Delicate, the Depressed, the Despised and the Disunited), by passivity (the Melancholics, the Malingerers, the Maltreated and the Moderates), by danger (the Ambitious, the Angry, the Ardent, the Argumentative and the Audacious) or by their very benightedness (the Occult, the Occluded, the Obstinate, the Otiose).

Silence was, however, almost total when it came to certain semi-clandestine academies. Perhaps these were destined to develop under water, like that of the Fluctuators; or perhaps even secretly to accept non-human members, like the most mysterious Academy of the Amphibians.

Not unnaturally, such fervid activity did occasion some expenses; however, a prestigious seat in some patrician palazzo, money for refreshments, for the printing of the best (of the rare) works written by the academicians, together with the extravagant (and somewhat less rare) junketing and festivities, were as a rule all bestowed by some benevolent patron, to whom the academicians dedicated their poetic, scientific or doctrinal offerings. Normally, this would be a cardinal or the scion of some wealthy family of the highest standing, when it was not indeed a pontiff who, for reasons of state or out of simple affection, took an interest in the arcane activities of this or that group of studious gentlemen. When the generous patron moved on to a better life, the academy, bereft of its benefactor, would typically opt for its own dissolution; as when the death of Queen Christina of Sweden in 1689 turned dozens, indeed perhaps hundreds of artists, musicians, poets and philosophers onto the streets. They all had to abandon Christina's palace on the Via della Lungara post haste and swiftly seek some other way of earning their keep. With the demise of their Maecenas, the ingenious activities of the Sterile, the Vague or the Aggravated Ones were all too prone to peter out; but their members usually belonged to several academies and kept on found-ing new ones. Human Knowledge was safe.

Whether they dealt in games for the *bon viveur* or serious scientific discussion, one thing was clear: Rome had become a unique Uni-versal Forum for Chatterboxes, in which at least one of the noblest of human faculties was guaranteed *ad libitum*: talk, talk, talk. It goes without saying that the speaker of the moment would set forth the most high-flown concepts and the most learned of meditations.

I was just thinking that I would, that evening, be attending such an event: a series of discussions for the finest and most select wits, held by academicians invited to the Villa Spada for the express pur-pose of enlivening the conversation, in whose presence I expected that I would, in all humility, have to struggle from beginning to end to keep myself from yawning. Matters, however, went somewhat dif-ferently.

Hardly had I donned my daytime uniform when a familiar voice caught my attention.

"We are terribly late, the guests are waiting! And it should be nice and warm, not all murky and muggy! Did you add almonds, hazelnuts and orange water? And half an ounce of carnations?"

It was Don Paschatio, who was rebuking two of the Steward's as-sistants for what he saw as the mediocre quality of the chocolate. The two stared at him with insolent, bovine eyes, as though he were some silly old uncle.

"Mmm. . ." said Don Paschatio, raising his eyes to heaven as he licked a finger coated with chocolate. "It seems to me that he has forgotten to add the two reals of aniseed. The Steward! Call the Steward!"

"To tell the truth. . . He has taken half a day's leave," said one of the assistants.

"Leave? With the guests still arriving?" exclaimed Don Paschatio, growing pale.

"He said he was offended by your latest reprimand."

"Offended, says he. . . As though a Steward had any right to take offence," he moaned disconsolately to himself. "It no longer counts for anything to be Major-Domo. *O tempora, o mores!*"

He turned around suddenly and saw me. His face lit up.

"Signor Master of the Fowls!" he exclaimed. "How very fortunate that you should be here, at the service of the most noble House of

Spada, instead of shirking your duties like so many of your fellow servants."

Before I could even begin to answer, he had placed a heavy silver tray in my hands.

"Take this tray. Let us at least make a start!" he commanded the other two.

So it was that I found myself holding up with the tray a great jug of fine pink-onion-coloured porcelain full of hot chocolate, surrounded by twelve clinking cups, as well as little jars of vanilla to sweeten the bitter potion. As I set off, I found before my eyes the lovely undulating buttocks of a Diana, painted on the jug, who with her bow and quiverful of arrows was chasing through the woods some poor stag destined for the spit. With the cups tinkling against one another, I was already entering the great salon on the ground floor of the great house where the shade extended calm to fugitives from the heat of the day, inviting palates to enjoy the exotic refreshment.

Once I had made my entry into the great hall, I found before me a scene very different from that which I had expected. There was in fact no academy whatever. Or, to put it better, no orator was to be seen, as the tradition of intellectual confraternities demands, before an audience of silent and absorbed listeners. The salon was full of little groups of guests, randomly gathered: some standing in tight knots, others seated in a semicircle; while yet others wandered around, congregating then going their separate ways, greeting the new arrivals and attending first to one speaker, then another. It reminded me of those clouds of summer gnats which one sees against the light in clearings; they seem at first to form a community, but when one looks more closely, they turn out to be nothing but a mass of chaotic singularities.

One could, however, hear outbursts from the liveliest speakers who, before that undulating and disorderly sea of heads and bodies, discoursed upon the immortality of the soul, the movement of the planets, the latest maps imported from the New World and the antiquities of Rome.

All that great conflation of scientific and philosophical discourse, amplified by the echo of the huge room, blended into a dense, milky cloud in which it was possible to distinguish only one or two sentences at a time.

"For, as Jovius opined in Book Four of his opus. . ." one pedant was proclaiming to my left.

"Thus, as it is written concerning Dionysius of Halicarnassus. . ." some eloquent fellow was opining to my right.

"Your Excellencies cannot be unaware that the sublime doctrine of Aquinas. . ." bellowed a third speaker.

In actual fact, no one was listening, for in Rome they assemble for no purpose other than vain chatter as a pretext and garnishing for food and drink. Romans have always been inclined to judge human events by the immemorial measure of the Roman Empire or by the eternal paradigm of the Catholic Church. Erroneously believing themselves to have title to those temporal or spiritual powers, of which they are merely adventitious offshoots, they end up by regarding all matters quotidian as less than nothing, and look down on all things from on high.

Atto came to meet me, perfectly at ease in the midst of that bedlam of noise and confusion.

"'Tis ever so: they all eat and drink and no one listens," he whispered in my ear. "And yet there's a Jesuit behind those people," said he, pointing towards a nearby group, "who is holding forth in a most interesting discussion concerning the problem of obedience to or rebellion against princes. Quite in vain, for they are all talking with their neighbours about their own little affairs. 'Tis quite true, if the Parisians meet a strumpet, they take her for a saint and go down on their knees before her. As for the Romans, if they meet a saint, they take her for a strumpet and ask her how much she wants."

Hardly had I shown my tray and laid it on a serving table in order to fill the cups than a crowd of gentlemen flocked around me with jovial exuberance.

"Look Marchese, there's chocolate!"

"Come, Monsignor, they are serving us."

"And what of the dissertation on the *Decades* of Livy?" protested one prelate who was taking part in an academic discussion.

"If you'll not let your *Decades* be bygones, 'tis the chocolate itself that will be gone," retorted another, and the whole company roared with laughter.

Leaning on the table, I had barely time to fill the cups than they had all been snatched up and the contents of the great jug vanished down the maws of the bystanders. Fortunately, other servants were by then arriving in reinforcement, taken by storm in their turn by new groups of guests, while yet others were besieged by princes and archpriests, secretaries and chamberlains.

While before me one such free-for-all was taking place, I heard behind me a brief conversation which intrigued me no little.

"Have you heard? It seems they intend to resurrect Monsignor Retti's project."

"The plan to reform the police, from back in the days of Pope Odescalchi?"

"Precisely. And I am all for it! It is high time that all those infamous corrupt catchpolls were taught a lesson."

Out of the corner of my eye, I saw that those exchanging these remarks were two middle-aged prelates. The topic was of no little interest to me: where there are catchpolls there will be thieves, and anything that enlightened me on that subject might be of use for my purposes and those of Abbot Melani. Soon, however, the two prelates were lost from sight (and hearing); hoping to retrace them, I promised myself that I would mention their discussion to Atto.

The lofty and majestic vault which, moments before, had resounded with chatter now echoed with sounds of sipping, sucking and the smacking of tongues. None could bear to forego the taste of chocolate which the Steward – regardless of whatever Don Paschatio might have to say on the matter – had prepared with perfect judgment and mastery.

Suddenly, a space opened up in the formless throng of revellers. Cardinal Spada made his way forward, accompanied by the bridal pair. The master of the house had preferred to let talk die down before making his appearance, thus taking advantage of the gaiety produced by the refreshments.

"Hurrah! Long live the bride and groom!" All turned to applaud the couple, rushing forward to exchange compliments with Spada and to kiss his ring, while festive cheering broke out all around.

"A speech, Your Eminence, a speech!" cried several guests, beseeching the Cardinal.

"Very well, my friends, so be it," he replied with a smile, benevolently calming the hubbub with a clap of the hands. "But faced with such an assembly of the learned, my contribution will inevitably be scanty. You will, I hope, pardon me if, in the modest verses I am about to recite, the topic of which is certainly familiar to you, I should fail to measure up to the science which I have heard in these chambers, but, as the poet puts it, *non datur omnibus adire Corinthum.*"

He begged silence and with jovial expression recited a sonnet.

> *He am I who through the unknown essence*
> *On fasting entered such an argument*
> *That to the schoolmen's great astonishment*
> *None knows to which of us to 'ward the sentence.*
> *One argues taste, the other, abstinence,*
> *Both to the Jesuit discipline assent;*
> *If, saith the one, to liquors we consent,*
> *We err, for then there is incontinence.*
> *Balm for his scruples, t'other then suggests*
> *Of amity a civil rite wherein the chalice*
> *Containing no vanilla, each ingests.*
> *Thus, betwixt innocence and malice*
> *A wondrous middle way he then invests,*
> *Which reconciles the fast with gusto and with avarice.*

This gave rise to laughter and yet another burst of applause. Cardinal Spada had brilliantly exposed, and resolved, a burning question much debated among Jesuit doctrinal experts: does the drinking of chocolate constitute the breaking of a fast? Spada's proposal was, in keeping with the best style of the Society of Jesus, a sensible compromise: by all means drink chocolate, but let it be bitter, without vanilla, thus reconciling appetite, abstinence and thrift. Meanwhile, the academic chapels whose activities had been disrupted by the arrival of the chocolate were again forgathering. Around single orators or pairs engaged in verbal duels, idle knots of listeners were forming, some still sipping from their cups, some deep in conversation with their neighbours, others gesticulating in the direction of some acquaintance glimpsed in a nearby group. In the motley multitude of ladies, prelates and nobles, it was child's play to discern political allegiances; to identify the partisans of France, Spain or the Empire, one had but to look at where pocket handkerchiefs were placed, the colour of stockings or on which side of their bosom the ladies had pinned some little flower.

With the pretext of removing cups and jugs left on the tables, I moved away from my place to rejoin Abbot Melani whom I saw chatting somewhat disconsolately with a pair of elderly ladies while scanning the whole assembly for the least event worthy of interest or, better, suspicion. Seeing me approach he promptly left the two ladies and with a furtive gesture indicated that I was to join him outside, on the balcony above the stairs leading directly from the main salon down to the gardens.

The sun was still blazing, and we found ourselves providentially alone. I told him briefly of the conversation between the two church-men and the planned reform of public order in Rome which I had overheard.

"Those two spoke the truth," he commented. "The Roman police have always been both corrupt and utterly shameless."

At that moment, a number of high-ranking prelates emerged from the salon onto the balcony, to take a few pinches of snuff. Some of the faces were known to me, but I could not put names to them. Only one did I remember perfectly and it was that, in fact, which startled me. It was His Eminence Cardinal Albani.

At a glance, Atto took in the situation. He continued what he was saying, gradually raising his voice as he spoke.

"No one is more corrupt than the catchpolls, my boy," he de-clared, speaking with mounting passion, turning now to address the cardinals who had just appeared.

There shone in his small eyes, perceptible only to those who knew him well, who knows what project or desire.

"And above all, than the judges," he continued, "because in our mad and supposedly modern times, which are nevertheless still the sucklings of a very recent past – times which I would call the Univer-sal Republic of Verbiage – facts count only on the basis of the name they're given. The judges are honorary citizens of this republic, be-cause their task is to satisfy the thirst for revenge of the powerless and the victims of injustice who have ever and will ever crowd their antechambers; antechambers which one leaves with few real facts in hand and many words, for it is precisely of words that this republic consists, as their eminences will be readily aware."

Atto's sally had cast all in the blackest embarrassment. He was at one and the same time addressing the highest wearers of the purple and myself, a mere plebeian. But such insolence, already grave and unusual, was as nothing beside the factious content of his discourse, which sounded like a hymn to mischief making.

"Through the judges' hands passes the world's future," he contin-ued, "for when man counts for little, as in our times, the law is trium-phant. Being intrinsically void of any substance, like insanity, it takes up whatever free space it can find. If you should read in a gazette, 'The Judges have ordered the arrest of the alleged swindler Such-and-Such', you will at once think that good has triumphed over evil, for the judges are called judges and the newspaper has called the man they've arrested a swindler. This being said, even before his trial, the death blow against Such-and-Such has already been struck, for fame has plenty of breath and immense wings and aims the darts that are placed in its quiver at whomsoever it will, without paying the slightest attention to any poison in which they may have been dipped. So no one will tell you that those Judges often lie or accept bribes, that they are marionettes, dolls, dummies created out of nothingness and manipulated so as to strike at adversaries, to create diversions, to subvert and to distract public opinion."

I looked around me. The cardinals present during Atto's rash *coup de théâtre* were grey in the face with consternation. The afternoon was supposed to be dedicated to academies, not the justification of revolt.

"Take careful note, however, the Universal Republic of Verbiage is certainly populated by puppets and marionettes, yet it is built of stones as massive as those of the walls of Ilium; these are called justice, truth, public health, security. . . Each one of these is a cyclopic mass that can neither be discussed nor moved, because the power of words is the only sovereign in our times. Whosoever stands up against seeming truth and seeming Justice will always be called deceitful and dishonest, whoever resists public health will be labelled a spreader of the plague, and if they take on security, they will be damned as subversives. Any attempt to convince others, many others, that behind those words there often, oh so often, lies concealed their very opposite, will be as effective as trying to lift those walls and transport them over a thousand leagues. Better by far to put one's hands over one's eyes and simply keep going, like those who have always decided the fate of nations, the sovereigns and their occult counsellors: well they know that perverse wheel of fortune, and indeed they encourage it, for they want the judges, the catchpolls and all the other marionettes of that sad and grotesque Republic of Verbiage to remain their slaves, and our butchers. Until, perhaps, one day they too are hanged on the orders of a judge."

"Abbot Melani, you are challenging the order of things."

It was Albani. As on the evening before, Atto was being menacingly called to order by His Holiness' Secretary for Breves.

"I am challenging nothing and nobody," Atto replied amiably, "I am merely meditating on. . ."

"You are here to provoke, to stir up trouble and confusion. You are promoting disorder, inviting people to mistrust judges, to disobey the police. All that, I heard quite clearly."

"Stirring up trouble? Far from it, Your Eminence. As a French subject. . ."

"That you are on the side of the Most Christian King, that, everybody knows by now," Albani interrupted him yet again, "but there are limits you should not overstep. The Papal See is not some land to be overrun by this or that power. The Holy City is the universal haven of peace, open to all men of goodwill."

His tone admitted of no reply.

"I bow down to Your Eminence," was Atto's sole response as he made a deep bow to his contradictor, and attempted to kiss his ring.

To complete the insult, however, Albani did not see (or wish to see) the gesture and turned sharply towards the rest of his company, commenting harshly on what had just taken place.

"Incredible! To come here, to the home of the Secretary of State, making propaganda for France, and then spreading ideas. . ." he exclaimed indignantly to his fellow cardinals.

Atto was thus left kneeling before Albani's back. Someone among the latter's friends noticed this and sniggered. The humiliation was as grave as it was comic.

Moments later, Melani had returned to the salon; I followed him discreetly. His rash speech had been made in my presence too. It might appear to be the ravings of one beside himself, which I had witnessed by pure chance. But one must not go too far: we must avoid word getting around that I was in his service, otherwise I too would come under a cloud of suspicion and mistrust. I did not want to protect his interests but my own. What if Cardinal Spada were to decide that I was mixed up with with a troublemaker? I ran the risk of dismissal.

We crossed the salon, still crowded with guests, keeping our distances. Melani gestured that I was to follow him to his lodgings on the upper floors.

"So, have you understood how the Republic of Verbiage works?" he resumed, as though his speech had never been interrupted.

"But Signor Atto. . ."

"You have doubts, I know. You would like to say to me: if what you say is really true, how do you know, and how do others like you know, that the police are not to be trusted and that judges too are sometimes corrupt, and at the service of the powerful?"

"Well, if, among other things. . ."

"These are clandestine truths, my boy, banished from the Republic of Verbiage and thus utterly worthless. And remember," said he with an admonitory grin, "if order is to be maintained in states and in kingdoms, the people must never know the truth about two things: what there really is in sausages and what takes place in the courts of law."

I had no time to contradict him and prolong the discussion, for by then we had reached his doorway. He opened the door, telling me to wait outside a moment, then returned with a basket of soiled underwear.

"Now I have an important meeting, I want to change my shirt. I must put myself in order, I am in a disastrous state. Count Lamberg, the Ambassador of the Empire, is on the point of returning to the villa and I shall approach him. He is a little late, soon he'll be here. I want to ask him to receive me. You, meanwhile, take these clothes and have them washed and ironed for me, otherwise I shall soon be left without any clean apparel. Now, leave me."

As I made my way to the laundry with Atto's dirty clothing in my hands, a swarm of thoughts crossed my mind. Melani's words accused sovereigns and the highly select circle (counsellors, ministers of state. . .) to which he was so proud to belong. It was almost as though with those words he really did mean to excite, to provoke, to stir up rebellion, as Albani said. With the Cardinal's double reprimand, Atto had acquired for himself the reputation of a rash fellow and an agitator to boot, all of which was what he least needed to be able to manoeuvre in peace. He was a spy and spies need discretion. Whatever could have got into him that he should have made such an exhibition of himself while, what was more, bruiting abroad his connections with the French party? Surely, those who had been present during the second clash between him and Albani must have spread that tasty piece of gossip among the other guests. The damage was done.

Strangely, Atto seemed oblivious of this. Hardly had we been alone than, instead of commenting on the humiliation he had suffered at Albani's hands when the latter had turned his back on him as he knelt at his feet, he had resumed his bizarre discourse on the Universal Republic of Verbiage.

Perhaps I had got everything wrong, said I to myself. No longer was I to expect from Abbot Melani the implacable lucidity I had found in him seventeen years before. He had aged, that was all. With the loss of his intellectual and moral faculties, imprudence, poor judgment and intemperance had taken over. From being sharp-witted he had grown quarrelsome, from being prudent, he had become rash, instead of coldly calculating, confused. I knew that men rarely improve with age. That he should have worsened somewhat should not, I thought, come as a surprise to me.

Meanwhile, I observed from afar a large company of persons entering the great house, accompanied by an impressive escort of men-at-arms. I heard the other servants being told that Cardinal Spada was coming to receive an important personage. I knew who this must be.

Moments later, the guest made his entrance into the salon, while Fabrizio Spada, accompanied by the bridal couple, advanced to meet him with obsequious and benevolent pomp. Many among the guests were those who rushed to meet the new arrival: the Count von Lamberg, Ambassador of the Emperor.

Cardinal Spada, so I subsequently learned, had sent one of his personal carriages to fetch him, preceded by that of the Cardinal de' Medici. In order to avoid grave problems of form, the other two representatives of the powers, the Spanish Count of Uzeda and the French Prince of Monaco, had tacitly arranged with their imperial counterpart that they were to be present at the same time only on the wedding day and to make a second visit on different days from one another. This would avoid conflicts of honour and precedence, as well as violence and brawls (such as occurred daily in Rome) between their respective lackeys, ever on the lookout for the best places to station their master's carriage.

The ambassadors of the other two great powers (France and Spain) would therefore not be present on that day, so that all attention would focus on Lamberg.

Because of my modest stature, obstructed as I was by the dense barrier of backs, heads and necks, I was obviously unable to witness the fatal moment of Lamberg's arrival in the salon. Nevertheless, the guests formed almost at once into two wings, between which the

Imperial Ambassador made his way forward. He was accompanied by a great retinue of lackeys in yellow livery and men-at-arms in dress uniform. Cardinal Spada was at his side, respectfully leading him to the centre of the salon. Ladies and gentlemen, to show their respect, bowed as he passed, seeking to attract attention by paying tribute to him and heaping blessings upon his head.

"Excellency. . ."

"May God preserve you!"

"May Your Excellency always keep as well."

Amidst the psalmody of obsequious expressions accompanying bows and curtsies, an unexpected note however arose.

"*Si Deus et Caesar pro me, quis contra?*"

I had no difficulty in recognising the voice which had pronounced that Latin phrase. It was Atto. He too must have knelt in homage to the powerful Austrian diplomat. "If God and the Emperor are with me, who'll be against me?" he had said. I tiptoed as far as I could, staring over some churchman's shining pate and at last I was able to witness the scene.

Atto was indeed on his knees before Lamberg, but in an elegant, controlled posture which manifested the desire to be courteous without indulging in self-abasement.

Before him stood the Imperial Ambassador, whose face I was able to see distinctly better than the day before. His eyes were coal-black; not deep, but cold and shifting. His expression was tenebrous, evasive and full of disquiet, as though indicative of a soul given to lies and dissimulation. The forehead was high enough, the oval of his face, regular, yet his complexion was ashen and dull, as though it had been rendered opaque by a surfeit of lugubrious cogitations. A slender, well-trimmed moustache gave his visage an airy touch of almost extreme elegance, designed only to mark off the distance from his inferiors. All in all, his presence inspired deference and respect but, above all, suspicion.

"Those are wise words," replied Lamberg, visibly intrigued. "Who are you?"

"An admirer, desirous of expressing to Your Excellency the most profound and sincere of praises," said Atto, handing him a note.

Lamberg took it. A murmur of surprise and curiosity ran through the crowd of guests. The Ambassador opened the note, read it and closed it. He gave a little laugh.

"Very well, very well," said he, nonchalantly returning the note to Atto and moving on.

Abbot Melani promptly returned to his feet with a satisfied smile.

I returned to my place, standing near the fireplace, in the hope of gleaning other interesting snippets of conversation from the lips of the two prelates I had overheard previously. Now, however, a different pair was seated beside me, in the same armchairs.

"Now really, to have gone so far as to serve chocolate. . ." one young cleric was hissing through tight lips.

"But you are unwilling to face up to the facts: this is a pro-Spanish Pope, he is a native of the Kingdom of Naples, which is a Spanish possession, and Spada is his Secretary of State," replied the other, a young man of excellent appearance who seemed to be of noble origin.

"Agreed, Your Excellency, but to have offered chocolate at a time when there may be a conclave within the year, what a shameless piece of Spanishry. Why, 'tis the favourite beverage of King Charles II of Spain. . ."

"It does seem like some partisan signal, I know, I know. You'll see that there will be talk of this in the next few days."

I did not know that chocolate could be regarded as a political sign of Hispanophilia. I did, however, know that the idea of serving the cacao-based beverage had been Don Paschatio's and that Cardinal Spada had consented to it, going so far as to jest on the matter by declaiming a graceful sonnet. Yet, I thought, laughing to myself, once tidings of such criticism and suspicions reached his ears, it would be easy to foresee the Secretary of State's reaction and his latest reprimand to his unfortunate Major-Domo.

Suddenly, my attention was caught by a movement on the right-hand side of the room. One of Cardinal Spada's lackeys was moving towards Cardinal Spinola, who was surrounded by a small knot of guests. I realised this only because in making his way through the assembly he had bumped into the back of the Marchesa Bentivoglio, Lady in Waiting to the Queen of Poland, who had spilled a good deal of still hot chocolate on her corsage. The lackey, bitterly rebuked by the Prince of Carbognano, had after a thousand apologies gone on his way and delivered a note to Spinola. The latter read the billet with ostentatious nonchalance, as though to stress its unimportance to those present, and returned it to the messenger. It was too far off for one to be able to hear, in that infernal hubbub, what the Cardinal said to the lackey, moving towards him in the most rapid of movements as he sent him on his way. With a supreme effort of all my senses, overcoming for an instant all that festive noise and my own impotent immobility, I somehow thought that I could read on Spinola's lips, taken together with his gesture of complicity in sending the lackey on his way, a few eloquent syllables: ". . . outside, on the balcony."

Seeing and moving were as one single motion. The urgency could not have been clearer: a message, sent in all probability from Spada to Spinola, was now being sent on to a third recipient. On the terrace, I already knew who might be present, as he had been a few moments earlier: Cardinal Albani. Communications were running unseen between the three members of the Sacred College who had met at the Vessel.

If we could only guess at the content of that message (for there could be no question of intercepting it), we should have made a considerable step towards understanding the manoeuvres taking place with a view to the conclave. We would perhaps be able to understand what point had been reached (and where and how) in the secret negotiations concerning the choice of the new pope, as suspected by Atto, and perhaps also why the three cardinals had chosen to meet at the Vessel, that place of a thousand mysteries. We must not fail.

I moved away from the wall and, taking care not to attract the attention of the other lackeys, I too made my way towards the balcony. The sun's glare was still blinding. As I drew near to the great window giving onto the terrace, I could descry against the light, like those figures which it seems the Jesuits know so well how to project against the backcloth in their theatrical performances, the dark silhouettes of the guests conversing in the open. Intuition, that indispensable ally in all difficult situations, enabled me at once to identify Cardinal Albani. There he was, to the left, still in the place where he had humiliated Atto, surrounded by that little congregation of friends and boot-lickers which always accompany every cardinal, just as cows are surrounded by flies. The only person to leave the group was a servant of the Spada household who had just finished refilling the cups with piping hot chocolate.

As I approached the door leading out from the salon, pushing my way between legs, chairs and tables, and praying the Most High that

I should not be intercepted by Don Paschatio, I became aware that Melani had not missed what had transpired. Buvat who, giving up his usual attempts to find a glass of wine, was acting as lookout whenever Atto was engaged in conversation, had drawn close to him and whispered something in his ear. Atto had instantly taken his leave of a cordial trio of gentlemen, leaving them there without so much as a by-your-leave. Then, in his haste, he collided heavily with one of the secretaries in Lamberg's retinue, somehow managing to avoid falling headlong.

The lackey had too great a start on us for it to be possible to catch up with him. It was thus through the window, I to the left and Atto to the right, that we witnessed the delivery of the note. Unfortunately, the company surrounding the Cardinal hid from our sight the moment when he opened and read the billet. A moment later, we reached the threshold of the balcony, breathless but taking care not to betray any signs of haste. At that very moment, I saw all the guests present on the balcony turn towards me. Every one of them bore on his face an expression of hilarious, amused curiosity. The sun, whose rays struck me frontally, hurt my eyes cruelly, preventing me from seeing the features of those near to me.

I turned towards Atto. He too looked at me in some surprise, but only for an instant, for at that precise moment Albani was folding the note and was irresistibly distracted from it. The look of wonderment on the faces of the others, still fixed on me, showed absolutely no sign of fading. Someone pointed at me, nudging his neighbour. I was purple with embarrassment. I dared not so much as ask what in my person might arouse such interest in them, but nor did I wish to move, now that I had reached Albani.

"How graceful," said Cardinal Albani looking towards me. "Cardinal Spada truly has exquisite taste."

Then he placed the cup of chocolate on the little wall of the balcony, using the hand in which he still held the note. As he did so, some chocolate spilled and wet the piece of paper. The Cardinal at once snatched back his diaphanous hand, unaccustomed to contact with vile kitchen matter, and boiling hot to boot. The note fell from his hand, ending up on the wall, next to the cup. At once I felt a familiar swishing above me, accompanied by a sort of caress on the top of my head. A swift shadow came between me and the sun. With just a couple of sharp movements of its feathers, the being skilfully swerved and landed on the wall, like some animated spinning top, just next to Albani's cup of chocolate. I was unable to restrain myself.

"Caesar Augustus!" I exclaimed.

The events of the following instants were among the most convulsive of the day and surely the strangest thing that the Villa Spada had ever seen.

Until a few moments before, Cardinal Albani and his friends, together with all the guests present on the balcony had been rapt in admiration, not of myself but of the majestic plumage of Caesar Augustus, perched just above my head on a projection from the villa's outer wall.

As I have had occasion to tell, the parrot was prone to an insane, overpowering passion for chocolate. Every now and then, I would procure him a little, filching it from the kitchen. It was, however, the first time that the whole Villa Spada had been invaded by that inebriating aroma. It was thus no accident that the bird had, that day, at last overcome its shy and retiring nature and come to join in the festivities, in the hope of finding something good to drink.

At the very moment when Albani had lost control of his cup, the fowl had seen and, true to his haughty and scornful nature, seized the ideal solution: theft. Even before landing, he had dipped his beak into the Cardinal's cup. Albani and the others smiled, a little embarrassed.

"How very charming, eh?. . . Really amusing," they just had time to comment before Caesar Augustus, under the somewhat shocked eyes of those who had just arrived on the scene and were gathering around, grasped the paper in one of his talons.

Albani reached out and tried to regain possession of the note which was less than a foot away from him. Caesar Augustus bit the back of his hand. The Cardinal withdrew it with a cry of disappointment. All the other persons present took an imperceptible step back.

"Your Eminence, let me help," I ventured, stepping forward in the hope that Caesar Augustus would not use violence against an old friend. I reached out with my hand and delicately took the note from him. Then came the terrible shock.

Someone had thrown me to the ground, or rather had fallen on top of me. From the protests which I heard I understood confusedly that at least two or three of us had fallen. Someone took the billet from my hand while other hands shoved clumsily against my ribs.

"Oh Your Eminence, excuse me, excuse me, I tripped," I heard Buvat's unmistakeable voice.

"Stop this madman!" echoed another voice.

I understood Atto's plan at once: to create confusion, perhaps even a brawl, by tripping that gangling Buvat so that he fell headlong against the group, while he himself got hold of the paper.

"Oh damnation, no!" I heard Melani utter immediately after that. I freed myself of someone's leg and rose to my feet.

Almost everyone had got up, including Buvat, who was putting himself in order under the irate glares of about a dozen people. Caesar Augustus was still there, on the same little wall as before, but with one important difference: the note was in his beak. He had snatched it directly from Atto's hands. Melani now stood before him imploringly, without however daring to ask him to return the paper: Albani was staring with a glazed expression at the bird and his paper.

"Caesar Augustus. . ." said I softly, hoping to catch his attention.

He replied with a gurgling sound. He was sucking the note, with its coating of chocolate. Then he spread his wings, looking obliquely at me. At length, with a whirring of white feathers, he rose, flying off at great speed.

Cardinal Albani flinched involuntarily.

"Truly a strange bird," said he with an imperceptible break in his voice, struggling to recover his dignity.

I noticed distractedly that the Cardinal was wiping pearls of sweat from his forehead with a handkerchief. My whole attention was focused on the direction in which the fowl was flying. There could be no doubt about it. As I had feared, he was leaving the villa in the direction of the San Pancrazio Gate.

It was not easy for me to find a way of disengaging myself. Muttering an excuse, I left the balcony. Atto joined me almost at once in the salon, in which dozens of heads were still turned towards the curious scene that had just taken place outside. We succeeded in melting sufficiently into the crowd. I had, however, to calculate carefully when to slip out of the salon and then the villa without being seen by Don Paschatio or other members of the staff; all that, while taking the time to exchange the livery for my own clothes. For that purpose, I was able to take refuge in Abbot Melani's apartments.

"Hurry, hurry, damn it, by now that wretched bird could be anywhere," said he as I hastily pulled on my breeches.

To pass unobserved there was no other solution but to creep through the cane-brake behind the main avenue of the villa and then to double back through the part of the garden behind the house. Fortunately, the summer sun was already sheathing the fiery daggers with which it was so fond of tormenting both objects and living things; the pursuit was thus less disagreeable.

After skirting the chapel, we crossed the drive that led to the theatre and came to the rear entrance. We got ourselves a little dirty but at least we had avoided being seen by the other guests or by the guards watching over the main entrance. We must make sure that Albani, Spinola and Spada should know nothing of our search.

Atto had commanded his secretary to remain at the reception and, most discreetly, to keep an eye on the three eminences, even though he did not expect to obtain much information.

We both knew that, if we could lay our hands on the note, we would learn the details of their next appointment, and perhaps of their plans. It was true that Caesar Augustus would have chewed up the paper thoroughly where it was steeped in his beloved chocolate. That was precisely why I knew that he would not have got rid of it, but would have held on to it carefully so that he could from time to time return to lick its sweet surface with his pointed black tongue.

We had just passed the San Pancrazio Gate when Atto grabbed me by the shoulder.

"Look!"

It was he. He was circling almost directly above our heads. He had surely heard us. He swerved at once to the right and then flew straight ahead. This was just what I had been expecting. Whenever he set out on his solitary adventures, abandoning the villa for days, sometimes even weeks on end, I would see him fly off towards the tallest, most forbidding trees; and that was what he now did. Leaving Rome, he had not much choice. The most majestic pines, the proudest cypresses, the most hospitable plane trees in the neighbourhood were all gathered in one place, and there we saw him disappear, shooting like a brilliant white and yellow comet, into the green gardens of the Vessel.

Evening the Fourth
10TH JULY, 1700

✠

As we slipped into the park of the Vessel, once again undisturbed, our gaze scanned the heights rather than what lay before us. Without a shadow of a doubt, Caesar Augustus was somewhere up there, perched on some high branch, perhaps even keeping an eye on us.

The late afternoon was at last free of the burning influence of the summer sun but, as had happened on the occasion of our previous visits, no sooner had we entered the Vessel than the evening shadows, which seemed already to be lengthening over Villa Spada, vanished, swept away, together with the few clouds, by a sharp little breeze that left the field open to a pure, shimmering golden light. In short, twilight seemed to be an unwelcome guest at Elpidio Benedetti's villa.

After crossing the entrance courtyard, we moved towards the espaliered citrus trees, in the neighbourhood of which we began a cautious investigation. The vivid tints of oranges and lemons, the splashes of colour of vases of roses, the leopard-like shadows of the chequerboard pergolas and the little wood confounded not only the sense of sight, but of smell, and indeed all the senses. Light breaths of wind caused every leaf to murmur, every flower to vibrate, every stem to sway. After a few minutes, I seemed to be seeing Caesar Augustus everywhere and nowhere. We walked the length of the drive, which was covered by a barrel-vaulted pergola ending with the fresco of Rome Triumphant. We found nothing. Even Atto seemed discouraged. We changed direction and headed for the house.

"Damned bird," he murmured.

"I confess that in my view we are most unlikely to find him. When Caesar Augustus does not want to be found, there is usually nothing that can be done about it."

"Nothing to be done? That we shall see!" said he, brandishing his silver-pommelled stick at the heavens, as though he were admonishing some deity.

"I tell you that if he does not want to be found, not even if. . ."

"I know what we shall do and what we shall not do, my boy. I am a diplomat in the service of the Most Christian King," said he, silencing me.

I held back briefly, then decided to answer.

"Very well, Signor Atto, then explain to me why you tore the note from my hand when I had just got hold of it. If Buvat had not performed that clever trick, if he had not fallen on top of me, perhaps we should now have the note in our hands. Instead of which, you took it and allowed it to be snatched from you by the parrot!"

I awaited his response with my chest tight with emotion. As usual, my sallies against Atto caused me a fine bout of anxiety.

For a second he stayed silent, then he answered me with a cruel hiss.

"You really haven't got a whisper of a clue, and what's more, you've never had one. You would never have been able to hold onto that note. Albani was right there in front of you. They would all have seen you, you'd have had to return it to him. Only I and Buvat could have made it disappear, if your idiotic parrot had not been there to ruin everything."

"In the first place, the parrot is not mine but was left to the household by the late lamented Monsignor Virgilio Spada, Cardinal Fabrizio's uncle, may God keep him in glory. And besides, it was thanks to the parrot that I was able to take the note from Albani."

"I could have distracted Albani. In the meanwhile, Buvat would have taken advantage of the opportunity."

"Distract Albani? But you've done nothing except to make an enemy of him. For the second time today you have caused a scandal in his presence with your verbal excesses. They'll all be talking about nothing else at the Villa Spada."

"Silence!"

I became furious. This was the straw that broke the camel's back. I knew that my outbursts were thoroughly justified. Atto could not reduce me to silence that easily. But this was about something else.

He was looking behind me, tense and on his guard, as though studying a wild beast at close quarters.

"Is he behind me?" I asked, thinking of Caesar Augustus.

"He is moving away. He is dressed in the same way as last time."

"Dressed?"

I turned.

He was a little over ten yards off. Under his arm, he held a heavy bundle of papers tied with a red ribbon and was walking swiftly, with an absorbed frown, in the direction of a young girl with a complexion as white as ricotta and with thick, curly brown hair. With a bow, to which the maiden responded with a broad smile, he then handed her a purse full of money and some papers.

I just had time to recognise them before they both disappeared behind a large vase containing a lemon tree. There was little room for doubt. It was the same pair again: the mature gentleman and the maiden with whom I had seen him in conversation on the first day when we had entered the Vessel. She was (identical to) Maria Mancini. He, now that I had seen him a second time, reminded me of someone; but who?

Just as they had appeared, the two vanished. Already instructed by the previous apparitions, we made no attempt to follow them or to understand how they had disappeared. I looked at Atto.

"*Ahi, dunque c'e pur vero,*" he murmured.

Now I knew whom we had seen.

⇛⇘

It would take too long to go over all the facts to which that phrase – "Ah, so it really is true" – referred. Suffice to say that seventeen years earlier, it had been uttered at the point of death by a guest at the Donzello, the inn where I was then working as an apprentice and where, in those same days, I came to know Melani.

The dying man who had pronounced those words was Nicolas Fouquet, the former Superintendent of Finances of the Most Christian King, who was imprisoned for life following a palace conspiracy and had, after untold hardships and turns of fate, found refuge in Rome: at the Donzello, to be precise. Atto knew full well that I had a perfect memory of those events, since the memoir which he had taken from me and then paid for in cash recounted them in detail.

"It was the same gentleman as the other day, with Maria. . ." I murmured, still shaken by that enigmatic manifestation.

He did not reply, letting silence assent in his stead. Our altercation of moments before by now forgotten, we kept looking here and there, sticking our noses between leaves and branches, hiding from one another the fact that we were no longer looking for Caesar Augustus but into the abyss of memory in which the apparition had, through some necromancer's arts, cast us. I was thinking of the time when I had come to know Abbot Melani. He, however, was thinking of yet earlier times, of his friendship with Fouquet, of his tremendous destiny and of his tragic end. That was why, I said to myself, the first apparition we had come across at the Vessel had shaken Abbot Melani even more than the subsequent ones. He had in one moment beheld that apparition of Maria, to whom he was tied by such a tangle of feelings, and of Fouquet, whose terrible death he had both witnessed and had a part in.

Merely by looking at him, I could clearly perceive the powerful clash of opposing emotions which was taking place in Atto's soul. He had seen his old friend, not old and exhausted by years of imprisonment, but in the flower of strength and maturity. The bundle which he carried under his arm must contain working documents which he, an indefatigable worker in the service of the kingdom, even brought home with him – that I knew from Atto – before the machinations of the court of France stripped him of his minister's place, his honour, his liberty and his life.

With erect carriage, determined gait, distinguished features, a frowning expression, but only because his mind was turned towards matters high and noble: such had been Fouquet's bearing when Atto had known him in his own youth. Seeing him again, the Abbot was once more cast back into the depths of a thousand remote events, a thousand motions of the soul and of history, into an agony of infinite pain, and perhaps no less remorse. In that villa, as in a limpid and placid pool, the past was wondrously mirrored and, arranging its hair, almost coquettishly said: I am still here.

I saw Atto walk awhile, no longer with the gay movements of a lively old man, but with the uncertain gait of a young man precociously aged. I felt incapable of confronting those ordeals of the heart and the spirit; if I were in his place, said I, my whole body would be all shaken with sobs. Yet, he was resisting, still pretending to look for the parrot. I could only pardon him, and I thought that his many defects (rashness, duplicity, arrogance) must be forgiven if I truly wanted to call myself his friend. This meant perhaps deluding myself about many things: for example, that he might be capable of sincere friendship and trust. "You are my truest friend": alas, that phrase, which I had heard during the first apparition of Maria Mancini and

Fouquet, I could certainly never have uttered in relation to Abbot Melani. Yet, is not friendship perhaps the constant companion of illusion, an illusion which, nurtured for its own sake, thus prolongs the joys, ephemeral but necessary, which it brings to our lives?

"I do believe that you are right. Caesar Augustus is not here, or else it is too difficult to find him," said Atto tonelessly.

"If he does not want to be found, this is perhaps the ideal place," I completed his reasoning, no less distractedly.

"Yet it is truly curious that he should have flown to this exact spot," observed Melani. "The three cardinals, the Tetràchion, your parrot: this place is becoming somewhat crowded."

"In the case of Caesar Augustus, I think that is fortuitous. He likes tall, leafy trees, and here there are the finest ones on all the Janiculum."

"Well then, let us try to establish whether all the others came here fortuitously."

"The others?" I retorted, thinking apprehensively of the apparitions.

"Starting with the Tetràchion," Melani hastened to make clear, directing his steps towards the entrance of the building.

Once again, however, he had to stop. The sweetest of melodies spread by an utterly aerial violin was softly filling the park. It was impossible to tell whence it came or for whose pleasure it was intended.

"Again that music. . . the *folia*," murmured Atto.

"Would you like to walk around the house and see where it is coming from?"

"No; let us stay here. We have done enough running for the time being. I would not be averse to a little break."

He sat down on a little marble bench. I thought he was about to justify himself with some pretext like "We all grow old" or "I am no longer a boy", but he said nothing.

"The *folia*. Like that of Capitor," I ventured.

"Did you too think of it?"

"It was you who explained it to me: Capitor, the Spanish lunatic, whose nickname 'Capitor' is, you said, only a deformation of *la pitora*, which is supposed to be Spanish for 'the madwoman'."

"*Tout se tient.** This, however, is a *folia* that seems never to come to an end. Every time we hear it there are new variations, while Capitor's folly did come to an end."

---

* "It all holds together." (Translator's note.)

"Do you mean that she left France in the end?"

"Yes, one day she and the Bastard did go. But nothing was ever the same as before."

"What happened?"

"A series of unfortunate circumstances which may have led to the scene which we have just witnessed," Atto whispered, at last deciding to utter some words on the apparition of Maria and Fouquet.

❧

After Capitor's spectacle, Abbot Melani told me, the Cardinal's attitude changed radically. The madwoman's obscure prophecy, "A virgin who weds the crown brings death", was breathing down his neck and terror's trumpet resounded in his ears: the union between Louis and Maria must be eradicated, crushed, prevented by all means. Frightened, the Cardinal thought, "My head depends upon it," hiding behind his usual pallor his new unavowable fear.

Thus, over the next two months, in the spring of 1659, ever more fearful obstacles came between the two lovers. In June, Mazarin formally decreed that Maria must leave the court. The Cardinal, who planned to travel to the Pyrenees in order to discuss a number of details of the peace treaty with Spain, would take his niece with him and separate from her during the journey, sending her on to La Rochelle, where she was to reside with her two younger sisters Ortensia and Marianna. The departure date: 22nd June.

The Queen, fearing Louis's reaction, took care not to break the news to him. Mazarin therefore charged Maria with announcing her departure to the King. Louis's wrath exploded: he threatened Mazarin with disgrace, and Maria's despair immeasurably increased his rage and thirst for revenge. For three days, he would not let his mother speak; in utter desperation, he cast himself at the feet of Mazarin and the Queen, begging them in tears to allow him to marry Maria. With consummate rhetoric and in a firm voice, Mazarin reminded the young King that he, the Cardinal, had been chosen by his father and mother to assist him with his counsel, that he had served him with inviolable fidelity and that he could never have done anything that might damage the glory of France and of the crown; and finally, that he was the tutor of his niece Maria and would rather have killed her than consent to such a betrayal.

The King, in tears, gave way. When they were alone, Mazarin said to the Queen: "What are we to do? In his place, I'd do the same thing."

Even after that day, Louis kept telling Maria that he would never consent to marry the Infanta of Spain, that he expected to overcome the resistance of the Cardinal and his mother and that only she would one day sit on the French throne. As a pledge of his faith, he gave her the most precious necklace which he had acquired from the Queen of England and which he had set aside for the day of his betrothal.

Maria, however, had no more illusions: deeply wounded by her loved one's weakness, she even went so far once as to urge Louis to wed the Infanta.

Louis tried to reassure her, swearing that he had thoughts for none but her and would surely find a solution. Such promises could no longer satisfy the woman who received them, nor even the man who pronounced them.

The days that followed were nothing but an alternation of contrasting sentiments and humours: of Maria's love for the King, on the one hand, and love for her honour, on the other. At court meanwhile, Louis constantly repeated that his pain at the separation was unbearable. But words no longer sufficed.

"Few men, my boy, have seen what I then saw, and none will ever speak of it, of that you may be sure," said Atto.

So that the looseness of his tongue would not cause his legs to grow heavy, Atto and I took a brief promenade under the pergolas of the park. In that place populated by the phantasms of the past, every drive seemed to elicit from him an episode, every hedge a phrase, every flower bed a detail.

On the eve of Maria's departure, the King was far from resigned. On 21st June, the day before the separation, the Queen Mother and her son had a long private conversation in the bath chamber. Afterwards the King was seen to leave with swollen eyes. Maria was to depart; Louis had lost a battle, yet hoped somehow to win the war.

On the next day, suffering from an exceptionally violent lovesickness, he was bled twice, on the foot and on the arm (in the days that followed he was subjected to four purges and to another six treatments with leeches). Sobbing unrestrainedly and promising in a loud voice that he would make her his wife, Louis accompanied Maria to her carriage.

"She, obviously, could not understand. He was the King, he could do what he wanted; and yet he was yielding to his mother and to the Cardinal."

"And what did Maria say to him?"

"'Ah Sire! You weep: but you are the King, and it is I who am departing!'" said Atto with a thin smile on his lips.

"But why did the King not impose his will?"

"You should know that only the absence of the beloved reveals her importance. Louis felt in love but precisely because it was the first time he did not realise that it would be the only one. Queen Anne convinced her son that with time he would forget and one day he would be grateful to her for the hurt she was inflicting on him. He believed her. And the damage was irreparable."

We again sat down on a marble bench.

Once Maria had gone, there began between the two an intense, impassioned exchange of letters. She chose to leave her sisters at La Rochelle and to take refuge at the nearby fortress of Brouage.

It was August. Louis, with Queen Anne and the court in his train, set out for the Pyrenees where the treaty between France and Spain was to be signed; and the seal of that accord was to be the marriage between Louis and the Infanta.

"As I think I have already mentioned to you, I was part of that expedition which played an important role in the history of Europe," said Atto with ill-concealed pride.

On the 13th and 14th the Mazarinettes went to greet the King and his mother who were passing through those parts. Although they all spent the night in the same palace, Maria and Louis were not permitted so much as to exchange one word. And he, the King, put up with this in silence.

"It was then that the thought crossed my mind: His Majesty will never be any better than that weakling of a father of his, Louis XIII! The Cardinal can sleep quietly in his bed. . ." said Atto scornfully.

It was on that very occasion, when the young King was mounting his horse to continue the journey, that Melani was the bearer of a most secret letter from Maria: the last farewell.

"No one but me has ever known of the existence of that letter. It was long and heart-rending. I shall never forget the words with which it ended."

Atto recited from memory:

Des pointes de fer affreuses, hérissées, terribles, vont être entre Vous et moi.
Mes larmes, mes sanglots font trembler ma main. Mon imagination se trou-
ble, je ne puis plus écrire. Je ne sçais ce que je dis. À Dieu, Seigneur, le peu
de vie qui me reste ne se soutiendra que par mes souvenirs. Ô souvenirs
charmants! Que ferez vous de moy, que feray je de vous? Je perds la raison.
*Adieu, Seigneur, pour la dernière fois.**

"And this was truly her last farewell to their love," he concluded.

"But," I suggested, "did you secretly read that letter?"

"Eh?" murmured Atto, embarrassed. "Silence, and do not interrupt me."

While I laughed inwardly at having caught Melani out (it was clear that he had taken a discreet look at Maria's letter before delivering it to the King), the latter continued his narration.

Mazarin strove to persuade Maria to accept the proposal of marriage from the Constable Lorenzo Onofrio Colonna, a member of the noble and most ancient Roman family which the Cardinal's own father had served. Mazarin himself had served Filippo Colonna, Lorenzo Onofrio's grandfather. It had been Filippo Colonna who had dissuaded Mazarin from marrying the daughter of an obscure notary with whom he had fallen in love and who had instead set him on the way of the soutane – the prelature – wherein he had, as his patron had predicted, found great good fortune. The young King's way seemed thus to be traced by and modelled on that of the Cardinal, who pitilessly bestowed on his ward the broken web of his own destiny.

In order to persuade Maria to have herself married off to Lorenzo Onofrio, Mazarin was prepared to make concessions. Maria then requested to be allowed to return to Paris at once. Thus she did return to the capital. There, however, her uncle ordered her to be immured in his house. Destiny, however, so arranged matters that, while the Cardinal was busy elsewhere in France, Maria and her sisters had to leave the Palais Mazarin because of some rebuilding works. And where did they take up lodgings? In the Louvre, in the Cardinal's own apartments, while the latter learned the news in letters from one of his informants and was unable to do anything about it.

---

* Awful iron spikes, bristling and terrible, will stand between you and me. My tears, my sobs, cause my hand to tremble. My imagination clouds over, I can write no longer. I know not what I say. Adieu, my Lord, the little life that remains to me will be sustained only by memories. O charming memories! What will you make of me, what shall I make of you? I am losing my reason. Adieu, my Lord, for the last time.

In the Louvre, Maria was once again the object of new, unexpected intrigues: she was passionately courted and received a proposal of marriage from the heir to the Duchy of Lorraine, Charles, the future hero of the Battle of Vienna. He was an eighteen-year-old, handsome, enterprising and brimming with ardour. She was prepared to marry him, far preferring him to Colonna, whom she had never seen and who would lock her up in Italy, where a husband's power over his wife was absolute. Mazarin, however, finding all manner of pretexts, vehemently refused. He feared that, even married, Maria would still be dangerous in Paris.

Meanwhile, preparations were proceeding for the marriage between Louis and the Infanta of Spain. There were seven months of negotiations and preliminaries before the ceremony could take place, in two stages, as required by custom, on either side of the frontier (all sovereigns being forbidden to set foot in the neighbouring kingdom, since that would be equivalent to a declaration of war).

The first act of the treaty was the solemn renunciation of her hereditary rights to the throne of Spain pronounced by the Infanta Maria Teresa. On the following day, still on Spanish soil, the proxy marriage was celebrated with the Most Christian King. Louis was represented here by Don Luis de Haro, the Spanish negotiator. No Frenchman was admitted, except for Louis's witness, Zongo Ondedei, Bishop of Fréjus and Mazarin's evil genius.

Anne of Austria and the Cardinal could not bear the delay. A thousand times they had repeated to Louis that his Spanish fiancée was beautiful, far more beautiful than Maria Mancini. It was thus essential that she really should be beautiful. Madame de Motteville, a lady in waiting to Queen Anne and Mademoiselle de Montpensier, a cousin of the King, were therefore sent incognito on a mission: to evaluate the bride's womanly qualities.

On their return to the French camp on the frontier, they knew they would have to answer only one question: "Well, what is she like?"

"They did all they could to appear satisfied," Atto laughed derisively, "but it was enough to look at their faces, their drawn smiles, their assumed expressions. . . We knew the truth at once."

"In fact, she does not seem to be very tall: on the contrary, somewhat on the small side. To put it briefly, she's short," they confessed in unison. "But she is quite well made. Her eyes are not too small, her nose is not too big," they forced themselves to say, the one interrupting the other. "Her forehead is, in truth, somewhat ungarnished," a roundabout way of saying that the spouse was bald in the temples and her hair anything but orderly.

Madame de Motteville concluded brazenly: "If she had more regular teeth, she would be one of the most beautiful women in Europe." Mademoiselle de Montpensier, more scrupulous, seeing that very soon everyone would be able to judge the Infanta with their own eyes, allowed herself to let slip, "It hurts one to look at her." Then she hurriedly corrected herself, explaining that she was referring to that horrible coiffure and to the "monstrous machine": the enormous farthingale into which Maria Teresa's poor little body was forced.

"At that point, we were all terrified by how Louis might react on the next day, when he saw the Infanta for the first time."

"And what happened?"

"Nothing of what we feared. At the meeting with his future bride, he went through the ceremonial like a perfect actor. Under his mother's doting eyes, he followed her innumerable recommendations and acted out the ritual part of the lovelorn suitor consumed with impatience, as is the custom at royal weddings. He even galloped rather gallantly along the riverside, with hat in hand, following the bride's boat. Louis was splendid, so manly and ardent on his steed, and sent poor Maria Teresa into ecstasies.

Abbot Melani adjusted the buckle of one shoe, then the other, after which he raised his eyes to heaven.

"Poor wretched Infanta," he murmured. "And what a wretch, he."

By that impeccable conduct, Louis was striving to obey the exhortations of the Queen Mother: to silence the heart and lock his senses in a drawer. He venerated his mother and was confident that she and the Cardinal had made the best choice for him. Such was the outcome of the inexperience of life and love to which the pair had condemned him. Yet, from the moment he saw his bride, he began silently to be consumed by the worm of doubt and suspicion, the burning fear of having been deceived.

From that moment on, the fire within him burned down to cold ash. The young Sovereign's face gave nothing away, nor did his actions or words, although a thousand eyes watched and a thousand ears listened at every moment. It was not possible to detect any weakening in the man who, at barely twelve years of age, surprised by the fury of the populace during the Fronde uprising had, when on the point of fleeing the royal palace with his mother, gone to bed still dressed and managed not to open an eye all night, while the furious mob passed near his feet, silenced only by a sacrosanct respect for the innocent sleep of the boy King. What would have happened if someone had raised the coverlets a little and seen the deception?

To his companions who, after the visit to Maria Teresa, went to him in the hope of persuading him to open his heart, asking him what was his impression of the Infanta, he replied simply: "Ugly." And not another word could be got out of him.

"Who knows how much he was suffering," I ventured.

"Because his future wife was not as he expected her to be? No, not as much as you think. For him that changed little or nothing. He was awakening to the fact that his heart was not docilely following his mother's reassurances, as he had for a time wanted to believe. He had been warmed by the sun of a fine pair of black eyes, lost in the heather scent of Maria's wild brown hair, enchanted by her witty barbs and silvery laughter."

Nothing of this showed in the King's behaviour during the nuptial celebrations and festivities, except one single detail: for the liveries at the reception, Louis chose the colours of Maria's family crest.

He absolved his first conjugal duty without batting an eyelid, but on the very next day, with the court by now journeying back to the capital, the King abandoned his bride for two days. Where did he go? No one voiced the least allusion to this, but everyone knew: Louis suddenly made a deviation from the planned route and galloped to-wards Brouage, the castle where Maria had stayed in the Charentes, a region where she is still fondly remembered. At Brouage, Louis wept by the seashore. He asked to be shown the bed in which she had passed the night without closing an eye.

"But if no one spoke of this, as you yourself have said, how come you know all these details?" I asked in astonishment.

"In that chamber, Maria's bedchamber, I myself saw him. I had come with others on the orders of His Eminence. We found him overcome by a sort of agony. He was, I thought, like an image of the Deposition: the blankets torn from the couch, and he, crouching in a corner under the window, trembling with pain in the cold dawn of the Charentes."

We again took the avenue leading to the courtyard before the entrance, crossing it from end to end, accompanied by the murmur of the fountain at its centre; Atto measured the space with slow and measured paces.

"At Brouage, Louis at last tore his heart from his breast. There he wept all the tears he had to weep; there he bade farewell to love forever, without knowing that in so doing he was saying farewell to himself, to that quiet and calm self which I had known and appreciated, and which was now lost forever. I shall never forget him. The face which looked up at me was that of a pillar of salt under the grey light of that dawn at Brouage. That was the last act. The rest is. . . a morass."

"A morass?"

"Yes. The slow sinking of that love, its weary agony, the painful series of attempts by the King to forget Maria."

Back in Paris with his Spanish bride, Maria Teresa, who knew nothing of all this, Louis was informed by the perfidious Countess of Soissons that the young and passionate Charles of Lorraine was courting Maria amiably and probably with success. The King grew furious with Maria, despised her, mistreated her. She in her turn grew cold; then he returned to the fold and began to visit her at the Palais Mazarin in the rue des Petits Champs.

"In other words, just in front of my present home," said Atto with calculated nonchalance. "And the courtiers, led by those two gossips Madame de La Fayette and Madame de Motteville, who still detested Maria out of envy, insinuated that Louis was going there more for the beauty of Ortensia, the youngest of the Mancini girls, than for love of Maria."

"Was that true?"

"What did it matter? Louis XIV was now married. The promises had been broken, the dream had vanished. Only a year before the love-lorn couple competed with poetic verses, now they went for one another with barbed, venomous remarks. They had become the eidolon, the phantasms of themselves. They had let life slip away from them, and the loss was final."

"Excuse me, Signor Atto, but you mentioned the Countess de Soissons?" I asked, wanting to be certain of the name.

"Yes, so you know her?" replied Atto with irony, irritated by my interruption. "Now listen and keep silent."

So I did keep silent, but my thoughts were straying elsewhere, to the letter from Maria in which she had spoken of the dangerous poisoner, the mysterious Countess of S., the memory of whom was so painful to the Connestabilessa. Was she perhaps this Soissons? The Abbot's tale, however, was already galloping on its way and distracted me from my reflections.

It was in the year between the marriage with Maria Teresa and the death of Mazarin, explained Melani, that Louis understood his error, and what was more tragic, that there was no remedy for it. His mother's prophecies had not come true: happiness had not come. But there could be no turning back.

"All or nothing – that was the King of France. And still is. Maria was his all and they took her from him. Since then Louis has been nothing."

"What do you mean?"

"The dissolution, the destruction, the systematic and deliberate dismantling of the monarchy and of the figure of the King himself."

With a grimace, I betrayed my dissent. Was not Louis XIV, the Most Christian King of France, not the most feared sovereign in Europe?

❧

I did not contradict Atto. Other thoughts were racing through my mind.

"Signor Atto, what has all this to do with the apparitions of Superintendent Fouquet and Maria Mancini?"

"It has indeed plenty to do with them. Louis was almost twenty-two years old in 1660, when he married Maria Teresa. He was still an indecisive, inexpert young man, incapable of opposing Mazarin and his mother. Barely one year later, as you well know, he celebrated his twenty-third birthday on 5th September by having poor Nicolas arrested; then he imprisoned him for life in the remote fortress of Pinerol, inflicting a thousand torments on him. Now, I ask you, how is it possible that the timid, dreaming young man he had been twelve months before should have suddenly become such a fury?"

"The answer, in your opinion, is the loss of Maria Mancini," I anticipated him, "yet the meaning of the two scenes we have just witnessed still remains obscure to me."

"What you and I saw a little while ago? Nicolas handing a purse full of money to Maria. And, in their first apparition, Maria saying: 'I shall be grateful to you for the rest of my life. You are my truest friend.' Well, you should know that today's apparation explains why Maria expressed those words of affection and gratitude to Fouquet."

"Meaning?"

"I shall take it step by step. When Cardinal Mazarin died, Maria found herself unable to obtain payment of her own dowry from the universal successor to His Eminence's fortune, that dangerous madman the Duc de la Meilleraye, the husband of her sister Ortensia. This was a painful situation, because apart from that money, Maria possessed absolutely nothing. She went for help to Fouquet, who had admired her and valued her company since her arrival at court. And it was directly owing to the Superintendent's timely intercession that Maria at last gained her dowry from her brother-in-law."

"So that bag of coins and all those papers were Maria's dowry?"

"Yes, the papers will have been letters of exchange or things of that sort."

"So that is why Maria, as we saw on our first visit here, said to Fouquet: 'I shall be grateful to you for the rest of my life. You are my truest friend.'" I concluded with passion.

I realised at that moment that the Abbot and I were now talking about these visions as though they were utterly normal phenomena.

"Signor Atto, it seems almost as though the facts which you are narrating to me here in the Vessel are actually congregating in this very place and. . . they are in fact restoring the past to life."

"The past, the past, if only it were more simple," groaned Atto with a sigh. "That past never happened."

I was shocked.

"That meeting between Fouquet and Maria about the dowry, and even Maria Mancini's thanks to Fouquet are not just the manifestation of some past event, do you understand? For it was not thus that Fouquet delivered her dowry to Maria, nor did she ever pronounce those words to the Superintendent."

"How can you be sure of that?" I asked dubiously.

"Because Maria wrote those very words of thanks and esteem in a letter which, moreover, the Superintendent never read: the letter was intercepted by Colbert, who had already plotted Fouquet's downfall, with the King's complicity. As you know, when the news of

Fouquet's arrest came, Maria and I were already in Rome; I received the dreadful news in a note from my friend de Lionne, one of His Majesty's ministers.

"And the dowry?"

"Likewise. Maria was already on the point of leaving for Italy, driven from Paris and destined to wed Constable Colonna by the Cardinal's will, albeit posthumous: the dowry was sent directly to Rome, such was the haste of the Queen Mother and the court to be rid of her."

"In other words, the Superintendent never gave Maria her dowry in person, nor could he ever have heard or even read those words: 'I shall be grateful to you for the rest of my life. You are my truest friend.'"

"Exactly."

"So we have then witnessed two events which never took place."

"That is not quite correct, or rather, it is incomplete. If Maria had not been driven from Paris, if Fouquet had not been arrested, then they might perhaps have been able to meet: he would have delivered in person that legacy of her uncle's and she would have expressed those thanks directly to him. Maria's departure was, moreover, a matter of great pain to Nicolas, who foresaw the disastrous consequences to which it would sooner or later lead; even if he, I think, could not imagine that he would be the first victim of the new King's vengeance arising from the ashes of that love."

"So we have seen what *should have* happened between Maria and Fouquet if malign conspiracies had not wrecked the natural course of their lives. . ." I understood in a flash, while the breath stopped in my breast.

"Seen, seen. . ." the Abbot corrected me, abruptly changing his tone, and suddenly denying the turn our thinking was taking. "How you let your mind run away with you. I'd say that we simply imagined these things. Do not forget that we might simply be the victims of vapours released from the ground, and perhaps encouraged by my tales."

"Signor Atto, what you say may certainly be true of the second of the three episodes we have witnessed: Maria Mancini in the company of the young King. But neither for the first nor for the last: how could I have imagined with such exactitude circumstances of which I did not even know the existence? Or do you mean to tell me that our hallucinations have the quality of clairvoyance?"

"Perhaps: rather, you have simply shared a hallucination *of mine.*"

"What does that mean?"

"Well, it might have been an episode of transmission of thought. Recently in France and England, a number of treatises have come out, like that of the Abbé de Vallemont, which explain that this is a real phenomenon readily explicable by the laws of reason. This takes place through the action of the most subtle and invisible corpuscles emitted by our thoughts, which sometimes meet with those of others and impregnate their imagination."

"So they say, then, that we are surrounded by invisible parcels of others' thoughts?"

"Exactly. A little like the exhalations of quicksilver."

"I know nothing of that."

"Nothing better than quicksilver demonstrates the subtle nature of vapours and exhalations. This metal, which is both liquid and dry, exhales fumes so subtle and penetrating that if you move it with one hand, you will see that a piece of gold tightly held in the other hand will be all covered with quicksilver. The same thing will happen to the piece of gold even if you hold it in your mouth. If then you place it in contact with gold, silver or tin, you will see that these metals soften and are reduced to a paste known as amalgam. If you place quicksilver in a leathern tube and heat it a little, it will penetrate the leather and emerge as though through a sieve."

"Really?" I exclaimed in astonishment, having never heard anything of the sort.

"Yes, and I have read that exactly the same thing may happen with the imagination."

"So I may simply have witnessed some unconscious fantasising on your part?"

Atto nodded in confirmation.

☙◦❧

We walked a while longer, one beside the other, in silence. From time to time, I would glance at him out of the corner of one eye: frowning, Atto appeared to be plunged in grave meditations, in which he did not, however, include me.

I meditated for a long time on the explanations furnished by the Abbot. So we had seen, not what happened between Maria Mancini and Fouquet, but what might have happened if Maria's destiny and

that of the Superintendent had followed their natural and benevolent course. If I had had the leisure and the means to philosophise, I
should have asked myself: does a chaste hand restore in some utopian
place the broken threads of history? Does some merciful refuge give
shelter to events which will not take place? All these were questions
which, like the pikes of an armed battalion, seemed to point to the
place where we were.

"Look at this," said the Abbot suddenly, stopping abruptly before
a fine, broad flower bed. "Look at these plants: each one of them has
a plate before it with its name."

"Hyacinth, violet, rose, lotus. . ." I read mechanically. "And what
of it?"

"Just go on: ambrosia, nepenthes, panacea, even moly," he insisted,
growing pale.

My attention wandered from those names to Melani's face, questioningly.

"Do these mean nothing to you?" he insisted. "These are the
plants to be found in the mythical gardens of Adonis."

I remained silent and perplexed.

"In other words, they do not exist!" exclaimed Atto in a strangled
voice. "Ambrosia is the food of the gods of Olympus, which gave immortality; nepenthes is a legendary Egyptian plant which, according
to the ancient Greeks, gave serenity to the soul and made one forget
suffering. The panacea. . ."

"Signor Atto. . ."

"Silence, and listen to me," he interrupted me brusquely, while
fear at last appeared on his face. "The panacea, as I was saying, but
perhaps you too know, is a fantastic plant which the alchemists have
been seeking for centuries; it is capable of healing all diseases and
preventing old age. As for the moly, it is a magic herb which Mercury
gave to Ulysses to make him immune to the potions of the witch
Circe. Do you understand now? These plants do not exist! Tell me
what they are doing here, on show, with their names before them?"

He turned suddenly, hastening nervously towards the villa. I
moved to catch up with him. Hardly had I done so than we witnessed
a spectacle which made the hairs stand up on our heads.

A waxen spectral figure, playing the violin, hovered in the air behind an arcaded open loggia on the battlements of the villa's outer
wall. An impalpable mantle of black gauze billowed capriciously from

his shoulders, moved by a sudden, turbulent wind. The music which sprung from his bow was none other than the *folia* which had so many times accompanied us on our peregrinations through the Vessel.

We drew back instinctively, and I felt my flesh grow as cold as marble. A moment later, however, the Abbot, ashen faced, advanced again. He then stood awhile staring open-mouthed and tense with shock, almost as though transformed into a tragic mask.

"Oh thou!" cried Melani at length to the apparition, stretching out his arms in front of him as to an apocalyptic vision and brandishing his walking stick at it. "Whence comest thou and what is thy race? What troubles bring thee here? By the Numina, I beseech thee and by all that is dearest to thee: respond to my request, hide nothing, that I may know at last!"

"I am an officer of the armed forces of Holland!" thundered the being up above, without putting down his violin, and in no way put out by our presence or by the Abbot's singular manner of addressing him.

Melani seemed to be on the point of fainting. I rushed to support him, but he at once resumed his speech.

"Thou Flying Dutchman!" cried Atto with all the breath that remained in his body, almost as though these must be his last words. "From what spectral world didst thou come to embark here in this phantom Vessel?"

The stranger stopped playing and said nothing, scrutinising us attentively. Suddenly, he bowed, disappeared behind the loggia and reappeared immediately after with a rudimentary rope ladder which he unrolled on our side of the wall.

Atto and I stood silently with bated breath.

The being who had appeared before our eyes in such spectral guise and who had seemed to float freely in the air now, however, to our great wonderment came down to us, violin and bow tucked under one arm, prudently stepping on the rope ladder like any other mortal.

"Giovanni Henrico Albicastro, soldier and musician, at your service," he introduced himself, bowing slightly to Abbot Melani, and showing no sign of noticing our pallid expressions.

Atto, after the great shock he had suffered only moments before, could not find the strength to do or say a thing, and stayed silent, leaning heavily on his walking stick.

"You are right," said the curious stranger, addressing the Abbot. "This villa is so faded and tranquil that it seems a phantasm. That is why I like it. When I come to Rome, I take refuge here, on the cornice of that little loggia. To play standing up there is not very comfortable, I must confess, but the panorama which one can descry does, I guarantee you, provide the best of inspiration."

"A cornice?" said the Abbot, shivering.

"Yes, 'tis a little walkway, on the other side," said he, indicating with his eyes the outer wall from which he had just descended.

The Abbot lowered his eyes, looking exhausted.

"Was it yours, the *folia* which you were playing a moment ago?" he asked in a broken voice.

Albicastro replied only with a questioning look.

"Sir, you have the honour to be speaking to Abbot Atto Melani," I intervened, overcoming my reticence.

Having at last learned the name of the person before him, Albicastro added: "Yes, Signor Abbot, 'twas I who composed it. I hope that I have not unduly offended your ears. You seemed to be in a state of great agitation when you addressed me."

"Far from it, far from it," replied Melani weakly, while the pallor of fear gave way to the purple of shame.

"I would not wish to detain you, Sir," said Albicastro. "You seem to me to be rather tired. With your permission, I shall take my leave of you. We shall be seeing each other later: after all, you too are visiting the villa, is that not so? There's no end to discovering it."

Accompanying his words with a slight bow, the musician strode away from us.

ৡৢ

Alone once more, silence reigned between the Abbot and me for several moments. I resolved to go and see. I scaled the rope ladder which Albicastro had left hanging down the outer wall and, reaching the loggia, clambered over to the far side.

"Is it there?" asked Atto, with a vague, nervous air, without taking his eyes off his fine shoes.

"Yes, it is there," I replied.

The cornice was there, obviously. Nor was it even that narrow. Albicastro was anything but a flying Dutchman.

The Abbot said nothing. The thought of the scene of terror which he had imagined only moments before filled him with shame.

"That Dutchman is, nevertheless, a trifle eccentric," I observed. "It surely is not every day that one finds a violinist playing up on a shelf."

"And those mysterious flowers, which made me. . ." continued Atto.

"Signor Atto," I interrupted, "with all due respect, permit me to say that those flowers are by no means as mysterious as you believe them to be."

The Abbot started, as though I had stung him.

"And what do you know of that?" he protested, visibly annoyed.

"It may indeed be true," I replied with all the modesty of which I was capable, "that ambrosia, nepenthes, panacea and moly were, as you say, all present in the mythical garden of Adonis; that I do not doubt. And perhaps that is precisely why Elpidio Benedetti chose these plants. But it is quite untrue that they do not exist. Of course, I speak only in my capacity as an assistant gardener, and on the basis of such humble experience as I have gained over the years in the plantations of the Villa Spada, as well as from a few manuals on flowers which I enjoy reading from time to time. Nevertheless, I can tell you that ambrosia, if it was once the food of the gods of Olympus on whom it conferred immortality, I know today as a mushroom which the ants are gluttons for. The same with nepenthes: it is described as a carnivorous plant which the Jesuit fathers brought back from China; whether it comes rather from Egypt and, as the ancient Greeks believed, makes the soul serene and enables one to forget pain, that, I'm afraid, I do not know. The panacea may have been sought for centuries by alchemists, but I know it as a medicinal plant that cures warts. As for moly, 'tis merely a form of garlic, which does not of course mean that it could not immunise Ulysses from Circe's magic potions. Everyone knows the infinite virtues of garlic. . ."

I broke off, when I became aware of the grave humiliation painted in dark tints on Atto's face.

Poor Abbot Melani. In the face of the mysterious apparitions which we had repeatedly witnessed in the Vessel, he had always espoused scepticism, attributing those inexplicable apparitions to corrupted vapours, corpuscles, imaginings and who knows what else. Yet tension and fear had grown in his breast no less than in mine, of this I now had the certain proof.

These had, however, materialised at precisely the wrong moment: before the plants in the flower bed in which the Abbot had thought to see the legendary flowers of the gardens of Adonis, and immediately after that, through a bizarre set of circumstances, before the image of that singular individual Albicastro, musician and soldier, seemingly suspended in mid-air. Atto had, in other words, given in to fear of the unknown just when there was nothing unknown involved. He had deceived himself several times over and now the shame of it was gnawing cruelly at his liver.

"That is what I meant to say," he commented at last, perhaps sensing my thoughts. "All this confirms what I have been preaching to you since the very first day we set foot in this place: superstition is the daughter of ignorance. Every single thing in this world can be explained by the science of things and phenomena; had I possessed sufficient knowledge of floriculture, I could not have made so dreadful a mistake."

"Of course, Signor Atto, but permit me to point out to you that, in my modest opinion, we have not yet found a convincing explanation for the apparitions we have seen here."

"We have not found one because of our ignorance. Just as we thought we saw a flying man, when he was simply walking along a cornice in a strong breeze."

"Do you think that someone has been playing tricks on us?"

"Who can say? The scope for disguising the truth is infinite."

❧

A few moments later we had entered the ground floor of the building.

"After the shock which Buvat gave us yesterday, you should have put a few questions to me," said Atto.

"That is true. How the deuce did Buvat manage to locate and get to us without being either seen or heard? He appeared so suddenly that he seemed to have descended from heaven."

"I too could not believe my eyes, but then I found the explanation," said he, drawing me into a little room to the right of the main door.

"Now I understand," I exclaimed.

The room was in fact the base of a minuscule service staircase. Unlike us, Buvat had not taken the main stairs on the opposite side of the building (in other words at the end and to the left, for those entering it) but these little service stairs. That was how he had appeared unexpectedly just in front of us, at the end of the first-floor salon that gave onto the Vatican. Although we could hear them, we could not understand where his footsteps were coming from, and this was not only because of the echo produced by the high vault of the gallery but because we were quite unable to conceive of the presence of another way up, of which we knew nothing.

So we went up to the first floor by the service stairs which were, like their more spacious counterpart, of spiral construction. We were just climbing the last steps when we were transfixed by a powerful siren, accompanied by a deep and menacing reverberation. Instinctively I brought my hands to my ears to protect them from the powerful shock.

"Damn it," cursed Abbot Melani. "Again that *folia*!"

Upon reaching the first floor, we found ourselves facing Albicastro. He had begun to play just at the top of the little spiral staircase which thus acted as a sound box, amplifying the violin and transforming the bass into gigantic lowing sounds and the treble into vertiginous whistling. The music ceased.

"It seems that the theme of the *folia* gives you more joy than any other music," said Melani, plainly enervated by the latest shock.

"As the great Sophocles put it, 'life is more beautiful when one does not reason'. Besides, this music is suited to the Vessel, the *stultifera navis*, or Ship of Fools, if you prefer," he replied with Dutch brio, dusting down his instrument and then beginning to tune it, thus emitting a series of mewing sounds at once comical and irritating.

Atto's sole response was to begin to declaim:

> *On streets or highways you can find*
> *A pack of fools who vaunt their shame*
> *And yet prefer to shun the name.*
> *Thus have I thought this was the time*
> *To launch a ship of fools in rhyme:*
> *A galley, bark, skiff, ketch or yawl*
> *– But one ship wouldn't hold them all.*

Atto, with those verses, seemed plainly to be calling Albicastro a madman.

"So you know my beloved Sebastian Brant?" asked the Dutchman, surprised and in no way offended.

"I have been received too many times at the court of Innsbruck or that of the Elector of Bavaria not to have understood your allusion to Brant's *Stultifera Navis*, the most widely read book in Germany over the past two hundred years. One cannot claim to know the German peoples if one has not read that book."

Once more I was taken aback by Atto's encyclopaedic knowledge: seventeen years ago he had admitted to having few clear notions of the Bible, but when it came to matters political and diplomatic, he always knew everything.

"You will therefore agree with me that the *Stultifera Navis* goes well with the villa in which we now stand," replied the musician, who then recited:

> *Know, foolishness is ever bold*
> *And fools themselves for wise men hold,*
> *But should a man himself despise,*
> *Why then, at last, a fool's made wise!*

And Abbot Melani responded:

> *But what fools are, we plainly see,*
> *The fools themselves don't want to be.*

Whereupon, Albicastro, eying with amusement the thousand pleats, leather embroideries and tassels and decorations on Atto's ceremonial dress:

> *Right now I will not mention those*
> *Who gad about in foolish clothes;*
> *Indeed, were I to count the same,*
> *I'd anger legions by the name.*
> *They have no taste for wearing twill*
> *Or simple jerkins void of frill*
> *Prefer to wear the Holland stuff*
> *With slitted sleeves and bright enough*
> *With colours woven in, befurred,*
> *And on the sleeve a cuckoo bird.*

"Nevertheless, 'tis quite true, many strange things do happen here," I swiftly interposed, fearing that the tourney might all too easily degenerate, what with the pair calling one another mad. "I mean," said I, correcting myself at once, for Atto was showing signs of impatience at my observation, "that 'tis said that corrupt vapours circulate here, or other strange exhalations able even. . . how can one put it?. . . to produce hallucinations."

"Exhalations? Perhaps. That is the beauty of this place. Did not nature's prudence perhaps bestow upon children the seal of folly wherewith to increase the pleasure they can give their educators and to soften the latter's trials? Likewise, this villa lightens the cares of travellers who find solace therein."

As he spoke, he placed the violin in its case, from which he drew a series of sheets of music.

"Do you perhaps mean that the Vessel possesses magical qualities?" I asked.

"No more than love possesses."

"What do you mean?"

"Did not Cupid, the god of love, take on the guise of a thoughtless and crazy little child with flowing locks? And yet love, as the poet puts it, moves the sun and the other stars."

"You speak in riddles."

"No, no, 'tis quite simple. One needs only a child's innocence to move the world. Nothing is more powerful."

Abbot Melani raised his eyebrows smugly, looking at me through half-closed eyes as though to tell me that Albicastro seemed to him somewhat touched.

Meanwhile, the musician continued:

> *The world was Alexander's fief:*
> *A poisoned drink brought quick relief;*
> *And likewise King Darius fled*
> *His troubles: Bessus struck him dead;*
> *And Cyrus' pride had no duration:*
> *His blood supplied his last potation.*
> *On earth no ruler comes so high*
> *That termination isn't nigh.*
> *In history, at least my version,*
> *The realms Assyrian and Persian,*
> *And Macedonian and Grecian,*
> *And Carthage and the Roman nation,*
> *They all have come at last to dust.*

The verses recited by the Dutchman struck me no little; they seemed closely to echo what Melani had told me of the powerful Cardinal Mazarin's fear of dying.

"Again your Brant. You speak always of folly, you love playing the *folia*," the Abbot intoned with ill-concealed scepticism.

"Scorn not folly, for 'tis no defect. Do you not, too, concur with my ancient compatriot of Rotterdam that to pardon one's friends' errors by trying to hide them, deceiving oneself about them and doing one's best not to see them – even going so far as to appreciate their vices as great virtues – is all too similar to folly? Is that not the greatest wisdom?"

Atto almost imperceptibly lowered his eyes: Albicastro had struck home. He seemed almost privy to the talks between Melani and me and my musings concerning our tormented friendship.

Meanwhile, the Dutch musician, turning back to rummage among his sheets of music, began to recite to himself:

> *We don't find friendships like the one*
> *That David had with Jonathan,*
> *Or of Patroclus and Achilles,*
> *Orestes and his friend Pyládes,*
> *Like Pythias, to Damon true,*
> *And King Saul's armour-bearer too,*
> *Or Laelius and Scipio.*
> *Self-seeking is our chiefest sin,*
> *Ignoring friendship, kith and kin.*
> *No Moses now among our brothers,*
> *Who, as himself, could love all others,*
> *No Nehemiahs to be found;*
> *And pious Tobits don't abound.*

The Abbot raged inwardly, but uttered not a word.

"And if folly is the highest wisdom," resumed the Dutchman, turning again to us, "where could it find better lodgings than in this Vessel which, as you yourselves acknowledged yesterday, is literally plastered with proverbs of wisdom?"

"Did you spy on us?" exclaimed Atto with a movement of surprise and disdain, beginning to suspect that all Albicastro's uncomfortable allusions to friendship might not be a matter of pure coincidence.

"I heard you when you raised your voices. Your words resounded up into the tower," he replied without any loss of composure. "But you will have other matters with which to occupy yourselves, so permit me now to leave you."

დილ

He descended the spiral staircase and within instants we had lost even the echo of his footsteps. Abbot Melani's features were livid.

"Quite insufferable, that Dutchman," he muttered.

"Holland is no country for you, Signor Atto," I could not help observing. "Why, once, if my memory does not betray me, you could not bear even the presence of Flemish cloth."

"Now, thanks be to heaven, that is no longer the case, ever since that people of stingy heretics improved their techniques for dying cloth, at long last attaining the quality of France's royal manufactures. But this time, I'd rather have been assailed by three hundred sneezes than have to put up with that Albicastro's nonsense."

We took the main stairs then to the floor above, where we were setting foot for the first time and where no few unforeseen events awaited us. The first surprise in truth found us even as we were making that ascent. The spiral stairs were carpeted with inscriptions:

So many friends. No friend
Be a friend to your own soul
Correct the friend who errs, but abandon the incorrigible
Believe only the friend with whom you've old acquaintance
Place not new friends before old
To adulate friends does more harm than to criticise enemies
Amity is immortal, enmity mortal
Attend to your enemies, but fear them
Be slow to form new friendships. Once forged, be steadfast
. . .

As I climbed, and those proverbs ran before my eyes, I was once more assailed by the bizarre impression that something in the Vessel, like an obscure and impersonal sense organ, had read my thoughts concerning fr.. lship and was now dictating, if not the answer, at least an acknowledgement of my secret ponderings. I remembered: had I not already, during our first incursion, read sayings about friendship carved on the pyramids in the garden? The series of events that had unfolded was coherent, it was perfectly clear. First, the quarrel with Atto; then Albicastro's words and verses on friendship; the latter were perhaps more a consequence of having listened to the music than some enigmatic manifestation of cause and effect, but here now were new phrases which seemed to be trying to rub salt into my inner wound.

Climbing those stairs, I felt myself like Cardinal Mazarin persecuted by the nightmare of the Capitor: the more I rejected the hints implicit in those proverbs, the more they obsessed me.

So many friends. No friend. With so many at the Villa Spada I exchanged pats on the shoulder; yet I could in truth count none as true friends, least of all the Abbot. *Be a friend to your own soul.* Atto and I shared the same soul – was that not so? – thought I sarcastically, the Prince of Dupes and the King of Intriguers. . . *Correct the friend who errs, but abandon the intriguer.* Yes, that was easy enough to say, but was not Abbot Melani the classic exemplar of the friend who is as incorrigible as he is skilled at not allowing one to let go of him? He too, climbing those stairs in front of me, must surely have read all those proverbs. As I expected, he made no comment on them.

On reaching the second floor, we found one other detail that called attention to itself. Above the arch through which one entered that floor was an inscription more singular than all those which had preceded it.

For three good friends, I did endeavour
But then I could not find them ever.

"'Tis just as well this inscription did not escape us," commented Atto to himself.

"What did Benedetti mean?"

"The inscription says '*I did endeavour*': that seems to explain why he built the Vessel."

"Who are the three friends?"

"You should not necessarily think of three persons. They could also be. . ."

"Three objects?"

Atto responded with a satisfied smile.

"Capitor's gifts!" I deduced excitedly. "Then you are right to seek them here."

"Obviously, it would be excessive to interpret the proverb literally and to regard the Vessel as having been built specifically for the three objects. In my opinion, the phrase means only that the building is, or was, the natural receptacle for Capitor's presents."

"It still remains for us to understand the meaning of '*I could not find them, ever*'," I retorted.

"That too will emerge, my boy. One thing at a time," he replied as we left the stairs behind us.

The second floor was subdivided very differently from the two lower floors which we had already visited. From the grand staircase we entered a vestibule, which to the left gave onto a terrace facing south, onto the road. This was the flat roof of the covered loggia on the first floor, and the generous gurgling of the fountain at its centre was clearly audible. For an instant we regaled our eyes and our spirits with the view, which encompassed and dominated all the surrounding estates and vineyards and reached in the far distance the silvery shimmer of the sea.

"Fantastic!" commented Atto. "In all Rome I have not enjoyed so generous a panorama. The Vessel is incomparable. So recondite within its walls, so free and airy without."

We returned indoors and followed a corridor towards the opposite, northern, end of the building. In the middle of this floor, there was an oval room, with windows lining its two longer sides. Beyond this room, the corridor continued, leading to a little room with a balcony giving onto Saint Peter's and the Vatican; in a corner was the top of the service stairs. We returned to the oval room.

"This room must have been used for meals during the cold season: there are four stoves in it," observed Atto.

"I do not understand why the proportions are smaller than those of the first floor, just underneath. We must have missed something."

"Look here."

My intuition was correct. Atto returned to the first of the two corridors and then to the other one. In each of these were two doors which we had at first failed to notice. We discovered that they led to four apartments, two in each corridor, each with a bedchamber, a bath and a little library.

"Four independent lodgings. Perhaps Benedetti had his friends sleep here, as Cardinal Spada does for his honoured guests at the festivities," I ventured.

"That is possible. However, it is clear now why the main room, here on the second floor, is markedly smaller than those on the two floors below. It is in fact merely the place where the four apartments meet."

While we were exploring those dusty premises, wherever our eyes came to rest, they were amiably assailed by the sentences, maxims and proverbs which Benedetti's extravagant mind had capriciously disseminated on the walls, columns doorposts and window frames. I read at random:

Lose not your peace of mind for others' gossip
Nobility's of little worth unaccompanied by wealth
Not to the Doctor for every ill, not to the Lawyer for every quarrel, not to the
    bottle for every thirst

Even above the doors of the four apartments a number of witty aphorisms met the eye:

All things are contained in commodious freedom
Little and good are worth more than much and bad
The sage knows how to find all in little
One cannot call little that which suffices

I sought Atto with my eyes: He had gone off to inspect one of the four apartments. I entered after him.

He was leaning against a doorpost. He greeted me staring, without a word.

"Signor Atto. . ."

"Silence."

"But. . ."

"I am thinking. I am thinking, how the Devil is it possible?"

"What do you mean?"

"Your parrot. I have found him."

"You have found him?" I stammered incredulously.

"Here, in this apartment," said he, pointing to a little adjoining room, "along with Capitor's presents."

కోపఈ

It was true. They were covered with a fine layer of dust; but there they were. Caesar Augustus was there, too. Time had not spared him. Covered with that immaterial shroud, he had been waiting for who knows how long to be rediscovered and, given his nature, admired.

"My boy, yours is a great honour," said Atto as I entered the little room. "With your hand you are touching one of the greatest mysteries of the history of France: Capitor's gifts."

A picture. We had found a picture. It was big: over four foot six high and six feet wide. It had been placed on the ground in the little room, unbeknownst to all save the walls and inscriptions of the Vessel.

The subject of the picture consisted of various fine objects harmoniously arranged with a clever mixture of order and disorder. In the lower part of the centre of the picture, in the foreground, there was a large golden dish rather richly worked in the Flemish style, placed obliquely on a step. On it two silver statuettes could be distinguished: Neptune, the god of the sea, trident in hand, and the Nereid Amphitrite, his spouse. They were seated one close to the other on a chariot drawn over the waves by a pair of Tritons. I knew already what this was: one of Capitor's presents, that in which she had burned the pastilles of incense.

Further to the right, depicted above the step, was a golden goblet, the stem of which was in the form of a centaur, the equine half of which was in gold and the human half in silver. This was obviously the image of the goblet which Capitor had handed to the Cardinal filled with myrrh.

Behind the first two objects stood a great wooden terrestrial globe with a golden pedestal: the third gift. Before this the madwoman had recited the sonnet on fortune which had so indisposed His Eminence.

In the painting one could also admire other exquisitely fashioned objects, whose images provided the pictorial key to its meaning. In the background, one could descry a table on which were placed a red carpet, a lute, a viol, a cymbal and a book of musical notations, open on who knows what page, perhaps that lugubrious *Passacaglia of Life* which Capitor had made Atto sing and which had so terrorised the Cardinal. On the far left, elegantly bending its paw, a hound of noble breed was nuzzling the great red carpet with shy curiosity.

But proudly showing off, right in the middle of the whole composition, was quite another animal: a splendid white parrot, its head surmounted by a great yellow crest, perched on the wooden globe, likewise with one foot raised and its head turning towards the dog, almost as though it were mimicking it and marking its own indifferent superiority. It was the faithful portrait of Caesar Augustus, perfect even down to the somewhat derisively haughty expression.

"This is the painting that Mazarin had made by that Dutch painter before getting rid of Capitor's three gifts. . ." I remembered, attaching the thread of what Atto had narrated to the web of recent events.

The Abbot fell briefly silent, utterly absorbed by the singularity and significance of the moment.

"Boel. He was called Pieter Boel. Years later he was to become an official court painter. I told you that he was good and now you see that I did not deceive you."

"The picture is. . . really splendid, Signor Atto."

"I know. They told me of it, but I myself never saw it. You can see that even the description of Capitor's presents which I gave you was faithful. My memory does not betray me," he added with ill-concealed satisfaction.

"I had, however, thought that the painting had remained in Paris. Did you not say that Mazarin kept it with him?"

"I too thought that it was in France. But as we explore the Vessel, I am becoming more and more convinced of one fact."

"And what would that be?"

"That Capitor's gifts are not here, or rather that they are no longer here."

"What do you mean?"

"I too believed that they had been entrusted to Benedetti to be kept here, at the Vessel. The picture was to stay with Mazarin as a surrogate. Instead, here I find the surrogate and no trace of the presents. That is not, of course, what we hoped to find but it is still better than nothing. As one of the maxims we have just read put it, 'The sage knows how to find all things in little'."

Once again, I reflected in astonishment, the Vessel had had the bizarre capacity to foresee (and to respond to) the intimate questionings of persons visiting it.

"The presents must have been sent to some other place," Abbot Melani was meanwhile thinking aloud. "But where? The Cardinal never left anything to chance."

We again turned to the painting, at once sublime, enigmatic and ill-omened.

"It is unbelievable. The parrot really does seem to be Caesar Augustus," I observed.

The Abbot looked at me as though I were an idiot.

"It does not '*seem*'. This *is* Caesar Augustus."

"What are you saying?"

"I did not remember you as being so slow of understanding. Do you think it possible that there could exist two parrots like this, one painted on canvas and a second, identical one, in two almost neighbouring cities without the one being a portrait of the other?"

"But this picture was painted in Paris," I protested, irked by the Abbot's sarcasm.

"It cannot be a coincidence. If you remember properly, I told you that the madwoman Capitor had a passion for all things feathered. She always had a flock. . ."

". . . of birds that kept her company, 'tis true, that you told me. Then you yourself, many years ago, perhaps saw Caesar Augustus! Many years have passed since then, but parrots are rather long-lived."

"Of course, I may have seen him then – who knows? She had so many parrots around her, the madwoman. Besides, I have never been too fond of those beasts. To tell the truth, I have never understood the vogue for keeping them in one's house, as so many do, what with the filth, the stink and the noise they make. I may even have seen your bird, but my memory would not hold such things today."

"It is simply impossible to believe that Caesar Augustus could have ended up in the aviary of the Villa Spada!" I exclaimed, still sceptical in the face of the Abbot's reasoning.

"For heaven's sake, it could not be clearer. Evidently, Capitor left Caesar Augustus in Paris, perhaps as a present for someone, or else she somehow left him behind, who knows? You can well imagine what Mazarin decided to do as soon as he learned that the madwoman had also left that wretched bird on his hands, in his city."

"Well, he'll have. . . sent it as far away as possible."

"Together with the three gifts. So much so that he had his portrait painted alongside them. And now, you tell me, what do you know of the creature?"

"I know only that the parrot was once the property of Cardinal Fabrizio's uncle, the late lamented Monsignor Virgilio Spada. It seems he was a strange man, a lover of antiquities and various sorts of curiosities. I do know that he also had a collection of natural curios."

"I know that too. I had been in Rome for about a year when Virgilio Spada died. He was very keen on castrati. I think he had studied with the Jesuits and they wanted him in their order; but Virgilio chose the Congregation of the Oratory of St Philip Neri because he was in love with the voice of the great Girolamo Rosini, the famed cantor of the Oratory. Virgilio was also friendly with Loreto Vittori, the castrato who was master of Christina of Sweden, and he personally took another young singer, Domenico Tassinari, into his service, who however abandoned music in the end and became an oratorian like his patron."

While Atto was complacently boasting of Spada's friendships among his castrato colleagues, I was reflecting.

"There is one thing I do not understand, Signor Atto: how come Caesar Augustus changed owners, passing from Benedetti to the Spada family?"

"Elpidio Benedetti and Virgilio Spada knew one another very well: I heard at the time that the Vessel contained many of Virgilio's ideas, for instance the fact that the villa should contain far more curiosities than luxuries, and that it should be a fortress of deep speculations on the Faith and on knowledge, whereby to attract the visitor and induce him to reflect."

"The Vessel as an Ark and school of wisdom, in other words," I commented, with a touch of surprise at the bizarre correlation. "So, in exchange for Monsignor Virgilio's suggestions, Benedetti may have given him his parrot to place in his aviary."

"Or perhaps that extravagant creature, instead of flying away from the Villa Spada to the Vessel was wont in those days to flee in the opposite direction and may have ended up by being adopted by the Spada household, with Benedetti's consent. On our own, we have no means of knowing, and Caesar Augustus will not tell us, all the less so as we've not yet succeeded in catching him. But his time will soon be up."

"How do you think you'll capture him?" I asked, perplexed by the Abbot's certainty.

"What a question. . . For example, with a parrot caller, if such a thing exists. Or with with the help of his favourite titbits, like chocolate. Or perhaps with a fascinating female parrot made of straw, why not?"

I avoided commenting on Atto's complete incompetence in the matter of fowls.

Meanwhile nightfall, to which the Vessel too had at last yielded, made it necessary to get back to the Villa Spada. As were retraced our footsteps, we heard Albicastro's voice in the distance:

> *Who would be wise by reputation*
> *But isn't blessed with moderation*
> *Engages in pursuit absurd;*
> *His falcon is a cuckoo bird.*

Melani turned sharply in the direction of the voice. Then, taken with a sudden idea, he smiled and set off once more on his way.

"How are we to capture Caesar Augustus? We shall need a little help. I already have an idea of how to begin, and with whom."

❧❦

We were both utterly worn out when we reached the gates of Villa Spada and without the least desire to get involved in the festivities and their trivial sophistication. All the way back, Atto had uttered not a word. He seemed weary of prying and meddling among the guests and desirous of retiring as soon as possible to his own chamber, there to meditate upon the many and surprising events of the day, which had multiplied unceasingly until our latest discovery of the painting by Pieter Boel.

We took leave of one another almost in haste, agreeing to meet the next day, but without specifying any time. Better thus, thought I. Perhaps I might tomorrow wish to take another solitary walk, as I had that morning. Or I might at long last get a chance to see my Cloridia and our two little ones. Or again (but this secret preference, I dared not admit even to myself), seeing that my adored consort and the little ones were in no danger, and Cloridia was surely rather busy, I wished I could find the time and the means to reflect deeply by myself upon all that was happening. The day which was now drawing to an end had dispensed a series of strange and suggestive occurrences which needed to be sorted out, yet the means of understanding them all were still missing; just as children know that they have human faculties of understanding and reasonably enough ask to be treated like adults, forgetting that they are still infants.

First, before awakening, there had been the nightmare of the old mendicant; then the procession of the Company of Saint Elizabeth, the brief conversation with the priest and the longer one with the innkeeper and the shoe-vendor about beggars true and false. After that came Atto's new revelations about the Most Christian King and Maria Mancini, the pair of encounters with Albicastro, the inscriptions in the Vessel which seemed to appear in unison with my thoughts, and the picture with the three presents: what was more, containing the image of Caesar Augustus. . . Of course, the parrot had disappeared along with with Albani's note, and now we had returned to the Villa Spada empty-handed.

It was too much, really too much, said I to myself as I went to sleep in my bivouac at the casino of the villa. Only the new day could bring me light and counsel, a clear picture of things, or at least a semblance of greater clarity.

As it turned out, I was mistaken.

Day the Fifth
11TH JULY, 1700

✠

"On your feet, curses! On your feet, I said!"

It could not have been a worse awakening. Someone had seized me and was shaking me, yelling unpleasantly and dragging me back into the world of the awake, but at the cost of a great headache.

My eyes were still half-closed when I heard the words which made clear to me the identity of my assailant.

"I've been waiting for you to wake up for centuries! Someone here is in possession of the most important information. You must act, and act at once. This is an ord. . . Well, this is my firm will, and not just mine."

Abbot Melani's words (for it was obviously he) alluded to the menacing and iron-willed figure of the Most Christian King, whom he had by now learned to evoke astutely, sometimes dressed for the part of Maria Mancini's ill-starred suitor, sometimes, as now, present-ing the inflexible tyrant to whose will all must blindly bend.

"A moment, I am just. . ." I mumbled in protest, my mouth still all gummed up, turning over in the blankets to get away from his tugging.

"Not one second more," said he, seizing my clothes from a nearby chair where I had left them and hurling them at me.

While freeing myself from his grasp, the first thing I looked at in the light of day was Atto, and he in turn stared at me with fiery, stabbing eyes. I noticed with no little curiosity that he had not come empty-handed. Against the chair he had leaned a bizarre collection of wooden and iron tools which seemed to me as familiar as they were out of place in a bedchamber.

Dressing hurriedly, I opened my eyes properly and realised what this was all about. Among the long-handled tools, I recognised a rake, a shovel, a hoe and a broom. In a heavy box with a handle, there were piled up a trowel, a bucket, a dibble, a pronged grubber, a sickle, shears, knives, a few pots and brushes. I recognised them.

"These gardening tools belong to the Villa Spada. What do you want to do with them?"

"What matters is what you will do," said he, rudely shoving all that hardware into my hands, so that it was a miracle that I did not drop the whole lot, and motioning me to follow him out of the door. "Now, however, there's an emergency. Today is Sunday and the first thing we must do is go to mass, otherwise our absence will be noticed. Get a move on: Don Tibaldutio is about to begin the service."

Villa Spada was astir with preparations for the fifth day of celebrations. On the evening before, dinner must have gone on until all hours, for when I was going to sleep one could not hear the sound of guests' carriages leaving the villa. Nevertheless, that morning the servants were already busy going about their duties: sweeping, cleaning, tidying, cooking, preparing, decorating, repainting and retouching. As we left my little room, all around us maidservants, ushers and menservants were rushing. Some of them looked at me enviously, since for days now that mysterious Frenchman had been relieving me of a great deal of work. Atto spurred me on, poking the pommel of his walking stick painfully between my shoulder blades. By a mere hair's breadth we avoided encountering Don Paschatio (whom we heard a short distance away, lamenting the disloyalty of an absent seamstress), thus avoiding the command to execute some urgent duties. Laden down as I was with all kinds of implements, I proceeded clumsily, at the risk of falling, tripping on the rake I was carrying or being knocked over by some weary scullion.

Once I had laid down the box of tools in the garden hut, we both at last entered the chapel, curiously full of all kinds of worshippers, from the eminences lodging at the villa down to the humblest menials (discreetly to one side), just as Don Tibaldutio's service was beginning. I took part in the rite wholeheartedly, inwardly begging the Lord also to pardon Abbot Melani, who was present at holy mass out of pure self-interest.

Once out of the chapel, Atto nonchalantly bestowed salutations right and left, but at the same time he had resumed poking me cruelly in the back.

"Get a move on, damn you," he hissed at me while smiling sweetly at Cardinal Durazzo.

"Now, would you kindly tell me what has got into you?" I protested while, once more burdened with the equipment, I followed him to the flower beds at the entrance to the villa. "What the deuce is it that's so urgent?"

"Shhh! There he is, 'tis just as well he has not gone," whispered Atto while inviting me to remain silent and indicating with his nose an individual bending over one of the two rows of flower beds lining the avenue giving access to the villa.

"But that is the Master Florist," said I.

"What is his name?"

"Tranquillo Romaùli. He is the grandson of a famous gardener, and works here at the Villa Spada. I know him well. His late lamented spouse was a great midwife, who taught Cloridia and who presided over the birth of our two daughters. I have often been commanded by Don Paschatio to act as his assistant.

"Ah, yes, I was forgetting: you too are an expert on plants. . ." muttered the Abbot, recalling the humiliation he had suffered at my hands at the Vessel the day before, over the supposed flowers from the mythical garden of Adonis. "Well, be prepared for a surprise, Tranquillo Romaùli knows of the Tetràchion."

In overexcited tones and employing lofty phrases, Abbot Melani explained to me how, that morning, he had awoken rather early, when Aurora was stretching her arms with a yawn and abandoning the conjugal bed she shared with Sunset. All night, he had been assailed by a thousand questions to which the previous day had given rise and left unanswered. The entire villa was still blessedly sleeping; the bluish first light of morn was penetrated only by the light of some furtive lamp issuing from the windows of those who, like Melani, wished to spy on the day in its secret youth. Atto had then descended to the garden in order to take a salutary walk and inhale the innocent and perfect air of the dawning day which only the idle despise.

"I wandered through the entire garden, without noticing anything suspicious," said he, thus betraying that the purpose of his walk was to spy and stick his nose into others' business. "I had reached the little grove when I saw him there, a few paces in front of me. He was busy using a pair of shears on a flower bed."

"That is his trade. So, what of it?"

"We spoke of this and that: the weather, the humidity, how lovely these flowers are, how I hoped it would not be so hot today, and so on and so forth. Then he named it."

"What, the Tetràchion?"

"Shhh! Do you want everyone to overhear you?" murmured Atto, darting nervous looks in all directions.

After the brief colloquy which he had described to me, Abbot Melani had moved on. He was only a short distance away when he had heard the Master Florist, no doubt thinking himself alone and therefore unheard, murmur a number of confused phrases. Then, still sitting, he had turned his eyes to heaven and had clearly pronounced the words which had thrown Atto into a state of such extreme alarm.

"'. . . and then the Tetràchion.' He said *that*, do you understand?"

"But this is incredible! What can he know of such things? The Master Florist has always seemed to me a spirit far removed from the things of politics. Not to speak of such. . . unusual matters as that of the Tetràchion."

"Usual or unusual, there's something behind this," Atto cut me short. "However unbelievable it may seem, he does know something. Perhaps he even *wanted* me to overhear him. It cannot be pure chance that he should have uttered those few words a few paces away from me, today of all days."

"Are you quite sure that you heard correctly?"

"Absolutely sure. Indeed, do you know what I think? This brings to mind the secret password of which your wife spoke."

"Cloridia did tell me that sooner or later she would have further information."

"Excellent. Except that, instead of reaching her, the information has come directly to us, in other words to the real interested parties, through the Master Florist."

"Passing Cloridia by? I find that hard to believe. In her circles, she is venerated. She assists at births all over Rome, and the women have no secrets from her."

"Yes, so long as they are mere women's gossip. But in an affair like this, no one would prefer some midwife to a diplomatic agent of His Majesty the Most Christian King," retorted Atto with ruffled pride.

"Perhaps I could try talking with the Master Florist, in order to see whether. . ."

"You could? Why, you *must* find out what he knows about the Tetràchion. Now, I shall be on my way. It is a fortunate coincidence that you should already have worked for him," said he, pointing at him and meaning that I was to commence my investigations there and then.

"Signor Atto, we shall need time to. . ."

"I do not wish to listen to ifs and buts. You are to begin forthwith. Stand next to him with all these implements and pretend that you mean to work. We shall meet at lunchtime. I must settle some rather urgent correspondence. I expect you to do your duty."

He set off at a determined pace for the great house. He had left me no choice.

In truth, I should have preferred to go first to the kitchen and get myself something to eat; but Master Tranquillo had already caught sight of me and I did not wish to give him the impression that I had something to hide. I therefore went up to him, wearing the least hypocritical smile of which I was capable.

Tranquillo Romaùli, who had been named after his grandfather, that most skilled and distinguished of floriculturists, welcomed me benevolently. His physical presence contrasted curiously with the silent and sober art of gardening. He was a great fat bear of a man with a thick, bristling beard, black hair and vaguely obtuse little eyes surmounted by a pair of tangled, bushy eyebrows. He had a strong jaw and a big stomach, swelled up by many and generous bouts of eating, and this made him at once imposing and comically ridiculous when he reached out his great paws to prune the leaves of some tiny sick seedling. Above all, owing to some previous illness of the auditory organs, he had become rather hard of hearing, and his booming voice made every conversation an exchange of shouts, at the end of which the person speaking to him was left no less deaf than the Master Florist. To find out from him what he knew of the Tetràchion, if ever he was prepared to reveal that, would be no easy matter. A conversation with Romaùli could practically never be settled in a few easy exchanges; although his character was exquisite, he was the most verbose individual, garrulous to the point of being insufferable and obsessed with one exclusive, all-embracing, mind-dulling topic: flowers and gardening. His science was so vast and profound that he had come to be regarded as a sort of walking encyclopaedia of flower cultivation. It was said that he could recite the whole of Father Ferrari's *De florum cultura* and that he knew by heart the origins, history and design of every vegetable or flower garden in Rome.

After a few brief exchanges of pleasantries, he asked me if I had nothing to do that morning.

"Oh well. . . nothing in particular, to tell the truth."

"Really? Then you must be the only person here at the Villa Spada without some business to attend to. I imagine, however, that all those implements which you are holding in your arms must be there for some purpose," said he, pointing at the tools which Atto had heaped onto me.

"Of course. . ." said I guiltily. "I was hoping to be able to make myself useful in some way."

"Very well, your wish has already come true," he replied with satisfaction, picking up a wooden case full of other tools and motioning that I was to follow him.

We were, he explained, on our way to the flower beds near the chapel of the villa. It was a fine day; the fresh early morning breeze seemed to be holding an amiable dialogue with the twittering of the birds and with the multiform ranks of clouds which observed placidly from on high the eternal round of terrestrial vanities. Our footsteps echoed softly on the fine gravel of the drives while the sun, still low on the horizon, warmed us with its first timid rays.

This delightful arrangement of the natural elements, however, completely escaped Tranquillo Romaùli who was, as ever, utterly preoccupied with the concerns of his art and had already begun to instruct me.

"Don Paschatio has ordered me to plant jasmine," he began in querulous tones. "Yet, I had told him quite clearly that the noblest garden has no place for jasmine. Neither our own yellow home-grown variety, of course, nor the common white lily. And even if there were any place for suchlike, they should take second place to the vermilion or orange Turk's head lily. These days, all sense has been lost of what is to be cultivated in a garden. 'Tis a veritable scandal."

"You are right, it is the most serious matter. So, you were saying that jasmine is unworthy of the best gardens?" said I, feigning interest.

"Let us say that pride of place is to be accorded to the 'silver goblet' or white narcissus, whichever one prefers to call it," he resumed, raising his voice. "Or to the double narcissus of Constantinople, which produces a set of ten or twelve flowers, to the Ragusa narcissus, the yellow narcissus or the starry variety; or again to the *frasium*, which resembles a rose, or a lettuce, to the ultramontane, which has the virtues of a double yellow rose, or to the sweetest smelling jonquils, with a perfume like that of jasmine, tempered by and mixed with the scent of orange blossom."

"I understand," said I, smothering a yawn and trying to see how I could place a word about the Tetràchion without arousing suspicion.

Meanwhile, we had moved around to the far side of the great house and had almost arrived at the flower beds near the chapel. The weight and bulk of my load was causing me to sway; inwardly, I was cursing Atto.

"I know that what I am about to say to you will sound obvious," added the Master Florist, "yet I shall never tire of repeating that it is a mistake of the moderns to neglect the false narcissus, also known as the trumpet lily because of its long, trumpet-shaped calyx. Likewise, greater use should be made of Indian narcissi, especially the Donnabella, which first became acclimatised to Italy in the gardens of the Prince of Caserta, and the spherical lilied narcissus which could not flower in France but, becoming at last a guest of Rome's amenity and majesty, here opened its flowers, almost like a sweet smile, in the happy plantations of my grandfather. And then, let them choose the crocus, the colchicum, the imperial crown, the iris, cyclamens, anemones, ranunculus, asphodels, peonies, fritellaria, lilies of the valley, carnations and tulips."

"The Dutch tulip?" I asked, if only to avoid the dialogue turning into a monologue.

"But of course! In no other plant does nature jest so freely or with so great a variety of colours, so much so that, years ago, someone enumerated over two hundred different colours. But take care," said he, stopping and looking me fixedly in the eyes with a severe mien.

"Yes, Master Florist?" I replied, stopping dead, dropping all the hardware I was carrying and fearing that I must somehow have said or done something displeasing.

"My boy," he admonished, in fact quite oblivious of me and absorbed in his own train of thought, "be sure not to forget that, alongside those I have named is the passion fruit, which is a native of Peru and is to be trained on cane trellises, Indian yucca, jasmine from Catalonia and Arabia and, lastly, the American variety which, it seems, some call quamoclit."

From this last assertion I realised that Tranquillo Romaùli, even when he fixed his eyes on yours, had the eyes of his mind focused solely upon the sole true interest of his life: the loving care of plants and flowers.

"And now, to work," said he, handing me his box and beginning to scoop at the earth of the flower bed with his bare hands. "Hand me the implements one at a time, as I request them. First, the straight-edge."

I rummaged in the box and almost at once found the long stick which was used for aligning the sides of the flower beds. I gave it to him.

"Give me the little jar with the seeds."

"Here you are."

"Sprinkler."

"Yes."

"Pruning knife."

"By your leave."

"Pronged grubber."

"Yes."

"Dibber."

"Yes."

"Cannon."

"Take it."

He turned the tool around in his hands and stood up with a start.

"I don't believe it. 'Tis not possible!" he said to himself, biting on the knuckles of his right hand: I had made a mistake.

"But my boy!" he exploded, opening wide his arms and addressing me in the grave, commiserative tones of a priest lecturing a sinner. "How many times must I tell you that this is an extractor, not a cannon, which is four times bigger?"

I durst not reply, conscious of the gravity of the misdeed.

"Forgive me, I thought. . ." I struggled to justify myself, hastily returning the extractor to the box and pulling out the cylinder for transplanting known as a cannon.

"No excuses. Let us attend to our work now. I see that you have already brought some pots with you," said he, regaining his composure and preparing to extract the seedlings which he meant to transplant.

While Tranquillo dug up and replanted, delicately moving the soil, carefully watering the turf and lovingly positioning the new bulbs, I searched my mind desperately for ways of steering the conversation away from flowers towards what concerned me.

"Abbot Melani told me that you had an interesting and profitable conversation today."

"Abbot who? Ah. . . you mean the gentleman from Pistoia; or France, was it not? He quite appreciated the way in which I had placed colours in my flower beds," said he, while cleaning the plants bordering the beds with a little brush and ridding them of the specks of earth scattered during the transplanting.

"Exactly, 'tis of him that I speak."

"Very well, 'tis no surprise that he should have expressed such pleasure. One must always so arrange matters that colours respond symmetrically to one another, and that I have done, as we did in the good old days at Duke Caetani's gardens at Cisterna: each bed must be filled with at least two or three sorts of flowers, differing among themselves in nature and in colour, and so arranged, frontally or sideways, that those which resemble or are the same as each other, although separated, correspond with one another."

"Precisely, and Abbot Melani said that. . ."

"But mind you!" he warned, brandishing the copper watering can severely. "One can never, I repeat, never, mix ranunculus, Spanish jonquils and tulips, for that would produce disharmony and deformity. My grandfather, Tranquillo Romaùli of blessed memory, who kept one of the finest gardens in Rome (ah yes, indeed, one of the few true exemplars of the art, such as are no longer to be found nowadays), as I was saying, my grandfather would always insist particularly on that point." Here, he sighed with exaggerated melancholy.

"Ah yes, you are quite right," said I, at the same time holding back another yawn, disappointed at my inability to break through the Master Florist's verbal wall.

A couple of servants passed behind us with as many baskets full of freshly killed and plucked poultry. They groaned, discreetly casting sardonic smiles of sympathy in my direction, for the Master Florist's terrible logorrhoea was well known at Villa Spada, and justifiably feared.

It only remained for me to risk my all.

"Well, Abbot Melani told me that he greatly appreciated his conversation with you," said I as rapidly as I was able to, "and he would be glad to renew the pleasure at your earliest opportunity."

"Ah yes?"

He had at last responded: a good sign.

"Yes, you know, the Abbot is very troubled. Death is hanging over El Escorial. . ."

He looked at me pensively, without uttering a word. Perhaps he had understood the allusion: the King of Spain's sickness, the succession to the throne, the Tetràchion. . .

"You are well informed," said he, speaking in unexpectedly grave tones. "The Escorial is drying up, son, while Versailles. . . and now Schönbrunn too. . ." he hinted, leaving his sentence unfinished.

That was the signal, said I to myself. He knew. And he had also referred to the most famous gardens of France and the Empire, the two contenders for the Spanish succession.

"We have a heavy burden to carry," he concluded enigmatically.

He had spoken of "we"; he was probably also referring to others: the order passed on by word of mouth, as suspected by Abbot Melani. And now he wanted to free himself of the secret that weighed upon his soul.

"I agree," I replied.

He nodded with a mute smile of secret understanding.

"If the Abbot, your protector, is truly so concerned for the fate of the Escorial, we shall surely have much to talk of, he and I."

"That would be truly opportune," said I, taking my tone from his last words.

"Provided that he is correctly informed," Romaùli made clear. "Otherwise, it would all be just a waste of breath."

"You need have no doubts," I reassured him, without, however, having understood the meaning of his warning.

As I walked towards the great house, mentally repeating the conversation with the Master Florist, I had just turned a corner when I heard the sound of two persons' footsteps behind me on the gravel, accompanied by as many voices.

". . . And what Abbot Melani dared to do was quite unheard of, on that point I am completely in agreement. But Albani's reaction was even more surprising."

Someone was talking about Atto. The voice was that of an old man of high birth. I could not miss the opportunity. I hid behind a hedge, preparing myself to listen to the content of that conversation.

"So many suspected him of being excessively Francophile," the voice continued, "and yet he gave Melani a good drubbing. So now he passes for a moderate, equidistant between the French and the Spaniards."

"'Tis incredible how quickly a man's reputation can change," echoed a second voice.

"Ah, yes. Of course, for the time being, it will not profit him much. He is far too young to be made pope. But everything is useful for keeping afloat, an art of which Albani is a past-master. Heh!"

I almost crawled behind the hedge, thus stalking unseen the pair who were out taking their morning walk. These were clearly two guests who had spent the night at the villa; they might, in all probability, be two cardinals, but their voices were, alas, not sufficiently familiar for me to be able to identify to whom they belonged. The reconnaissance was also made more difficult for me by the rustling of the nearby shrubs, which from time to time made perfect vigilance impossible.

"And what about the note they were passing to one another? Is what I was told yesterday true?"

"I checked and they told me that, yes, it was quite true. The parrot stole the message and went off to read it in his nest, heh! Albani did not show it, but he was desperate. He charged two of his servants with searching for the bird high and low, without showing themselves, for no one was to know how important the matter was. One of the two was, however, seen by the Major-Domo climbing up a tree in the garden and ingenuously explained to him what he was up to, so that the news was bruited abroad. No one knows where the bird is."

Although I pricked up my ears as much as I was able to, I was unable to overhear anything else, for the hedge along which I was moving turned to the right, while the two turned off to the left. I remained a while crouching on the ground, waiting for the pair to move away. I was already recapitulating with secret euphoria all the urgent news to be reported to Atto: the Master Florist who had promised, however obliquely, to reveal to him all that he knew about the Tetràchion; Albani desperate at the loss of his note, which therefore did contain really precious information, for no one else's eyes; and lastly, the political speculation on the two altercations between Atto and Albani who, it seems, had, precisely as a result of this, rid himself of his uncomfortable reputation as a vassal of the French.

What I did not know was that I would not be telling him any of these things in the immediate future.

". . . to read it in his nest, heh!"

I was already on my feet and gave a violent start. I crouched down once more, terrified of being caught spying. It was the voice of one

of the two cardinals overheard a few moments earlier. How could he
have turned around without my realising it?

"Everything's useful for keeping afloat, eh?!"

I grew pale. My ears could not betray me. The cardinal was behind me.

I turned around and saw him just as he was opening his wings and
taking off, insolently showing me the plumage of his tail, his talons
and the piece of paper which for many hours now had been held
tightly in their grasp.

࿐

I rejoined Atto in his apartment, where he awaited news of my conversation with the Master Florist; as soon as he knew of the most
recent development, namely the appearance of Caesar Augustus, we
rushed into the garden, exploring above all the area around the tool
shed where I had seen the bird not long before. There was no trace,
however.

"The aviary," I suggested.

We hastened there with our hearts in our mouths, anxious to pass
unobserved among the servants at work and the eminences out walking. In the aviary, too, there was no sign of Caesar Augustus. Helpless,
I looked at the flocks of nightingales, lapwings, starlings, partridges,
francolins, pheasants, ortolans, green linnets, blackbirds, calandra
larks, chaffinches, turtle-doves and hawfinches. Blissfully unaware,
they pecked away at seeds and salad leaves, without a care for our
concerns. Even if they knew where the parrot was hiding at that
moment, they could do no more than stare at us with their vacant
eyes. I was already regretting the fact that the wretched parrot was
the only one among them to have the gift of speech when I noticed
that a young francolin kept looking upwards, apparently worried by
something. I knew that vivacious and impertinent bird perfectly
well, for often, when I was feeding the aviary, it would perch on my
arm, pecking in the palm of my hand at the dry bread of which it was
inordinately fond and which it hated me to distribute to its companions. Now it was showing the same signs of disquiet, twittering away
with its beak pointing upwards. Then I understood and I too looked
up there.

"Everything's useful for keeping afloat, eh?!" repeated Caesar
Augustus when he saw that he had been found out.

He was perched at the very top of the aviary, but on the outside: above that graceful little cupola of metal netting which crowned the entire structure of that prison for birds. Since the moment of his flight, obviously, Caesar Augustus' regular ration of food had not been placed before his personal cage. He must therefore have stolen somewhere the piece of bread which he was pecking at on that pinnacle, while the francolin looked enviously on.

"Come here at once, and give us that piece of paper," I ordered him, taking care, however, not to call too loud for fear of being overheard by the other servants.

His sole response was to fly off and perch on a nearby tree, but without his usual nonchalance. It was quite clear that he meant to provoke us; he had probably taken a dislike to one of us and it was not hard to see who that might be.

"He seemed to have some trouble perching, he must still have that note hooked onto one of his claws," I said to Atto.

"Let us hope that it does not fall who knows where, and that the solution soon comes."

"The solution?"

"I have sent Buvat to find a specialist. He went on horseback with one of the servants. Fortunately, your colleague had all the necessary details but I hope there will be no delay, otherwise we shall soon have everyone gathering around us, starting with the Major-Domo."

I was on the point of asking him what he meant by the term "specialist" when events anticipated my words. Buvat appeared behind a hedge, announcing his arrival.

"Thank heavens!" exclaimed Melani.

Thanks, perhaps, to some obscure premonitory faculty, Caesar Augustus flew off at precisely that moment in the direction of the vegetable garden of the excellent Barberini estate, which shared a long border with the Villa Spada.

"Do the Barberini have armed guards in their garden next door?"

"Not to the best of my knowledge."

"Very well," said Atto, "our friend will not go far."

Just at that moment, in the opposite quadrant of the sky, there appeared a sharp and rapid shadow which, although distant, appeared to be aiming menacingly at the fluttering outline of Caesar Augustus. The latter must have become aware of this, for he turned suddenly downwards to the left, perhaps in the direction of some thicket. The fast-moving shadow then disappeared from the luminous blue bowl of the sky.

"Come, I shall introduce you to the specialist," said Atto, "or rather, to employ the correct term, the falconer, for that is what he prefers to be called."

We found him waiting for us as soon as we left the Villa Spada. He was a truly strange and singular individual: tall and thin, with long crow-black hair, black, rapacious eyes and an aquiline nose. Across his shoulders, he carried a big sack containing all his equipment. He was accompanied by a fine big hunting dog which looked keen to see action.

I looked questioningly at Atto while we accompanied the falconer towards the aviary and the place from which Caesar Augustus had just taken flight.

"*Engaging in no hunt absurd, we'll use a falcon, not a cuckoo bird,*" he jovially declaimed, miming the pose of a bard. "I got the idea from that mad eccentric Albicastro with his endless quotations from that moral poem on madness."

Just at that moment, the falconer glanced up at the ample vault of heaven and whistled twice. At once there plunged from on high a whirlwind of feathers, plumes and talons which, slowing its descent with an acrobatic turn, landed among us, coming to rest on its master's arm, stretched upwards to show the hawk where to land. The man's right arm bore a coarse leather glove to protect it from being maimed by the bird's talons. I looked at the creature with a mixture of admiration and horror, as it settled comfortably between the wrist and the elbow, contentedly testing its solid perch with its talons, while its master covered its head with a leather hood. The falconer had trained his bird well, for, after freeing it who knows where, he had only to call it to bring it back to him.

"Rather than going after cranes, we shall hunt the parrot," announced Atto, "and with the best of arms, a falcon."

❧

We returned to the villa, silently hoping that no one would ask us what we were doing or why. Fate was friendly to us. We met only one of Sfasciamonti's friends, on guard, who let us pass without posing any questions, although he did look at us somewhat curiously.

"It is horrible," I protested, as we straddled the wall bordering the Barberini estate, towards which Caesar Augustus had flown. "It will massacre him."

"Massacre, massacre. . ." chanted Atto smugly as we got him over the wall with the help of a stool. "Let us say that we shall teach him a lesson. The note belongs to us, the parrot knows that perfectly well. I could, to tell the truth, have used this method from the start, but you would never have agreed."

"What makes you think that I shall agree now?"

"The emergency. The parrot is no longer obeying any orders, the situation is out of control. Remember, my boy, emergencies call for uncomfortable decisions. And if there is no emergency, one must await, or even, if needs be, create one. That is an old technique employed by all men in government, which I have often had occasion to observe during the course of my career as a counsellor," said Atto with a disarming little smile, betraying a certain contentment that Caesar Augustus' petulant disobedience allowed him recourse to strong measures.

We jumped down from the wall; this was the natural continuation of a Roman wall, fortified with towers further to the left, which extended down almost as far as Piazza San Cosimato. Scrambling from the stool, the dog followed us over the barrier.

"Say what you will, the fact remains that the falcon is bloodthirsty," I protested. "I know perfectly well what it is capable of. Once I saw one during training catch a hen and split it asunder, tearing its heart from its breast still beating."

Meanwhile, the falconer had unhooded the falcon and released it. The hawk had climbed rapidly to a considerable height where it appeared as little more than a dark spot in the sky.

"Perhaps it won't ill-treat him too much," sniggered Melani. "In any case, the only thing that matters to us is the note. If he lets go of it, he'll come to no harm."

"You speak as though the falcon could understand what he's doing. Birds are beasts. They have neither intellect nor heart," I replied.

"Enough of that, boy," the falconer broke in.

He spoke with a northern accent, perhaps from Bologna, or Vicenza, where I knew that falconers had always been in abundance.

"Your ignorance is equalled only by the courage of my falcon," he told me in a harsh voice. "You say that birds have no pity. Do you not know that the great Palamedes, imitating the flight of cranes, which fly in V or A formation, or grouped to form many other letters, composed the characters from which came the alphabet, as Saint Jerome writes, and that from the imitation of the wise living of these cranes, or *grues*, comes the latin verb *congruere*, which means literally to be congruent, or coherent."

"No, I did not know that, but. . ."

While he imparted these notions to me, above our heads the falcon traced a series of threatening circles in search of his victim. We advanced cautiously through the long grass, looking for traces of Caesar Augustus. Atto and the falconer were sure of tracking him down. I was rather less sure, but I thought that if that were to happen, I should be able to make the parrot understand that it would be in its best interests to return Albani's note, on pains of suffering the cruellest of combats. We all stood there with our noses pointing up in the air, waiting for something to happen. The hound sniffed feverishly at trees, looking halfway up, watching the slightest movements.

"And how can you say that birds have no heart? They practise gratitude, fidelity and justice far better than men. The sparrowhawk captures a little bird to help with its digestion and keeps it alive all night close to its belly, whereupon, out of gratitude, it frees it instead of devouring it. Geese are even more modest than a young maiden: they couple only when they know that no one can see them and, afterwards, they wash thoroughly. Crows practice only marital love. Widowed, a turtledove will never mate again. Swallows always feed each of their fledglings fairly and equally. Are human beings capable of that? Furthermore, among fowls, the males are loquacious and the females taciturn: the contrary of men and, when one comes to think of it, far better. Lastly, geese, although rather inclined to gossip, when they know that an eagle is approaching, resist the temptation to honk and thus be discovered by putting a stone in their beaks.

"They even assist us when we are ill: there is no better way of ridding oneself of stomach ache than to place on it a live duck. For pains in the ribs, you need only eat an Austrian parrot; those with weak stomachs should eat swan's, eagle's or cormorant's meat; the dropsy is treated with powder of burned bats, while for many distempers one takes swallows' nests dissolved in water, nor is there an end to the remedies which poultry breeders generously offer us, and. . . One moment."

The falconer had at last broken off. Everything happened suddenly. The dog barked loudly and pointed: he had found the quarry. From a nearby shrub we heard a loud rustling, then the beating of wings. Caesar Augustus, brilliantly white and fluffed-up with his yellow crest, escaped from the thicket and took to the air. The dog barked loudly but the falconer held him back from following and cried out:

"Look! Look!"

Hearing that call, the falcon knew that its time had come. Instinctively, it directed its beak downwards and plunged towards Caesar Augustus who had fortunately, although three times slower than his aggressor, gained a good start. He was flying towards the fortified Roman wall; the raptor corrected the angle of its attack as it drew closer. It was like a projectile, ready to plant the tip of its beak into the flesh of its victim, or to brake at the last moment, then turn and wound it with its deadly talons. It would only remain then for it to follow the disorderly fall, diving at last onto the poor injured and defenceless body on the ground and slaughtering it with two or three decisive blows to the breast.

The parrot hastened towards the great wall, behind which it presumably hoped to find shelter at least from the first attack.

"Caesar Augustus," I cried, hoping that he might hear me, but then I realised that everything was happening too fast for human senses.

The falcon was drawing ever closer. Twenty yards; fifteen; ten; seven. All of us, three men and a dog, stared breathlessly at the scene. The wall was too far off. The parrot could never make it that far. Only an instant and it would all be over. I awaited the impact.

"No," the falconer hissed angrily.

He had made it. At the very last moment, Caesar Augustus had opted for a nearer refuge. He had hidden himself in a group of trees thick enough to discourage the falcon, who slowed down and at once regained height.

"Caesar Augustus!" I called again, approaching at a run. "Let go of the paper and all will be well!"

We tried but failed to find the outline of the parrot among the branches. He had hidden really well, as the falconer, too, was forced to admit.

"You promised that you would give him time to ponder," I protested vigorously to Atto.

"I am sorry. I did not realise that things would go so quickly. Nevertheless, he has had all the time he needed for thinking."

"Thinking? But he'll be utterly terrified."

The events that followed proved me to have been utterly mistaken.

While we were exploring around and under the thick clump of trees, a sudden, lacerating double whistle broke the silence. We looked at one another. It was the falconer's whistle, yet he seemed as astonished as we.

"I did not. . . did not do it. I never whistled," he stammered.

Instinctively, he looked upward.

"The glove, damn it," he cursed, seeing that his faithful pupil, hearing the call, was promptly returning and was looking for his forearm. So the falconer had to pull on his leather glove in furious haste and only just caught the flying beast in time. It was then, out of the corner of my eye, that I saw the white and yellow spot gliding silently to the left, once again in the direction of the Roman wall. Atto too realised this a few (important) moments later.

The parrot had imitated the falconer's whistle perfectly, thus causing the predator to return to its master, down below. Caesar Augustus had thus gained enough time to get away, before his enemy could gain height and, with that, the ability to attack.

"That way!" exclaimed Melani, turning to the falconer.

The wasted time had given Caesar Augustus a distinct advantage. The falcon was once again freed and once again had to gain height. The dog was barking wildly.

"Can your bird not attack at once?" asked Atto, running towards the point where Caesar Augustus had disappeared from sight.

"He has first to gain height. He does not attack horizontally like a goshawk!" replied the falconer, as offended as if he had been asked to attend a wedding dressed in rags.

This gave rise to a wretched, disorderly chase downhill along the Roman walls, following the road that traverses the Barberini property up to Piazza Cosimato. Behind the ancient walls, rhythmically punctuated by antique watchtowers, Caesar Augustus's yellow crest would reappear from time to time. He could not fly higher than the falcon, as herons do to dodge such attacks. He had, however, perfectly understood the enemy's weak points and was employing delaying tactics: flying low and passing very rapidly from a tree to a crack in the wall, then vice versa, alternating brief but lightning sorties with the repeated whistle which he had heard the falconer use and had at once learned to imitate to perfection. The falcon could only obey the commands which he had been taught from his very first training, and with every whistle he came back to his master, who was, understandably, almost out of his mind. A couple of times, Caesar Augustus also used the falconer's "Look! Look!" hunting signal, throwing the adversary into such confusion that, if its master had not got it away from there with yells and curses, it might have turned its warlike attentions to a couple of innocent sparrows fluttering in the vicinity.

The last part of the road was flanked on both sides by two ordinary walls and no longer by Roman ruins. I turned around to look for Atto: we had lost him. Caesar Augustus, too, was nowhere to be seen. I did, however, hope that he would have continued along the same trajectory as he had followed hitherto. In that case, as soon as we reached the first open space, we might perhaps have caught sight of him. It was thus that we came to the front of the convent of the nuns of Saint Francis, in Piazza San Cosimato. Abbot Melani arrived some time later, completely out of breath (despite the fact that he had left off running very early on) and sat down by the roadside:

> *The hunter wastes much time at stalking*
> *The game he's after, riding, walking,*
> *He combs through hill and dale and hedge,*
> *Conceals himself among the sedge,*
> *Oft scares away more than he gets*
> *If he's been slipshod with his nets.*

"Thus Albicastro would have mocked me with his beloved Brant, if he had seen the state I am in," Melani sighed philosophically, huffing and puffing like a pair of bellows.

I noticed that the Abbot, as I had discovered many years previously, had a taste for citing quotations on the most varied occasions. Only, especially at difficult moments like this, he no longer had breath enough to sing them; and so, instead of the little songs of Le Seigneur Luigi, his one-time master, he preferred to quote verses.

I then turned to contemplate the piazza. To my surprise, notwithstanding the fact that it was very early on Sunday morning, Piazza San Cosimato was full of people. His Holiness (but this I was to discover only later) had decided freely to grant the little boys and girls of Rome the Jubilee indulgence and the remission of sins, subject only to visiting the Vatican Basilica. For this reason, the children of various quarters were preparing to visit the Vatican in procession, with so many little standards, crosses and crucifixes. The maidens were all dressed in the most splendid lace surplices, and with garlands on their heads, each decorated for some particular devotion. The affecting little procession was attended and guided by the parents and by the nuns of the Convent of Saint Francis, all of whom were crowding into the piazza and witnessed our arrival, all dusty and fatigued, with no little surprise.

The falconer was at his wits' end.

"He is not coming back, I cannot see him," he blubbered.

He had lost sight of his falcon. He feared that he might have been abandoned, as sometimes happen with raptors apparently tamed by their masters yet still in their hearts wild and proud.

"There he is!" cried Atto.

"The falcon?" asked the falconer, his face lighting up.

"No, the parrot."

I too had seen. Caesar Augustus, who must have been rather tired too, had just left a cornice and begun to glide in the direction of the nearby Piazza San Callisto. Atto was by now exhausted, while the falconer had thoughts only for his pupil. Only I and the dog were prepared to follow the parrot, with the opposite intentions: I, to save him, he, to slaughter.

The dog barked like mad and charged to the attack, terrifying and scattering all the children from the ranks of the procession, amidst whom I too plunged in pursuit of the parrot, sowing further confusion and provoking the anguished reproofs of the nuns.

By now Caesar Augustus was flying wearily, perching ever more frequently on windowsills, little shrines and balconies, then flying off only when fear of the dog, which bared its teeth angrily, forced him to seek some new refuge. I could not even ask him to land on the ground and give himself up. The dog was always ahead of me, barking wildly and leaping up furiously, simply longing to get its teeth into the poor fugitive. The passers-by watched in shock as our screaming scrimmage, an extraordinary chimera composed of fleeing wings, biting fangs and legs coming to the rescue, made its way forward.

Several times, I narrowed my eyes, peering into the distance: the bird still seemed to have that wretched scrap of paper hanging onto a talon. After covering a considerable part of the Via di Santa Maria in Trastevere, our bizarre trio turned left and came at last to the bridge of the San Bartolomeo island.

Caesar Augustus landed on a windowsill at the corner, just where the bridge begins. He was quite high up, and the dog (which had perhaps realised by now that it had lost all trace of its master) was beginning to tire of that exhausting, absurd circus. It looked at the parrot, which nothing now seemed likely to shift from its position of safety. To my left stood the San Bartolomeo bridge and, beyond it, that beautiful island, the one single piece of insular territory which completes and embellishes the impetuous flow of fair Tiber. The dog at last turned on its heels, not without one last outburst of rage and disappointment.

"So, do you want to come down? We are alone now."

In the parrot's eyes, I read his willingness to surrender at last to a friend. He was on the point of coming down. Instead, one last cruel reversal intervened.

An old woman who lived in the house had come to the window. She had seen him. Taken aback by the unusual features of that bizarre and beautiful creature, yet incapable of appreciating such splendour and rendered nervous by her own stupidity, the hag tried brutally to drive him away, threatening to strike him. The poor fowl fled, borne on the wind which in that place generously accompanies the current of the river.

I saw him successfully gain height, like some new falcon, dipping and again rising, until he gave way at last to the caprices of the eddying winds and disappeared from view, a drop in the sea of lost desires.

I returned to the Villa Spada covered in sweat, worn out and embittered. I was to report at once to Abbot Melani with the bad news. He, however, had not yet returned. He must surely be resting, on the way back, from the exertions of the parrot hunt: an ordeal at his age, exacerbated by his painful arm. I decided that, rather than endure a discussion and Atto's complaints, it would be best to slip a note under the door of his apartment reporting on the negative outcome of the hunt. However, even before leaving him that message, I knew as soon as I set foot in the villa that the afternoon would be filled with chores, and yet more occasions for over-exertion.

The wedding festivities included a ludic entertainment: a great game of blind man's buff in the gardens of the villa. Eminences, princes, gentlemen and noble ladies were to challenge one another in joyous competition: hiding, following, finding and getting lost once more among the hedges and avenues of the park, vying for who was to show the greatest sagacity, speed and skill. The game could be played only in a place where vision, access and even hearing were obstructed, making for ease of concealment and difficulty in discovering those hiding: the magnificent gardens of Villa Spada, now rendered almost labyrinthine by decorations ephemeral and floral.

I was advised that my services would be required by Don Paschatio on this occasion, in view of a temporary shortage of staff. No fewer than four servants had deserted the Major-Domo, giving such more or less imaginative excuses as a fit of melancholy humour and the sudden death of a dear aunt.

The day had grown cloudy, the temperature had gone down a little and so the game was to begin not too late. I hastened to find some sustenance in the kitchens; it was by now time for luncheon and the hunt for Caesar Augustus had left me ravenous. I found some leftovers of turkey and toasted eggs, by now grown cold, but a delight both for my taste-buds and for my stomach.

I was still chewing on some little bones when one of Don Paschatio's assistants instructed me to don livery and report to the junction between the avenue alongside the secret garden and that which led through the vines down to the fountain. At that crossroads, a place of refreshment had been set up, with fresh waters, orange juice, lemonade, selections of fruit and vegetables, freshly cut bread and good preserves, all in the shade of a great pentagonal white and blue-striped pavilion, the pilasters of which were decorated with great wooden shields bearing the family arms of the spouses' families, the Rocci and the Spada. All this had been provided to slake the thirst of the players of blind man's buff, overheated by all that running around, but also for the sake of those taking no part in the game and preferring to stay idly stretched out on the great white canvas armchairs in the shade of the pavilion.

Making my way to my post, I could but admire once more the infinite caprices granted by the good architect of nature, of which, now that the work of gardening had been completed, I kept discovering new and admirable details. As in every garden all things must be pleasant, in the Villa Spada, every element had been bent to the pleasure of the eye and the intellect, starting with the order of woods and vegetation; for the art of building is a matter of more than the architecture of walls and roofs and comprises hedges, walks and avenues, meadows, porticoes, pergolas, palm trees, flower beds and kitchen gardens. The greatest villas possessed splendid tree-lined avenues, and it is true that we had none such. Therefore, to give a better tone to the walks, along the edges were aligned rows of noble box shrubs, privets and acanthus.

Barrel-vaulted pergolas gently introduced the shy, admiring visitor to the confluence between one avenue and another, or to crossroads under verdant bosky cupolas. Espaliered laurels were trained as canopies, symmetrically tonsured and seven or even fifteen feet high, vying with sheltering holm-oaks, myrtle bushes shaped like umbrellas or sugar loaves, as well as with complete ephemeral wooden buildings, all covered with a mantle of vegetation, and rows of columns in green with festoons and wreaths providing a frame for the orchestra. From a semicircular platform, a small ensemble of string players filled the air with a melodious counterpoint, a joyous game of hide-and-seek between trills and pizzicati that seemed to anticipate the game to which the guests had been invited.

Here, a few paces distant from the platform of the little orchestra, I had been detailed to serve, mixing orange juice and lemon, slicing bread, taking care of the armchairs and providing whatever else might please the excellencies and eminences present or passing by.

As soon as I arrived, I began boldly mixing juices and filling glasses, running from one guest to another like a bee buzzing from flower to flower in the morning.

Once I had done my duty waiting upon them, I placed myself at the gentlemen's service, standing beside one of the wooden pillars of the pavilion before which the other waiters stood like so many Lot's wives. Under the white and sky-blue wing of the great linen tent the guests stood and chattered, laughing and joking, or sat ensconced in armchairs. A few paces away from me, a few middle-aged monsignors calmed with lemonade tongues over-exercised with gossip.

It was at that moment that I realised I was in luck. Next to me stood the two monsignors whom I had, during the Academy, overheard discussing a certain plan to reform the corps of sergeants. From what I could gather, the discussion was continuing:

". . . And so now, things should get a move on."

"But this idea is twenty years old, surely they do not intend to implement it now?"

"On the contrary, that does appear to be the case. I was told by my brother who is still an auditor of the Rota but is close to Cardinal Cenci."

"And what does Cenci know of it?"

"He knows, he knows. Here in Rome, at a certain level, the matter is common knowledge. It seems that the time is ripe; if the Pope lives a few more months, the reform will be carried through."

I listened to those two like Diana drawing her bow against a fleeing stag.

"But it is absolutely just that this should be done," continued the first speaker. "You and I, who are decent persons, have never seen the proud cohort of catchpolls entering a tavern or wine-shop at night, for at night we sleep and do not go out winebibbing in taverns. But everyone knows perfectly well what takes place. First the catchpolls get roaring drunk, befoul everything and create pandemonium, then off they go without so much as a goodnight. And if the innkeeper is so ill-advised as to ask to be paid, they spit in his face as though he had committed *lèse-majesté*, treat him worse than some back-street assassin and the night afterwards they return to take their revenge. They arrange for some strumpet to enter the hostelry, or a pair of ruffian friends of theirs, and get them to play cards with unstamped playing cards. Then they enter, pretending to be there for a police check, find the cards, or the strumpet, and everyone is thrown into prison: the host, the waiters and anyone who happens to be in the tavern at the time, thus ruining the establishment and the innkeeper's family."

"I know, I know," replied the other, "these tricks are as old as the world."

"And do you think that a trivial matter?" insisted the first speaker. "It appears that the catchpolls exact a tithe, 'the gratuity', they call it, not only from all traders and hawkers but even from artists. What is more, they take a cut from all the harlots, and not only that. They rent rooms and sublet them to the same women of the town at a high price, so that they take money off them twice over. If the harlots refuse, they lose all their advantages."

"Advantages?" repeated the other, somewhat confused.

"Those protected by the catchpolls can work, if you will pardon the improper term, even on feast days. The others they keep checks on, obliging them to rest during religious festivals, in accordance with the law. So those ones lose earnings. Do I explain myself clearly?"

"Well, that's a fine one," said the other, wiping his forehead with a white lace handkerchief in a voice that expressed a mixture of surprise, curiosity and a hint of prurience.

"Come," said the first one. "Let us go and take a look at the game of blind man's buff."

They rose from their armchairs and took one another by the arm with familiar courtesy, moving towards the nearby outer wall bordering the Barberini estate; there, they would certainly be turning to the left, towards the little grove where the game would be at its height.

I looked around me. There could be no question of leaving my post and abruptly or suddenly abandoning the other waiters in the tent. Don Paschatio would certainly receive notice of such a thing; hitherto, I had enjoyed almost complete freedom of movement, except for those occasional duties as a supernumerary, whenever there was a shortage of personnel. If I were to be counted among the deserters, that would only be the start of my troubles. Perhaps the matter might even be brought to the attention of Cardinal Spada in person and I would lose my job; or else the permission to serve Atto might be revoked.

Just as I was reviewing all these pessimistic prospects, I found the solution. A lady with a *décolletage* after the French style, with a great white veil on her shoulders, was being served a generous portion of blood orange juice in a crystal bowl. Next to her, the Marchese Della Penna awaited his turn. Swiftly I took a carafe of lemonade from the table and rushed to serve the Marchese.

"But what are you doing, boy?"

In rushing to serve the gentleman, I deliberately jogged my colleague's arm, with the result that he sprinkled red juice on the lady's immaculate veil. Surprised and angered, the lady promptly protested.

"Oh heavens, what have I done! Permit me to remedy this, the veil must be washed at once, I shall see to this in person," said I, snatching the veil from her shoulders and rushing towards the great house; a move executed with such rapidity that the victim and the onlookers were left with no time to react. The school of Atto, master of false accidents, had yielded its first fruit.

A few moments later, I placed the veil in the hands of a maidservant, with the request to wash it and return it to me in person. That task was the pretext I needed to abandon my post at the pavilion.

Immediately after that, I was in the vicinity of the little grove, on the trail of the two monsignors overheard moments before. How, I wondered, was I to spy on them without being discovered? At last I caught sight of them walking between the box and laurel hedges and continuing their earlier conversation. I was jubilant: the good old rules of Master Tranquillo Romaùli had offered me the solution. Near the statues, the hedges had been left not more than a yard high. Elsewhere, they were higher. The precise height of those hedges, neither too low nor as high as those in a maze, provided me with a decisive advantage: they concealed even the top of my head, while leaving the others uncovered from the shoulders upwards. I could see without being seen, spy without being spied on.

I stopped behind a hedge, ready to listen, when a voice made me jump.

"Cuckoo! You are here, you naughty girl, I know."

"Hee hee hee hee!" responded a feminine laugh.

The Penitentiary Major, Cardinal Colloredo, was groping his way, impeded by his voluminous cassock, with his eyes covered with a big red bandage and his hands, adorned with huge topaz and ruby-incrusted rings, stretched out before him in search of his prey. A few paces beyond, hidden behind a little tree, a young highborn maiden wearing a lovely cream-coloured gown and with a heavy diadem of emeralds around her neck awaited Colloredo's approach with trepidation.

"That is not fair! You are breaking the rules," the young woman chanted, for the ancient wearer of the purple, pretending to wipe the perspiration from his brow, had raised the blindfold a little from his eyes.

Suddenly, a nobleman wearing a showy French periwig, whom I was able to identify without a shadow of a doubt as the Marchese Andrea Santacroce, burst out from the surrounding bushes. He grasped the maiden firmly, pressing his chest hard against her back, and kissed her passionately on the neck, like a gander covering a goose and biting her sensually from behind.

"You are mad," I heard her moan, as she freed herself from the embrace. "The others are coming."

Just then, indeed, another blindfolded player was approaching that part of the wood, driving the other players before him, as happens when the prey is driven forward by the beaters on a hunt. Santacroce disappeared as rapidly as he had materialised. The damsel cast one last languid glance at him.

I concealed myself even more thoroughly in the grass, terrified of the prospect of being discovered and taken for a spy on clandestine trysts.

"I know that you're nearby, ha ha!" came the happy chant of the Chairman of the Victualling Board, Monsignor Grimaldi, blindfolded with a big yellow handkerchief.

Before him moved a little group of guests who were enjoying themselves provoking him, keeping very close but never allowing themselves to get caught. The ladies caressed him with fans, the men tickled his belly with a little finger, then were gone in a trice, some under the sheltering foliage of loquat or marine cherry bushes, some taking refuge under the friendly fronds of a young example of those strange trees, the palms, which were for the first time planted by Pope Pius IV in the garden before the Villa Pia and had since made such an impression that their exotic mops were now to be found throughout the Holy City. Grimaldi bounded forward, sure of surprising the nearest player, the Cardinal Vicar Gaspare Carpegna. Instead, he collided with the trunk of the palm tree, causing great mirth in all the group.

The Cardinal Vicar, who had escaped the assault by a hair's breadth, leaned contentedly against a wall, when from this came a spray of water which caught him straight in the face, soaking his collar and his purple cape. An even heartier burst of general laughter followed.

In order to make the games richer in surprises, Cardinal Spada had arranged that little water devices were to be scattered throughout the property, which would be activated by the unwitting passerby, unleashing sprays, spouts, buckets and downpours for the joy of gay, fun-loving souls. The wall on which Carpegna had leaned, inadvertently pressing on a lever, was in reality a wooden panel leaning against a tree and covered with bricks, behind which was concealed a hydraulic machine equipped with a spout aimed at the activator.

"Cardinal Carpegna was hoping to get away, and instead. . . he got a wetting, ha ha!" commented Cardinal Negroni who, however, promptly tripped over a vertical cord which tipped a bucket of water on an overhead branch onto his head, giving him abundant copious cold shower.

More laughter followed and I took advantage of the diversion to move a little further away. I was on the point of giving up my bold project of espionage and returning to the great house when I recognised the two monsignori whom I sought, as they distractedly observed that jovial pastime. As I expected, they did not notice me, absorbed as they still were in their discussions.

"The catchpolls protect fugitives and persons who have been served summons," said the first, as they slowly strolled towards the fishpond under the fountain, "yet they imprison people with a mere civil debt for insolvency. And what is one to say of those convicted in absentia who are arrested and arrive in prison half dead? All the doctrinal texts make it quite clear that torture is licit, but at the end of proceedings, not the beginning."

"And how about illegal arrests? No one says anything about these but they are exceedingly frequent. People are arrested in the middle of the night, interrogated, maltreated and thrown into the cells for no good reason. I tell you roundly that, as long as all this remains unchanged, pilgrims and foreigners are bound to leave Rome scandalised, ascribing the crimes of the sergeants to the persons who worthily preside over public administration."

"The Pope, the Secretary of State, the Governor. . ." added the other, stopping by the feet of the Triton to admire the water-lilies, the marsh marigold with its yellow double flowers and the white-petalled trefoil, all limply abandoned on the surface of the waters.

"Of course, and they will spread the word everywhere in foreign countries, to the great dishonour and discredit of the Holy Apostolic See."

Prolonged and forced immobility behind a mere box hedge, although thick and as high as a young boy, was both risky and uncomfortable. The danger of being found out by some player of blind man's buff entering the walk where I was eavesdropping gave me cold sweats. Such was the tension in my legs, what with my concern not to make the slightest sound on the gravel, that my calf muscles were close to cramp.

Suddenly, my heart stopped: the hedge was no longer there. Or rather, it had shifted. It had gradually moved out of alignment and it was now extending to my left, leaving me without cover. By pure

luck, the two monsignors were facing away from me, and so did not
see me. I felt as desperate and defenceless as a pig at the gates of
a slaughterhouse. Leaping, I took refuge in the shade of a jasmine
espalier. I saw the two monsignors break off and look in my direction
with an amazed expression on their faces; I prayed to the Lord and
lowered my head.

I raised my eyes. They were not looking at me but at the hedge
which, to their astonishment, was trotting off in the direction of Cardinal Nerli, an individual who was, as I have had cause to mention,
disliked by many. We followed the scene from a distance. Nerli was
blindfolded and following a lady.

Then it happened. From the upper half of the promenading bush
came an iron tube which sprinkled Nerli with a light jet of water,
eliciting from him a cry of alarm. Then the ball of leaves and bushes
ran off, trotting out of the wood. All the company was convulsed with
hilarity. The Cardinal tore the blindfold from his eyes.

"What a splendid joke, Eminence, do you not think?" cried a
number of members of the Sacred College, running up to congratu-
late Nerli, who was as white as a sheet. Judging by their laughter,
they had taken a malicious pleasure in the game.

"Ah yes, really a delightful trick," commented one of the ladies
present, "and how elegant that little squirt was, so well done!"

The Cardinal, scarlet with embarrassment and irritation, did not
seem to share this view.

"Eminence, do not be a spoil-sport," said one of the damsels
present. "Put back your blindfold at once, for the game must go on."

Lost in all that great verdant sea and in the smile of the lady
who was speaking to him, Cardinal Nerli's eye and mind willingly
resigned themselves to sweet shipwreck. The magnificence of the
gardens softened his soul, its perfumes loosened his heart and lightened his head. The prelate allowed himself to be gently blindfolded
and the game resumed without a care.

The two monsignori commented on the innocent pastimes of the
other guests with mute disapprobation. I in the meantime made sure
that the espalier of jasmine which I was hiding behind was not also
equipped with a tenant and legs. Soon, however, the pair resumed
their promenade in order to get away from the noise of the players.
For a while, they walked in silence. They went through immense
pergolas, mounted on cross-beams and pilasters, so that those passing

underneath saw almost a brand new sky, viewed through green-tinted lenses. For brief instants, their eyes caught sight of nearby peach trees, artichoke plants, pear trees, rows of lemon trees, orange groves, cypresses and holm-oaks which played hide-and-seek with the visitor's eyes since, as Leon Battista Alberti puts it, without mystery there can be no beauty. Dodging behind lemon trees and box hedges, I did not let them out of my sight or hearing.

"But let us get back to our subject," resumed the second of the pair, emboldened after listening to his companion's arguments. "What you tell me is true, and you are quite right. I shall even go further: because of the catchpolls' abuses, or simply their incompetence, the courts of law and the protocols of the civil notaries are full of cases that have had to be dismissed. When they do on occasion catch someone who deserves to end up behind bars, they ill-treat him so brutally, neglecting to collect evidence correctly, that the defence lawyers manage to get the proceedings suspended or even halted. Nevertheless, I do not hold out any high hopes for this reform. You know better than I that there is no point in trying to reason with these catchpolls."

"Of course there's no point in reasoning with them; but by now, we are no longer talking of catchpolls but of common thieves paid by the Apostolic Chamber! Every one of them is wretchedly poor before enrolling. The wages they receive are not enough to live on; a corporal receives six scudi, a catchpoll, four and a half. Now, let us suppose that with some honest work the corporal can earn another three scudi and the catchpoll another two."

"Very well, let us suppose that for the sake of argument."

"How do you explain, then, that if you enter their homes you will find it filled with luxury furniture? Their wives rival great ladies in their apparel and jewellery. And if they have no wife, you will find them surrounded by a brace of harlots, to which you may add gambling, drinking, gluttony and all manner of vices: not even forty scudi a month could pay for all that. It is quite plain that all that money can only come from robbery, do you not think so?"

"Of course I think so and I second your every word."

Meanwhile, we could hear the distant cries of the ladies, calling for an end to the game and inviting everyone to come and picnic, and rest, before dinner. The pair went through the gate to the secret garden, in search of quiet. I waited for them to move a little further in, among the elms and Capocotta poplars, and then I too entered, concealing myself to one side, behind a row of zibibbo vines.

"And so, this reform project?" asked the same one as before.

"It is simple and sensible. First, by means of a special bull, abolish all the functions of the Bargello, of every tribunal, both in Rome and in the country. Dismiss lieutenants, corporals, ranks of standard bearers and clerks and the like, all of which offices are usually also conferred on the sergeants."

"You are an optimist. Do you really believe that so crude and radical a reform will be approved by His Holiness, given his present state of health?"

"We shall see, we shall see. But you have not heard the rest. In the first place, the number of catchpolls will be reduced. Then the Mantellone, or President of Justice, if you prefer that title, will command sergeants from several tribunals, which, as you well know, is not at present possible. For the purposes of patrols and arrests, the catchpolls could be accompanied by a few soldiers, as is already the practice in many kingdoms and republics. All in all, about two hundred catchpolls will be dismissed."

"And in their place?"

"Perfectly simple: replace them with soldiers."

While I was returning to the great house to fetch the noblewoman's veil, cleansed of orange stains and ready to be returned to its owner, innumerable thoughts rushed into my mind. Of course, I was not unaware that the catchpolls were in part a miserable, ill-born and unfortunate rabble. Never, however, had I heard all the depraved commercial activities of the officers of the law listed all together, one after the other. Corrupt they were, indeed. But that was the least of their iniquities. The sergeants, so I had heard, practised far worse outrages, which reduced the law to the theatre of deceit and order to the handmaid of abuse.

My thoughts turned to Sfasciamonti: it was no surprise that he had to encourage his colleagues to investigate the *cerretani*. Why, I wondered, should they go out of their way to discover the secrets of the sects of mendicants if they already had to go to such lengths to conceal their own?

Of course, Sfasciamonti had shown himself to be familiar with the worst practices: falsifying police reports, arresting people unjustly, lying, threatening those detained for questioning. He would even have been prepared to have Il Roscio kept illicitly in prison. But all that was, I thought, in order to arrive at a goal that was in itself praiseworthy: to combat the *cerretano* scum and find out what had become of Abbot Melani's manuscript, the telescope and the relic. If these were the methods necessary to arrive at the truth, they were perhaps less than ideal; but they could doubtless be accepted.

જ્જ

When I arrived at Atto's lodgings, I was already awaited for my report. "It is about time. Where on earth have you been?" he asked me, while getting Buvat to spread an ointment on his arm.

I then told him of the many vicissitudes which had kept me busy, including those before the hunt for Caesar Augustus which I had not yet had occasion to report on: the conversation with the Master Florist, Albani's desperation at the loss of his note, stolen by the parrot; and finally, the scandal caused by the repeated argument between Atto himself and Albani, thanks to which the Secretary for Breves was ridding himself of his inconvenient reputation for fidelity to France.

The Abbot received these three items of news with excitement, amusement and thoughtful silence, respectively.

"So the Master Florist is prepared to talk. That is good, very good. Only, he said that I should be correctly informed before meeting him: in what sense? He will surely not be of the imperial party."

"Signor Abbot," Buvat intervened, "with your permission, I have an idea."

"Yes?"

"What if the Tetràchion, which Romaùli mentioned, were the flower of some household? The arms of noble houses are full of beasts with the most singular names such as the dragon, the gryphon, the siren and the unicorn, and it may be that plants follow the same pattern."

"Ah yes, it could come from some family coat of arms!" Atto jumped up, bespattering his poor secretary's clothing with the ointment from his arm. "All the more so in that the Master Florist knows all about flowers. You are a genius, Buvat. Perhaps Romaùli hoped that I should be well informed before I meet him because he does not wish to name names and so he expects that, when I go and talk with him, I should already know what family is hidden behind the Tetràchion."

"So," I asked, "would this provide the proof of the heir to the Spanish throne, as Ambassador Uzeda's maid said? And if that is the case, what would that have to do with the fact that Capitor named the dish after a heraldic flower?"

"I have not the faintest idea, my boy," replied Melani, over-excitedly, "but Romaùli does seem to intend to provide us with useful information."

Having said this, Abbot Melani sent his secretary off to search through the official registers of recognised arms for a hypothetical noble shield bearing a flower named Tetràchion.

"You can start at once in the library of the villa. You may be sure that they will have the precious opus of Pasquali Alidosi, which is illustrated with woodcuts of the arms, and that of Dolfi, which has the advantage of being more recent. After that, Buvat, you will resume work on that other matter."

"When am I to copy your reply to the letter from Madama the Connestabilessa?" asked the secretary.

"Afterwards."

Once Buvat had left, not in truth that keen to set to work again at that hour (which he ordinarily dedicated to repose in the company of a fine bottle of wine), I would have liked to ask Atto what else he had in mind for his secretary, who had, for a couple of days, been largely out of sight. But the Abbot spoke first:

"And now let us pass from the *vegetalia* to the *animalia*. So Albani is much troubled through the fault of your parrot," said he, referring to what I had told him not long before. "Ha, so much the worse for him!"

"And what do you think of the comments they have been making on him?"

He looked at me with a grave expression on his face, but uttered not a word.

"We must be vigilant in all directions, without excluding anything," said he in the end.

I nodded, at a loss for words, without understanding what he might mean by that all-embracing phrase which clearly said all and nothing, like most political statements. He had not wished to comment on Albani's new public image. Perhaps, I thought, he too did not know where that might lead, but did not wish to admit it.

Ignorant as I was of matters of state, I was mistaken.

Evening the Fifth

11ᵀᴴ JULY, 1700

✠

I had a bone to pick with Abbot Melani. Who was the Countess of S., the mysterious poisoner to whom the Connestabilessa referred so reticently in her letter? Had she something to do with the Countess of Soissons mentioned by Atto, who had spread trouble between Maria and the young King? And who was she? When I asked him, the Abbot, engrossed in his own narration, had not deigned to answer.

While Atto enjoyed himself at dinner in the gardens with the other illustrious guests, once again I plunged my hands amidst his dirty linen and found the ribbon binding his secret correspondence with the Connestabilessa. Unlike previous occasions, however, I was unable to find either the message from Maria Mancini or the reply which the Abbot had recently penned and which, as I had just heard, he had not yet sent. Where were they then?

Meanwhile, I felt myself drawn to the bundle of reports, and that brought to mind what I had read on the previous occasion about the unfortunate King Charles II of Spain. I thought that, if I were to read on, I might be able to find other traces of the Countess of S. and understand what she might have to do with Abbot Melani's business. I opened the report from the Connestabilessa which Atto had marked in a corner with the number two:

OBSERVATIONS
CONCERNING MATTERS SPANISH

Given the state to which the Catholic King is reduced, and the absence of an heir, in Madrid they could think of only one explanation: witchcraft.

For a long time now there has been talk of this. Two years ago, El Rey in person turned to the powerful Inquisitor-General, Tomás Rocaberti.

The Inquisitor, after consulting with His Majesty's confessor, the Dominican Froilán Díaz, put the question to another Dominican, Antonio Alvárez de Argüelles, the modest director of an obscure convent in Asturias, but an excellent exorcist.

It is said that, when he received Rocaberti's letter, Argüelles nearly fainted. In his letter, the Inquisitor-General explained the matter to him in detail, asking him to implore the Devil to reveal what evil spell had been cast on the Sovereign.

Argüelles did not need to be asked twice. In a chapel, he summoned one of the sisters whom he had earlier freed from a diabolical possession. He made her place her hand upon the altar, then recite the spells suitable for that purpose.

From the mouth of the sister, he heard the Evil One speak thus. The voice revealed that King Charles had been the victim of a spell at the age of fourteen, cast by means of a bewitched beverage. The purpose was ad destruendam materiam generationis in Rege et ad eum incapacem ponendum ad regnum administrandum: *in other words, to make him sterile and incapable of reigning.*

Argüelles then asked who had cast the spell. Through the nun's mouth, the Devil replied that the potion had been prepared by a woman called Casilda, who had extracted the malefic liquid from the bones of a condemned man. This juice had then been administered to the King mixed with a cup of chocolate.

There was, however, a way of curing the diabolical infection: El Rey was once a day to drink half a quart of holy oil on an empty stomach.

Action was taken at once. Only, the first time that Charles swallowed a little oil, he was at once convulsed with such dreadful bouts of vomiting that the little group of monks and nuns, exorcists and physicians feared for his life. Thus, they were compelled to use the oil externally, on his head, chest, shoulders and legs; after which the relevant formulae, litanies and antidotes were recited.

Just a year ago, however, Rocaberti died suddenly. Obviously, everyone feared that this might be revenge on the part of Satan. Froilán Díaz, the King's confessor, had to go ahead on his own. Help arrived from an unexpected quarter: in Vienna, the Emperor Leopold had also taken an interest in the question, for something unheard of had occurred in the Imperial capital. In the Church of Saint Sophia, a young man, possessed by evil spirits and subjected to exorcism, had revealed that the Catholic King was a victim of witchcraft. The boy (or the spirits which spoke through him) had even explained that the magical instruments employed were concealed in a certain place in the Spanish Royal Palace.

In Madrid, a furious search began. Squads of workmen unscrewed planks, drilled through panels, demolished party walls, tore away marble plaques, and in the end something was indeed found: a number of dolls and a pile of paper scrolls.

There could be no doubt about it: dolls are fetishes used for the casting of spells. On the scrolls, however, no one knows what was written.

The Emperor then sent a Capuchin Father to Madrid, a famed and feared exorcist, to eradicate the influence of the Evil One from the apartments of El Rey. There, however, matters became more complicated: not a day passes without rumours of the discovery of some other malefice, which some priest is said to have been taken on to combat, and so on and so forth. The situation is beginning to get out of hand. It even happened that a madwoman entered the Palace screaming and shouting; yet, so obscure and tormented is the atmosphere these days that no one had the courage to stop her, for fear that she might be a messenger of powers supernatural.

The madwoman succeeded in getting past the guards and even entering the royal apartments, screaming that El Rey was the victim of black magic, that the spell had been cast by means of a snuff box, and that the person behind the sorcery was none other than his wife.

The revelation was immediately accorded much credit, because the King's second wife, Maria Anna of Neuburg, is very ill-tempered and has sometimes behaved as though she were out of her mind.

Whenever Charles denies her some little favour, she tells him that this was in fact destined for someone capable of casting the evil eye (of which El Rey is terrified) and, if the King does not give in to her, the mysterious person will take revenge; not condemning him to death or sickness, but making him evaporate into nothingness, like a withered flower. Trembling with fear, the Catholic King invariably gives in to her.

When the rumours of sorcery and exorcisms got around, the Queen decided to act against the person responsible for all that chaos, who in her view was none other than poor Froilán Díaz. In short, he has been arrested.

Now, in this Jubilee Year, every day in Madrid new lunatics emerge, witches and maniacs overcome by their own nightmares. They scream and tear their hair out or roll on the ground, crying out in public places, under the anxious gaze of the populace, supposed revelations about the ensorcelment of the royal family. There seems to be no way of defending the Catholic King and his consort, and above all the honour of the Kingdom, from the defamatory attacks of those possessed by demons.

Tired and confused by this infernal round, the King is struggling to cope with a sense of guilt, shame and profound sadness. He is visiting the crypt of the Escorial ever more frequently, where he has the tombs of his ancestors opened in order to look upon their faces, thus condemning those regal corpses to immediate decomposition. When they opened the coffin of his first wife, Marie Louise of Orleans, he suffered a fit of desperation, kissing the corpse and wanting to take it away with him, caring nothing for the fact that it was crumbling in his hands. They had to drag him from the crypt by brute force, invoking the name of Marie Louise and screaming that he would soon be rejoining her in Heaven.

In this, El Rey is a true Habsburg, an epigone of Joan the Mad who could not be separated from the coffin of her husband Philip the Fair; or of Charles V who, after abdicating and withdrawing to a monastery, was wont to have himself enclosed in a sarcophagus naked and swaddled in bandages, to listen to his own requiem mass. Philip II slept with his coffin by his bed, with the Crown of Spain surmounted by a skull; and, like his son, Philip IV, was wont to visit the crypt of the Escorial, sleeping every night in a different tomb.

Queen Maria Anna, too, is desperate. For her the one solution would be to become pregnant. If the Monarchy has an heir, there will at long last be some hope amidst its dark future prospects. Only a couple of years ago, the Queen underwent the special cures of a monk of the Order of Jerusalem who was granted free access to her apartments.

It was in fact never clear what these exercises against sterility may have involved. It has, however, come to light that the monk, in the ecstatic fervour of prayer, suddenly made a great leap into the air, whereupon the Queen, who lay under the bedclothes, took fright and in turn leapt out of bed. The ambiguous event caused such a stir at Court that the monk had to be sent away forthwith. No few persons insinuate that the Queen, in her frenetic desire to become pregnant, may have imposed upon her own body acts redolent of the most unrestrained concupiscence.

Everything, alas, is possible. The Queen is weighed down by too much bitterness. Her soul, already suffering from years of conjugal disappointment, is exasperated by the sinister and unsettling atmosphere that pervades the Court. Maria Anna needs sympathy; it is well known that she sends tormented letters to her German correspondents, in which she attempts to explain and justify the madness into which what was once the greatest and most feared Kingdom in the world has descended, becoming the object of universal pity and derision.

But she writes in vain. Suffering poisons her thoughts and makes her unable to express them in writing. It is said that she often confides by letter in the Landgrave of Hessen. The Landgrave, however, hesitates to answer her; from what one can gather, the Queen's letters are a meaningless nonsense, the product of a disturbed mind, in which verbs and subjects wander without rime or reason, like the possessed who go howling through the dark night of Madrid.

Here the Connestabilessa's report, which continues and expands upon the desolate picture of the wretched Catholic King, came to an end.

I tried again to find those two last letters, which the Abbot had evidently placed elsewhere. Why, I wondered, had he done that? Was he perhaps beginning to get wind of my incursions?

I looked briefly among Buvat's papers, but found nothing. Then I looked among his clothes. There I discovered a curious series of sheets of paper, carelessly folded and placed in the pockets of his breeches, each filled with a different letter. One sheet was full of the letter *e*, another of *o*s, yet another, the letter *y*, and finally, a page of *l*s and one of the letter *R*. Perplexed, I turned those pages over in my hands. They looked like the kind of exercises one does when learning to write. It was certainly no fine handwriting: the hand was heavy and uncertain. I laughed. It looked like some weird exercise undertaken by Melani's secretary in order to rid himself of the fumes of wine before returning to the Abbot's service. Such overindulgence was, indeed, not rare in those days in which not only the noble guests but those accompanying them were spoiled.

A little later, in a coat, I found without too much difficulty the two letters that I sought. I calmed down: perhaps the Abbot had simply handed them to Buvat to remind him to prepare an archive copy of the reply to the Connestabilessa before sending it. So I sat down to read.

Rather than clarifying my ideas, the Connestabilessa's letter left me even more confused.

My dearest Friend,

My fever shows no signs of abating and I am rather sorry to have to delay so long my arrival at the Villa Spada. The physician does, however, assure me that I should be able to resume my journey within a couple of days.

Here, meanwhile, I continue to receive news. It seems that Charles II has employed the most heartfelt tones in begging for a mediation by the Pope. The poor Catholic King is caught in a dilemma. As I had occasion to tell you, he asked his cousin Leopold I to send his youngest son, the fifteen-year old Archduke Charles from Vienna. El Rey wants him in Madrid. He even had a naval squadron made ready in the port of Cadiz to go and fetch the Archduke. It is clear that El Rey means to make him his heir. But, as you well know, the Most Christian King now comes into the picture. As soon as he learned of this move, he instructed Ambassador Harcourt to inform El Rey that such a decision would be regarded as a formal breaking of the peace and, following up this message, he immediately had a fleet rather stronger than the Spanish one put out from the port of Toulon, ready to intercept and bombard the ship carrying the Emperor's youngest son. Leopold dared not make his son run such a risk. El Rey then proposed that the Emperor should send him to Spain's Italian territories, but Leopold is temporising. After years of fighting against the Turk, the Empire is unwilling to spill its subjects' blood in its defence, and that the King of France knows.

The Most Christian King has indeed determined that now is the time to strike the decisive blow: as you know, in order to frighten the Spaniards even more, a month ago he made public the secret pact into which he had entered with Holland and England a couple of years ago, pursuant to which Spain is to be partitioned. Upon hearing the news, they royal couple hastened back to Madrid from El Escorial in a state of shock. The Queen flew into a

*rage and smashed everything in her bedchamber. Even I could not calm her.
There is a state of emergency at Court: the Council of Grandees fears France
and is ready to welcome a nephew of the Most Christian King if that will
spare the country an invasion.*

*El Rey, for his part, wrote at once to his cousin Leopold, thanking him
for having had nothing to do with the pact of partition and begging him to
have no part in it in the future.*

*Pardon me if I have recounted here facts already known to you, but I
must repeat that the situation is quite serious. If His Holiness Innocent XII
is unable to bring the Most Christian King to reason, it will be the end for
all of us.*

*Now, will the Holy Father be in a position to attend to so grave and
delicate a task? We all know that he is seriously ill and that a conclave may
be imminent. I have even heard that he may not wish to have anything to do
with the matter. What do you know of that? It seems that he may no longer be
very much his own master and that, to every question, he replies: "And what
can we do about that?" It seems that even in those moments when he is most
lucid, he likes to repeat: "We are denied the dignity which is due to the Vicar
of Christ and there is no care for us."*

*It would be unheard of for someone to dare really to force the hand of
His Holiness, taking advantage of his illness.*

*Silvio, 'tis right to pay the gods their homage due, but then I can't allow
their ministers should be disturbed.*

*Lastly, courteous Silvio, why do you kneel to Dorinda since you're her
lord? Or, if you be her slave, obey her words.*

My spirit was weighed down by conjectures. I tried to take matters in order. In the first place, the Connestabilessa again spoke of
a mediation. The King of Spain, or so she said, had requested the
Pope's help so that he could make Archduke Charles his heir and
have him brought from Vienna to Madrid without starting a war. The
Most Christian King, however, was threatening to send the Archduke's ship to the bottom of the sea.

I did however recall that, in his first letter, Abbot Melani had
clearly written that the Pontiff was to have provided the King of
Spain with an opinion as to whom he should choose as his heir:
the Duke of Anjou, nephew of the Most Christian King of France
or the Archduke Charles, younger son of the Emperor of Austria.
This was a very different matter from the mediation to which the
Connestabilessa referred in a letter which closed on what looked
like a veiled rebuke to the Abbot, whom as usual she addressed as
Silvio, for the pressures which were said to be being·exercised on
the Pontiff.

Only, why ever should the Connestabilessa be angry with Atto? Was the old castrato then really so influential at the pontifical court?

Lastly, the Connestabilessa was answering Atto's earlier letter, in which 'midst a thousand reverences, the Abbot reminded her of his eternal platonic love. And here came the new mystery. Maria too was replying from behind a pseudonym: Dorinda.

Dorinda: now, where had I heard that name? Unlike Silvio, Dorinda was far from being a common name. And yet I seemed already to have heard it, or perhaps read it. But when?

At that juncture my soul was beset by too many questions. My curiosity was by now well and truly whetted and I hastened to read Abbot Melani's reply.

Here, however, I found myself having to read a honeyed and painfully interminable preamble of lamentations for the Connestabilessa's delays, which were said to endanger the Abbot's very life, and countless other such sickly-sweet protestations, as well as a description of the wedding between Maria Pulcheria Rocci and Clemente Spada, in which the Abbot did not spare the unfortunate bride with the most irreverent comments on her flatfish face.

Then at long last I came to what I was looking for:

Do all that you can to recover your health as soon as possible, I beg of you! Do not allow yourself to be beset by pointless worries. His Majesty King Charles II of Spain has rather wisely decided to defer to the Holy Father. The choice of the right pair of hands into which to confide his magnificent Kingdom, which unites no fewer than twenty Crowns, is surely one that calls for divine Counsel.

Fear not: Innocent XII is a Pignatelli. His is a family of faithful subjects of the Kingdom of Naples, and thus, of Spain. He will not fail to honour the Catholic King's request, of that you may be sure. His decision, even if it may be slow in coming, will be carefully weighed up and will certainly be dictated by love for the Spanish Crown.

All of us here are sure that whatever His Holiness may decide will, for the King of Spain, be sacrosanct; nor will anyone in Europe dare disregard the Pope's opinion. Against the fulminations of Heaven the Potentates of this world can do nothing. The hand of the Almighty which extends its protection over the successors of Saint Peter in accordance with the words qui vos spernit, me spernit, *will attribute a rightful triumph to the word of His Holiness.*

I could not understand a thing. It was as though Abbot Melani and the Connestabilessa were conversing together in two different languages, caring not whether they understood one another. Had the Catholic King not decided for the Archduke, as the Connestabilessa said, and was he not imploring the Pope's support? Or did he not know which heir to back and was accordingly making his decision dependent upon the Papal opinion?

Melani's letter ended thus:

And you, most clement one, do not worry about the Pontiff's health: he is surrounded by excellent persons who take good care of him and his needs, but would never dare to interfere with the pastoral role which His Holiness holds in his grasp by divine right. First among these is the Cardinal Secretary of State Fabrizio Spada, whom you too appreciate so greatly and who is anxiously awaiting your arrival at this his marvellous Villa on the Janiculum.

My friend, from this hill one dominates Rome, all Rome and perhaps a little beyond. Tarry no more.

Shall we not be meeting in two days time, then?

And, at the foot of the letter:

So, be Dorinda. You, Silvio, what more can you expect? What can Dorinda afford you more? But you, Dorinda, goddess who dwell'st on heav'n's high summit, show Silvio now eternal pity, not eternal anger.

Atto yielded to the Connestabilessa's invitation not to bow down before her, even symbolically; indeed, said he to himself, whatever could he lay claim to any more? His love for her was hopeless. Nevertheless, Abbot Melani, replied with gentle supplication to the rebukes which the Connestabilessa regularly reserved for him when she called him Silvio. He begged her henceforth to show pity, not fury.

I had to admit that Abbot Melani had a rather fine poetic vein, in the matter of love.

I again turned over the name Dorinda in my mind but was still unable to remember where I had seen or heard it before.

Soon, moreover, I returned to graver considerations: Atto had still said nothing to me about the Spanish succession, yet his letters to the Connestabilessa spoke of nothing else (love apart). This I had realised from the day when the Abbot arrived at the villa. From that time until this, however, I had established nothing. I had not even managed to find out anything more about the Countess of Soissons, always supposing that she and the enigmatic poisoner, the Countess of S., were one and the same person.

I shook my head disconsolately: the enigma remained intact, nor was there any sign of the fog that surrounded it dispersing. One thing was certain: the Cardinal my master was in some way involved in the matter. Both the Connestabilessa and Melani reported that the Secretary of State had been to see the Spanish Ambassador about the King of Spain's request to Innocent XII and, in view of the Pontiff's dreadful state of health, the Cardinal was dealing with the matter personally on his behalf. I therefore felt it to be all the more my bounden duty better to clarify my ideas about this series of mysteries. I therefore promised myself that I would, on the morrow, at last question Atto at least about the identity of the Countess of Soissons.

❧

Il Roscio's directions were accurate enough. The place could not have been more uninviting; yet, according to the instructions we had received, we were to go there by night, so as not to be seen. This was an essential precaution: we were, after all, trying to take the inscrutable German by surprise.

To tell the truth, I was expecting some out-of-the-way, solitary place, perhaps in the midst of market gardens or woodland, far removed from men and merchandise. Instead, Il Roscio had sent us into the heart of the Holy City. "I have never been there," he had warned, "but I do know from the others in my company that there's where he lies low."

We did not have far to go: from the Villa Spada, we came to Monte Cavallo, passing before the sacred and imposing walls of the Apostolic Palace. There, we turned off to the right, then into Via San Vitale. To the left, behind the high walls which lined the way on either side, stood the campanile of the Jesuits of San Vitale. Its graceful outline reminded me of the little church which, on very clear days, one could sometimes, from our little field, catch sight of in the far distance; and I prayed God to keep me in good health, not only for my own sake but for that of my Cloridia, whom I mentally implored, seeing all the dreadful risks I had run in recent days and was likely to encounter in the coming ones, to pray not only for my soul's salvation but for that of my body.

We came at last to the Via Felice which, with its harmonious alternation of ups and downs, takes one from the steep pile that is Santa

Maria Maggiore to the gentle heights of Monte Pincio. There, we turned to the right, leaving the Quattro Fontane behind us. A little before the church of the monks of San Paolo l'Eremita and the Premonstratensi Fathers' church of San Norberto, a few paces away from Santa Maria della Sanità de' Benfratelli, a nameless side street ran off to the right. We took it, walking between a little group of houses on the right and an isolated house to our left. Beyond these habitations, the road bent leftwards, petering out into a track amidst uncultivated fields.

It was precisely at that point that, following Il Roscio's instructions, we left the road and turned right. Here the terrain became steep, almost vertical, forming a sort of great elongated mound which stretched out rather like the back of a buried giant. As we skirted this mound, we noticed in its flank, below and to our right, first, a slit, then a more generous opening, and lastly, a grotto, then yet another. It was a series of artificial caverns, originally faced with well-cut stones, but by now covered in earth and overgrown with trees, bushes, creepers, fungus, lichens and all kinds of mildew.

The caves were arranged in two parallel rows, one on a lower level, where we were. The other, consisting of larger grottoes, was higher up and set further back, so much so that before it there was a sort of corridor several yards wide. At the right-hand end of this group of caverns there was yet another group on a third level, above which rose a rustic house with a turret. Behind that, stood the convent of the nuns of San Francesco alle Therme. The name of the convent was no accident.

"Whoever could have imagined that?" said Atto, whose familiarity with antiquities I had known since the time of our first encounter. "The Baths of Aggripina. I'd never have expected that I might have to look for people as foul as the *cerretani* in so noble a place."

He was moving among those ancient imperial ruins almost on tiptoe, as though he feared that he might, by tripping up, damage some centuries-old brick; he looked all around him with caution and an imperceptible strain of melancholy in his voice. Seventeen years previously, I had seen him recognise and admire a subterranean Mithraeum and I knew that he had written a guide to Rome for lovers of fine antiquities. Despite all the time that had passed, he had not, it seemed, lost his former predilections.

"We have arrived," said Sfasciamonti, pointing in front of us. "Here is the place."

At the end of the row of caves, before the last stretch of the convent wall, dark and impassive, there stood a tower.

This was one of the numerous pinnacles that had once made of Rome an *Urbs turrita*, in other words, a city adorned with many towers, steeples and turrets: lookout and defence positions from the Middle Ages, which gave the place an old-fashioned, warlike look. This one was not high: it must have been topped, as often happened during the barbarian invasions, or else the upper part had collapsed in some fire.

"No one will stop you," Il Roscio had added enigmatically when furnishing us with details of the German's lair. "If anything, it is you who will decide to go away."

We had a first confirmation of these words when we arrived in front of the tower. We circled it, looking up at all the walls. The windows were all barred. At the foot of the structure, we found a sort of hut which contained the entrance. It was made of wood, creaking and decrepit. We pushed on the door. It was open.

Once inside, we found ourselves in a large, dark, evil-smelling space. Rats and strays of all sorts seemed from time immemorial to have chosen the place for their dejections. The light of our lantern enabled us to avoid the colossal cobwebs which hung throughout the length and breadth of that dungeon, and the foul matter (scrap, rubble, rubbish) that covered the floor.

Suddenly I came close to tripping heavily against a solid mass, well secured to the ground. I rubbed my sore toe. It was a step.

"Signor Atto, a staircase!" I announced.

I shone light on the place with the lantern. A stairway climbed the right-hand wall towards a door.

Here too, neither lock nor chain barred the way.

"Il Roscio was right," observed Sfasciamonti, "there are no obstacles or security measures to impede us. How very interesting."

Behind the second door, another stairway awaited us; this time, exceedingly steep. Melani often stopped to catch his breath.

"But when are we going to get there?" he wondered disconsolately, trying in vain to look behind him and see how far we had come.

"We are climbing to the top of the tower," I answered.

"That, I had surmised for myself," retorted Atto acidly. "But tell me where the deuce the German's lair could be. On the chimney-pots?"

"Perhaps the German is a stork," joked Sfasciamonti, stifling a laugh.

I in the meanwhile was returning in memory to that time, years ago, when Atto and I had spent entire nights exploring galleries and catacombs in the dark underbelly of the city, encountering all manner of perils and fending off dangerous ambushes. Now we were back in the same pitch darkness, but climbing heavenward, not down into the bowels of the earth.

For several minutes, we continued in a straight line, by the faint light of our lantern, until we reached a little quadrangular cavity. The floor was covered with an iron plate. In front of us, a few steps led to a little door which looked very much as though it led to an even higher level. We looked at one another suspiciously.

"I do not like this one bit, corps of a thousand bombards," commented Sfasciamonti.

"Nor I," echoed Melani. "If we go up there, it will be impossible to beat a quick retreat and get out again."

"If only there were a window in this tower, even a slit, perhaps we might be able to work out how high we've climbed," said I.

"Come, come, 'tis pitch dark outside," retorted the Abbot.

"What are we to do?"

"Let us go on further," said Atto, advancing into the little room. "How strange, there's a smell here like. . ."

He broke off. It all began at that moment and happened too fast for us to have any control over events. As we followed Melani, we felt the platform resound slightly and, with a discreet but quite distinct click, descend about half a palm.

We started, aware of imminent danger.

"Get back! 'Tis a trap. . ." screamed Sfasciamonti.

It was already too late. A massive and immensely heavy wooden and iron trapdoor slammed thunderously behind us, cutting us off from the stairway from which we had come and brutally striking the ground, like a peasant's hoe biting into the bare and arid earth. Fortunately, the lantern had not gone out, but what the light was about to reveal to us was enough to make us wish for the blackest darkness.

Tongues of infernal fire flickered before and around us, illuminating us with their horrid light and making our faces seem like those of damned souls. Once they touched our skin those fiery daggers would surely inflict unspeakable suffering upon us.

"God Almighty help us! We have ended up in hell," I exclaimed, overcome by panic.

Atto said nothing: he was trying to keep those demonic fireflies from his face, hitting out at them as one strikes at mosquitos, but with thrice the force and thrice the desperation.

"Damnation, my feet!" cried Sfasciamonti.

At that moment, I felt it too: unbearable heat burned as though within my shoes. I had to raise one foot, then the other, then again the first, for keeping them on the ground was quite intolerable. Atto, too, and the catchpoll were leaping like madmen, brushing off the tongues of fire and struggling to keep each foot on the ground as little as possible.

"Out of here, damn it!" screamed Atto, rushing with Sfasciamonti towards the little door that we had not wished to pass through but which had now become our only way out.

Fortunately, like the other doors before it, this too was open. This time we were confronted by a series of rusty iron rungs. The catchpoll entered first. The opening was so tight that we had to bend almost until our noses touched our knees. We advanced breathlessly, one stuck to the other, our feet still half burned, while some of the malignant droplets of fire mockingly invaded our little hole. Thus, I found myself caught between Sfasciamonti's powerful bulk and Atto's more scrawny and weary body, trembling with fear and imploring Our Lord to have pity on my soul.

"No!!"

It was then, just when Sfasciamonti let forth that desperate scream, that I saw him disappear, engulfed by a sudden abyss and felt him grasp at my right arm, dragging me down the precipice with prodigious force.

The invisible and natural mechanism that governs human actions in such upheavals moved of its own accord and caused me, willy-nilly, to grasp at Atto, who thus fell with me. Hanging onto one another in a wretched bundle of flesh and bones, we were sucked by an invincible force into a vertiginous and endless fall.

"*Et libera nos a malo*," I had the presence of mind to gasp as the alien vortex almost robbed me of my breath.

༺❀༻

The fall seemed to last forever. We were piled up one on top of the other as though Lucifer's pitchfork had cast us among the damned and was bringing us before the judges of the Inferno.

Sfasciamonti, motionless under me, was hunched up in terror as well as under the combined weight of Atto and myself. Melani was overcome by shock and pain and moaned, barely moving. With an immense effort I struggled out from under that double human carpet and gave thanks to the Lord that I was able to sit on the ground. The floor was no longer burning hot. A pungent and familiar odour, disquieting under those tragic circumstances, impregnated my skin and my clothing. I became aware of the environment surrounding me, and anguish gripped my soul.

The lantern, of course, was broken. It was, however, possible to descry everywhere a weird luminosity, a mixture of fog and bluish half light, like that which glow worms dispense in gardens after nightfall, subtly pervading all things.

Was I still in one piece? I looked at my hands and trembled. They emitted light, no, they seemed even to be made of light.

I was no longer a man. An opalescent glow issued from every point on my body, as I could see when I looked at my legs and my belly. My mortal remains were elsewhere. In their place was a poor lost soul, a wretched effigy wandering in the Underworld, of substance translucent and immaterial.

At that moment, Sfasciamonti rose to his feet and saw me.

"You. . . you are dead!" he whispered in horror, his eyes fixed on what remained of me.

He looked all around him with mad, bulging eyes. Then he looked at himself, his hands and his arms. He too emitted that bluish light which was everywhere, within us and without.

"Then I too. . . all of us. . . oh, my God," he sobbed.

Then came the apparition. A being of darkness, enveloped in a menacing black shroud, his face hidden by a great mystic cowl, was watching us from a niche in the wall, closed with an iron grate.

Atto too rose from the ground and saw him. All three of us were suspended for long, interminable moments between breathing and breathlessness, between desperation and hope, between life and death. Other hooded figures appeared behind the figure in the niche, which must have been, or so it seemed, a little gallery. Evil emissaries of the infernal regions, they would soon be upon us. It was clear that they were about to seize and devour us.

The grate rose. Now nothing separated us from the demons. Their leader, he who had appeared to us first, took a step forward.

Instinctively, we drew back. Even Sfasciamonti, or rather the great bluish phantom who had taken his place, trembled like an autumn leaf.

It all happened in moments. The satanic being extracted from his shroud a long, lurid orange object. It was a glowing dagger, in keeping with the white heat of the flames of Hades. This he pointed at us, as though casting an anathema. Soon, said I to myself, from it would issue the tongue of flame that consumes every residual mortal atom, reducing us (if our luminous manifestation still possessed any substance) to poor wandering ectoplasms.

He pointed the dagger in my direction, in a gesture of condemnation. Whatever had I committed, I asked myself blubbering, to merit, not purgatory, but the irremediable horrors of hell? Four devils ran to me, seized me and forced me to the ground on my back, nailing me down with their horrid clawed arms. I did not scream: terror itself, choking my throat, prevented that. Besides, said I to myself in a flash of desperate humour, who can hear the lament of the damned?

Their leader came to me. Even now, his face could not be seen, only the macabre hooked hand (likewise bluish and phosphorescent) brandishing the fiery dagger. Meanwhile, I knew not what had become of Atto and Sfasciamonti; I heard only an indistinct scuffling. Probably they too had been overcome in their turn.

The angel of evil leaned over and was upon me. With his dagger, he aimed directly at my forehead. He directed the tip just above my eyes, in the middle. He was about to penetrate the bony covering (or its appearance) with the overwhelming force of fire. Then, twisting the blade in the hole, he would stir and fry the grey matter of my brain.

"No," I implored, I know not if with thought alone or with the whisp of voice that I had been allowed to retain from my earthly life.

In the lightless abyss which was my executioner's hood, I thought I saw (the powers of darkness and their agents) a malign smile, which heightened my terror at the approaching end. The absurd heat of the blade dried my eyeballs (had I still any?). Only an animal lust for life still kept them open.

The point of the incandescent blade was less than a hair's breadth from my forehead. It was about to strike. Now, in less than a second. Now, yes, Cloridia my love, my sweet little girls. . .

It was then, as though in a gentle prelude to death, that I lost consciousness. Before fainting, heart and soul beat together for one last instant. Just long enough to hear:

"One momentary: periculous blunderbungle."

"What? Wretched imbecile, I'll blast you to bits!"

Then, violent noises, as of a struggle, and the shot.

ဆာင်္

"Take courage, hero, stand up."

A smack. Rapid, violent and alarming as a bucketful of water in the face. It had awoken me, recalling me from the torpor of my swoon. Now I heard Atto's voice addressing me.

"I. . . I do not. . ." I stammered, still prone, while my head seemed to be on the point of exploding. I coughed several times. There was a smell of burning, and smoke everywhere.

"Return among the living," Melani chanted to me. We must leave here before we are asphyxiated. First, however, let me present you Beelzebub. You will, I think, be surprised to find that you have already met."

Still trembling, I sat up. The bluish light no longer pervaded the cavern. Now all was yellow, red and orange: a torch had been lit, which illuminated the surroundings. I looked at my hands. I too no longer emitted that arcane phosphorescence.

"I have reloaded," I heard Sfasciamonti announce.

"Good," replied Atto.

I opened my eyes wide. The scene moments before, faced with which I had believed myself to have bid life farewell, had changed utterly.

In his right hand, Sfasciamonti brandished the dagger with which I was on the point of being put to death. He was pointing it at a little group of hooded demons, all huddled oh so quietly against the wall, without giving the faintest sign of resistance. Such discipline was not without cause: in his left hand the catchpoll held his ordnance pistol. Atto, for his part, grasped an improvised torch: a cone made up of sheets of paper which he had lit with the incandescent dagger and which now illuminated the narrow space in which we stood, while however spreading fumes that rendered the air unbreathable.

"Up, you wretch, and get us out of here," said Atto to the chief of the demons, placing a handkerchief across his nose in order not to breathe in too much smoke.

It was then that I recognised the leader of the infernal company. That foul, oversized covering, the odours of filth and decay spreading all around, those clawed hands. . .

The cowl shifted a little. Once more I beheld that crumpled parchment of a face, that miserable patchwork of bits of skin held together only by inertia, that tumescent cankered nose like a mouldy carrot, the evasive eyes, bloodshot and deceitful, the few broken yellow-brown stumps of teeth, the wrinkles deep as ploughed furrows, the skeletal cranium and the yellowish scalp from which hung resignedly a few rare tufts of rust-coloured hair.

"Ugonio!" I exclaimed.

It is necessary that I should at this juncture make clear the nature and history of the personage in question, as well as his companions, with whom it was my fate to share no few adventures many years ago.

Ugonio was a *corpisantaro*, one of those bizarre individuals who spend their lives searching Rome's subterranean innards for the relics of saints and of the first martyrs of the Christian faith. The *corpisantari* are truly creatures of darkness, whose time is spent grubbing with their bare hands underground, separating dirt from shards, earth from stones, splinters from mould, and exulting whenever this stubborn and meticulous labour of filtering reveals a mere fragment of a Roman amphora, a coin of the imperial age or a piece of bone.

They are wont to sell for a high price the relics (or *corpi sanctorum*, whence their name) which they find in the subsoil, exploiting the good faith, or better, the unpardonable ingenuousness of buyers. The piece of amphora is sold as a fragment of the cup from which Our Lord drank at the Last Supper; the little coin becomes one of the thirty pieces of silver for which Judas Iscariot betrayed the Son of God; the sliver of bone is palmed off as part of Saint John's collarbone. Of all the vile substances that the *corpisantari* glean under the ground, nothing is thrown away: a half-rotten piece of wood is sold dear as an authentic splinter of the True Cross, a feather from a dead bird is auctioned as a plume from an angel's wing. The mere fact of spending a lifetime grubbing, piling up and archiving all that disgusting material has endowed them with a reputation as infallible hunters after sacred objects and thus guarantees them a large number of readily hoodwinked customers. Over a long period of time and thanks to the astute bribery of servants, they have accumulated copies of the keys to cellars and store rooms throughout the whole city, thus gaining access to all the most recondite recesses of subterranean Rome.

Surprisingly enough, the *corpisantari* combine their execrable practices with a genuine, intense, almost fanatical religiosity, which surfaces at the most unexpected moments. If my memory does not betray me, they have asked several pontiffs for the right to form a confraternity; but there has never been any response to that request.

So, Ugonio was one of their number. Being a native of Vienna, he spoke my language with inflections and accents which often made it difficult to discover any coherent sense behind the verbiage; hence his nickname, the German.

"The German. . ." I exclaimed, utterly astonished, turning to Ugonio. "So 'tis you!"

"I recognate not this disgustiphonous appellation, from which I dissocialise myself with my entire personage," he protested. "I commandeer the Italic tongue, not as an immigrunter, but as if 'twere my own motherlingo."

"Silence, beast," cut in Atto, who had already heard many years before how Ugonio loved to boast about his disastrous gibberish. "Just to hear you talk gives me nausea. So you have made your fortune with this Jubilee, cheating the pilgrims with your so-called relics, perhaps selling some ham bone at a good price as the tibia of Saint Calixtus. I hear that you have become a big noise. And now you've sold yourself to Lamberg, eh? But, what am I saying? Far from selling yourself, you are a true patriot. After all, you're Viennese and, as such, a faithful subject of His Imperial Majesty Leopold I, like that damned ambassador of yours. Bah, who would have guessed that I'd ever again in my life have to put up with your disgusting presence?" concluded Melani, spitting on the ground in disdain.

I, meanwhile, looked at Ugonio and a thousand memories raced around my head. Certainly, the Abbot's suspicions seemed utterly justified: if the infamous German was in cahoots with the *cerretani*, it followed that they too would all have been in the pay of Vienna and conspiring against us. Nevertheless, I was content to see the old *corpisantaro* again, with whom I had shared so many adventures, and I sensed that the Abbot too was not displeased, despite his indignant reaction.

"What have you to tell me about the stab wound in the arm which I got from that *cerretano* accomplice of yours? Was it perhaps meant for my breast? Speak!"

"I deny, redeny and ultradeny your absurdious inculpations. Nor was I beware that someone had stubbed your member with a messerblade."

"I see, you don't mean to collaborate. You will regret it. And now, get us out of here," Atto continued. "Show us the way. Sfasciamonti, give me the pistol and keep Ugonio covered with the dagger. Anyone who makes a false move will end up with a hole in his belly."

The group of hooded beings, whom in my momentary panic I had taken for devils, filed back through the niche whence they had come. We followed, keeping them under the threat of pistol and dagger and, obviously, Sfasciamonti's muscular bulk. Thus, we entered a fetid and narrow burrow which led out from what we'd taken for a *bolgia* from Dante's *Inferno*, once again towards the unknown.

"But... we are underground!" I exclaimed at one point, as I became aware of a certain strange humidity and recognised the *opus reticulatum*, the brick structure typical of ancient Roman walls.

"Yes," Sfasciamonti assented, "where did the tower end and this begin?"

"We are in some secondary conduit of the Baths of Agrippina," replied Abbot Melani. "Who knows, perhaps this was once a corridor on the second floor, with windows and balconies, and one could breathe the fresh air. The rest, I'll explain to you later."

As will by now be quite plain, the ambiguous arts of the *corpisantari* meant that they had *de facto* much in common with another execrable group, the *cerretani*. It was no accident that we should have run into them in the course of our search for the famous German.

As we proceeded along the tunnel, faintly lit by Atto's torch (which he revived by adding a little piece of canvas found on the ground) Sfasciamonti began to interrogate Ugonio.

"Why do they call you the German? And why did you order the theft of Abbot Melani's text and of the relic?"

"'Tis a vilethy, iniquilous falsehoodie. I am pletely innocuous, this I perjure now and forever, indeed almost never, I mean."

Sfasciamonti fell silent for an instant, taken aback by the *corpisantaro's* garrulous and ramshackle jargon.

"He said that it is not true. Anyway, they call him the German because he was born in Vienna and his mother tongue is German," I explained.

Meanwhile, we had passed from the corridor to a stairway. I was still affected by the experiences from which I had just emerged, shaken through and through by having passed from life to death (or so it had truly seemed to me) and then back again. I was exhausted and in pain from the innumerable kicks, shoves and bruises I had received. My clothing stank of a thousand strange essences and, what was more, I had the inexplicable feeling that my back was covered with a fine layer of lard. Last but not least, I was burning with shame at having been the one member of the group to have fainted from fear, and what was more, at the very moment when Atto and Sfasciamonti had brought the situation under control.

Atto's torch had ended its brief life; we found ourselves suddenly proceeding in the most stygian darkness, testing the terrain with our feet and groping along the walls with our hands. I trembled at the thought that another battle might break out on that airless staircase, with unforeseeable and surely bloody consequences. However, the hooded troop proceeded up the stairs in good order; Atto and Sfasciamonti needed to suppress no insurrection. That was in the nature of the *corpisantari*: shamelessly deceitful cheats, up to all manner of scheming and chicanery, yet incapable of harming anyone or offering violence; except, of course, when (as I had seen seventeen years earlier), it came to aiding some high-ranking ecclesiastic, on which occasion their Christian zeal inspired them to act with a courage and audacity worthy of true heroes of the Faith.

"Accursed ragamuffins," Atto railed. "First of all that hoax with the Inferno and now these infernal stairs."

"Signor Atto," I found the courage to ask him, "we were enveloped in a strange blue light. How the deuce did they manage to make us look like spectres?"

"That is an old trick. Indeed, if I remember rightly, two tricks were involved. In the first room, where we seemed to be under a rain of fiery droplets, there was an iron platform, under which they had placed hot coals. The platform was burning hot, but that we realised only after the heat had penetrated our shoes. Under the iron plate, on the coals, they will have placed a vessel, probably made of enamelled terracotta, containing wine spirits, together with a piece of camphor, which will have filled that small space with its exhalations."

"I see! That is why I smell so strange. I thought that it was. . ."

"It was just what you thought: camphor," Atto cut me short. "What they use against moths. But let me continue: at a certain point in our advance, we tripped against a mobile step which lowered and, in so doing, activated some machinery. That in turn caused a trap door to fall vertically, making a hellish noise. Meanwhile, the flame from our lantern penetrated that den full of the vapour of spirits and camphor, which immediately caught fire. The surprise and the tremendous burning under our feet worked perfectly. What with all that dancing fire and the heat coming up from below, we thought we were in hell. Then we escaped through the little door, taking the only way out, down the iron rungs, when we were sucked down as not even Scylla and Charybdis could have engulfed us."

"Quite! But how was that done?"

"I and Sfasciamonti worked that out while you were taking your little nap. At the end of the iron rungs, there was a metal slide, smooth and well greased with abundant kitchen fat."

I touched my backside. Yes, it was just the same lard I had used when I was an apprentice at the inn, when I greased the pots and pans before cooking chicken in a wine sauce with walnuts, or preparing some poultry in broth.

The grease, Atto continued, caused us to rush down the slide at great speed, descending the whole height of the tower in an instant.

"The whole height? What does that mean?" interrupted Sfasciamonti who had listened open-mouthed to Atto's explanation.

"The tower is not really as low as we had thought; on the contrary, it is very high, but over the centuries it has been partially buried. We entered through a sort of lean-to hut that was built quite recently and led, not to the ground floor of the tower, but about halfway up its original height. The slide, however, hurled us down, down to the original, ancient base of the tower, which is today many feet under the ground."

"And deep down, the tower communicates with a whole network of tunnels," I concluded, drawing on the strength of my old acquaintance with subterranean Roman galleries, all joined up to one another.

"Yes, and here the second trick awaited us. As soon as they saw us arrive at the Baths of Agrippina – what was more, at a late hour, which gave away our intention of entering their rabbit warren – they burned a glass of spirits or some similar liquor in this second space. And in the spirits, if I recall the recipe correctly, they dissolved a little common salt."

"One moment," I interrupted, "how do you know all these details?"

"These things are child's play. In France, everyone knows them; one need only purchase some suitable book, like that of the Abbé de Vallemont, which I think I have already mentioned to you."

"The one of which you spoke to me at the Vessel?" I asked, vaguely troubled.

"Exactly."

The artifice that followed, Abbot Melani went on to explain, worked, not in the presence of fire, but if one lit a candle and then extinguished it. And our lantern, as those who organised all that machinery could easily foresee, reached the bottom of the slide still lit but was smashed upon contact with the ground. If the room had been well impregnated with the vapours of the mixture of spirits and salt, faces seen through that artificial atmosphere would take on the pallid, livid, deathly semblance of exhumed corpses, or lost souls. And that is what happened.

"Excuse me," I then asked, realising that our ascent through utter darkness was practically at an end, and we were again walking on flat ground. "Why did you not realise at once that this was all an artifice?"

"Surprise. They organised everything to perfection: first, the dancing fire, then our faces turned into spectres, and lastly the army of devils and the flaming sword, in reality heated up on some stupid fireplace. . . Unfortunately, in a state of shock, I too was slow to recognise the smell of camphor, otherwise I'd have warned you in time."

"Then, what made you realise what was happening?"

"When that idiot Ugonio, alias the German, opened his mouth. It was impossible not to recognise him, even after all this time. He, too, knew you. He said 'periculous blunderbungle', realising that he was on the point of committing a dangerous blunder. I'd say that his eyes and his memory are better than yours, heh!" guffawed Atto.

"Was that why he did not strike me?"

"I never bestrike," interrupted Ugonio's offended voice from the end of the line.

"Never?" I asked, not without a trace of anger in my voice, recalling those terrifying moments at the mercy of the incandescent dagger.

"All trespissers emergency profoundamentally pissified," grunted Ugonio, stifling with great difficulty an outburst of malign, conceited laughter.

He was right. Before fainting, I too had involuntarily wet myself like a terrified infant.

The purpose or all that infernal theatre was quite plain. Down there among the tunnels in and around the Baths of Agrippina, the German had his lair and no one was to enter there uninvited; the point was that anyone foolhardy enough so to do was to be subjected to that carousel of terror so that he would run for his life, ejected like a dog, soaked in his own urine.

It was the first time for seventeen years that I had ventured into the subterranean city beneath Rome, and here again I had found Ugonio, just as when I last emerged from that labyrinth. What had brought me there? The investigations into the theft perpetrated against Abbot Melani: loot consisting of papers, a telescope and the relic of the Madonna of the Carmel with my three little Venetian pearls. Yes, the relic. I had almost forgotten it. I should have realised earlier, I thought with a little smile: relics and tunnels. . . the daily bread of the *corpisantari*. Now it only remained for us to find the place where the stolen goods were stored.

By this time, we had come to the end of the stairway that had led us away from the second infernal chamber. Here we met with a surprise.

We found ourselves in a spacious storeroom, at least thirty yards long by thirty wide, with a good level floor and walls reinforced with bricks, equipped with a number of exit doors (leading, presumably, to other tunnels) and a spiral staircase leading to a trapdoor in the ceiling. Here reigned indescribable chaos: piles and piles of objects of every imaginable and unimaginable shape and form made of the storeroom a mad pandemonium of knicknacks, remnants, relics, trifles, hardware, ornaments, toys, souvenirs, sweet nothings, playthings, scrap, builders' waste, shards and splinters, antique junk, food leftovers, bagatelles, detritus, rubbish and much other vile material regurgitated from burglaries and robberies in the city's most sordid back streets.

Thus, I saw heaps of coins half-eaten by time, immeasurable piles of paper pressed together and tied up with string, baskets of filthy, greasy clothes, moth-eaten furniture piled up to the ceiling, dozens, indeed hundreds of pairs of shoes of all kinds, from rustic boots to courtesans' finest slippers, sashes and belts, books and exercise books, pens and inkstands, pots and pans, distorts and alembics, stuffed eagles and embalmed foxes, mousetraps, bear skins, crucifixes, missals, sacred vestments, tables large and tables small, hammers, saws and scalpels, entire collections of nails of all sizes, and then arrays of wooden planks, bits of old iron, brooms and brushes, rags and cloths, bones, skulls and ribs, buckets of oil, balsams, ointments and innumerable other disgusting things.

All these, however, were mixed with vases full of rings, bracelets and golden pendants, boxes of Roman medals and coins, frames and ornaments of the finest quality, silverware, porcelain dinner and coffee services, jewel cases, carafes, bowls and glasses of the finest Bohemian crystal, tablecloths from Flanders, velvets and upholstery materials, arquebuses, swords and daggers, entire collections of precious paintings, landscapes, portraits of ladies and of popes, nativities and annunciations, all roughly piled up one against the other and covered in layer upon layer of dust.

"Good heavens," exclaimed Sfasciamonti despite himself. "This seems almost like. . ."

"I know what you are about to say," interrupted Atto. "The proceeds of the last three hundred thousand thefts committed in Rome during the Jubilee."

"It turns one's stomach," replied the catchpoll.

"What they said about you was true," continued Atto, addressing Ugonio. "During the Holy Year, your business prospers even more than usual. You will, I imagine, have made some special vow to the Blessed Virgin."

The *corpisantaro* did not respond to the Abbot's irony. I, meanwhile, was looking around prudently in the midst of all that vile chaos, taking care not to knock anything over. One had to proceed down narrow aisles between one heap and the next, without disturbing anything. Failure to do so might result, not only in breaking a vase but getting oneself buried under an avalanche of books, or a pyramid of amphorae, clumsily stacked on top of some rickety old cupboard. Something in a dark corner, half hidden beneath a tumulus of old sheets and a precious golden pyx, attracted my attention. It was a strange ironwork device, like a bush made up of curved pieces of tin and iron sheeting. I took it in my hand and showed it to Atto, who was approaching. He picked up the tangle of iron and his eyes opened wide as he examined it. "This once was two armillary spheres. Or perhaps three, I cannot tell. These beasts have succeeded in reducing it to mere wreckage."

There were in fact two or three of these special devices in the form of a globe, consisting of several iron hoops rotating concentrically around an axis and fixed on a pedestal, which are used by scientists to calculate the movement of heavenly bodies.

"The expropriament was complicationed by an unforesightable," said Ugonio in an attempt to justify himself. "Unfortuitously, the objectivities got jammied one against t'other."

"Yes, jammied," murmured Atto in disgust, casting aside the little tangle of metal and exploring the mass of junk. "I have no difficulty in imagining what happened. After the theft, you will have gone off and got drunk somewhere. I suppose that here there will also be. . . Oh, here we are."

It was a row of cylindrical objects, standing vertically on the flagstones, one beside the other. Atto picked up one that seemed a little less dusty and ill-used than the others.

"Excellent," said Melani, dusting the cylinder down with his sleeve. "Those who don't die, meet again."

Then he handed it to me with a triumphal smile.

"Your spyglass!" I exclaimed. "Then it is true that the German was behind this."

"Of course he stole it. Like the others in this collection."

On the ground there stood a little forest of telescopes of all shapes and sizes, some brand new, others filthy and falling to pieces.

Sfasciamonti too drew near and began to rummage about near the telescopes. At length, he picked up from the ground a large device that seemed familiar, and showed it to me.

MACROSCOPIUM HOC
JOHANNES VANDEHARIUS
FECIT
AMSTELODAMII MDCLXXXIII

"This is the other microscope stolen from the learned Dutchman, as reported to me by the sergeants my colleagues, do you remember?"

said he, "it is the twin of the one which I and you recovered from the *cerretano* a few nights ago."

The hooded troop looked on powerless and embarrassed at the unmasking of their trafficking. We all looked at Ugonio.

"You also stole my handwritten treatise," hissed Melani spitefully.

The *corpisantaro*'s hump seemed even more bent, as though he were struggling to become even smaller and darker in his desire to escape the consequences of his misdeeds.

Sfasciamonti drew the dagger and grabbed Ugonio by the collar of his filthy greatcoat.

"Ow!" he cried, at once loosening his grip.

The catchpoll had pricked a finger. He turned the collar of Ugonio's jacket and drew out a brooch. I recognised it at once: it was the scapular of the Madonna of the Carmel, the *ex voto* stolen from Abbot Melani. And above it were still sewn my three little Venetian pearls which Atto had so lovingly kept on his person all these years.

The catchpoll tore the relic from Ugonio's breast and handed it to Atto. The Abbot took it between two fingers.

"Er, I think it would be better if you held onto this," said he with a hint of embarrassment, turning away as he handed it to me.

I was happy. This time, I would hold jealously onto my three little pearls, as a keepsake of that Abbot Melani who was from time to time capable of an affectionate gesture. I grasped the relic, not without a grimace of disgust at the dreadful odour emanating from it after its prolonged sojourn close to the *corpisantaro*.

Sfasciamonti, meanwhile, had returned to work and was holding the dagger against Ugonio's cheek.

"And now for Abbot Melani's treatise."

Atto grasped the pistol. The *corpisantaro* did not need to be asked twice:

"I have not stealed anyfing: I executed a levy on commissionary," he whispered.

"Ah! A theft on commission," Atto translated, turning to us. "Just as I suspected. And on whose behalf? That of your wretched compatriot the Imperial Ambassador Count von Lamberg, perhaps? Now, tell me, do you also have people stabbed on commission?" he asked emphatically, showing Ugonio the arm wounded by the fleeing *cerretano*.

The corpisantaro hesitated an instant. He looked all around, trying to work out what the consequences might be for him if he were to remain silent: Atto's pistol, the dagger in Sfasciamonti's grasp, the corpulent bulk of the latter, and, on the other hand, his band of friends, numerous, but all more or less halt or lame. . .

"I was commissionaried by the electors of the Maggiorengo," he replied at last.

"Who the Devil are they?" we all asked in unison.

Ugonio's explanation was long and confused, but with a good dose of patience, and thanks to some recollections of his extraordinary gibberish, retained from the events of many years ago, we did manage to grasp, if not all the details, at least the main message. The matter was simple. The *cerretani* elected a representative at regular intervals, a sort of king of vagabonds. He was known as the Maggiorengo-General and was crowned at a great ceremony of all the sects of *cerretani*. We learned among other things that the previous Maggiorengo had recently passed on to a better life.

"And what has all this to do with the theft which they commissioned you to carry out?"

"Of that I am iggorant, with all due condescendent respect to your most sublimated decisionality. Ne'er do we ejaculate the why-andwherefore of a levy. 'Tis a problem of secretion!"

"You are not speaking because it is a matter of secrecy between you and your client? Do you imagine you are going to get away with it that easily?" threatened Melani.

The dusty and suffocating storeroom in which we stood was lit by a few torches set into the wall, the smoke from which escaped through channels set above the flames of the torches themselves. Atto suddenly grabbed one of these torches and held it next to a nearby pile of papers, which seemed to me to consist of legal and notarial deeds stolen from who knows where by the *corpisantari*.

"If you will not tell me to whom you have given my manuscript treatise, as true as God exists, I shall set fire to everything in here."

Atto was serious. Ugonio gave a start. At the idea of all his patrimony going up in smoke, he grew pale, at least as far as the parchment pallor of his face permitted it. First, he tried blandishments, then he tried to persuade Melani that he was placing himself in some ill-defined danger, this being a particularly delicate moment as the milieu of the *cerretani* had been shaken by a grievous robbery perpetrated against them.

"A grievous robbery? Robbers aren't robbed," sneered Atto. "What have they stolen from the *cerretani?*"

"Their novated lingo."

"Their new language? Languages cannot be stolen because they cannot be possessed, only spoken. Try inventing something else, you idiot."

In the end, Ugonio gave in and explained his offer to the Abbot.

"Agreed," said Atto in the end. "If you keep your side of the promise, I shall not destroy this wretched place. You know full well that I can do it," said Atto, before having us accompanied to the exit. "Sergeant, have you anything else to ask these animals?"

"Not now. I am curious to see whether they will keep their word tomorrow. Now, let us go. I do not wish to remain too long absent from Villa Spada."

"Ugonio recognised me as soon as he saw me from close up. Do you think it possible that he did not know from whom he was stealing the treatise and the telescope?" I asked Melani.

"Of course he knew. Rascals like him always know where they're sticking their hands."

"And yet, he didn't think twice about doing it."

"Certainly not. Evidently, the pressure from whoever commissioned him was too great. They must have offered him a great deal of money; or perhaps he was too afraid of failing."

"Now I understand! That was why I always had the feeling of being watched at the Villa Spada," I exclaimed.

"What are you saying?" asked Atto in astonishment.

"I never told you this, because I was not sure of what I was seeing around me. We have already encountered so many strange things," I added, alluding to the apparitions at the Vessel. "I didn't want to make it look as though I'd become a visionary. Yet, several times in the past few days, I have had the feeling of being spied on. It was as though. . . well, as though they were constantly keeping an eye on me from behind hedges."

"Obviously. Even a child could see that: it must have been Ugonio and the other *corpisantari,*" said Atto, irritated by my slow thinking.

"Perhaps," I thought aloud, "they may even have been following us on the evening when we were drugged. Some rather strange fellows came into the wine shop where we had stopped, some mendicants who seemed to be spoiling for a fight. There was even a brawl which forced us to abandon our table. They almost knocked over the jug of wine."

"The jug of wine?" exclaimed Atto, wide-eyed.

I told him then of the scuffle that had broken out in the wine shop, which I and Buvat had witnessed, and how we had momentarily lost sight of our table. Atto exploded:

"Only now do you think of telling me this?" he groaned impatiently. "For heaven's sake, did you not realise that you and Buvat were put to sleep by pouring a little sleeping draught into your wine?"

I fell silent, humiliated. It was true, it must have been done like that. The mendicants (obviously a group of *cerretani*) had organised what looked like a brawl in order to create confusion in the place; thus, they had caused us to leave our table and got in our way while they poured the narcotic into our wine. After that, they had gone off without any further ado.

"Once they had put you to sleep," concluded Atto, calming down a little, "Ugonio and his companions in crime will have entered your house and Buvat's bedchamber. Then, as soon as they were able to, they tried again with me."

"It is a miracle that they crossed the villa boundary and managed to leave with their loot without being seen by anyone," I commented.

"Yes, indeed," said Atto, looking askance at Sfasciamonti, "it really is a miracle."

The catchpoll lowered his eyes in embarrassment. Yes, while I had cut a poor figure, Sfasciamonti ran the risk of passing for an incompetent. Atto, on the other hand, by finding Ugonio, had found out not only who had put me and Buvat out of action with the sleeping draught, but the thief of his treatise on the Secrets of the Conclave and of the relic and the telescope, which he now held tightly in one hand, fuming in equal measure with disdainful rage and warlike satisfaction.

No sooner had we crossed the Tiber than Sfasciamonti announced that he would hasten on his way in order to get back as early as possible, leaving us the advantage of proceeding at a more convenient and moderate pace.

"I shall go on ahead of you, it is getting really late, corps of a thousand maces. My absences from the villa cannot last too long.

I do not want Cardinal Spada to think I am shirking my duty," he explained.

"Better, far better thus," commented Atto, as soon as we were alone.

"And why?"

"As soon as we get back, we shall have things to do."

"At this hour of night?"

"Buvat should have completed the task I set him."

"What? Searching for the flower among the arms of noble families?"

"Not just that," replied the Abbot laconically.

Yes, Buvat. The evening before, I had seen him again after a prolonged absence, and Melani, after setting him to work searching for traces of the Tetràchion among the noble arms, had requested him also to see to an unspecified "other matter". What could he be up to? During the first few days, his presence had been constant and assiduous. More recently, he would appear briefly, then absent himself again for a long period. Now I knew that Atto had assigned him some task to which the scribe was obviously attending outside the villa. I realised that the Abbot had, for the time being, no intention of revealing to me what was going on behind the scenes.

When we reached the villa, however, Atto's secretary had not yet returned.

"Good! Plainly, the trail which I suggested he should follow has proved fruitful. Perhaps the final details are still missing."

"Details? What of?" I insisted.

"Of the accusations whereby we shall nail Lamberg."

Day the Sixth

12TH JULY, 1700

✠

"But you *never* close the door, do you?"

I opened my eyes. I was at home. The daylight flooded in through the wide-open door of the bedroom, blinding me. Nevertheless, I recognised beyond any doubt the voice which had so disagreeably awakened me: Abbot Melani had come to pay me a visit.

"Charming, this little house of yours. One can see the feminine touch," he commented.

That night I had reached my bed dead tired, with just enough strength left in me to make sure that my two daughters were sleeping placidly in their bed, seeing that Cloridia was still spending the night in the apartments of the Princess of Forano.

"Come on, come on, get up, I am in a hurry. We have plenty to do: Buvat found absolutely nothing about that damned Tetràchion in the books on heraldry. We must interrogate Romaùli at once."

"No, that is enough, if you please, Signor Atto. I want to sleep," I replied somewhat brusquely.

"Are you quite mad?" trilled Atto's castrato voice.

I had no time to tell him to lower his voice so as not to disturb my little ones who were sleeping on the floor above. They rose at once and were soon looking in curiously. They stared in astonishment at this curious gentleman, the like of whom they had never seen before, red-stockinged, bewigged, all bedaubed with ceruse and bedizened with lace, braiding and knick-knacks after the French fashion, from his periwig down to his shoe buckles. The little one, who was also the less shy of the pair, ran straight to him, wanting to touch all the marvels with which Abbot Melani's apparel was bedecked.

"Oh fathers!" exclaimed Atto delightedly, as he took the little one in his arms. "When you return home afflicted by business, what could be sweeter than to see your dear little daughter at the top of the stairs, awaiting you with such a loving, joyful welcome, receiving you with kisses and embraces, telling you so many thoughts and so many things that you are at once freed from all the dark ponderings that weigh down your mind and become jocular and gay even despite yourself?"

Rising in haste, I rushed to tell my daughters not to disturb the Abbot, but Atto halted me with his hand.

"Stop! Do not think that playing with little children is no matter for serious men," he berated me with a feigned air of reproof, already forgetting his reason for being there, "for I reply to you that Hercules, as we read in Elianus's works, was wont after the heat of battle to amuse himself playing with little ones; and Socrates was found by Alcibiades playing with children, while Agiselaos would ride a cane to entertain his sons. You should take advantage of my presence to get dressed while I act as nurse for these two little angels. You know what awaits us."

Whereupon, he let my little ones' curious tiny fingers tug at all those bows and tassels with a seraphic joy and patience of which I would never have imagined Abbot Melani to be capable.

I knew full well what awaited us: the search for the Tetràchion; or better, for the dish donated by Capitor to Mazarin, and which the madwoman had called "Tetràchion". According to Cloridia's friend, the maidservant at the Spanish Embassy, that name denoted an "heir", not further specified, to the throne of the Catholic King of Spain. The same name, however, Atto had heard on the lips of Tranquillo Romaùli, Master Florist of the Villa Spada; which was distinctly curious, since Romaùli never seemed willing to speak of anything but petals and corollas. Nevertheless, seeing that his late spouse had been a midwife, there was a suspicion that the secret feminine password of which Cloridia had heard tell might come down to us from the lips of the Master Florist himself. When prompted, Romaùli had permitted himself a few hints: the Escorial was, he said, growing arid, and he had even let slip an enigmatic reference to Versailles, the residence of the Most Christian King, and to the Viennese Schönbrunn. All this, I had reported in detail to Abbot Melani, and Buvat had advanced the theory that Tetràchion might be the name of a flower present in some noble coat of arms. However, as the Abbot had just informed me, research in heraldic tomes had turned up no such flower, so that now Atto could not wait to take the conversation with Romaùli further.

A dish, an heir, a Master Florist: three tracks, every one of which seemed to lead in a different direction.

"Seeing that your Romaùli appears to be the only one to know what or who the Tetràchion is," said Atto, as though following the thread of my cogitations, "I should say that we must start from there."

On our arrival at the villa, I constrained the Abbot to make a little deviation before rejoining Tranquillo Romaùli, whom I knew to be intent at that hour on raking the gardens in preparation for the afternoon's festivities. I had to escort the little girls to Cloridia at the great house, so that they could assist her in her midwife's duties with the new mother and infant and, at the same time, receive her loving motherly care.

We found Master Romaùli leaning over a flower bed, wielding a pair of shears and a sprinkler. Upon seeing us, his face lit up. After the exchange of the usual pleasantries, it was Atto who came straight to the point.

"My young friend has informed me that you would be glad to pursue discussion of a certain matter," said Melani with calculated nonchalance. "But perhaps you may prefer the two of us to remain alone, and therefore. . ." he added, alluding to the possible desirability of sending me away.

"Oh no, not at all," replied the Master Florist, "for me 'tis as though my own son were listening. I beg of you, allow him to stay."

So Romaùli had no hesitation whatever about discussing delicate matters, like that of the Tetràchion, in my presence. All the better, said I to myself; obviously, he felt so sure of his own arguments that he had no fear of the presence of witnesses.

Since the Master Florist had shown no sign of any intention to move from his working position and was still on his knees, in order to facilitate conversation, Atto too had to sit, choosing a little stone bench which was fortunately just in the right place. I looked around; no one was observing us or walking in the vicinity. The conditions were right for squeezing from Romaùli all that he knew.

"Very well, honourable Master Florist," Atto began. "You must in the first place know that at this present moment, the fate of the Escorial is almost closer to my heart than that of Versailles, of which I have the honour to be a most faithful admirer. Precisely for that reason. . ."

"Oh, yes, yes, how right you are, Signor Abbot," broke in the other, working on a low rosebush. "Could you hold the shears for me one moment?"

Atto obeyed, not without a grimace of surprise and disappointment, while Romaùli handled the stem of the plant bare-handed; then he resumed his speech.

". . . Precisely for that reason, as I was saying," continued Melani, "I am sure that you too will be aware of the gravity of the moment and that it is therefore in the best interests of all. . . in this field, shall we say, to succeed in resolving this grave, nay this most grave crisis, as painlessly. . ."

"Here we are," the other interrupted him, placing in his hand a rose just cut from the bush, "I know what you want to get down to: the Tetràchion."

For a moment, the Abbot fell silent with astonishment.

"The Master Florist is most intuitive and a man of few words," Atto then said in amiable tones, yet looking swiftly all around to make sure that no one was watching us.

"Oh, it was so obvious," came the reply. "Our common friend told me that you wished to resume the matter upon which we touched in our first conversation, in which I referred to the Tetràchion and in which I also mentioned the Spanish jonquil and Catalan jasmine. And now you speak to me of the Escorial: one does not need to be a genius to understand what you are leading up to."

"Ah, yes, of course," Atto hesitated, somewhat troubled by the rapidity of the other's deductions. "Very well, this Tetràchion. . ."

"Let us proceed step by step, Signor Abbot, step by step," said the Master Florist, pointing at the rose which he had just placed in Atto's hand. Now, smell it!"

Somewhat taken aback, Atto twirled the rose a little in his hand; at length he raised it to his nose, breathing in deeply.

"But it smells of garlic!" he exclaimed with a grimace of disgust.

Tranquillo Romaùli laughed delightedly.

"Well, you have just demonstrated that, as with the palate, so with the flower; if the smell is not good, every beauty is insipid and as though 'twere dead. Thus, giving a good odour to a flower that has none, or only a bad one, is as beneficial as the miracle of giving it life."

"That may be so; but to this. . . er, impertinent flower," objected Melani, dabbing his nostrils with a lace handkerchief, and again shivering with disgust, "death was given, not life."

"You are exaggerating," said the Master Florist amiably. "It is only a medicated flower."

"Meaning?"

"To treat flowers, one takes sheep's manure, which one then macerates in vinegar, adding musk reduced to powder, civet and ambergris, and in this one bathes the seeds for two or three days. The flower born of this process will smell of fresh and delicious aromas, those of musk and civet, which tone up and revive the nostrils of whosoever brings it to his nose."

"But this rose stank of garlic!"

"Of course. It was in fact medicated in another way, to make it resistant to parasites. For, as Didymus and Theophrastes teach, it suffices to plant garlic or onions close to any kind of ornamental flower, especially, close to roses, for the latter to be instantly impregnated with a garlicky stink."

"Disgusting," Atto muttered to himself. "However, what has that to do with the Tetràchion?"

"Wait, wait. By means of medication," continued Romaùli, quite unperturbed, "one can completely remove the bad smell of flowers that are rather disagreeable to the nose, such as the African marsh marigold or Indian carnation, whichever you prefer to call it. One need only macerate the seeds in rose water and dry them in the sun before sowing. Once the flower has been grown, one must take the seeds and repeat the operation, and so on."

"Ah, and how much time does it take to arrive at the result?" asked Atto, growing vaguely curious.

"Oh, a trifle. No more than three years."

"Ah yes, a trifle," replied Atto, without the other becoming in the least aware of his irony.

"And even less time is needed for these little ones," said Romaùli, utterly unruffled, jumping lightly up and tiptoeing as he invited Melani to lean over and look into a damp, shady corner behind the bench, between the trunk of a palm and a little wall.

"But these flowers are. . . black!" exclaimed Atto.

He was right: the petals of a group of carnations, hidden in this little cranny (where I had often noticed the Master Florist busying himself of late) were as black as anything I had ever seen.

"I made them grow there so that they should not be overmuch in evidence, said Romaùli.

"How did you do it?" I asked. "In nature, there are no black flowers."

"Oh, that is a bagatelle for one versed in the secrets of the art. You take the scaly fruit of the alder, which must first be dry on the tree, reduce it to a very fine powder, and incorporate it in a little sheep's manure, tempered with wine vinegar. You must add salt to correct the astringency of the vinegar and the whole thing will grow soft. Thereupon, you incorporate the roots of the young carnation, and there you have it."

Atto and I, although bored by the Master Florist's explanations, were both astounded by the amiable and ingenious perversion whereby he obtained floral miracles. Not even to me, his faithful helper, had he revealed the existence of the black carnations. Who knows, I wondered to myself, how many such prodigies he had sown in the flower beds of the Villa Spada. He did in fact confide to us that he had just planted an entire bed with lilies the petals of which were painted with the names of the spouses (SPADA and ROCCI) in letters golden and silver; another, with roses medicated with the rarest of oriental essences, and a third with tulips from bulbs soaked in colours (cerulean, saffron, carmine and suchlike), thus tinted with striations of myriad hues, almost as though a rainbow had come down to earth; yet another, with monstrous plants, born of heterogeneous seeds planted in the same ball of manure, as well as parsley with its leaves infolded in the form of cylinders, obtained by pounding the seeds in a mortar and squashing their meatus, and a thousand other wonders of his art.

"I cannot wait for the moment," he concluded, "when Cardinal Spada brings the guests to take a look at my little productions."

"Ah, good. But I still do not see why you no longer wish to speak of the Tetràchion, and I am beginning to wonder whether I may not be wasting your time," said Atto, his tone betraying his real meaning, namely that he was wasting his own time; having said which, he rose from the bench with a decided air.

I too looked around me in confusion. Was the Master Florist having second thoughts?

"Yet, we are getting there," he replied. "The gardens of the Escorial are withering miserably, as I had occasion to mention last time we spoke."

"The *gardens* of the Escorial, did you say?" Atto asked with a slight start.

"Many, who are wrongly informed, maintain that those Spanish gardens, which were once so splendid, have no future, because of the climate, which has become icier in winter and more arid in summer. I have read much about those unfortunate gardens, you know. They need only a Master Florist and they would be saved. I have never been in Spain, nor indeed have I ever set foot outside Rome. I do, however, love to make comparisons with the gardens of Versailles, which I know to be quite hardy, despite the damp, unhealthy air of the region, and with the many-coloured flower beds of Schönbrunn, which, I have read, were only recently reclaimed from the harsh conditions of the Vienna woods."

Abbot Melani turned and looked at me with hatred in his eyes, while the Master Florist carried on with one of his gardening tasks.

"And I," I tried in a whisper to justify myself, "when I told him that you were worried because death was hovering over the Escorial, thought he might not have understood. . ."

"So that is what you said to him. What a refined metaphor, eh?" hissed Atto.

"I have the solution for saving those gardens," continued Romaùli, without realising a thing, "and it is indeed fortunate that you should be here, given your deep interest in the matter, as I have learned from your protégé."

"Yes, but what about the Tetràchion?" I stammered, still hoping to learn something useful from the Master Florist.

"Precisely. But let us take this step by step. It is a delicate matter," announced Tranquillo Romaùli. "Think of anemones. If one wants them to be double, one must select the seeds from flowers which are not early- or late-blooming; they must have suffered neither from heat nor from cold, and thus will produce completely perfect seeds."

"Double flowers, did you say?" I asked, beginning to imagine, and to fear, what he was getting at.

"But of course, from a single carnation will come a double one, if a seedling of the former is planted in excellent soil within the thirty days beginning on the 15th of August, Feast of the Assumption of the Virgin Mother of God, in a warm place that is well protected from the extremes of the summer. From a double carnation will come a quadruple one if one takes two or three seeds of the double species and, having enclosed them in wax, or in a feather that is wider at the base than at the tip, placed them in the ground. That is what I have done, you see."

Lovingly, he pointed to a few flowers with rather bizarre characteristics: they were carnations of the purest white, with four flowers on the same stem, which bent almost in an arc under their sweet-smelling load.

"Here is my secret recipe for saving the Escorial. These flowers can resist every variation in temperature and climate; I invented them. These are my *tetràchion* carnations."

"Do you mean. . ." stammered Atto, blanching and stepping back a little, "that your Tetràchion is. . . this plant?"

"Yes, indeed it is, Signor Abbot Melani," said Romaùli, rather surprised by Atto's evident disappointment. "They are so noble, these quadruple inflorescences, that I wished to give them an unusual name: *tetràchion*, from the ancient Greek *'tetra'*, meaning 'four'. But perhaps you do not share my opinion and my hopes for the Escorial. If that is so, I beg you to tell me at once, lest I bore you any longer; perhaps you might have preferred to visit my elaboratory of flower essences. I myself can take you there. You will come and visit me one of these days, will you not?"

❧

The conversation with Tranquillo Romaùli had cast us into the deepest gloom.

"A bane on you and your wife!" Abbot Melani began, the moment that we left him. "She promised us heaven knows what information through her supposed network of women, and here we are with a fistful of dead flies."

I lowered my head and said nothing; Atto was right. In fact, I was beginning to suspect that, after having risked my life to serve Abbot Melani, Cloridia might secretly have changed her mind about the assistance she had at first promised me and decided to provide me with little or no further news, in case such information might spur me to undertake perilous courses of action. Obviously, I said nothing to the Abbot about my suspicions.

"Clearly, the Master Florist has nothing to do with the women's password," I retorted; "yet he did give us one useful piece of information: Tetràchion means quadruple."

"But tell me, what the Devil has that to do with Capitor's dish?" cried Melani, hammering each syllable and laughing hysterically.

"Nothing whatever, Signor Atto, as far as I can see. But, as I said, at least we know now what the word means."

"I certainly did not need your Master Florist to know that '*tetra*' means 'four' in Greek," the Abbot rejoined angrily.

"Yet you did not know that Tetràchion means simply 'quadruple'..." I hazarded.

"I had simply forgotten, at my age. Unlike Buvat, I am not a librarian," Atto corrected me.

"Perhaps there was something quadruple in Capitor's dish."

"As I told you, it represented Neptune and Amphitrite driving a chariot through the waves."

"Are you quite sure that there was nothing else?"

"That is all I saw, unless you regard me as completely senile," protested Atto. "However, we shall know for sure the moment that we find Capitor's three gifts. And you know well where we must look."

So, at a tired, funereal pace, we moved yet again towards Elpidio Benedetti's arcane Vessel. I then recalled that I had something urgent to ask Abbot Melani: whoever was that Countess of Soissons, who had sown trouble between Maria and the King? Was she in fact the Countess of S., the mysterious poisoner to whom the Connestabilessa had so reticently referred?

I was suddenly overcome by a bout of acute resentment for the Abbot: he still had made no mention to me of the Spanish succession, yet the Connestabilessa's letters spoke of nothing else. Atto spoke to me of another Spain, that of fifty years ago, the Spain of Don John and Capitor with her mysterious gifts to Mazarin. Might there be a connection between these two Spains? Perhaps there was one, contained in the mysterious essence of the Tetràchion.

"You are lost in thought, my boy," observed Atto, who had in truth until that moment been more absorbed than I.

The Abbot was observing my frowning, pensive face with some anxiety; like all professional liars, he was forever worrying that someone might sooner or later piece together the broken threads of his half-truths.

"I was thinking of the Tetràchion and, now that we are again approaching the Vessel, of Maria Mancini," said I with a great sigh.

This was, of course, a lie. It is true that I was thinking of Maria, but only because in the letters which she had sent to Atto, and which I had by now inspected several times over, there were still a number of things that eluded me.

"To be specific, I was wondering about the court's cruelty to that young woman; for instance, about the Countess of Soissons – by the way, who is she?" I asked with false ingenuousness.

"I see that even the intense events of the past few hours and even the lack of sleep have not caused you to forget all that I have been telling you," replied the Abbot with some satisfaction, probably believing that I had been so moved by his narration of the amorous vicissitudes of the young King of France that I was now begging him for more details. He had expected no less of me.

The Countess of Soissons, explained Abbot Melani, was none other than Maria's elder sister. She was called Olimpia Mancini and, according to some, she had been among the young King's initiators in the arts of love.

In the spring of 1654, when she was seventeen and Louis fifteen, they would often dance together on festive occasions; and she nursed the kind of hopes that might be expected in the circumstances. . .

However, her uncle, the Cardinal, promised her early on to the Count of Soissons, a member of the House of Savoy related to the royal family. They married in 1657.

"Olimpia was rather envious by nature," croaked Atto, bringing up what was plainly a disagreeable memory. "She had a long, pointed face with no beauty about it other than dimples on her cheeks and two vivacious eyes, which were unfortunately too small. The court wondered: 'Was she ever the King's mistress?'"

"Well, was she?" I interrupted, in the hope that Melani would let drop some detail of interest for my research.

"That is not the right question. One cannot speak of mistresses in connection with a fifteen-year-old boy. The most that might be asked is whether they may have given in to their urges. And the answer is: what does it matter?"

According to Atto, one thing was certain: whether platonic or not, the time passed with Olimpia left absolutely no mark on the young King: nothing that touched his soul. And when Maria and Louis's hearts first beat for one another, Olimpia was already expecting her first son.

"Alas, pregnancy did nothing to curb her terrible jealousy for her sister, who had succeeded in the most natural way in the world in obtaining what she had vainly but deliberately set out to win: the heart of the young King."

Spite thus spurred Olimpia once more to flirt with the Sovereign, between her first and second pregnancies; but this time, in vain. She then gained the secret support of the Queen Mother, who feared the love between Louis and Maria, and took pleasure in troubling her sister by showing her letters in which the King's mother expressed her opposition.

"So it was she who calumnied Maria in the King's ear, as soon as she returned to Paris after the Spanish wedding!" I realised in surprise.

Given my condition as a foundling who had never had brothers and sisters, I had always dreamed of and liked to imagine myself with many, many siblings. And in my dreams, I always saw them as the truest and most trustworthy of friends.

"Are you surprised? Since the times of Cain and Abel, things have gone thus," replied Atto with a complacent air, whereupon he recited:

> *Blood brothers often will ingest*
> *Dame Envy's fatal venom best:*
> *First Cain, then Esau, and Thyéstes,*
> *And Jacob's sons and Eteocles,*
> *For they were fired much more than others*
> *As if their victims weren't their brothers,*
> *And consanguinity incited*
> *Will burn up stronger when ignited.*

"As you heard, it is no accident that Sebastian Brant, who is so dear to that Albicastro, should have dedicated verses in his *Ship of Fools* to fraternal hatred. Fortunately, however, there is no infallible rule. Maria always kept up the closest of ties with another of her sisters, Ortensia."

Ah, yes, I thought. Was not Atto himself a living example of fraternal love? He had all his life been tied to his brothers by an unbreakable mutual aid pact. I had heard of this many years before, at the Locanda del Donzello, when a lodger hissed disapprovingly that the brothers Melani always moved "in a pack, like wolves".

"So Olimpia, as I was telling you, whispered malevolently in the King's ear that, while he was away at the Spanish border getting married, Maria had allowed herself to be courted by the young Charles of Lorraine and was even prepared to marry him."

"And what was she supposed to do, poor thing?" I commented.

"By now, the King had taken a wife."

"Precisely, Maria was looking for a French match. She had no desire to return to Italy where women of high rank are compelled to rot at home as mere ornaments."

With malign joy, Olimpia saw her calumnies bear fruit. It happened when Maria was presented to Louis' new bride. This was the first time she had seen the King after a long absence: that time had seen their separation, Mazarin's violence and Louis's tears at the fortress of Brouage. Love, and with it jealousy, had not come to an end; it had simply been cast in chains.

Well, when Maria again came before him, Louis, eaten up by jealousy, looked at her with such coldness and scorn that she was barely able to complete the three ritual reverences. Olimpia's wickedness had triumphed.

Mazarin, on his deathbed, richly rewarded Olimpia's zeal in separating Louis and Maria: he appointed her superintendent of the Queen's household, to the great displeasure of Maria Teresa herself, who was anything but pleased to have her still hopefully hanging around her husband.

"Poor Maria Teresa. Olimpia took advantage of her closeness to the Queen to be the first to reveal the King's adulterous affairs to her."

It happened with Louis XIV's first official mistress, Louise de la Vallière. Olimpia, who stuck her nose in everywhere, offered her to the King as a screen, to cover his nocturnal promenades with his sister-in-law Henriette, secretly delighted that the man she could not have was now deceiving his own consort.

But the fence that separates the power of sovereigns from their desires is easily swept aside, and thus in the end it was Louise who became the King's real mistress. Then Olimpia became her bitterest enemy, putting another of the Queen's maids of honour, Anne-Lucie de la Motte, into the fiery Sovereign's bed and then informing the naive Louise by means of an anonymous letter. Unable to separate the two lovers, Olimpia obtained an audience with the Queen and told her everything: from the King's escapades to the steady relationship with Mademoiselle de la Vallière. Then she sat back and enjoyed the spectacle: torrents of tears, a memorable scene between the King and his mother, and finally a palace scandal involving all the maids of honour.

The King himself remedied all this. In his exasperation, he took advantage of the opportunity to break away from his mother's influence and impose Mademoiselle de la Vallière on her, on his wife and on the whole court as his first official mistress.

"Olimpia was now hoist of her own petard," laughed the Abbot, "and that was the beginning of her ruin which, after all she had got up to, was not long in coming."

"Look!" I exclaimed, interrupting the narration.

We had passed the San Pancrazio Gate and had almost reached the Vessel. Before the entrance of the villa stood three magnificent carriages.

"One of them is Cardinal Spada's," I noticed.

Suddenly, the three carriages moved off and turned to the right. As they drew away, we could clearly see that they were empty. Their passengers (Spada, Spinola and Albani) had descended at the Vessel, where, presumably, their lackeys would later be returning to collect them.

"Take courage, my boy, perhaps this time we're in luck: the trio are 'on board'," commented Melani.

So the three cardinals had returned to meet at Benedetti's villa. The time before, we had attempted to trace them, but in vain. Now we had found them by chance: perhaps it would go better this time.

Seeing that we had almost arrived at our destination, Atto rapidly completed his tale.

"Olimpia was ruined by her own jealous fury. She ended up by commissioning anathemas and poisons for the lovers of the Most Christian King and love potions for Louis himself. All these intrigues came to light with the Affair of the Poisons, which cost her an arrest warrant and compelled her to flee in all haste to Brussels. To this day, she still hops from place to place throughout Europe, a prey to an irreducible hatred for France, striving by all the means in her power to harm the reign of the Most Christian King. She is suspected, among other things, of having poisoned her husband, and even Madame Henriette and her daughter."

"Madame Henriette and her daughter?" I repeated hesitantly.

"For heaven's sake, here we go again, must I always repeat *everything* to you? Henriette, I have just told you, was the King's sister-in-law; what is more, we have seen her portrait on the ground floor here. She was the mother of Marie-Louise of Orleans, the first wife of King

Charles II of Spain. But that is another story," said the Abbot, cutting short his account. Curiously, he was always in a hurry to terminate our conversation whenever it touched in some way on the present state of Spain.

Now at last I had discovered the identity of the mysterious Countess of S.: the Countess of Soissons was a sister of Maria Mancini. The Connestabilessa had in fact hinted at the suspicions of poisoning hanging over her head after the death of the Queen of Spain, Marie-Louise of Orleans. Her discretion in speaking of her was due, not to any involvement on Olimpia's part in the present state of affairs, but to the fact that she was her own sister. That was why Maria had, when referring to her, expressed such pain at her evildoing. In other words, I had made another fine blunder, the second of the day, after that with the Master Florist: the mysterious Countess of S. was in fact far from mysterious, nor had she anything to do with the dangers which seemed now to hang over Abbot Melani's head.

As Atto was ending his narration, although I was concerned not to show any sign of it, I once again became a prey to anger. For days and days now, I had been spying on the correspondence between Atto and the Connestabilessa concerning the Spanish succession, yet had found out absolutely nothing. What was more, Melani still had not uttered so much as a word on the matter of Spain, nor did he seem to have any intention of ever doing so. All his attention seemed to be taken up with investigating the meetings between my master, Cardinal Spada, Cardinal Albani and Cardinal Spinola di San Cesareo, with a view to the forthcoming conclave. And these meetings were taking place at the Vessel, or so it seemed, for, when all was said and done, despite our repeated visits to that strange villa towards which we were now directing our footsteps, we had never found anything to confirm that. The Vessel, however, with its disquieting and inexplicable apparitions, had led the Abbot to follow the thread of distant memories: Maria Mancini, the youthful King of France, even Superintendent Fouquet, all leading up to Capitor, Don John the Bastard's madwoman (and here we were, back in Spain) who forty years ago gave Mazarin three presents, among them the dish which she called Tetràchion.

The Tetràchion. As though lost in a circular labyrinth, here I was, again thinking of it. The chambermaid at the Spanish Embassy, on whose lips this obscure name had surprisingly appeared, had been skilfully interrogated by Cloridia to help me cast light upon a whole series of intrigues: the stab wound to Abbot Melani's arm, the death of Haver the bookbinder and the exchange of letters between Atto and Maria Mancini on the Spanish succession, in which my master Cardinal Fabrizio was, moreover, also mentioned. The letters reported that the Cardinal Secretary of State Fabrizio Spada had visited the Spanish Ambassador in connection with the King of Spain's request to Pope Innocent XII for assistance and, given the Pontiff's poor state of health, Spada was personally looking after policy in his place.

And here we were back at the start: the Spanish succession, in which the Tetràchion, an indefinable, faceless and formless entity, was said to be the legitimate heir.

Ever since the Abbot and I had set forth together on this adventure, I had kept returning again and again to the same considerations, yet without ever getting anywhere. Everything seemed to be connected – but how? Perhaps the solution was there, close at hand, yet I could not get at it. That tangle of clues was rather like the *folia*: a circular motif, pervasive yet intangible, a sort of sea serpent, at once evasive and insinuating, which in the end holds the innocent listener in its hybrid embrace, immobilising him in its coils.

The *folia*: the Abbot and I were crossing the threshold of the villa and already that music was enveloping us in the Lethe of its warm, spicy embrace.

❧

Once again, we found Albicastro perched on his cornice, drawing from the magic quiver of his violin the scintillating sounds of the *folia*.

"Does he always have to be in the way?" muttered Atto. "He has no fear of making himself ridiculous!"

Albicastro left off playing and looked at us. I started, fearing that the musician had overheard the Abbot's unflattering remark, despite the fact that he had uttered it under his breath.

"Human affairs, like the Sileni of Alcibiades, always have two faces, each the opposite of the other. Did you know that, Signor Abbot Melani?" the Dutchman began enigmatically. "Like those ridiculous and grotesque statuettes which contained divine images, what seems from the outside to be death, when examined from within, proves to be life; and vice versa, what seemed alive, is dead."

The musician had, alas, heard Atto's acid words.

"In human affairs, what seems beautiful turns out to be deformed, what seems rich, poor, what seems infamous, glorious; the learned man may prove ignorant, the strong weak, the generous ignoble, the joyful sad; prosperity may reveal itself to be adversity, friendship hate, the enjoyable harmful. All in all, when you open up the Silenus, you find everything suddenly transformed into its opposite."

"Do you mean that what to me seems ridiculous, is perhaps divine?" said Melani teasingly.

"I am taken aback, Signor Abbot, that you, who come from France, should have difficulty in grasping my meaning. Yet you have the perfect example before your eyes. Who among all you Frenchmen would ever say that your king is not rich and master of all that surrounds him? But if he's in thrall to many vices, is he not perhaps equal to the most ignoble of slaves? And above all, if his heart is devoid of the soul's wealth and he dies without having been able to satisfy it, should he not be called most poor? You doubtless know what Solon said to Croesus, King of Lydia: "The richest man is no happier than he who lives for the day, unless, having enjoyed a life in the midst of great wealth, he has the fortune to end it well.""

Upon hearing these last words, Melani gave a start and walked off disdainfully, without deigning so much as to salute the Dutchman.

As I followed him, I too grew pensive. Croesus, King of Lydia: the name of that famous monarch of ancient Greece reminded me of something. The pallor I found on Atto's face when I cast a sidelong glance at him, walking tense and silent beside me, made me suspect that the musician had touched a tender place on his heartstrings. I strove for some resonance from another string, that of memory. Where had I heard the story of the sage Solon and the Lydian Croesus? I strove in vain. So I said to myself that, where memory would not reach, reasoning could. Albicastro had compared Croesus to the Most Christian King. . .

It took only a few seconds, then, for that name to come to mind: Lidio, which kept cropping up so enigmatically in Atto's correspondence with the Connestabilessa. Croesus was King of Lydia – another "Lidio". That mysterious personage was sending Maria messages through Atto, and through the same channel, she was replying to him. What was the Connestabilessa conveying to him? "In every matter it behoves us to mark well the end: for oftentimes God gives men a gleam of happiness, and then plunges them into ruin." And, yet again: "With respect to that whereon you question me, I have no answer to give, until I hear that you have closed your life happily." Thinking about this, it all sounded as though these were quotations from some ancient book. What was more, did not these phrases resemble what Solon told Croesus, as quoted by Albicastro? I promised myself to seek out the episode between Croesus and Solon as soon as I possibly could in the library of Villa Spada.

I joined Atto and we looked all around us. Of the three cardinals, there was no trace.

"No, they are not here. Otherwise, we'd hear some sound, or at least some secretary would emerge."

It was as though the trio had vanished into nothingness.

"There's something wrong here," said Atto, pensively pinching the dimple on his chin. "Let us get a move on. Standing around here will get us nowhere. And there's much work to be done."

Our goal was the charger. Judging by the picture depicting Capitor's three presents, which we had found at the Vessel two days before, this must be a rather bulky object. It was made of gold, exquisitely wrought and magnificent in appearance. It would have been in Benedetti's interest to show it for all to see in some fine room; however, seeing the state of abandonment of the Vessel, it was not unlikely that someone had put it in a safe place to preserve it from being stolen.

"We found the picture on the second floor," said Atto. "We shall begin there."

This was the floor with the four apartments with a bath chamber and a little shared salon. Our search could not have been more thorough. We inspected beds, wardrobes, dressers and little rooms, all to no effect.

In the process of checking every possible nook and cranny, we had to rummage through each of the four little libraries with which the four apartments were equipped. Climbing onto a chair, I began to look behind every row of books, swallowing some of the dust which had gathered there over who knows how many years. This phase in the search brought me no luck either, apart from a single detail.

As I was inspecting the books in the fourth and last library, my eyes settled on the third shelf from the top. This was a long row of volumes which were all the same, with their spines engraved in gold letters:

HERODOTUS
THE HISTORIES

On the first volume, under the title, I read:

Book I
LYDIA AND PERSIA

Obviously, I knew the name and works of the famous Greek historian. But what struck me was the title: here was Lydia, the land of Croesus.

"I am going down to the first floor, there's nothing here," called Atto, as he descended the stairs.

"I've still something to do up here, I'll join you in a moment," I replied.

Indeed, I did have something to do. I climbed down from the chair on which I was perched and settled into an armchair. I opened the book to search for the passages containing the story of Croesus.

As I turned the pages, I offered up my silent thanks to the walls within which I sat. Once again, the Vessel had, through ways obscure and ineffable, perceived a request for explanations, a yearning for knowledge. This time, however, it had not replied with its inscriptions but had placed a book before my eyes.

The search was more successful than that for the dish. The passage which explained everything began at the twenty-seventh chapter.

The immensely wealthy Croesus, King of Lydia, received one day a visit from Solon, the Athenian sage. Croesus said to him: "Stranger of Athens, we have heard much of thy wisdom and of thy travels through many lands, from love of knowledge and a wish to see the world. I am curious therefore to inquire of thee, whom, of all the men that thou hast seen, thou deemest the most happy?"

Croesus, who was extraordinarily wealthy, venerated and powerful, obviously thought that Solon would say that it was he, great Sovereign of the Lydians, who was the happiest of men. Instead, Solon spoke of someone unknown, a certain Tellos of Athens, who had had a prosperous life, many sons and grandsons, and had died in battle against his city's enemies. The second prize, he accorded to the Argive brothers, Cleobis and Biton, two athletes who took the yoke of their old mother's chariot on their shoulders for a good forty-five furlongs to the temple in which the festival of the goddess Hera was being celebrated. Upon reaching the temple, their mother prayed Hera to grant her sons the best fate a man could have. After banqueting and performing the sacred rites, Cleobis and Biton lay down to sleep in the temple and never again awoke: such was their end. The people, looking on them as among the best of men, caused statues of them to be made.

Croesus then broke in angrily, "What, stranger of Athens, is my happiness, then, so utterly set at nought by thee, that thou dost not even put me on a level with common men?"

Solon answered with these wise words:

> *I see that thou art wonderfully rich, and art the lord of many nations; but with respect to that whereon thou questionest me, I have no answer to give, until I hear that thou hast closed thy life happily. For assuredly he who possesses great store of riches is no nearer happiness than he who has what suffices for his daily needs, unless it so hap that luck attend upon him, and so he continue in the enjoyment of all his good things to the end of life.*
>
> *. . .If he end his life well, he is of a truth the man of whom thou art in search, the man who may rightly be termed happy. Call him, however, until he die, not happy but fortunate. . .*
>
> *. . . He who unites the greatest number of advantages, and retaining them to the day of his death, then dies peaceably, that man alone, sire, is, in my judgment, entitled to bear the name of 'happy'. But in every matter it behoves us to mark well the end: for oftentimes God gives men a gleam of happiness, and then plunges them into ruin.*

"Boy, are you coming or not? Our work is only beginning!"

Atto's voice called me back sharply to the present; the volume of Herodotus jumped in my hand.

I had read enough, I thought. Now I was beginning to understand.

If my reasoning was correct, the name Lidio must conceal no less than the Sun King in person, just as he was hidden behind the metaphor of Croesus in Albicastro's speech. Besides, had not Atto mentioned to me that Herodotus was among Louis and Maria's favourite authors?

Here was the secret I had sought in vain: the Connestabilessa and the King wrote to one another secretly, and Atto was their go-between!

Of course, they were no longer Maria and Louis, the ivory-skinned maiden and the timid youth of the apparitions at the Vessel; their writings were no longer murmurings of love. Nevertheless, the King of France still held the counsel of Maria Mancini in high esteem, so much so that he was prepared to run the risk of a clandestine correspondence in order to enjoy the benefit of her wit. I well remembered that in a post scriptum Atto had written to her:

You know what value he sets upon your judgement and your satisfaction.

Atto had in truth written in the same letter that he had something to deliver to the Connestabilessa: something which, he asserted, might cause her to change her opinion of Lidio. Whatever could that have been?

After the first moments of enthusiasm, however, doubts surfaced: the reference to Herodotus was obvious, but it was less evident that Lidio was the pseudonym for the Most Christian King. Of course, it was not perhaps an accident that Louis should have loved to read Herodotus together with his beloved. Besides, Albicastro had made an all-too-facile comparison between Croesus and the King of France. All in all, one could not completely rule out the possibility that, in Atto and Maria's correspondence, someone quite different might be hidden behind the disguise of the King of Lydia. What was more, I knew too little about Maria Mancini's life since her departure from Paris to be able to find out who this mysterious personage might be.

In other words, I still needed to confirm the identity of one of the personages. I already knew which one: Silvio.

Maria Mancini had written to Atto, sometimes calling him Silvio, and in those passages in her letters she sent him warnings, recommendations and even reproofs, the meaning of which remained thoroughly obscure to me.

And what, I asked myself, if these too were literary quotations, just like the Lidio referred to in Herodotus? I began to imagine that Silvio too might also be a character from some book, perhaps a messenger of love, even one drawn from mythology.

There, I said to myself, if only I could discover where that name, Silvio, came from, perhaps I might obtain a few more clues as to who Lidio might be or even, I hoped, definitive proof that the King and the Connestabilessa were still engaged in amorous conversations.

I soon grew discouraged; I had only one name: Silvio. It was like looking for a needle in a haystack. Where was I to begin my search?

A hand fell heavily on my shoulder, dragging me from my reflections.

"Will you stop meditating with that book in your hand like Saint Ignatius? Come and help me."

The Abbot, covered in dust and perspiration, had come to get me back to work.

"So far, I have found nothing. I mean to continue searching the first floor. Come and help me."

"I am coming, Signor Atto, I am coming," said I, climbing onto the chair and replacing the little volume of Herodotus.

My meditations would have to wait until later.

એન્જ

So we descended to the first floor, with its gallery of mirrors and its distorted perspective and, on either side, the little chapel, the bath chamber and the two little chambers dedicated, the one to the papacy and the other to France.

Suddenly, I found myself facing the delightful image, woven into a tapestry, of a lovely nymph dressed in a wolf's skin, who had been wounded in her flank by the arrow of a young hunter. The nymph's gentle appearance, from her ivory complexion to her soft ebony curls, were in sharp contrast to the blood that gushed from her side and the desperation written on the young man's face. The floral frame punctuated with scrolls and medallions in relief completed the tapestry with exquisite elegance.

Then I recognised it. This was one of the two Flemish tapestries before which Abbot Melani had stood, lost in ecstatic admiration, on our previous visit to the Vessel. Atto had explained to me that it was he himself who had persuaded Elpidio Benedetti to purchase it when the latter was visiting France some thirty years previously.

What else had the Abbot said to me? This I pondered, while my thoughts began dancing in my head like Bacchantes moving in procession towards some exciting, yet unknown goal. Originally, there had been four tapestries – that, Melani had told me – but two of them he had made Benedetti present to Maria Mancini, because the scenes depicted in them were drawn from an amorous drama, *The Faithful Shepherd*, much appreciated by her and the young King (but this detail I had almost had to drag from him, so reticent had Atto become at that juncture). A drama of love. . .

Turning to Abbot Melani with an ingenuous smile, while I struggled to feign a bad bout of coughing, brought on by all that dust,

I begged his leave to absent myself awhile from our search. Then, without even awaiting his permission, like some new Mercury flying on winged heels, I dashed up the stairs to the second floor and in a matter of seconds I was again visiting the four libraries, in one of which I had left the *Histories* of Herodotus.

Perched on a chair, my fingers almost scratching at the spines of the volumes, I scanned their titles, as though my eyes needed help from the sense of touch to confirm what they were reading.

At last I found it: tiny, no more than a booklet, some six inches high and less than half an inch thick. It was bound in black leather patterned with golden squares, its spine decorated with Florentine lilies. I opened it:

I then placed my trust in the book-mark, of fine maroon satin, by now faded; opening at the place where it had lain since time immemorial, I read at random:

> *Happy Dorinda! Heav'n has sent to thee*
> *That bliss you went in search to find.*

I exulted. Dorinda: that was the name of the wounded nymph whom I had just seen in the tapestry. Abbot Melani had told me when we saw it for the first time. And Dorinda was also the name which the Connestabilessa had given herself in her last letter, in which she addressed Atto as Silvio.

I had found what I was looking for. Now it only remained for me to seek the name Silvio. If, as I thought, he was one of the characters from *The Faithful Shepherd*, I had succeeded. So, with my breast trembling with emotion, I began to leaf through the pages of the little book, in search of a Silvio who might perhaps be a messenger of love between Dorinda and her beloved, just as Melani was perhaps the go-between linking the Connestabilessa and the Most Christian King.

Very soon, I found it:

> *Know you not Silvio, son to famed Montano?*
> *That lovely boy! He's the delightful swain.*
> *O prosp'rous youth. . .*

This Silvio was, then, no go-between, as I had hoped, but a wealthy and beauteous youth. Apart from his wealth, he seemed hardly a portrait of Abbot Melani. . .

What I then read surpassed all my imagining:

> *O Silvio, Silvio! Why did nature give*
> *Such flower of beauty, delicate and sweet,*
> *In this thy Spring of life, to be so slighted?*

It was a dialogue between Silvio and his old servant Linco, who reproves the youth for his hard-heartedness. I turned more pages:

> *O foolish boy, who fly to distant hills*
> *For dang'rous game, when here at home you may*
> *Pursue what's near, domestic and secure?*
> . . .
> *SILVIO:*
> *Pray, in what forest ranges this wild creature?*
> *LINCO:*
> *The forest is yourself, and the wild creature*
> *Which dwells therein is your fierce disposition*
> . . .
> *Shall I not say thou hast a lion's heart*
> *And that thy hardened breast is cased with steel?*

No, it could not be Atto who hid behind the nickname Silvio. Rather, someone else came all too readily to mind when I read of that scornful, rich young shepherd:

> *Now, Silvio, look around, and take a view*
> *Of all this world; all that is fair and good*
> *Is the great work of love. The heav'ns, the earth,*
> *The sea are lovers too.*
> . . .
> *In short, all nature is in love but you.*
> *And shall you, Silvio, be the one exception,*
> *The only soul in heav'n and earth and sea,*
> *A proof against this mighty force of nature?*

I thought once more of all that Abbot Melani had told me: was not that series of reproofs perfectly suited to His Majesty the Most Christian King of France? Had not the Sovereign's heart turned to ice after his separation from Maria Mancini?

> *Thou art, my Silvio, rigidly severe*
> *To one who loves thee ev'n to adoration.*
> *What soul could think, beneath so sweet a face*
> *A heart so hard and cruel was concealed?*

And, yet again:

> *O cruel Silvio! O most ruthful swain!*

I turned to the frontispiece. I wanted before all else to read the foreword and the initial *argumentum* or résumé of the drama, so as to discover what part was played in it by the nymph Dorinda who provided the Connestabilessa with her nom de plume. Thus I learned that Silvio was betrothed to Amaryllis, but did not love her. He loved no one. He wanted only to go hunting in the forest. Then, however, he accidentally wounded in the side a nymph who was in love with him – Dorinda, to be precise – having mistaken her for a wild beast because she wore a wolf's skin. At that point, Silvio fell in love with her, broke his bow and arrows, cured the wound and the couple married.

Was the tale not perhaps very like that of the young King of France, betrothed to the Spanish Infanta but in love with Maria Mancini? Only the denouement of their love story, as well I knew from Atto, was very different from that of *The Faithful Shepherd*, for which they themselves so yearned.

Time was growing short. Atto would soon be coming up to look for me. I entered the spiral staircase. There, I heard a strange buzzing. Cautiously descending a few steps, I peeped out to glance at Abbot Melani. Tired, Atto had slumped into an armchair to await my return, and had gone to sleep.

I sat down on a step and drew my conclusions: not only the name of Lidio but also that of Silvio were screens concealing the Most Christian King. Thus, the Connestabilessa was not only what Solon had been for Croesus; she still remained Dorinda, Silvio's lover. . .

Many things in Atto's and Maria's letters had at last become clear to me. What lay hidden in those letters was not state espionage, not obscure political manoeuvring, not the turbid depths of international diplomacy, as I had suspected all that time when I so ignobly spied on Atto and Maria. No, those letters concealed an even greater secret, an unimaginable, yet purer one: Louis and Maria were still writing to one another forty years after their last farewell.

At last I understood why Atto spoke to me with such confidence of the French Sovereign's sentiments for the Connestabilessa and how his suffering at the loss of his beloved had hardened his heart. I understood, too, why he told of these things as though they were alive and kicking today; he was constantly dealing with the most confidential first-hand details of the undying love between the couple!

That was why Atto had come to Rome: to meet Maria Mancini, after an absence of thirty years, and to bring who knows what embassy of love on behalf of the Most Christian King. I would have given anything to know at that moment what the King was sending through Abbot Melani. Whatever could necessitate a meeting *en tête à tête*? A signed letter from the King? A pledge of love?

I could also understand why Abbot Melani had hesitated so much when answering my questions the first time we had seen those tapestries at the Vessel. *The Faithful Shepherd* had not only been the favourite reading of the two old lovers: it still was. It was their secret code. And Atto acted as their go-between, now as then.

Yet, what kind of love can there be between two old persons who have not seen one another for forty years? The answer was to be found in a letter from Atto to Maria, which I recalled at that moment:

> *Silvio was proud, 'tis true, but he venerates the gods, and was one day vanquished by your Cupid. Since then he has ever bowed down before you, calling you his.*
> *Altho' his you were not.*

A love made up of memories and lost opportunities, such was the King's for Maria Mancini.

And I who had believed that Atto was referring there to his wretched castrato's estate! No, Atto was referring to the unbroken chastity of that love, and to how present it still was in the old Sovereign's soul.

I then thought of all the passages in Maria's letters in which she wrote addressing Silvio, and I understood at last the meaning of the warnings and reproaches which she borrowed from *The Faithful Shepherd*:

> *O, Silvio, Silvio! who in thine early years hast found the fates propitious, I tell thee, too early wit has ignorance for fruit.*

These words, which were impenetrable when I believed them to be addressed to Abbot Melani, now calmly revealed their meaning to me. The Most Christian King had indeed ascended to the throne very young; thus, his destiny had matured "when still unripe". But he who comes to power too early must, "on attaining maturity, surely reap the fruit of ignorance", in other words remain arrogant throughout his whole life. And now that the burning question was that of the Spanish succession, Maria was warning Louis XIV to act wisely.

In the same way, was Maria Mancini not perhaps accusing the Sovereign of being somehow himself responsible, through his own arrogant conduct of both life and government, for the series of disasters which had befallen France's friends in Spain?

> *Vain boy, if you imagine this mishap*
> *By chance befell, you widely are deceived.*
> *These accidents so monstrous and so strange*
> *Befall us mortals by divine permission.*
> *Don't you reflect the Gods by you were slighted,*
> *By this your haughty pride and high disdain*
> *Of love and ev'rything the world deems human.*
> *They cannot abhor, although it be in virtue.*
> *Now are you mute, who were but now so haughty!*

Very soon, the game had become perfectly clear to me. The Connestabilessa, writing with consummate skill, spoke to Atto of Lidio in the third person, sending messages and replies through the Abbot; and then addressed Atto, calling him Silvio, the message really being for the King's eyes. Two identities, to confound unwelcome readers and thus to protect the writers from any spies. With me, the trick had worked perfectly. Never could I have discovered the truth, had it not been, first, for Albicastro, then, the Vessel, both of which had showed me the way that led to Lidio. The Flying Dutchman and his Phantom Vessel, as Melani called them. . .

Yes, indeed, I observed, turning *The Faithful Shepherd* over and over in my hands. All these illuminations had come to me through the Vessel. First, there was the phrase of Albicastro, the eccentric occupant of the villa, which with singular clairvoyance compared Croesus to the King of France. That explained why Atto had given such a start and turned rapidly on his heels without replying to the Dutch musician; he himself had been perturbed by that arcane oracle. Then came the book of Herodotus, followed by that of the Cavaliere Guarini, thanks to which my ideas were made completely clear. Benedetti's mysterious villa had once again proved its fathomless faculties.

Suddenly, I smiled to myself: it was, when one came to think of it, most probable that the villa's one-time owner, Abbot Elpidio Benedetti, in his capacity as an agent of Cardinal Mazarin in Rome, had collected in his villa books, pictures, works of art and everything that a fashionable Francophile could not fail to have or know.

One thing was by now certain: neither the conclave nor the Spanish succession was the matter or purpose of the meeting planned between Atto and Maria, but love. Political manoeuvres were the basis, not the heart of their epistolary conversations. They were just a cover, and might arouse the interest of those keen on intrigue, but no more.

That was why Atto became so heated when, in our incursions to the Vessel, he told me the old story of that broken royal romance. For him it was something still alive, and one might even posit that the apparitions and phantasms of the past which we had witnessed at the Vessel were none other than the spiritual emanations of that long-distant (yet still potent) passion between the Connestabilessa and the aging Sovereign.

This, in all probability, was the true motive behind Melani's presence at the Villa Spada during that time: he and the Connestabilessa were taking advantage of the invitation extended to both to attend the Spada wedding to meet once more. All of this was, I thought, far removed from the conclave or the Spanish succession.

Maria, however, was late arriving. She had already missed the day of the ceremony. Whatever could be keeping her? Perhaps she really was suffering from a persistent fever, as she declared in her letters; or perhaps, I came to imagine, she was held back by a natural reluctance to engage in amorous skirmish, leading her to play hard to get, almost as though Atto himself were her former love, rather than his ambassador.

I heard Abbot Melani's footsteps. He had woken up and was coming up to see what I had done.

I looked again at *The Faithful Shepherd*. The book was really tiny, I thought. It would be child's play to slip it into my pocket and take it with me without the Abbot seeing. I would return it later. Now, it was useful to me. I would read Maria's letters in the light of those verses.

๛

"At long last! May one know what you are up to?" he exclaimed, seeing me at the top of the stairs.

"As you had gone to sleep, I thought I'd let you rest awhile."

"And that was wrong of you, for without your help I have been able to get practically nothing done," retorted Atto, trying to hide his embarrassment.

It was an elegant way of confessing that, as soon as I had left him alone, he had dozed off.

"Now it will be enough to feel our way," the Abbot continued. "I mean to explore the Vessel systematically, from top to bottom. The dish must be somewhere here. We have already searched the second floor more than enough. We shall therefore begin with the ground floor, then we shall go up to the first floor and, lastly, to the third floor, where the servants' quarters are."

As he descended the spiral staircase in front of me, I scrutinised from behind his bent and age-worn figure, still, however, made vibrant by the call to action. Looking at him, I was moved by the thought of the nature of his mission. For once, Melani had surprised me, revealing sentiments and ideas nobler than those I had ascribed to him, rather than the base ones which had, alas, all too often driven him in the past.

It was thus, with my soul overflowing with emotion, that I entered the other parts of the villa, to help Atto in his search for Capitor's three gifts, and above all, the dish.

We inspected the great hall on the ground floor: the shelves, the dressers, the drawers. Every single object (cutlery, glasses, ornaments) was where we had found it on our first visit. It was in that room that were exhibited, as we knew, a number of portraits of lovely and noble ladies of France (including the portrait of Maria which I had admired on our first tour of the premises).

As I was rising after pointlessly stirring up the dust under a divan, I found myself face to face with one such portrait to which I had not previously accorded any attention.

"Madame de Montespan," announced Melani as he too approached that face of extraordinary, disturbing beauty. "One-time favourite of the King of France. A relationship which lasted ten years and produced seven children; almost a second Queen."

I had just enough time to admire the abundant flesh of her bosom, the blue eyes fired with the will to elicit desire, the lips ready for kisses, the well-rounded arms. Atto had already passed to the next portrait.

"Louise de la Vallière," he announced. "His Majesty's first official adultery, as I have already told you," he added, pointing to that face of singular purity, crowned by thick silvery blonde tresses, a veritable synthesis of finesse, elegance and ethereal refinement, so much so that she seemed to have been formed by the Lord to manifest to humanity the blessed triad of grace, modesty and tenderness and almost magically, through her sea-coloured eyes, to win hearts and fidelity.

"How different they are!" I exclaimed. "This one is so pure, and the other so. . . how can I put it?"

"Turbid and sinful? Come straight out with it: that la Montespan was no angel one can see at a glance," laughed the Abbot, "but almost importantly, they are both far removed from the frank and impetuous temperament which radiated from Maria's person. These are two Frenchwomen, even if the one's the opposite of the other. Maria is Italian," concluded Atto, emphasising the last words, while his eyes lit up with renewed ardour at the thought of her.

Now at last I realised from what a privileged and intimate observer I had hitherto had the good fortune to hear the tale of the drama which had so perturbed the soul of the Most Christian King. Thus, I trembled with the desire to hear the remainder of that old, unhappy story, now that I knew it to be still going on. Above all, I was by now convinced that Atto was on the point of meeting Maria to bear her some important embassy of love from the Most Christian King, and I was determined to discover what this might be.

"The King of France had many loves after the departure of Maria Mancini, if I remember correctly," I remarked, while the Abbot guided me into the salon with the portraits of kings and princes.

"He had many favourites," Atto corrected me, "and never fewer than two at a time."

"Two? Is that the custom among French sovereigns?"

"No, of course not," smiled the Abbot, opening a huge dresser full of Venetian crystal and Savona porcelain and rummaging inside it; "far from it." Never had such a thing been seen in France: a Queen and two titular mistresses, all three condemned to live shoulder to shoulder. Without counting the fact that Madame de Montespan was already married. Henri IV, Louis's grandfather, had a mistress, but he never thought of imposing her on the Queen."

"I imagine that you see this as yet another unfortunate consequence of his abandoning Maria," said I, holding out the bait in my impatient desire to satisfy my curiosity about the present relations between the Most Christian King and the Connestabilessa.

"The deluge of pain that rained down on the heart of the young King, he transformed into a universal deluge, capable of submerging entire peoples for generations and generations," intoned the Abbot. "So Louis could not have Maria for his Queen? Then, let the other Queens pay! He could not have Maria as a woman by his side? So he surrounded himself by women without number, and all at the same time."

The King, explained Atto, always had at least two mistresses at the same time, who were in turn betrayed and abandoned for others, and this was a continuous process; nor could they ever be sure of the King's feelings or of what he intended for them. "The Three Queens" was what they called that constant triad.

"He who has suffered an injury needs to inflict it in turn upon others, *ad infinitum*," Melani summed up. "As he could not belong to Maria, Louis chose to share his time among many, and so to belong to none. With cold calculation, and at the same time, icy wrath, he divided his life among his many women: his wife, the long-term mistresses, the thousand lovers of a month or of a night, causing them all immense pain. Help me to lift this carpet, please."

He kept them all on tenterhooks, continuously, and not even the court could ever be sure whether the ladies with whom Louis loved to show himself off were really the favourites of the moment or if their star was already setting and their only use had become to serve as foils to divert attention from some new, secret preference. All submitted to the Sovereign's scourge; and none dared raise her head.

"The drastic change in the King's character was evident at court from the day after his marriage," said the Abbot. "Louis bundled all Maria Teresa's Spanish retinue off to Madrid."

The Queen, Atto continued, by now in full spate of recollection, opposed not the least resistance, but in exchange requested a boon from her spouse: to be able always to remain with him. Always. Louis granted her that. He ordered the Grand Maréchal des Loges never to separate them. He kept his promise until her death: at the Louvre, at Fontainebleau, at Saint-Germain and even Versailles, he always slept beside her, abandoning his mistress's bed in the middle of the night and returning to the bedchamber of his legitimate consort where he remained until daylight. All this, without exception, without a word of explanation and without any excitement; even when Maria Teresa's bedchamber was crossed by wet-nurses bearing a bundle in their arms, the latest bastard of the King's mistresses, delivered in one of the adjoining rooms. Even the concession which had seemed to the poor Queen to be a boon, Louis transformed into a perverse and cruel reprisal.

"But how is that possible? The King's mistresses occupying rooms adjoining the Queen's bedchamber?"

"Here comes the best bit," replied Abbot Melani with sad irony. "His Majesty's favourite hunting grounds were among the Queen's maids of honour. And correspondingly, when Louis grew weary of some concubine, he would often cover his withdrawal by granting her a position in his consort's retinue. So much so that Maria Teresa always sighed 'I am fated to be served by my husband's mistresses.'"

The Abbot glanced curiously into a huge light-grey soup tureen, decorated with pomegranates of shining green and crimson porcelain.

"For two decades, the King sired a child a year, and I speak only of those who were recognised; but of these only six were children of the Queen. Seven came from la Montespan, the rest from other mistresses," Atto explained, arching his eyebrows. "Colbert, his Minister, for as long as he lived, was the King's dumb slave. He served as his intermediary, procuring wet-nurses, babes' clothing and compliant chirurgeons to assist at his mistresses' deliveries. He even found among his old servants adoptive families in which to raise the secret bastards, or in other words the children of the concubines of the moment," added the Abbot, prodding the stuffing of an armchair.

The King did not stop at imposing upon the Queen this painful cohabitation with mistresses and their brats. When he travelled, he put them all in the same carriage and even compelled them to eat elbow to elbow. Then came the worst: Louis made his new bastards legitimate and even declared them Bourbon princes. For them, he arranged royal weddings, going so far as to inaugurate the unheard of mixing of bastards with the legitimate Bourbons. He even wedded one of his bastard daughters to a "nephew of France", forcing the son of his brother Philippe to marry the last daughter he had fathered on Madame de Montespan. The court grumbled; the young man's parents were desperate, there were scenes, tears and very public scandals. The King exulted.

"Where will it all end, at this rate?" hissed Atto vehemently.

"If I have understood you, there is reason to fear for the future of the throne."

He stopped to catch his breath after detaching from the wall a large picture, the frame of which had seemed to him (erroneously) too massive not to hide a hidden chamber in its backing.

"I am afraid that one day the King may place his bastards in the line of succession to the throne. And that will be the end. It will mean that no longer will the Queen's son become King but anyone, just *anyone*, can do so. At that point, any plebeian will ask: Why not me?"

ॐॐ

"Let us be seated a moment," suggested Atto, slumping onto a daybed. "Let us rest awhile, then we shall resume our search."

I sat down too, in a great armchair, and at once gave a great yawn.

"Of course, the Most Christian King," I observed, picking up where Atto had left off, "consoled himself soon enough with all those mistresses after Maria's departure."

It was a provocation, in the hope that he might betray something of the current contacts between the Sovereign and the Connestabilessa. Atto took the bait.

"But what are you saying? Do you not listen when I am speaking? His first mistress, Louise de la Vallière, he used only to take his revenge on the Queen Mother, who had separated him from Maria by making him believe that he would soon forget her. But this affair with Louise was a triumph that came too late, a pointless reprisal against his old mother, the fruit of posthumous courage, a vindictive libation offered upon the sepulchre of his own heart," he declaimed with heartfelt pomposity.

What vain satisfaction, continued the Abbot, could the King gain from forcing the Queen his consort and the Queen Mother to dine at the same table as his mistress? Or by such behaviour as bringing her surreptitiously into his mother's apartments, or making her sit with him at the gaming table, together with his brother and sister-in-law, then making that known to the old Queen, like an insolent child? Yet Louis XIV was concerned to defend his own reputation, when he forced Louise to give birth with a mask over her face, assisted by chirurgeons who had been brought to her blindfold.

Poor Louise was a docile instrument, unambitious and naturally modest, in the hands of a King with only pride where his heart should have been. Louis meant to impose her on his mother for as long as she lived, in a confrontation in which the real object of his vengeance – as with the hatred with which he persecuted Fouquet – was the looming shade of Mazarin.

When there was no longer anything to fight about, he dismissed her, already bored, despite the three children she had borne him.

"Louise was not made for the sophisticated social round, games and gossip, intrigues and all the coquetry and capriciousness of life at court," sighed Atto, yawning and stretching on his day-bed. "She was far from stupid, she loved reading, but she had no repertoire of jokes, no witty repartee, she coined no epigrams. In other words, she was not Maria," he concluded with an insolent little smile.

We rose and continued our hunt for Capitor's dish. We began by searching the room where there was a billiard table. On the walls it was adorned with various framed prints: some represented antique bas-reliefs, others were after the manner of Annibale Carracci, and included various portraits of famous men. We took them off the wall to see whether there might be a secret compartment behind them, but were disappointed. The felt of the billiard table, all covered in dust, had turned from bright green to the colour of dew. One solitary white ball lay in the middle of the table, abandoned and imprisoned, almost a metaphor for the heart of Louise de la Vallière, a hostage in the wilderness of Louis's indifference. Atto gave it a sharp tap, causing it to bounce on the opposite cushion, then continued his account.

Thus, the King very soon went to see Mademoiselle de la Vallière only to delight in the coquetry and provocations of another lady, Madame de Montespan, known as Athénaïs. One day, having to depart for the wars in Flanders, he left Louise alone at Versailles, four months with child, and took Madame de Montespan with him, in the Queen's retinue.

"Ladies of the court at war? And even the Queen?"

"But with all that you have read on your own account, did you not even know that?" he asked, as we left the billiard room and turned to the great dining hall.

Thence, we entered a room that led to the back of the garden, facing east. We went out. Here began a drive which led, as we were soon to discover, to a gracious little grotto.

"I tell you once more, I have been reading books, not false, lying newspapers," I replied, irked and trying to cover a certain embarrassment.

"Very well, like the Turks, the King enjoyed dragging with him to the wars all the conveniences he enjoyed at court: the finest furniture of the crown, the porcelain, the golden cutlery and all that was needed to organise ballets and firework displays in every town he came to; and, of course, women.

What a strange experience for villagers and country folk, I thought, to witness at close quarters that mad mixture of war and the festivities of the royal court, with plumed cavaliers escorting gilded carriages, unreal jewel cases concealing the most beautiful women in the realm!

"If only from the mud that spattered the decor, and from the King's face, thin and sunburnt," continued Atto, "and lastly from the tiredness of his women, exhausted by the voyage and the inhuman hours they were forced to keep, it was plain enough that this was no promenade in the park of Versailles. I remember one journey in particular. Passing Auxerre, where the women are rather good-looking, the inhabitants had all come out to see the royal family and the ladies in the carriage with the Queen. The ladies themselves put their heads out of the carriage windows to look. It was then that the good people of Auxerre burst out laughing: '*Ah, quelles sont laides!*' – 'How ugly they are!' The King laughed long and loud and spoke of nothing else that day," laughed the Abbot.

The Most Christian King brought the whole court with him during the War of Devolution, which Louis started after the death of Philip IV, his father-in-law, to claim a part of Spanish Flanders as Maria Teresa's inheritance.

"He brought just about everyone, except Louise, you said. And what about the Queen?"

"Maria Teresa was the first to be compelled to go, seeing that, at least nominally, the war was being fought on her behalf. And whenever a city fell into French hands, she had to go and take possession of it officially."

But Louise, a simple, passionate heart, decided to risk her pregnancy and brave the King's wrath by joining the court in Flanders. She arrived exhausted. The King, in no way impressed – on the contrary, much amused – listened to the description of the scene when the poor pregnant maiden slumped half dead, together with the ladies accompanying her, on the benches of Maria Teresa's antechamber, while the latter vomited out of fury and vexation.

Meanwhile, we had reached the little grotto. Surely, Capitor's dish could not be there, but we both felt the need to breathe clean air after all the dust with which we had filled our lungs.

In the purity of the breezes which my breast inhaled in the garden, I seemed to find the description of la Vallière: Louise the ingénue, the enthusiast; a timid zephyr soon swept aside.

"Was the King furious that his mistress had disobeyed him?" I asked as we left the grotto and continued along a little path.

"Apparently not; on the contrary, invited by the Queen to mount her carriage, he refused and went off to ride with Louise. And what was more, on the next day, going to mass, poor Maria Teresa found Louise entering her carriage, although everyone had to huddle together in order to make room for her, after which she had to put up with her presence at dinner that evening. On the next morrow, caring not a whit for his consort or for his mistress, he spent almost all day locked in his chamber. La Montespan did likewise. And it so happened that the two bedchambers were communicating."

The Queen did not yet know that, with the arrival of Athénaïs, she would have to resign herself to the most painful proximity: journeys in a carriage with her consort's two favourites became the rule, and in all things an official cohabitation was imposed upon all three.

The mistresses were no better off than the Queen. Louis, continued the Abbot, kept them strictly sequestered under lock and key, and even if the one enjoyed ascendancy over the other, he took good care to keep them in a permanent state of anxiety, with herds of nameless concubines coming and going through their apartments. Every day, the official favourites suffocated in uncertainty, and the wretched spectacle of spite and squabbling somewhat calmed Maria Teresa's jealousy.

The path had brought us to an amphitheatre, far smaller than that which had been prepared at that time at Villa Spada for the spectacles accompanying the wedding, but graceful and delightfully mysterious. It was surrounded by a little portico decorated with antique bas-reliefs and with many vases of flowers; in the middle there was a little fountain, so that the portico, between one arch and the next, echoed its gentle splashing and gurgling.

"Around his heart, the King had built a tower of ice," continued Atto, deeply absorbed in his narration and almost completely unmoved by so much beauty. "Only great suffering could shake him a little, as on the death of children, and many of them did die. Of the six legitimate children, only one, the Grand Dauphin, is still living. When, about thirty years ago, his youngest son, the little Duc d'Anjou, died, I saw him utterly broken: I feared that this might be a sign of God's wrath, but it did not last long. Even when Louise de la Vallière decided to enter a convent, the King was incapable of reacting with any sentiment other than anger.

"A convent?" I asked, as I slaked my thirst, gulping down great mouthfuls of good fresh water from the fountain.

"Yes, poor woman, hers was a sincere heart, and she had really asked nothing more than to love the King and be loved by him in return. She was the only favourite who loved Louis for himself alone, which greatly flattered him, but no more than that. She, however, had taken that feeling very seriously indeed; when she decided to take the veil as a Carmelite, she publicly begged the Queen's pardon. "My sins were public and so must be my penitence." She knelt at Maria Teresa's feet; deeply moved, the Queen raised her and kissed her. A multitude of persons were present. It was a moment of intense emotion. Only the King was absent."

❧

We returned to the house, and in a very short time we completed our search of the ground floor. The Abbot looked disconsolately at our reflections in a great mirror. With our apparel whitened with dust and all the cobwebs in our hair, we looked like a pair of rag-and-bone men.

"What are we to do now, Signor Atto, shall we go up to the first floor?"

"Yes, and not only to look for the dish."

Once on the first floor, Atto guided me to the bath chamber near the little chapel.

"*Hic corpus*," exclaimed Atto, repeating the motto over the entrance, which we had already read three days earlier. "We shall take advantage of the wonders of hydraulics, if they still work."

So he opened the tap marked *calida*, hot water, but nothing came out. He tried the tap marked *frigida* and was more fortunate.

"Open up those chests: perhaps there are still some towels."

Atto had guessed correctly. Although old and dried up, the cloths had remained free of dust. I even found some hard lumps of soap. Thus we were able, first he and then I, to wash and cleanse ourselves to our heart's content.

Yet again, we set out in search of Capitor's treasures, but above all the dish.

On the first floor, composed of four little rooms and the great gallery which lines of mirrors seemed to prolong all the way to the Vatican palaces, there was indeed much to inspect. We opened the drawers of massive ebony chests inlaid with ivory and brass, or oak roots with inlays of briar, full of old porcelain cups; we turned back shutters painted in bright colours and with great difficulty shifted huge dark cupboards, carved with spirals and leaves, with stags' heads on either side, or columns carved in the form of satyrs; we moved grim chests and dusty crystal mirrors.

We removed the imposing mirror above the mantelpiece, first taking from it a multitude of statuettes in the finest porcelain, such as a blonde and delicate shepherdess with a pannier on her shoulders and, among the more bizarre ones, a young chimney-sweep complete with beret and ladder, and even a Chinese mandarin with the index finger of his right hand (visibly broken and glued back on) raised in warning. In the chests beneath the windows, we rummaged among blackened silver teapots, cords and braiding for curtains, even a pack of playing cards from Paris. Abbot Melani even stuck his head into the stoves, emerging stained with soot.

Coughing at all the dust, we unrolled carpets and French drawings and lifted enormous tapestries with scenes mythological and pastoral, always hoping to discover some secret hiding place or a concealed entrance to some intimate little room (after all, it is not easy to hide a globe!), in our dogged search for Capitor's presents.

After Louise de la Vallière, continued Melani with his lips curled in a supercilious little smile, there began the reign of Madame de Montespan. Exceptionally beautiful, witty and always at the height of fashion, with a seething sensuality and a heart of ice, la Montespan meant to conquer the King at all costs, and this was quite obvious. He knew at once, but resisted her. He went further and teased her: "Madame de Montespan desires me to desire that which I do not."

Then, however, the King's senses, and his intellect, the orphans of his heart, gave in. The ascent of Madame de Montespan coincided with the death of every feeling or appearance of such a thing. Not only was Louis no longer capable of loving; from Madame de Montespan onwards, he was unloved.

"Only much later did the Most Christian King come to understand that no woman had really loved him," said Atto enigmatically.

With Athénaïs there began the ten years of the apogee of Louis XIV, the era of splendour and arrogance, which was to end with the Affair of the Poisons, when the King realised that he was the prey of his mistresses, not they his. Years in which he gave the worst of himself, bedding hosts of other damsels with high hopes, ever ready and ever different. Not all of them deserved censure; some acted under the illusion that they could save a young husband or fiancé from being sent to the wars or in an attempt to recover for their father the family fortune unjustly confiscated by the treacherous Colbert. Louis never failed to take special pleasure in crushing the latter in his bare hands.

"My boy," the Abbot addressed me, perceiving the horror painted on my face, "the Most Christian King had suffered one day in a far distant past as he could never have imagined it possible to suffer; he who had already known the terror of the Fronde."

Now, like a cruel boy who inflicts unspeakable suffering on a little bird, the King watched the shipwreck of those wretched women's illusions to see whether they were suffering as *he* had suffered, and whether indeed it was possible to suffer so much. He wanted to tear from those hearts the secret of their pain, the only thing that once defeated the magnificent Sun King.

"But all that happened in the secrecy of the King's bedchamber," warned Atto, as we proceeded along the gallery, with the great vault echoing our footsteps.

At court, however, Athénaïs reigned undisturbed: the "reigning Mistress", they called her, paraphrasing the title of "reigning Queen" which distinguishes the King's consort from the Queen Mother. They were not so mistaken. With Madame de Montespan, Louis had presented the court with a surrogate Queen: here at last was one who possessed the exceptional beauty and wit needed to enhance the splendour of the French court.

"She radiated luxury and magnificence, just like the *Aurora* of Pietro da Cortona," said the Abbot, pointing to the splendid fresco on the ceiling of the gallery.

Atto's attention was suddenly drawn to the fresco of Midday which, between Aurora and Night, occupied the middle of the gallery. It depicted the fall of Phaeton, struck down by Zeus's thunderbolt for having dared drive the Sun's chariot.

"The first time I came here, I passed over this: to celebrate the culmination of the day, Benedetti chose an event of pride punished. On the walls below, he placed sayings praising the King of France. How very singular."

"Yes," I acknowledged in surprise, "it seems almost a warning to the Sun King."

"'Thy destiny is to be mortal, Phaeton, but what thou desirest is not for mortals,'" Atto quoted from Ovid's *Metamorphoses* in confirmation of my remark.

The Abbot then continued his tale. Without being one, Athénaïs played the part of a Queen: she received, she entertained, she fascinated all the ambassadors. The King showed her off with extreme pleasure and gloried in her: all in all, she was a service to the monarchy.

"She knew perfectly well that the King did not really love her," said Atto with a certain bitterness, "but he had great need of her 'to show himself loved by the most beautiful woman in the kingdom', as she herself liked to say. An ornament like so many others, when all's said and done."

"In common with Maria, Athénaïs had the courage to stand up to the King," added Atto. "She was not afraid to speak her mind, and she had good taste, like a true Queen."

During the decade of her 'reign', the Palace of Versailles became what it is today. The papier mâché of ephemeral architecture which, in Louise's day, lasted for the duration of some fête, was transformed into rocks, travertine, bronzes and marbles, arranged according to the secret order of surprise and the unexpected, bringing to life new groves, fountains and flower beds. The Grand Canal was populated by a tiny fleet of gondolas and feluccas, brigantines and galleys. The park, stifling under the mantle of the summer heat, was dotted with the white and azure of Chinese pavilions.

But above all, Athénaïs dedicated herself to her personal residence, not far from Versailles, repeating the splendour of the palace in miniature: the great Le Nôtre (the sublime genius of architecture, he who had laid out the palace gardens and, before them, those of Vaux-le-Vicomte, Fouquet's ill-starred château) was called upon to surpass himself, with gardens of tuberoses, narcissi, jasmine, violets, anemones, and basins of tepid water perfumed with aromatic herbs. . .

"And that which you simply cannot imagine if you have not seen it. Alas." ·

"Why do you say that?" I asked, hearing that melancholy moan.

"Because all that grandeur came to no better end than Fouquet's château. It all fell in ruins with the disgrace of its patroness, just as Vaux was wrecked when its lord was arrested. And this too confirms what I am telling you."

"Why? What happened?"

"The Affair of the Poisons broke out, my boy, the greatest trial of the century, as I have already mentioned to you. Almost everyone had a part in it; and, after Olimpia Mancini, Athénaïs was the most deeply involved. Witnesses emerged who had seen her participate in black masses, in which children were sacrificed, all to keep the King's love. All this was hushed up, but for her it was the end. And the hunter understood at last that all along he had been the quarry."

Learning of what iniquities his mistresses were capable, hearing of satanic rites and of witchcraft performed to gain orgasms in his bed, Louis understood that in all his amours there was very little love. From that revelation he never recovered. He had imagined that he had reversed the roles since the time of Maria Mancini, when he himself had been sacrificed on the altar of power. Instead, his destiny had been repeated: once again he had been a pawn on the chessboard of those who swore fidelity to him. And this time, he was alone; he had not even the consolation of sharing his sad fate with the woman of his life. It was thus that the doors of old age opened up for him.

࿇

We had completed our exploration of the first floor and we were now climbing the grand staircase. We continued right to the top, coming to the third floor, where the servants' quarters had once been. By comparison with the rest of the villa, this was another world: there was no furniture, no mouldings on the walls and ceilings, no embellishments. There were a number of mezzanines for the servants, others for the saddlery, and various service rooms. Spiders, flies and mice were the undisputed lords of those sad, empty rooms. It seemed just the squalid image of the Most Christian King's old age.

We began patiently to beat on the walls with our knuckles in search of secret rooms and to check whether some floorboard concealed a trap door, or if a windowsill contained a strongbox.

We then moved on to a chest of drawers. It would not open; unlike all the furniture we had hitherto inspected, it was locked.

"Ah, here, perhaps, we have it!" exclaimed the Abbot, recovering his good humour. "Go down to the first floor and find me a knife in the cutlery drawers. I seem to have seen some in that great cupboard held up by old Generalissimo Goatleg," he sniggered, alluding to the imposing and severe wooden satyr carved on it.

I went down to the first floor but found nothing. I then went down to the ground floor and there I found a knife. Before returning, my attention tarried a moment on one of the portraits of women hanging on the walls which had hitherto escaped my attention.

It was a lady no longer young, a little too plump, with features that were not repugnant, yet so wan and ordinary that they contrasted no little with the pomp of the portrait, from which one gathered without the shadow of a doubt that this must be a person of great consequence. I read below, on the frame:

Madame de Maintenon

It was the fourth time that I had come across that name. Was she not the lady whom the Most Christian King had secretly married, as Atto Melani had told me? She was. I looked once more at the portrait: the face was absolutely anonymous, contrasting oddly with the vivacity and aristocratic grace of the other royal favourites depicted beside her. I returned to the third floor.

"Madame de Maintenon," I murmured. "How could the King of France have married her? I mean, after all those fascinating women. . ."

"You saw her portrait down below? Incredible, eh?" commented Atto as he grasped the knife I held out to him. "The King married her one October night seventeen years ago, just two months after the death of Queen Maria Teresa."

"Secretly," I repeated. "You told me that a few days ago, the first time we visited the Vessel. However, I fear that I did not fully grasp your meaning. Is she some kind of a wife but not the Queen? I seem already to have heard of this kind of royal marriage in which the king's wife does not reign beside him and her children have no right of succession to the throne. . ."

"No, that is a morganatic marriage: you are not on the right track. Madame de Maintenon is, more modestly, an 'undeclared' wife, in other words, an unofficial one. Everyone at court knows of the marriage, and the King is happy with that. He simply wants it never to be mentioned. *Tamquam non esset*, as though it did not exist."

"But who was she before?" I persisted, recalling that the Abbot had described her as "socially unpresentable".

"A governess who, as I said, had as a child begged for alms," he said to me, raising his eyebrows and looking at me with a little smile while, having slipped the blade into the crack, he tried to open the lock.

Françoise d'Aubigné, later invested by the King with the title Madame de Maintenon, Abbot Melani continued, had for ten years been the governess of the many children Madame de Montespan bore the Most Christian King. There was not a drop of noble blood in her veins. She was an orphan of the humblest birth, born in a porter's lodge where her mother, the wife of a Huguenot whose life was spent passing from one prison to another, had been granted lodgings out of pity. She had spent her childhood with her two brothers dressed in rags, begging for a bowl of soup at the gates of convents. Fortune so arranged matters that, at the height of the Fronde, she met an old cripple, Scarron, an unseemly satirical poet who was fashionable in those days of barricades. Scarron, confined to a wheelchair, was not capable of looking after himself and was a dreadful sight to see. Unceremoniously, he asked the sixteen-year-old to be his nurse, in exchange for which he would marry her. She accepted without thinking twice.

After the fires of the Fronde, however, Scarron fell on hard times. He was reduced to writing eulogies on commission for various personages. His young and fresh little wife served as a lark's mirror. She attracted potential patrons, allowing them to entertain hopes, but without (it seems) giving in to their entreaties. In exchange, he fed and instructed her.

When he died, she was barely twenty-five years old. She inherited only a mountain of debts. After selling her few pieces of furniture, the young widow was left on the street. But she had gained something. Now she had to her credit the art of coquetry, and the education necessary to tell tales to some rich protector who might save her from indigence.

Proof of this was her friendship with Ninon de l'Enclos, an influential bawd to high society," sneered the Abbot, "from whom she inherited a pair of fiery lovers, thanks to whom she came to the attention of Athénaïs de Montespan."

The latter had just borne the King her first child, a daughter. Having to bring her up in great secrecy, she offered Françoise a post as governess. Subsequently, more children followed and, after a few years, a stroke of luck: the bastards were made legitimate. By the will of the King, Madame de Montespan moved to court with all her baggage and all her children; needless to say, governess included.

"She then proved sly enough to pass herself off as a very pious lady, even a zealot," commented Atto bitterly. "A fine piece of effrontery when one considers that a few years earlier Madame de Montespan had unleashed her on Louise de la Vallière to dissuade her from becoming a Carmelite, trying to scare her with the life of privations into which she would be entering."

"But she could surely not hope to please the King in a saint's guise!"

"She was far-sighted. For years, the clergy and zealots at court had been grumbling about la Montespan and the King's excesses. She became their mouthpiece, working in the shadows. For years, she had been living side by side with Athénaïs: the classic serpent in one's bosom. When the Affair of the Poisons culminated, her time came. Madame de Montespan was by now ruined and the King had undergone a sudden awakening."

"Do you mean that the King converted to a more sober life?"

"Not exactly," Atto hesitated. "In fact, the King's conduct was never so libertine as at the time when the Affair of the Poisons concluded, almost as though he hoped thus to exorcise his fears. He would move from one strange woman to the next, a different one every night, all of them, it was rumoured, very young. It was then that he suffered another grievous blow, too soon after the previous one. His most recent favourite, the beautiful Angélique de Fontanges, gave birth to a stillborn child and herself died very soon after that, suffocated by a flood of blood from a horrible pain in the chest. She was only twenty: she could have been his daughter."

The King's health reeled under all these blows. What was more, in those years, he was suffering from continual boils in the loins after a fall from horseback, which were removed with red-hot irons, so that he was constrained to promenade along the avenues of Versailles on an armchair with wooden wheels. He felt surrounded by hostile forces: first betrayal and now death, along with his own illness, cried out to him that he was dramatically alone.

"In the midst of all those poisoners and shrews, whom was he to trust? He desperately needed someone. But he had had enough of beautiful favourites. In middle age, they had proved too dangerous a game."

Meanwhile, we had opened the chest of drawers, only to find that it contained nothing whatever. We threw open all the windows to let in some clean air and the sweet sounds of the Roman afternoon. We sat briefly on a windowsill facing west. The soft and gentle foliage of the tallest trees was spread out below us. I again turned my eyes to the servants' quarters: after Abbot Melani's narration, they no longer seemed so squalid to me. Like the face of Madame de Maintenon, they were extremely plain, which was precisely why they showed more signs of wear and tear. But the absence of pomp and splendour gave the visitor's soul a rest from sentiments of emotion and wonderment, inspiring instead peace and familiarity.

Françoise de Maintenon, continued Atto, had in the meantime become a true mother to the royal bastards and that gave the King an unparalleled feeling of security. She was the only one, in those restricted court circles, of such ordinary origins that she could not aspire even to the role of official favourite, as the latter must always be chosen from among the families of the best nobility. Her conversation, too, was pleasant, without being brilliant. The King, in other words, felt himself in no way either attracted or threatened, which pleased him greatly. Thus, he took to enjoying ever more frequently a few hours chatting with her, talking of the children and about other subjects, none of which were ever too demanding. He could relax with this governess, who did not physically excite him in the least, while neither did she displease him.

"Françoise, in other words," Abbot Melani summed up, "gave him peace without taking up any room in his soul. His senses were tired; his spirit, mistrustful. What was more, when he became a widower, he was horrified by the idea of being pressed on all sides to remarry and give France a new Queen. He had already been subjected to one forced marriage. So he decided that the time had come to take his revenge: as I told you, he imposed that tramp of an ex-prostitute on the same kingdom that had imposed Maria Teresa on him and taken Maria from him. And he took no little pleasure in the scandal to which his choice gave rise at court; his minister, Louvois, even threw himself at his feet, begging him not to marry her."

We came down from the windowsill on which we had been sitting and continued our search.

"But this time too, a nasty surprise awaited the Most Christian King. His spouse was far less placid than he had thought. . ."

"What do you mean?"

"A few years ago, the King discovered that Madame de Maintenon had for years been passing information, obtained in confidence from himself, to her own private circle of priests, bishops and miscellaneous *dévots*, of whom a number were even suspected of heresy. The purpose of all this: the King's 'conversion'; or, to put it more clearly, the infiltration of the clergy into government."

I was left open-mouthed. Of course, I reflected, one could hardly say that the King of France had been fortunate with women: first Madame de Montespan with her black masses, and now this Madame de Maintenon, whom he was even so good as to marry, was betraying state secrets to churchmen in order to bring them to govern the land.

Once more, the place we were in seemed squalid and hostile and I wanted to return to the magnificent rooms below. Likewise, perhaps, the King of France may have missed la Montespan's beautiful face when he found that his colourless wife was in reality no less poisonous than she had been.

"Just think of it," continued Atto, "the King had already had quite enough of Cardinal Mazarin. The blood went to his head. How dare this nondescript little woman whom he had amused himself imposing upon the court as his wife, conspire behind his back and reveal to that handful of zealots the most secret affairs of state; she whom the King had never even permitted to eat at his table! She who to this day occupies a mistress's apartments in the Palace of Versailles. She who, if she may be addressed as 'Your Majesty' in private, must in public be content with taking last place."

"And why did he not dismiss her, as he did with Madame de Montespan?"

"He would have had to have her put on trial. The accusation in the air was one of political conspiracy. But that would have meant exposing to ridicule he who had insisted on flouting all good sense by marrying her."

What did the King then do before the court, which awaited his reaction with bated breath? He surprised everyone by pretending that nothing had happened; instead of exiling the traitress, he moved his daily meetings with ministers. . . to her bedchamber!

King and ministers, seated, faced each other. Behind the latter sat Madame de Maintenon, crouching in the shadows of her "niche", the padded wooden cabin she had had built for her, hypochondriac that she had always been, to shelter from draughts. Every now and then, the King would even ask her opinion. But this was only for show. The proof of that is that she had perforce to answer in the most general terms. And there would be trouble if she spoke without having been asked explicitly for her opinion by the Sovereign. She would at once be confronted with her spouse's most extreme fury.

"His Majesty is not prepared to admit before the court that he allowed himself to be hoodwinked by that counterfeit saint, so he has chosen to impose her even more than before," the Abbot concluded.

৵৽৻

Behind an old stove, we found an improvised palliasse, with next to it a box of fresh figs, some of which were still intact, a canvas bag with a few slices of bread and another bigger one full of cheeses. Next to that, stood a half-empty bottle of red wine, with a fine goblet of historiated blue glass. A fat, half-consumed candle completed the refuge.

"So our Flying Dutchman sleeps here," observed Atto scornfully. "That is why he's always in our way. Look at how much cheese he eats. Too much, like all Dutchmen. Can one be surprised that he rants so much after that?"

Hunger, however, took the upper hand. The Abbot indolently reached out for a fine piece of *caciocavallo*, placed it on a slice of bread and added half a fig (for nothing is more pleasant than sweet fruit, offsetting the saltiness of the cheese) and greedily bit into it. I too felt the pangs of hunger, so I took the same ingredients and imitated him, sharing with him both wine and glass. But while I had soon devoured that meagre dinner, I saw Atto chewing more and more unwillingly until, in the end, he threw away the cheese and contented himself with the bread and fig.

"I cannot bear cheese any more. In France, too, they serve it up with everything. I have come to detest it."

While I was finishing my picnic, Melani rummaged under the palliasse, drawing out a comb and a jar of salted sardines.

"Stuff bought from street vendors," observed Atto without disguising a certain disdain for Albicastro's frugal habits.

At long last we moved on. At the northern end of this floor, we found a great walnut table, with an enormous drawer set in it which, like the previous one, looked somewhat suspicious to us.

"'Tis truly massive," observed Atto. "There might be something inside it."

The Abbot tried with the knife.

"It is not locked, only jammed," said he.

We then tried to get it out with our bare hands, which cost us much time and trouble.

"What with poisons, conspiracies and betrayals," I commented, "the gallery of the Most Christian King's wives and mistresses really does him scant honour."

"Despite that, even to this day, I have to put up with hearing the court speak with disdain and scorn of my Maria," Atto replied hotly, as he puffed and panted, trying to extract the drawer from the table by brute force. "They say that the shipwreck of her life has unmasked her for the cold, ambitious, scheming and calculating woman they suspected her of being all along. The most indulgent among them maintain that she has proved less intelligent than her brilliant conversation let one suppose. 'She had wit,' they laugh, 'but no discernment. Ardent and impulsive, her angry outbursts drew one to her for a while, but ended up provoking disgust.' All this I have had to hear from those ferocious slandering tongues. Their spite for Maria has never died down. Not even now, after fifty years and many more than fifty lovers in the King's bed."

"How do you explain that?"

"Because Maria was a foreigner, and what was more, Italian, like Mazarin. And the French had had enough of the Italians imported *en masse* by the Cardinal. Add to that the fact that his niece made the Sovereign fall for her!"

"But as you were saying, the King has had so many lovers since then! Is it possible that the court should still remember the Connestabilessa to this day?" I insisted, in the hope of gleaning some hint of the current secret contacts between the King and Maria Mancini.

"And how could one forget her? To take just one example: only once did Queen Maria Teresa and Madame de Montespan join in alliance. This was about thirty years ago, and the alliance was against Maria Mancini. Maria, fleeing her husband, asked for sanctuary in Paris. The King, however, was not at court. He had gone off to war with Holland and, according to custom, had entrusted the regency to Maria Teresa. Maria's request thus fell into the hands of the Queen, who turned it down. But it was Athénaïs who convinced her to do so. She had understood everything: Maria had not only been the King's first love, but his last; some flame might still have remained alight."

Meanwhile, we had completed our (somewhat violent) examination of the walnut table. In our attempt to force its more intimate parts, we had grazed our hands and wrists. Inside, as we found in the end, nothing was hidden.

"By the time that news of Maria's request reached the King's ears," continued my companion, bandaging his scratches with a handkerchief, "it was already too late to revoke Maria Teresa's veto.

"But Louis did not decide to return Maria to her husband, although the latter was claiming her. He instructed Colbert to place her in a convent far from Paris and assigned her a pension. Maria, who knew nothing of the manoeuvres of Maria Teresa and Athénaïs, exclaimed:

'I have heard of money being given to women to see them, but never *not* to see them!'"

"But you said all this happened thirty years ago," said I, egging him on.

"Then listen," countered Atto, irritated by my caution in the face of his passionate assertions, "I know for certain that Madame de Maintenon has for some time been trying to persuade the King officially to invite Maria to Paris. Now, why do you think she should do that, she who is so jealous?"

"I would not know," I replied, with feigned hesitation.

"She is doing this because he is more and more frequently muttering half-phrases, or half-sighs, calling for Maria, now that at sixty-two years of age he is wearied and disillusioned and drawing up the balance sheet of his life. Maria is the same age as he. If the King should see her now, or so la Maintenon hopes, perhaps his angelic memory of her will be shattered. Only, she has not taken account of Maria's timeless fascination," Atto exclaimed pompously, despite the fact that he could know little of Maria's physical appearance, since he too had not seen her for thirty years.

"Presumably Madame de Maintenon has never seen her?"

"On the contrary, they knew one another and were friends. Maria even brought her with her to watch from a balcony the triumphal entry of the King and Maria Teresa into Paris, immediately after their wedding. But one must live shoulder to shoulder with Maria in order to understand that not a thousand years in time or a thousand leagues in space could ever make her memory pale," said the Abbot, all in one breath.

"Such an irony of fate: the first woman and the last in His Majesty's life, both together on the same balcony," I commented. "But Signor Atto, I must insist. Is it possible that the King's feelings should have remained unchanged for thirty years? After all, he never saw her again." This I added in the hope that he might at last give something away.

He hesitated for a moment, looking pensive.

"Nor have I seen her for thirty years," he answered quietly.

"Now at last she is coming," I encouraged him.

"Yes, so it seems."

❧

The minutes that followed passed in total silence. Atto was musing.

"I shall go outside again to catch a breath of air," said the Abbot all of a sudden. "I cannot take all this dust any longer. You, do whatever you feel like; we shall meet here in twenty minutes."

I looked at him questioningly.

"Of course, you have no watch," he remembered. "Come, let us go downstairs."

We stopped on the second floor where Melani began to open the drawers of a tallboy.

"I saw a carriage clock somewhere around here. Ah, there we are."

He placed it on the edge of a nearby desk and began to wind it up. Then he set the time and handed it to me.

"There, this way you can make no mistake. I shall see you later."

Atto was exhausted. We had spent hours rummaging. But the true reason for his going out was the rush of memories which had swelled his chest. He now needed a little solitude in which to calm his emotions.

Thus it was that I soon found myself in complete silence, holding the clock in my hand like a lantern.

I sat down on an old cordovan leather stool and set to thinking once again about Abbot Melani's long narration. Three were the Sun King's women of whom he had spoken to me, and three the storeys of the Vessel which we had inspected. This might have seemed too bold a leap of fantasy, but as I had already sensed, the three floors of the Vessel were just like the three women: the gardens on the ground floor, the secret garden and the little grotto, airy and graceful as la Vallière; on the first floor, the deceptiveness and sophistication of the splendid gallery of mirrors and the magnificent, breathtaking *Aurora* of Pietro da Cortona were like la Montespan, "the most beautiful woman in the kingdom", the "reigning mistress", while, next to the *Aurora*, the fresco of Midday with the fall of Phaeton from the Sun's chariot seemed to be a warning against the arrogance of Louis XIV who, at the time of Madame de Montespan was at the very height of his reign. Finally, the third floor was as bare and ordinary as the face of Madame de Maintenon, as sad as the King's life beside her, as empty as the Sovereign's old age.

By now, I knew everything, or almost, about the Most Christian King's intimate life, with the exception of what mattered most to me: his current relations with the Connestabilessa and the purpose of the love mission which the King (as I had by now guessed) had confided to Atto. It was just then that I discovered I was not alone.

Does the day the night surpass?
And can a human make an ass?
Did Socrates or Plato run?
Such learning's in our schools begun.
He is a fool who doesn't falter
At trying what he cannot alter.

I turned sharply: the voice which had recited those verses was Albicastro's and he stood on the threshold with his violin hanging from one hand.

"Are you calling me mad too, now?" I asked him, surprised by that speech. "Have I perhaps offended you in some way?"

"Far from it, son, far from it. I was only joking. On the contrary, I wanted to pay you a compliment. Does not Christ thank God for having hidden from the wise the mystery of beatitude, manifesting it rather to the little children, that is, to the fools. For in Greek, *nèpiois* means both little child and fool and is the opposite of *sofòis*, or sage."

"Perhaps, Sir, my small stature makes me like a little boy, but you should know that you and I are about the same age," said I with a certain embarrassment. "You should also know that you have not offended me in this."

"I thank you, son," insisted Albicastro, nonchalantly installing himself on a porphyry console, "but I was referring to your spirit, which I find to be still as pure as a child's. Or a fool's, if you prefer," he added with a little laugh.

"In that case, I'd be in the best of company. Was not Saint Francis called 'God's buffoon'?" I replied, by now completely distracted from my previous meditations.

"Even better, as the apostle said: 'Has not God made foolish the wisdom of the world?' and 'God has chosen the foolish things of the world to shame the wise.'"

"What should one then do, become mad?"

"No, not become it, just simulate it."

"I do not understand you."

"In the first place, everyone is agreed on the well-known proverb: 'Where reality is missing, the best thing is simulation.' That is

precisely why our children are taught early on the verse: 'To simulate folly at the right time is the highest wisdom.'"

"Simulation does not seem to me to be a great virtue."

"It is, however, when used to save oneself from cunning schemers. And pretending to be mad is a sign of the greatest wisdom, as
well the young Telemachus, Ulysses' son, knew. He was the author of
his father's triumph, and do you know how? He simulated madness
at the right moment."

I did not understand what he meant, but just then something else
was on my mind.

"Signor Albicastro," I broke in, "please be so kind as to answer my
question: why do you always speak of folly?"

To this, the Dutch musician's sole response was to shoulder his
violin and start playing his *folia*.

"Said Saint Paul in the First Epistle to the Corinthians," he recited slowly, as he produced the first slow sounds with his bow. "'Let
no man deceive himself. If any man among you seemeth to be wise in
this world, let him become a fool, that he may be wise.' And do you
know why? Because, through the mouth of the prophet Isaiah, the
Lord warned: 'I will destroy the wisdom of the wise and the discernment of the discerning I will set at nought.'"

I was intrigued and fascinated by this good-humoured and bizarre
disputation on the topic of folly, into which the Dutchman seemed
to be taking pleasure in dragging me, while in the background he
continued to play the notes of the *folia*. Perhaps Atto was right: he
ate too much cheese.

"So, in your opinion, true wisdom is masked under the semblance
of folly. And why ever is that?" I asked, standing up and approaching
him.

"As Sertorius demonstrates so well, it is impossible in one go to
tear out a horse's tail, but one can perfectly well attain that aim by
pulling out the hairs of his tail one by one," Albicastro candidly
answered, giving three light touches of his bow to the strings of his
violin, as though to reproduce the sound of horsehairs pulled out one
by one.

I could not restrain myself from laughing at that funny idea.

"If during a play someone were to tear off an actor's mask to reveal his true face, would he not perhaps spoil the whole show?" the
violinist went on to explain, "and would he not deserve to be driven

from the theatre with brickbats? To raise the veil on that deception means to ruin the spectacle. Everything on this earth is a masquerade, my boy, but God has determined that the comedy be played in this manner."

"But why?" I insisted, while in my soul there awakened a sudden and impatient thirst for knowledge.

"Just imagine: if some sage, fallen from heaven, were suddenly to start clamouring that, for example, one of the many whom the world adores as lord and master is in truth no such thing and that he's not even a man, because he's nothing more than a piece of living flesh in thrall to the basest passions, like a beast; or worse still, he is nothing but one of the vilest slaves, because he spontaneously serves other infamous lords and masters above him, whom we down here cannot even imagine; tell me, what else would he obtain thereby, save to become odious to all peoples and, what is more, ignored and unheard? There is nothing more damaging, for oneself or for others, than untimely wisdom."

Having said which, Albicastro descended from the porphyry console and, whirling to the notes of his *folia*, moved towards the spiral staircase.

And well we can with Terence state:
Who spawns the truth gives birth to hate.

After declaiming those verses which I guessed must come from his favourite poem which he was forever reciting, Sebastian Brant's *Ship of Fools*, he turned once more to me:

"The world is one enormous banquet, my boy, and the law of banquets is: 'Drink or begone!'"

❧

I heard Albicastro go down the stairs. I stayed still for a while, with his words still humming in my head.

"We must yield to evidence."

I raised my head. Atto Melani had returned.

"The gifts are not here," he chanted.

"Perhaps we have not searched thoroughly enough, we should try to. . ."

"No, no use. It is not a matter of searching. It is the very idea that's mistaken."

"What do you mean?"

"You told me that Virgilio Spada, the uncle of the Cardinal your master, was the first owner of the parrot."

"Yes, and what of it?"

"The good Virgilio, as you too know very well, had a collection of curiosities."

"That is true, yes, at Villa Spada, everyone knows of it. Virgilio Spada was very religious, but also a man of learning, a sage, and he had this collection of *mirabilia*, of curious and rare objects, which was rather famous, and. . ."

"Quite. I think that it must by now be clear to you too: when Benedetti decided to rid himself of the three presents and to give them to someone, Virgilio Spada was the ideal candidate."

"But why should Benedetti have wanted to give away the presents? Was he not instructed by Mazarin to keep them here at the Vessel?"

"To keep them, yes, but. . . there is a detail I've not mentioned."

It was thus that Atto disclosed to me what he had passed over in silence four days before, when we came to the Vessel for the first time and he spoke to me of Elpidio Benedetti, the builder and master of the Vessel, and his relations with Atto himself.

"Well, my boy, every person of influence must every day confront the most varied and unforeseeable intrigues," said he, as a prelude, "and so, he needs faithful and trusted men who accompany him through the myriad uncertainties of daily business."

"Yes, Signor Atto, and so?" I replied, without concealing overmuch my irritation at that verbose introduction, which served no other purpose than to distract attention from Atto's past reticence.

"Well, Cardinal Mazarin had, in addition to his official secretaries and officials, a host of. . . staunch and trusty factotums shall we say, among whose number I myself had the honour to serve."

These factotums, as Atto explained with a series of elegant circumlocutions, were in fact nothing but spies, straw men and schemers whom the Cardinal used for handling the most delicate and secret personal matters. Money was one of these; indeed, it was the main one.

"If I told you that the Cardinal was rich, I'd be lying to you. He was. . . how shall I put it?" said Atto, turning his eyes heavenward. "He was wealth incarnate."

Years and years spent in power over the kingdom of France had enabled him to amass a mad, vertiginous, outrageous fortune. Moreover, an illegal one. The Cardinal had nibbled away here, there and everywhere: at taxes, tenders, grants, exports. He had mixed his own property freely with that of the crown and, when separating the two, much money from the royal coffers had remained stuck to his fingers.

Obviously, this enormous estate (at the death of Mazarin, they spoke of tens of millions of *livres*, but no one will ever know exactly how many) had to be invested with the greatest discretion.

"My poor friend Fouquet was calumnied, arrested for embezzlement, torn from his family and all he loved and incarcerated for life. Meanwhile, the Cardinal, who was really responsible, was never made to pay for his depredations, which were both heinous and innumerable," the Abbot commented bitterly, "but he must be credited with having succeeded in keeping completely out of trouble."

Mazarin concealed his clandestine, illegal assets. This secret capital was entrusted to a network of bankers and men of straw, largely abroad, so as to prevent anyone from setting traps for His Eminence. The money was not deposited only with bankers. Mazarin instructed his henchmen to invest in pictures, precious objects and property. They had only to choose. There was nothing His Eminence could not permit himself, and his host of acolytes operated throughout Europe.

"Here in Rome, for example, Mazarin acquired sixty years ago from the Lante family the grandiose Palazzo Bentivoglio on Monte Cavallo, which thus became the Palazzo Mazzarino. For the past twenty years the Rospigliosi family has rented the palazzo, and my good friend Maria Camilla Pallavicini Rospigliosi has from time to time extended me the exquisite favour of receiving me there as a house guest."

"So the Palazzo Rospigliosi is really Palazzo Mazzarino!" I exclaimed, a little shaken, thinking of the splendid building near Monte Cavallo which I had again seen when I accompanied Buvat to collect his shoes.

"Exactly. He paid seventy-five thousand scudi for it."

"Quite a sum!"

"That is just to give you a small inkling of what was possible for the Cardinal. And do you know who convinced him to buy that palace?"

"Elpidio Benedetti?"

"Bravo. On the Cardinal's behalf, he bought books, pictures and valuables. Among other things, I recall some fine drawings by Bernini, which he made him buy, but at rather too high a price. What are we to say, then, of the Palazzo Mancini on the Corso, where Maria passed her childhood? Benedetti had it restored and enlarged at huge expense; all charged to Mazarin, obviously.

"When His Eminence sent Monsieur de Chantelou here to buy a few fine works of art, it was Elpidio Benedetti who sent him to Algardi, Sacchi and Poussin, whom you may remember."

"Of course, the famous artists."

"Quite. Then he recruited musicians on his master's behalf, to send to Paris, like that simpering Leonora Baroni."

This time, Atto did not ask me whether I knew that name, but I recalled that many years ago he had told me of this lady, a highly talented singer who had been his bitter rival.

"Elpidio Benedetti also acted as a secret go-between on Mazarin's behalf. On the latter's death he found himself endowed with funds of which no one knew the real ownership. The Vessel is too large and fine to have been paid for out of Benedetti's pocket. It is no accident that he had it built immediately after the Cardinal's death."

"So, the Vessel is. . ."

"It was built with Mazarin's money. Like everything that Elpidio Benedetti possessed, including his little house in town. It is, as I have already told you, no accident that Benedetti bequeathed it to the Duke of Nevers, Mazarin's nephew and brother to Maria."

"He returned the ill-gotten gains."

"Come, let us not get carried away: is one a thief if one robs another thief?" laughed Melani.

So, when the Cardinal had entrusted Benedetti with keeping Capitor's presents, he had imposed an additional condition: those three ill-starred objects were not to be kept on his properties. Forever a prey to his guilt, and to the phantasms which it evoked, he had the obscure presentiment that not only his person but also his property should be kept physically separate from those infernal devices.

All this, Elpidio Benedetti executed to the letter. He himself was not insensible of the need to ward off evil influences. Thus, when the time came to choose the place to keep the three gifts, he gave up the idea of placing them in his own town house, which in reality also belonged to Mazarin. The Vessel did not yet exist (it was to be completed six years after the death of His Eminence), so that Benedetti had no other choice but to give the presents to someone else: Virgilio Spada.

"Do you recall the inscription that we read here? 'For three good friends, I did endeavour, but then I could not find them ever.' We already suspected that the three friends might be Capitor's three gifts, but that 'then I could not find them ever' refers perhaps to the fact that only their portrait is here, while the objects themselves cannot be found."

"Because they ended up in the hands of Father Virgilio," I concluded briefly.

"Of course, this will not have involved a sale but the placing in trust of the objects," Melani made clear. "For, as I told you, the Cardinal wanted to keep the three objects available for all eventualities. That is why it is possible that the gifts may still be among Virgilio Spada's things."

"But where?"

"Villa Spada is small. If Capitor's great globe were there, you would certainly have seen it."

"True," I agreed. "But wait: I know for certain that Virgilio Spada did possess a large terrestrial globe, among other things, and that, unless I am mistaken, it was made in Flanders."

"Just like Capitor's."

"Exactly. It is now in Palazzo Spada. I have never seen it but I have heard tell of it. I know that visitors come from all the world over to admire the rare and precious collections in the palace; Cardinal Spada is very proud of that. If the globe is in Father Virgilio's museum of curiosities, we shall also find Capitor's dish there. But you should know all this. When we met at the Donzello, I seem to recall that you were writing a guide to Rome. . ."

"Alas," sighed Atto with a grimace of displeasure. "Do you remember when I broke off writing it? Since then I have not added a word. And, among all the palaces I have visited in Rome, that of the Spada is one of the few that I had still to see. Of course, I know from books and from other guides to Rome of the architectural treasures in which it is so rich, but no more than that. Now we shall have to find a way of getting in there."

"You could take advantage of the visit to the Palazzo to which Cardinal Fabrizio has invited all the guests next Thursday, the last day of the festivities."

"For the purpose of completing my guide to Rome, that would suit well; but not for finding Capitor's dish. Only three days remain until Thursday. I cannot wait that long. And then, what an idea! Can you imagine me fluttering from room to room like a butterfly, rummaging in chests and opening cabinets, with the house overflowing with guests?" said the Abbot miming with his arms the flight of a curious butterfly.

"Palazzo Spada, did you say? That would be no problem!" said a familiar, silvery voice.

The Abbot started.

"At last we have found them, Signor Buvat! I told you that they would both surely be here, my adorable little husband and your master."

Cloridia, followed by Buvat, had come looking for me, and had found me.

She had news for us. She had obtained all the information that she needed about where Atto and I were going from our two little ones (who, in their Mama's absence, always kept their ears well pricked up, ready to report all that they had heard in the finest detail), had co-opted Abbot Melani's secretary, who was also looking for us, and had entered the Vessel.

Such were the strange circumstances under which Cloridia and Atto, after having avoided one another several times over, met at last. Melani was about to repress a outburst of impatience upon hearing her voice when, turning towards her and seeing her face after so many years, his face suddenly changed its expression.

"Good day to you, Monna Cloridia," Atto greeted her, bowing, and with unexpectedly good grace, after a few moments of silence.

At the Locanda del Donzello, the old castrato had left a provocative, shameless courtesan of nineteen, and now he found himself facing a radiantly beautiful spouse and mother. My wife was very beautiful, far more so than when he had met her, but it was only at that moment, through the Abbot's admiring look, that I really saw her in all her splendour for the first time, free of the veil of conjugal habit, sweet though that might be. Her locks, no longer blonde and curled with an iron, but naturally brown, fell simply on her neck, freely framing Cloridia's face. Her eyelids free from cosmetics and her pale pink lips gave her a freshness which Atto did not remember in the young harlot of many years before.

"Forgive us for bursting in on you like this," began my consort, returning Atto's salutation with a curtsy. "I have news for you. The day after tomorrow, there will be a meeting in these parts between the three cardinals who interest you," she announced, coming straight to the point.

"When, exactly?" Atto asked at once.

"At midday. Take care, I beg of you," said Cloridia, with a slight hint of anxiety in her voice.

I smiled to myself. The news was too important for my wife not to pass it on to me. At the same time, my suspicions about Cloridia were now confirmed. Her initial impulse to help us had already cooled: she feared for me.

"Fear not, I shall watch over your husband," said Melani in honey-eyed tones, lying brazenly.

"I thank you," replied my wife, bowing her head slightly. "How magnificent! This is the first time that I have set foot in the Vessel," she added at once, looking all around her in astounded admiration.

Fortunately, the beauty of the villa had distracted her from her fears.

"Our Buvat cannot say as much. After all, I do not think he saw very much last time he was here," laughed the Abbot, remembering how Buvat had come to us covered in blood from the Princess of Forano's childbirth.

Atto's secretary did not hear what was said; he was already engrossed in reading the inscriptions on the walls of the room in which we stood.

"This villa is in rather good condition for one that has been abandoned for years: one would say it belonged to the Fortunate Isles, also known as the Isles of Folly, for there that goddess was born, there everything grows without sowing or ploughing, nor is there weariness, old age or disease; not, at least, according to my countryman, the learned Erasmus," added Cloridia quite spontaneously.

Atto and I gave a start. I was shocked by Cloridia's bold observation. I had not yet had occasion to tell her of the extravagant Dutch musician or his obsessive playing of one tune, the *folia*, spiced with curious maxims on folly. Yet she seemed to have guessed at all that, and what was more, as though it were the most natural thing in the world: the Vessel and folly. Not only that, she too, who had grown up in Amsterdam, had, like Albicastro, often heard of the encomium which their countryman from Rotterdam had composed in honour of madness. Certainly, I thought, my spouse's long familiarity with the arts of divination must have played its part. Atto seemed of the same opinion:

"You were once a past-mistress at reading the lines of the hand, if I remember rightly," said he, hiding his unease. "May I ask you what, in your opinion, bestows eternal youth on this uninhabited villa?"

"Simple: it is what the Greeks so rightly called a 'good state of mind' and which we for our pleasure may call folly."

"So you possess some arcane art which enables you to judge that the place in which we stand has a soul, a mind of its own?"

"What woman worthy of the name does not possess that art?" replied Cloridia with a facetious smile. "But now, tell me, I hear that you want to enter Palazzo Spada."

I summarised for her the complicated situation in which we found ourselves (and she listened with many expressions of wonderment); then I explained to her that we should need to search in the museum of the late Virgilio Spada.

"You happen to be talking to the right person: within a few days, the wife of the Deputy Palace Steward is due to give birth. For months now, I have been going regularly to check on her. It will be a long, difficult thing, the woman is very fat and I shall certainly need her husband's help. Thus, the palace will be unguarded."

"But there will be other servants around," I observed.

"You seem to have forgotten that they have all been transferred to Villa Spada as reinforcements for this week's festivities," retorted Cloridia with a sly smile. "Indeed, I'll tell you more: the Deputy Steward and his wife are temporarily lodging in a room on the ground floor, the better to keep watch now that the palace is empty. They, too, were supposed to be sent to Villa Spada, but because of the pregnancy they were left in the caretaker's lodge. That opens up a golden opportunity for us," she concluded confidently.

How sure of herself my Cloridia had become, I thought with some amusement. She feared for me when I was going around without her, but if, as now, she could accompany me or be nearby, she became emboldened, almost as though she felt herself to be a powerful goddess whose presence alone sufficed to make me invincible.

"And is there really no one else in the palace?" Atto asked dubiously.

"Of course, the guards are still there, but they make their rounds outside the palace, and that's all," explained Cloridia.

"We, however, need to enter Palazzo Spada as soon as possible," objected Atto. "We cannot wait for your delivery to arrive at its term."

"And where's the problem? I'll go and visit her today for a check on her progress: a few tisanes with good stimulating herbs. . . and 'tis done."

"Do you mean that you can make her give birth earlier?" I asked, taken aback, for my wife had never told me that midwives had that ability. "How is that possible?"

"Easy. I shall make her womb sneeze."

Atto and I fell silent, fearing that Cloridia was mocking us.

"Do you mean that a woman's uterus can sneeze?" the Abbot asked circumspectly.

"Of course. Just as though it were the nose. Take a dram of marjoram, half a dram of love-in-a-mist, add a scruple of very finely pounded cloves and white pepper for luck, half a scruple of nutmeg, white hellebore and castor and mix it all to prepare a fine, almost impalpable powder. One must blow several times into the woman's womb with a quill, and that will provoke sneezing marvellously. If that should not prove sufficient, one can throw a paste prepared by mixing the same powder with fat onto hot coals so that it produces smoke to make the womb sneeze. Obviously, it will first be necessary to open up the passage as wide as possible in advance, and that can be done by attaching a sheet tightly to the woman's navel."

"Excuse me," interrupted Abbot Melani anxiously, "are you sure this is not dangerous?"

"Of course not. On the contrary, these are remedies greatly appreciated by women's wombs, just like bringing odours of musk and amber before them: they have the effect of pulling them downwards, for they are attracted by such odours. I am sure that, thanks to such stratagems, the Deputy Steward of Palazzo Spada will soon be calling for me with all haste, as the infant will be about to come into the world."

"And what if it should not work?"

"It will work. Otherwise I shall make use of some simples which work extremely rapidly because of their occult properties, such as the aquiline stone tied to the thigh, or the doeskin, or seed of porcelain to be drunk mixed with white wine, or even a bitch's placenta pulverised and spread on the vulva; or the skins that serpents leave in March, to be fed into the womb. But this last remedy is less prudent."

Abbot Melani paled on hearing Cloridia list all those venereal manoeuvres so insouciantly.

"When would you expect that. . ." I began.

"Judging by appearances, as she's so fat, labour should not begin before tomorrow afternoon. Is that too late?"

"No, that will do well. Only, how shall we manage to enter and leave the palace?" asked the Abbot.

"Today, when I go to Palazzo Spada, I shall discreetly gather information and study the situation; tomorrow morning, I shall be able to tell you. There is only one thing you will have to see to on your own: the keys to the rooms."

"That will not be a problem," answered Atto with a little smile.

I knew who he had in mind.

Evening the Sixth

12ᵀᴴ July, 1700

✠

This time, my work place was in the garden, of course, need I say dressed as a janissary, setting up the artificial lights for the *opera galante* which was about to be staged. I was to work under the guidance of the Major-Domo, Don Paschatio Melchiorri, who in his turn had been well instructed by the architect of the scenery. The latter had in fact had a rather original idea: to make of these preparations, which were in fact quite unusual, a spectacle in its own right, to attract and entertain the guests while they awaited the start of the performance.

The area had been provided with a work table and, in the middle, a fire, on which a cauldron of water had been put to boil. A group of cardinals drew near, intrigued by these activities.

"We shall now put up various transparent colours for the embellishment of this evening's scenic jest, and first of all the colour sapphire, or sky-blue, which is also the most beautiful," announced Don Paschatio, resplendent in dress livery, in town crier's tones. I, meanwhile, followed him with a barber's basin and a brass vase under my arms, as well as a shoulder bag.

"Master of the Fowls, take a piece of sal ammoniac from your bag. Rub it on the bottom and the sides of the basin until it is all used up, then add a little water, but very little. The more the salt, the more splendid the colour."

I obeyed, after which he made me filter the water with a felt pad and pour it into the brass vase. I was astounded to see that the water which came out of this was sapphire-coloured. He then made me pour part of this into two large glass jars of a curious half-moon shape, one half of which was convex, the other concave.

"And now," proclaimed Don Paschatio, "we shall make Emerald Water." Thereupon, he drew from the bag a little jar containing a certain yellow powder which looked just like saffron.

He poured a little of this into one containing sky-blue water, stirred it quickly with a spoon and the liquid at once changed colour, becoming green.

We then dissolved some rock alum in the cauldron of boiling water, made it foam and decanted it through a piece of felt into five different containers, the last of which was almost as big as a cauldron.

"And here is the colour ruby," declaimed Don Paschatio to the bystanders, pouring into the first jar a few drops of highly coloured vermilion wine, which promptly dyed the water a rather bright red.

"And now for the Afghan red!" exclaimed the Major-Domo, pouring red wine and white together into the second jar.

Into the last two containers, he poured a Frascati wine and a little bottle of Marino red.

"And here for you, last but not least, the colour page-grey, and topaz!" said he smugly, while stupefaction was painted on the faces of all those lords and eminences.

"And this?" asked Cardinal Moriggia, pointing at the biggest receptacle.

"This remains as it is: it will reproduce the colour diamond, which is that of the sun in the Greek Islands," said Don Paschatio, who had never been to Greece and was with some success repeating parrot-fashion the instructions passed down to him by the scenery designer.

With this, the spectacle of the preparation of the colours came to an end. What we were about to accomplish next, explained Don Paschatio, was to be kept out of sight of prying eyes.

"Otherwise, if they discover the trick, there's an end to the wonder of it," said he, talking furtively.

With the help of other servants, we took the jars behind the painted backcloth, representing the countryside in Cyprus. There, we found a wooden panel with holes in it. We positioned the jars so that they filled these holes with their convex sides, standing them on tripod supports. On the concave side, so as better to receive the light, we placed a lamp designed to provide light of constant intensity.

"Lift the biggest container up there," the Major-Domo ordered me, "and instead of a lamp, put a big torch behind it. Then, behind that, place a well-polished shaving bowl so that the light from the flame is reflected forward as much as possible."

Great was my surprise when, emerging from the wings to admire the results of all these preparations, I beheld a lusty sun sparkling like a diamond in the painted Cypriot sky of the backcloth and shining paternally on fresh, luminous greenery and flowers coloured ruby, red and topaz, while the sapphire glint of the distant sea was capped by the page grey foam of the waves.

The stage had, moreover, been decorated with trees, hills, little mountains, grasses, flowers, fountains and even rustic huts, all fashioned from the finest of many-coloured silk. Thus, the liberality of the munificent Cardinal Spada and the art and skill of the architect, both enemies of ugly parsimony, had led to the destruction of much of the work of the Master Florist, so that all these things might be recreated in silk, making them even more praiseworthy than if they had been natural. The sea was rich in little cliffs, conch shells, sea snails and other creatures, coral trunks of every colour, mother-of-pearl and marine crabs nestling between the rocks, with such a variety of beautiful things that were I to attempt to describe them, I should expatiate for far too long.

The stage was simply lit with pairs of hanging torches, since the spectacle was to begin in the late afternoon when daylight is still bright and generous. Other lamps also gave both actors and spectators not only splendid lights but superb perfumes: bowls of camphor water were suspended above chandeliers or torches, so that, in accordance with the architect Serlio's formulae, they spread gentle glimmers and soft effluvia, thus preparing the hearts and minds of those present for the pleasures of the performance.

In the meanwhile, the terraces, furnished with comfortable sateen-upholstered armchairs, had filled with the noble public. I too stopped briefly to admire the stage: obviously, sitting on the ground. From my awkward position, far too much to one side, I could however overhear some of the comments of the guests seated in the front rows. A trio of gentlemen was particularly voluble; I heard them exchanging jokes while the actors were coming on stage.

"The last performance I recall attending was in March, at the Palace of the Chancellery: Scarlatti's oratorio '*La Santissima Annunziata*'," said one of the three.

"That for which Cardinal Ottoboni wrote the text?"

"That one."

"What was the Cardinal's verse like? Was it good?"

"Terrible. Far from an Ottobonbon, 'twas truly awful – just a load of Ottobombast," replied the other.

The three gentlemen laughed heartily as they joined the audience's applause welcoming the actors.

"Apropos things terrible, what do you think of Giovan Domenico Bonmattei Pioli's play?"

"The one that was published in January last year?"

"A real horror. It was commissioned by Ottoboni, who is a member of the most learned Academy of Arcadia, but Pioli's plays are really quite nauseatingly crude."

Smiles all round. It goes without saying that the Scarlatti oratorio in March, a good four months earlier, was by no means the last spectacle the gentleman "remembered" attending. . . What was, however, abundantly clear was the trio's scant sympathy for the Ottoboni faction. This cardinal enjoyed a considerable following at that moment and they were – like all good theatregoers and participants in the Roman social round – enjoying the opportunity for malicious gossip, with an elegant exchange of salacious jokes at their victim's expense.

"His Holiness must again be suffering from poor health," said the third gentleman, changing the subject. "Today was the ninth anniversary of his accession. At the Quirinale, they held a service in the Pontifical Chapel, but he did not attend."

"I can tell you what was wrong with him: he was suffering from the jostling he's been given by the Spanish Ambassador and his cronies."

"Really?" said one of the other two. "Do you mean that they have at last succeeded in convincing him?"

"A sick old man like him could hardly stand up for long to sly foxes of that calibre."

"Poor man, the thing must have lasted until lunchtime," added the third speaker. "His Holiness came out only in the afternoon, when he went forth into the city and received much applause."

"All merited, for that poor saintly, martyred Pope."

"Let us hope that the Lord will soon call him to his glory, to put an end to his sufferings; after all, there's nothing to be done now. . ."

"Quiet, *lupus in fabula*," said the third, pointing towards the drive from which Cardinal Spada was arriving, followed by the bridal couple, greeted by a renewed salvo of applause.

With a brief gesture, the master of the house called for the play to begin. This was a farce from the pen of the Roman Epifanio Gizzi, entitled *Love, the Prize of Constancy*. Both title and content were consonant with noble sentiments and with the gifts of fidelity and perseverance called for by the sacred bonds of matrimony.

The stage, still empty of actors, opened onto a series of effects most pleasing to the spectators. The architect had arranged for a number of sets of little lay figures to be prepared, cut out from thick cardboard and coloured, and these crossed an arch placed on stage, running along a wooden rail placed on the ground with a dovetail joint. The operator, who was none other than the architect himself, remained hidden behind the arch and the scene was accompanied by quiet music both vocal and instrumental. At the same time and by means of the same cardboard cut-out technique, the moon and the planets crossed the heavens, pulled invisibly by a black wire.

The operetta was well made and the public enjoyed it no little. The scene was set on the Isle of Cyprus. The protagonists were two gentlemen, Rosauro and Armillo, the latter accompanied by his coarse servant Barafone. With numerous ups and downs, the pair vied for the favours of two damsels, Florinda and Celidalba. After innumerable tricks and turns of fate (duels, shipwrecks, famines, disguises, fires, attempted suicides) it was revealed that Armillo was really called Alcesti and that he was Celidalba's brother, while her real name was Lindori. Florinda, meanwhile, after several times disdaining Rosauro's attentions, gave in at the end and even married him, thus showing that love is indeed always the prize of constancy.

The cavaliers wore splendid costumes, made of rich cloth of gold and silk, and even the servant's jerkin was lined with the finest skins of wild beasts. The fishermen's nets which appeared on the beach were of fine gold and the apparel of nymphs and shepherdesses, too, threw down the gauntlet to meanness.

While the actors drew the applause and laughter of the noble public, I cooperated backstage with the other servants in producing the most varied scenic effects. We simulated a stupefyingly realistic shipwreck. For thunder, we ran a large stone across the wooden floor; for lightning, we reeled across the stage a spool covered with sparkling gold which flashed just like the real thing. For sheet lightning, I stood behind the wings holding a little box in my hand with powdered paint in it and a lid full of holes; in the middle of the lid, there was a lit firework, of the kind that creates rather good effects of lightning. We put all the effects – thunder, lightning, flashes – together at the same time, with the greatest possible success.

The shipwrecked voyagers landing on the beach in Cyprus were warmed on stage by means of a fire which we lit using a firework and the most potent aqua vitae, and it lasted a long while, to the amazement of the spectators.

While I was thus working backstage, my mind was busied with very different matters. To what were the gentlemen referring whom I had overheard saying that the Spanish Ambassador, Count Uzeda, had at last succeeded in convincing the Pope? By the sound of what they were saying, it seemed that he and others had put pressure on the dying Pope to induce him to do something of which Innocent XII was clearly not convinced. Concerning Uzeda, I knew only what I had read in the correspondence between Atto and the Connestabilessa: the Spanish Ambassador had transmitted to His Holiness the request for help from Charles II.

Whatever could they have wanted to convince him of? And who were the other "sly foxes" who were supposed to have worked so unscrupulously with Uzeda to persuade the old Pontiff to yield? The three gentlemen whom I had just overheard were sincerely sorry for the Pope, who was suffering and seemed no longer to have any power. Did not these words bring to mind similar considerations on the part of the Connestabilessa? She had written that the Pope was often reported as saying, "We are denied the dignity which is due to the Vicar of Christ and there is no care for us." Who dared thus ill-treat the successor of Saint Peter?

Lupus in fabula, one of the three gentlemen had whispered when Cardinal Spada appeared, whereupon the conversation had broken off suddenly. What did all that mean? That my most benign master, Cardinal Fabrizio, was perhaps one of the "sly foxes" in question?

෧෨ඏ

"I am delighted to find that what the most learned Father Mabillon said about the libraries of Rome is still true, for they are still in the same excellent condition as when I first came to Italy many years ago," said Buvat enthusiastically.

After the performance, Abbot Melani had returned to his apartments, followed by myself, and had asked his secretary to report to him on what elements he had succeeded in gathering in the course of his research. The time had at last come to know what Abbot Melani's faithful servant had been up to in the course of his peregrinations across the city.

"Buvat, forget that Father Mabillon and tell me what you have succeeded in doing," Atto urged him.

The secretary examined a little pile of papers hastily annotated in minuscule handwriting.

"In the first place, I obtained the advice of Benedetto Millino, the former librarian of Christina of Sweden, who. . ."

"I am not interested in what he advised you. What did you find?"

Buvat said that this was precisely what he was on the point of explaining: he had been to the library of La Sapienza, to the Angelica, to the Barberini Library at the Quattro Fontane, to those of the College of the Penitentiary at Saint Peter's, the College of the Minor Franciscan Fathers at San Giovanni in Laterano, then the Penitentiaries of the Basilica of Santa Maria Maggiore; to the Vallicelliana near the Chiesa Nuova, the library of the Collegio Clementino, the Colonna or Sirleta, the libraries of Sant'Andrea della Valle of the Theatine Fathers and of Trinità dei Monti, belonging to the Minim Fathers of San Francesco di Paola, to that of the most Eminent Cardinal Casanate of happy memory, now taken over by the Dominican Fathers, as well as. . .

"Go on, go on. The main thing is that you have not set foot in the Jesuits' or the Vatican libraries. They are nests of spies and they would have registered and checked on everything."

"I did as you ordered me, Signor Abbot."

"And I hope that, in the third place, you abstained from visiting the private libraries of cardinals, like the Chigiana or the Pamphiliana."

"Yes indeed, Signor Abbot. That would have been far too visible, as you yourself did not fail to point out to me."

That triple abstinence had in fact cost him no little trouble, since in the Apostolic Vatican Library or that of the Jesuits, as well as in the libraries of cardinals' families, Buvat would have had far less difficulty in finding the manuscripts which he was looking for.

Fortunately, showing his accreditation as a scribe at the Royal Library in Paris, he had at once been well received at the other great libraries which he had visited. He had been able to touch and even to turn the pages of a Greek codex eight centuries old containing

the famous *Commentary on the Dream of Nebuchadnezzar* composed by
Saint Hippolytus, Bishop of Oporto; then he had for the first time
been able to consult the famous *Antiquities* of Pirro Ligorio in eighteen
volumes; and also, the works of sacred and profane erudition of the
Cavaliere Giacovacci and a Latin codex with the Acts of the Council of Chalcedon emended from the original. His palms had then
touched with trembling the personal library of Saint Philip Neri at
the Biblioteca Vallicelliana, in which are to be found the *Life of Saint
Erasmus, Martyr* written by Giovanni Soddiacono, a monk at Monte
Cassino, who subsequently became pope under the name of Gelasius II
(of which, Buvat stressed, the eighteenth volume contains, as is well
known, the ancient *Collation* of Cresconio), a most important codex
of the Venerable Bede on the Lunar Circle and the Six Ages of the
World and the collections of Achille Stazio Portoghese, Giacomo Vol-
poni da Adria and Vincenzo Bandalocchi, not to mention the famous
repertories of the lawyer Ercole Ronconi.

But the most moving visit had been that to the library of the College of the Propaganda Fidei, famed for its printing press where, with
magnanimous and providential zeal, and for the benefit of all nations,
books are printed in no fewer than twenty-two languages. A special
glory of this library, recounted Abbot Melani's secretary, is the most
accurate set of indexes of the books in its possession, including the
most unusual books printed in foreign nations, listed by languages,
varieties of customs, strange religious usages and habits; writings in
the most exotic characters, emblems, ciphers, hieroglyphics, colours;
and those with mysterious lines traced on elephant's leather, pork
rind, fish membranes and dragon's skin.

"Enough, Buvat, enough, damn you!" cursed Atto, beating his fist
on his knee. "What do I care about books printed on fish skin? How
is it that, whenever you have to do with books or manuscripts, you
always allow yourself to be distracted?"

Silence descended upon our trio. Humiliated, Buvat said nothing. I was impressed by the number of libraries which the French
scribe had visited; within a short space of time, he had been through
a great part of the bibliographic resources of the city – admittedly
situated a short distance from one another – which were universally
known to be immense, thanks to the accumulation over the centuries of books both printed and manuscript by dozens of popes and
cardinals. Clearly, only a boundless passion for letters and scripture

could have inspired so extensive and detailed a search. What a pity, then, that Atto's secretary found it so difficult to pass from analysis to synthesis.

"Buvat, I sent you out to search through books because in this city, everyone talks about certain things yet no one knows what they are talking about. Report to me only on what I ordered you to investigate: the *cerretani*," the Abbot requested. "So, what have you to tell me about their secret language?"

"It is very difficult," answered Buvat, this time in a distinctly less enthusiastic tone of voice. "The catchpolls can, it is true, learn a few rudiments, but only regular daily practice can enable one to understand correctly what it is that they mutter to one another. It is an ancient language but, from time to time, when they realise that it is no longer impenetrable, they renovate it a little, with minor changes, just the minimum necessary to make it completely incomprehensible once more. Rigid *cerretano* tradition requires that their king, or Maggiorengo Generale, and only he, may dictate the new rules. He writes them with his own hand (for which reason he cannot be illiterate) and the script is read at a general meeting with representatives of all the sects, who then arrange to spread the new codex far and wide. Thus, for centuries, only they have spoken their language, nor can anyone inform against them, not even when they steal the military secrets of the realm and pass them to an enemy."

"Espionage!" snarled Atto. "There, I knew it! That accursed Lamberg!"

"But how do they obtain secrets?" I asked.

"First of all, they always pass unobserved. No one pays any attention to an old, seemingly half-witted, beggar slumped by the roadside," said Buvat, "and yet he always sleeps with one eye open, observes when you enter and leave the house, sees who's with you, listens to your conversations from under the window and, if the opportunity presents itself, steals things from under your nose. What's more, there are so, so many of them, and word gets around very fast among them. Supposing one sees something, ten will know of it at once, then a hundred. No one can tell them from one another, for they all look the same, ugly and dirty, and above all no one can understand a word of what they say when they talk. Their sects. . ."

"Hold on: did you look in that book which I told you of?"

"Yes, Signor Abbot. As I thought, Sebastian Brant's *Ship of Fools* contains a chapter on German canters. They too have a secret language and are in close contact with the Italian *cerretani*. So much so that among Italian vagabonds there are groups known as *lanzi*, *lancresine* or *lanchiesine*, probably because those names come from the German *landreisig*, meaning stray and homeless. What's more, every group of. . ."

"Ah, so they're in close contact. Good, excellent; go on."

"Yes. *The Ship of Fools* is an excellent historical source for the study of canters and *cerretani* and their customs, 'tis perhaps even the first such book since it was published in Basel for the Carnival of 1494, while the so-called *Liber vagatorum*, which is regarded as the oldest surviving document on canters, was already circulating at the end of the fifteenth century but was printed only in 1510. . ."

"Get to the point."

Buvat hurriedly drew a sheet of paper from his pocket and read:

> *They speak a sort of pedlars' French;*
> *They beg and thus their thirst they quench,*
> *Their* doxies *clothe and bed and board 'em*
> *By* mumpin', filchin' *and by whoredom.*
> *They limp their way across the city,*
> *In robust health, arousing pity.*
> *And what they win, the canter* soaks,
> *Then rolls false dice the* bens *to hoax.*
> *He'll* beat his heels *and begone quick*
> *As soon as he has* pinched the wick –
> *He always plays it fast and loose –*
> *He'll snitch a hen or swipe a* deuce,
> *Which he* unleashes, grins *and sells*
> *To please the* heels, *and charm the* dells.
> *In the* wide-open, *in the mud,*
> *He'll cheat the* chewers of the cud.
> *Every which where, through town and village,*
> *These beggars scrounge and steal and pillage.*

"Here at last we have the gibberish, their secret language. Translate!"

"The *doxies* are the bawds, *mumping* and *filching* are begging and stealing, to *soak* is to drink, a *ben* is a fool, *pinching the wick* means to defraud, *to beat one's heels* means to run for it, the *wide-open* means the countryside, *deuce* is a goose, *to unleash* means to strangle, *to grin* means to cut off someone's head, the *heels* are the accomplices in crime, *dells* are buxom young wenches, and lastly *chewers of the cud* are the bumpkins and riff-raff."

Buvat had rattled all this off in one long breath, without the Abbot or I understanding a word of what he had said.

"Good, good," commented Atto. "Excellent, my compliments. So now, at least, the cant language is no longer a secret to us."

"Ummm. . . to tell the truth, Signor Abbot," stammered the secretary, "I did not translate the gibberish quoted by Brant: the edition which I consulted was annotated."

"What? Are you saying that you found no other terms for the cant language. . .?" Melani assailed him.

"No dictionary, manual or list. Nothing whatever, Signor Abbot Melani," confessed Buvat with a sigh. "So the language of the *cerretani* remains completely undecipherable. I guarantee you, no glossary exists which. . ."

"Are you telling me that you have been loafing at my expense for days on end in libraries," roared Atto, "sifting through old papers and scribbling, wasting precious time on Greek codexes, the acts of Church councils and other such idiocies, all to come up with *this?*"

"Really. . ." the secretary attempted to object.

"And I, who went so far as to intercede on your behalf to get you an increase in pay from that miser of a chief librarian of yours!"

"In any case, he did not grant me any. . ." Buvat dared contradict with a quavering voice. "But, getting back to the dictionary which you requested of me, Signor Abbot, you must believe me. . ."

"There's no time: we must act now."

❧

Ugonio had kept his word. As agreed, through a filthy little boy who acted as his courier, he had informed Sfasciamonti where we were to meet him.

The ride on horseback was initially free from danger or discomfort. The rendezvous was in a place outside the city walls, beyond Piazza del Popolo, at the cemetery of the harlots.

As we rode, I was able to question Atto without being overheard by Sfasciamonti, who went some way ahead of us, while Buvat trailed wearily behind.

"Yesterday, you said that Buvat was collecting evidence with which to entrap Lamberg. I must confess that your words were something of a mystery to me."

"It is quite straightforward. Unless one has a burning desire to arrive at the truth, one will never get at it," he replied with a smile, as though challenging me. "Anyway, it really is simple; just listen to me. The *cerretani* ambushed the bookbinder who, whether it was fate or something less, died as a result. What did they want from poor Haver? My treatise on the Secrets of the Conclave. This was a theft on commission, for those tramps would certainly not know what to do with such a thing. From Haver, the *cerretani* took all that they could. But afterwards, examining the stolen goods, the person who ordered the theft found that my treatise was missing."

"Because you had already withdrawn it from the *coronaro*."

"Exactly."

"And you are quite sure that Count Lamberg is behind all this."

"But of course. The prime mover, as one can see from the whole context, has excellent connections in Rome – men, money, protectors – and is interested in matters of high diplomacy. He knows full well that Abbot Melani too enjoys discreet support from several quarters and knows facts and persons that could prove decisive at the next conclave. All of this fits in perfectly with Count Lamberg."

While the clip-clop of the horses' hooves echoed between us, I chewed over Atto's explanation. I thought of the grim figure of the Imperial Ambassador, of his sphinx-like expression and the sinister fame that accompanied the Empire's meddling in Spain's affairs: the conspiracies, the mysterious deaths, the poisonings. . .

"The break-in at Haver's place was carried out by the *cerretani*," Atto resumed, "and just bear in mind the coincidence that in the German-speaking lands there also exist other canting sects which are somehow linked to the Italian ones. Lamberg may perfectly well be familiar with suchlike rascals who, thanks to their accursed skills, are capable of getting up to just about anything. Add to that the fact that our dearly beloved tomb robber Ugonio, alias the powerful German, who is in cahoots with the *cerretani*, also happens to come from Vienna. And this brings us to the next stage. Since the move against the bookbinder failed, Ugonio came to look for my treatise at Villa Spada. And this time, they found it."

"And the wound to your arm?" I asked, already guessing at the explanation.

"Easy. Lamberg wanted to intimidate me; and seriously. He hoped that I'd take fright and run away."

"So he did not mean to kill you. There is, however, something I do not understand: why, among all the diplomats and agents of His Most Christian Majesty present here in Rome should Lamberg have taken aim at you?"

"But it is quite obvious, my boy! He knows that my words and writings are heard and read by influential persons and that I can act on some of the most eminent members of the Sacred College, who are preparing. . . well, they're preparing for the next papal election, a matter which is obviously close to Lamberg's heart."

I was struck by Atto's hesitation in explaining why Count Lamberg should have wanted to filch his treatise. I had my own good reasons for this. From my clandestine reading of the correspondence between Atto and Maria, I knew that the conclave was not the only game involving the Pope, as Atto was trying to get me to believe. There was also the matter of the Spanish succession.

And precisely that aspect of the question remained unclear to me. Why had Atto, in reconstructing all that had happened to him (the theft, the wound to his arm) failed to make any reference whatever to the Spanish succession? Yet Lamberg, the Ambassador of the Habsburgs, must take a lively interest in the question, seeing that the House of Austria aspired to place one of its members on the Spanish throne!

I pretended to be satisfied with Abbot Melani's explanation and for the rest of the way we rode in silence.

Gloomy and sinister was the place where our meeting was to be held, and perfectly in keeping with Ugonio's lugubrious cowled silhouette which awaited us in the midst of the expanse of tombstones. Some nocturnal raptor disturbed the air with its eldritch screeches; the air of that warm night, almost as though impregnated with some black secretions from mortal remains, was in that neglected churchyard even denser, murkier, more torrid. Ugonio had chosen well: for a clandestine meeting, there could be no better place than the harlots' cemetery.

The *corpisantaro* approached, staggering under the weight of a great jute sack which he bore on his shoulders.

"What have you in there?" asked Atto.

"A merest ineptitude of nothingnesses. Jubilleous objectitions."

Atto circled him and prodded the sack with his hands. The loot creaked and clattered as though the bag had been crammed to the limit with all manner of objects: wooden, metal and bone.

"So business is thriving now that there's the Jubilee?"

Ugonio nodded with false modesty.

"This is a lady's hand mirror," Abbot Melani diagnosed, groping at a corner of the sack, "stolen from some poor dame as she prayed in church. The little purseful of coin just next to it will be the proceeds of alms obtained from the ingenuous by one of your dirty tricks, or else your ruffian's fee for taking a group of pilgrims exhausted by their travels to some overpriced doss-house. This must be a most holy sacrament filched from some distracted parish priest; and this must be a crucifix, perhaps lifted off some confraternity during their visit to the four basilicas, am I not right?"

The corpisantaro could not suppress a bestial half-smiling grimace which betrayed shame at the unmasking of his evildoing and gloating delight at the opportunities which the Jubilee offered him for satisfying his base appetites. He then drew a little book out from his greatcoat and handed it to Melani. It was in rather poor condition, and poorly bound; judging by its size it could not contain more than eighty pages. Atto opened it at the frontispiece as I craned over and read:

> *A new way of*
> *understanding the cant lingo.*
> *Or how to speak St Giles' Greek*
> *newly brought up to date*
> *in Alphabetical Order.*
> *A work no less pleasant than useful*
> *MDXLV*
> *In Ferrara by Giovanmaria di Michieli*
> *and Antonio Maria di Sivieri, Companions.*
> *Anno MDXLV*

"Aha!" the Abbot jubilated, flourishing it under Buvat's nose.

"What is it?" I asked.

"What my good secretary was supposed to find: a glossary enabling one to understand the canters' language – or Saint Giles' Greek, if you prefer. It will help us to understand what the *cerretani* are saying. 'Tis a good thing that I also asked Ugonio to find this somewhere," replied Atto, slipping a couple of silver coins into the *corpisantaro*'s claws.

"I bestole it off a goodlious old friendly," declared Ugonio with a mean snigger.

"From what I can see, it is an old edition; I doubt if it will be very reliable," interjected Atto's secretary, nervously scrutinising the book.

"Silence Buvat, and read it to me," the Abbot cut him short.

We began to leaf through the pages:

A

Abduct, to	To spirit away
Abscond, to	To pike, to scuttle off, buy violets
Allure, to	To spirit away
Almighty, the	Anticrot
Ambassador	Anticrot
Angels	Saint Uponhigh's heels
Anxious	A-gog, all-a-gog
Apothecary	Clyster pipe, Gallipot
Apprentice	Rum bob
Asking, or begging	Maunding
Assafoetida	Devil's dung
Attend to what I'm telling you	Rebecca the counterpoint
Avaricious	Fat, overweight
Ave Maria	The hurdy-gurdy song
Astrologer	Saint Uponhigh's paper dragon

AND CONTRARIWISE

Abbess, or Lady Abbess	A bawd, the mistress of a brothel
Abram	Naked
Abram Cove	A cant word among thieves, signifying a naked or poor man; also a lusty, strong rogue
Abram Men	Pretended mad men
To sham Abram	To pretend sickness
Academy, or Pushing School	A brothel
Accounts; to cast up one's accounts	To vomit

Agog, all agog	Anxious, eager, impatient
Air and exercise	He has had air and exercise, i.e. he has been whipped at the cart's tail, or, as it is generally, though more vulgarly, expressed, at the cart's a-se
Albert	Egg
All-a-mort	Struck dumb, confounded
Altitudes	The man is in his altitudes, i.e., he is drunk.
Amuse, to	To fling dust or snuff in the eyes of the person intended to be robbed; also, to invent some plausible tale, to delude shopkeepers and others, thereby to put them off their guard.
Anticrot	Ambassador
Anglers	Pilferers or petty thieves, who, with a stick having a hook at the end, steal goods out of shop windows, grates, &c.

B

Babes in the Wood	Criminals in the stocks, or pillory.
Basket-making	The good old trade of basket-making: copulation, or making feet for children's stockings.
Bawdy Basket	The twenty-third rank of canters who carry pins, tape, ballads, and obscene books to sell, but live mostly by stealing.

There followed all the letters of the alphabet, each with its double list of words from ordinary language and a translation into the jargon of the *cerretani*, and vice versa.

"'Tis a truly strange glossary," insisted Buvat, looking sceptical. "It mixes words with phrases, and then it makes for all kinds of confusion.

'Albert', the name of a person, means 'egg'. 'Anticrot' means 'God' and 'Christ', but also 'Ambassador'."

"It is still better than nothing," said Melani, silencing him. "Come now, let us test it. What did that *cerretano*, Il Marcio, cry out when we went to get him and Il Roscio?"

"'The saffrons. . .' and then 'buy the violets'," I said.

We leafed through the book and soon found what we were looking for.

"There, do you see?" Atto gloated, turning to his secretary. "As I thought, the saffrons are the police. To buy violets means to make a run for it. Il Marcio warned Il Roscio that we were in the vicinity. This book is by no means useless. But there's something else you must lend me. I'm sure you must have many copies of what I need," said Atto to the *corpisantaro*, miming with his hand the gesture of someone turning a key in a lock.

Ugonio understood at once. Nodding with a sordid, knowing smile, he pulled out from the old greatcoat a huge iron ring from which hung, clinking against one another, dozens and dozens of old keys of every kind, shape and size. This was the secret arsenal of which I have already spoken, giving the *corpisantari* access to all the cellars of Rome for their subterranean searching for the sacred relics from the sale of which they lived; but often, they were also used to enter and rob private residences.

"Good, very good," commented Atto, inspecting the heavy bunch. "In Palazzo Spada these will surely prove useful."

Out of the corner of my eye, I saw that Sfasciamonti, like every good catchpoll, could not wait to squeeze some information from the *corpisantaro* in his turn. He was still somewhat disoriented by that animal-like being, half mole and half weasel, so different from the ordinary criminals he had known; he came to the point, confronting him brutally.

"So, what did you learn?"

"I parleyfied with two Maggiorenghi," replied the *corpisantaro*. "The treaticise is to be presented to the Grand Legator, who in turn will present it ad Albanum."

I saw Atto grow pale. The tidings were doubly grave. Not only had the *cerretani* given Atto's treatise to a mysterious Grand Legator, but the latter would be presenting it to a certain Albanum. And who might that be if not Cardinal Albani, His Holiness's powerful

Secretary for Breves, the man with whom Atto had already had two venomous verbal clashes at Villa Spada?

"Until Thursday, where will they be keeping my treatise?"

"In the Sacred Ball."

"The Sacred Ball?"

I looked at Sfasciamonti. His face wore the same astonished, dumbfounded expression as Atto Melani's.

"Thus have they verbalised," continued Ugonio, hunching his shoulders. "Then the Grand Legator will exposition ad Albanum the insinuation, accusation and perquisition against the treaticise."

"Who is this Grand Legator?"

"I know not. I scented that they do not want to verbalise this to me."

Some coins (no few of them) moved rapidly from Atto's hands into those of Ugonio. As he slipped them clinking into a greasy little purse, the *corpisantaro* pulled his cowl well over his forehead, preparing to disappear into the shadows.

"Your treaticise corroborates a periculous and suspifect sapience," said he to Atto before leaving.

"What do you mean?"

"When they affabulate thereupon, the Maggiorenghi become tempestiphilious and agitabundant. . . almost neuromaniacal. Have a care, Your Enormity. And kindly refract from requestifying me to reference more and more news and ulteriorities to you: I don't want to end up with a broken colon-bone."

❧❧

On our way back, I dared not so much as address a word to Atto. This was no time for such things. From what we could glean from Ugonio's tortuous account, the *cerretani* did not care one bit for what Atto had written in those pages. We gathered that they intended on Thursday to bring the matter to the attention of a mysterious Grand Legator. The latter would go and see Albanum, in other words Cardinal Albani, with a formal summons against Atto.

So, who was this Grand Legator, if not Count Lamberg? A person of such elevated lineage could, after all, only be referred to obliquely; just as the *cerretani* had done.

What would Albani then do? Would he in turn report Atto as a French spy? After the arguments which had flared up between the two at Villa Spada, nothing would be easier for the astute Cardinal than to denounce Abbot Melani, his political adversary (for as such he could now be described) and crush him, causing him endless trouble, including perhaps an immediate arrest for espionage and political conspiracy.

More and more questions beset us: what the deuce could the Sacred Ball be, in which, according to Ugonio, Atto's treatise was to be kept until Thursday, and where was it to be found? Sfasciamonti was silent: he too seemed quite unable to help us resolve the enigma.

"I was forgetting. Lamberg has agreed to receive me," announced Melani.

"How did he inform you?"

"Did you see me hand him a note when chocolate was being served?"

"Yes. I remember that he replied, 'Very well, very well.' So, in that little note, did you request an audience?"

"Precisely. Subsequently, I asked his secretary, and he arranged the appointment: I shall visit Lamberg on Thursday."

As he pronounced that last fateful word, the day on which Atto would perhaps learn the truth about his stabbing, I heard a slight tremor in his voice. Watching him as he rode his nag, I knew that his soul was weighed down by yet another great anxiety. He felt himself to be at the mercy of two giants, Count Lamberg, the Imperial Ambassador, and Cardinal Albani, the Secretary for Breves.

And to think that he had come to Rome (or so he had told me) to take the helm at the conclave and to make his mark on the fate of the papacy! The navigator had become a castaway; and destiny, which he had meant to tame, was crushing the barque of his soul as cruel Scylla had done with the ship of Ulysses.

Day the Seventh

13ᵀᴴ JULY, 1700

✠

"Mistress Cloridia, I seek Mistress Cloridia! Open up at once!"

I know not for how long they had been knocking at the door of my little house. When I at last opened my eyes, I saw that it was still pitch dark. My wife had already put on her gown and was on her way to the door.

I dressed with all speed, while the sparkling freshness of the air suggested that we were in the hours immediately before first light, when the temperature sinks to its lowest. I rejoined Cloridia. In the doorway stood a little boy who had just alighted from a barouche; the wife of the Deputy Steward of Palazzo Spada needed her midwife: her waters had broken.

"Please hurry, quickly, Mistress Cloridia," the boy insisted. "One of the palace guards has paid me to come and fetch you. The lady's alone with her husband and doesn't know what to do. You're needed urgently."

"This we could have done without, we really could have done without," muttered my wife, stamping on the ground, while she gathered her equipment in a furious hurry. "Go and wake up the little ones," she ordered me, "and join us at once at Villa Spada."

"At *Palazzo* Spada, you mean," said I, correcting her.

"At the villa," she said. "We shall meet by the back entrance; and be sure to bring your big sackcloth cape with you."

"But I'm not cold."

"Do as I tell you and stop wasting my time," Cloridia retorted angrily, literally beside herself at my sluggishness in emergencies.

Still dazed and somnolent, I stared vacantly at my wife as she moved from side to side of the room, picking up a towel here and a jar of oil there. She stopped one moment to think, then took from the trunk a camisole and petticoat which she herself had worn when pregnant, wrapped them up in a bundle with a pair of clogs and other articles of clothing and in the twinkling of an eye leapt onto the barouche and urged the boy towards Villa Spada.

∂∾∾⊚

"The knitted stockings, too? Ah, no, that I cannot bear. Find another solution, Monna Cloridia."

"Do you want the Deputy Steward to ask me how it is that my assistant is wearing fine red abbot's stockings under her skirts?"

When I arrived at my appointment with Cloridia, I could not believe what the moon's grey reflection presented to my eyes: Atto, with his smooth, flaccid face half concealed under a white midwife's bonnet, and dressed in large women's clothes left over from my wife's last pregnancy, was mounting a last, vain resistance to Cloridia's expert hands as they lifted the skirts of his disguise.

Cloridia had dressed him well for the part of an old midwife and now, having discovered that under that attire the Abbot had secretly kept his favourite red stockings, was making him change them for a pair of knitted hempen ones of the kind worn by women of the people. It was these that had provoked Atto's rebellion. The old castrato, who had sung the most varied feminine roles in half the world's theatres, was not so ill at ease dressed up as a midwife; but, like a real prima donna, could not bear the vulgarity of those knitted stockings of the sort worn by any common woman.

"Would you rather go barefoot in your clogs, like a beggar woman?" Cloridia rebuked him impatiently.

"Good idea, you'd make a perfect *cerretana*," I interrupted, making fun of Atto by way of greeting, whereupon we exchanged winks.

While the barouche waited outside the gates, my consort rapidly summed up the situation. Unfortunately, her herbs had acted earlier than expected: Cloridia had counted on having the morning free in which to inform us about what she had been able to see and study at the palace the day before.

"So now we have no time," said she anxiously. "Anyway, I have learned that on the first floor there's a gallery, which is kept locked, and which Father Virgilio in person had built. It contains various objects, including the Flemish globe you mentioned to me yesterday. Perhaps you will find what you are looking for in that gallery. The Deputy Steward's lodgings are on the ground floor, on the right-hand side of the vestibule with its three small aisles; you'll find the stairs immediately after that. The rest I shall show you when we get there."

We moved towards the gates, followed by the little girls. During the ride, Cloridia explained her plan to me.

"I shall tell the Deputy Steward that, as his wife is fat, I have had to bring a trusty old midwife with me, as well as my daughters," and here she pointed at Atto, "because I need someone who, together with the husband, can hold the woman down while I induce her to give birth, while our two little ones look after the instruments, towels and all the rest."

From her little smile, it was, however, quite clear that Atto would need to make no great effort to mimic a woman's voice and movements more than convincingly.

Atto, then, was to pretend to be an assistant midwife; the thing was far from being without danger, even without considering the disgust which it caused the Abbot. How the deuce had Cloridia persuaded him to attempt this masquerade? I regretted not having been present when my consort was using her powers of persuasion.

"This is all very well," retorted Melani, "but you still have not explained to me how I am supposed to get away from the Deputy Steward's lodgings. I'd not want to run the risk of having to provide real assistance throughout the delivery and then having to return empty-handed."

"Trust me," murmured Cloridia, for we were already approaching the gate. "There's no time to explain it to you now, but I'll make sure you know when the time comes to leave me."

"But. . ." Atto tried to say.

"Hush, now."

"And what about me?" I asked.

"You, pretend to take your leave of us and, while I distract the boy who's driving the barouche, put on your cape and get onto the back axle."

My sweet wife had not thought any disguise necessary for me; ah yes, I thought with a trace of melancholy, my small size made it easy for me to slip in concealed. . .

❧

Once they had all got down from the barouche, I leapt up as swiftly and stealthily as possible and hid myself behind it. Fortunately, I thought with a smile, the presence of my two little ones in the barouche, well behaved but not without vivacity, created so much noise that it helped keep my presence hidden from the young driver.

When the carriage entered the palace courtyard, I stretched the cape even further over my head. The guards let us pass with a nod.

As Cloridia had advised us, the Deputy Steward and his wife, who had come from Milan not long before the pregnancy to take up service with the Spada family, were temporarily lodging in a small room on the ground floor, which enabled them to keep an eye on the entrance to the palace, now that the servants had all been sent to the wedding at Villa Spada.

I waited hidden in the coach-house. As agreed, Cloridia soon announced that she had left a purse in the carriage and, while the Deputy Steward and Melani took the service entrance to go to the woman in labour, she brought me surreptitiously in. We went up to the first floor. First, I tried out the key ring lent to us by Ugonio. As expected, I did not need to try many times and soon found the right keys. The locks on the doors yielded quietly one after another.

"Wait here and don't make a sound," my wife commanded me, kissing my forehead. "Soon I shall send you Mistress Midwife Melani. Keep a lookout here," said she, opening a window in the wide corridor which gave onto the inner courtyard still sunk in darkness. "Here's what I thought when I came to this place yesterday."

From this window, Cloridia showed me, I could see almost everything that was happening in the room where the woman was giving birth. This would be extremely useful. While we were searching, we could keep a constant check on the Deputy Steward's presence near his wife and thus be sure that the coast was clear. I had a quick look: Atto and the Deputy Steward were down there and I could descry the woman lying on the bed. I smiled seeing Abbot Melani got up like that: he must be on tenterhooks waiting for Cloridia. To keep up appearances, he was removing the equipment from the bag and arranging it by the woman's bedside. Yet he held each item disgustedly with his fingertips, as though he were picking up dead rats.

Cloridia returned downstairs, leaving me in the dark, and entered the Deputy Steward's lodgings. I saw her take three bolsters and arrange them on the floor. Then, to my great surprise, she made the pregnant woman lie down there on her back. She arranged the three cushions carefully under her so that her head hung back towards the floor.

The posture was quite uncomfortable and the poor woman was complaining, but Cloridia made matters even more difficult for her, or so it seemed to my untrained eyes, by bending her knees so that her feet ended up under her back, as in the drawing which I am reproducing below:

"How hot it is in here!" exclaimed Cloridia, opening the window of the room, so that from my lookout I could hear as well as see all that was taking place within.

"But is it really necessary for my wife to give birth in that position?" moaned the Deputy Steward, who could not bear to see his wife bent in such a horrid posture.

"'Tis surely not my fault if your wife is so fat. All the lard in her paunch compresses the womb and makes it even tighter. Only thus can the woman's uterus be dilated sufficiently for her to be able to give birth easily, however fat and corpulent she may be."

"And how is that?" asked the husband dubiously, turning also to Atto, who at once turned his eyes elsewhere with a vague expression on his face.

"Simple: the fat on the body spreads towards the sides," my wife replied, as though this were all perfectly obvious, "so that the infant is not prevented from coming out, as would happen if the birth seat were used, because the belly and the full weight of the fat and the intestines would compress the womb below and restrict the opening for the child no little, thus obstructing the delivery."

With the groaning woman lying thus arranged, Cloridia ordered the Deputy Steward and Abbot Melani (who, however, kept his gaze well averted from the woman's private parts) to hold her firm by both arms while she herself knelt between her legs, with a cushion under her own knees.

She covered the woman's pudenda and got our eldest daughter to hand her a terracotta jar full of oil of white lilies, with which she anointed both her hands and forearms and began to smear her patient's genitals and belly. Then with the greatest care, she thrust her right hand into the woman's privates and abundantly softened the insides with oil. Lastly, she ordered her to be turned on one side and also anointed the point four fingers above the ending of the back, known as the little tail or coccyx, which in childbirth sticks out no little, as I had occasion to observe when Cloridia gave birth to our two little daughters. She then made a movement with her hand which drew a resounding howl from the poor mother-to-be.

"Heavens, the canal really is narrow," complained Cloridia. "My friend," she then commanded, turning to Abbot Melani. "Go and get me the oil of yellow violets which is inside that glass jar."

She continued as before and then thought the time ripe to give our daughters a little lesson in obstetrics.

"If the woman in labour has a tight womb, one anoints freely and unrestrictedly with oil of yellow violets. And since one or ten applications of ointment cannot compensate for natural defects, one may use up to twenty or thirty, until – as Hippocrates and Avicenna proposed – art corrects nature. Avicenna also favours squirting a few drops of oil right inside the womb, the better to relax the internal parts."

The children paid attention, while the Deputy Steward and his wife, with her face all covered in perspiration, looked at one another full of admiration and gratitude for the knowledge of so fine, and renowned, a midwife.

I was beginning to fume: Cloridia had promised to free Abbot Melani, but as yet nothing was happening. And I could see that Atto, too, was in a state of growing agitation, casting eloquent winks in my consort's direction.

"Alas, there is not enough of this oil," said Cloridia. "My dear, please go and fetch the other bottle which I left in the bag."

Atto obeyed. When he returned, Cloridia looked at him with a worried expression.

"M'dear, you seem unwell."

"Well, I really. . ." whined Atto who did not know what Cloridia was getting at.

My wife began to scrutinise him attentively and asked: "Are you aware of any slight feelings of faintness? Lassitude? Do you feel confused?"

Abbot Melani returned Cloridia's inquiring gaze with an uncertain expression and answered her fusillade of questions vaguely. Then suddenly my consort rose and put her hands around his neck. Atto, taken by surprise, opened his eyes wide and tried instinctively to defend himself, while Clorida energetically opened his blouse and plunged her nose in, pretending to observe the breasts.

"Those red spots. . ." she murmured, lost in thought, prodding first the one, then the other breast, which I knew to be only stuffed with rags, while even the Deputy Steward's wife had left off complaining about her pain and was looking on with bated breath. ". . . and these purple ones here. . . My unfortunate friend, I fear that you may be suffering from the *petechiae!*"

"The what?" the other two both asked in unison.

"The spotted-fever; in Milan, they call it *segni,*" Cloridia announced to the couple, who looked frightened.

Upon hearing that phrase, Atto at last realised what had already been clear to me for several minutes. I saw him change expression and restrain a sigh of relief.

"This distemper is caused by the excess of heat and dryness," continued my wife, "and it tends to affect cholerical temperaments, as I know that of my colleague here present to be. My poor dear, you must go home at once and try to keep calm. Eat cold food, which will cool down the choler, and you will see that you will soon recover. We here shall manage without you."

"You can take my mule, which is in the servants' stables," said the Deputy Steward, exceedingly worried about the risk of contagion. "It is the only one left in there, you cannot go wrong."

"And the guards?" Atto asked in a weak voice.

"You are right. I shall accompany you."

"Of that, there can be no question!" Cloridia promptly cut in. "I need you here. Besides, you must avoid any possible infection. There must surely be some way out using a service door to which you will, I imagine, have the keys. . ."

My astute consort had seen and foreseen everything. The Deputy Steward opened a drawer and pulled out a key.

"I only have one copy of this," said the Deputy Steward to Atto, "but I beg you to. . ."

"You'll get it back promptly enough, of that you can be sure," my wife cut him short, snatching the key from his hand and giving it to the Abbot.

In reality, we had no need of that key: there would certainly be a copy in Ugonio's bunch, but that we could certainly not tell the Deputy Steward.

With a warm and amused wink, Melani lit a candle and, going to the door, left in great haste.

I leaned out an instant down the dark stairway to make sure that Atto had not forgotten Cloridia's directions and taken the wrong way.

"Your wife really enjoys a good joke," he commented as soon as he rejoined me. "She took me by surprise with that story of *petechiae*, but I must say that she does have an excellent memory."

Cloridia had in fact, in her little charade with the *petechiae*, merely quoted the sentences she had heard seventeen years before in the mouth of Cristofano, the Sienese physician and chirurgeon who had been shut in with all of us in quarantine at the inn where I was working, and where I had first met Atto. What he said had remained unforgettable for us; we all hung on every word from the lips of the doctor who was looking after us in those days when every moment was alive with the fear of contagion.

Since she had not had time to prearrange anything with Atto, my wife had therefore used those words to give him a clear signal; it was certain that, on hearing them, Abbot Melani would obey without thinking twice.

I guided Atto to the window on the corridor and explained that from there we could easily keep a check on the situation and thus avoid being discovered.

"And now," Cloridia was ordering imperiously, "avoid like the plague the ill wind that blows in draughts! Let us place your wife near the open window so that she may breathe the good sweet-smelling air of early dawn. But close the door tight, so that there are no draughts. We shall open up only once the child has been born."

"But I have to do my round every half-hour," protested the Deputy Steward.

"There can be no question of that."

"But. . ."

"You will appreciate the importance, if one is to avoid all risks of contagion, of avoiding all agitation and over-activity. The distemper dessicates and in a short space of time extinguishes the body's radical humidity, and that can in the end kill," declaimed our brave Mistress Cloridia, yet again quoting, this time solely for her own pleasure, the words which the physician had uttered so many years ago in the Locanda del Donzello.

Upon hearing those words, the Deputy Steward, suddenly as pale as death, hastened to close the door of the room, accompanied by my tenacious spouse's seraphic smile, as she again knelt between her patient's legs.

∽∝⦷

"Here we are."

Thus Abbot Melani commented on the swift movement of the door which, with a short squeal, swung open on a dark space.

We entered, immediately closing the door behind us. We did not know how much time we had in which to operate: everything depended upon the pregnant woman's labour, after which Cloridia was to be accompanied home by the Deputy Steward. By that time, we would have had to complete our own search and take the mule away from the stables, otherwise the Deputy Steward might become suspicious.

We tried to make sense of the dark space which now enveloped us. We shed light with Atto's taper, which I myself brandished, turning it here and there, in an attempt to reconcile our tentative footsteps with the frenzy of our eyes. The room in which we stood seemed enormous.

"This does not seem to be the gallery of which your wife spoke," commented Abbot Melani.

"Anyway, there are no globes here," I observed.

We crossed the room, then another one, then yet another. All the walls were covered with rich frescoes and paintings which filled the Abbot with enthusiasm and wonder.

"Ah, I recognise these paintings, they're by a Flemish artist, Van Laer; I saw them years ago in the collection of Cardinal Casanate, peace be on his soul," said he, stopping to contemplate four pictures depicting a cow, a tavern and two scenes of assassinations in the woods. "The Cardinal has been dead these four months only and the Dominicans of la Minerva to whom he left everything have already begun to sell off his legacy," said he with a bitter laugh.

While Atto kept stopping before every canvas, taper in hand, I made my way rapidly back, like a cat in the night, to spy on Cloridia through the window.

The woman's labour pains were becoming more and more excruciating and the poor thing was suffering greatly, but, as my wife had predicted, the birth was proceeding extremely slowly.

Seeing how the situation was slowing down, and despite his wife's entreaties that he should hold her hand, the Deputy Steward had not forgotten his custodian's duties and had, alas, returned to his desire to do the rounds of the palace's rooms.

Thus, on one of my incursions to check up on developments, I saw and heard through the window that, in order to detain him, Cloridia had took up her favourite argument: breast-feeding.

"You want to hire a wet-nurse, did you say? Ah, you must have money to waste! And what objection does your wife have to giving suck herself?"

"But Mistress Cloridia," stammered the Deputy Steward, "my wife must soon return to service. . ."

"Yes, to earn enough to pay the wet-nurse! Would it not be better to keep the infant at home?"

"We shall speak about that later, if we must. Now I must go out on my rounds. . ."

"'Tis incredible," my wife attacked, rising from her position near her patient and barring the Deputy Steward's way. "Now even the wives of artisans yearn to send their new-born infants to wet-nurses outside the home, as though we were all princes and most delicate princesses, while those folk, yes, 'tis true that they cannot afford the luxury of babes crying in the house as they are always weighed down by public business."

The Deputy Steward was speechless.

"Who does not know, after all," continued Cloridia, "that in every state and condition of persons, it is far better to raise one's children at home than to give them out to wet-nurses? Aulus Gellius confirmed that centuries ago!"

The man, who surely had not the least idea who Aulus Gellius was, seemed intimidated by the citation.

"In this, women today are truly more inhuman than tigers or other cruel beasts," she continued, "for, apart from women, I know of no animal that is unwilling to give suck to its young. How can a mother, after carrying it in her belly and feeding it with her own blood, not yet knowing whether it was a boy or a girl or a monster, once she has seen her child, recognised it and heard its cries, sobs and sighs calling on her for help, then exile it from her bosom and from her bed, pleased with herself for having given that child its being yet denying it all *well*-being, as though her breasts had been given her by God and nature as a mere ornament of the torso, as in males, and not to feed her children?. . ."

I had heard enough. I knew from experience that once she had launched into that subject, Cloridia would without difficulty detain the Deputy Steward for a long, long time.

I returned to Atto and we resumed our search as the first light of dawn filtered into the palace. Soon we had left behind us a long series of rooms superbly decorated with mythological and historical subjects: the room of Amor and Psyche, the room of Perseus, the stucco gallery, and then the rooms of Callisto, Aeneas and the feudal era.

"'Tis no good. There's no trace of the globe you spoke of."

At that juncture, we heard a series of screams, followed by a lacerating, interminable howl which almost caused Abbot Melani to faint. We ran to see: the Deputy Steward's wife had given birth. The herbs administered by Cloridia to stimulate delivery had worked more swiftly than our search.

"A bane on your wife and the day when we placed our trust in her," muttered Abbot Melani. "Now we are stuck here and we have discovered absolutely nothing."

At that moment, Cloridia looked up to the window, holding the squalling babe in her arms, already wrapped in a towel, and made a rapid signal in our direction, as though to say, "Go ahead, do not worry."

So we returned to our search, uncertain and cautious. We visited the Achilles room, that of the Tales of Ancient Rome and those of the Four Elements and the Four Seasons, moving on to the Great Gallery, the study and even the chapel.

"There's something here that doesn't square up properly," said Atto. "Let us return to the staircase."

"Why?"

"When we first came up from the ground floor, we turned right. Now, I want to turn left. Then I'll tell you why."

The Abbot, as I was soon to see, had his good reasons. Retracing our footsteps, we realised that, turning left immediately after climbing the stairs, there was a gallery which we had not yet explored. The daylight, which was growing brighter moment by moment, enabled us to see not only the walls, doors and windows, but also the very high ceilings which the eye should enjoy on the first floor of every noble palazzo.

As soon as we entered this new space, we stopped before a great candelabrum on the floor, whose candles we lit with our taper so that there was light all around us. Great was my wonder when we found ourselves facing a broad gallery, with a wealth of all kinds of frescoes, all kinds of works of art and the most precious furnishings.

It was quite clear even to untrained intellects that this room was one of the most splendid and eminent treasures of the entire Palazzo Spada, one that could not fail to be shown to the benevolent guest in the course of a humble visit.

It was a fairly spacious gallery, in the form of an elongated rectangle. On the one side, the walls were covered with frescoes and paintings, while the opposite side was subdivided into a series of great windows which in the daylight hours brightly lit the whole space, with, between them, a series of fine marble busts. The ceiling consisted of a curved vault which was adorned with an imposing fresco, the order and meaning of which I would, however, have been unable to understand at first glance, were it not for Abbot Melani's explanations.

Atto explained that the magnificent imagery on the ceiling stood for Astronomy and Astrology. I saw cherubs holding up a white velarium on which were drawn lines intersecting on the surface of the earth; at one end of the fresco, one saw Mercury bearing a meridian in the heavens, while the whole assembly of the pagan gods looked on in wonderment. At the opposite end were four female figures representing Optics, Astronomy, Cosmography and Geometry who were also intent upon creating a catoptric meridian, 'midst many other splendid and praiseworthy anthropomorphic figures.

On the walls there was an extensive and unusual series of splendid paintings, for the most part faithful and highly realistic portraits of illustrious men. Although I could not yet make out the details, it did seem almost as though there were a multitude of real faces looking down upon us. A great whitish crab was perched above our heads on the vaulted ceiling and seemed to be sternly observing us.

"Good heavens, Signor Abbot, look up there. Never have I seen so huge a crab, and what's more, creeping along a ceiling. And all white!"

"Well, my boy, here now is an opportunity for you to learn something. This is Palazzo Spada's celebrated Gallery of the Anacamptic Astrolabe."

"Ana- what astrolabe?. . ." I tried in vain to repeat after him, still keeping a wary eye on the great white crab which did not, however, for the time being show any sign of leaping on us.

"Or catoptric dial, if you prefer, to use the terminology of the learned Father Kircher."

For a moment, I fell silent.

"Did you say Kircher?" I asked, recalling how we had come into rather close contact with that personage in the course of our adventures seventeen years ago.

"If you were to read newspapers from time to time," was his only reply, "you would sooner or later learn something about the marvels of your city."

"Yes, I knew that Palazzo Spada abounded in architectural marvels and that people come to admire it from all the world over, but. . ."

"I imagine that you at least know what a sundial is," said the Abbot, cutting me short.

"Of course, Signor Atto. It is a clock in which the shadow cast on given points by a certain object, like a stone or a piece of metal, enables one to tell the time."

"Correct. This, however, is a special dial: it functions catoptrically, to employ Kircher's terminology. In other words, not thanks to the sun's rays but to reflection. Do you know what there is down there, outside?" said he, pointing to a sort of little window that gave onto the courtyard.

"I do not know."

"A stand with a mirror on it which reflects the light of the sun and the moon. The Spada household has mirrors of various forms and designs which reflect sun or moon-rays and project luminous images like your white crab. This, as you can now see, is nothing but light refracted onto the ceiling of the gallery, which thus gives the exact time."

I looked up again: he was right, the beast was white because it was drawn on the ceiling by a ray of light.

"And it tells the right time?" I asked incredulously.

"Certainly. You too can surely see those lines marked on the vault, which permit anyone who can read them to follow the hours and minutes on the ceiling of the gallery, so long as the light is a little stronger than this candelabrum. For the whole thing is an immense sundial, but upside down. The light does not reach it from above but rather from below. That crab is reflected moonlight, and I suspect that it takes the form it has because in these July days we are in the sign of Cancer, the Crab. This is probably done by using a mirror of the right shape."

Atto's explanation was interesting, but it was I who interrupted it with a cry of surprise.

"Look, there's the Flemish globe! Indeed, there are two of them."

We drew near the better to examine our find. Further down the gallery, there were in fact two wooden globes, one representing the terrestrial regions, the other, the heavens. We read the name of their maker, a certain Blauew of Amsterdam.

"Alas, if this is indeed a terrestrial globe like that of which you have heard tell, it has nothing to do with Capitor's globe," said he in weary, opaque tones.

"It is not the one?"

"No."

The globe which stood before us did not in fact much resemble that in the picture, and it did not even have a golden pedestal.

"So, what now?" I asked.

"It is no good. We have made a mistake. Once again, we have got everything wrong," groaned Atto, sitting wearily on a chest.

I raised my eyes, drawn by something on the wall opposite. My gaze drew near to the series of portraits decorating the window-less wall and stopped deep in thought at one of them. This was the likeness of an individual with a severe face, whose expression was strong but gentle, his forehead broad, the mouth decisive and the beard bristling. He wore a tricorn hat similar to those of the Jesuits, and an embroidered surcoat with on its breast a heart betwixt two branches.

"There he is. I present to you Virgilio Spada. As I have told you, he was a member of the order of the Oratorians, followers of Saint Philip Neri, and the portrait here is in accordance with their precepts. He was a wise soul, and quite pious. He helped his order in many ways, above all materially."

All around, I saw portraits of other members of the family, but Atto barely deigned to spare them a glance. For a while longer, he remained pensive, then he shook his head.

"No, we are mistaken. This is not it."

"What do you mean?" I asked, without knowing where to turn my thoughts.

"Have you looked around you, my boy? Where the Devil is Virgilio's collection of curiosities? I can see no trace of it here. We've not even found one tiny bit of it here. And yet it must be clearly displayed somewhere, seeing that the family loves receiving distinguished visitors and showing them its possessions."

"And so?"

"This portrait tells me something."

"What?"

"I do not know. I must think on that, now I am too tired. Let us go, Cloridia may have finished."

After saying this, the Abbot moved slowly towards the door, bent by the weight of years and fruitless searching.

As I followed him, I continued to feed greedily on the marvellous, but to me, incomprehensible, decorations of the catoptric sundial.

"Signor Atto, all those signs and numbers painted up there, what are they?"

"Those numbers are the houses of the zodiac with the astrological tables for the compilation of the celestial figures, or the birth chart and horoscope, while the other lines that you see show the times in various parts of the world," explained Atto, stopping and looking up.

"Was Father Virgilio also interested in all these things?" I asked perplexed, being well aware of the deadly risks that a churchman could run for showing an interest in horoscopes, especially half a century ago.

"Oh, if that's all you want to know, the Spada have always had a passion for the celestial sciences. Virgilio and his brother loved astrology, including the forbidden forms of it. As I have already told you, I was in Rome when Virgilio died in 1662. It is said that he even possessed books placed on the Index by the Holy Office, as well as some writings regarded as heretical, which, however. . ."

The Abbot broke off and stood there staring at me as though seized by a sudden thought.

"Boy, you are a genius!" he exclaimed.

I gazed questioningly at him.

"I know where we shall find Capitor's dish," said he.

So it was that Melani explained to me, in a barely audible voice, that Virgilio's great passion had been for judicial astrology, or that which dealt also with horoscopes and predictions; he had studied his own celestial chart and his father's, and many others too. In 1631, however, this science had been condemned by the Barberini Pope, Urban VIII.

"I remember that well, from the tales I heard at the time when we met, at the Donzello."

"Then you'll remember the ugly death that Abbot Morandi met with when they discovered all those books on astrology in his possession."

I repressed a shiver as I recalled what I had learned at that time.

"When that happened, many prelates with an interest in the subject took fright. Among their number were Father Virgilio and his brother Bernardino: it was said that Virgilio had moved a number of dangerous books by night from Palazzo Spada to the Oratory, where they were kept under lock and key in a great chest until his death."

"In other words, it is at the Congregation of the Oratory that we shall have to search."

"Yes. It will be pretty difficult to evade the surveillance of the Philippine Fathers, and I really do not think that your Cloridia can be of any help to us this time."

After leaving the Gallery of the Catoptric Sundial, we returned to the window whence we could espy my sweet consort. We found her still in full flow of her sermon, while she collected, cleaned and put her things in order together with our two little daughters; while so doing, she turned her sanguine prose to the ever more perplexed Deputy Steward who, in the meanwhile, to regain something of his composure, was caressing and consoling his exhausted spouse.

"It is even worse when, in order to avoid paying a wet-nurse, or because she has grown weary of giving suck, a mother makes her little one drink the milk of beasts. You may be certain that, once her child has tasted of that poison for body and soul which is animals' milk, it will have difficulty digesting and will thus be too full to be drawn to its mother's breast, which it will come to forget."

We waved our arms from the window to let Cloridia know that our search was at an end, that she need trouble herself no longer and could put an end to that flood of words with which she was holding back the Deputy Steward, but all in vain. Caught up in the whirl of her pleading, my wife did not notice us. What was more, we had to take care not to be seen by my little ones who might, in their innocence, give us away.

"The truth is that goat's milk makes children into goats, and cow's milk makes them into oxen. Now, what father or mother would want a child as feeble-minded as a calf or horned like a goat? Or both together? The animal spirit twines itself around the radical humidity of the infant's little body and will not abandon it until it dies. Take a good look at the faces of children who have received cow's milk: the acqueous, bovine stare, the hooded eyelids, the fat head, the swollen members and the flaccid, pallid skin. And what of the nature of these little unfortunates? If it is not tetchy and taciturn, like that of a goat, it will be placid and temperate, like that of a calf. And how proud their stupid mothers are of them! They can do what they will without being bothered by their stolid, bastardised little ones, while they look on with disgust at other mothers, exhausted by giving suck and weary with caring for their tireless, lively little earthquake of an infant."

At long last, Cloridia caught sight of us.

"In conclusion, have a care before giving animals' milk to a being whom God had endowed with a soul!" said she with a voice almost broken by her bombast, while she began to put her equipment back into her bag. "Until three years of age, no child should touch a single drop of the milk produced by beasts. And even after the age of three, this will be most harmful. So everyone, both fathers and mothers and their little sons and daughters, should keep well away from beasts' milk throughout their lives, if they mean to live in good health and clarity of mind. *Deo gratias*, we have finished."

She crossed herself, as she did after every birth, and we heard her impart her last recommendations to the new mother as Atto and I rushed to the stables and the mule which was to take us back, weary and disappointed, to the Villa Spada.

We were already in the inner courtyard, still asleep under the mists that herald the early morning, when we heard a grim, disquieting sound. It came from our left, where there stretched out an immensely long gallery of singular magnificence, followed by an equally long avenue, flanked by hedges and terminating in a garden.

It was then that we caught sight of a dreadful colossus, a quadruped higher than two men and as long as a carriage, as black as night and covered with thick, disgusting hair. For a few interminable moments (at least so it seemed to me) I was paralysed with terror, almost hypnotised by that infernal monster. I saw it leap over the hedges in the avenue and rush at an unimaginable speed towards us, again emitting the thunderous roar which we had just heard.

With a superhuman burst of speed, I fled, forgetting even Abbot Melani, and in the twinkling of an eye I had shut myself into the stables.

Atto was already there: unlike me, he was clearly unperturbed and had got out of the way at once.

"The monster. . . the colossus. . ." I panted, my face contorted with terror.

I looked at Melani. He had a grin imprinted on his face.

"What do you find so funny?" I asked, thoroughly irritated.

"What you too will soon see. Follow me."

A few minutes later, Atto was at the opening of the gallery, seated on the base of one of the columns, tranquilly caressing the colossus. For it was no colossus at all, but a nice little dog. The creature had been sleeping out in the garden beyond the gallery and, surprised by my arrival, had reacted with a typical canine growl, then drawn near to challenge the invader. What had seemed to me a monster of incredible proportions was in reality a little animal that came up to my knee.

"Do you understand?" asked Melani.

"I think so, Signor Atto."

Yet it still seemed incredible to me. The gallery from which the dog had emerged was a masterpiece of the great Borromini, whom the Spada had often employed to improve and enlarge their palace. It was so constructed as to delude the observer, through a clever play with perspective which only someone who knew the trick could detect. As the visitor entered the gallery, it grew steadily smaller: the pairs of columns by either side became lower, the black and white chequerboard paving went upwards and grew narrower, while the squares themselves became smaller, imitating the flight towards infinity which painters know so well how to simulate in their creations when they depict roads, cities and temples.

Even the stucco mouldings on the semicircular vaulting were formed into an ever smaller quadrangualar grid, so as to keep in proportion to the shrinking of the vault itself. Beyond the other end of the gallery, there was no spacious garden stretching out to infinity, but a modest little courtyard in which, however, imitation box hedges had been carved from stone and painted with two coats of green. With their regular parallelepiped form, these became ever lower and narrower as the distance from the gallery, and thus, from the observer, increased, thus creating the irresistible impression of a distant avenue running to meet the sky. The sky itself, which I had thought I saw behind the hedges, was in fact painted with clever chromatic counterfeiting a few paces beyond, upon the wall that concluded the whole illusion.

I entered the gallery and timidly caressed the first pair of columns, then the second, then the third. . . each time narrower and lower. Borromini's optical illusion was so cleverly designed and carried out that it had tricked me to the extent even of terrifying me. Besides those sham hedges, even that little dog had seemed to me gigantic. Its growl, distorted and amplified by the echo of the vault, had seemed on reaching me to be the roar of a wild beast.

"We fear what we cannot understand: here, as in the gallery of mirrors at the Vessel," said Melani in paternally admonitory tones as we trotted on our mule back to Villa Spada.

"I had heard tell of Palazzo Spada's gallery in perspective and of its marvellous optical illusion: princes and ambassadors come to visit it from all the world over. But I did not know what it might be and, caught unawares, I took fright. . . You know, I am very tired. . ." said I, trying to justify myself and to cover my shame.

"You saw an immense portico, which in reality was very small. Within a small space, you saw a long road. The more distant they are, the larger small objects can appear, rightly placed," Atto philosophised. "Greatness is but an illusion on this earth, the wonder of art and the image of a vain world."

I knew what he really had in mind: the Vessel. But not the gallery of mirrors. Rather, he was meditating upon those mysterious apparitions which we had witnessed, and upon his faint hope of finding a rational explanation for them in the end.

I therefore said nothing, while we wended our weary way across the Holy City, meeting the first passers-by, still half wound in the coils of sleep, and formless nocturnal cogitations made way for clear thinking.

❧

On our return to Villa Spada, we found a letter for Abbot Melani: the usual one. Atto's reaction upon opening and reading it was no different from the times before: he became sombre and dismissed me hastily, on the pretext that he wanted to take a rest. In reality, he had to reply to the letter, in which the Connestabilessa announced her latest delay.

In the hours that followed, I was unable to enjoy so much as one moment of rest. The programme for the day consisted of a rather demanding entertainment, and Cardinal Spada had repeatedly insisted to Don Paschatio that he was counting on him to ensure its complete success, informing him that any servants who failed to fulfil their duties would be most severely punished. Don Paschatio had for his part ensured that, this time, none would dare absent themselves: he had, of course, sworn as much on all previous occasions, without being proved right. This time, too, a pair of waiters had let the Major-Domo down, on the pretext that they were ill (whereas they had in fact gone fishing on the island of San Bartolomeo, as I had gleaned from their conversation the day before).

There was indeed a great deal of work to be done, nor was it easy to carry out. For the guests' entertainment, there had been laid on a shooting party, the game being birds. This outing was open not only to the gentlemen and cavaliers present but to ladies too, since the hunt for fowls involves no dangers, only joyous recreation. This was, in other words, to be a pleasure party, consisting of many and various kinds of hunting merriment, as had been announced to the guests the day before by no less than Cardinal Spada in person.

The territory of Villa Spada was, however, too small for the beat, which would require much space in which to hide, set up ambuscades and entrap birds. It had therefore been agreed with the excellent Barberini household that the entertainment could also take place in the plot of land adjoining the Spada estate (where, two days before, the falconer had tried in vain to catch Caesar Augustus with his hawk).

The guests were to be organised into groups, according to the means they would be employing. The first squad, consisting of about ten people in all, was to be issued with special bird traps: sham bushes within which had been set a Y-shaped wooden stick. This stuck out from the top of the bush and at either extremity were placed two pieces of iron rather like scissor blades which, operated from a short distance by means of a long, thick cord, would snap shut, crushing the bird's legs.

The second group of huntsmen received a number of artificial trees, to be planted in the earth with the sharp point at the base of their trunk. At the top of these little trees was fixed a horizontal stick which would look quite inviting to birds seeking a perch. At the base of the bush was hidden a great crossbow, pointing upwards, into which was notched a sort of big rake with many sharp points. If fired at the right moment (even from a short distance, by activating the trigger of the crossbow with a stout brown string) the bizarre mechanism would shoot up and impale any unlucky fowl perching on top of the tree.

For other participants, special arquebuses had been prepared, to be set into the ground (by means of a handle with an iron point) to be aimed at some clearly visible branch and fired the moment some passing bird came to rest there. Here too, the arquebuses were to be operated at a distance by means of an invisible thread.

Those cavaliers gifted with sharp eyesight were given fine crossbows of the highest quality with which to shoot at birds in flight.

The most able-bodied gentlemen were equipped with real portable trees, capable of concealing a whole man and his arquebus. These were made from papier mâché covered with bits of bark and mounted on an iron frame. They were furnished with false branches covered with an abundance of twigs. So that these could be worn, they were equipped internally with leather belts which made it possible to carry the simulacrum of a tree on one's shoulders while leaving the arms free. The guest could look through two little apertures and freely approach his victim, take aim with his arquebus, slowly pointing the barrel through the appropriate slit, and fire with assured success. This ingenious invention, designed on the basis of the advice of Gioseffo Maria Mitelli, from Bologna, son of an artist and painter of frescoes who had done much work at Palazzo Spada, gave rise to such praise and wonderment that I am providing a drawing of it here:

Others, who were more adventurous, were to attempt the so-called hunt with an ox. In other words, they used imposing sham cows, painted in oils with the greatest verisimilitude on canvases mounted on wooden frames, to be used as screens behind which to stalk the prey without frightening it off, and then shoot it with an arquebus. To paraphrase more noble examples, one might call these real Trojan cows. I have also provided a drawing of this expedient, but I have other reasons for so doing:

In fact, the cow, as soon as it was set up in the field, scared all the animals on the Barberini estate, and some ladies too. This was because the bovine effigy, being painted in oils, shone with such lucent splendour in the sun that it seemed almost like a burning mirror. It had therefore to be rapidly withdrawn, otherwise all the birds would have flown off in terror.

Of course, in order to be able to attract a sufficient prey, it was necessary to stock the area of the merry hunt with a great number of song birds, so that their warbling would attract their fellows. For this purpose, many cages had been purchased full of chaffinches and goldfinches. Given my occasional role as Master of the Fowls, Don Paschatio had entrusted me with the important task of placing these cages at strategic points on the Barberini estate, making sure that each group of hunters should have the same number of these baits and that they should be uniformly positioned throughout the hunting grounds. To reinforce the effect, I was also to tie other song birds to the stems of plants and to trees, securing their legs with thread.

As I was gathering the cages and carrying them two by two to the Barberini estate, I encountered Don Tibaldutio. As often happened, he felt like conversing a little with me. I have already mentioned that he lived apart from the rest of the villa in a little room behind the chapel, and often felt somewhat lonely. I therefore proposed that he should keep me company while I laid out on the ground, on the trees and in the midst of bushes and shrubs the cages containing the birds which were to serve as bait.

Hardly had the chaplain begun to speak of this and of that when his upright and chaste presence revived like an invisible flame the burning memory of the night before.

Atto's memoir was, I thought once more, to be brought "ad Albanum": thus, behind all these shady affairs there was a cardinal, no less! What malign force, what infernal ladle was capable of mixing in the cauldron of the Holy City a highly placed cardinal, the right-hand man of His Holiness, and the diabolical sects of the *cerretani*? I then remembered that the *cerretani* had originally been defrocked priests. How was that possible? Only an ecclesiastic could enlighten me on this point.

As a good pastor, Don Tibaldutio listened to my questions without batting an eyelid. I pretended that I had heard rumours in the street concerning the religious origins of the sects of mendicants.

"Age-old is the scourge, and wrapped in mystery, its origins," the Carmelite began gravely.

It all began after the barbarian invasions which put an end to nine centuries of Roman domination of the world. In those days, men were for the most part poor peasants and lived in small, isolated rural communities. The roads were unsafe, many the bandits and masterless soldiers, and the bears and wolves on the lookout for prey. Friars and monks remained in the safety of their monasteries, often built on inaccessible heights. Apart from the merchants, who had to travel for their trade, everyone lived in villages, working the land and praying God for the next harvest. But they were not alone: regularly, visitors would arrive.

They were dressed in rags, haggard and dirty, and they asked for charity. They came from obscure places on the edge of villages, abandoned lazarets, little gaggles of hutments, almost a parallel civilisation devoted to filth. They were known as vagrants, degenerates, knaves, rascals, or tricksters and swindlers, if you prefer. But they were not poor: their poverty was only a disguise. They knew well how to profit from the words of the Evangelist, which call on all good Christians to practise charity: "Give *alms* of such things as ye have; and, behold, all things are *clean* unto you."

"Some, perhaps, had been priests," said Don Tibaldutio, "but instead of honouring the Lord with prayer, they had given their souls to the Evil One."

They would choose the humblest among the peasantry, ignorant of the world and its snares, and present themselves to them in unusual guises, with wild eyes halfway between folly and wisdom. They pretended to be all at once healers, magi and prophets, saviours of body and soul. They sold talismans, relics, miraculous orations, magic spells against the evil eye, ointments and panaceas; they announced miracles or divine punishments; they interpreted dreams; they miraculously found hidden treasures and rich inheritances which had been concealed; they exorcised and cast anathemas, thundering against sinners and promising heaven to the just. In the course of all this, they asked for and invariably received offerings in money.

Begging for alms (which was thus both their purpose and their method) they were past-masters of suggestion, illusion and swindling, as the learned Gnesius Basapopi tells so well. When they practised flagellation, from their wounds gushed false blood – that of cats and chickens. But invariably they took alms and tribute in plenty from the credulous and simple, who were legion. Besides, did not the Sophists, too, have a reputation for being jugglers and charlatans, and, moving beyond them, even Socrates and Plato? None of those peasants remembered the admonition of the Bishop of Hippo, that one should give to the poor, but not to play-actors.

"But were they never unmasked?" I objected, as I took a goldfinch from a cage, tied its foot to a piece of twine and secured this with a nail to the trunk of a young acacia.

"Of course, from time to time, a victim would react. But this was rare, and in any case, when it did happen, those rascals would change their skins like serpents and return to their former trades as tumblers, rebeck players, even tooth-pullers because, as that verse of Theocritus puts it, *paupertas sola est artes quae suscitat omnes:* poverty alone gives rise to invention."

Then he sang:

> *By lies and by tricks*
> *You can live half a year;*
> *By tricks and by lies,*
> *Live the other half too.*

"What's that?" I asked, as we moved on to the area where the arquebuses had been placed.

"An old rhyme of false beggars: just to help you understand how corrupted their minds are."

But there was more to it. Insistent rumours had it that the *cerretani* had all united in a single sect. Following this, their high priest had founded the various subdivisions, not so much in order to organise them according to their specialisations as for a satanic purpose: the imitation of the religious orders of the Catholic Church.

This hypothesis was not to be underestimated, for Bernardino of Siena tells how one day Lucifer, surrounded by all his demons, manifested to them his desire to start a church in contraposition to that of Christ, an *Ecclesia malignantium* wherewith to cancel out or at least mitigate the effectiveness of the other, celestial Church, upon which it was modelled. Even Agrippa of Nettesheim, who did not much believe in witches' spells, was so certain of the malefic powers of the canters that he went so far as to accuse them of practising black magic.

With time, matters got worse, explained the chaplain, as I checked on one of the arquebuses planted in the ground, to make sure that it was indeed well aimed. Even the genuine religious orders were infected by the scandal. The monasteries got wind of the freedoms enjoyed in the world: it was necessary only to serve up a little nonsense to the ingenuous. The body came then to prevail over the spirit, eating and drinking over prayer, sloth over works consecrated to the Lord.

"Wearing black vestments, as Libanius writes in *Pro Templis*, the monks ate more than elephants. They were men in appearance, yet they lived like pigs, and they publicly tolerated and committed acts of the foulest, most unspeakable turpitude. As Saint Augustine well knew, the enclosed orders of friars were reduced to an ignoble, muddy Gehenna," he exclaimed, casting a compassionate glance at a robin I had found dead in one of the cages, perhaps killed by the strain of being carted around thus.

Monks and pseudo-monks, excommunicated by their own bishop, swarmed out from the cloister and began to wander unpunished on the highways, perturbing the peace of the Church and spreading further corruption amongst the good people. They joined the multitudes of true and false tramps, ragamuffins, layabouts, lepers, gypsies, vagabonds, cripples and paralytics lying in front of church doors, and made them their impure flocks.

Now all doors were open to their cunning. Yet none could do anything about them, because they were poor, or at least, so they seemed and, as Domingo de Soto teaches in his *Deliberatio in causa pauperum*, in case of doubt, one should nonetheless give one's coin to those who beg. *In dubio pro paupere.*

"Not only does the practice of charity cancel out sin but, as Saint John Chrysostom puts it: the poor beggars piled one on another in church porches are the physicians of the soul. Indeed, Peter Chrysologos preached that, when the poor man stretches out his hand to ask for charity, it is Christ Himself who does so."

"But, if it is as you say, then roguery is the daughter of compassion and thus, indirectly, of the Church itself," I deduced with no little surprise as I placed a few crumbs in a cage.

"Oh, come now. . ." Don Tibaldutio stumbled, "I really did not intend to say such a thing."

There was, he nonetheless admitted, something disquieting about all this. The Hospitalier Friars of Altopascio, for instance, who begged unrestrictedly at castles and in villages, were an official grouping authorised by the Church of Rome. By their preaching they frightened the people, threatening excommunication or promising ingulgences. And, in exchange for money, they would absolve anyone.

Had not the pontiffs too succumbed to the ambiguous fascination of superstition and charlatanry? Boniface VIII always wore a talisman against the urinary calculus, while Clement V and Benedict XII were never separated from the *cornu serpentinum*, an amulet in the shape of a serpent which John XXII even went so far as to keep on his table, stuck into a loaf of bread and surrounded by salt.

"But, some say," he added, lowering his voice by an octave, "that even the *cerretani* themselves originally enjoyed official sanction."

"Really? And what kind of sanction?"

"There's a tale that I heard from a brother originating in those parts. It would appear – but beware, there is no proof of this – that at the end of the fourteenth century, the *cerretani* had a regular authorisation to beg, at Cerreto itself, on behalf of the hospitals of the Order of the Blessed Antony. A permit, in other words, emanating from the ecclesiastical authorities."

"But then the *cerretani* were officially tolerated. Perhaps they still are to this day."

"If such a permit ever existed," said he, prudently, "it would have had to be registered in the statutes of the city of Cerreto."

"And is it?"

"The pages concerning this begging for alms were torn out by someone," he remarked impassively.

Besides, he added in the same breath, if one really wished to pay attention to gossip, it was even said that they had a friend in the Vatican.

"In the Vatican? And who could that be?" I exclaimed, matching my intonation to my incredulity.

On his face, I read regret at having pronounced one word too many, and displeasure at being unable to row back.

"Well. . . They speak of someone from the Marches. But perhaps it is all a matter of envy because he has an important post in Saint Peter's factory, so they slander him behind his back."

So, I thought in astonishment, someone at Saint Peter's Factory (the permanent workshop for the repair and restoration of the most important church in Christendom) was in contact with the *cerretani*. This was obviously a matter to be looked into, but not with the chaplain, who had given himself away and would certainly provide me with no further details.

It was time for us to part. I had completed my task of setting out the birds which were to act as bait, and I had checked on the fixed arquebuses; furthermore Don Tibaldutio had answered quite exhaustively my questions concerning the links between the Church and the *cerretani*.

How much like the skilled and crafty trade of scoundrels and swindlers was all that proliferation of Holy Years, decade after decade, which had reduced the Jubilees from a rare act of collective devotion falling only every hundred years to a vehicle for constant money-making! Was this not perhaps a consequence, however distant, of the errors and misdeeds committed or tolerated when the *cerretani* first came into the world, even before the first Jubilee, born from a rib of Holy Mother Church and fed with the sacred milk of pity and charity? Sfasciamonti was right, said I to myself, we were surrounded. The seat of the papacy was a fortress into which the Trojan horse had long since been introduced.

Don Tibaldutio blew his nose in conclusion, staring at me thoughtfully through the folds of his handkerchief. He understood that I had on my mind something that I did not mean to reveal to him.

I thanked him and promised that, should I need further clarification on the subject, I would certainly seek his advice.

A moment before taking my leave of the chaplain, I remembered a question over which I had been brooding a long time:

"Excuse me, Don Tibaldutio," said I with seeming nonchalance. "Have you ever heard tell of the Company of Saint Elizabeth?"

"But of course, everyone knows it," he answered, caught out by the ingenuousness of my question. "It is the one that gives money to the catchpolls. Why do you ask?"

"I saw them passing the other day and. . . Well, it was the first time I had ever seen them, that's all," said I, clumsily disguising the matter.

I simply could not see clearly into the doubt that was slowly gnawing away at my insides but had not yet reached my brain.

ॐ

Thank heavens, the merry hunt turned out well and happily. After a few hours of lying in wait and laying ambuscades, the ladies and gentlemen had exhausted their lust for the chase and had returned to the great house, bearing almost empty baskets containing a meagre, pitiable haul (starlings, swallows, rooks, a few toads, two moles and even a bat) and with everyone falling about with laughter. In the end, once I had withdrawn all the cages with the bait, I could see that these were far more numerous than what had been caught.

Only a few minor incidents (all of them fortunately resolved by the prompt intervention of the servants, who had come running en masse) had momentarily disturbed the entertainment, causing poor Don Paschatio's heart to jump into his mouth. Prince Vaini, reckless as ever, had for a joke aimed his crossbow at the hat of Giovan Battista Marini, Bargello of the Campidoglio, whereupon the shot had gone off by accident. The arrow had narrowly missed Marini's cranium and had stuck into a nearby tree, taking his hat with it. Cardinal Spada, backed by his Major-Domo and a host of lackeys, had had to plead long and hard to avoid Vaini and his victim coming to blows. Challenges to fight a duel, several times uttered, had fortunately come to nothing.

In the meanwhile, Monsignor Borghese and Count Vidaschi, for want of nobler prey, had fired their arquebus at a large rook. The black (notoriously inedible) fowl had fallen to the ground, apparently badly wounded. When, however, the two aggressors had advanced to catch it, it had taken off, flying rather haphazardly among the other players and ending up perched on the fine, flowing tresses of Marchesa Crescenzi who exploded into screams of pain and panic. When at last the bird let go of her, the whole group took aim at it with arquebuses and crossbows. The poor creature, being wounded in one wing, could not gain height. When at last it landed on the ground, it was ingloriously finished off with a shovel.

The third incident was not the fruit of an excess of audacity, as in the case of Prince Vaini, but of total incompetence. Marchese Scipione Lancelotti Ginetti, who was notorious for his lack of wit, and even more so for his short-sightedness, shot a bolt from his crossbow at what he believed to be a bird perched on the topmost branch of a tall pine. The bolt struck a bough, causing it to shake violently. Out of the branches fell a whitish sphere which shattered on the ground.

"An egg," exclaimed the first.

"One does not shoot at nests, it is both pointless and cruel," exclaimed the other, turning to Marchese Lancelotti Ginetti.

Others gathered, all keen to stress the Marchese's error, at a time when the latter was pulling strings to be appointed Colonel of the Roman People (an ancient and noble office of the city's communal institutions), while many nourished the hope that he would fail in this. Moreover, any pretext was good for distracting attention from the hunt, which was yielding such meagre results. The Marchese tried to disculpate himself, claiming that he had been shooting at a big bird, while everyone was trying to hide their laughter, knowing full well that Lancellotti Ginetti could not see a yard beyond his own nose.

With their noses pointing skyward, many guests – all claiming themselves to be expert hunters – tried to understand to which bird the egg that had fallen to the ground might belong.

"Riparian swallow."

"Pheasant, in my view," proposed Monsignor Gozzadini, Secretary for His Holiness's Memorials.

"But, Excellency, on top of a tree. . ."

"Ah yes, that is true."

"A partridge," said another.

"A partridge? Too small."

"Excuse me, it must be a turtle dove, or at most a pigeon, that's quite clear."

"But even a white dove. . ."

"Perhaps it is a jay," ventured Marchese Lancellotti Ginetti, who seemed to regard it as somehow dishonourable not to pronounce his opinion on the egg which he himself had brought down.

"Come, come, Marchese!" butted in Prince Vaini with his usual insolence. "Can you not see that the egg is white, while jays' eggs are speckled? Even the dogs in the street know that!"

The entire group ganged up on poor Lancellotti Ginetti, stressing the gravity of his mistake with a series of "Ah, yes!", "But what's got into his head?", "Utterly absurd" and so on and so forth, all accompanied by allusive little coughs and the clearing of throats.

Suddenly, the ear-splitting report of an arquebus was heard. Everyone, including Lancellotti Ginetti, immediately ducked to the ground to avoid any further shots.

Fortunately, there were no dead or wounded. A quick check revealed that none of the gentlemen present had an arquebus. Moving further afield, none of those handling one admitted to having fired in the previous few minutes. Some of those present still had goose pimples from the experience, and moved away to resume the beat.

This incident, which I had fortuitously witnessed as I was in the process of moving one of the cages to a better position, filled my soul with a dense cloud of disquiet. At point blank range, an arquebus shot could only kill.

Out of a sense of duty, I at once reported what had happened to Don Paschatio; his face was marked in equal measure by anguish and terror. The one thing not needed at the festivities which he was overseeing was a dead man, perhaps one high born. He began lamenting that this hunting party was most inappropriate at the present time when a conclave was imminent, with so much mutual detestation in the air. Someone might give in to the temptation to settle old accounts.

I had, however, cooled down after the initial shock. I had my suspicions; but I could not yet imagine whether there were any grounds for them, nor did I know whether it would be wise to investigate the matter. In any case, urgent business now occupied my mind, calling me to action.

The business of spying, to be quite precise.

Evening the Seventh
13ᵀᴴ JULY, 1700

✠

I found Atto in his lodgings. He had not taken part in the merry hunt: the hunt for Caesar Augustus had been quite enough for him, said he. In fact, he was too busy replying to the letter from the Connestabilessa. Now that he had accomplished that task, it was time for him to go down with Buvat for dinner in the gardens of the villa. I told him what I had learned from Don Tibaldutio: the *cerretani* even had a friend at Saint Peter's, whose name the chaplain had not, however, revealed.

"Ah yes? Very good, very good," he commented, "I shall ask Sfasciamonti to check up on this at once."

Half an hour later, after making sure that the Abbot and his secretary were at table, I again plunged my hands into his dirty linen and took out the little envelope of secret correspondence.

From my pocket, I drew the little book of *The Faithful Shepherd* which I had borrowed from the library at the Vessel: now I was ready to read Maria's letters in the light of those verses. As on the previous occasion, I could find in the folder neither the Connestabilessa's letter nor the reply which the Abbot must just have penned. I searched among Buvat's effects, hoping to find an interesting letter, as had happened during my previous inspection, but this time I found nothing.

I rummaged everywhere, to no avail. I grew worried. Perhaps Melani was beginning to harbour suspicions of my incursions. Alas, Atto must have taken the letter with him.

It only remained for me to read the third and last report from Maria Mancini on the court of Spain, the only one which I had not yet read. Who knows, said I to myself, perhaps now that I had discovered the truth about the correspondence between Atto and Maria, now that I had got to the very heart of it, which had to do not with politics or spying, but with love, I might be able to retrace in those reports allusions and quotations which had at first escaped me. Glancing out of the window to make sure that Atto was a long way off and otherwise occupied, I opened the packet.

Attached to the report was a covering letter from Maria. It had been sent from Madrid two months before. The Connestabilessa was replying to a letter from Atto and confirming that she would be coming to Rome to attend the Spada-Rocci wedding.

My friend, I understand the point of view shared by Lidio and yourself, but I repeat my own opinion: it is all pointless. Moreover, what today may seem good will tomorrow turn out to be a disaster.

Nevertheless, I shall come. I shall do as Lidio desires. So we shall meet at the Villa Spada. This I promise you.

Here again was an allusion to Herodotus. She wrote of Lidio, in other words of Croesus, King of Lydia, the name by which, I had the day before discovered, Atto and Maria referred to the Most Christian King.

I collected my thoughts. So it had been Lidio, the Most Christian King in person, who had asked Maria to accept Cardinal Spada's invitation! And why should he have done that?

I read and reflected, until I had an intuition: the Sovereign wanted to convince Maria to return to France. That was what Abbot Melani's mission must be about. And the backdrop to all this was provided by the nuptials at Villa Spada.

The King of France was filled with nostalgia for the Connestabilessa. Had not Atto himself given me to understand this the day before, during our last visit to the Vessel? He had even revealed to me that Madame de Maintenon wanted the King to see Maria again now that she was old, in the hope of blotting out once and for all the memory which the King retained from the years of their youth.

I imagined that the Sovereign might, through Atto, be pulling strings to persuade Maria to meet him again; perhaps by accepting the official invitation to court which Madame de Maintenon was so keen on, or perhaps a secret meeting, far from inquiring eyes.

But the Connestabilessa, judging by the letter I had before me, had no intention of accepting. She considered that by now it was "all pointless", even that "what today may seem good will tomorrow turn out to be a disaster". She was probably referring to a possible meeting with the King; the joy of embracing once more would be followed by a bitter confrontation with the truth: the withering of bodies, the faded lineaments, the wilting of every charm.

Ah yes, I reasoned, the Connestabilessa would never show herself aged to the love of her whole life.

Anchored to these certainties, I continued the letter. I frowned: the Connestabilessa seemed suddenly to have changed the subject. She was speaking of Spanish affairs:

> *Have you heard of the jingle that is doing the rounds in Madrid? Charles V was Emperor, Philip II was King, Philip IV was but a man, Charles II is not even that.*
>
> *My friend, how have we descended into such decay? The worms that infest the old trunk of the Monarchy are myriad but do not believe all you hear: many, far too many of them come from beyond the Pyrenees. Who inoculated in Spain's weary members the toxin of spies, plotters, artificial terror, misinformation, corruption? Who wants to see Spain voided from within, poisoned, intoxicated and made to rot like the walking cadaver of her King?*
>
> *I am Italian by birth, I grew up in France and I chose Spain as my new fatherland; I can see when the shadows of the Great Jackals stretch over Madrid.*

I left off reading; who were the Great Jackals? Probably the other European kingdoms. The report continued with a list of all the defeats of the past half century, starting with the bloody battle of Rocroy, when the Spanish forces who were winning ended up massacred by the French. The leader of the Spanish forces, Francisco de Melo, had thrown his victory to the winds, yet for this he received no sanction but a purse of twelve thousand ducats. How better, the Connestabilessa wondered, could one have fostered the decay and subversion of all values?

Since then, everything had fallen apart: the humiliations in Flanders had been followed by the defeats at Balaguer, Elvas and Estremoz, the rout of Spain's armies at Lens and the shameful retreat from Castel Rodrigo. Then came the loss of Portugal after twenty-four long years of war and the uprising in Naples, put down only with the greatest of difficulty. (They had even proclaimed a republic). How could one be surprised by the continual military reversals when one knew that, to compensate for their lack of equipment, the Spanish armies had (as at the expedition against Fuentarrabía) been reduced to using antique arms from the collection of the Duke of Albuquerque, which had been rejected by the King himself a century before. How could one be surprised, knowing that Charles's father, Philip IV, had for his most trusted counsellor a nun from an enclosed order who knew nothing of the world?

Passing from battles to diplomacy, matters became even worse:
the Peace of Westphalia had humiliated Spain, while that of the
Pyrenees had made her an object of ridicule in the eyes of all Europe.
Meanwhile, the members of the dynasty had been dying like flies:
the first wife of Philip IV, Isabella, had died at the age of forty-one,
followed two years later by her first-born, Balthazar Charles; the little Prince Philip Prosper had died before reaching the age of five and
Charles II's first wife had died of suspected poisoning when she was
not yet thirty.

*Now, at the end of this long Calvary, here in the capital we are reduced to
utter chaos. The secret agents of both parties, all hired or held to ransom,
circulate rumours of defeat, foment revolts, make every government hated
by the people.*

*My friend, do you think they have not realised? The order is peremp-
tory: let the Minister be corrupt, let the magistrate be arbitrary and let the
priest sin.*

*The Grandees of the Kingdom have all been set at one another's throats,
so that no joint action is any longer possible. Let every government be short-
lived, so as to increase uncertainty. Let robber Ministers be dealt with clem-
ently, or not at all, so as to convince honest citizens that Evil pays. Let the
rulers tarry at ceremonies and festivities, indifferent to the fact that their
country is falling to pieces. All hope must be lost: for the morrow, for justice,
for humanity.*

*Only then, impelled by the powerful force of evil examples, will the plan
of the Great Jackals come to fruition: the police will rob, the merchant will
cheat, the soldier will desert, the honest mother will prostitute herself. Children will grow up without love and without illusions to sow disorder and
unhappiness among future generations. Let Herod's test be renewed, may
every seed of love die out; let madness flourish.*

*Every Spaniard's claim to rights, respect, dignity, must be destroyed.
He must be convinced that his destiny matters to no one and that he can
therefore count on no help. He must feel betrayed by everything and everyone, and he must hate.*

*In the face of his dismay, his hunger, his fear, Palace protocol must
remain sumptuous, the privileges of the rich, shameless. Every day must,
for Spaniards, bear the colours of disillusionment, the odour of betrayal, the bitter taste of rage; until, one morning, they will rise cursing
their rulers, but with resignation. When that day comes, the time will
be ripe.*

*The ruin or fortune of Kingdoms depends not upon finances, not upon
armies, but on the soul of the people. Even the most sanguinary tyrant can
in the long run do nothing against the hostility and mistrust of his fellow-
countrymen. This is more powerful than cannons, swifter than cavalry, more*

indispensable than money, for true power (and every Minister knows this) proceeds from the Spirit, not the Flesh.
The people's scorn is a hot wind that no wall can stop. It will in the end dissolve the hardest stone, the most solid bastion, the sharpest sword.
That is why tyrants have since time immemorial yearned to crush the people, but not without first obtaining their assent.
For that purpose, however, the lie is essential, the mother and sister of all despots. They invoke dangers which they themselves have secretly created, magnified by newspapers, and to which they claim to hold the solution. To achieve this, they will demand and be given full powers. And with those powers, they will reduce the people to desperation.
What will then happen? The Great Jackals will exult. Oh, how stupid they are! For this will also be their own end: all will fight one another, to divide the spoils of dead Spain. A great fratricidal struggle, a new Pelopponese war, after which there will no longer be any possibility of peace, only more wars, this war's daughters.

Not knowing Spain's political affairs, I could not understand to what the Connestabilessa was referring. I therefore passed on at once to reading the report itself and thus learned what had quite rightly given rise to so much discomfiture:

OBSERVATIONS
WHICH MAY BE OF USE IN RELATION TO
SPANISH AFFAIRS

When King Philip IV died, Charles II was still a child. The Regency thus went to his mother, Maria Anna. Incapable of governing the fate of the Kingdom on her own, Philip IV's widow appointed to the head of the government a Jesuit, her confessor Father Nidhard. Very soon, however, he was ejected by a conspiracy headed by Don John the Bastard. A few years later, the post was taken by Valenzuela, an unscrupulous adventurer whom Charles II, now an adolescent, had made a Grandee of Spain in order to make up for a banal hunting accident (when he had shot him in a buttock). But the Bastard instigated a second plot, exiled the Queen Mother and had Valenzuela arrested too. The latter's wife was arrested, incarcerated and raped. She ended her days begging and died mad. When, however, the Bastard died too, the Queen Mother returned and appointed a new Minister, the Duke of Medinaceli.
Medinaceli worked all day long, apparently exhausting himself in the process, but never achieved a thing. Despite this, he resigned because the task was too wearying. In the end, the Count of Oropesa took the reins. His health was delicate. He was tormented by constant attacks of Saint Anthony's fire and spent more time in bed than on his feet. After barely three years in office, he was thrown out by a palace coup and sent into exile. King Charles then appointed a new Junta without any chief minister. This, however, was soon nicknamed the "government of swindlers". Its failure gave rise in turn to a

quadrumvirate consisting of three noblemen and a Cardinal. They achieved absolutely nothing, so there was yet another change of government: the Duke of Montalto came to power, but he too was soon dismissed. The King then recalled Oropesa whom he particularly liked, but the people rose in revolt and swept him away: disguised as a monk, he made a miraculous escape with his wife and son when the rebels came for him.

The public accounts are so disastrous and confused that no one can manage to reconstruct the State budget. Taxes are kept high by public officials so that they can make money out of them, milking surreptitiously the entries in the Exchequer or else exacting bribes. The Royal finances are in such a parlous state that even the staff of the Alcázar go unpaid. At the same time, they increase the taxes on meat and oil for three weeks in order to pay the actors who celebrate the King's birthday.

The French burst into Catalonia. The Spanish army was routed on the river Ter; Palamos and Gerona are under occupation.

El Rey, who looks upon government as the Devil looks on holy water, spends his days in the gardens of the Buen Retiro picking punnets of raspberries.

In the streets, the host of wretches, beggars, petty thieves and homeless people has grown out of all proportion. The people are on their knees. The humblest foodstuffs are paid for with their weight in gold. Thefts, homicides and rapine are the order of the day. Taxes on bakers' goods are raised and the bakers go on strike. Madrid, already famished, is breadless. Flour can be found nowhere. To obtain a little, the English Ambassador has had to send out a squad armed to the teeth, or else his servants would be attacked. To work as a baker means running a daily risk of being robbed and killed.

The only thing that the hungry people get for a reply is the latest in a long line of announcements that the Queen is with child and Spain will soon have an heir to the Throne, but no one believes the Palace's lies.

The darkest day was a year ago, on 29th April 1699, when the furious mob came to the Alcázar, under the windows of the Royal Family. The Sovereign had to come out onto the balcony in person and only by a miracle did he succeed in calming the insurgents. At Court, all is turning to catastrophe.

The King is paralysed by fear and ready to do anything he is told. But no one can or will offer him counsel. The factions into which the Court is divided are so many hornets' nests in which everyone, even good friends, can expect nothing but ruin from the others. France and Austria blow secretly on the fire of wrath, ambition and envy.

I broke off my reading: footsteps seemed to be approaching in the corridor. In a flash, I put everything back in its place and rushed to the door, ready to make my escape. Alas, I was too late: Atto Melani was returning. Fortunately, he was alone.

I took refuge in Buvat's little room, praying God that the secretary would not return too soon, and from there I watched through the half-closed door. The first thing that the Abbot did was to remove his heavy grey wig, which – seeing how little cool there was even at that late hour – he snatched off with a grunt of satisfaction. He placed it on the appropriate stand which he put on his bedside table. Then, moaning with fatigue, he rapidly undressed. The hectic day which had just come to an end had sapped the Abbot's strength: he had retired to his apartment without waiting until the end of dinner, and now he had not even called a *valet de chambre* to remove his shoes.

Hidden in the little room, I had perforce to witness Atto's undressing. When he had stripped, I was surprised to observe a body which was, it is true, extremely mature, yet in excellent condition. His skin sagged and in several places fell into folds; his shoulders, however, were straight, and his legs, which were tense and agile, seemed to belong to one twenty years younger. Nowhere on his lower limbs were there those bluish marks which old age inevitably brings. Well, I thought, were it not so, Abbot Melani could not have borne the strain of those intense days of action.

"The Abbot is afraid of dying forgotten. But if he goes on like this, he will live a great deal longer and will do much. Surely, he will have all the time he needs to go down in history," I concluded, laughing inwardly.

Atto extinguished the lamp and, bathed only in moonlight, went to bed without even scraping off the ceruse, the beauty spots and the carmine red on his cheeks. Very soon, he began to snore loudly.

I was about to go on my way when I remembered that I still had not managed to find the most important thing: Atto and Maria's two last letters. The Abbot must have kept them on his person. What better time to find them?

I searched his clothes from top to bottom, even the heels of his shoes, but found nothing. Melani's teachings, together with the many and singular experiences which I had lived through at his side, had, however, sharpened my senses and my wits. Thus it was that, looking attentively all around me, I noticed a curious detail. Atto had placed his foppish periwig, not on the dressing table, as he should normally have done, but on his bedside table; as though he meant to keep watch over it even in his sleep. . .

Straining to avoid making the slightest noise, an effort which caused me to break into a copious sweat, I succeeded in my undertaking:

the letters were in an unlikely secret pocket inside the wig, in the starched web to which were attached the curled locks of artificial hair. The elaborate choice of hiding place left no room for doubt: the Abbot feared greatly that someone might get at these letters. Of course, said I to myself, how could one blame him after all the misadventures with the *cerretani*? So much care might, however, mean that the content of those letters was far more delicate than the previous messages, and perhaps even too hot to handle.

To my surprise, there were not two but five letters. At a snail's pace, cursing the creaking wooden floor, I at last moved away from the bed in which Abbot Melani was sleeping.

Three of the letters seemed rather old. Curious, I opened one of them. It was the ending of a letter written in Spanish, penned by a rather uncertain hand. Imagine my astonishment when I read the signature:

yo el Rey*

It was a letter from the King of Spain, poor Charles II. It was dated 1685, some fifteen years before. Despite the extreme similarity between the Spanish language and Italian, the Sovereign's contorted and tortured handwriting did not allow me to understand anything of what he had written. I opened the two other papers, in search of the beginning of the letter, in order to be able to understand to whom it was addressed. Instead, to my astonishment, I saw that each consisted of the ending of a letter written many years ago. Both were signed by the King of Spain, and here too I was unable to understand the contents.

What was the meaning of those truncated pages? And why ever were they in Abbot Melani's hands? They must be very important if he kept them hidden in his periwig.

Alas, I had very little time in which to reflect. There was something far more urgent to be done: to skim through Atto and Maria's two epistles and put them back in their place before Buvat's return.

Hardly had my eyes settled on the first page than I gave a start.

My dearest Friend,

I have learned the most surprising news which I am sure will surprise and interest you as much as it has me. His Holiness Pope Innocent XII has set up a special congregation for consultation on the Spanish question. It

* "I the King". (Translator's note.)

seems that the Pontiff, after a long period of hesitation, has at last given in to the pressing requests of the Spanish Ambassador Uzeda to give his opinion on El Rey's request, and has charged the Secretary of State, our benign Fabrizio Spada, together with the Secretary for Breves, Cardinal Albani, and the Chamberlain, Cardinal Spinola di San Cesareo, to study the situation with a view to preparing the Papal reply.

My heart was beating hard. Spada, Albani and Spinola: the same three eminences who had for days and days been meeting secretly at the Vessel and whose trail I and Atto had been trying in vain to follow. So the Spanish succession was the real reason they were meeting, not the conclave!

I raised my eyes from the letter, frowning. Why had not Atto run to tell me as soon as he had learned the news from Maria?

Feverishly, I skimmed through the letter. I stopped a little further on:

Thus, His Holiness has yielded to spirits more tenacious than his own. Will he have the necessary clarity of mind to act effectively on the King's behalf? Here, my friend, I begin once more to have my doubts. What does the Holy Father mean when, as you wrote, he is heard to moan: "We are denied the dignity which is due to the Vicar of Christ and there is no care for us"?

I switched rapidly to Atto's reply, which gave me even more food for thought:

Most Clement Madame,
*   I have known for some time of the congregation of the three cardinals responsible for drawing up an opinion on the Spanish Question. The matter is common knowledge here in Rome, at least in well-informed circles. If you were among us here at the festivities, you would already have learned of it. . .*

I doubted those words. Did Atto perhaps want to make Maria believe that he had prior knowledge of everything, so as not to lose face? Melani's letter continued:

In reality, His Holiness had originally chosen Cardinal Panciati instead of Spinola, which would have been better for France, since Spinola is openly in favour of the Empire; but then the former was obliged to decline on grounds of poor health, so much so that he has not even been able to attend the delightful wedding at Villa Spada.
*   You were however informed most promptly, since the assignment will only be made officially tomorrow, on the 14th July.*

No, Atto was pretending nothing to the Connestabilessa. He was telling the truth: to me, however, he had lied. From all these details, which he was setting forth with such confidence, it was clear that Atto had for some time been fully informed of the three cardinals' diplomatic manoeuvres following Charles of Spain's request for the Pope's assistance. But all this he had deliberately kept from me, and that, for a long time.

Then suddenly I remembered: what was it that I had heard those three spectators saying the evening before, just before the play began? The Spanish Ambassador, Count Uzeda, with the help of others, had at long last succeeded in convincing Pope Innocent XII. To do what, however, that they had not said. Nor had they mentioned the names of those who were supposed to have helped Uzeda by influencing His Holiness: they had only referred to "four sly foxes".

Now the Connestabilessa's letter made everything clear: plainly, Innocent XII did not wish to involve himself in the question of the Spanish succession, but he had in the end given in to pressure from the Spanish Ambassador. And who were the other "sly foxes" like him if not Albani, Spada and Spinola? That was why one of the trio, whom I had overheard the evening before, had silenced the others with the words "*lupus in fabula*" as soon as he had realised that Cardinal Spada was approaching.

In other words, the three eminences had used every means at their disposal to put pressure on the dying Pontiff to assign them the task of dealing with the question of the Spanish succession. But worst of all was the fact that when, on the day before – the 12th – Pope Pignatelli had let himself be convinced to set up the congregation, the three cardinals had already been meeting secretly at the Vessel for a week! Perhaps they were deciding on the tactics to adopt with the Holy Father.

To keep their meetings well hidden, what better cover than the wedding at Villa Spada? No one would become suspicious seeing them together, since Spada was the master of the house and both Albani and Spinola were among the guests. All that without counting the fact that they were so skilful in their manner of slipping away to the Vessel that the Abbot and I had never managed to catch them *in flagrante* during their meetings there.

All in all, it seemed that the poor old Pope no longer counted for anything, as the three guests had commented the evening before.

I felt bitter about this: alas, it meant that Spada, in his capacity as Secretary of State, was in all probability one of those (together with the Secretary for Breves, Albani, and the Chamberlain, Spinola di San Cesareo) about whom the Pontiff complained that he was denied the dignity due to the Vicar of Christ and treated inconsiderately, as the Connestabilessa had mentioned on no fewer than two separate occasions in her letters to Atto.

What was the Abbot's role in all this? Now that was clear: Melani's purpose was to spy on the trio, not with a view to the conclave but in order to know whether or not what they decided for the Spanish succession was favourable to France; and perhaps to hold himself at the ready to act on his King's behalf. Had I not read his correspondence with Maria, I would have remained in the dark about all this.

Discouraged and humiliated, I continued reading:

> *. . . and yet you must not think that His Holiness is in bad hands. From such information as I have been able to gather, he is perfectly and disinterestedly assisted by the Secretary of State, by the Secretary for Breves and by the Chamberlain, who look after all affairs of State with the greatest of care and solicitude. As I have already had occasion to write to you, they have in no way taken the crosier from His Holiness's hand but are only carrying out the difficult task with which the Pontiff has been so good as to entrust them, a task which they accepted humbly and with joy. Fear not.*

So tense did I become at this juncture that I came close to crushing the letter between my fingers, leaving the mark of my clandestine reading. Such impudence! Not only did Atto know perfectly well what those three cardinals were up to during their secret meetings at the Vessel (despite the fact that he had never succeeded in finding them there) but he was speaking of it in unctuous, mellifluous terms. And this despite the fact that among the three was Cardinal Albani, in other words one of the Abbot's bitterest enemies: the one who, only the evening before, thanks to Ugonio's information, we had discovered to be in cahoots with Lamberg. The whole thing was really rather strange; what was Abbot Melani hiding?

Continuing my reading, however, I found that the subject changed suddenly:

> *But enough of this futile chatter! You know all too well how easily I immerse myself in vanities social and political when she who speaks (or writes) to me of such matters is the sweetest, noblest and most enchanting of Princesses one could ever desire to serve. You ought to amuse me with the most superficial of*

stratagems, even then you would effortlessly ensnare me, for all that issues
forth from your mouth, as from your pen, is sublime, enchanting and worthy
of love.
  But now it is time to pass on to serious matters. Most clement and dearly
beloved Madame, how much longer will you deny yourself the delights of
Villa Spada? Barely two days remain before the withering away of the fes-
tivities, and still I have not been vouchsafed the Grace of kneeling at your
feet. Nor do you even tell me now whether you have been restored to health
or when you will be arriving. Do you want my death?

> *But if, with your compassion*
> *All the dear softness which was born with you*
> *Be not extinguished quite, deny me not*
> *This one request (although thy soul be cruel,*
> *'Tis lovely too) to my last farewell sigh*
> *Return but one, and then will death be pleasing.*

  What envious god causes you to turn your back on Lidio and disdain
his requests? You know full well: if I am here, 'tis only because you promised
Lidio that you would come.

Here was the truth. How could I have doubted it? He loved her
and his love was mingled with that of his king, of whom Atto was but
the old messenger. And when he returned to the subject of Eros, the
Abbot betrayed the fact that all other things were merely a pretext
for conversing, even if only on paper, with the object of his feelings.

No, there was no mystery here, save that of the lasting love that
joined three old persons. The Abbot, it was true, had been reticent
with me about the question of the Spanish succession, persuading
me that the three cardinals were meeting to prepare the next conclave.
Yet it was also true that the matter was extremely delicate, and Atto
had therefore preferred to keep me in the dark. I well remembered
from the days when we had met at the Locanda del Donzello, how
the Abbot had been prodigal with the most stupefying revelations
concerning events distant in time, while he carefully kept the truth
about his manoeuvres and projects of the moment to himself. When
all was said and done, what else could I expect of a veteran spy? I
had to yield to the facts: Abbot Melani would always keep something
from me, if only out of his inborn mistrustfulness and the complicated
workings of his mind.

So it was with new eyes that I reconsidered Melani's letter which
I had just read, and now I no longer found it so suspect. For example,
might not the obsequious tone employed by Atto when speaking of

Albani be due to the Abbot's fear that someone might read his letters and realise that he was spying on the three cardinals for the Most Christian King?

Now it was time for me to be on my way. I left the three letters where I had found them, in the Abbot's wig. The love verses, however, by their very nature resistant to all human will, accompanied me far on my way. They perpetuated the motionless dance of the rhymes along the way home to my bed, where I took out one last time the Cavaliere Guarini's *Faithful Shepherd* and sought those lines. When at length I found them playing on the lips of Silvio and Dorinda, I smiled at that final confirmation of the truth, for once kinder than my fears. Atto, Atto,

although thy soul be cruel, 'tis lovely too,

I found myself repeating this in that confused whirlpool which precedes sleep, and later, in the mystery of the night hours when the soul feeds on shadows and vain images and loves to discover itself immortal.

Day the Eighth

14ᵀᴴ JULY, 1700

✠

"And what do you mean to say? That I'm an ignoramus?"

Poor Buvat fell silent at once, shocked by Atto's acid tone.

That morning Abbot Melani was really beside himself. Buvat had just returned from a walk in town and had found us in close conversation, trying to think up a way of getting into the Congregation of the Oratory while eluding the surveillance of the Philippine Brothers. The moment that he attempted to contribute to the discussion, Atto set to berating him.

"Never would I dare suggest such a thing, Signor Abbot," the secretary hesitantly defended himself, "only. . ."

"Only what?"

"Well, there's simply no reason to elude the surveillance of the Philippine Brothers because, as I was saying, there is none."

Abbot Melani and I looked at one another in consternation.

"What is more," Buvat continued, "Virgilio Spada himself arranged for his collection to be displayed in an accessible place. It is indeed a genuine museum, so arranged as to satisfy the curiosity of many visitors."

Buvat went on to explain that Virgilio Spada, although he had in his youth soldiered under the Spanish flag, was a most religious, cultivated and erudite man, a good friend of the great architect Borromini whom he had introduced to the court of Pope Innocent X half a century previously. Spada had at the time been instructed by the Pontiff to restore order to the great hospital of Santo Spirito in Saxia, and had subsequently been appointed Privy Almoner to His Holiness. Besides this he had, thanks to his spiritual qualities, been invited to join the pious Congregation of the Oratory, so called because its founder, Saint Philip Neri, had held its first spiritual meetings at the Oratory of San Girolamo della Carità and later in that of Santa Maria in Vallicella, where the seat of the Congregation of the Oratory is now to be found, along with Virgilio's collection.

"How the deuce do you come to know all this?"

"You will of course remember that, when I was recently visiting libraries in search of information on the *cerretani*, among other things, I went to the Biblioteca Vallicelliana, which happens to be just next to the Oratory of the Philippine Brothers. So it was that I got into long and pleasant conversations with them. At that time, I could even have taken a look at the collection of Virgilio Spada, if only you had told me that you thought you might find there these objects which interest you so much."

Melani lowered his eyes and muttered furious obscenities under his breath.

"Very well, Buvat," he then said. "Take us to your Oratorian friends."

❦

"And this must be what you are looking for," said the young monk, turning the key in the lock of a great two-panelled chest.

The room was gay and luminous, but rendered severe by the display cabinets, walnut chests of drawers and bookcases full of all manner of objects which covered it and made it rather like a sacristy.

"No one knows that these objects, the ones you're looking for, are here. Perhaps there's someone in the Spada family who remembers," added the monk, with an expression that betrayed the desire to know how we came to be informed of this.

"Quite. I believe that is precisely the case," replied Atto, in terms that did not address the Oratorian's observation, who was therefore left no wiser.

We were in the room at the Oratory devoted to the museum: a corner room on the second floor giving onto the Piazza della Chiesa Nuova (that of the church standing next to the Oratory itself), and a narrow alley called the Via de' Filippini.

We had begun with a detailed visit to the entire collection of Virgilio Spada: Roman coins; medals from every epoch; busts antique and modern; sundials; concave mirrors; convex lenses; gnomons; volcanic rocks; crystals; precious stones; solar sponges; the fangs of monstrous beings; teeth and bones of animals mysteriously turned to stone; the ravenous mandibles of unknown beings; elephants' vertebrae; gigantic conch and mussel shells; seahorses; stuffed birds and hawks; horns of rhinoceros and stags' antlers; turtles' shells; ostrich eggs; claws of

crustaceans; and in addition, oil lamps of the first Christians found in
the catacombs; tabernacles; Roman, Greek and Persian vases and amphorae; goblets; huge oil jars; lachrymal vases; bone calyxes; Chinese
coins; alabaster spheres and a thousand other oddities which kept us
suspended between wonderment and impatience.

After a guided visit lasting half an hour (tiresome but necessary,
for if we had asked at once to see what interested us, that would have
attracted too much attention), Atto put the fateful question: were
there by any chance three objects which the good Virgilio Spada had
not integrated into the collection but for which he cared no less, and
which were of such and such a kind?

The Oratorian then led us into an adjoining room, where we at
last stopped in front of an orotund and triumphal globe, that of
Capitor. The Abbot and I concealed our enthusiasm and examined it
with polite interest, as one might any fine product of human crafts-
manship.

"We have it, my boy, at last we have it!" Abbot Melani whispered
in my ear, controlling his joy with some difficulty, while our guide led
us to the second object: the goblet with the centaur. Once again, we
dissimulated.

"It looks just the same as in the picture, Signor Atto, there can be
no doubt about it," I murmured in his ear.

The crucial moment came only at the end, when the great black key
turned in the lock and the mechanism which had guarded the third gift
since who knows when gave way at last. The Oratorian opened both
doors of the cabinet wide and extracted an object measuring about
three feet by six, weighing a great deal and covered with a grey cloth.

"Here we are," said he, laying it carefully on a little table and
removing the cover, "we have to keep it under lock and key because
it is particularly valuable. It is true that no one enters here unan-
nounced, but one never knows."

We barely heard the words of the courteous Oratorian father; the
blood beat hard against our temples and we would willingly have exchanged our eyes for his hands the better to discover the object so
long and ardently coveted: the Tetràchion.

Here it was at last.

"It. . . is so beautiful," gasped Buvat.

"It is the work of a Dutch master, so at least we are told, but we
do not know his name," the priest added laconically.

After the first moments of emotion, I was at last able to enjoy the refined forms of the dish, the exceedingly fine decoration of the edge, the exotic seashells and most capricious arabesques, and then the wonderful central marine scene, in which a pair of Tritons ploughed the waves drawing a chariot surmounted by a couple of deities seated one beside the other, their pudenda lightly covered by a golden veil; Neptune was grasping a trident, and, entwined in an embrace with her spouse, the Nereid Amphitrite was holding the reins. The pair were embossed in silver and stood out strikingly, being statuettes in the round set in the golden bed of the charger. Just as I was pausing to view the divine couple, Atto drew near to examine a minute inscription.

I too approached, and read in turn. The inscription was carved at the feet of the two deities:

MONSTRUM TETRÀCHION

"Would you like to see anything else?" asked the Oratorian, while Atto, without even having asked his permission, took the dish in his hands, and with Buvat's help, closely inspected the two silver statuettes.

"No thank you, Father, that will suffice," the Abbot answered at length. "Now we shall take our leave. We simply wished to satisfy our curiosity."

తురోు

"The correct meaning of *monstrum* is 'marvel' or 'a marvellous thing'. But what sense does it make to write *monstrum Tetràchion*, or 'quadruple marvel'?"

No sooner were we on our way, moving from the Oratory of the Philippines towards the Tiber than Atto set about trying to work out what that inscription might mean. We had to hasten towards the Vessel. It was almost midday and, as Cloridia had announced to us two days earlier, another meeting between the three cardinals was due to take place, perhaps the last one on which we might have a chance to spy, or attempt to spy, seeing that all our attempts to date had failed miserably.

"Permit me, Signor Abbot," interrupted Buvat.

"What is it now?" asked Melani nervously.

"To tell the truth, *monstrum Tetràchion* does not mean 'quadruple marvel' at all."

Caught off balance, Atto stared at his secretary and uttered a faint murmur of protest.

"*Tetràchion*, as you obviously know, is a word of Greek origin, but the Greek word for quadruple is *tetraplàsios*, not *tetràchion*. On the other hand, *tetràchion* is not to be confused either with *tetràchin*, an adverb that means 'four times'," explained the secretary, while humiliation painted itself in dark colours on Atto's forehead.

"And what does *tetràchion* mean then?" I asked, seeing that the Abbot lacked the breath to put the question.

"It is an adjective, and it means 'with four columns'."

"Four columns?" Melani and I repeated incredulously in unison.

"I know what I am saying, but you can always check in any good Greek dictionary."

"Four columns, four columns," murmured Atto. "Did you not notice anything curious about those two statuettes, the marine deities?"

Buvat and I reflected a few moments.

"Well, yes," said I at length, breaking the silence, "they are in rather a strange position. They are sitting on the chariot, one beside the other, and Neptune has his left leg between those of Amphitrite, unless I am mistaken."

"Not only that," Buvat corrected me, "but it is not clear which is the right leg of the god and which is the left leg of the nereid. It is as though the two statuettes were actually. . . fused together. Yes, they are joined, by a hip, or a thigh, I know not which, so much so that when I first saw them, I thought, how strange, they look like a single being."

"A single being," repeated Atto thoughtfully. "It is as though they had – how can one put it? – four legs shared between the two of them," he added in a low voice.

"So the four columns are the legs," I deduced.

"That is possible. Oh yes, in terms of language, it is certainly possible, I can confirm that," Buvat pronounced. His intellect may perhaps have been lacking in daring, but when he took the bull of erudition by the horns, he would not let go.

"So, Buvat, if I may take advantage of your admirable science, I ask you whether, instead of 'quadruple marvel', I can translate *monstrum Tetràchion* as 'four-legged' or even 'four-pawed monster'."

Buvat reflected one moment, then gave his ruling: "Yes, definitely. *Monstrum* in Latin means both 'prodigy' or 'marvel' and 'monster', that's well known. Still, I do not understand where all this is leading up to. . ."

"Good, that will do," commented Atto.

"Still, what is this Tetràchion?" I questioned him. "If it really is the heir to the Spanish throne, it seems almost to be an animal, Signor Atto."

"What the Tetràchion is, I do not know. What's more, to be quite honest, I know even less than I did before. Yet I feel that the answer is at hand, if we can but take one step forward. It is always like that: whenever one is close to the solution of some mystery of state, everything seems confused. The closer you approach, the more you stumble in the dark. Then suddenly, it all becomes clear."

While he was commenting on our progress, we passed the bridge over the Tiber and by now we were already climbing the Janiculum Hill and rapidly approaching our goal.

"Only one piece is missing from the mosaic," Atto continued, "and then perhaps we shall find what we seek. I want to know: where the deuce does this word Tetràchion come from? We must go and put a couple of little questions to someone. Let's hope he's already arrived at Villa Spada. We have very little time left before Spada, Albani and Spinola return to the Vessel. Let us get a move on."

Our initial search through the gardens of Villa Spada proved fruitless. Romaùli, said the other servants, was doing his rounds, but no one knew exactly where he was. Since he spent most of his time bending over, he was easily concealed by hedges and shrubs.

"Damn it all, I have it," cursed Atto. "We need some help."

He guided our trio to his apartment. No sooner had we entered than he rushed to the table and grasped a familiar object: the telescope. He pointed it out of the window, to no avail.

We then went outside and crossed to the other side of the villa. This time, after a swift scan, Melani whistled with satisfaction:

"I have you, wretched gardener."

Now we knew where he was.

Tranquillo Romaùli, punctual in his activities as the rising of sun and moon, could certainly not fail to water the Saint Antony's lilies which he had planted not long before and which required constant and intensive care. He was carefully sprinkling the diaphanous lanceolate calyxes bunched in lovely racemes when we appeared before him, greeting him with the greatest courtesy that haste and emotion permitted.

"Do you see? With lilies, the ground needs generous watering, but it must never be drenched," he began, almost without responding to our greeting. "In this period, they should really be resting, but I have succeeded in developing a hybrid which. . ."

"Signor Master Florist, be so kind as to permit us to ask you a question," I asked him amiably, "a question concerning the Tetràchion."

"About the Tetràchion, my Tetràchion?"

"Yes, Signor Florist, the Tetràchion. Where did you find that name?"

"Oh, that is a rather sad story," said he, as he put down his watering can, his face marked by some distant memory.

Fortunately, his explanation was not too lengthy. Years before, Romaùli had not dedicated all his time to flowers: he had been married. As well I knew, his late spouse had been a great midwife; indeed she had taught the art to Cloridia, and had attended the birth of our two little ones. From his tale one understood that it had been the premature death of his wife that had caused him to devote himself body and soul to gardening, in a vain attempt to banish the indelible shadows of mourning. Not long after the sad event, the poor woman's parents had asked Tranquillo if he could leave them some personal belonging of hers as a memento.

"I gave them a few jewels, two little pictures, a holy image and then her work books."

"So these were books for midwives," said Atto to encourage him.

"They are used by midwives to acquaint themselves with the possible accidents arising from difficult deliveries, or to instruct themselves on the different kinds of womb, and other such matters," he replied.

"And from which book did you take the term Tetràchion?"

"Ah, well, that I really cannot remember. It was so many years ago. I do not recall the details. The use of that name is in fact a memento, just a memento of my dear wife."

We had learned enough.

"Thank you, thank you for your patience, and please pardon us for having troubled you," said I, while Atto was already hurrying away, without so much as a farewell, towards the gate of the villa. Romaùli stared at us in surprise.

Running as fast as I was able to, I rejoined Atto, who had charged out of Villa Spada without even a nod towards a pair of cardinals, who had themselves turned to greet him. Buvat meanwhile had obeyed his master's orders to remain in the villa and had turned back towards the great house.

"I have sent him to look for your wife," explained Melani. "We must find the book from which the Master Florist took that name. I want the author, the title, the page number, the lot."

He and I moved rapidly away from the Villa Spada. The Vessel awaited us.

❧

"A curse upon Tranquillo Romaùli and his chatter. I knew it: they've disappeared again."

It was midday. We had entered Benedetti's villa, but as on the previous occasions, of the three cardinals there was not so much as a shadow.

"It is noon. The appointment was fixed for precisely this hour," I observed after we had carried out our usual swift but careful preliminary reconnaissance.

We were on the second floor. Near us, on the ground, lay Pieter Boel's picture.

"It looks very like a gross error of workmanship," commented Atto.

The Abbot leaned over the canvas, intent upon comparing the depiction of Capitor's dish with the original which we had just examined so avidly at the Oratory.

"It is just as I had already observed: what at first sight appears to be Amphitrite's right leg comes from Poseidon's left side," continued the Abbot, "while what looks like the god's left leg comes from the nereid."

"Then it is as I said," I intervened, "there's just one leg placed over the other."

"That was my own first impression," he retorted, "but look carefully at the toes."

I leaned over in turn to examine the detail.

"It is true, the big toes. . ." I exclaimed in surprise. "But how is that possible?"

"From their position, it is clear that the two legs cannot be crossed:

the nereid's right leg really is her own and Poseidon's left leg really does belong to him."

"It is as though, through the goldsmith's carelessness, they'd been wrongly attached to the statuettes."

"Quite. But do you not find that rather strange for an artist capable of producing a masterpiece like this?"

"We shall have to return to the Oratorian Fathers and ask to be shown the original again."

"Alas, I fear that would not be of much use. Unfortunately, it is impossible to verify to which statuette the legs are in fact attached. I already tried to look on the dish itself, but do you see the little strip of gold that runs horizontally across the flanks of the two deities, covering their pudenda?"

"Yes, I'd already noticed it."

"Well, the goldsmith soldered it to the statuettes, so it is no longer possible to raise it and resolve the mystery. Only, I wonder why ever. . ."

Melani broke off with an irate grimace of vexation.

"Him again, that demented Dutchman. But when will he stop?"

Re-emerging once more from who knows where, Albicastro was at it again: once again the theme of the *folia* echoed, proud and indomitable, through the halls of the Vessel. A little later, he entered the room where we were.

"I thank you for the compliment, Signor Abbot Melani," the violinist began placidly, showing that he had heard Atto's comment. "Telemachus, the son of Ulysses, overcame the suitors thanks to his madness."

Melani snorted.

"If you will kindly excuse me, I shall be on my way," said Albicastro amiably in response to Atto's rude gesture. "But remember Telemachus, he will be useful to you!"

It was the second time that the Dutchman had spoken of Telemachus, but on neither occasion had I grasped his meaning. I knew Homer and the *Odyssey* only in outline, having read it thus some thirty years before in a book of Greek legends; I remembered that Telemachus had feigned madness in the assembly of the suitors who had invaded his father Ulysses' palace and had thus delivered them up to the death which Ulysses planned for them. Nevertheless, I could not fathom the meaning of Albicastro's recommendation.

"Signor Atto, what did he mean?" I asked when he had left.

"Nothing. He's mad and that's all there is to it," was Melani's only comment as he shamelessly slammed the door behind the Dutchman.

We returned to the picture. A few seconds later, however, we again heard the penetrating sound of Albicastro's violin and of his *folia*. Melani rolled his eyes in vexation.

"Of the inscription on the dish, there's no trace in the painting," said I, in an attempt to bring his attention back to bear on the image of the Tetràchion. "It is too small for it to be possible to paint it correctly."

"Yes," Atto assented, after a few instants; "or else Boel did not *wish* to paint it; or perhaps someone ordered him not to do so."

"Why?"

"Who knows? Likewise, the goldsmith may have perhaps made that mess with the legs deliberately, because he was commissioned to do so."

"But why?"

"For heaven's sake, my boy!" shouted Atto, "I am only airing suppositions. It exercises the intellect, and one finds an answer every now and then. And above all, tell that Dutchman to stop that racket once and for all, I need to reflect in silence!"

Thereupon, he put his hands over his ears and moved towards the staircase.

It was rather rare for Abbot Melani to become angry. Albicastro's music was certainly not so loud as to disturb or annoy. I had the impression that more than the volume of sound, it was the music itself, the *folia*, which was getting on Atto's nerves; or perhaps, I thought to myself, Albicastro, that curious soldier-violinist, and his bizarre philosophising were even more irritating for him. It was very rare for Atto to call an adversary mad. With Albicastro, who was no enemy, he had done just that: as though the other's thinking set off some hidden inner rage in him.

"Signor Atto, I agree, I shall go down and tell him. . ."

But the Abbot had already disappeared from my sight.

"Forget it. I shall look for somewhere better," I heard him say from some adjoining room.

I followed him at once. I expected to find him in the central salon giving onto the four apartments. When, however, I got there, I found myself alone. Yet Atto had not gone downstairs: I checked the main staircase and not a sound reached me from below. I then went to the service stairs, and there at last I heard his footsteps. He was not going down but up.

"It is quite intolerable," he grumbled as he climbed the stairs to the top floor.

When I followed him, I understood why. As had already happened the first time that we met Albicastro, in the little spiral staircase, the sound of the violin was amplified beyond all measure and embellished by echoes which transformed that agreeable melody into an infernal jumble. The sonorous reverberation produced by the spiral cavity made it seem like, not one violin, but fifty or a hundred all playing the same tune, but one note out of time, so that the plain linear theme of the *folia* sucked one down into the all-enveloping vortex of a musical canon which wound in vertiginous coils ever more tightly around the hearer, like the coils of the stairway itself which I and Atto were now climbing a few paces apart, he fleeing the music and I, following him.

"Where are you going?" I yelled, trying to drown with my voice the deafening orchestra of a thousand Albicastros twisting like restless spirits in the stairwell.

"Air, I want air!" he replied, "I'm suffocating here."

As the stairs wound upward, I heard him cough once, then twice, and in the end came one long, tremendous outburst, a hoarse, painful attack like that brought on by a dreadful cold, suffocation, strangling or burned lungs. True, the Vessel was dusty in the extreme, but that feverish fit, that violent and malignant expiration bespoke a grave alteration of the humours. Atto's soul was in sore travail, his body was struggling to rid itself of all that was weighing it down by fleeing the *folia*.

"But Signor Atto, perhaps if you open a window. . ." I called out to him.

There was no response. Perhaps he had not even heard me. I realised then that, as I climbed, the music was getting louder, despite the fact that the sound of Albicastro's violin seemed to be coming from the ground floor.

"Upstairs there's nothing but the servants' quarters, and they are empty," I called again, as I tried to catch up with him.

Almost at once, I reached that level; but Atto had gone on higher.

Two days earlier, we had reached that third floor, but to do so we had taken the grand staircase, which went no further. Unlike those stairs, the servants' ones went right up to the very top: to the terrace crowning the Vessel.

At last I too climbed those last narrow steps and, like a soul welcomed to paradise, fled the darkness of the stairwell and the unnatural thundering of the *folia*, emerging into the blessed, airy light of the terrace.

I found Melani slumped on the ground, still coughing, as though he had been almost asphyxiated.

"That accursed Hollander," he murmured, "damn him and his music."

"You have been coughing badly," I observed as I helped him to his feet.

He did not even answer me: he had raised his eyes and was staring, dumbfounded by the beauty of the space in which we stood, bounded by a wall surmounted by many fine vases decorated with floral motifs. In this wall were a number of wide oval openings through which one could enjoy an immense panorama dominating all the surrounding villas. At the four corners stood the four little cupolas crowning the Vessel and characterising it even from a distance. Covered with majolica tiles, over the four little domes stood weathervanes in the form of banners, each ending in a cross, which beautifully completed the terrace.

"With all the searching we've done here, we never discovered this belvedere. Admire it, my boy, what a gem! And such peace!"

His walking stick trembled. The fit of coughing, although short-lived, had shaken him badly. He seemed to me again the old, worn Atto I had found on the first day. He turned his back on me and walked towards the short end of the terrace, facing south and overlooking Via San Pancrazio, the street from which one enters the Vessel.

We allowed ourselves a few minutes in which to stare wide-eyed, leaning on an iron balustrade wrought to resemble foliage, at the splendid panorama surrounding the Vessel, with its vineyards and its pines, the solemn walls of the Holy City, the San Pancrazio Gate, and lastly, distant and discreet, the silvery glint of the sun on the sea.

We then moved to the head of the terrace, facing north. Here stood a rather lightweight structure, a sort of penthouse, crowned by a suspended balcony decorated at the corners with the fleur-de-lys, to which one gained access by two iron staircases set at either end.

We climbed the stairs on the left, and here our view opened up even more. We were simply overcome by the magnificence of the vistas which, both to the left and to the right, revealed to the spectator the triumphal grandeur of the Eternal City: in a pageant of symbols of the Faith, there stood before us a host of blessed cupolas, a forest of holy crosses, giddy pinnacles, venerable campaniles and the pink roofs of noble palaces, crowned by the hills which have always protected the cradle of Christianity. I remembered what Monsignor Virgilio Spada had suggested to Benedetti, and which Atto had mentioned a few days before: the idea of building a villa as a fortress of wisdom which would stimulate the visitor to reflect deeply on the victories of the intellect and the mysteries of the Faith.

My eyes then turned to the gardens of the Vessel and to the great pergola of grapes over the avenue leading from the entrance: as the Abbot had observed, Benedetti welcomed his visitors with grapes, the Christian symbol of rebirth.

"We're standing on the prow," said Atto.

In the naval architecture of the Vessel, that hanging balcony did indeed correspond to the upper deck.

Like two admirals on the bridge, we looked towards the Vatican Hill, that custodian of things imperishable. The Vessel dared point its bows towards the apostolic palaces, as though it were claiming: I too possess a fragment of eternity. Then I thought to myself, was not the Vessel perhaps a place of rebirth, where the broken threads of past and present again came together? Had this not perhaps happened when I had been able to witness the apparation of the young Louis and his beloved Maria and their dalliance? Likewise, when we beheld in the garden the image of Superintendent Fouquet, serene, free, untouched by disgrace or calumny. Those apparitions in that garden had recreated for us what history had denied them. The theatre of what should have been but never was: such was the Vessel.

It was on the strength of that very high office that this galleon claimed its place near the Vatican Hill. Saint Peter's, rock of the Faith and, near it, that other guardian of things eternal: the Vessel, fortress of justice, banished from the pedestal of history.

So it was that, standing on that little terrace suspended above infinity, with the wind raising the laces of my shirt, for an instant I felt like an intrepid sailor on the deck of a new Ark, a miraculous craft able to salvage just Fate and to stand guard over it in another time. While I was thus wandering off into my daydreams, Atto suddenly called me back to things present.

"Perhaps you will have formed a precise image of it."

I knew at once to what he was referring.

"No," I replied. "It is a monster; that is the only thing I have understood. If the forecast is correct, a monster with four legs is about to succeed to the Spanish throne. That really doesn't seem to make much sense, does it?"

"I know. I've not stopped thinking of it for a moment, but nothing else comes to mind. Until your wife gets hold of the book that Romaùli saw, I fear we shall not be able to make head or tail of it."

"I hope that Cloridia is as quick as usual."

"Let us go back down," said Atto at length. "I want to go and take another look at the picture."

It was then that we made the discovery.

"Look!" said Atto. "That is where they get through."

It could be seen only from there, at that particular angle. No other observation point anywhere in the Vessel was high enough or faced in the right north-westerly direction like the steps on which we stood. From here we could descry a little gate in the boundary wall of the garden through which one could pass unseen into a street adjoining the Vessel. This exit was cleverly concealed by a barrier of plants and brambles. It was quite impossible to locate unless one already knew of its existence. Once out, where did one go? That, we could see for ourselves: a furtive little group, perhaps the escort of one of the three cardinals, was entering a similar gate in the wall of a villa further down the road, the property of a Genoese nobleman by the name of Torre.

Peering more closely, I could make out a little further off the three cardinals of our acquaintance as they strolled undisturbed in Torre's garden.

"So that's why Spada, Spinola and Albani always make their appointments at the Vessel," said Atto. "They confound anyone who might wish to follow them, including us, by entering here then mysteriously disappearing. In actual fact they meet at Torre's villa. For

your master Cardinal Spada, that is an ideal solution. At a short distance from his own estate he has a safe house in which to hold secret
meetings, Torre's villa, and a place to muddy the waters, namely the
Vessel. It is not by chance that until this moment he has always succeeded in shaking us off."

As he spoke, Abbot Melani did not take his eyes off the trio for
one moment. I saw him suddenly stretch out his neck and screw up
his eyes as though trying to see better what was going on; but the
distance was too great. Our lookout point may indeed have been exceptional, but it would soon be useless. It was then that the Abbot
suddenly slapped his forehead.

"What a fool I am. Fortune assists me and I neglect it!"

He reached into his jacket and drew out a long, fine cylinder: the
telescope. He had kept it on his person ever since we had located
Romaùli in the garden of Villa Spada, as thence we had gone directly
to the Vessel.

He looked briefly, then handed me the spyglass.

"Take a look yourself; it will be a useful experience."

I brought the eyepiece to my pupil and looked.

Cardinal Spinola was shaking his head gently, as though he were
hesitating, while Spada and especially Albani were deep in conversation. The thing really did not last long; following a few words from
Albani, Spinola assented with a somewhat unwilling nod, or so it
seemed to me from that distance. Then Albani took him by the arm
with visible pleasure and the three continued their stroll. Atto then
took the telescope back from me and resumed his observation.

In the light of what I had learned the evening before from reading
the exchange of letters between Atto and the Connestabilessa, the
episode had no more mysteries, even for me. The three cardinals had
to provide His Holiness Innocent XII with an opinion on the question of the Spanish succession, so that the Pope could respond as
best he could to the request for help put to him by the King of Spain,
Charles II. The three eminences had therefore to agree on a common
line: a gesture of immense political importance which could make
the fortune of the trio or be their ruin. It was quite clear that Spinola
was not of exactly the same opinion as the other two prelates.

I looked once again at Atto as he spied avidly on the meeting between the three cardinals. He was worried, and I knew why. Were
those meetings, at which the election of the future Pope would almost

certainly be decided, impartial? Barely two days before, we had learned that Albani was in cahoots with the Imperial Ambassador, Count von Lamberg. As for Spada, being the Secretary of State of a Neapolitan pope, he was naturally pro-Spanish. Spinola, as I had read in the Abbot's last letter, was pro-Empire. French interests, or so it seems, were not represented. This could certainly not please Atto. As though that were not enough, Lamberg and Albani had got hold of the treatise on the Secrets of the Conclave and probably intended to use it against Atto.

"And now, what are we to do?" I asked.

"There's no point in sticking our noses in over there and being seen by Torre's guards."

"So?"

"I declare myself defeated. By now the festivities at Villa Spada are at their last gasp and tomorrow all the guests will leave. We shall never know what those three were confabulating about."

The seraphic resignation with which Atto had replied to me only reinforced my conviction. I already knew that, opinion or no opinion, conclave or succession, something quite different lay behind his presence at the Villa Spada: the mission of love with which the Most Christian King had entrusted him, in the hope of persuading Maria Mancini to see him once more.

"Let us go and take one last look at the picture," said he at last, "even if I despair of getting anything more from it; then let us go and see whether Buvat has found Cloridia."

We descended the little iron staircase, but just as we were about to enter the service stairs once more and descend to the second floor, we heard that voice:

> *This work I call a looking-glass*
> *In which each fool shall see an ass.*
> *The viewer learns with certainty;*
> *My mirror leaves no mystery.*

It was Albicastro's inimitable timbre, although slightly muffled. It came from within the little penthouse from which the balcony was suspended.

"Again that Dutch lunatic," moaned Abbot Melani. "As if that fiddle were not enough, now he must needs pester us again with his damned Sebastian Brant. But what's Albicastro up to in there and how did he get in?" he asked, thoroughly vexed.

"Oh, to the Devil with him," said Atto, opening the door to the little penthouse which we had not even noticed before that. It was then that it all happened.

৵৽

The penthouse was empty. Albicastro was not there. Curiously, the light was very dim. It came from two windows on the side facing Saint Peter's. The glass was partially blackened, so as to reduce the light drastically and – so I suspected – to make the visitor's steps uncertain. The space was quadrangular, with two pillars in the middle, perhaps supports for the little balcony. We were just next to one another and it was comforting in that strange place to feel Atto's by my side. Then we heard the Dutchman once more.

> *Whoever sees with open eyes*
> *Cannot regard himself as wise,*
> *For he shall see upon reflection*
> *That humans teem with imperfection.*

A disembodied voice, quite impossible to place. True, those verses were typical of Albicastro's usual inane ramblings, yet it was as though, in order to reach us, they had passed through some alien dimension in which sound is drained, washed free of its very properties. It was (to give the reader a fair idea) the voice of Albicastro's ghost. It seemed to come from the left.

We therefore turned to the left, and we saw.

It was there, or rather, they were *both* there looking at us. What cruel comedy there was in that sharp vision, I thought in a sudden flash of humour, as I beheld the being both one and double, and he looked at us. After Albicastro's ghostly voice, the Tetràchion overwhelmed us with the evidence of its utterly carnal presence, its stolid bestiality.

They stared at us as one, both with that dazed expression which only the Habsburg chin, that monstrously protruding jaw, can confer upon a human visage. Moreover the eyes were mismatched, the one sticking out, the other caved in, while the neck was twisted, the bodies deformed: one was stunted, as so often happens to beings ill-favoured by nature, the other, bloated. The flanks fused together, the legs wavering and horridly twisted one against the other, almost like the tentacles of some marine monster, gave that being the miserable destiny of twins who share the same body.

Incapable of opening my mouth, I raised my hand to shield my sight, and saw that the wretched creature (or one of them, but which?) gestured towards me, greeting me or begging perhaps to be left in peace. Then their features, as though made of quicksilver, became even more distorted, so that the chin of the one protruded absurdly, while the other collapsed on itself, and one chest was contorted in a horrendous spasm, while the raised hand of the other became a paw, a hoof, a stump. What nauseous and horrifying force dominated that flesh, those skins, those bones, and deformed them with the same cruel mastery as a taxidermist exercises upon the cadavers of the beasts which he stuffs?

Without a care for the sad spectacle of the *monstrum Tetràchion* and the horror it inspired, Albicastro's voice rang out as mockingly and ferociously as those paintings in which Death, a walking skeleton shouldering a scythe, walks calmly amongst the plumed knights and ladies whom he is about to harvest:

> *He's stirring at the dunces' stew;*
> *He thinks he's wise and handsome too,*
> *And with his mirror form so pleased*
> *You'd think he had a mind diseased;*
> *Indeed he cannot see the ass*
> *That's grinning at him from the glass!*

Then there remained nothing, only horror, folly and desperation, my scream, our disorderly, precipitous flight down the stairs and then down the road, each paying no attention to the other, and at last the pain of having found in the mysterious abyss of the Vessel a second abyss peopled by monsters, sad morbidity, incest and death.

"Do you know who Ulisse Aldrovandi is?"

"No, I do not," I heard my distant voice reply, as pale and empty as my face.

We were in Atto's apartments at Villa Spada, where Buvat had summoned Cloridia. My legs were still trembling, but I had come back to myself sufficiently to hear others' voices, or at least to pretend that I heard them.

"But what ails you, husband?"

"Nothing, nothing," I answered, indicating Atto's frowning forehead with my glance and gesturing that only later would I be able to explain. "Now, tell us."

Cloridia had found out at once. She had found, not the book, but something better: now, at last, she could explain to us what the Tetràchion was.

"'Tis a very curious business indeed that your secretary has asked me to advise you on, Signor Abbot Melani," she began.

"Why curious?"

"It is something reserved for the very few, a matter that's almost obscure, I'd say. These are things which midwives are in fact not even obliged to know; even if we do, in the end, learn a little of everything: medicine, anatomy, natural philosophy. . ." said she with a knowing grimace.

"And what is this subject that's so unusual?"

"It is the science of abnormal foetuses and the generation of prodigies and portents: the science of monsters."

"Monsters?" asked Atto, on whose face I could for an instant descry the same terified expression as it had taken on when faced with the Tetràchion.

Cloridia then explained that the literature on the subject was most extensive. Among the most exhaustive works, one must mention the *Deux livres de chirurgie* by Ambroise Paré, first chirurgeon to the King of France, published over a century ago, and the more recent *Monstrorum historia* by the learned Bolognese Ulisse Aldrovandi, which listed the most famous cases of monstrous births and unnatural features.

"There is, for example, the celebrated case of an Ethiopian born with four eyes, one next to the other, or that of a man who came into this world with the neck and head of a crane, and there was another born with a dog's head. . ." said Cloridia, apparently savouring our reactions.

The list of monstrous births, in nature and in man, continued with hairy little girls, infants with horse's legs, new-born babes like fishes enveloped in a monk's habit, creatures in the form of scorpions, with two hands on each arm and huge asses' ears, or with the face of a wolf; or others with the features of a goat-like biped, raptor's talons, flaccid breasts, demon's wings, eagle's claws and canine chest; with mermaid's characteristics (but masculine) and with a devil's head, horns, goat's ears, great bestial fangs, protruding tongue, hands with thumbs but no other fingers, crested fins on the arms and back, seal's tail; or again, creatures with a woman's belly, one foot a pig's trotter and the other made like a hen's, or with the whole body covered in feathers; even gruesome entities formed like fish-pigs, with webbed and clawed fins, human eyes emerging from their scaly sides and a mouth full of fangs; and, to end with, a fine exemplar of the *monstrum cornatum & alatum*: with a bear's head, no arms, an enormous spindle-shaped penis ending in a point, one leg feathered, eagle's wings, an eye on the knee and the left foot webbed.

"Enough, enough, that will do for me," Atto protested at length, as disgusted by the descriptions as I. "So, what then is the Tetràchion?"

"The Tetràchion, Signor Abbot Melani," replied Cloridia in a subtly sarcastic tone of voice, "might prove somewhat indigestible for you, like some of those poor beings of which you have just heard, almost all of which miscarried or were stillborn."

"And why is that?"

"It is another kind of misfortune of nature. In the language of the specialists, it concerns a well-known case that occurred in Paris in 1546: a woman six months pregnant gave birth to a creature with two heads, four arms and four legs. Doctor Paré, who carried out the autopsy on the child, found that it had only one heart. From this he concluded, on the basis of Aristotle's well-known statement, that it must really be one infant, not two. The malformation was probably caused by a material defect, or by something wrong with the womb, which was too small, so that the seed was hard pressed and coagulated into a globe, producing two infants connected and united."

"And those two beings, or rather, that being, had. . . four legs?" asked Atto.

"Two heads, four arms and as many legs."

Atto lowered his eyes and scratched his forehead, while with the eyes of thought he returned to the infernal vision he had shared with me.

"But," continued Cloridia, "there have been less grave examples of a Tetràchion."

"What do you mean?"

"There have been cases of twins, perfect in every way, but united in some part of the body solely by their skin; or joined by a member, an arm or a leg, which is thus deformed. Both such cases cannot, however, be distinguished at birth from the more severe cases, for they cannot be separated as that might kill them. They must be allowed to grow. If they attain adulthood, they may be operated on with little harm. At most, they will be crippled."

I could not have said whether the being (or beings) which we faced in the little house on the terrace corresponded in all details to the image cited by my wise spouse: too great was the horror that had seized me upon seeing it. At least one detail did, however, correspond: the number four; the four contained in the Tetràchion, the being that stands on four columns, as in the (clearly stylised and beautified) image of the two marine deities on Capitor's dish.

"In any case, there are worse things," commented Cloridia.

"Worse things. . ." repeated Atto, somewhat shaken. "What do you mean?"

Cloridia explained that she was referring to unheard of entities like the *Monstrum triceps capite Vulpis, Draconis & Aquilae* which was for some time to be found near the banks of the Nile and which, besides having an arm and limb like an eagle's, a horse's tail, feathered legs ending in two feet, one fin and one dog's paw, had three heads. There was also the *Monstrum bifrons* born to a Frenchwoman in Geneva in 1555: it had two faces, like the god Janus, with a head, arms and legs, both in front and behind; or again the *Monstrum biceps caudatum* born on 26th October 1598 in a citadel between Augeria and Tortona: two boys with two backs, but joined on the right side so that they had one arm and one leg for each head but, in the middle, instead of the other two legs, an enormous, horrendous fleshy excrescence.

"Tell me just one thing, Monna Cloridia," Atto interrupted her. "What causes such monstrosities?"

My wife explained that, if it was not to be defective, childbirth must satisfy five conditions: the infant must be born in the right position, at the right time, easily, with no sickness that cannot be cured by means of purges, and with complete, perfect limbs. Any delivery which fails to satisfy one of these conditions will be defective. If the infant is partially imperfect, it will be called a monster; if it is completely unsound, it will just be a formless piece of flesh.

But the principal cause lies in the mother's imagination. If the woman imprints the vestige of something desired in the unborn infant's body, it will come to pass, because she desires that greatly. Yet, what foolish woman would ever desire to have monstrous children? The answer is that one does not need desire to generate monsters, it is enough that the expectant mother should see something monstrous, even without desiring it.

"This comes of something natural which we see almost every day of our lives. If someone yawns, you too will yawn; if you see wine running from a barrel, you will want to urinate; if you see a red cloth, your nose will bleed; if you see someone else drinking medicine or buying it from the grocer, you will evacuate your bowels three or even four times. For the same reason, if you place a killer before the body of someone he has killed, more blood will gush from that corpse."

Atto made no negative comment on Cloridia's discourse. After all, he too had attributed to a similar theory (that of flying corpuscles) the apparition of Fouquet, Maria and Louis at the Vessel. Why, then, should he not admit that a mother's imagination, which is so intimately involved with the fruit of her womb, could determine so many mutations in the foetus?

"The midwife must, in any case, baptise monsters at once," continued Cloridia, "because most of them survive only a very short time. To be precise, a monster with two heads or two torsos should be baptised twice, but only once if it has only one face and four arms and four legs."

If in the monster one can recognise one distinct body, said she, completing her explanation, but the other cannot be clearly discerned, the first to be baptised will be that which clearly belongs to the human race, then the other, but *sub conditione*, meaning that, for the baptism to be valid, God must recognise the second one as being endowed with a soul, which only He will be able to see beyond the appearance of the deformity.

"As you have seen, I was not lying when I said to you that the subject of monstrous foetuses is somewhat curious," commented Cloridia; "and, what is more, rather an entertaining matter to tell of to women who have just given birth to fine, healthy infants. After all the travails of childbirth, while they are resting before the afterbirth and the purges, they'll be cheered up by tales and theories about monsters."

"Cheered up?" muttered Atto, whose greenish pallor gave us cause to fear an attack of nausea.

"But of course," trilled my little wife. "When they're resting under observation, we give them rather amusing descriptions of monstrous creatures, with dog's, calf's, elephant's, deer's, sheep's or lamb's heads or with goat's legs or other members resembling those of some animal. Or those with more members than usual, like two heads or four arms, as with your Tetràchion. Or monsters resulting from the crossing of two different species, like centaurs, half man and half horse, minotaurs, half bull, or onocentaurs, half donkey. Then there's the legend of Gerion, King of Spain, who had three heads, and. . ."

"What's that?" Melani interrupted her again. "A King of Spain with three heads?"

"Exactly," she confirmed, noticing Atto's interest. "It is said that they were triplets born joined together, and that they reigned in great concord."

"Tell me more about this Gerion, Monna Cloridia," Atto requested, wiping the perspiration dripping from his forehead with a handkerchief.

"There's no cause for surprise," said my wife. "Have not the kings of Spain a two-headed eagle on their arms? That is simply a memento of a defective birth of that kind which took place among the Habsburgs in long bygone days."

I held my breath. This would have been the time to talk and tell Cloridia what had happened.

But Atto said nothing. I understood that he was overcome by shame and even diffidence at the prospect of telling Cloridia of such an incredible event. In any case, in order to explain himself, the Abbot would be constrained to admit our dishonourable flight. For my part, I did not wish to break his silence: the secret belonged to us both.

It was no accident that Spain, continued Cloridia, was a land where all manner of extraordinary and anomalous births had been thoroughly studied. The Iberian Antonio Torquemada, in his book, *The Garden of Curious Flowers* writes, for example, that from bears and baboons, if they mate with women, perfect men may be born with their wits well about them. He tells of a Swedish woman who mated with a bear and of a Portuguese one who, condemned to death and driven into the midst of a wilderness, was with child by a baboon: both gave birth to perfect men. The same thing happened between a woman and a dog who were the only survivors of a shipwreck in the East Indies. Marooned in a desert place infested with wild beasts by the name of Tartary, the dog defended the woman from attacks by the wild beasts and love grew up between them. She became pregnant and gave birth to a perfect boy. He in turn lay with his mother and they gave birth to so many perfect and wise men and women that they peopled the whole kingdom. The dog's descendants preserved the memory of their ancestor and to this day they can find no finer title for their emperor than the Great Khanine.

"If this were the case," commented my wife, who was becoming more and more amused by the bewilderment she was causing me and Atto, "the Scaligeri, the lords of Verona, might also be of canine origin, for many members of that family are called Cane della Scala or even Cangrande della Scala."

Soon, Abbot Melani dismissed us all. I looked at him. He had reached the limit of his strength. The tremendous vision we had seen at the Vessel had profoundly shocked him and he now urgently needed to rest. What was more, that evening was to be the final one in the series of festivities; and Albani would be present.

When I was left alone with Cloridia, I was able to bring her up to date with the latest disconcerting events. She became pensive, and when I asked her for her opinion on the matter, she would only venture: "You are digging too deep: some matters are best left alone. You should rather be busying yourself with obtaining the girls' dowry from Abbot Melani."

❧

While awaiting the final spectacle, which was to begin only after dark, the afternoon had been dedicated to various amusements and entertainments.

A real tennis court had been set up. For the players there had been acquired from Horatio at the Piazza di Fico, a noted real tennis player, the most perfect racquets and the best "flying balls". A short distance away, another space had been prepared for the game of bowls.

The participants, however, were few. Many guests preferred to save their strength for the long night of entertainments and carousing ahead of them. Cardinal Spada had arranged for a number of Turkish pavilions to be set up decked in the finest, lightest, opalescent silk gauze which, it seems, was sent specially from Armenia (and was something that had never before been seen in Rome), all in the most vivid colours, richly ornate and most pleasant to behold. Those who so desired could open up the roof onto the starry sky. Meanwhile, braziers would be lit to fill the night with sweet-smelling smoke. Here, those guests who did not wish to abandon themselves to sleep could take their ease on generous day-beds where they would be served until the break of day with all manner of delicacies by lackeys attired in gorgeous Saracen uniforms, enjoying both the exotic decor and that rare opportunity capriciously to take their ease.

In view of the small numbers of persons playing real tennis and bowls, Don Paschatio soon exempted me from serving those gentlemen and sent me instead to help prepare the Turkish pavilions: unrolling tapestries and carpets, setting up the braziers, polishing brass bowls and filling them with perfumed water for washing hands, providing each pavilion with napkins and towels in abundance, *et cetera*, *et cetera*.

While busying myself thus, I thought of Abbot Melani. As we had learned from Ugonio, his treatise on the Secrets of the Conclave was due on the morrow, Thursday, to pass from the hands of the *cerretani* into those of Cardinal Albani. What might the Secretary for Breves, who had clashed so bitterly with Atto, do with it? Perhaps he might approach the Abbot that very evening to propose some sordid exchange that would compromise him even more: I shall refrain from ruining you, provided that you do me this small favour. . .

Or perhaps tomorrow, for instance, during the guests' visit to Palazzo Spada, he might take advantage of the situation to create a public scandal, casting the manuscript at the feet of the Pope's other ministers, starting with Cardinal Spada. Then, everyone would be able to read the most recondite information on conclaves, France's secret intentions, the Abbot's true opinion on dozens and dozens of cardinals, concerning whom Atto, in that secret report (intended for the eyes of the Most Christian King only), had revealed who knows what sins.

Abbot Melani's career, an entire lifetime devoted to tricks, insults, threats and dissimulation, was on the point of coming to an end. His vocation as a political acrobat, walking a tightrope between espionage and diplomacy, was within a hair's breadth of failure. Within a few hours, at the very latest on the next day, all the discretion he had employed for decades, all the prudent stratagems, the subterfuges. . . Yes, everything would collapse under the weight of infamy and betrayal, as well as in the eyes of the senior hierarchy of the Church of Rome: those of whom he boasted that he knew them as well as the contents of his own pockets. Could one imagine a worse epilogue?

Evening the Eighth
14ᵀᴴ JULY, 1700

✠

After so many celebrations and festivities, it had all come to an end. We were on the final evening of the entertainments which were, or so Cardinal Spada had ordered, to attain the highest peaks of gaiety and wonder. For the solemn leave-taking, a great pyrotechnic spectacle, or, as others would call it, a display of fireworks, had been laid on. Ephemeral machines, rockets and dazzling Catherine wheels were to light up the Roman night, arousing admiration and wonderment in the four corners of the Holy City. Had he been in good health, even the Holy Father would from his window have been able to admire the enchantments which the artificers hired by Don Paschatio were preparing on the lawns of the villa. The noble guests were already comfortably seated on the lawn, where plentiful chairs, armchairs and day-beds had been arranged so as to be able to seat even late arrivals.

Despite all the adventures I had lived through that day with Atto, the huge number of questions in search of an answer, the knots to be loosed, and all the excitement to which that had given rise, I suddenly gave way to sadness and weariness. The fatigue caused by too many efforts consumed my limbs and my thoughts were tinged with the bitter ink of melancholy.

On the next afternoon, the guests would have packed, I thought, and would be returning to their homes and business, some at the other end of Rome, some outside the city, some even beyond the confines of the states of the Church. That great event, the nuptials of Clemente Spada and Maria Pulcheria Rocci, was by now behind us. Two souls were concluding their existence as youngsters and setting out on a new life as spouses. However joyous the occasion, it was but one chapter giving way to the next. Thus every single thing in this world, mean or glorious, must pass, leaving in its wake only the volatile stuff of human memory. Once the lights had died, darkness would return to my modest life as a rustic and a servant.

"*Tenebrae factae sunt*," I murmured to myself, greeting the coming of night, when a great explosion made me jump.

The artificers had set off the deafening sarabande of fireworks. At a nod from Cardinal Spada, a whole series of cannon salvoes had begun which shook the whole company, to the great (but well dissimulated) amusement of the master of the house.

After the salvo came the first scenic apparition. In those days, there had been brought to Rome from the Orient a being that had rarely been seen in the city, larger and more terrifying than any animal described in living memory: an elephant. He was led by his keepers through the streets of the centre, to the astonishment of the children, the fascination of natural philosophers and the terror of old women.

Well, they all turned in amazement when such a colossus entered the gates of Villa Spada. This was another exemplar of the same race, no less mighty than its fellow, accompanied by four janissaries, and it was now advancing towards the spectators, panting savagely as it came.

"His Lordship, the Elephant!" announced the Major-Domo proudly, while some ladies uttered little cries of dismay and a number even stood up to take flight. A moment before fear got the better of the amiable gathering, something unimaginable happened. A white, red and yellow flame burst from the back of the beast, then a series of little flames began to issue from the tip of its curved tusks; following which, a volley of firecrackers exploded from the tip of its trunk, almost as though it had been transformed into a musket. Everyone then knew: it was an artificial elephant made of wood and papier mâché, a perfect imitation of the real thing, equipped to display fireworks. One could see that it was, after all, moving on a float, behind which the artificers were pushing, half hidden. Hearts beat more easily; as the great beast advanced along the main avenue, even the most fearful returned to their seats. All that huffing and puffing (one could now see) was produced by a small boy working a pair of bellows placed behind the sham monster, which released compressed air into a tube that emerged from its mouth. The company, however, especially the ladies, was still more fearful than entertained.

"Poor ladies, what a scare! As the Cavalier Bernini put it, pyrotechnical machines are made to impress, not to amuse."

It was Abbot Melani, who had discreetly come to my side as I helped a monsignor to his feet who had fallen as he attempted to flee. Atto was quivering and tense as a palfrey just before a race. "I have asked. Albani is not here. He will be coming tomorrow, perhaps," he whispered curtly.

Just when it came near to where we stood, the luminous elephant was extinguished like a burnt-out taper. With perfect timing, the chaos of brilliant rockets began. First came a green comet, followed by three yellow shooting stars, then three red ones, then again a green one, after which came special ones which broke up into a stream of sparks, a deluge of light, a dazzling explosion of a thousand incandescent meteors.

"Do you like the spectacle, Your Eminence?" Prince Cesarini asked Cardinal Ottoboni, who was that evening attending the celebrations for the first time, between one explosion and the next.

"Oh, 'tis not bad. But I am not made for such noise. Just to give you an example, I recall with greater pleasure the silent light spectacle with torches on the cupola of Saint Peter's ten years ago, to be exact, when Saint John of God was canonised," replied the Cardinal with a hint of melancholy in his voice, perhaps because ten years ago his uncle, Alexander VIII, had been Pope.

This amiable chatter was interrupted by the arrival of another float, on which was seated no less than Lucifer in person. The guests laughed. It was by now clear that each apparition, however frightening, was for their entertainment. The moving figure of the Devil, complete with horns and infernal sneer, was half hidden behind a bed of reeds and held coiled in his arms the malefic serpent of Genesis. Suddenly, from the reptile's mouth shot a tongue of fire that could not have been more real. Then the head of the Evil One exploded with a tremendous bang and his body rapidly caught fire, which gave rise to a great burst of applause even from the most fearful trembling ladies. To the guests' utter astonishment, when the smoke cleared, we saw in the place of Satan a noble angel, with shining wings and immaculate vestments, while at the four corners of the float joyful flames appeared, illuminating the victory of light over darkness; which everyone commented upon with great pleasure amidst great and general applause.

In every corner of the garden, then, including the most recondite, the Catherine wheels lit up: spirals of yellow, pink, violet and the colour of lightning, hanging from trees, hedges and the boundary wall, spitting fire everywhere and transforming the scene (except for those parts set aside for the guests) into an infernal forest, racked by Vulcan's darts. Hammering salvoes of firecrackers deafened the company and filled the air with acrid, stinging smoke, so that the eyes of many were filled with tears. At the same time, rockets were again launched, filling the sky with multicoloured flashes, so that all around us seemed to be a circle of hell from whose burning talons Atto and I, standing one beside the other like Dante and Virgil, miraculously escaped only by the will of the author who had brought us there.

The deluge of fire and lightning, although breathtaking, was not without consequences. A spark from a Catherine wheel set fire to the periwig of Count Antonio Maria Fede, a resident of the Duchy of Tuscany. We all heard the Count's cries of horrified surprise and his impassioned complaints to Don Paschatio. The Major-Domo sent at once for the head of the artificers who, however (or so his acolytes said), had had to absent himself owing to a prior engagement.

"So Count Arselick almost caught fire," commented Atto with a happy grin, his fun spoiled only by the wait for Albani's arrival.

"I beg your pardon?"

"That's Count Fede's nickname, for 'tis said that he made his career licking the arse of the Grand Duke of Tuscany, and later that of His Holiness. He did not deign to greet me because he knows that in April the Most Serene Republic of Venice granted me the status of Patrician, so that now we are both nobles, only he began life as a porter, and I did not, heh!"

There was not much cause for laughter, I thought to myself, for Atto too had been born poor: he was the son of a humble bell-ringer at the cathedral of Pistoia, as I remember learning many years ago, at the time when we met. It was no accident that, of the seven brothers, no fewer than four were destined for castration by their father, in the hope of replenishing the family's coffers.

"Oh!" exclaimed the Abbot at that moment, "what a pleasant surprise!"

An elegant and rather stiff gentleman was moving towards Atto, accompanied by his fine lady and a servant.

"'Tis Niccolò Erizzo, Ambassador of the Republic of Venice," Melani whispered to me before going to exchange greetings.

"Prince Vaini has just been seen running like mad from a little wood," Erizzo announced with a wink after the ritual salutations.

"He was amusing himself there in the bushes with a beautiful lady, married to a marchese whose name we unfortunately don't know."

"Ah yes, and what were the two conversing about amidst all that verdure?"

"That, I leave to your imagination. Suddenly a giant Catherine wheel lit up and Vaini was so scared that he was almost reduced to ashes."

"Vaini the vain reduced to ashes or to. . . vanilla?" Atto replied, causing all three to burst out laughing. "Oh, please do excuse me, here is an old friend. . ."

I understood the subterfuge at once. Pretending that he had seen some other influential personage, he took his leave of the couple, who were already joining others. From behind a bush, Sfasciamonti had been gesturing to him. They spoke briefly, whereupon Atto turned back and came to fetch me.

"Sfasciamonti has obtained that information," said he, passing me a piece of paper.

I opened it at once and read.

Nicola Zabaglia.
Saint Peter's Factory. Head of the School.

శ్రీ

"There can be no question of this, Signor Atto. I am telling you for the last time."

Abbot Melani said nothing.

"Do you know Saint Peter's? Have you been there?"

"Of course I have been there, but. . ."

"Then you will know that the undertaking you propose is utterly insane!" I exclaimed, quite beside myself.

We met again at a late hour in Atto's apartments, when the smoke from the fireworks had cleared and the guests were busy feasting in the Turkish pavilions.

"Albani did not put in an appearance," the Abbot began, with his mien somewhat restored. After that, we discussed the information obtained from the catchpoll.

"There is no point in insisting, Signor Atto, you will never succeed in convincing me."

Thus far, I had resisted his insistent pleas with success. Then, however, came the argument I feared.

"Even if you will not do it for me, if I were in your place I'd do it for my daughters."

"Our agreement laid down explicitly that I was not to risk my skin."

"But that you would do all that was *possible* to favour my interests."

"And how about you?" I retorted. "The festivities are over: tell me when you intend to keep *your* promises. Where is my daughters' dowry? Let us hear that!"

"I have already instructed a Capitoline notary," Abbot Melani answered tersely. "He is drawing up the deeds. We shall go and see him the day after tomorrow."

A smile of embarrassment and relief escaped me.

"If you respect our agreement," he added icily.

I felt cornered. Here was a veiled threat that he would not pay the dowries if I refused to do what he asked of me.

"I do not understand," I murmured disconsolately. "What makes you think they are in that place? Just because we now know that this friend of the *cerretani*, this fellow called Zabaglia, is employed by Saint Peter's Factory."

Atto explained. I had to admit that the idea made sense. I did not argue the point; and that was a sign of my giving in.

"In any case, I shall not be able to accompany you," Atto concluded.

"And why not? The treatise on the Secrets of the Conclave is yours, it is you above all who. . ."

"This will call for agility, swift reflexes, the ability to hide promptly," said he with a rather hoarse voice.

Without saying it, he had nevertheless said it: for an undertaking such as that which he was proposing, Atto was simply too old.

"Then I shall go with Sfasciamonti," said I resignedly.

Atto thought for a moment.

"Take Buvat with you, too. And above all, take these."

"I had already thought of that, Signor Atto," said I, taking from his hands Ugonio's heavy, jangling bunch of keys.

❧

We departed not long before daybreak to minimise the risk of being seen by guards or catchpolls of any sort. Abbot Melani had told

Sfasciamonti and Buvat that they were to climb up high, but without specifying *how* high.

The Sacred Ball: as we moved away from Villa Spada, I laughed to myself at that rather clumsy name used by the *corpisantari* and the *cerretani*. It was, however, a name which, once one knew the object to which it referred, turned out to be quite accurate. There were many tales about that ball and even I had heard some of them, since it was famed for being almost impossible of access, and brave was he who made it that far.

The undertaking was absurd. But for that very reason, I knew that I should need all the courage I could muster. Not only must I prove bold and reckless like Abbot Melani, I must feel myself so to be. Like Saint George, a dragon stood before me, which I must slay. The fear that might prevent me, however, lay within me. The most redoubtable adversary sleeps between our two ears.

I could already hear my lovely Cloridia's voice when the time would come to tell her of this venture, and she would interrogate me about all that had taken place, pulling me to pieces with her steely logic, forcing me to tell of all the difficulties, hazards and madcap schemes planned by Atto but executed by myself.

At first, she would be overcome by pity: she would embrace me and cover me with kisses at the thought of all that I had risked. Soon, however, her invincible lucidity would get the better of her; she would hear me out with her eyes bulging from their sockets and her hair standing up on her head like some new Gorgon, commenting with growing scorn on my account of what I had done. Finally, holding back her deadly anger, she would call me irresponsible, a bad husband and father, a beast and a megalomaniac and, what was worse, an idiot. True, the future of our little daughters was at stake, and I had agreed to a lavish recompense for my services; but for death there can be no recompense.

While I received this dressing-down from Cloridia, our two daughters would nod in agreement with severe expressions on their little faces, before laughing behind my back. Perhaps my spouse would even banish me for a few days from the family home, to save herself from the temptation of hitting me over the head with a ladle or striking me with one of her massive and dangerous obstetrical instruments.

The risk was there, nor was there any use denying it; but if the venture were to succeed, I could claim a bonus from Atto, and a big one too. Now, however, it was premature to think of all that. We must place our trust in Sfasciamonti's massive shoulders and in the merciful hands of the Saviour, whom I implored to watch over me and keep me from harm.

Ugonio the *corpisantaro* had said that until Thursday the treatise would be kept in the Sacred Ball. Don Tibaldutio had added that the *cerretani* were said to have a friend at Saint Peter's. The information from Sfasciamonti completed the picture, giving a name to the friend of the ragged scoundrels.

Nicola Zabaglia was a member of the venerable factory of Saint Peter's, the centuries old institution that looked after the construction, maintenance and restoration of the basilica built over the tomb of the first Pope. He even enjoyed a position of some eminence, being regarded as a genius in the construction of machines for the transport of large objects (stones, columns, *et cetera*) and he had been appointed director of the school for future members of the factory, who were known as *sampietrini*.

Only the *sampietrini* had access to the most secret places of the basilica: from the mysterious crypts (where Peter's tomb lies) to the aery pinnacles of the cupola.

All this had suggested to Atto where we should find his treatise on the Secrets of the Conclave. The problem was only how to get there, especially at that hour.

The way from the villa to Saint Peter's, skirting the northern slopes of the Janiculum Hill, was rapid and free from difficulties. After crossing the crowded streets of the suburbs approaching the piazza, we slipped under the great colonnade with its two mirrored semicircles, decorated with no fewer than one hundred and forty statues of saints, which extends around the great Saint Peter's Square in a faithful image of the merciful arms of Mother Church, offering shelter and consolation to her beloved children.

The square was constantly watched over by guards and it was obvious that, sooner or later, we must encounter them, ideally as late as possible. We therefore penetrated the great complex of the basilica through an arch on the far right of the façade, leaving to our left the great entrance portico and the adjoining Door of Death. We then passed through a small courtyard which led through a narrow corridor open to the sky to yet another little courtyard under the north face of the sacred edifice, next to the Vatican gardens.

Thence, through a great door, we passed through the sacred walls of the basilica. We found ourselves in a small, dark vestibule. To our right was a wide spiral staircase. At the foot of this, we were, however, stopped by a guard. Fortunately, Sfasciamonti knew what to do. With easy, brisk explanations he confused our interrogator, using the banal pretext that he was looking for one of the *sampietrini*, which was, after all, almost the truth (as it was Zabaglia's name that had brought us there). We passed the guard nonchalantly and disappeared rapidly up the stairs.

Thus, we climbed the great spiral. The curving vault of the rising shaft was dimly lit by torches and punctuated by great windows behind robust iron grilles. We advanced cautiously, almost clinging to the fine balustrade. Every now and then there would be little doorways leading from the outer wall of the staircase with inscriptions above them that remained obscure to us, such as "First Corridor", "Second Corridor", "Octaves of St Basil and St Jerome", presumably leading to passages used by the *sampietrini* to gain access to the most secret anfractuosities of the enormous construction.

A few minutes later, we encountered another individual, who in turn asked what we were doing there at that hour. This time, Sfasciamonti made use of his sergeant's title, making it clearly understood that he was under no obligation to say a thing. The other nodded and did nothing to oppose our passage. We could breathe again.

After no little climbing, already panting from fatigue and anxiety, we came to a long level corridor, then a short spiral staircase. This we climbed.

At the end of this came the surprise. These stairs had brought us to a terrace, indeed to the one real terrace in Saint Peter's: the great flat area behind the statues of the Redeemer and the Twelve Apostles which dominate and embellish the façade. Before us, we found a colossus: the great drum and then the monumental ogive of the cupola.

I looked behind me. We had emerged onto the terrace from a cupola with an octagonal base, which seemed minuscule beside its great companion. Since the plan of the basilica is that of a great cross, the terrace covered the surface of the longer arm from the end all the way up to the point of intersection with the shorter arm. The space was punctuated by cupolas terminating in the great lanterns which give light to the side chapels, and was divided in the middle by a long shed with a sloping roof.

Above our heads, night spread its dark veil. The moon gave only the vaguest of glimmers from a fine crescent; just enough, I thought, to distinguish the colossal outline of the basilica and to instil a true fear of God, so that, whatever might happen, our visit would not be in vain. But while these thoughts were crossing my mind, events took the turn I most feared.

"There they are," we heard clearly pronounced in the dark. I knew at once: the second guard we had met had not trusted us. Someone had been sent to intercept us.

I could distinguish a small group of persons, at least two and not more than four advancing from the end of the terrace giving onto the square, where the statue of Our Lord turns his holy face towards the multitudes of the faithful.

"What shall we do?" I asked Buvat.

"I could try to persuade them by throwing them a coin," said Sfasciamonti, "even if I don't really think that. . ."

But I already lacked the ears to hear and the patience to wait. I had made my own calculations. If I was quick enough, I had a good chance of making it.

"Eh, boy, look here. . ." I heard Sfasciamonti say as I ran like mad and took a stairway with two separate flights which climbed up the outside of the drum of the cupola and led to an entrance.

Then there were no more words: to my rapid footfalls responded those of Buvat and Sfasciamonti and those of the surprised and angry people on our heels.

"Dear Cloridia," I murmured with my voice broken by breathlessness, "when I tell you of this, I hope you'll forgive me."

The disadvantage was our scant, indeed non-existent knowledge of the place. The advantage was surprise, and the head start that had given me. My small stature seemed, on the face of it, to be a drawback, but I was later to find that, all in all, this was not the case.

I was running at breakneck speed, but with the secret (unreasonable) hope that I was not taking excessive risks: the worst thing that could happen to me would be to end up being caught by the guards of Saint Peter's, but I could always attribute the whole thing to audacity. I was stealing nothing, I was damaging nothing. To avoid trouble with the law, Sfasciamonti would make use of his many acquaintances, and Buvat would be able to get help from Atto who could get me out of trouble through his wide network of influential connections: all silly ideas mechanically repeated, only to urge me on.

Once I had entered the drum, another spiral staircase took me even higher. I could hear Sfasciamonti's wild footsteps closer and closer behind me, and behind him, those of Buvat and the guards. No one spoke: our lungs were for running, the guards' for pursuit.

At the top of the spiral staircase, I found myself at a junction; I chose at random and went to the left. I crossed a threshold with no door and suddenly found myself suspended above infinity.

I was inside the cupola, facing a chasm of incalculable immensity. A corridor ringing the vast drum stretched to the right and to the left: at my feet, a fathomless vision of the inside of the basilica. There lay the colossal central nave of Saint Peter's, precisely at the point where it intersects with the transept. Just there, but many, many yards below, I knew there stood the Cavaliere Bernini's grandiose baldaquin, the glory of the basilica and of all Christendom. Above me, the immeasurable vault of the cupola, an abyss standing over an abyss, made me feel like an atom of dust lost in interstellar space.

At my height, on the walls of the great tambour supporting the cupola, were colossal mosaics with tender little cherubs the size of five men seated on cornucopias as big as two carriages.

All that, I could, however, see only with the eyes of the imagination: the interior of the church was dimly lit by a handful of torches; a boundless dark cavern echoing only to the desperate rhythm of my feet.

The threshold whence I had emerged into that vertiginous observatory was one of the four entrances to the annular corridor, which were placed diametrically opposite one another at the cardinal points.

Right or left? Left again. This time, the threshold contained a door. I pushed: it was open. Left again: I banged my nose against the handle of a door, which was closed. Now there was no light at all, only moonless night. Left again, then.

A stairway. Stairs going straight up, then winding, but the broadest of steps. From the wall on the left, a glimmer of light, almost none. There was a large window giving onto the outside. Through it one could descry the roofs of the basilica, tranquil and indifferent to my desperate agitation. The spiral staircase kept climbing, then became rectilinear. Once again I collided with an obstacle: before me was a tight, airless little spiral staircase climbing vertically. I took it. The others, too, must have been in some difficulties; I heard a cry. I appeared to be going fast. The noise from them seemed a little further away. But, where was I? I prayed that my calculations would not run up against hard facts. Escape was even more important than attaining my goal. Negotiating the labyrinth of the cupola was like dismantling a delicate piece of clockwork, but Atto had shown me all the details. Fortunately, in the library of Villa Spada we had found all we needed and we had made use of the night hours before my departure to refine our tools. The tome we studied was *The Vatican Temple and its Origin* by the learned Carlo Fontana, rich in tables and illustrations and published in Rome six years earlier, in 1694. It contained plans, sections and prospects of the basilica and, of particular interest to me, the cupola. In a couple of hours' close study, I had memorised the arrangement of corridors and stairways in the upper part of the basilica. Although approximate, my memory had guided me well.

The stairs again began to wind. Strangely, both walls, the outer and the inner, leaned frighteningly to one side, leaving hardly any room to advance. I wondered how Sfasciamonti would manage to get through those absurd bowels: the air was dense, heavy, almost unbreathable. Every now and then a window provided a little relief and less torrid air, but there was no time in which to stop for breath.

Only then did I understand: I was in the cavity between the two layers of the cupola. The spiral stairs were installed between the outer surface and the inner one, which was only visible from within the basilica. But almost at once the vertiginous sensation of walking inside a body suspended over the void came to an end. The spiral no longer led upward, there was a brief level passage. From below, more cries.

"Sfasciamonti, Buvat, where are you?" I called.

In response, only voices and vague noises. My legs trembled a little, not only from fatigue. I tried to go faster, but slipped and fell heavily. I tumbled down several steps, hurting my thighs and knees severely. I stood up, still in one piece. I returned to the horizontal corridor, dragging myself forward who knows how far. No stairs, no way out, nothing.

Then I sensed it: something was missing, two or three paces in front of me: the floor. I tried to stop, lost my balance, held on with my right arm to the inner wall. And I felt it.

It was a stone step, an absolutely enormous one, almost up to my neck. I stretched out my arms and touched it. Yes, there was another step above it, and one above that, too. It was more or less as I had imagined it, and I felt confident: from that point on one climbed further. It was one of four stairways with huge steps, one at each cardinal point leading to the summit of the cupola within its cavity wall. The stairs began again. At last I realised with joy that being small meant one weighed little, and those who are light can move fast.

Initially, the huge steps were higher than they were wide; then, gradually, as one approached the very top of the cupola, the proportions were inverted. In the end there were only three more steps, then two, then one. Exhausted, but again on my feet, I pulled myself onto a horizontal platform, while from above a weak gleam of light came down to me – or perhaps one might better describe it as darkness less total. I fumbled to the right, to the left, in all directions, finding, first, a wall, then an opening. I stumbled, perhaps on a step, and my right hand found a banister. I no longer knew where I was going but I followed through without hesitation and at last I felt fresh air on my skin, found the outside world, the sky: I had emerged into the open.

My feet were treading the circular walkway that runs all around and above the cupola. On the inside, there was a double row of columns, under which one could pass through a series of arches. On the outside, however, the paving sloped downwards to allow rain water to run off, and this made the visitor feel continuously drawn towards the abyss. The only protection was a handrail, beyond which my eyes reeled, intoxicated by the invisible panorama of nocturnal Rome, lethargic and sunk in passivity. Wherever I looked, a plunge to death threatened.

"My sweet wife, from this point on I shall tell you nothing," I murmured, as my legs stiffened with fear and emotion.

Again I heard the panting of the guards. Whoever was hunting me down could not be far off now.

There was almost no time left. I looked for it, knowing from the book I had read with Atto at Villa Spada that it did exist. Halfway around the platform, I found it. A dark corner, an iron grate, two hinges: there it was. A little doorway that seemed almost to have been scraped with fingernails from the hard stone of the cupola. I pulled off my sweat-soaked shirt and drew from my breeches Ugonio's jingling bunch of keys. I looked for the right one. A big one, a slightly smaller one, another, the right size. Seconds passed, I was losing my advantage. I turned the key in the lock, needlessly: the door was already open. No time for cursing; a few rapid strides and I was inside.

The moment I passed through that door, I found myself on a narrow circular platform very similar to that which I had just left, but far smaller, with a handrail surround punctuated by great mushroom-shaped stone supports, even more perilously clinging to the top of the cupola. If only I had had the time, I would have delighted in the sprinkling of lights which the stars scattered across the black vault of heaven, indulging the fantasy that I could reach out and touch them with my hands.

In the midst of that disc-like upper platform, there was a small circular building. I immediately looked around it; there was no door. I was on the point of despairing, for I had heard any number of times that one could get in there, and then I saw it: a sort of low window was set into the wall at about the height of my stomach. I bent down and entered, and just as I did so I heard footsteps on the platform below.

Surprisingly, it was not completely dark inside this structure: a faint dawn light glimmered through the window I had just entered.

I heard a slight reverberation above my head. A ladder stretched upward towards the goal: the bronze ball that rises above the very highest point of Saint Peter's, immediately beneath the great cross which surmounts the basilica.

Leaping forward, I grasped a rung and hauled myself up, giving the wall a few kicks to help me on my way. As I clambered up, I saw that the vague light was growing stronger.

It is said that the ball of Saint Peter's can hold up to sixteen people, so long as they are suitably placed. However numerous those chasing us might be, there would, I knew, be no chance to put that report to the test.

At last, I poked my head into the ball, then my shoulders, at last resting on my elbows inside the great bronze sphere. Only then did I realise that I was not alone.

Perched with his great backside on the concave inner surface of the ball was Sfasciamonti, sweating like a donkey and panting, utterly winded. He had made it before me, probably taking another of the four stairs with huge steps that reach up to the top of the cupola within its cavity wall. In one hand, he was holding a little tome: the treatise on the Secrets of the Conclave; in the other, a pistol.

In the middle of the spherical cavity in which we stood, just next to the hole through which one gained access to it, there was a stool. The book must have been deposited on it and the catchpoll had been quicker than me in getting to it. Suddenly, he handed it to me.

"Put it in your breeches, they're coming!"

I heard a noise coming from below. Sfasciamonti's finger curved around the trigger. We seemed to have no way out.

"We can't fire, we are in a church. . . And besides, they'll arrest us," I observed, in my turn gasping for breath.

"If anything, we're *on top of* a church," the catchpoll sniggered.

It was pointless to try getting down from the ball: someone had entered the little structure and was about to climb the ladder. Sfasciamonti and I looked at one another, uncertain what to do next.

Then it all happened: our eyes were struck by a blinding flash which burned our faces like a whip, while our bodies contorted in shock.

Suddenly I understood why. As I penetrated, first, the little building, then the ball itself, I had been vaguely aware of a diffuse glimmer, growing ever clearer. Years back, I had known an old butcher whose son was employed in Saint Peter's Factory, and he had described to me what was now happening. The ball in which we stood had four slits in its sides, placed as high as a man at the four cardinal points: thrusting an incandescent blade into that facing east and flooding all with its presence, the sun had made its joyous introitus among us.

It was dawn.

Day the Ninth
15TH JULY, 1700

✠

As though it were a sign of destiny, the ray directly struck Atto's tome, which refracted its luminous flood into a thousand blinding white rivulets.

Indifferent to this curious event, Sfasciamonti pointed his pistol downwards.

"Halt or I fire, I am a sergeant of the Governor!" he cried.

Then (or so it seemed to me) he tripped over the stool, which fell through the hole in the ball with a great and general clangour. Perhaps the catchpoll fell after it. Perhaps, in his struggle to break his fall, he dragged me with him.

Time was no more. From light I passed to darkness, the world and the ball whirled drunkenly and suddenly I was elsewhere.

While they were carrying me away, a bag of worn-out, weary members, my eyes strove to catch one last fragment of those sacred pinnacles, that eyrie consecrated to the Lord.

I was head down; but by one of those curious algorithms of consciousness that enables some to read perfectly from right to left or to compose impromptu anagrams, before I again lost consciousness, it appeared to me, and I recognised it.

Proud and enigmatic, anchored on the heights of the Janiculum, the Vessel was observing us.

☙❧

"Behind every strange or inexplicable death there lies a conspiracy of the state, or of its secret forces," pronounced Abbot Melani.

My head was throbbing. My neck was hurting. To tell the truth, I was hurting all over.

"But also those cases of persons who disappear, or are kidnapped, or suffer incredible accidents, then miraculously reappear from nowhere safe and sound, all these things are clear signs of subversive plotting. No one can escape death like that save with the help of an assiduous practitioner."

Atto's voice was suspended in a naked crystalline void. My eyes were still closed and there seemed to be no urgency about opening them.

Some memories came to me: the sensation of my body, lying heavily in the back of a cart; the cold of daybreak; then the return to warm, familiar surroundings.

A few hours passed (or were they only minutes?) until I was awoken by the sound of the door handle opening and closing, and of footsteps in the corridor. My eyelids at last decided that it was time to wake up.

I was lying on Abbot Melani's bed in the casino of Villa Spada, still fully dressed. Atto sat nearby, on an armchair, lost in who knows what thoughts. He had not realised that I had come to my senses. Only after a few minutes did he detach his gaze from that imaginary point in mid-air on which he had fixed it and turn to me.

"Welcome back among the living," said he with a smile at once satisfied and ironic. "Your wife was very worried, she waited up for you all night. Even though it was dawn, I made sure she was informed that you had returned safe and sound.

"Where's Sfasciamonti?" I asked anxiously.

"Fast asleep."

"And Buvat?"

"In his little room. And snoring, to boot."

"I do not understand," I said, sitting up for the first time; "why did they not arrest us?"

"From what your catchpoll friend told us, you have been extremely lucky. Sfasciamonti threw himself at the *sampietrino* who was about to get into the ball, knocking you down in the process. After that, he disarmed him and, with a few kicks and punches, left him very much the worse for wear. Then he hoisted you onto his shoulders and carried you back down, without too much trouble, seeing his size. When he got there, nobody saw him. It was daybreak and there was not a soul about. Probably all the guards on duty had run after Buvat."

"After Buvat?"

"Yes, indeed. He took to his legs the moment they began to follow you, up on the terrace."

"What?" I exclaimed in astonishment, "I thought he had come up with us all the way to the. . ."

"Despite himself, he was quite brilliant. Instead of following you when you ran up the stairs towards the cupola, he turned and ran back down the stairs you had come from. One of the *sampietrini* who had been following you, a little fellow – oh, pardon me – followed him," explained the Abbot, excusing himself for his gaffe about my height. "But Buvat has long legs and he couldn't see him for dust. He ran out of Saint Peter's like greased lightning and no one even managed to get a glimpse of his face, he left them all standing. Then, typically enough, he got lost on the way back from Saint Peter's and arrived only a little while before you."

I was shocked through and through. I was convinced that I had two allies in my perilous rush up to the ball of Saint Peter's, but one had shamefully deserted while the other had collapsed on top of me.

"I know you bore yourself magnificently, you attained your goal."

"Your treatise on the Secrets of the Conclave!" I burst out. "Did Sfasciamonti give it to you?"

Atto's features became gently disconsolate:

"That was not possible. When he was carrying you, the book slipped out from your breeches and flew down. If I have understood correctly, it landed on a part of the terrace too far off to risk going there. He had to choose between safety and my treatise. He could not, I imagine, do otherwise."

"I don't understand. . . It had all gone so well, then. . . It is absurd," I commented, thoroughly distressed. "And then, why did he bring me here instead of taking me home?"

"Simple: he does not know where you live."

Still somewhat groggy, I had to wait for the stupor and disappointment beclouding my soul to settle. That dangerous chase, the fatigue, the fear. . . All for nothing. We had lost Atto's book. Then a vague memory came to me.

"Signor Atto, while I slept, I heard you talking."

"Perhaps I was thinking aloud."

"You said something about unexplained deaths, conspiracies of state. . . well, something of the sort."

"Really? I don't remember. But now you must get some rest, my boy, if you so desire," said he, standing up and moving towards the door.

"Will you be going into town with the other guests to visit the Palazzo Spada?"

"No."

"Will you really not go?" I asked, imagining that Atto might be afraid of meeting Albani. By then, some *sampietrino* at Zabaglio's orders might have recovered Atto's tome and be handing it over to the *cerretani*, who would in turn give it to the Grand Legator, namely Lamberg, who would hand it to the Secretary for Breves.

"It is not the moment for that," Atto replied. "I should love to examine the marvels of Palazzo Spada by the light of day, but we have other far more urgent matters to worry about."

છે‍જ

The weather turned a little grey. A sudden gust of hot wind lashed our faces as soon as we entered the spiral staircase to the terrace of the Vessel.

Our preparations for this incursion had taken quite some time. Among the many possibilities, we had in the end opted for the essentials: Atto's pistol, a long dagger, which I had stuffed into my breeches; and, last of all, a net, one of those used during the merry hunt three days before. Thus we were equipped to hold the creature at bay, to injure him if there should – oh horror! – be hand-to-hand fighting, or even act like *retiarii* in the gladiatorial ring, trapping him under the net.

We stood outside the little penthouse, our legs almost rigid with fear. After exchanging looks of reciprocal encouragement, Atto advanced first, turned the handle and pushed the door open. Within, shadows and silence.

For a moment we neither spoke nor moved.

"I shall go ahead," said Melani at length, drawing his pistol and making sure that it was ready to fire.

I responded by brandishing the dagger and, spreading the net lightly across my left shoulder, I readied myself to throw it at the first opportunity.

Atto entered. Hardly had he crossed the threshold than he backed against the left door jamb, so as to reduce the number of directions from which he could be attacked. With one arm, he motioned me to advance. I obeyed.

So it was that I found myself once more in the monster's den, shoulder to shoulder with Atto. Panting and by no means any longer feline in his movements, the Abbot was, despite his advanced age and declining eyesight, as leonine as ever, behaving like the foremost among the King's musketeers.

The light was faint because of the smoked glass, and this time the passing clouds made it even dimmer than on the previous occasion. In the middle of the little building there were, as I remembered, two small pillars.

If it was there, it was well hidden.

A sharp pain made me jump. To catch my attention, Atto had jabbed me in the side with his elbow.

Then I saw it.

In the opposite corner, beyond the two pillars and close to the right-hand window, something had moved on the wall. Something rather like an arm, horribly deformed, and covered with a sort of scaly, serpentine skin seemed to emerge from the wall and had reacted to Atto's dig in my ribs. The beast was there.

Our view was partially obstructed by the two columns; we would need to get closer in order to understand what part of the monster had really moved and, above all, what it was doing so bizarrely stuck into the wall.

"Keep still. Don't make a move," whispered Abbot Melani, almost inaudibly.

A minute passed, maybe two, in total immobility. The Tetràchion's arm had ceased to move, as had its monstrous hand. The door was open. Both we and the creature could have broken and run. Whether out of courage or fear, neither dared resolve so to do. The air was humid because of leaks in the ceiling and the whole of the tight space seemed to be incrusted with saltpetre. Our bated breath seemed to make the atmosphere even damper, as did the heavy all-pervading silence, the materialised, fleshed-out fear.

While all this was happening (in reality, nothing whatever, save the storm in our hearts) I was fighting another battle. I was doing all I could, yet, despite the gravity of the moment, I knew that sooner or later I would have to give in. I absolutely had to, and yet I could not. In the end, I surrendered. I simply had to scratch my nose if I wanted to avoid something even worse – a sneeze. And I did so.

Never could any expression in human language convey the feeling of desperate amazement which seized me when I saw the monster's hand imitate mine in perfect synchrony, rising to its horrid face, which remained hidden behind the two small pillars. A terrible doubt came over me.

"Did you see?" I whispered to Atto.

"It moved," he replied in alarm.

I wanted to perform a second test. I freed the fingers of the same hand and made them flutter gaily. Then I moved a leg back and forth, rhythmically. At length, under Atto's stupefied gaze, I left my place and advanced towards the two pillars to look, free from all obstacles material or of the spirit, upon the mystery which had so cruelly enchained us.

⁖

"It is absurd. My boy, I forbid you to tell this to anyone," said Atto, without removing his eyes from the looking glass. "I mean, of course, not until we have made clear all that remains obscure," he prudently corrected himself to cover up the cause of his peremptory command: shame.

He again touched the gibbous surface of the deforming mirror, admiring how it alternately swelled up, hollowed out, curved or straightened his fingers, knuckles, palm and wrist.

"I saw something rather like this in Frankfurt a long time ago, when Cardinal Mazarin sent me there for some secret negotiations. But it did not have such a. . . tremendous. . . effect as this."

We had seen no Tetràchion. At least, so it seemed. Witty Benedetti, the ingenious creator of the Vessel, had for the greater amusement of his guests placed a number of distorting mirrors along the wall of the little penthouse which, thanks to the dim light and the dark, grim atmosphere of the place and the fact that they reflected one another, transformed the visitor's image into something like a monstrous being.

When I scratched my nose, I noticed that the presumed Tetràchion imitated my gesture with inordinate promptness. Likewise, my other little movements were mimed by the monster with quite incredibly exact timing. It could not be anything other than my own image reflected in some unknown distorting surface.

During our first incursion into the penthouse, our minds were full of the image of Capitor's dish, with Albicastro's voice, transmitted up there who knows how, and with the tales which Atto himself had recounted about Capitor. Faced with the absurd and alien features of a creature with four legs and two heads (in reality, myself and Atto, standing closely side by side) we thought we saw the Tetràchion. Instead, we were merely surrounded by curved mirrors. I heard Atto repeat:

> *This work I call a looking-glass*
> *In which each fool shall see an ass.*
> *The viewer learns with certainty;*
> *My mirror leaves no mystery.*

"Those are the verses we heard Albicastro's voice declaiming," said I.

"Quite. He knew of the distorting mirrors and he was taunting us," Atto replied, as he continued reciting:

> *Whoever sees with open eyes*
> *Cannot regard himself as wise,*
> *For he shall see upon reflection*
> *That humans teem with imperfection.*

"But where did his voice come from?" I asked dubiously.

Instead of replying, Atto began to feel the walls where there were no mirrors.

"What are you looking for?"

"It should be here. . . or a little further along. . . Ah, here we are!"

With his face full of the cheer engendered by his regained sagacity, he showed me a brass tube which ran vertically down the wall and then curved towards us, ending in a trumpet.

"How idiotic not to have thought of that earlier," he exclaimed, slapping his forehead in frustration. "Albicastro's voice, which we heard on that occasion, and which seemed like that of a phantom, came from this: the old tube used to pass orders to the servants on other floors and which I showed you on the ground floor. That mad Hollander must have been on one of the lower floors near to one of the mouths of the tube. When he realised that we might be in this wretched place full of distorting mirrors, he began chanting the verses of that damned Sebastian Brant and his *Ship of Fools* and froze the blood in our veins," Atto concluded, revealing how frightened he had been last time.

Atto's conclusions were incontrovertible. The "mirror of folly" cited by the bizarre Albicastro fitted in perfectly with the perverse

game whereby the Tetràchion mentioned by the madwoman Capitor relived in the mirrors of the Vessel. What was more, did not
the Dutchman's little song warn that what appears in a looking
glass is not always worthy of our confidence? At that moment, Atto
recited:

> *He's stirring at the dunces' stew;*
> *He thinks he's wise and handsome too,*
> *And with his mirror form so pleased*
> *You'd think he had a mind diseased;*
> *Indeed he cannot see the ass*
> *That's grinning at him from the glass!*

"Do you understand those verses now?" he asked. "Albicastro
made idiots of us, and took great pleasure in so doing. I really want
to look him in the face, that insolent Dutchman, and demand an
apology," he added, with a warlike expression on his visage, as he
motioned me to follow him downstairs.

Armed to the teeth, we had been defeated by a few mirrors and
our imagination. Now Abbot Melani wanted to unload his anger and
shame on the only other occupant of the Vessel. The only flesh and
blood one, at any rate.

৵৽৶

Of course, we could not find him. Albicastro belonged to that rare
class of persons who appear by surprise ("to make a nuisance of
themselves," Atto added) and never when one looks for them.

Atto insisted on searching bath chambers, store rooms and the
like, but it very soon became quite clear that there was no trace of
the Dutchman in the whole of the Vessel.

"We fear what we cannot understand," I recited, reminding the
Abbot of his own philosophising two days previously when I had tak-
en the little dog in Borromini's perspective gallery for a colossus.

"Shut up and let us return to Villa Spada," he muttered, his face
dark with anger.

We made the brief journey without exchanging a word. I was
thinking. Every single one of the mysteries which we had encountered, and which had caused Abbot Melani or myself (or both) to
tremble, had become clear in the end: the Dutchman had been walking on a cornice hidden from our view; the flowers from the mythical
gardens of Adonis had turned out to be common plants like garlic and

castor bean; the gallery of the Vessel which seemed to extend as far as the Vatican Hill was just a clever trick with mirrors; the infernal tongues of flame and the faces of dead souls which we had seen in Ugonio's den at the Baths of Agrippina, and which had succeeded in convincing me that I myself was dead, were the mere product of camphor vapours; the roaring monster which I feared was about to devour me at Palazzo Spada was in reality nothing but a lapdog, whose dimensions had been made to appear gigantic by the false perspective of the Borromini gallery; and, last of all, we had taken our own reflections in distorting mirrors for the Tetràchion. For one thing only we had found no explanation: the apparitions of Maria, Louis and Fouquet in the gardens of the Vessel. The Abbot had invoked his theory of corpuscles and hypothetical hallucinogenic exhalations, but nothing more; unlike all the other mysteries, we had found no concrete solution to this one.

While these thoughts were turning around in my mind, Abbot Melani continued to hold his peace. Who knows, perhaps he too was asking himself the same questions, I thought, glancing at him out of the corner of my eye.

Here, my reflections were brought sharply to an end. I saw Abbot Melani grow pale, paler than the ceruse on his face. We had come by now to the gates of the Villa Spada and Atto was staring at something in the distance.

Amidst the perfume of the flower beds, there reigned a great confusion of valets, porters, secretaries, with trunks and travellers' baskets of provisions being hauled onto departing carriages, and a going and coming of eminences and gentlemen amiably taking their leave of the master of the house, making appointments to meet at a degree ceremony at the Sapienza University, at some consistory, or at a mass for the repose of somebody's soul.

I was just wondering what could have so altered the Abbot's humour, when I saw one of Sfasciamonti's catchpolls pointing out a stranger to us. The shock to my heart was tremendous. I could already see myself accused by the parish priest of Saint Peter's of breaking into the basilica, identified by the Bargello's men, tried and cast into a dungeon for twenty years. Terrified, I looked at Atto. I did not even attempt to flee. At Villa Spada, everyone knew where I lived. The stranger's face was tense, tired, quivering. Soon he confronted us.

"An urgent message for Abbot Melani."

"He stands here before you, speak up," said I, feeling greatly relieved, while the Abbot said nothing, his face drawn, staring fixedly before him, almost as though he already knew – and feared – the message which the man was about to deliver to him.

"Madama the Connestabilessa Colonna: her carriage is a short distance from here. She begs you not to leave; within an hour, you will meet."

Rooted by my own legs, I expected some reaction from Atto, some free expression from his soul, some genuine impulse from the heart.

But the old Abbot did not open his mouth. He did not even quicken his footsteps; on the contrary, he seemed slower and more uncertain.

We reached his apartments without a word. Here, he took off his wig, slowly stroked his forehead and sat down, suddenly very tired, before the dressing table.

He began to whistle an unknown tune. His whistling was short of breath and uncertain, often breaking off in his throat as he looked sadly at his own naked, hoary and almost bald head reflected in the looking glass.

"This is a tune from the *Ballet des Plaisirs* of Maestro Lully," said he, continuing to explore his face; then he stood up and donned his dressing gown.

I stood open-mouthed. That messenger had just announced the imminent arrival of the Connestabilessa, and Atto was not getting ready?

Did Melani no longer believe in her coming? He was not entirely to be blamed; too many times already, he had awaited her in vain. This time, however, there seemed to be no doubt about it: Maria was already almost at the gates of the Villa Spada, there were no more impediments. Of course, what she was coming for now that the festivities were over may have been somewhat less than clear. Perhaps she was coming to offer her tardy tribute, and her apologies, to Cardinal Spada.

"Everyone at court was astonished when, a few months ago, they suddenly heard His Majesty sing this same music from memory. An air which he and Maria had sung together for a whole season during their amorous promenades forty years ago. Everyone was surprised, except me."

I understood. In fact, I knew perfectly well for what purpose Maria Mancini was coming: she was obeying the wish of the Most Christian King, as she herself had written to Atto; and she was prepared to listen to Atto's entreaties on the King's behalf and his offer that she should return to France. To assure himself of her attention, to move her, and lastly, to persuade, Atto must therefore call upon memory. He must be able to recall and report to the Connestabilessa, looks, moments, words pronounced by the King, of which she could not know but which the Abbot must at all costs be able to give life to in her eyes and in her heart.

"Since the time of the Affair of the Poisons, when he thought that the world was collapsing on his head, His Majesty has increasingly asked his ministers to request my services," Melani explained, "and ever more frequently in the missives which I received Madama the Connestabilessa Colonna was mentioned: How was she? What was she doing? And so on."

Maria, he continued in a bitter tone of voice, had for some time taken refuge in Spain, persecuted by her husband, the Constable Colonna, whom she had abandoned when she fled Rome. The poor woman spent her time in and out of convents and prisons.

"During all those years, I did not fail in truth to bring her news to the attention of the Most Christian King."

I held my breath. Melani was at last beginning to confess to being the King's go-between with the Connestabilessa. Perhaps he would soon tell me the whole truth, which secretly I already knew.

"Until one day," Atto continued, "when the King, after being compelled to suppress the Affair of the Poisons, began to show more vividly on his face that old secret trembling whenever he heard the name Colonna."

Colonna: that name, the Abbot revealed, bore more of a sting for Louis XIV than the familiar "Maria". "Colonna" carved into his regal flesh, always as though for the first time, the knowledge that their separation was forever: she belonged to another; and then there were the three sons by that prince, the Grand Constable Lorenzo Onofrio Colonna, whom Maria had conceived and given birth to.

"And above all, the cruellest torment was to know that she had never forgotten him, so much so that she fled from the yoke imposed upon her by that husband, despite the strong passion of the senses which, as I had not failed to inform the King, he aroused in her."

Thus Atto concluded, his mouth watering as one compelled ever to live such passions vicariously, with his nose glued to the monastic grate which separates his unfortunate kind from ordinary men and women.

"Signor Atto, you've told me nothing about Prince Colonna, Maria's only husband."

"There is not much to be said," said the Abbot, cutting me short, thoroughly irritated.

Atto, too, I thought with a snigger, hated to speak of the man who had fathered Maria's children and had made her flesh thrill, if not her heart. Nevertheless, I had already heard a great deal about the stormy ten-year long marriage between Constable Colonna and his indomitable consort.

"Did you not fear the King's ire, passing him news that might injure his feelings?"

"I have already told you, word by word and blow by blow, how Louis lived in the twenty years that followed his marriage with Maria Teresa: his heart was sunken into a deep, disturbed sleep. I did no more than to throw pebbles of light, sharp crystal splinters which, cutting through that torpor with the stiletto of jealousy, for a brief instant struck the King's heart and veins with the blinding lightning of Maria's memory, more brilliant than all the brocades and jewels with which he covered his mistresses, all that astounding machinery with which his pageantry and fêtes, his plays and ballets were filled and all those deafening orchestras with which he surrounded himself. Dreams, moments, soon upset by the magnificent hubbub of the court, too brief for him to become fully aware; and yet there they lay, lurking in a corner of his soul, whispering to him, perhaps on nights when he lay between waking and sleep, that she existed."

I was moved by the fidelity with which Abbot Melani had humbly sacrificed his impossible love for Maria Mancini. For twenty years, alone and in secret, he had maintained the silver thread which still joined those two unfortunate hearts, without them so much as realising it.

Perhaps the Abbot would now reveal to me his current task as go-between; but he remained silent, overcome by his memories.

Then he drew forth from his pocket a richly wrought little box shaped like a golden seashell. He opened it and took out a few citron pastilles which he threw into the carafe of water in order to make a refreshing beverage. As soon as the pastilles had dissolved, Atto drank deeply.

"Ah, this citron-juice is truly delicious," he commented with a sigh, wiping his lips. "Marchese Salviati sends me these regularly. And don't you find my little seashell lovely, eh?" said he, alluding to the box which I was in fact admiring. "It comes from the Indies and it is as fine and pleasing as can be, do you not think so? Maria sent it to me as a present a few years ago."

The Abbot's voice was tinged with emotion.

There was a knock at the door: a valet asked if the Abbot required anything.

"Yes, please," Atto answered, clearing his throat. "Bring me something to eat. And what about you, my boy?"

I accepted willingly, seeing that hunger was causing my stomach to complain, as no little time had elapsed since lunch.

"Just think how different France and all Europe might have been," Atto resumed, "if Maria Mancini had reigned happily at Louis's side. The invasions of Flanders and the German principalities, the brutal destruction of the Palatinate, hunger and poverty within France's borders to finance all those wars, and who knows what else might have been spared us."

"Well," I could not help provoking him, "you regret so much what happened, yet were matters not as they now stand, France would have no claim to the the Spanish throne."

The Abbot was cut to the quick.

"There is no contradiction whatever," said he, rising to his full height. "The past is the past and can be altered only in our imagination, as happened at the Vessel. We can only so arrange matters that past events should not have been in vain."

"What do you mean?"

"If His Majesty's separation from Maria Mancini were now to bring Bourbon blood to the throne of Spain," Atto declaimed pompously, waving his index finger as he spoke, "their suffering, from the blind and pointless torment of forty years ago, would be sublimated into a supreme sacrifice for the good of the royal household of France and, plainly, to the greater glory of God from whom the monarch's power emanates."

At first, I found it difficult to grasp what he was getting at in that obscure oratorical display. One thing, however, was perfectly clear to me: for the first time since his arrival at Villa Spada, Atto was talking with me of the succession to the Spanish throne.

"Only thus will they not have been separated in vain," he added.

The war in Flanders, for example, Melani continued, could only have been undertaken by the Most Christian King in his capacity as consort of Maria Teresa, seeing that the purpose of that conflict was to claim his wife's dowry from the Spaniards.

"In other words, then as now, the Most Christian King has been determined to extort, if needs be by violence, all that he could lay his hands on which might serve to avenge him of the violence which he himself once suffered. The violence of which I spoke to you: once suffered, then inflicted upon others, do you remember?" the Abbot reminded me.

"Yes, from what you've told me, I know that his favourite ways of getting his own back have been through women and wars."

"Queens and *raison d'Etat*: the very things which once separated him from Maria Mancini forever."

That was why, Atto continued in a hoarse voice, Louis XIV never held back whenever there was any opportunity to make women suffer; even better if he could mix the matter up with politics, as in the case of the Princess Palatine and the Grande Dauphine.

"These were two women whom the King admired greatly. They were not fragile and forever sighing like Louise de la Vallière or social climbers like Athénaïs de Montespan. Worse, they were independent spirits, fighting for their ideals with all their strength, just as he himself had once tried to do against his mother and his godfather."

Louis identified no little with those two rather masculine and idealistic young women. But he, in his own time, had lost his battle; and now he could not allow them to win theirs. The King was unhappy: at court, none could allow themselves the luxury of being happy, or even serene. The King was small of stature: none dared wear heels or more imposing periwigs that would make them taller than he.

"The King is small? But you told me that he was tall and good looking, and. . ."

"What does that matter? I told you what they all say and always will say and what will always be depicted in court portraits. Besides, with those red heels and those towering wigs, I challenge you to find a single monarch in Europe taller than he. The Most Christian King, my boy – and this is really in confidence between the two of us – when he takes off his shoes and that false hair, is not very much taller than you."

They brought us a dish with two pairs of roast francolins accompanied by green beans, artichokes and sour fruit, with wine and little flat breads with sesame. Atto started with the greens, while I immediately got my teeth into the francolins' breasts.

So, heaven help anyone whom the King found to be at peace for too long, even if this were out of resignation. And such was the character of the Princess Palatine (so called, because she came from the Palatinate): young, ugly and perfectly aware of the fact, the King's German sister-in-law was the second wife of Monsieur, in other words, his younger brother Philippe, and, unlike his first wife, the restless and unlucky Henrietta of England, she had been able to find a peaceful *modus vivendi* with that strange husband of hers. He did not like women, but she was sufficiently masculine not to disgust him. And, with the miraculous help of some holy image in the right place at the right time, he had even managed to make her pregnant and thus to provide the male heir his luckless late wife had been unable to conceive. Thereafter, the couple separated their beds by common accord and to their mutual satisfaction, united only by their love for their children. Madame Palatine's serene resignation was, however, to be short-lived.

"The dirty trick that was played on her, a little over ten years ago, was one of the most horrendous crimes of French military history," Atto stated, without mincing his words, by now engrossed in his tale. "The methodical and ferocious sacking of her land, the Palatinate, and of the castle of her birth, perpetrated in her name but without her consent. This was a masterpiece of devilish perfidy."

As he had once done with Maria Teresa and her supposed right to receive Spanish Flanders as part of her dowry, Louis claimed the Palatinate on behalf of his sister-in-law and against her will. She begged him desperately for an audience, but he would not receive her. Meanwhile, he ordered the French troops to conduct a scorched-earth campaign, but in the towns rather than the countryside, where that had previously been military practice. Thus, instead of a few scattered peasants' hutments, he had whole cities razed to the ground: Mannheim, and especially Heidelberg, where the magnificent pink sandstone castle was thrown into the waters of the Neckar.

"Years have passed since then, but the thing was so unheard-of that the French officers who took part in the campaign are still ashamed of it. It is only thanks to the spontaneous compassion of the Maréchal de Tessé that, at the very last moment, when the fires were already burning, the gallery of the princess's family portraits was saved, in an effort to mitigate the desperation which he knew would overcome her when she heard of the disaster."

In vain did Louis' confessor whisper such expressions as "love for one's neighbour" in his ear, in the shadow of the confessional: the King would rise angrily, muttering "Chimaeras!" and shrugging his shoulders, before brusquely turning his back upon the father confessor without so much as a farewell.

On the contrary, the King continued in the same vein quite un-perturbed. He inflicted the same torments upon the other German in his family: the Grand Dauphine, his daughter-in-law.

"She had it in her to become a queen one day, the real queen whom France had so long lacked. She had both the qualities and tal-ents which could one day have enabled her to bear the weight of government. I still remember the King's admiring stare whenever she spoke."

Quite by surprise, however, Louis XIV told her that she was no longer to be informed of matters pertaining to government and, shortly after that, he did not disdain to enter into conflict with the Grand Dauphine's native land, Bavaria, rejecting with subtle pleasure every one of the young woman's attempts at mediation. For her, this was the end. Melancholy undermined her spirit and pervaded her whole body: from the waist downwards, it swelled up and within a few days she died amidst convulsions.

"This was a nemesis for the kingdom," moaned Abbot Melani. "With the death of the Grand Dauphine, France was left without the figure of a queen: no longer was there a queen mother or a reigning queen, nor was there a dauphine. The past, present and future of the royal family are the sphere of women and the force behind this destruction was in great part the King himself. Nor does he show any sign of regretting what he has done. Indeed, by marrying Madame de Maintenon, not only has he removed any possibility of seeing a new sovereign on the throne, but he has even gone so far as to exhort the Dauphin, now a widower too, to marry an old mistress of his, an actress," said Atto, list-lessly fishing in his plate for a few scraps of artichoke.

"In other word, the Queen has been. . . abolished," I exclaimed, depositing on the tray the well-picked skeleton of the francolin and helping myself to another one.

"Only the old man who stands before you knows the origin of these excesses, in those remote, bitter days long, long ago. They go back to that dawn at the fortress of Brouage when the supreme pain of the separation from Maria suddenly engendered the need for hardness of heart: a mask which the King donned then and has never since removed. Only in these last few years, with advancing age, His Majesty has no longer been able completely to conceal that ancient, unassuaged suffering. Madame de Maintenon's confessor, to whom she complains every morning, knows all about this."

"And what do you know of it?"

"The confessor complains to me," laughed the Abbot. "What everyone can see is that the King goes to see Madame de Maintenon three times a day: before mass, after lunch and in the evening on his return from the hunt. What very few, however, know of is the mysterious bouts of weeping that regularly seize him at the end of the day, when he goes to bid his wife goodnight: he becomes sad, then his temper flares up, and ends up weeping uncontrollably. Sometimes, he even faints; and all this, without the couple exchanging so much as one word."

"Surely Madame de Maintenon must nevertheless have guessed what it is that so worries him?"

"On the contrary, that is precisely the source of her own worries: 'I am quite unable to get him to talk,' she is wont to repeat when she feels worn out by the struggle to communicate. For Madame de Maintenon, the King is a sphinx."

That is why, Abbot Melani continued, the King's enigmatic goodnight to his wife has become for her a cause of anger, even disgust. The King likes to conclude his sentimental and lachrymose outpourings with brief outbursts of quite another, far more vulgar nature which she, given her age, finds repugnant. "These are painful moments," she confides to her confessor. Only after obtaining physical satisfaction does the King go on his way, with his cheeks still lined by tears and without uttering a syllable.

"On the next day, however, he is the same tyrant as ever. Indeed, with age his tyranny has become ever harsher; so that, by now, life at Versailles, especially for the women of his family, has become a torment. Whenever His Majesty undertakes the smallest journey, even only to go to Fontainebleau, he insists on taking daughters and nephews with him in the same carriage, just as he was once wont to drag a party of mistresses in his wake. He treats them all with the same hardness of heart, deaf to their lamentations, blind to their fatigue; he makes them eat, converse and be gay on command. Pregnancies do not exempt women from having to travel in the King's retinue, and so much the worse if there is a miscarriage. None dares keep count of the pregnancies which never reached term because of those unreasonable journeys by carriage."

I was horrified.

"And what is one to say," the Abbot continued with a smile, "of the torments to which he subjects Madame de Maintenon? He has made her travel under conditions which one would not impose on a servant. I well recall one such journey to Fontainebleau when we feared she might die on the road. Supposing that Madame de Maintenon has a fever or a headache, what does he do? He invites her to the draughty theatre where the icy blasts and the glare from a thousand candles reduce her to a wreck. Or she's lying sick in bed, all muffled up against her proverbial draughts. He visits her and throws all the windows wide open, even when it is freezing outside."

"One would not think that for the past forty years he has been the greatest king in the world," I commented in some perplexity after a few moments of silence.

"The Most Christian King is still struggling against the old defeat inflicted upon him by his mother, Queen Anne; while torturing all the women of his family, it is on her that he would really like to turn the tables. But the King's is a lost battle. The dead, my boy, are quite invincible in that one can't answer them back."

Atto's long narration, which had seemed like a river in full spate, came now to a halt. He had meant to tell of the love which Louis XIV still bore Maria, and in speaking of her, to re-live it. Instead, he had ended up expatiating upon the old King's misdeeds. Yet the essence of the tale remained unchanged: the wives, mistresses, rancours and revenges of the Most Christian King all tended towards her: Maria. That name encapsulated forty years of European history. For that woman, invoked so belatedly and so vainly, *le plus grand Roi du monde* had put Europe to fire and the sword. A heart torn to shreds had fed on the hearts of entire peoples, even the King's own kith and kin. And now she, the innocent cause of it all, would soon be among us.

Someone knocked at the door. It was Buvat. The Connestabilessa had arrived.

❧

"She is walking in the garden," said the secretary with ill-concealed embarrassment.

"Very well," replied Atto, dismissing his secretary without asking him for further details, as though he were reporting the arrival of just any visitor.

But it was hard for him to pretend. He had the slightly stifled voice of one unwilling to admit an upheaval of the soul, and striving at all costs to show equanimity.

"How stuffy it is today," he commented, as soon as the door had closed. "Rome is always too hot in summer. And it is so humid. I remember that in the first years when I came here I suffered tremendously from that. Do you not feel hot too?"

"Yes. . . I do feel hot," I answered mechanically.

He went over to the window, looking into the distance, as if pausing for thought.

I was astounded. Maria was there outside; he could join her at any moment. It was unquestionably up to Atto to go and look for his friend. Yet he was doing nothing. After all the tales I had heard, after he had told me of all the stages in the love between Maria and the Most Christian King and indeed of his own castrato's crippled love for the selfsame woman, after waiting for her for days on end, after all those letters overflowing with passion, after thirty years' separation. . . After all this, Atto was not moving an inch. He was looking out of the window, still in his dressing gown, speaking not a word. I looked at his plate: he had left the delicious meat of the francolins untouched, eating only some greens. His stomach must be beset by very different ferments.

I stood up and went to his side. It was as I thought. There was no risk of mistaken identity, for all the guests from the week's celebrations had left. Accompanied by a lackey and a maid of honour, she moved gracefully through the garden, admiring Tranquillo Romaùli's flower beds with bemused wonderment, from time to time caressing some plant, observing with pleasure the luxuriant and refined ambience of Villa Spada, even now that the festivities were over and there was much disorder all around. She seemed untroubled by the goings and comings of servants and porters, dismantling platforms or carrying sacks of rubbish. She must be rather weary after her journey but this did not show.

"Even if we're to judge only by the number of people working there now, these celebrations must have cost your Cardinal a fortune," said Atto with a hint of irony.

"Perhaps we should. . . I mean, perhaps *you* should. . ." I stammered.

But Abbot Melani ignored the suggestion. He wandered wearily over to the wardrobe, opened it and began carelessly to review all the rich apparel within. Then he opened a little medicine chest and looked, with a sceptical expression that I had never before seen in him, at the whole collection of balms, ceruses and little boxes of beauty spots. Turning again to the wardrobe, from the darkness of the interior he brought forth a few pairs of shoes into the light of day. Rather scornfully he turned them over with his foot, rolling these beribboned creations onto the floor in disorder. Atto examined them impotently, as though he knew they could do nothing to satisfy his desires. He then began unwillingly to pull out suits of clothes.

"With the dead, 'tis too late to cry out 'You were wrong!'" said he suddenly.

As he stared at all those rich materials, Atto's mind was still dwelling on the phantasms of the past. Maria awaited him in the gardens, but he remained glued to his memories like a limpet clinging to a rock and (the image was his own) refusing to let go.

"The Queen Mother was mistaken in her plans, but it was Mazarin who did the greatest wrong," he continued, distractedly caressing a tabby shirt hanging in the wardrobe. "If the Cardinal had not been there, Louis would certainly have overcome his mother's resistance and married Maria, and the Queen of England's necklace would have been his gift for their betrothal, not their parting."

"The greatest wrong, did you say?"

"Indeed. A wrong for which the Cardinal paid with his life."

"What are you referring to?"

"Do you recall what I told you about Capitor and her enigmatic warnings to His Eminence?" he asked, while his interest was aroused by a waistcoat with a ruffle in pleated Venetian lace.

"Yes, if my memory does not deceive me, Capitor said 'A Virgin who weds the Crown brings death.'"

"You have not remembered the whole message. She added that death would take place when 'the moons join the suns at the wedding'," he recited, feeling his way through breeches, cuffs, caftans, collars and tunics.

"Ah yes, I remember but, to tell the truth, you never explained that last riddle to me."

"At the time, it was not understood, so that not much attention was paid to it. Everyone was concentrating upon the 'virgin', Maria, and Louis's 'crown' which would, supposedly, bring death to the recipient of Capitor's vaticination, namely Mazarin. They all wondered how he would react to that dark presage."

"That was why Mazarin separated Maria and the King," I remembered.

"Exactly. Louis married Maria Teresa, the Infanta of Spain, on the *ninth* of June. But, like lightning falling from a blue sky, *nine* months later, on the *ninth* of March, Mazarin died. Capitor's prophecy had come true."

"I do not understand."

"My boy, with age, you seem to have grown slower on the uptake," said the Abbot, mocking me. The contact with his precious treasures of apparel seemed to be restoring his good humour: "Nine, nine and nine."

I stared at him, perplexed.

"Come, do you still not understand?" said Melani, growing impatient. "The number of 'moons', or months, was equal to that of 'suns' or days, from the wedding. The number of suns of the nuptials was nine, for the marriage between His Majesty and Maria Teresa was celebrated on the *ninth* of June. *Nine* moons (or nine months) later, the Cardinal died, on the ninth of March, the very day of the ninth moon."

While my face showed plainly how disconcerted I was by all this, the Abbot tried to match a pearl-coloured sash with a pair of violet-red stockings.

"In that case, Capitor's prophecy did not come true," I then objected. "She said that Mazarin would die if 'the virgin' married 'the crown', but that did not happen."

"On the contrary, it did," retorted Atto. "The virgin was not Maria but the King himself, and do you know why?"

"The virgin. . . the King?"

"Tell me, on what day was His Majesty born?"

"In September, if my memory does not fail me; you told me that on his birthday he had Fouquet arrested. . . Yes, that would have been the 5th September."

"And in which sign of the zodiac is the 5th September?"

"In Virgo?"

"Bravo, you're getting there. The King is a native of Virgo, the sign of the virgin. On the other hand, 'the crown' is that of Spain which Maria Teresa brought with her in her dowry and which now enables France to advance claims to the Spanish throne."

"How did you deduce that?"

"I was not alone in doing so," Melani retorted, trying on a blackish Brandenburg cassock, then a mother-of-pearl-coloured Bohemian cape and a short *gris castor* cloak, which, worn too long in front of the mirror, were making him almost die of heat. "What was worse, the Cardinal himself realised that, by separating Maria and Louis and compelling the latter to marry the Infanta, he had signed his own death warrant. But that came too late; he was already on his deathbed. With the little strength that remained to him, he cried out and struggled, suffocated by the revelation and trying to tear off his sweat-soaked clothes, as though he could thus undo the fatal nuptials for which he had striven so hard. With my own eyes, I saw him despair. I remember that at one point his eyes, which by then had grown opaque, stared intensely at me and I read in his terrified look how he and I had struggled side by side during the negotiations at the Isle of Pheasants to obtain Maria Teresa's hand despite the claims of the Emperor Leopold. He did not survive that last lightning bolt of memory: his poor body was shaken as by a thunderbolt and Cardinal Jules Mazarin, Italian by birth, Sicilian by blood and French by adoption, gave up the ghost."

"From your manner of speaking, it seems you placed the greatest possible trust in Capitor's words," I remarked with a hint of sarcasm, while in my mind the horror of that lugubrious tale was mixed with no little irony for the Abbot, who was as sceptical about the apparitions at the Vessel as he was convinced of that Spanish madwoman's prophetic powers.

"One moment, one moment," Atto hastened to correct me, tottering on a pair of high-heeled shoes which his swollen feet would not fit into, "I never said that I believed in Capitor's magic."

"But if now. . ."

"No," he interrupted me haughtily, "listen to me carefully. Do you know why Mazarin died on the ninth of March? Because he had realised that on that day there fell the ninth moon after the ninth of June, the day of the Most Christian King's wedding."

"I don't understand."

"He was already very ill, that's true; but this revelation, together with the fated date, brought about a renal colic which cut his life short in the small hours. In other word, Capitor's prophecy was indeed the cause of the Cardinal's death, which was, however, brought about by his superstition, not her powers," declaimed Abbot Melani, with a huge blond periwig sitting askew on his head and another chestnut brown one in his hand, undecided as to which to choose. "For better or for worse, we are, my boy, affected only by what we believe."

Atto imagined that he had silenced me with his exegesis. He wanted at all costs to avoid any close contact with the kind of occult phenomena which had so irritated and confused him during our incursions to the Vessel.

This was not, however, the truth: I well recalled how enthusiastically Melani had, when he first spoke of Capitor, described the prophetic powers of that Spanish madwoman who had come to court in the retinue of Don John the Bastard. However, I held back and refrained from pointing this out to him.

"And yet," he himself admitted after a moment's silence, without, however, breaking off his minuet of trying out new periwigs, "I must confess that something else in Capitor's words really came very close to being prophetic."

This was, Melani explained, the sonnet about the globe as the wheel of fortune, which we also read above one of the doors at the Vessel. Atto recited the last lines:

Behold, one to the heights hath risen
Et alter est expositus ruinae;
The third is stripp'd of all; deep down, to waste is driven.
Quartus ascendet iam, nec quisquam sine
By labouring he gained his benison,
Secundum legis ordinem divinae.

"This happened after the Cardinal's death," said Atto, grasping a perfume for periwigs and rapidly perusing a belt and two pocket watches: "Colbert's ascent must inevitably bring to mind, 'Behold, one to the heights hath risen', while the brewing storm that preceded the fall of Superintendent Fouquet seemed to fit perfectly with '*et alter est expositus ruinae*' or, 'the other is exposed to ruin'. The fourth prefigured the coming to power of the Most Christian King in person who '*ascendet iam*' or, 'is now ascending'. In fact, the young King did gird up his loins immediately after His Eminence's death and take personal control of the government of the state, as the sonnet says, '*nec quisquam sine* / By labouring he gained his benison', in other words, on the strength of his own efforts, but also, '*secundum legis ordinem divinae*' or, 'according to the order of divine right' precisely upon which the King's power rests."

"In your interpretation of the sonnet, the third personage is, however, missing, the one who's 'stripp'd of all; deep down, to waste is driven'."

"Bravo. I see that you may be slow on the uptake, but you are by no means inattentive. The third character is Mazarin himself."

"Did he really die poor?" I asked, utterly astonished. "When we first met, I seem to recall you telling me that he left a fabulous inheritance."

"Your memory is absolutely correct. Only, he chose his heir badly. Armand de la Meilleraye, Ortensia Mancini's husband, was mad," he exclaimed, trying out all sorts and colours of capes, cloaks and cowls, in all materials from jujube-red Ormuz muslins to scarlet ferrandine silk and wool blends, brocaded cloth of gold and silver, bicoloured moiré satins, and so compulsively that it truly seemed he too had taken leave of his senses.

Armand de la Meilleraye: almost indifferent to the dubious spectacle which the Abbot, by now almost naked, was making of himself, I was deep in thought. I already knew from Buvat that, when Maria left Paris, Atto had transferred his attentions to Ortensia, thus enraging her mad spouse, who sent out ruffians to hunt him down and give him a beating and thus caused him to flee from France. Melani had taken advantage of this to go to Rome and, with the King's blessing and financial assistance, to seek out Maria, newly married to the Constable Colonna.

"'Tis almost risible," continued the Abbot, by now lost in his dance of the costumes which, from a graceful minuet, had degenerated into an unseemly sarabande: "Mazarin had sought far and wide the best match for the most beautiful and sought-after of his nieces and had decided to make him his universal heir. The choice fell upon a nephew of Richelieu, the Duc de la Meilleraye, who thus became master of the Cardinal's boundless and ill-gotten fortune. They married barely ten days before the death of Mazarin, who thus had no idea of the sad individual to whom he had abandoned his fortune."

Armand de la Meilleraye, Atto narrated with acid sarcasm for his one-time enemy, was without question utterly mad. He was ashamed to have inherited from Mazarin, whom he regarded as a thief destined for hellfire. He therefore took an extreme pleasure in accepting the inheritance with the secret intent of destroying and delapidating it. He sought out the victims of the Cardinal's depredations and exhorted them to sue his heir, namely himself. In this way, he collected over three hundred lawsuits and did his very best to lose them all, thus restituting the great man's ill-gotten gains.

For that purpose, he obtained the advice of the best and most costly lawyers, and then did exactly the opposite of whatever they recommended. One morning, what was more, he put paints and hammers into the hands of a group of servants and led them to the gallery where His Eminence had lovingly collected extraordinary works of art: and there he began violently to strike Greek and Roman statues, because they were naked, and ordered the servants to cover the paintings depicting nudity with black paint: Titians, Correggios and who knows what else. When the King's minister, Colbert, arrived distraught, hoping to save those masterpieces, he found the madman, exhausted but calm at last, in the midst of all the wreckage; midnight had struck: it was Sunday, the day of rest. The destruction had come to a halt, but almost nothing had survived.

"As cruel irony would have it, in the last days of his life, Mazarin was seen wandering around his gallery, caressing those very statues and those marvellous paintings, sobbing and repeating over and over: 'And to think that I must leave all this! To think that I must leave all this!'"

"It seems almost as though he was struck down by a curse," I observed.

"The schemes whereby great men try to make their memory eternal, are utterly ridiculous," exclaimed Atto in response.

He fell silent, shaken by the very phrase which he himself had just pronounced.

"Ridiculous. . ." he repeated mechanically while, despite himself, his lips drooped, forming a tragic mask.

The old castrato lowered his gaze to his chest. He looked at the breeches, the sash, the Venetian lace jabot and all the other things he had put on – more than one would ever place on a tailor's dummy. He moved slowly to the window and glanced into the park, where, I supposed, the Connestabilessa must still be waiting.

Suddenly, there came flying capes and cloaks, sashes and jabots, the Bohemian cape, the cuffs, the pleated silk cloak and the stockings. The precious silks, the shining satins, the amber fur, the cloths enriched with gold and silver thread, the moiré satins, the Milanese *salia* and the Genoese sateens, all flew into the air, flung by Atto in handfuls. There followed what looked like a bewitched aerial army of empty costumes: tabbies, grograms, striped and flowered linens, muslins, ferrandines and doublets all flew menacingly upwards. My eyes were confused amidst the colours of pearl, fire, musk, dried roses, ginger, scarlet, maroon, dove-grey, grenadine, berrettino grey, nacre, tan, milky white, moiré and *gris castor*, and blinded by the gold and silver braiding and fringes which Atto was hurling to the floor in a silent, desperate frenzy.

I was utterly at a loss in the face of Melani's assault on his sartorial masterpieces; all the more so when I recalled how, many years ago, he had cursed in the honeycomb of underground galleries beneath Rome every time a splash of mud dirtied his lace cuffs or his red abbot's stockings.

When at last the curious army of costumes lay lifeless on the ground and the entire wardrobe was scattered far and wide, Atto's old body lay, like that of a half-naked satyr, slumped on the divan at the foot of the bed. Hardly had I overcome the icy grip on my members and rushed to the Abbot's assistance than the latter suddenly raised his face from his hands where he had plunged it and, standing up once more, moved away from me and slipped on his dressing gown.

"Now do you understand the verse in the sonnet on fortune recited by Capitor?" he asked me, as though nothing unusual had taken place.

He went to the console and poured two glasses of sweetened red wine, one of which he handed me.

"The third is stripp'd of all, *deep down*, to waste is driven," said he, seeing that he was unable to get a word out of me: "Hardly was he dead, than Cardinal Mazarin lost all that he had intrigued for."

"Yes," was all I was capable of saying.

I gulped down the wine in one go. My hands were trembling. Atto poured me another glass. He was avoiding my eyes. Fortunately, the fumes of alcohol soon dispelled those of emotion and I found myself once more at peace.

"That was a true prophecy," I exclaimed, once I had digested the Abbot's revelations concerning Capitor's words.

"Either that or a diabolical coincidence," he replied.

I smiled. The old castrato was irredeemable; he would not admit in my presence to the inexplicable nature of certain phenomena; I would leave him that little satisfaction.

"There is one so-called 'prophecy' of Capitor's that certainly has not come to pass," the Abbot insisted, for any such flaw corroborated his convictions. "That which she pronounced before the charger with the Tetràchion: 'He who deprives the crown of Spain of its sons, the crown of Spain will deprive of his sons.' What does that mean? Who has deprived Spain of heirs? King Charles II has no heirs; no one has been deprived of any. Capitor was talking nonsense, and that is the fact of the matter."

"But, if I remember well," I objected, "Capitor, when she presented the dish, said first of all 'Two in one'. And in doing so, she pointed first to the couple formed by Neptune and Amphitrite, then to the sceptre in the form of a trident, is that not so?"

"What are you getting at?" Atto grumbled, sounding as though he wished to set the matter to one side once and for all.

"Does it not seem to fit in rather curiously with the monstrous Tetràchion of whom Cloridia spoke?"

"I do not see how," the Abbot retorted drily.

"Perhaps the Tetràchion is a pair of twins attached to one another at the side, like the two deities on the charger, and like the image we saw reflected in the mirrors," said I, illustrating my idea, myself surprised by the theory which had suddenly arisen in my mind. "After all, Capitor did say 'Two in one', did she not?"

"Yes, but she was referring only to the figures on the charger; and that, my boy, is the one and only Tetràchion in this tale, for what we thought we saw in the penthouse at the Vessel was merely an optical illusion – or have you forgotten?"

He turned his back on me, signifying that the conversation was at an end, and returned to the window.

"Is she still there?" I asked.

"Yes. She always loved gardens, man's hand bending the beauties of nature to his will and surpassing them," said he with a tremor in his voice.

"Perhaps it is time for you to go down. . ."

"No. Not now," he retorted at once, revealing which thoughts had triumphed in that cruel inner battle which had taken place before my eyes; "I shall see her tomorrow."

"But perhaps you could. . ."

"My mind is made up. Please leave me alone now. I have many things to deal with."

Evening the Ninth

15ᵀᴴ JULY, 1700

✠

"One moment, please, all of you, one moment. Let us leave off from chewing, let us hold our tongues, let us curb our appetites! Let none rest on the laurels of their ill-conquered lunch! And let no one forget our kind Lord who, in offering us such a treat, is lavishing all these good things on us without a thought for the morrow, thus demonstrating with wise liberality the splendid generosity of his soul. Permit me then to raise my glass and dedicate this toast to our master, the most eminent, munificent and excellent Cardinal Spada, and to wish him the most magnificent and ever-increasing good fortune!"

While a gay concert of clapping, cries of jubilation and the sound of clinking glasses accompanied the end of this short speech, he who had pronounced it, namely the Secretary for Protocol of the Spada household, Carl' Antonio Filippi, sprawled on one of the day-beds in the garden, then rolled up his sleeves and began to gorge himself on fried trout covered with lilies and stuffed with apricocks, candies, sugar and cinnamon and triumphally garnished with slices of lemon.

The wine flowed fresh down my throat, but I wanted to keep my lips wet with it and pressed them against Cloridia's; while the two little ones who are the fruit of our union played at our feet, I kissed her tenderly, whispering sweet nothings, love pleasantries and other secret things.

All around us the servants' banquet was in full, free and joyous progress: Cardinal Spada had allowed the servants to celebrate and enjoy themselves in the august park of the villa and even to pass the night in the Turkish pavilions, caressed by Armenian silks, which had until a few hours previously received the noble guests invited to the nuptial celebrations. This generous decision had provided Secretary Filippi, the author of the speeches given in the Spada household on important occasions, with yet another opportunity to display his mastery of impromptu eloquence and the whole company with a rare chance to feast like lords.

I had not yet told my sagacious little wife the truth about the mad night at Saint Peter's: doing my very best to gloss over the dangers to which I had exposed myself, I strung out a sketchy, improbable account of that adventure, which she pretended to believe out of the kindness of her heart, aided and abetted by the festive atmosphere. From time to time, she would innocently pose me some trick question and I would invariably fall into the trap. But such was her joy to have me back by her side that she showed no great keenness to dig any deeper with her questioning: on that evening she took delight in using her tongue to caress rather than to scourge.

The Secretary for Letters of the Spada family, Abbot Giuliano Borghi, was seated at a sumptuously laid table with Don Tibaldutio, Don Paschatio, the Venerable Dean Giovanni Griffi, Master Cup-bearer Germano Hondadei, Auditor Giovanni Gamba and Aide de Camp Ottavio Valletti, all busily engaged in devouring a dish of soles pan-fried in butter and stuffed with pulped fish, marzipan, tellins and *mostacciolo*. True, these were leftovers, but marinated in gravy and their own good juices, they can sometimes taste even better.

Footmen, lackeys, sub-deacons, coachmen, assistant coachmen and grooms, sitting around a simpler table, were sipping with evident pleasure and surprise at a soup of prawns, truffles, prunes, mantis crabs, lemon juice, muscatel wine and spices, with bread crusts garnished with prawns' shells stuffed with *foie gras* interspersed with little pastries *alla Mazzarino*, coated with pistachios.

Another yet more humble group comprising porters, wardrobe servants, gardeners, prentices and assistants was gaily assembled around a soufflé full of pulped bass, tench and eel, pork crackling, capers, asparagus tips, prunes, poached egg yokes and slices of citron.

All the servants, even cooks and scullions, were seated under the stars or under cover in the Turkish pavilions, freely commenting on all the effort they had expended during those days.

As though the world had been turned upside down, the servants were the gentry and the gentry were bereft of assistance: all the illustrious guests had departed or were taking their leave, and none was any longer paying any attention to goings-on at the villa. Cardinal Spada, for his part, had returned to affairs of state.

After a week's unremitting labour, the humble company was relaxing and gossiping, commenting on all that had happened in town

– whether important or frivolous – during the past few days. At the Apostolic Palace of the Quirinale, with the pontifical choir in attendance, mass had been sung by Cardinal Moriggia (whom by now everyone at Villa Spada knew well, especially Caesar Augustus, who had liberally covered him with insults); during Vespers in the church of the Madonna at Monte Santo, a beam had collapsed, killing a member of the choir; His Holiness, on the occasion of the ninth anniversary of his pontificate, had received the Sacred College of Cardinals and the ambassadors, who had proffered him their wishes for a long reign (knowing full well that this could never happen).

Some of the chatter smacked of a return to normality. Everything, not only the celebrations, seemed to be over and done with. Maria had come but, thanks to Abbot Melani's eccentric behaviour, we had been able to descry her only from afar. If she had never come, might it not have been the same? Atto's treatise on the Secrets of the Conclave had remained in the hands of the *cerretani*, and perhaps it had already been handed over to Lamberg, if not to Albani in person. Thus, Atto was under the sword of Damocles. What was more, the three cardinals whom we had so carefully stalked had always evaded us and only on the last occasion had we been able to understand why: but too late.

Lastly we had, it was true, tried to understand what the Tetràchion was, but the arcane atmosphere at the Vessel and the apparitions we had witnessed there had misled us; instead of the monster announced by popular prophecies and Capitor's bizarre charger, we had seen our own effigies, reflected in distorting mirrors. We had tried everything, and nothing had succeeded. We had been defeated by adverse conditions, our own incapacity and by human weakness.

Lastly, and worst of all, the Abbot had hidden the truth from me about the three cardinals and what they up to when we followed them: the dying King of Spain had requested the Pope's assistance in resolving the problem of the succession to the throne and the Pope had instructed the three to draw up the reply. I had taken part in a hunt without knowing what quarry we were pursuing.

Of course, I understood perfectly well that, given his prudence and his mistrustful nature, Atto could not always reveal to me what he was plotting: all the more so in that his principal reason for coming to Villa Spada concerned something very different: the secret correspondence between the Connestabilessa and the Most Christian King.

Nevertheless, his stubborn silence on the Spanish question had made me feel like a marionette who could not be trusted with secrets. The worst of this was that I could not even blame him for his behaviour: I myself had betrayed his trust by reading his correspondence with Maria, and that forced me to remain silent.

We had amply fed at the gentlemen's table. Cloridia absented herself briefly to put the little girls to bed alongside the children of the other servants. Returning to me, she took me by the hand and guided me towards the pavilions. There, under cover of the late hour and guided by the braziers giving off their odours of pungent spices – and protected by the fact that most souls were overcome by so much imbibing of sugary liqueurs – the chaos of the domestics' chatter had given way to conspiratorial whispers and amorous murmuring. My spouse and I made our way between stockings and shoes abandoned on the lawn and bare feet echoing on the thresholds of those silken kiosks.

We settled down some way off, on the edge of that curious village, by now silent, yet full of activity. There, under a fluttering tent of Armenian gauze softly interwoven with gentle shades of amaranth red, we prudently unrolled the hangings to close the entrance and, far from prying eyes, my members sank amidst plumed cushions and my memory dissolved utterly in my lady's melting, rounded warmth, while the aromatic perfume of the braziers blended with other secret and ineffable fragrances.

"To what do we owe the honour?" said Cloridia, smiling in the most natural way in the world to someone behind my back.

I gave a violent start and turned sharply, as a hand was laid on my shoulder.

"I have news," said Abbot Melani, without so much as a hint of embarrassment. "Get dressed. I shall wait for you at the gate. My respects and my most profound apologies, Monna Cloridia," he added; then, just before pulling the entrance curtain behind him, "and my compliments. . ."

"How dare you!" I shouted, quite beside myself, after dressing and joining him.

"Calm down. I did call you from outside the tent, but you were too busy to hear me. . ."

"What do you want?" I cut him short, purple in the face with indignation.

"I have spoken with Lamberg."

"And?" I rejoined, hoping that some light had at least been cast on the assault suffered by Atto.

After a long wait, Abbot Melani had at last come face to face with the powerful Count Lamberg, scion of one of the Empire's most glorious families of ambassadors.

Exercising the greatest possible caution, he had come accompanied by Buvat. But the sombre Lamberg had begged the servants to leave him and his guest in private. Consequently, the secretary had remained in the ante-chamber.

"I know you by reputation, Signor Abbot Melani," Lamberg began.

Atto was instantly alarmed: was this an allusion to his treatise on the conclaves? Had he perhaps received it by some oblique route, perhaps from Cardinal Albani himself, and already perused it from start to finish?

"When the Emperor sent me here from Ratisbon," the Ambassador continued, "I expected to find benign influences here in this Holy City where the Jubilee is now taking place. Instead, I found Babylon."

"Babylon?" repeated Atto, growing even more circumspect.

"I find myself caught up in a sea of confusion, of horrible wars, of partisan struggles," he continued, scowling grimly.

"Ah, yes, I understand: the difficult international situation. . ." said Atto in an attempt to bring some calm to the conversation.

"Wretch!" Lamberg screamed suddenly, banging his fist on the table.

Silence descended on the room. Innumerable pearls of sweat ran down Abbot Melani's forehead. Such threatening and violent behaviour might even presage an attack. Without giving any sign of doing so, Atto had begun to look around him: he feared the sudden attack of assassins ordered to murder him. Damnation, why had he not thought of that? It was too long since he had been on mission in the Empire and he had forgotten how different the Germans were from the French. "Those damned Habsburgs, mad and bloodthirsty every one of them, from Spain to Austria, ever since the time of Joan the Mad." Before the meeting, he had promised himself that he would accept nothing from Lamberg's hand, not even a glass of water; but the possibility of an ambush had not crossed his mind.

"No one would ever find me. Only you knew that I had gone to visit Lamberg, but no one would ever have believed you," observed the Abbot.

He began to curse himself for having brought Buvat; they might kill the pair of them and both would simply disappear from the face of this earth.

At that point in the Abbot's narration, I remembered the Bezoar stone which, as I had secretly read a few days earlier in his correspondence, the Connestabilessa had sent him for its powers in warding off poisons. Atto had promised to keep it in his pocket during the audience, but it would be of little use in the event of an ambush. . .

As these dark thoughts rushed through the Abbot's mind, Lamberg remained silent, looking him straight in the eye. Melani returned the stare, not understanding whether the Ambassador intended to continue the conversation or to pass from words to action.

A sudden thought consoled him: too many people had seen him enter the Medici palace, which was the Roman property of the Grand Duke of Tuscany, his protector. Atto was well known there. If he were to die of stab wounds, it would be difficult to hush the matter up for long.

Still Lamberg said nothing. Atto dared not move a muscle. He remembered an old story – who knows whether it was true or not? A minister of the Emperor who had apparently died of a heart attack had in fact been killed with an invisible inoculation of poison behind the ear. There were any number of poisons that simulated a natural death: some could be sprayed on clothing, in one's hair, vapourised in the air, poured into the ear, dissolved in baths and foot-baths. . . All this, Atto knew perfectly well. The serpent of fear again crept up his back.

"Wretch. . ." hissed Lamberg once more, betraying in his trembling voice anger of an intensity approaching madness.

Fear or no fear, Atto could not allow himself to be insulted like that. Calling up all the audacity of which he was capable, he replied as his honour demanded.

"I beg your pardon."

Lamberg's eyes, which had for a moment wandered elsewhere, again fixed his own with unbearable intensity. The Ambassador stood up. Atto did likewise, fearing the worst. He grasped his walking stick firmly, ready to defend himself. Lamberg, however, moved to the window, which was ajar. He opened it wide.

"Are you happy in Rome, Signor Abbot Melani?" he asked, suddenly changing the subject.

"That's an old trick," thought Atto to himself, "continually changing the subject to confuse the person with whom one is speaking. I must be on my guard."

Meanwhile, Lamberg was looking out of the window, with his back to him: an unusual, and somewhat embarrassing situation. Atto waited awhile, but as the Ambassador continued to show him his back, which was in terms of diplomatic protocol quite unprecedented, he felt entitled to move so as to be able to see and hear him better. However, hardly had he taken a step forward than he realised the Austrian's chest was shaking rhythmically. Atto could hardly believe his eyes, yet there could be no doubt about it.

Lamberg was weeping.

"Wretch," he repeated for a third time, "he did not leave me so much as a scrap of paper. But the Emperor will make him pay for this, ah yes, that he will! He will pay for every one of his misdeeds," said he, turning and wagging his finger menacingly at Melani. "That wretched dog Martinitz," he sobbed, with a crazed expression contorting his face.

Count Martinitz, Atto explained to me, had been Lamberg's predecessor. A few months previously, he had been relieved of his post as Ambassador and hurriedly replaced because he had made himself too many enemies in Rome. Everyone in town had heard of this.

What no one, however, knew of and Lamberg angrily explained to Atto, was Martinitz's revenge. On his arrival in Rome, poor Lamberg had found in the Embassy archives, as he himself had confessed, not one single scrap of paper. His predecessor had carried off the entire diplomatic correspondence with him.

The new Ambassador (who in fact knew neither the city nor the pontifical court) was thus deprived of all the information essential for his work: the contacts upon whom he could count, the list of paid informers, the cardinals with whom there were good relations and those of whom one must be wary, the character of the Pope, his preferences, the details of pontifical ceremonial and so on and so forth. Of course, when he was appointed, he had, as was common practice, received instructions from the Emperor; but the situation really obtaining at the Rome embassy he could only learn from Martinitz, who had instead played this atrocious trick on him.

"I understand, Your Excellency, the matter is extremely grave," murmured Atto sympathetically.

Atto knew perfectly well: the representatives of the Empire were rigid and intractable and incapable of any spark of imagination. Without a written trail to follow, Lamberg was perfectly incapable of building up his own network of acquaintances and informers.

The Ambassador's outpourings continued like a torrent in full spate. Hardly had he set foot in Rome, he recounted, when he realised (but no one had forewarned him) that the pro-imperial party in the city was very weak indeed, while the French had it all their own way and obtained from the Pope whatever they wanted.

"Really?" I exclaimed in surprise.

"He even told me that he was unable to obtain an audience with the Pope, while Uzeda and the other ambassadors come and go freely every day in the Vatican."

In other words, the long-awaited meeting with the man suspected of being behind the wounding of Atto and perhaps even the assault which had brought about the death of the bookbinder Haver, had turned out to be nothing but a litany of whining and complaints. In the end, Lamberg had approached Atto, putting him on his guard against the malign forces which were abroad in the city and inviting him especially to beware of the Sacred College of Cardinals, that nest of every vice and iniquity.

"I expected to find here the government of the just, but I was all too soon forced to change my mind," said he in lugubrious tones. "What counts in Rome are reasons of state and in the pontifical court worldly affairs are handled with no respect for reason or rights, not even for the law. Religion counts for absolutely nothing!"

"I seemed to be hearing the music of that compatriot of theirs – what is he called? Ah yes, Muffat. A symphony so grave, so slow and severe as to be positively mournful," said the Abbot with perplexity written all over his face.

Faced with this outburst, Atto, once more sure of himself, had retorted: "But what did you expect to find in these parts, Signor

Ambassador? This is the city of deceit, dissimulation and eternal postponements, and of promises never kept. The Pope's ministers are past masters at spinning illusion, saying but not saying, intriguing, attacking from under cover."

The Abbot had continued freely to list the iniquities of the court of Rome, while Lamberg nodded disconsolately; until the Ambassador, perhaps because of another visit, sent him warmly on his way, honouring him with a sincere handshake.

Sincere? Once in the street with Buvat, Atto had regretted allowing himself to be dismissed so soon. He realised that Lamberg's behaviour bordered on the improbable. What if it had all been put on? If it had been he (as really had appeared to be the case until that moment) who had woven the thread of the assault on the Abbot and the theft of his treatise on the Secrets of the Conclave, then he must be malign and subtle indeed. If that were so, would he not be able even to act the part of the fool? The emotions displayed by the Ambassador had, however, been so violent and unexpected that anyone would have been caught out.

"In other words," I commented, "we are back where we started."

"Alas, yes. This Lamberg is either a soul whose true vocation was to be found in the peace of an Austrian cloister, or else he is a consummate actor."

"If I have understood, he got you to speak at length about the court of Rome while he himself told you little of any use."

"What do you think? Of course, I told him only what is generally known, nothing of any importance. Do you take me for a novice?" Melani retorted, somewhat piqued.

"I am not for one moment doubting your word, Signor Atto; however if Lamberg really put on a show for you but you were not pretending with him. . ."

"What of it?" he asked nervously.

"Then he knows your nature but you don't know his."

"Yes, but I do not think that. . . Buvat, what is this all about?"

Atto's secretary had arrived all out of breath. This was clearly an emergency.

"Sfasciamonti had caught the second *cerretano*, the friend of Il Roscio."

"Is that Il Marcio, the one we followed at the Baths of Diocletian, but who got away?"

"The very man. It was sheer luck: he made a false move. He was begging in church, in Saint Peter's itself. Seeing the protection enjoyed by the *cerretani*, he must have thought he could get away with it. Instead, Sfasciamonti was around and he caught him. He has already interrogated him using the same methods as last time: real prison, false notary. He enlisted the help of a couple of colleagues."

"Those are people who do nothing out of friendship," commented Atto. "I think I shall have to shell out another large tip. . . So, what did the *cerretano* say?"

"Sfasciamonti is waiting to tell us all about it."

"Let us make haste, then," Atto exhorted me, as I resigned myself to doing without Cloridia's company for the rest of the evening.

కుం

The catchpoll was hiding behind the toolshed in the garden. He was in a state of agitation and one could not blame him for that. It was the second time in a few days that he had laid hands on a *cerretano* and, if the sect were really that powerful, he was risking his skin. As he talked, he panted with excitement, as after a long run.

"They are holding it tonight, by all the daggers."

"Holding what?"

"They're meeting tonight for the new Maggiorengo-General. The leader of the scoundrels. They all get together, even those who come from far afield, to appoint the successor."

"And where?"

"At Albano."

"Can you repeat that?"

"At Albano."

I saw Atto Melani lower his eyelids, as though he had just heard a friend had died, almost as though he had been told that the Most Christian King had ordered him never again to set foot in France.

"It simply is not possible. . . Albano, a stone's throw from Rome. . ." I heard him gasp. "How could I not have thought of that?"

Albano. And not Albani. When Ugonio told us that the *cerretani* intended to bring Atto's papers *ad Albanum*, we thought that they meant to hand them over to Cardinal Albani. Instead the old tomb robber meant that they were to be taken to Albano, the little town near the lake of the same name, which has been a well-known holiday resort since the days of Cicero.

I saw Atto's face relax a little. At least there was no danger of Cardinal Albani covering him with infamy, as he had feared.

There remained the unknown factor of Lamberg, and the Grand Legator: why should the *cerretani* have to go to Albano to deliver the treatise on the Secrets of the Conclave to him?

"What will they do with my manuscript at Albano?"

"The vagabond knows nothing of that."

"What else did he say?"

"Besides electing the Maggiorengo-General, the *cerretani* have to change their way of speaking. But there's a problem. The new secret language appears to have been stolen."

"But by whom?"

"The ragamuffin does not know. If you want, I can read the record of his interrogation to you. As I did with Il Roscio, I changed a few dates and names, you know, in order not to run any risks; but the rest is exactly as I said."

"Not now. While we are on the road."

"While we are on the road?" I asked, without grasping what he meant by that.

਒ȣ਒

Geronimo. That was the real name of Il Marcio, the *cerretano* caught by Sfasciamonti. Now we had his words under our eyes, lit by the tremulous flame of a lantern, written in a tiny no-nonsense handwriting of which one could with a little intuition sense that it lent itself readily to lies: the hand of some catchpoll in the habit of falsifying, distorting or cutting statements. As we had been told, the date of the interrogation had been altered for safety, as had already been done with that of Il Roscio. Sfasciamonti had back-dated it by more than a century so as to be able to place it in the Governor's archives while making sure that it passed unobserved. So this second record of proceedings was dated 18 March 1595, as ever at the prison of Ponte Sisto.

It was not easy to read. Despite its being summer, the road to Albano was full of potholes and the bumps followed one another without a break. The carriage (despite the fact that it was an excellent vehicle, hired at the last moment at an astronomical cost) shook and jumped because of the road, swinging and sometimes tilting dangerously from side to side; but it kept moving. Atto, who sat to my left, had devoured Geronimo's statement. Now he sat there, silent and deep in thought, with his unmoving gaze fixed on the landscape, as though he were observing the rare lights from farmhouses, whereas his mind was implacably set on his anxieties.

To my right sat Buvat, as stiff as a poker, despite a passing bout of somnolence. Before we mounted the carriage, I saw him briefly confer with Don Paschatio. From their confabulation, we overheard only a few last recommendations which the Major-Domo imparted when Buvat was already on his way to the carriage: "Take care: avoid dampness and excessive movement, and make sure to keep them upright at all times." I had no idea what this was all about, but when Buvat got in, Atto asked him no questions, so I too asked none. On the front seat, there sprawled Sfasciamonti's exorbitant bulk, as though squeezed by force into the tight space. He too was locked in impenetrable silence. A short while before our departure, he had held a long conversation with Atto, probably to agree on the price of his forthcoming services. The journey to Albano by night was no joke. Even less reassuring was the place to which we were headed; the agreed price must have been high. Next to the catchpoll sat the passenger who must, at the time of our departure, have most perplexed our coachman.

As soon as the carriage arrived, Atto had ordered that we first be taken to the Baths of Agrippina. Objective: to pick up Ugonio. It was unthinkable to sneak into the meeting of the *cerretani* without a guide. As soon as we reached his hide-out, we brought him out simply by shouting his name at the top of our voices. Rather than attract the attention of the neighbourhood (for Ugonio, it was indispensable to have a discreet lair known to no one) the *corpisantaro* rapidly emerged and agreed to talk with us. At the outset, however, Atto treated him with obvious irritation. When he reported that the treatise on the Secrets of the Conclave was to be brought *ad Albanum*, Ugonio meant the town towards which we were now heading. If he did not make that clear, it was because, to him, it was perfectly obvious. He could of course have no idea that a certain Cardinal Albani might be involved in Atto's affairs or that this might give rise to confusion on my part and Atto's. He could not be blamed for the misunderstanding, but it had wasted a huge amount of our precious time. To increase Atto's impatience, Ugonio put up a strenuous resistance when he knew for what purpose we meant to recruit him: to guide us to the meeting of the *cerretani*. Only under the combined pressure of threats and abundant offers of cash did he end up by giving in and accompanying us, bringing with him all that would be needed for the undertaking. Just before the corpisantaro climbed into the carriage, there was, however, one last negotiation. Atto drew the new passenger aside and held an intense discussion with him. Finally, he poured an unusually large number of gold coins – or so they seemed in the darkness that enveloped us – into Ugonio's purse. Last of all, he passed him a book. I tried to ask the Abbot, but he would not tell me what all that business was about.

My thoughts turned once more to the curious meeting between Atto and Lamberg. Until that moment, we had acted on the assumption that the Imperial Ambassador was behind the assault and the theft suffered by Atto. But now we were stumbling in the dark: either Lamberg was a brilliant simulator, or else he really was a pious and fervent Catholic whose moral code had been afflicted by the cruel scourge of disillusionment. If that were the case, our journey to Albano was beset by even more unknown factors: the enemy towards which we were marching was faceless.

I saw that my mind was wandering and broke off from that review of the latest developments to return to my reading.

The record of the *cerretano's* interrogation, which I was subsequently able to transcribe almost in its entirety, began with the criminal notary's usual forms of words, followed by the arrested man's statement:

DIE 18 MARTIJ
Examinatus fuit in carceribus Pontis Sixti coram magnifico et Excell.ti Dño N. . . per me notarium infra scriptum Hieronymus quondam Antonij Furnarij Romani annorum 22 in circa, cui delato iuramento etc.

Interrogatus de nomine, patria, aetate et causa suae carcerationis, respondit:

"I was born in Rome, son of the late Antonio Fornaro of the Colonna ward near the Trevi Fountain. My name is Geronimo, I am twenty-two years of age, I have no trade, except that I go and work in the salt pans for four months every year, after which I return to Rome and go begging for alms. As you can see, I am very poor and sick, and for the past ten years I have been without father or mother, an abandoned orphan, trying to live as best I can, and I was arrested in Saint Peter's on Friday last March because I was begging in Church."

Geronimo was then asked what he knew about the mendicants' secrets. Here, the interrogation repeated all twenty-five sects already confessed by his predecessor to which the accused added several others: the Trawlers, the Mountebanks, the Hucksters, the Dormice, the Mandrakes, the ABCs, the Bloodsuckers, the Mumpers, the Itchies, the Palliards, the Marmots, the Bullies, the Sharpers, the Errants and the Sweeps.

"The Trawlers sleep at night and beg by day; the Mountebanks sell fake rings and pieces of earth of Saint Paul's Grace and fool the hicks most wonderfully; the Hucksters are dreadful charlatans, they always have some *grubs* or *crabs* with them – that's what they call the youngsters who work with them. They go to market and while they're at their huckstering or shopping, the *grubs* and *crabs* go stealing and cutting purse-strings, then in the evening they all share the spoils. They always have boys with them because they're all *back-gammon players*, which is what we call sodomites. The Dormice are crippled in all four limbs, they don't even have hands and feet, and they beg. The Mandrakes are cripples and get themselves pulled in little packing cases on wheels or carried on someone's shoulders, and they, too, beg. The ABCs are poor blind men, and they beg as well. The Bloodsuckers go from hamlet to hamlet selling chap-books of the lives of the Saints and Orations to Saints, which they sing, and then they all beg together for alms. The Mumpers are those who are well dressed and claim to have formerly been gentlemen or artisans and, with the most courteous, severe mien, off they go a-begging too.

"The Itchies are mangy, scabby lepers and the like, and they beg like all the others. The Palliards are those who cut their hands or feet and seem to be crippled, but there's nothing wrong with them at all. They make false wounds on an arm or a leg with a piece of bloody liver, and beg. The Marmots pretend to be dumb or to have no tongue, and beg. The Bullies are those who go begging dressed in mountain men's sheepskins. The Sharpers play in hostelries and inns with marked cards and loaded dice, they're as cunning as they come. The Sweeps are those who say they're Jews and they have families, and they've converted to Christianity. That way they collect plenty of alms. Last but not least, there are the Doxies and the Autem Morts, who are women that beg in various ways. The Doxies are young and good company, whereas the Autem Morts are good for the hospital or the tavern and for the most part they're old."

I skimmed through the statement rapidly until I came to the important information about Albano.

"I have heard said that in May many beggars mean to meet at the grottoes of Albano, because they want to elect the new Maggiorengo-General and to give out the new jargon for us to speak, but, as we've heard that this has been stolen, they mean to set things in order and to lay down penalties so that no one gives the game away. And whoever does give us away they'll *play Martin with* – in other words, he'll find himself on the wrong end of a dagger. And I've heard that some fellows found that Pompeo near Pescheria and started to beat him up, and if he'd not run to a Church for sanctuary with the priests, they'd have killed him, as everyone was so angry with him for having sold out on them."

So the *cerretani* would be meeting at Albano, as Sfasciamonti had told us (for safety, the statement spoke of May instead of July). They said someone had stolen their new secret language and they meant to restore order (though Geronimo did not say how they proposed to do so). What's more, they wanted to kill Pompeo, alias Il Roscio, because they had heard he'd blabbed. But who'd told them?

At the end, the criminal notary asked why the mendicant, who had made a full confession, did not abandon such bad company and such infamous practices and find a trade, as so many did in Rome.

"Sir, I'll tell you the truth. We like this way of living freely here and there, sponging for bed and board, without having to make any efforts, far too much and, in short, whoever once has tasted of the canters' way of life will never give it up that easily. This is true both for the men and the women. I hope that with God's help I shall be able to change my life, if I can get out of prison, 'cos I'd like to go and stay with the friars of San Bartolomeo on the island and take care of their donkey."

"In the end, of course, we had to let him go," laughed Sfasciamonti who, as had happened with Il Roscio, could certainly not have someone imprisoned who had not been legally arrested. "He'll surely go and take care of the donkey, so long as his comrades don't catch him first and *play Martin with him*, as they put it."

"But how could they know he's been questioned?" I asked, worried about the idea of another leak of this kind of information.

Sfasciamonti's visage darkened.

"In the same way as after Il Roscio's arrest."

"Meaning?"

"I don't know."

"Come now, what do you mean?"

"These *cerretani* are diabolical. One of them says something and suddenly they all know about it."

"It's true, damn it," Atto echoed him forcefully after a moment's silence, "they really are diabolical."

This time, Buvat was not there. "Who," I asked, "played the part of the criminal notary?"

"A real notary," the catchpoll replied.

"How can that be?"

"There's no more perfect forgery than an authentic object," Atto interjected.

"I don't understand."

"That's a good sign. It means the old law still works, and three centuries hence it will still be working," replied the Abbot.

"Now I remember that when we met you spoke to me of how false documents sometimes contain the truth. Is that what you meant?"

"No, this time I meant the exact opposite, and I'm not speaking only of papers but far more. I'll give you an example: who mints money in a state?" asked Melani.

"The Sovereign."

"Exactly. So the coin that comes from his mint, the state mint, will always be genuine."

"Yes."

"In fact, no. Or at least, not always. The Sovereign can always, if he wants, mint false money, and in large quantities: for example, to finance a war. All he need do is produce coin with a lower gold content than its nominal value. Now, will that money be true or false?"

"False!" I answered, contradicting what I had just said.

"But the King minted it. So it will be both true and false at the same time. To be precise, this money will be genuine but misleading. The trick's as old as the world. Four hundred years ago, when the King of France, Philip IV the Fair, wanted to finance a war against the Flemings, he reduced the *livre tournois* by half. Initially, it weighed eleven and a half ounces. But he also did the same thing with its gold content, lowering it from 23 carats to 20 carats. That way the King's coffers gained six thousand Parisian livres 'under the counter'. In the process, however, he reduced the land to extreme poverty."

"Does that kind of thing still happen today?"

"More than ever. William of Orange did it when he minted forged and suitably 'lightened' Venetian zecchini."

"How awful! False things that reveal the truth and true things that spread what's false," I sighed.

"That's the chaos of human society, my boy. That pain-in-the-proverbial, Albicastro, did say at least one thing that was absolutely right: 'Human affairs, like the Sileni of Alcibiades, always have two faces, each the opposite of the other.' That is and always will be the way of the world: open a Silenus, and you'll find everything transformed into its opposite," concluded Atto, surprising me by quoting the Dutchman whom he so detested.

The Abbot was speaking of the Sileni mentioned by the violinist, those grotesque statuettes which contained divine images within.

"Getting back to the subject," added Melani. "Friend Sfasciamonti had Geronimo examined by a real notary, who drew up a record of the interrogation that was in the correct form down to the smallest details, as not even Buvat could have done. It is not a false document. It contains information which is somewhat. . . imprecise, if you wish, like certain dates; nevertheless, it was drawn up by a genuine notary, assisted by genuine sergeants. It is not a faithful document, but it is an authentic one, indeed, most authentic. Is what I say correct?" asked Atto, turning to his travelling companion.

The catchpoll said nothing. He was not pleased that these methods should be spoken of openly, but he could not deny what had been said. Instead of answering, he looked away from us, thus giving his tacit assent.

"Remember, my boy," said Atto to me, "great falsifications call for great means; and these, only the state possesses."

❧❧

Following Ugonio's directions, we ordered the coachman, a mercenary used to all manner of missions (nocturnal fugues, adulteries, clandestine meetings) to take us to a quiet spot in the town. We were set down in a dark alley behind a big haystack. The houses were plunged in darkness. Only from rare windows did faint lights still glimmer, while the sole denizens of the narrow streets were cats and their customary victims.

The driver told us to take care, but carefully avoided asking us what we proposed to do in that God-forsaken place at that hour.

The streets were singularly free of any sign of life; yet it was a warm, comforting summer night of the kind beloved by insomniacs, clandestine lovers and adventurous boys. Judging by the deathly pall over all our surroundings, one might have thought we were in the midst of a blizzard in the dark lands of the far north of the kind so well described by Olaus Magnus.

The corpisantaro carried a big greasy sack on his shoulder. We took a lane that led out into the fields, split into two separate roads, then petered out amidst a group of ruins. Our march was long and tortuous. We crossed vegetable gardens, then an uncultivated field. The only counterpoint to our footsteps was the chirping of crickets and the petulant buzz of mosquitos. We had in truth to advance rather cautiously, to avoid falling into some hidden ditch.

"Is it still far?" asked Atto, somewhat impatiently.

"'Tis a particulable and secreted location," said the corpisantaro in justification, "that must remain incognito."

Suddenly, Ugonio stopped and drew from his sack three filthy hooded cassocks.

"Only three?" I asked.

The *corpisantaro* explained that Sfasciamonti could not come with us.

"These vestibulements would be overmuch too tight-knitted for him," said he, pointing at the cloaks. "He has an excess of corpulousness. Better that he should vegetate here until our retourney, decreasing the scrupules so as not to increase our scruples, naturalissimally."

The catchpoll grunted some discontented comment but did not protest. What a strange destiny for Sfasciamonti, I thought. He'd striven so long to investigate the *cerretani*, despite the opposition of colleagues and superiors, and here he was, reduced to doing so on Abbot Melani's behalf: in other words, as a mercenary. And now, after travelling by night all the way to Albano, he could not even come with us to the meeting.

I put on the smallest of the cassocks. There is no point in my dwelling upon the disgust that those vile, stinking rags inspired in me, worn for years by creatures accustomed to crawling amidst subterranean rubbish in a world utterly alien to the very notion of cleanliness. They reeked of stale urine, rotting food and acid sweat. I heard Atto cursing under his breath against Ugonio's companions and their filth. Buvat put up with these clothes uncomplainingly, faithful secretary that he was.

The undeniable advantage of the garments was, however, their disproportionately voluminous cowls which covered almost all one's face, the outsized sleeves which concealed one's hands and the way they trailed along the ground, so that one could walk without one's footwear or stockings being visible. Holding back a wave of nausea, I slipped my arms into the sleeves. I had been transformed into a smelly cocoon of clumsy, formless sackcloth. Only their stature rendered Atto and Buvat a little less awkward.

"What? No lantern?" Atto protested once more when he learned from Ugonio that we would have to proceed in the dark. The *corpisantaro* was adamant: from that moment on, we risked being discovered and unmasked by the *cerretani*. What was more, I remembered that the tomb robbers always moved without light, both by night and in the dark tunnels under Rome.

Like three faceless ghosts, Buvat, Atto and I followed Ugonio who guided us along a pathway visible only to him. In a hoarse whisper, Sfasciamonti wished us good luck.

As I walked, the stink of the caftan I wore cancelled out the smell of the effluvia of the countryside by night. I crossed myself mentally and prayed the Lord not to judge too severely the rash acts which we were surely about to commit. I sought courage in the thought that only the future dowries of my little girls could justify such recklessness.

After a long straight walk on the level, the path made a great curve and sloped gradually down into a damp ravine where only a few sinister and wavering glimmers reached us from the heavens.

Suddenly, as though magically exuded from the darkness, a few figures appeared nearby. An old cripple, supported by two companions, was coming towards us. Behind them, emerging from the nocturnal mists, other similar beings appeared.

Before us stood a great stone wall which seemed to be that of an enormous edifice. We entered through a narrow tunnel. A number of torches set into the walls at last cheered the soul and the eyes.

Suddenly, however, rock, moss and bare earth closed in on us, forming an impregnable fortress. The tunnel had come to an end. Ugonio
turned, showing us his broken, blackish teeth in a malicious smile,
taking pleasure in our discomfiture.

Buvat and I exchanged alarmed looks. Had we been led into a
trap? The *corpisantaro* gestured that we were to make sure that our
faces were well hidden under our cowls, so that no one could distinguish our features. Then he leaned against the wall to our left. The
rock swallowed him up: Ugonio had entered it like water absorbed
into a sponge.

Almost as though emerging from another dimension, he took a
step backwards and motioned us to follow him.

Obviously, Ugonio had not penetrated the substance of the rock.
The sharp noise of the painted wood forming the door set into the
rock face had escaped me. This was a secret passage which intruders would be utterly unable to find but which Ugonio had obviously
taken who knows how many times.

Once inside, it took a few moments for our eyes to become accustomed to the new situation. We looked all around us. Neglected for
centuries, enormous and powerful, and now crawling with *cerretani*,
the Roman amphitheatre of Albano lay before us.

"So we came in by a secret passage," I whispered in Ugonio's
ear.

"To bring about more benefice than malefice," he assented, "the
normal orifices have been blockified. No strangers or nose-insinuators
must get in here tonight."

"But no one stopped us."

"It is not necessitable. There are many guardians postified every-
whichwhere and any introoter will be visualised, compressed and suppressed."

So the amphitheatre was protected by a system of sentinels responsible for finding any intruders and rendering them harmless.
Thanks to the disguise provided by Ugonio, no one had suspected
us.

Along the internal perimeter of the amphitheatre, a long series
of torches lit up the scene. In that vast space, enclosed but open to
the sky, I felt simultaneously disoriented and imprisoned. Above our
heads, the star-studded black of the sky warned that there was no
hope of escape for those without wings. Waves of murmuring coming

from the arena maliciously tickled the senses and the spirit. The air was sickly-sweet, humid and loaded with sin.

"But yes, of course, the amphitheatre," said Atto under his breath, "it had to be here. . ."

"Do you know this place?" I asked.

"Of course. Back in Cicero's day. . ."

Ugonio silenced us with a sudden movement of his arm. A few paces behind us there was still that old cripple with his two friends who had escorted him from outside. The animal caution with which the *corpisantaro* was leading us seemed all but tangible; and already we could feel the dismal atmosphere of a secret meeting of brigands clutch at our shoulders like some rapacious lemur.

‽‽

From the centre of the arena shone the rays of several torches which, from what we could hear and see, lit up an assembly. At the same time, a confused babble of voices reached us. We approached, still following prudently in Ugonio's footsteps. After passing a heap of firewood, we could at last get a look at the scene.

A few paces ahead of us stood a huge brazier, as high as a man, in which a great flame burned generously, crackling and sending sparks high up into the sky. All around were small groups of *cerretani*; some were idly eating a wretched meal, others were gulping down cheap wine and yet others were playing cards. Then there were some who were welcoming new arrivals, raising their arms in salutation. The company was one great multitude of sordid, ill-dressed, mud-bespattered, evil-smelling people.

"We have arrivalled at the most suitful moment," murmured Ugonio, motioning us with his hand to follow him in single file.

From another part of the amphitheatre, we saw approaching us a sort of procession, upon seeing which those camped near the brazier stood up dutifully.

"The electrocution has just taken place. The Maggiorenghi are now entrifying with the Grand Legator," said Ugonio pointing to the procession and inviting us to stand aside. "The firstsome is the head of the Company of Mumpers. Behind him are all the adjuncts and conjuncts of the othersome companies: Dommerers, Clapperdogeons, Brothers of the Buskin, Abram Coves, Pistoleros and Tawneymen. . ."

"So these are the heads of the *cerretani* companies?" asked Atto, opening his eyes wide, as we prepared to join the procession.

I looked at that vile troop. On the basis of what Il Roscio had told us, I could identify the head of the Dommerers' company. Around his neck, he wore a huge iron chain and he was constantly murmuring "bran-bran-bran"; as I recalled, the speciality of his group was imposture: they claimed to have been prisoners of the Turks and so spoke Turkish. Of course, there was no pigeon to pluck that evening but the Dommerers, like all the other *cerretani*, had, after a manner of speaking, come to their general meeting wearing their company uniform.

"And where is the Grand Legator?" he added, looking all around (although the very idea was absurd) for Lamberg's face.

In lieu of an answer, Ugonio moved to the head of the procession of Maggiorenghi. He greeted the head of the Mumpers, an individual with a flowing grey beard and long hair that spilled out from under a showy plumed hat; in accordance with the practice of his sect, he wore the clothes of a nobleman, save that these were unbelievably dirty and threadbare. The Mumpers, as I had just read in Geronimo's statement, were those who begged, saying that they were ruined gentlefolk or artisans. Ugonio knelt in the most unctuous and servile manner, momentarily slowing down the little cortège of Maggiorenghi. Instantly, we pulled our cowls down even lower, fearing that our faces might be seen. Fortunately, we were helped by the intermittent, flaming light of the torches which illuminated the space somewhat irregularly. I looked around me again: the whole place was crawling with cripples and lepers, with men blind, mutilated or emaciated, their bodies half naked, twisted and limping, bearing the marks of flagellation, chains and torture. It was a veritable catalogue of the *cerretani*'s impostures: all those apparent lacerations, those pustules, that exhausted dragging of legs, were merely the tricks of the trade: not suffering, but art, of which the canters kept the signs even when they were not actually engaging in their scoundrelly activities. Observing more closely, I saw that they were strolling peacefully here and there, downing their cheap wine, laughing and joking without a care in the world. I wavered between horror, fear and wonderment, but there was no time to exchange any comment with Atto. After a brief muttered colloquy, Ugonio returned to us and the procession continued on its way.

"Bemark the Mumper posterior to the Maggiorengo," he whispered.

This was a bald, half-hunchbacked old man, wearing a badly torn artisan's apron and a pair of down-at-heel shoes. He, too, according to the dictates of his sect, begged, pretending to have been an honest workman who had fallen on hard times. On his shoulder, he carried an old bag in which one could just descry the white pages of a small tome.

"He is the Grand Legator," announced Ugonio.

"What!" hissed Atto, his eyes bulging out of his head with surprise.

"He is a brother from Holland. His name is Drehmannius and he's a bit gagafied, he can't even read the foliables he binds, but he is indeed an excellentissimus buchbinder. That's why he's a Mumper. He has the treaty," added Ugonio, with an imperceptible nod in the direction of the contents of the bag on the man's shoulder.

I saw Atto's jaws tighten. What Lamberg? What imperial plot? Now it was all crystal clear: the Grand Legator was no *legatus* or Ambassador but a *legator*; in the *cerretanis'* dog Latin, that meant he was an ordinary bookbinder! So the treatise on the Secrets of the Conclave, the key to Atto's destiny, was in the hands of that lousy insignificant old Dutchman.

"What's this Dutch bookbinder, Drehmannius or whatever he's called, proposing to do with my treatise?" asked Melani, on tenterhooks.

"To ungluify the binderings. The Maggiorengo has just secreted it to me."

"To unglue the binding?" repeated Melani, utterly at a loss for words. "What the deuce do you mean?"

But we had to stop talking. A tall, imposing *cerretano*, with filthy, stubby great hands, had drawn near to us, his right eye covered with a black bandage. He called Ugonio to one side and the latter followed him at once.

Thus, we were suddenly without a guide in the very midst of that demented, lawless mass, at the tail of a procession of which we knew neither where it was going nor why. In the middle of that cortège, a group of old men were fighting over a flask of wine. One of them, obviously drunk, came face to face with Atto and belched loudly. Melani turned away in disgust and rummaged instinctively in his overcoat in search of his lace handkerchief, then realised it would be wiser not to seem finicky.

Suddenly, the procession of *cerretani*, by now distinctly the worse for drink, struck up a bizarre song:

> *Doing nothing at all is the very best trade.*
> *And when winter comes,*
> *You just lie in the sun,*
> *While in summer, you lie in the shade.*
> *With a branch in your hand, you chase flies away*
> *And the fat meat you eat*
> *And you toss out the lean. . .*

A tramp, bare-chested and all covered in bruises, with filthy bag-pipes hanging around his neck and bare feet with long black nails, encouraged by the little chorus, began to sing loud and clear, caring not to keep time with the others:

> *By lies and by tricks*
> *You can live half a year;*
> *By tricks and by lies,*
> *Live the other half too!*

I recognised this: it was the same *cerretano* doggerel Don Tibaldutio had taught me.

Suddenly, an icy cold, sliding presence came between the cassock and my neck. I turned sharply.

I nearly fainted. A slimy serpent, held in the hand of a disgusting wretch with a fat, greasy, ill-shaven face had licked my defenceless neck. The *cerretano* roared with coarse laughter and gave me a slap on the shoulder that almost knocked me over. It was all a joke. He then put the serpent in a wicker basket and began to sing in a chorus with three or four of his mates:

> *We are scum, we are scum,*
> *'Tis for wenching we have come,*
> *From the house of Saint Paul we descend.*
> *We were born, we were born*
> *Far away from this land*
> *With a snake on the bum,*
> *On the bum, on the bum,*
> *And a snake in the hand. . .*

So this was a *sanpaolaro*, a healer and handler of serpents, like the one I'd seen at work a few days before. To make the meaning of his doggerel quite clear, he put his hand on his privates and accompanied the last verses with obscene rhythmic thrusts of the hips. If he and his companions were not drunk with wine, they surely were with bestial gaiety. A middle-aged tramp had seized a fiddle and was making it moan and whine like a cat on heat.

But there was no time to stop and stare. New participants kept arriving in the amphitheatre, multitudes of *cerretani* were crowding into the arena. Choruses, chaotic ballets, screams and coarse belly laughter resounded everywhere. When we arrived, it was a meeting, now it was one of the circles of hell. The procession had become enormous: there were hundreds and hundreds of vagabonds, almost all bearing torches, and it had begun simply to turn on itself in the arena, imprisoned by the amphitheatre like a mole whose nest has become too tight for it. Curious eyes focused on us. Although well covered by Ugonio's cassocks, we did not have the agile, bestial movements of the *corpisantari*, nor did we seem to be playing any great part in the carousing. But we had no time to worry. Our attention was distracted by a new development. Other swarms of beggars had gathered around the little procession of the Maggiorenghi, overcrowding the end of the arena where we stood. Elbows, backs and legs struggled like gladiators in agony. It was hard to keep close to Atto and Buvat and not to get dragged off into the crowd.

The chaos was such that, fortunately, no one seemed to be paying much attention to anyone else, and thus, not to us either. In the background, the whining of the fiddle was joined by the whistling of a group of rustic flutes and the nasal complaint of bagpipes.

"Look: just take a look at that one," said Atto, pointing out a gaunt-looking young man with a bushy beard and sunken eyes.

Standing on tiptoe, I could just make out this character's face.

"Does that face not seem familiar to you too?"

"Well, yes. . . I do seem to have seen him before, but I don't recall where. Perhaps we've seen him begging somewhere."

Just next to the young man, almost in the very middle of the throng, three Maggiorenghi suddenly appeared. They had mounted a platform, or perhaps some other kind of dais, hurriedly erected by a group of scruffy half-naked youths. The Maggiorengo in the middle was the head of the Mumpers. The other two raised his arms heavenward and the crowd cheered. We needed no interpreter to understand that this was the new Maggiorengo-General.

Beside the trio appeared the Grand Legator. He was holding a book in his hand. Both Atto and I recognised it: it was his treatise on the Secrets of the Conclave.

"Tut, tut, another Dutchman, what a coincidence."

"What do you mean?" I asked.

"Use one Dutchman to hunt the other," he replied with a wicked little smile.

While I was trying to understand the Abbot's enigmatic words, a fifth being mounted the platform: Ugonio.

"Take care not to lose us, we must stay close to the platform," Atto warned me.

Then silence fell – or almost.

"My wily, artful friends, you guys and you heels, hear me out, prick up your bells!" began the Maggiorengo of the Mumpers, speaking in a stentorian voice. He was, it seems, beginning his enthronement speech as the new Maggiorengo-General: a speech in Saint Giles' Greek, of which we would probably understand next to nothing.

Buvat, kneeling, well wrapped in his bedraggled caftan so as to avoid being seen, began rapidly to turn the pages of the glossary of cant. Atto and I did our best to shield him from unwanted attention.

The Maggiorengo-General asked the Grand Legator to pass him Atto's book.

"This breviar is by a froggy autem cull," the Maggiorengo continued, waving the book in the air; "an angler, and his falcon with the harness of little tapers, he wanted to make a razzia: to make up like a carp and whitewash the damned one."

A scandalised and hostile hubbub arose from the crowd.

"I think he said that the book which he's holding in his hand is by a foreign ecclesiastic who wanted to cause trouble and discover the language," Buvat muttered to Atto, continuing to leaf frenetically through the book.

"To discover a language?" repeated Atto. "The Devil, I've got it! The stupid, ignorant jackasses, may God curse them. . ."

At that moment, I noted with alarm that a young *cerretano*, barefoot and emaciated, almost completely bald and with his face horribly scarred, bare-chested and with the rest of his body covered only by an old blanket knotted around his waist, was staring perplexedly at Buvat and his little book. Atto, too, became aware of this and fell silent.

"Baste the cull, baste the cull!" screeched a horrendous old man in the crowd, with his face all covered in pustules.

"Siena! Si-e-na! Si-e-na!" the crowd responded, swaying with enthusiasm. Another round of applause followed and many bottles emptied by the mass of *cerretani* were hurled into the air in jubilation.

"Baste the cull means. . . Well, they're saying this foreigner should be punished, in other words, he should be killed," whispered Buvat worriedly, still feverishly turning the pages of his glossary. "*Si*ena means yes."

"What a clever idea," commented Atto sarcastically, as he pulled the grimy cowl down more closely over his head, taking care to touch it only with his fingertips.

The half-naked *cerretano* drew a companion's attention to us. By pure luck, at that moment the movement of the crowd blocked their view. Were they approaching us?

Meanwhile, the Maggiorengo of the Mumpers waited for the applause to die down a little. Moved by an almost primordial instinct, I checked our distance from the entrance, which I supposed must also be the way out. It was still very near.

"And now, my goodly heels," said the orator, "whereas We, Sacred Majesty, great and glorious Emperor, have duly been elected Emperor, King, Chief, Condottiere, Prince, Rector and Guide of the Canters; and whereas such authority as We enjoy appertains not only to His Most Scoundrelly Majesty but to the least canter among our select assembly, We are impelled by our scoundrelly nature to expatiate in this our speech on the pre-eminence and most condign worthiness of the Way of the Canters and all those who follow it."

An ovation resounded through the amphitheatre.

At this point, Buvat was fortunately able to leave off consulting his glossary. The speech was continuing in ordinary language since no strangers could be present to follow it (we, of course, being secretly present): the introduction in the cant language had served mainly to warm up the spirits of those present.

Someone handed a bottle to the Maggiorengo-General, from which he drank voraciously, in great gulps, until he let it fall empty at his feet.

"For a start," he continued, "the society of the canters is more ancient than that of the Baronci, of which Boccaccio speaks, older than the Tower of Nembrotto, and indeed that of Babel. Being ancient, it is of necessity excellent and perfect, and consequently, every single canter is excellent and perfect, so that it follows that its Sovereign will be most excellent and most perfect and almost immortal!"

Waves of applause greeted the eulogy which the new Maggiorengo-General, laughing complacently, heaped upon himself and his subjects. Atto and I exchanged worried glances. We were in the midst of a host of madmen.

"And let us, then, begin from the beginning of this great horrible world," continued the Maggiorengo. "Let us speak of the Golden Age, when Master Saturn was the King of men. What a scoundrelly life was ours back then! All lived in peace, considering the Sovereign as a good father, and he treated them like good children. All lived in freedom and safety, 'midst all manner of contentments and pleasures, eating, drinking and dressing after the manner of good canters, knowing not wealth or possessions, so that this epoch was called by the authorities of the people of canters the Golden Age. Then there were only goodfellows, purloiners free from all malice. Everything was held in common, there was no division of lands, no carving up of things, no separation of houses, no fences around vineyards. No force had ever to be employed in dealings with anyone, there were no disputes, no one stole chickens, no one contended for harvests. Everyone could work the land he wanted to, planting whatever seed he would and training the vines as it pleased him. Every woman was everyman's wife and every male was every woman's husband and of every thing the valiant canters made one great bundle. What a wonderful stallion our good scoundrel Biello would have made in that Golden Age!"

The Maggiorengo-General spoke these last few words turning towards a *cerretano* seated near him on the podium and pointing him out to the multitude, who applauded him long and loud.

"But then came that beard-splitter Jove, who forgot that he too was a canter, seeing that he'd been raised like a beast and given suck by nanny goats. Greedy for power and no longer having the slightest respect for the people of canters, Jove drove his old father Saturn from the Golden Age. Thus, life and conditions changed for everyone, freedom was lost and enmity, wrath, disdain, fury, cruelty, arson and rapine arose among men. Then they began to divide all possessions and goods, to enclose vineyards, gardens and houses, to lock gates, doors and entrances, to be jealous of women, to question each other and to fight even to the death, and so many other evil things that one loses all count of them."

One *cerretano* not far from us let out a great noisy fart, making all his neighbours laugh.

"Ah, Jove did plenty of damage," Atto commented to himself in disgust.

"Nevertheless, the tyrant Jove was not powerful enough to cancel out and extinguish the holy people of canters," continued the Maggiorengo-General, "who, being divine and immortal, even given this change and setback, gave that proud upstart clearly to understand that, king though he was, he could not do without us. For not only Jove, but all his relatives – and he had masses of them – lived in comfort and contentment only because they ate and drank what they extorted from the canters. . ."

"Si-e-na! Si-e-na!" bawled dozens of *cerretani* in a chorus of approval.

Atto motioned that I was to follow him: we moved to the left, doing our best to avoid the attentions of the half-naked *cerretano*. To no avail; when I turned around, he was still looking at us.

". . . And everything in which the gods took pleasure, they did using Canters'manners and tricks: dissimulating who they were, fooling and cheating everyone. Starting with Jove himself who, when he wanted to lay Europa, the maiden who looked after King Agenor's cows, had to get help from the Canters to dress up as chief cowherd. He'd never have had Europa if he hadn't fooled her with that disguise! And when he wanted to make the beast with two backs with Leda, he dressed up as a poultryman, and that's why, when she became pregnant, she laid eggs, ha!"

The adepts responded to the Maggiorengo's joke with a chorus of laughter.

"To do his dirty little things with Antiope, Jove dressed up as a goatherd; and when he wanted to screw Alcmene, he got himself up like a boatman to look like her husband, who plied that nasty trade. When he coupled with Danae, he dressed as a stonemason and with that huge prick of his drilled a hole in her roof, and once he'd got into her house, he reverently futtered her. When he wanted to piss into Aegeria, he dressed as a chimney-sweep. And to debauch Calisto, he had to dress up as a washerwoman, which was easy enough for him because in those days he was still as imberb as any nancy-boy of an ephebe, or as my dear old rascal Biagio, who sits here before me."

Biagio was the nickname of a beardless fatty with a bald, shiny pate who responded to the Maggiorengo's call with hoarse and hearty laughter, echoed by the uncontrollable screeches of the *cerretano* multitude.

"Although Jove's relatives were privileged, being his cousins, nephews and nieces, to get up to their dirty tricks, they all ended up embracing the Canters' way. How? They were gods, you tell me? Yet everyone knows that Vulcan was the lousiest failed blacksmith of all time – worse even than Bratti Old-Iron!"

Bratti was a toothless old man standing a few yards away from us who had been nicknamed after the well-known Tuscan popular figure of fun. I saw him snigger proudly when he was pointed out as an example to the rest of the company.

The Maggiorengo-General's harangue was really most effective and perfectly suited to that kind of gathering. Citing all manner of examples of mythical iniquity, adapted to meet the needs of the *cerretani*, he galvanised his listeners incomparably. I looked once more: this time, I could not see the half-naked canter.

"I've lost sight of him," I told Atto.

"That's a bad sign. Let's hope he hasn't gone off to spy on us."

"And Apollo? He was an even lousier hunter after other people's business than our arch-canter Olgiato," said the orator, winking at another fellow lost in the crowd. "Mars, when he was young, was a great bandit and assassinated thousands. Mercury was a sturdy, baby-minding steward, courier and ambassador or squire or summoner; meaning that he was in the business of extortion. Pluto was a baker and his Proserpine looked after the ovens. Neptune was a fishmonger, Bacchus, a wine merchant, Cupid, a little pimp. As for their womenfolk, some looked after the hen run, like Juno, some were washerwomen, like Mistress Diana. Of Venus, everyone knows she was an even bigger whore than that Pullica from Florence, and she'd let any man sow and plough her fields."

The vile mass of *cerretani* roared with boorish laughter, tickled by their new leader's obscenities.

"Plato, the granddad of all scribblers, lived and died a canter. Aristotle was born the son of a common-or-garden physician and never strayed from the Way of the Canters. Pythagoras came from the codpiece of a bankrupt merchant; that old tramp Diogenes slept in a barrel without any straw. But let's move on now from the Greek and barbarian kingdoms and talk of the Latins. Was not Romulus, the glorious founder of Rome, the wretched son of a common soldier who extorted his pay from the rich? His mother, as is public knowledge, was a nun who'd been thrown out of her order, and he himself was nothing but a lousy bricklayer who did a job or two on the walls of Rome. As long as he lived by the Canters' code, he was a great man and highly esteemed; when he betrayed it, as we all know, he ended up badly. A long, long time after Romulus, the Roman people became the masters of the world. But what does 'people' mean? The people are the Canters, the plebs and the ne'er-do-wells! And who were the captains of the Roman armies?"

"The canters!" the assembly thundered.

"And so, who fought, who smashed and subjugated the world?"

"The Canters!"

A burst of acclamations and applause followed the last exclamation. Calm returned only a while later. The Maggiorengo skilfully chose exactly the right moment to resume his harangue.

"Virgil, the imitator of Homer, was born in a shack near Mantua from the finest canters who ever lived in Piedmont; when he came to Rome, his only desire was to stay a Canter till he died, so he worked in the imperial stables, until the Emperor Augustus took him from there. And that was because the Emperor loved him, precisely for his virtues as a great rogue. Cicero was a canter; he always loved the canters and hated all forms of gentility and all things high class. Mucius Scevola was a baker and he never put his hand heroically into the fire to save Rome, as they tell you now. He was branded on the palm of the hand by the judges because, during the siege of the city, he mixed bean flour in with wheat flour to make his loaves weigh more. Marcus Marcellus was a lousy butcher, and Scipio, the one who killed him and took over from him, was a poultry farmer."

"What an erudite speech," commented Atto sarcastically. "Worthy of a real ruined gentleman. 'Tis no surprise he's a Mumper."

The words of the new Maggiorengo-General did indeed suggest that he had known better times. Meanwhile, he continued:

"And what of the great families? The Fabi sold beans, the Lentuli sold lentils, the Pisoni, peas; and the Papinii take their name from the candlewicks they sell on the market. Even Caesar, for as long as he stayed a canter like his peers, was feared and revered. But when he abandoned that way of life to become a tyrant and command all the others, they killed him like a dog. Augustus, born to a baker from Velletri, as the prophet Virgil was to tell him, followed the holy Way of the Canters, and the humbler he was and the better a companion, the higher he rose. His stepson was Tiberius, and as long as he followed in his stepfather's footsteps, all went well for him, because he who holds to the Way will be successful in all he undertakes and cannot possibly end up badly. However, he who despises and departs from it will become a vicious ingrate, bizarre and odious in everyone's eyes, and after his death he will fall into the greater hell!"

New rounds of applause arose, whistles, some raspberries and a belch. I saw Atto stand on tiptoe to scan the hellish horde of *cerretani*.

"It is time," said he to Buvat as the turmoil of acclamations continued to rage. "Take care not to be seen, or we're done for."

The secretary moved off towards the middle of the amphitheatre which, as I had seen, was full of old firewood and other rubbish and happened at that moment to be almost deserted, since almost all those present at the meeting had gradually gathered around the dais where the new Maggiorengo-General sat. It seemed to me that there was a kind of bulge under Buvat's cassock and I remembered that I had noticed something of the sort under his usual tail coat when we sat in the carriage.

"Caligula was more of a scoundrel than a canter," the Maggiorengo continued undaunted, "and that was his ruination. Nero was the great canter whose renown we all know, but as he was above all a glutton, he's not of much interest to us. Needless to say, all those other great emperors, the Tituses, the Vespasians, the Ottos, the Trajans, right down to our own day, were born and lived as canters. And the better they were at canting, the more dignified and valiant they were as emperors. He who is not, has not been and will not be a canter will never enjoy power, wealth or dignity. One cannot be virtuous nor can one excel in any science unless one follow the Way of the Canters. It is holy, because in it there is faith, love and charity; it is divine because it renders men immortal; it is blessed because it makes men rich and powerful. From the Way, all pleasures derive, all consolations and all amusements, right down to games like tarot and *piastrelle*. Remember! The real canter is loved, revered, courted, and desired by all, even if they don't all want to show it. Let everyone therefore embrace the Way of the Canters, place their trust in it and make it their capital. Let everyone exercise and refine how he does his canting, as does the rascal Lucazzo who's sprawling here just next to me, who cheats, steals and begs with the same art as the Cavalier Bernini designed his statues. Through the Way of the Canter, each of us can become a poet, an orator, a philosopher and, in principle, a gentleman, even a king or an emperor. Long live the canters! And you will see that destiny will soon send us a sign of its favours!"

"Don't worry, I'll send you that *now*," said Atto, as a deafening burst of cries, clapping and whistles greeted the conclusion of the speech.

"What's Buvat gone off to do?" I asked in a whisper.

"Telemachus."

Too late I understood what was about to happen; and that was just as well. The suspense of waiting might have been too much for me.

It all happened in a matter of moments. First came a terrifying explosion, almost like the rumble of an earthquake. I glanced at Ugonio, who was still perched on the platform, and our gazes met somewhere above the multitude of the *cerretani*, all excited by the speech which had just ended, then suddenly paralysed. Then came another, even more tremendous deflagration.

The noisome greyish mass of the *cerretani* spilled out in all possible directions, some jumping in the air for shock, some throwing themselves to the ground, the others scattering to the four winds.

Came the third explosion, which prevented the sordid mob from recovering their senses. This time, however, as well as the thunderous bang, there opened above our heads a marvellous purple flower, illuminating the *cerretano* horde, quite unworthy of such dazzling beauty, with great flashes of carmine and vermilion. The reddish globes which had multiplied in flight above the amphitheatre opened up into as many luminous corollas which descended gently to the ground, at last forlornly dying.

The name of the first two infernal machines said it all: Earthquake.

Before leaving, Atto had sent Buvat to Don Paschatio to ask whether any fireworks remained from the evening before. He had been far-sighted. Buvat had got the Major-Domo to explain to him in detail how to light the fireworks (fortunately, there was no lack of fire at the meeting of the *cerretani*) and how to handle them before use: no dampness, no excessive movement, and keep them upright at all times (as I had heard Don Paschatio say when we were on the point of leaving). Usually, the Earthquake is used to bring the pyrotechnical display to a triumphant close, by which time the ears are accustomed to the thundering noise of explosions. Buvat, however, had shattered the eardrums of the gathering, taking them by complete surprise, and the shock was redoubled by the funnel shape of the amphitheatre. After the two Earthquakes, Buvat had set off a real multicoloured firework.

Abbot Melani's technique, as he himself had just announced to me, had been that of Telemachus, the son of Ulysses who – according to what Albicastro had reminded us of the day before – had feigned madness before the assembly of his mother's suitors and thus had delivered them helpless and unprepared into his father's vengeful hand.

Atto's calculations had proved completely accurate. The *cerretani* were behaving just like the suitors of Homeric lore: despite the confusion, no one had come down from the dais, neither the Maggiorengo-General, nor his two colleagues, nor Drehmannius, the Dutch bookbinder. Faced with the fireworks, they were plainly unsure whether this was a joke, a pleasant surprise spectacle or a threat. Ugonio obviously was by their side and he was as rapid as he was precise. When the red rocket rose in the sky, followed by all the noses in the amphitheatre, the corpisantaro's clawed hands were already deep in the bookbinder's bag, removing his book and replacing it with the one which Melani had handed him in the carriage. The two small volumes were identical: it can not have been difficult for Atto and Buvat to find another book of similar dimensions with an unmarked vellum cover, just like the one which the Abbot had commissioned poor Haver to make for his treatise.

"Use one Dutchman to hunt the other," Abbot Melani had said enigmatically not long before. Now I understood: thanks to the words of Albicastro, we had taken the treatise on the Secrets of the Conclave from Dremannius's bag.

❧

In the festive but still somewhat stunned crowd of the *cerretani*, everyone was asking his neighbour who had had the fine idea of setting off fireworks.

"Let's go, Signor Atto."

"We can't yet. We must wait until. . . Buvat! There you are, damn it! Let's get out of here."

"What about Ugonio?" I asked.

I looked at the platform. The *corpisantaro* had turned his back on us. The message could not have been clearer. We must leave the amphitheatre on our own; he would take another route.

We hastened towards the secret door.

"Not like that, not like that," whispered Atto. "Look at me."

Instead of turning his head in the opposite direction from the crowd, Abbot Melani was walking backwards, with his face directed towards the platform, so as to merge in with all those around us.

Too late. The half-naked *cerretano* who had been keeping an eye on us had seen me and Buvat and was now trying to point out our position to a pair of ugly great brutes. The two stared intensely into the teeming multitude in search of our trio. In the end, they identified us and I saw them set off determinedly after us.

"Signor Atto, they've sent two fellows to catch us," I announced, as we continued our difficult task of making our way through the crowd while showing no signs of haste.

The distance between us and the pair who were hunting us down decreased rapidly. Forty paces. Fifteen. The door leading to the secret passage through the rock was in sight. Ten paces from the brutes. Eight.

A sudden violent movement caught my attention. It was behind the pair following us and a little to the right. The outline of Ugonio, advancing with great difficulty, tugged back from behind – then turning to free himself – a hand taking Atto's tome away from him – but he resists, grabs it back, again begins to flee – other hands grasping the book, the binding is torn. . .

"Buvat!" commanded Atto, apparently referring to something already agreed.

I did not understand what he meant. Meanwhile, we were only some six yards from the bully boys. Now I could see them better. They were as dirty as all the others but quite muscular and obtuse-looking. I could tell instinctively that they knew very well how to inflict pain.

"But where am I to. . . Ah, here!" exclaimed Buvat, practically throwing himself at a *cerretano* bearing a torch.

The flame was incredibly intense: red, white and yellow as well as some shades of light blue, then the Catherine wheel became animated and spun wildly, flying towards Ugonio and those chasing after him. Buvat had worked most skilfully, hurriedly lighting the fuse at just the right point and aiming the firework perfectly. The crowd split into two like the Red Sea dividing to let the children of Israel pass.

Meanwhile, after the ceremony and the sermon, the time had come for Bacchus to take to the stage. An enormous vat was being transported towards the speakers' rostrum, to enable the revellers to give full rein to their baser instincts. The container, which must have weighed as much as a pair of buffaloes, was being carried by a group of *cerretani* who were already tipsy and was just in the way of the pair who were after us.

I just had time, as we disappeared into the secret passage, to catch a glimpse of the first of the two brutes, his face contorted with pain and his leg shattered under the huge vat, while the other screamed at the bearers terrorised by our rocket, and tried to co-ordinate their efforts so as to extricate his injured mate. The smoke from the Catherine wheel, which had ended up goodness knows where, was making those nearest to it weep and adding to the confusion. The chaos was total, the panic of the *cerretani*, too.

I could see nothing else. As the door closed behind us, there blew on my face for the last time, like the breath of a sleeping dragon, the rank, foul stench of the *cerretano* gathering.

The next sensory impression was the invigorating caress of the night breeze as we took the road back: a long march across fields, on the bare grass, avoiding the path so as to spare ourselves any disagreeable encounters. We kept our ears pricked and our eyes alert for any sign of whether Ugonio had made it to the exit: an all-too-faint hope, as he had been found out. In fact, we heard and saw nothing.

Atto was swearing. His treatise on the Secrets of the Conclave, which had perhaps already caused Haver's death, was still in Ugonio's hands and the last time that we had seen him, he had been in those of the *cerretani*. The tomb-robber had betrayed them for Atto's money. They would by now have found it on his person and torn him to pieces.

We came to the place where we had left Sfasciamonti, by now exhausted, our nerves shattered by the danger from which we had just escaped, and depressed by the defeat we had suffered. For the last few minutes, Atto had trailed behind us, fiddling with something in his waistcoat, so much so that Buvat and I had had to incite him to catch up with us.

Sfasciamonti came towards us.

"Let's get a move on, it will soon be daybreak," he urged.

"Look out! Behind you!" Atto yelled at him.

The catchpoll spun around, fearing an attack from behind.

Atto approached and pulled something from his waistcoat. The report of the little pistol resounded sharply, almost stridently, in the night.

Sfasciamonti fell forward onto his face with a blind scream of pain.

"Let us go," was all that Abbot Melani said.

I had not the courage to look back and see the sad, corpulent figure of the catchpoll disappear amidst the grass of the field, covered in blood right down to his ankles.

☙◦❧

We were five when we left, only three returned. Ugonio was at that moment probably being murdered by the crowd in the amphitheatre, while Sfasciamonti must be dragging himself in search of help in a desperate attempt to survive.

At last, we reached the carriage which was waiting for us behind the haystack, and were on our way. In response to the questioning glance of the coachman, when he noticed the absence of Sfasciamonti (who had hired him) and Ugonio, Atto responded laconically: "They preferred to stay overnight."

Words accompanied by gold coin, which Atto forced into the postillion's hands, thus silencing any further questions.

Once again, as seventeen years before, I found myself surreptiously scrutinising the face of Abbot Atto Melani, one-time famous castrato singer, trusted aide to the Medici of Florence, to Mazarin and to a thousand princes throughout Europe, friend of cardinals, popes and sovereigns, and secret agent of the Most Christian King of France, and wondering whether I was not in fact facing a mere rogue, or worse, a professional killer.

He had shot poor Sfasciamonti coldly, cruelly and without showing the least sign of pity. In the face of such determination, no one had dared express the least opposition. Had I protested, perhaps I too would have met the same end.

Now, sitting in the carriage opposite the Abbot, my limbs felt as cold and rigid as marble. Buvat, overcome by emotion, had soon collapsed into heavy, infantile sleep.

Atto relieved me of the need to put questions to him. It was as though he had heard the sound of my thoughts and wanted to silence it.

"It was you who provided me with the necessary elements," said he suddenly. "In the first place, the ease with which the thief got into my apartment. It was you who pointed that out when we inspected the place immediately after the theft. After all, you said, Villa Spada was under close surveillance. And then I asked."

"Whom did you ask?" said I, without understanding what Atto was getting at.

"The thief, obviously: Ugonio. And yes, he told me that, yes, the *cerretani* had told him that his work would be facilitated, so to speak, by those working in the Villa Spada."

"Sfasciamonti betrayed us," I murmured.

I was unable to accept this. Had Ugonio and his accomplices really carried out the theft with Sfasciamonti's complicity?

"Ugonio might have said that he'd been helped by Sfasciamonti for the sole purpose of calumnying him," I objected. "After all, the catchpolls are the enemies of the *corpisantari.*"

"That's true. But I told him straight away that I suspected Don Paschatio, with whom the *corpisantari* have no bone to pick. Thus, I avoided the risk of a less-than-genuine answer."

"And what else?"

"Then it was you who again provided me with an interesting factor: the reform of the police, which you heard talk of during the celebrations. If that were to be put into effect, many catchpolls might lose their jobs, including Sfasciamonti. Our man's scared, he wants money, the future is uncertain. And then there's the incredible story of the ball."

"Do you mean when we went to Saint Peter's?"

"It was quite clear that it was he who prevented you from taking my treatise from the ball, where it was hidden – a weird idea but, I must admit, a rather charming one – either by Zabaglia, the foreman at Saint Peter's in cahoots with the *cerretani*; or, more probably, by one of them who'd done him some dirty favour. I pretended I believed him when he told me that he had picked up your inanimate body and carried you back to the Villa Spada all on his own, losing my treatise in the process – what a coincidence!"

"What do you think really happened?"

"He nearly killed himself to get to the ball before you because he wanted to stop you from getting your hands on his quarry. He did not fall accidentally, as it seemed to you, he must have thrown himself onto you with his full weight, knocking you down and giving you a good bash over the head to send you into the world of dreams. Then he took you away with the help of the guards, obviously in collusion with Zabaglia."

I remembered that when I came to my senses after Sfasciamonti had brought me home from the failed expedition to the ball above Saint Peter's, I had heard Atto pronounce certain obscure phrases. Now their meaning became quite clear to me.

"That was why you said, if my memory does not betray me, 'No one can escape death like that save with the help of an assiduous practitioner.' You meant that it was Sfasciamonti who saved me from death or capture."

"Exactly."

"You also said: 'Behind every strange or inexplicable death there lies a conspiracy of the state, or of its secret forces.'"

"Yes, and that's not just true of assassinations but of every single theft, every injustice, every massacre, every scandal about which the people complain to high heaven and yet, strangely, no culprits are ever brought to justice. The state can do absolutely anything, if it so desires. It doesn't matter whether it is the King or France, the Pope or the Emperor who's in command. The all-too-easy life of the *cerretani* here in Rome is a perfect example: they can get away with it only because of the corruption of individual catchpolls or their superiors, the Bargello or the Governor. Or perhaps the state may find it useful to manipulate the *cerretani* for its own purposes. Or they may hold them in reserve to do so when necessary. Remember, my boy, happy is the criminal who sows terror on behalf of the state: he'll surely never go to prison. But only for as long as he's not privy to too many infamous secrets; when that day comes, he'll meet a bad end."

"Yes, just recently I was told that the halt and the blind belonging to the Company of Saint Elizabeth bribe the catchpolls to be able to beg in peace."

"I'm perfectly aware of that. So why are you surprised if the *cerretani* pay Sfasciamonti?"

So here, I thought, was the suspicion which had been tormenting me ever since I had learned about the Company of Saint Elizabeth, and which I had never quite been able to put my finger on.

"But why did he help us to get as far as Zabaglia and so to understand that your treatise was inside the ball?"

"Because when I asked him to find the person of whom Don Tibaldutio had spoken, I did not tell him what I meant to do with that information. He himself was curious to know what we wanted it for."

I fell silent, licking the wounds in my soul.

"Sfasciamonti is no fool," the Abbot continued. "He's one of the many catchpolls who's short of money and tread the line between justice and crime. They're always on the lookout for a good source to exploit: assassins on the run, harlots occupying apartments illegally, embezzling tax officials, and so on and so forth. Anyone susceptible to a good extortion racket. Once he's identified his victim, the catchpoll puts on a terrifying face: he pretends that he means to investigate, to arrest or sequester property. Thus, he makes a good impression on his superiors, while in reality he always comes to a stop one step before reaching his supposed goal: when he has to arrest someone, he arrives two minutes too late, when he's interrogating, he conveniently forgets to put the right question; when he's searching premises, he doesn't look in the room where the loot is hidden. In exchange, obviously, the victim shells out a good deal of money. Rogues always set a good deal aside for such contingencies."

"But the *cerretani* are far too numerous to be afraid of. . ."

". . . of a fathead like Sfasciamonti? For those engaged in dirty business, every single catchpoll is like a mosquito: if you can't squash him, you try to make sure he stays outside. With money, you can do that, and there are no pointless risks involved. On the contrary, you'll make a friend of him forever, because he'll have every interest in leaving things as they stand. You know the saying: stir the shit and out comes the stink."

I felt bewildered, and said nothing. The coarse but honest catchpoll I thought I knew had turned out to be no better than an astute, corrupt rascal.

"Who knows how long Sfasciamonti's been on the heels of the *cerretani*?" Atto continued. "Whenever he got too close to the objective and threatened to cause them serious trouble, they'd give him something to keep him happy. And off he'd go back home with his tail between his legs. That's what he did when he interrogated Il Roscio and Geronimo: he falsified the data so that it could never be found and would never be used. What judge can accept evidence a century old? Yet the information contained in those records could not be hotter; these things are all taking place here and now: a thorn in the side of the *cerretani* who want to keep their sects secret and are prepared to pay generously to ensure that stuff does not get around. So he keeps blackmailing them and they keep paying. The catchpolls' pay is risible, you too know that from when you overheard those two prelates at the villa, and that's why the Rome police are so corrupt."

"But is Sfasciamonti not afraid that the *cerretani* may sooner or later grow tired of this and get rid of him?"

"Kill him? Forget it. A dead catchpoll can cause a whole load of trouble, while buying him off with money resolves everything discreetly and well. Besides, if you kill him, you don't know who may take his place. Perhaps it will be a hard man who takes no bribes and does his job thoroughly."

"When were you sure he was betraying us?"

"After you climbed up to the ball at Saint Peter's. But tonight I got the final confirmation: how do you think the *cerretani* knew that Il Roscio had talked, as Geronimo told us?"

"It was Sfasciamonti," I murmured disconsolately.

So, I reflected bitterly, the catchpoll had accompanied us during our investigations, even providing us with some help here and there, only in order to spy on us and keep a check on our activities.

"The funny thing is that, to keep him at my service for the past while I too had to pay him. So he was taking money from both sides: from Abbot Melani and from the *cerretani*," said he with a bitter smile.

"Did you plan to use the fireworks?"

"Only if our backs were to the wall, in order to create chaos and exploit it. It was Cardinal Spada's idea of rounding off the celebrations with a pyrotechnical display that saved us. Even you did not know what was going to happen in the amphitheatre: I couldn't risk the possibility that you might give something away to Sfasciamonti."

I felt myself blushing. Despite all his expressions of friendship and esteem, at the decisive moment, Atto had treated me like a troublemaker to be trusted with as few secrets as possible. There was nothing to be done about it, I thought: once a spy, always a spy, an outsider with everyone and an enemy to all forms of trust.

"Why did you bring him here with us?"

"To keep a check on him. He thought he was keeping an eye on us, but it was the other way around. I told Ugonio that Sfasciamonti was not to accompany us to the meeting. Thus, he wouldn't get in our way. Of course, he could not object: he knew perfectly well that he'd have raised too many suspicions, had he done so, because I paid him to do what I told him. He may perhaps have tried to get in and give us away, but he doesn't know where the secret passage is."

I stared out into the nothingness. How was it possible? Had I really understood nothing about the people around me? Was Sfasciamonti really *that* hypocritical and immoral? I called to mind the first time I had met that clumsy but courageous sergeant who claimed he was trying to convince the Governor to put those mysterious *cerretani* in the dock: the catchpoll who withdrew from the daily struggle only to go and find his mother. . .

"By the way," added Atto, "between visiting libraries, I sent Buvat to put a couple of questions to the parish priest where Sfasciamonti lives. He discovered something really funny."

"What?"

"Sfasciamonti's mother died sixteen years ago."

I fell silent, saddened by my own inadequacy. Atto had deduced Sfasciamonti's betrayal from observations and information much of which I myself had collected, and yet I had been incapable of collating it all logically.

"There is one thing I do not understand," I objected. "Why did you not unmask him earlier?"

"That is one of the stupidest questions you have ever put to me. Think of Telemachus."

"Again?" I exclaimed impatiently. "I know that the myth of Telemachus gave you the idea of creating a diversion to distract the *cerretani* with fireworks, but here, frankly, I can't see. . ."

"Homer called Telemachus 'wise'," Atto interrupted me, "'the equal of the gods' and even 'endowed with sacred strength'; he praises him in almost every verse. But what did the good Eumaeus, the swineherd who so loved him, have to say about him? That 'one of the gods has damaged his brain'. And what of his own mother, the faithful Penelope? She screamed at him: 'Telemachus, you are mindless and witless!' Thus was his behaviour judged by those who best loved him. They were unable to appreciate the subtle wisdom and extreme prudence of his apparently senseless acts. And do you know why?"

"He was pretending to be mad in order not to arouse the suspicions of the suitors who had occupied Ulysses' palace," I replied. "But, I repeat, I cannot see what this has to do with. . ."

"Just wait and hear me out. Telemachus himself masked as folly his boldest act, namely drawing the suitors into the fatal trap: the competition to draw Ulysses' bow. He said: 'Alas, Zeus, son of Cronos, made me mad and here I am laughing and joking like a madman.' And was he not, acting like a lark's mirror, the very first to try that bow which he said only his father could bend? He never gave away his own simulation until the moment when Ulysses seized the bow and massacred the suitors."

"I understand," said I at length. "You pretended to believe Sfasciamonti until we had an advantage over him."

"Exactly. If I had unmasked him earlier, we should never have learned anything from Il Roscio, nor would we have got as far as the German, in other words Ugonio, and so on and so forth. What's more," Atto concluded with a knowing grin, "it would have been complicated to get rid of Sfasciamonti earlier; I couldn't very well fill his buttocks with lead in the middle of the festivities at Villa Spada!"

❧

Meanwhile, the carriage made its way in the first light of dawn. Fatigue weighed down our eyelids inexorably, yet too many questions still beset me.

"Signor Atto," I asked, "why did you swear when Ugonio told you that the Dutch *cerretano* was going to unglue the cover of your treatise?"

"At long last, you're asking me. The whole thing hangs on that."

"What do you mean 'hangs on that'?"

"It was a matter of wrong targets. When you take aim at the wrong target," said Atto, "you get nothing but trouble."

The first mistaken target had been Cardinal Albani. As we now knew, he had nothing whatever to do with the theft of Atto's treatise on the Secrets of the Conclave.

The second wrong target had been Lamberg. We had believed that the Imperial Ambassador was behind the theft, supposing that he meant to get hold of the secret information which Atto intended for the eyes of the Most Christian King only. That was another mistake.

"Lamberg is nothing but a very pious believer who, instead of trying to be an ambassador, should be at court in Vienna, gobbling down haunches of venison and strudel with soft cheese like all his compatriots, and looking after his tranquil estates. It was not he who ordered the theft of my treatise."

"How can you be so sure of that?"

"I am sure of that because nobody ordered the *cerretani* to steal the book. It was they who decided to do it."

"They? And why?"

"Do you remember what Ugonio said when we entered his lair at the baths of Agrippina? The *cerretani* are nervous, he muttered, because someone has stolen their language. That was confirmed by Geronimo, the *cerretano* whom Sfasciamonti questioned today. At the time, Ugonio's reply made no sense, but that phrase of his kept buzzing around in my head. The new language: is it not true that the *cerretani* have a secret language or jargon, gibberish, Saint Giles' Greek or whatever you want to call it? As we know, it is something rather more serious than that ridiculous play on words which you heard when you were thrown off that terrace in Campo di Fiore."

"D'you mean. . . 'teeyooteelie'?"

"Exactly. Until now, their secret language was the jargon which we managed to understand a good deal of thanks to the glossary which Ugonio procured for us. Now, however, precisely because that was beginning to become too well known, they had decided to update it. Do you remember what Buvat told us? This is an ancient language. When, however, it ceases to be impenetrable, they modify it a little, using small tricks of speech, just enough to render it incomprehensible once more. This time, however, someone stole the key to their code, the rules governing it, or something of the sort; just as Geronimo told Sfasciamonti and his worthy companions. Now, that something might be no more than a simple sheet of paper with the instructions for speaking and understanding the revised jargon."

"Yes, I follow you," said I, beginning to understand.

"Well, once they'd suffered this theft, the *cerretani* would obviously have done everything in their power to recover that magic scrap of paper, do you not think so?"

"Of course."

"Right. And what were they trying with all their might and main to get from me and to hold onto until this very evening?"

"Your treatise! Do you perhaps mean that the secret language of the *cerretani* is contained in. . ."

"Oh, not in what I wrote. I know nothing of their language. The sheet of paper is, to be precise, *concealed* in the volume."

"How?"

"Do you know how they make covers like that with which I asked poor Haver to bind my treatise?"

"By gluing. . . old papers together! I have it. The instructions for the secret language were glued inside the cover! After all, Ugonio said that the weird Dutch *cerretano*, the bookbinder, was going to *unglue* a page."

"Certainly. He was to separate from my cover the page which describes the new rules of the secret language. In fact, the pages which are used for bindings are usually glued to the cover on their written side."

"So that's why they brought an expert all the way from Holland to unglue it. But there's something I still don't understand: how did it come to be there in the first place?"

"What a question! Haver, the bookbinder, put it there. Without knowing it, obviously."

"That's why the *cerretani* broke into Haver's shop and carried everything off: they were looking for your book!"

"And the poor man died of fright," Atto added sadly. "Only, as you'll recall, when they raided Haver, I had already withdrawn my book and so they got nothing. This they realised only after they'd gone through what they'd looted: mountains of old paper."

"Then they commissioned Ugonio to steal the treatise."

"Quite. The tomb robber went about it with a sure hand. There were no other freshly bound manuscripts in my apartment. Otherwise, it might have been difficult for him to be sure of taking the right book, seeing that neither he nor the *cerretani* knew what its contents were."

"Yes. But how did the sheet of paper come to be in Haver's shop? And how did the *cerretani* trace him?"

"You will have to use your memory. Do you perhaps recall that this evening, right next to the rostrum where the Maggiorenghi sat, there was a young man we seemed to have seen somewhere?"

"Yes, but I still can't remember where we came across him. Perhaps we saw him begging somewhere in town. Or perhaps he was among the other mendicants at Termine, that evening when we followed Il Roscio and Geronimo."

"You're wrong. But 'tis hardly surprising. We saw him only for a matter of seconds. Anyway, I saw him better than you, because he sliced up my arm."

"The *cerretano* Sfasciamonti was chasing in front of Villa Spada!"

"Precisely. It comes as no surprise that he should have been so near the Maggiorenghi this evening, together with Ugonio and that little monster, what was he called?. . . Ah yes, Drehmannius. That beanpole of a lad, all skin and bones, was carrying the paper with the secret language somewhere. He collided with us and the sheet of paper went flying off into the air and got mixed up with all the other papers. And it ended up in the binding of my book. For the *cerretani*, with the help of Sfasciamonti, finding Haver's shop will have been child's play."

"But why did the skinny *cerretano* stab you in front of the villa?"

"He didn't stab me. It was an accident. Sfasciamonti had seen him in the area and knew that he was up to no good. After trying to stop him, he ran after him. The catchpoll had an excellent intuition: after all, the lad was carrying on his person the code for the new secret language. He was probably a courier. We now know that the assembly of the *cerretani* was imminent and preparations were surely in hand. When he was being chased, the lad unsheathed his knife, in order to defend himself if they caught up with him. That was when he collided with me, causing the wound which still hurts me and losing his knife. In any case, Sfasciamonti took the weapon, probably to be sure that no one else should be able to snatch the investigation off him."

"But why, instead of complicating their lives by stealing your treatise, could the *cerretani* not simply obtain another copy of their code?"

"It does not even exist, I think."

"And how do you know?"

"You need only add two and two. Buvat told us that, traditionally, only the Maggiorengo-General can dictate the new rules. He writes them out in his own hand and the text is read to a general meeting of all the sects who then do whatever is necessary to spread it far and wide. But Ugonio told us that a new Maggiorengo-General was to be appointed because the previous one had died. So the only person who knew the contents of that paper, namely its author, was no longer there."

"At that point, however, the general meeting had already been convened, perhaps months earlier," said I, taking up the argument. "Swarms of *cerretani* were converging from all over Italy and a new code could not be drawn up because there was no time."

"Of course. Even if, given the emergency, they'd wanted to fashion a new secret language in the place of the late Maggiorengo-General, how do you imagine those beasts dressed in rags could have managed such a thing in less than a week?"

"It is quite incredible," I commented, after a brief pause. "I could never have imagined Sfasciamonti running like that after someone with whom he'd come to terms immediately afterwards."

"On the contrary, it is absolutely obvious. Corrupt catchpolls are always the first to arrive at the scene of a crime or where there's no more than a suspicion that something could take place; they're already counting the money they hope to extort."

He fell silent an instant, wiping the sweat from his forehead with one of his fine lace handkerchiefs.

"Do you think that he will make it?"

"Have no fear. Before shooting him, I got him to turn around for two reasons: because he's a traitor, and traitors are shot in the back; and also because I aimed at his backside, the only part of the body where there's nothing one can fracture and there's almost no likelihood of infection."

Abbot Melani's familiarity with infections caused by firearms caused me to suppose that he had in the past had no little experience of such matters. Like every true spy.

When we arrived, it was already daylight. We arranged to be set down not too near to Villa Spada, so as not to be seen by any of the staff of the villa when we were leaving the carriage.

Atto was exhausted. On his way to his apartment, he had to be supported by myself and Buvat. The servants of the villa, by now inured to our appearing and disappearing at the most absurd hours, pretended not to notice.

Laid on his bed like a dead body, Abbot Melani closed his eyes and prepared for a long sleep. I was on the point of slipping out the door when I saw Atto's nose curl up as it always did in the presence of a bad smell. At the same time, my eyes, no less tired than Atto's limbs, noticed a movement behind the curtains. Looking down, the folds of the curtain failed to conceal a pair of old down-at-heel boots.

"We'll never be free of all this," said I to myself, at once scared and exasperated. The intruder did not budge, perhaps fearing our reaction. Buvat, Atto and I stiffened in turn, waiting for him to make a move.

"Come out from there, whoever you are," said the Abbot, grasping his pistol.

There was a moment's silence.

"To be more medicinal than mendacious, I desiderate to submit to your most subliminal decisionality this most modest production of my hardput industrialising," mumbled a hesitant voice.

The sleeve of a sackcloth cassock stretched out from behind the curtain and held out the remnants of a book that looked as though it had been run over by a hundred carriages.

"My treatise!" said Atto, grasping it and sharply pulling aside the curtain.

Ugonio, in an even sorrier state than usual, wasted no time in idle chatter. He explained that he had escaped from the *cerretani* only thanks to the Catherine wheel which Buvat had lit just before we escaped from the fray. Once out in the open, he too had carefully avoided the main path, which was why we had not seen him. To return to Rome, he had adventurously purloined a horse from an unguarded stable, at the risk, however, of being caught and slaughtered by the irate owner who had followed him on a filly, armed to the teeth. Now he had come to deliver the promised goods and to receive a last, well-deserved reward.

Abbot Melani was paying no great attention to him, so overcome was he by emotion at recovering his treatise. He opened it and I could at last see with my own eyes the little book for which I had risked life and limb:

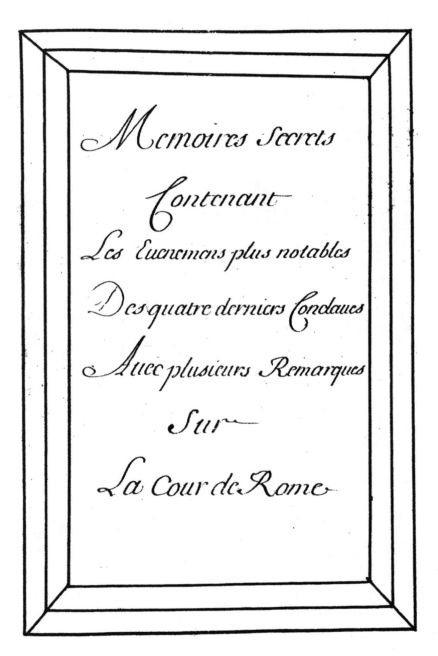

Atto proudly read me the frontispiece:

"Secret Memoirs containing the most notable Events of the past four Conclaves, with severall Observations on the Court of Rome."

"I am most factiously in urgent neediness of the ultimate parcel of my emollyment," Ugonio solicited, massaging one shoulder. One of his hands was bandaged and there were bloodstains on his face.

"What happened?" asked Atto, turning from his beloved opus. He was still incredulous that the exceedingly skilful Ugonio should have been caught with his hand literally in the sack when stealing the treatise back for him.

"A nothingness, an utteringly minimous snaggle."

The answer was too evasive not to get on Atto's nerves:

"What does that mean? With all the money I've given you, you let yourself be caught with my treatise in your hand and you call that 'a minor unforeseen contingency'."

The *corpisantaro* said nothing, but showed clear signs of embarrassment. His wounds spoke for him: when he was filching the book from the *cerretani*, something had gone askew, nor could he refuse to explain what had happened. He therefore spoke as though at one remove, explaining after his own fashion (that is, in terms somewhat colourful and bizarre) how the Grand Legator Drehmannius had been wearing a little chain around his neck with a most interesting relic hanging from it: a small wooden crucifix from which hung a small box containing a canine tooth which Ugonio, with his unfailing flair, had at once recognised as coming from the sacred jaw of the Dutch Saint Leboin.

"Who cares! You weren't there to. . ." Atto interrupted him, then suddenly clapped his hand over his mouth. His little eyes narrowed, becoming as sharp as two daggers about to strike.

"Go on," said he.

Amidst ambiguities and fragments of sentences, the confession painfully emerged. Ugonio, despite the fact that he had at great personal risk filched Atto's treatise from the Grand Legator's bag, had proved unable to resist temptation. With a feline movement, he had drawn close to the Dutch canter, whispering some empty compliments in his ear. The chaos provoked by the fireworks was still reigned, transforming the whole assembly into one wild, deafening crucible. With one hand, Ugonio had undone the little chain of the crucifix behind the other's neck, whereupon, pretending to lose his

balance, he had practically fallen on top of him ("a most hightly com-
mendable and productiferous technique!" he gloated) so that his
victim should not notice that he was being robbed. The crucifix had
fallen into the Grand Legator's lap, whereupon Ugonio had grabbed
and pocketed it.

"Just as I thought," muttered Atto, barely restraining his fury.

As Melani and I well knew, the *corpisantari* robbed, trafficked and
made use of everything they could lay their hands on, but their
ruling passion was for holy relics, whether true or false, (and we had
witnessed their insane appetite for these things when first we met
them seventeen years before). Unfortunately, their unbridled greed
for relics all too often got the better of them when there were far
more important matters at stake, thus ruining everything. Ugonio's
rapacity had all too soon been punished, as he went on to explain, his
voice growing more and more feeble with embarrassment.

When, a few minutes later, the Grand Legator scratched his foul
mangy chest, he became aware at last of the theft of Saint Leboin's
tooth and consequently that of the treatise on the Secrets of the
Conclave, which would otherwise have passed unobserved. That was
why Ugonio had soon had to run for his life, succeeding in escaping
his former allies only by dint of the strength which desperation lent
him and with the help of Buvat's Catherine wheel.

"Drehmannius is a silly absent-mindless fellow," the tomb robber
smugly concluded, betraying his genuine ape-like inability to forego
his favourite fun and games.

"Beast, animal, idiot!" Atto burst out. "I paid you a fortune to get
back my treatise, not to go hunting for your rubbish!"

Ugonio did not answer; his expression, which had suddenly become
contrite and cringing, hypocritically masked (of this I was certain)
that dull, bestial craving for possession which is the mark of primitive
natures.

"Just one question, Ugonio: where is the holy relic now?" I asked
in my turn, at once horrified and amused by the *corpisantaro's* extraordinary rapacity.

Like a peasant taking his best rabbit out from a cage to show buyers, Ugonio swiftly extracted a small box from his cassock: the reli-
quary containing the tooth of Saint Leboin. He had carried it off.

"But now the *cerretani* are looking for me very concentratively,"
said he, with a note of anxiety in his voice which I had never heard

before. "I must extrude me out of here pissed haste. I think I shall infibulate myself at Vindobona."

"You're returning to Vienna?" Atto asked in surprise as he slipped a full purse into the hand that was still sound; Ugonio estimated the value of this reward which was, after all, richly deserved, emitting a grunt of approval.

We knew that he came from the capital of the Empire, which explained his precarious grasp of Italian; but we could never have imagined that the *cerretani* might hunt him down so relentlessly as to make him return there.

"Still, I imagine that, after this Jubilee, you will not lack the means to settle down comfortably in your own land," observed Atto.

Ugonio was unable to suppress a self-satisfied grin.

"To be more medicinal than mendacious, the Jubiliary incomings have been satisfecund and abundiform. I shall low-lie in a quiet, refugious residence and trial not to wasten my economies."

Abbot Melani, despite being a champion cynic, seemed almost sorry to see him go: "Could you not find a temporary refuge in the Kingdom of Naples, a few hours distant from here, and return when the waters have grown calmer?"

"The cerretanici are rootless, murtherous and foxily cunningful," replied the *corpisantaro*, preparing to leave as he had probably come, through the window. "Most fortunitiously, they have baggered what they most ravened after."

Before making his exit, he pointed at the treatise which Atto at last held in his hands.

As the corpisantaro slipped out of sight (would I ever see him again?) I realised that the cover had in fact been torn off. Then I remembered that when Ugonio was trying to get away from his pursuers, the book had already been seriously damaged.

The *cerretani* had succeeded: the code of the secret language remained in their hands.

Day the Tenth
16ᵀᴴ July, 1700

✠

On the next day, Abbot Melani had Buvat summon me. I had allowed myself a few hours' sleep during which I had mostly relived the experience at Albano and, going back further, the arrival of the Connestabilessa, Atto Melani's incoherent emotions, and the tale of the sad old age of the Most Christian King who had never forgotten his Maria. On awakening, I had thought especially of the Tetràchion. And I had thought about it for some time.

Atto's secretary brought me a magnificent suit of clothes complete with patent leather shoes. At the end of his stay at Villa Spada, the Abbot was at last putting into practice his original intention to see me well dressed; and I knew why, or better, for *whom*.

I washed, dressed and combed my hair as well as possible, tying it with the fine blue bow that I had received with the suit.

As I was leaving, Cloridia caught sight of me: "My goodness, what extravagance! That Abbot of yours is really generous. Let us hope he at last pays out that blessed dowry for the girls."

"We are to go to the notary this afternoon," I informed her.

"At long last. I feel that you've more than earned it."

When I rejoined Atto, from his face one would never have thought that he had lived through the shattering events of the night before. He had recovered that state of nervous artificial calm in which I had left him in the afternoon. There was only one difference: he was, to my surprise, at last wearing that mauve-grey soutane with the hood and Abbot's periwig in which I had met him seventeen years before and which he had worn when he came to find me at the Villa Spada. Clothes which, although clean and well ironed, were somewhat outmoded and evoked bygone days.

This was, I thought, right. Was he not perhaps about to embark on a meeting with the past? I felt a surge of gratitude. He had at last decided to go to meet the Connestabilessa wearing the sober clothing which he had also worn when he presented himself to me.

The sole note of vanity was a French-seeming perfume which filled the whole room with a somewhat over-emphatic fragrance.

Atto was seated at his writing desk. He was placing a wax seal on the red ribbon enclosing a letter rolled into a tube. His old hand was trembling and seemed unable to get the better of the curved surface of the paper.

The day was already hot and rather stuffy. Through the window one could hear the chanting of a procession: that of the Arch-Confraternities, wending its way through the nearby streets of Trastevere to the church of the Madonna del Carmine.

Melani caught sight of me and sighed, already exhausted before he had even ventured forth, as always happens when one feels unequal to the task which awaits one or to others' expectations about oneself. He did not even greet me.

"This morning I announced that I would be visiting. We must be there in half an hour," said he laconically.

"Where?"

"At the nuns' convent on Campo Marzio."

"Why did she not stay at the villa?"

"From what I could gather, she thought it inopportune. The celebrations are over and Cardinal Spada has very different matters to worry about."

A carriage awaited us at the entrance. Once we had left, Atto's gaze was soon lost in contemplation of Villa Spada as it receded into the distance.

I guessed, or at least I thought I could understand intuitively, what must have been going through his mind at that moment: the feasting was over, by now the *cerretani* belonged to the past, he was returning to reality. After seeing the Connestabilessa, he would resume his personal battle, the desire to impose his own stamp on human affairs at the forthcoming conclave. At the same time, he must have been painfully aware of the inexorable passing of time, feeling how hard the springs of the carriage were on his loins, far, far harder than when, as a young castrato decades before, armed only with his own talent and the protection of the Grand Duke of Tuscany, he had looked out over the same city from another carriage, with grasping eyes and an ardent heart, as he came to play his part in the great banquet of music, politics, intrigue and, perhaps, one day, glory.

Within a few months, with the new conclave, he would know

whether a lifetime was sufficient to achieve those ambitions. In a few minutes, however, he would know whether a lifetime had been able to cancel out a great love.

When the horses passed in front of the Vessel, Atto leaned out instinctively, looking upwards. I knew what he was thinking of: the Tetràchion.

It was time to talk.

"Why, when Capitor said 'two in one', did she also point to Neptune's sceptre, in other words, the trident?" I asked without warning.

The Abbot turned towards me, surprised.

"What are you getting at?" he asked me, frowning.

"Perhaps she meant that those two figures were united with the sceptre, truly 'two in one'."

"But what sense would that make?" asked Atto, betraying his impatience at not, for once, thinking as fast as I. He could not know that I had turned that thought over a thousand times in my bed a few hours before.

"Do you recall what the chambermaid at the Spanish Embassy said to Cloridia? That the Tetràchion was the heir to the Spanish throne. And, as you yourself told me, what was the meaning of that trident in Neptune's hand? The crown of Spain, mistress of the ocean and of two continents. There, perhaps that is what Capitor meant."

"I still don't grasp your meaning."

"In other words," I resumed, while my thoughts galloped ahead and words found it hard to keep up, "in my opinion, the madwoman meant that twins like those of the Tetràchion were the legitimate heirs to the Spanish throne, and she issued a warning to Mazarin."

"To Mazarin?" exclaimed Melani, incredulous and impatient. "But what's come over you, my boy? Are you losing your senses?"

I continued without paying any attention to this.

"Capitor also said that punishment would be meted out to the sons of whoever deprives the crown of Spain of its sons. Perhaps. . ." Here I hesitated. "Perhaps those sons are the Tetràchion and, as we might have seen them at the Vessel, perhaps Cardinal Mazarin may have had them abducted from Spain. . ."

The Abbot burst out laughing.

"His Eminence ordering the abduction of that sort of octopus we thought we saw up there in the penthouse above the Vessel. . . Why, that's not such a bad idea, good for a picaresque novel. Are you quite insane? And why, for heaven's sake, should he have done that? To boil it and serve it up with carrots and olives? Perhaps with a sprinkling of fresh oregano, since Mazarin was Sicilian. . ."

"He did it because the Tetràchion is the heir to the Spanish throne."

"Might you be suffering from sunstroke, by any chance? Or could last night's trip to Albano have caused you to part with your senses?" the Abbot insisted; but he had grown serious.

"Signor Atto, don't think that I have not reflected long and hard on the matter. You yourself said to me that, before Capitor's prophecies, Mazarin seemed to have very different plans for making Philip IV sign a peace favourable to French interests, and those plans were not matrimonial. But can you explain to me why? You also said that Mazarin had no intention of marrying the Most Christian King with the Infanta; indeed he was blissfully allowing the relationship between His Majesty and Maria to continue and develop undisturbed."

Now Atto was listening without moving a muscle.

"Perhaps Mazarin had a trump card in his hand, a horrible secret, born of the rotten blood of the Spanish Habsburgs: the Tetràchion. All Philip IV's legitimate heirs died but those twins survived against all expectations."

"Do you mean that, before Charles II was born, Philip IV may also have sired twins like the Tetràchion?" he asked in a toneless voice.

"Perhaps this was one of the less serious cases, as Cloridia mentioned: those joined only by a leg," I continued. "They could not be separated when small, but if they reached adulthood, then the thing could be done. There was an heir, indeed, there were heirs to the Spanish throne. Mazarin had them abducted to use them as assets to be horse-traded in the peace negotiations. Then along came Capitor with her prophecy of the virgin and the crown, the Cardinal became scared and wanted at all costs to separate his niece from the young King. As for the Tetràchion, he did not know what to do with it, so he sent it to Elpidio Benedetti, who. . ."

"Halt. There's a serious logical flaw in all this," said the Abbot, stopping me with his hand. "If, as you assert, Capitor meant to warn Mazarin that he would be punished for having removed the Tetràchion from Spain, the Cardinal should have been beside himself with fear and therefore have returned the twins to Philip IV as quickly as possible. Instead, he sends them straight to Benedetti in Rome. Now, why?"

"Because he did not understand?"

"What do you mean?"

"You told me yourself. Mazarin was quite flattered by the gift of the charger with Neptune and Amphitrite. In the two deities who rule over the seas, he saw himself and Queen Anne, and in the trident sceptre of Neptune, the crown of France, held tightly in his hand; or perhaps that of Spain, mistress of the ocean and the two continents, exhausted by wars and by now in Mazarin's hands. This last possibility had sent him literally into raptures. Also, as you told me, the Cardinal had understood the mad seer's warning to whoever deprived the crown of Spain of its sons as being directed against Philip IV. In other words, he did not realise that Capitor's words concealed a threat aimed at him."

"My compliments for the fantasy, even if it is somewhat convoluted," said Abbot Melani scornfully.

"If Mazarin had not had those twins abducted," I continued, quite unshaken, "France today would not have any claim to the Spanish throne. With one deformed leg each, they would certainly have been crippled, but, unlike Charles II, they might have been able to procreate. Is there not in Spain the legend of King Gerion, who had three heads? And what are we to say of the two-headed eagle on the arms of the Habsburgs? Cloridia herself said this might be a memento of some defective birth which took place who knows when among the ancestors of Charles II. In other words, it does not seem that the Tetràchion is the first such case among the kings of Spain."

"And obviously, according to your theory, Elpidio Benedetti would have sheltered those two unfortunate children somewhere, then here in the Vessel, once the building had been completed," the Abbot concluded rapidly.

"It is not by chance that Mazarin then entrusted the three gifts to him as well as the picture depicting them," said I gravely.

"So, in that villa, as well as the apparitions of Maria, the King and Fouquet, and the picture with Capitor's three gifts, not to mention your parrot – what's he called? Caesar Augustus – we may also have seen the Tetràchion. Well, it all goes to make a fine stew, that Vessel, and there's no gainsaying that! It should have been called the Stewpot, ha!" he sniggered.

Atto went on laughing a long while. I looked at him without taking it badly. I knew that what I was saying was not at all as absurd as it seemed, and I was proud that for once it was I who was master, and he the disciple.

"You are forgetting one thing, however," the Abbot made clear after a while. "The Tetràchion that we saw up there was only the deformed reflection of ourselves."

"That's only what we've seen today. Besides, if we trust to those mirrors, we too must be monsters," I exclaimed with complete confidence.

My observation alarmed the Abbot: "Do you mean that the time before we might have seen those twins' reflections distorted by the mirrors?"

"Are you so sure you can exclude that?" I asked ironically. "We saw yesterday with our own eyes that those mirrors reflect one another. They may perhaps have sent us the reflection of the twins standing somewhere else in the penthouse, perhaps even confounding them with our own images. We were terrified by the distorted vision and fled for our lives without even looking around us."

Abbot Melani was drumming impatiently on the pommel of his walking stick.

"Why are you so unwilling to admit it, Signor Atto? There's nothing magical or inexplicable here. There's nothing to it but the physics of those mirrors and medical obstetrics which, for over a century, have described cases of twins born conjoined like the Tetràchion. And those twins we saw together had – just note the coincidence – the famous Habsburg jaw."

"And where are they supposed to have got to afterwards? We found no further trace of them at the Vessel."

"Once we'd found those distorting mirrors, we made no further attempt to find them. And that was a mistake. It was you who taught me seventeen years ago, with a wealth of examples: if one detail proves baseless, that does not mean the whole hypothesis is to be thrown out. Or, a document may be false, but tell the truth. In other words, as they say, we must be careful not to throw the baby out with the bath water. Now, however, we have fallen for all these errors."

"Then, listen here," retorted the Abbot, cut to the quick: "Yesterday I mentioned this to you. To be quite precise, Capitor said, 'He who deprives the crown of Spain of its sons, the crown of Spain will deprive of his sons'. This, if you want to know, does not, I believe, make any sense. Mazarin had no children, but his nephews and nieces had so many that the name of Mazarin is unlikely to die out at any foreseeable time. Do you know what I think? That all this is far too complicated to be true. I'm glad that I taught you never to trust appearances and to make use of suppositions, without censoring any, wherever evidence is lacking. But I beg you to calm down, my boy, to everything there's a limit. That madwoman was raving and she's making us lose our wits too."

"But think carefully about it. . ."

"Now, that will be enough of your nonsense, I'm tired."

Atto was looking out of the window at the heights of the Janiculum as we sped away: the villas, the verdant gardens, the gentle treetops; and then, at the city below, many-towered and abounding with the symbols of Christianity and the eternal power of the Church; and finally at the cupola of Saint Peter's.

I should have liked to have the Abbot's support for my reflections; but Atto had remained sceptical and had even laughed in my face and ended up by silencing me, even rejecting factual examples of what he had once taught me. I did not know whether he was incapable of understanding, envious, too old, or whether he really thought that, yes, he had for once listened to me drawing conclusions, only to find that I had come up with nothing but senseless ravings. Who knows whether mine were nothing more than the crude, ingenuous fantasies of a bumpkin who believes in monsters? Only one person could know that, perhaps.

ৡৢঌ

We were approaching our goal. The postillion stopped the horses. I descended from the carriage, went to the other side and helped Atto to step down.

We walked the last few yards on foot, unhurriedly. On arriving in front of the convent, we stopped a moment to contemplate the façade. Shielding his eyes with one hand, Atto looked up at the windows of the upper storeys which in convents are traditionally reserved for guests staying incognito. Perhaps she was behind one of these.

Melani remained motionless, with his gaze fixed on those windows, as though he had come this far only to contemplate them, nothing more.

"It seems you'll have to climb plenty of stairs," said I, to shake him from his torpor.

He did not answer. Instinctively, I held out my arm to him, I know not whether to incite him to knock at the convent door or to offer him comfort. He hesitated. Then he handed me the rolled-up, sealed letter.

"There. Give her this as soon as you see her."

"Me? What do you mean? She is waiting for you and you have so many things to say to her and so many questions to ask, do you not want to. . . ?"

Atto turned his eyes away, towards an old wooden bench, abandoned there by goodness only knows who.

"I think I shall sit down here for a moment," he said.

"Why, do you not feel well?"

"Oh, I am fine. But I should like you to go up."

I paused, disconcerted. "Do you mean that you will not be going?"

"I do not know," said Atto slowly.

"If you do not go, she will not understand."

"Go on, my boy, perhaps I shall follow you."

"But what will she say when she sees a stranger appear? And what am I to say? I shall have to tell her that you are a man of other times and you prefer to climb the stairs slowly. . ."

The Abbot smiled.

"Just tell her I'm a man of other times, nothing more."

I was unable to restrain a gesture of incredulity. My fingers closed around the letter.

"You are committing a folly," I protested weakly, "and besides. . ."

But Atto turned on his heels and made his way to the bench.

At that very moment (hard to say whether this was a coincidence, or because the nuns were secretly observing us) the convent door opened. A sister was looking questioningly at me, with her head peeping just outside the door. She was waiting for me to come forward.

I looked at Atto. He sat down. He turned towards me and raised one arm, a gesture combining a greeting and the order to go ahead. I just caught a glimpse of him as the sister closed the door behind me.

⊱⊰

I was in a corridor, enveloped in that unmistakeable aroma peculiar to women's convents, smelling of orisons, fresh novices and dawn vigils. I followed my guide up stairways, steps and along corridors until we came to a door. The sister knocked, then turned the handle and looked in. A woman's voice said something.

"Please wait a while. There, take a seat here," said the nun. "Knock again in a few moments. They will let you in. I myself must go at once to the Mother Superior."

What was there in the letter I held tightly in my hand? Was it a message from Atto to the Connestabilessa, or was it rather a note penned by King Louis of France for his Maria? Perhaps both. . .

Days before, Melani had written that, when they met again, he would deliver to her something that would make her change her mind about the King's happiness. What exactly did that mean? The answer was in the letter I held in my hand.

I had little time but my decision was already taken. Atto's seal was badly applied; it had not stuck properly to the paper.

Here I was, about to raise the curtain on the most intimate spectacle of the hearts of those three old people. I unrolled the letter.

When I read it, I could hardly believe my eyes.

❧

After I know not how much time, I knocked. My soul was serene, my spirit more lucid then ever.

"Come in," replied a pleasant feminine voice, mature but kind, gentle, well disposed.

She was, after all, as I imagined. I stepped forward.

After introducing myself and delivering the letter, I provided her with an explanation for Atto's absence, cobbled together in the most general terms. She was kind enough to pretend to believe me, nor were her words tinged with any note of reproach, only regret at have missed meeting Melani.

I bowed again and was on the point of taking my leave, when I thought that, all in all, I had nothing to lose. There was something I wanted to ask her; not about what I had just read – for that I needed no explanations.

The Tetràchion. Perhaps she would be surprised, but she would not have me thrown out. She might have thought I was acting on behalf of my master, that my mouth and ears were his.

I began directly, because she perhaps was alone in knowing the truth; and there was little time.

❧

My explanation had not taken more than a few minutes. During all that time, the Connestabilessa did not bat an eyelid. She remained seated, looking fixedly out of the window. She made no comment or gesture. She stayed silent, but hers was a silence that said more than thousands of words.

Here was the mute confirmation that what I was saying was not a figment of my imagination. That silence probably signified that at least a part of my reconstruction was mistaken, perhaps crude and ingenuous. But the kernel of it remained true and vivid, and Maria better than anyone knew how very real the case was. If I had just been raving, or if she had known nothing about all this, I would, at best, have earned myself a reprimand and been asked to leave. Instead, she had remained motionless and heard me out in total silence. She knew well of what I was speaking. It concerned that secret history against which all her hopes of happiness had been dashed and which had condemned her to a life of wanderings and misfortune. Her silence – explicit, yet prudent – was the best possible way of assenting to, confirming and encouraging my view.

I finished what I had to say, allowing the silence to fill the room and the space between us for a few more moments. She kept staring out of the window, as though she were already alone.

There was no more to be said. I took my leave with a bow, accompanying it with the same penetrating absence of words as that with which she had listened to my speech. This was the only possible farewell between persons who know that they will never meet again.

കൈ

It might have been simply the latest surprise, but I was expecting it: in the street, no one was waiting for me. Neither Atto nor the carriage. By now, I had understood the game.

As I walked towards Villa Spada, the bittersweet impressions of my meeting with Maria Mancini soon gave way to the violent emotion aroused by the letter I had delivered to her.

One single sheet of paper, blank. And in the middle, rather high up, just three words, written in an easy cursive hand:

yo el Rey

Even an idiot could understand. Since the Catholic King of Spain was certainly not in Rome, this was a forged signature. And as Charles II was about to die, what document could it be for, if not his will?

The more I thought of it, the more hatred and hilarity came together in my mind. What a fine little game Atto had used me in, without saying a thing to me! And what a fool I had been to suspect nothing. . .

The last will and testament of Charles II: the document in which the heir to the world's greatest kingdom would be named, the heir whom all Europe awaited.

Under the pretext of his nephew's marriage, Cardinal Spada invites both Atto and Maria to Rome. Atto brings with him the ideal person to forge the signature: a quite unusually refined forger.

After all, what had Abbot Melani said when he introduced Buvat to me? "He is at his best with a pen in his hand; but not like you: you create; he copies. And he does that like no other." At that moment, I had thought that he was referring to his secretary's work copying letters; but no. It was then, in a flash of memory, that I recalled what Atto had told me many years earlier, when first he mentioned his secretary's name. "Every time I leave Paris secretly, he looks after my correspondence. He is a copyist of extraordinary talent, and knows perfectly how to imitate my handwriting."

So *that* was what I had seen among Atto's secretary's well hidden papers: those strange proofs of *e*, *l*, *R*, *o* and *y*, which I had at first taken for badly performed calligraphic exercises, were in fact part of Buvat's preparations for forging a signature. He was practising to imitate that of Charles II, repeating over and over again the letters contained in the autograph *yo el Rey*. These exercises he had kept in order to compare them with authentic signatures of the Catholic King and to be able in the end to select the best copy.

I need only have put those letters together in the right order and I would have found out the truth. So that was why Atto kept so carefully concealed in his wig those three incomplete letters bearing the signature of the King of Spain: they were the models on which Buvat was to practise. They were, however, far too confidential to be left in his secretary's hands, and so Melani kept them on his person.

I resumed my reconstruction. Maria, then, had the task of bringing those forged signatures back to Spain, where they would be put to use in due course: when Charles II was dying and his will must be drawn up. A false will would be prepared, the last page of which would be that containing the signature prepared by Buvat. The blank space above would be used to set down the last part of the will. Obviously, a French heir would be appointed. That explained why Atto had never spoken to me of the Spanish succession, instead of which, he kept going on about the conclave! Poor fool that I am, I had not understood the real objective he was so doggedly pursuing.

Had the wait for Maria, then, been nothing but a charade? What a treacherous *mise-en-scène*, with all those sugary letters in which he spun out his yearning to see her again!

It had all been planned to perfection, so designed as to withstand any attempts at espionage. The Connestabilessa was to arrive at the wedding celebrations as late as possible, just in time to collect the paper with the signature from Atto and Buvat! It was important that she should not in fact attend the festivities: the presence of Maria Mancini, Mazarin's notorious niece who resided in Madrid, would at once have given rise to suspicions of an anti-Spanish plot.

How convenient it had been to make use of me to deliver the paper with the signature to the Connestabilessa! Atto need not even dirty his hands with the chore. He knew perfectly well from the outset that he would never meet her: he had deceived me up to the very last moment, making me think that he was too perturbed to see her after their thirty-year long separation.

The theft of Atto's treatise had been a mere complication which had frightened and impeded him but had only partly distracted him from his prime objective. Once the mystery had been resolved and the stolen good had (once more, thanks to my good offices!) been snatched back from the *cerretani*, Atto had been able calmly to conclude his shady business of espionage.

Having rapidly made my way back, driven by the force of my anger, I entered Villa Spada, already knowing what awaited me.

When I went to knock at the door, I found it already open. A few articles of clothing remained on the bed, and on the day-bed, a dry inkwell and a few scribbled notes. The scene matched perfectly my poor dismayed and bewildered spirits.

Atto and Buvat had gone.

Doing my best to dissimulate my rage and disappointment, I made a brief investigation, questioning the servants of the villa. I learned that the pair had departed post haste and that their destination was Paris. They had stocked up with provisions, and Atto had left a long letter of thanks for Cardinal Spada, to be delivered by Don Paschatio.

Now I understood why, that morning, he had donned his abbot's mauve-grey soutane and periwig which I knew so well: it was his travelling costume!

They had been gone for quite a while by now. They must have packed their bags in extraordinary haste, like refugees fleeing the onset of war. This was no departure; they had fled.

What from? I was quite sure it had nothing to do with fear of any further threats from the *cerretani*. It was not like Atto to fear what he had already experienced, once he was familiar with its nature. Nor was he fleeing any supposed political threats, as he had put it about earlier. No, it was something else: he was fleeing from me.

Not that he had any material fear of me – of course not. Nevertheless, at the last moment, having accomplished what he had set out to do and fearing that I might have guessed at the truth, he had not felt up to confronting me and answering for his lies and subterfuges.

He had turned up after an absence of seventeen years, asking me to act as the chronicler of his deeds with a view to the forthcoming conclave. Yet, he had not provided me with any further instructions, nor had he subsequently shown any interest in the matter.

The chronicle of those days at Villa Spada had been a mere pretext: the only thing that had mattered to him was that I should look, listen to and report everything that might be of use to him. Whether or not I wrote it down was quite indifferent to him. What had he said to me at the outset? "You will pen for me a chronicle in which you will give a judicious account of all that you see and hear during the coming few days, and you will add thereto whatever I may suggest to you as being desirable and opportune. You will then deliver the manuscript to me." He had persuaded me that I would be acting as a gazetteer. Instead, he had got me to spy. So much so, that he had left like a fly-by-night without even taking delivery of my work.

Nor did he give a fig for the conclave, of which he had initially spoken at such great length. We had seen, discussed and done all manner of things: from the alarums and excursions with Caesar Augustus to the insane climb up into the ball of Saint Peter's, from the ineffable experiences at the Vessel to the final nightmare when we narrowly missed being slaughtered by the *cerretani*. But we had hardly touched again on the subject of the conclave.

"What a stupid, ingenuous imbecile I have been!" I berated myself, torn between laughter and tears. He had kept me at his service, manipulating me without the slightest regard for my safety, just as he had done seventeen years before. He had pointed out one road to me, urging me on, while he himself tiptoed off in a very different direction.

This time, however, it was far more serious. Now he had played with the future of my little daughters. When I was on the point of withdrawing from his dangerous games, he had enveigled me with the promise of a dowry for them, and I had fallen for the bait, even risking my life for him. That very afternoon, we had been supposed to go to the notary for the endowment. One moment, however: I did have the document with his written promise.

Stung by a thousand scorpions, I rushed home, grabbed the paper and spurred my mule towards town.

I went from lawyer to lawyer, from notary to notary, in search of someone who might at least give me a glimmer of hope. To no avail. I met invariably with the same question: "Do you by any chance know whether this abbot owns property in the Papal States?" And when I shook my head the sentence was always the same: "Even if you sued and won your case, we would have no means of claiming what is owed you." So, what was to be done? "You should find out whether you can also sue in France. That would be a lengthy and expensive process and, what is more, my good sir, the outcome would be utterly uncertain."

In other words, I had no hope. Now that Atto was on his way to Paris, his promise was not worth the paper it was written on.

Returning to Villa Spada, I was tempted to hit myself with my own whip. I should have insisted on going straight to the notary, or at the very least, I should not have waited so long. The truth is that I had allowed myself to be swept along by events and I had let the Abbot use me like a slave, without any consideration for my family. What would have happened if I had died or become an invalid? Cloridia could not keep our household going on her own. What would have fed and clothed our daughters? Not their work as apprentice midwives. Farewell to those evenings when I had taught them to read and write and they had stared wide-eyed at the fine books bequeathed to me by my late lamented father-in-law. The children would have had to roll up their sleeves at once and slave away as scullery maids, probably in some foul tavern, unless Don Paschatio were magnanimously to find them some place in the Spada household.

I was boiling over with rage. Abbot Melani had deceived me. He had run off and instead of the promised dowry I was left with nothing. I myself felt like fleeing, leaving that place; indeed, leaving this cruel deceitful world. Had my duties as a husband and father not prevented me, I would have taken flight like some new Daedalus, or become like Icarus, but instead of falling to earth, I would fall into the sky, sucked forever into the azure abyss of the celestial spheres.

As I was cursing to myself, I ran into one last piece of trouble.

"Signor Master of the Fowls! Did you not see what a success our festivities were? And did you hear the enthusiastic comments of our master, Cardinal Spada?"

Don Paschatio had intercepted me at the gate. He wanted to talk about the success of the festivities. No doubt he would point out that if I had not been so frequently distracted by Abbot Melani, and had made myself more available, the triumph would have been even more complete.

This really was not the moment for such things. Anything, anything rather than suffer his logorrhoea.

"Signor Major-Domo," I replied bluntly, "since during the past few days I have absented myself on several occasions, I am sure that you will not be surprised if I interrupt this conversation and ask you to set me some useful task so that I can make up for my past failings and avoid time-wasting."

Don Paschatio faltered, stopped short by so brusque a response.

"Er, well. . ." he hesitated. "Yes, you could attend to the cleaning and provisioning of the aviary, as I was just about to instruct you to."

"Very well!" I concluded, turning sharply on my heels. "It will be done at once, Signor Major-Domo."

Don Paschatio stared at me, scratching his forehead in perplexity, while I marched nervously towards the kitchens to collect feed for the birds and the necessary to clean the aviary.

I could not know it, but I was never to accomplish that task. Hardly had I opened the big cage when an unusual noise, a sort of furtive fluttering, caught my attention. I looked up towards the cage of Caesar Augustus which had remained empty since the day of his escape, and suddenly, in a bewildering flash of intuition, the bizarre events which had involved the parrot during the past few days became quite clear to me.

As I have had occasion to mention, recently, in other words, just before disappearing with the note addressed to Cardinal Albani, the parrot's mood had been unusually unhappy and agitated. What was more, he would often return with a twig in his claws, for some unknown purpose, something he had never done previously. The bird's nervousness had come to a head with the theft of the note and his long absence. Later, during the course of the hunting party organised for the guests, a badly aimed crossbow shot had brought down from a nest on a pine tree an egg of unidentified provenance. With the oddity I now found staring me in the face, I recalled that another parrot of the same race as Caesar Augustus had recently arrived and came to a quite inconceivable (but correct) conclusion.

"Dismiss him! Dismisssss him!" screeched Caesar Augustus, mocking me from his comfortable perch in the middle of a fine nest of feathers and twigs.

"But you. . . you are. . . you have. . ." I stammered.

I could not even bring myself to say it. No one could easily have accepted, even if they had witnessed it with their own eyes, that Caesar Augustus was really a female parrot. . . with a nestful of eggs.

I was amazed, almost entranced, watching the new manifestation of that surprising being, by no means accidentally once the property of the mad Capitor: he – she? – had, as a calm spectator, traversed decades and decades of history; he had seen the decline of Mazarin, the advent of the Sun King, and then a succession of no fewer than five popes, and now, with his eternal, unbearable squawking, he was making a triumphal entry into the new century in the sacred guise of a mother.

I saw him rise briefly from the nest lovingly to arrange the surviving eggs with his beak. The hunters who had examined the egg that had fallen from that pine tree were all mistaken: it belonged neither to a riparian swallow nor to a pheasant, nor to a turtle dove or a partridge, but to a parrot.

"Doiiiiinnnnng," went Caesar Augustus, with a pair of accusing eyes, imitating the sound of a crossbow bolt embedding itself in a branch and making it vibrate: the same bolt which, shot by Marchese Lancellotti Ginetti during the hunting party, had caused Caesar Augustus's egg to fall from its nest and had obviously forced him to abandon the pine on the Barberini property for the relative safety of the familiar aviary of Villa Spada.

"I know, I know, for you it must have been quite terrible," I answered.

"One does not shoot at nests, it is both pointless and cruel," said he, repeating the words of the cavalier who, immediately after the incident, had derided Lancellotti Ginetti's bad shooting.

"Lancellotti did not mean to harm you," I tried to explain to him. "Of course, building a new nest and transporting your eggs must have been a terribly difficult job; but, after all, it was only an accident, and you shouldn't have imitated that arquebus shot that so terrified all. . ."

"Dismiss him!" he replied sharply, descending to cover with loving wings the little whitish spheres containing his brood.

Don Paschatio and the others at the Spada household would never have believed their eyes. I could already imagine the rush to find some other noble Latin name for the fowl: Livia or Lucretia, Poppea or Messalina? I had known that bird for so long that I had come to treat him almost as an equal, from one male to another. Instead, I had really been dealing with a scornful, rebellious, intractable lady clothed in feathers. I felt almost guilty for having developed these all but comradely feelings; the only extenuating factor was the fact that it is, as is well known, almost impossible to determine the sex of a parrot visually or by touch. To solve the mystery, the only possibility is to wait until, once the right company has been found, it lays eggs or becomes the vigorous defender of the nest.

After a few more moments of stunned surprise, I recovered my aplomb.

"If I know you, I'm prepared to bet that, in addition to the eggs, you transported something else. Do you not have a certain something to return to me, now that you have calmed down?"

He continued to turn his back on me, pretending not to hear.

"You know perfectly well what I'm talking about," I insisted.

The bird acted swiftly and apparently with utter unconcern, almost scornfully. With one foot, it scratched inside the nest, extracted it and let it fall. My request had been granted.

Like any other dead leaf, Cardinal Albani's message fluttered crazily down, making a few graceful pirouettes until my hands grasped it.

It was dirty, torn and stank of birds' droppings. How could it have been otherwise, seeing that the parrot, after sating itself chewing the corner dipped in chocolate, had used it for its nest? And, stubborn as he was, after building a nest inside the aviary, he had not failed to bring it with him.

With eager fingers, I opened the scrap of yellow paper. There were just three lines, but they rent my already lacerated soul even more:

Opinion ready.
Wednesday 14th at the Villa T., time to be confirmed.
Arrangements already made for scribe and courier.

My arms grew heavy and fell by my sides. What for anyone else would have been mysterious was for me as clear as daylight and as painful as a fiery arrow.

The Villa T. was obviously the Villa del Torre, where in fact on Wednesday 14th Atto and I had, from the terrace on top of the Vessel, seen the three cardinals. The ready opinion was clearly the document to be copied by the scribe and sent by courier to the King of Spain, whereby the Pope was indicating an heir to the throne.

As I already knew from what I had overheard just before the play at Villa Spada, on Monday 12th the Spanish Ambassador Uzeda and the three cardinals (those four "sly foxes", as they had called them) had convinced the Pope to set up a special congregation to be entrusted to the same Albani, Spada and Spinola. The Pontiff had formally created it two days later, on the 14th July. However, they had already made their decision even on the day when the message was stolen by the parrot, namely Saturday 10th!

It had all been a great sham. If the King of Spain was a dead man walking, the Pope too no longer counted for anything. Albani, Spada and Spinola had dictated the destiny of the world from the Villa Spada, between a cup of chocolate and a hunting party, without anyone knowing anything of it. Atto, the vigilant eye of the King of France, had kept an eye on them from a distance; and I, without knowing it, had seconded him.

Instilling in me a desperate feeling of impotence, Albicastro's words came back to mind: "The world is one enormous banquet, my boy, and the law of banquets is: 'Drink or begone!'"

Would I then never have any other choice? Did the authority invested by God no longer count for anything?

Autumn 1700

✠

About a month had passed since Atto Melani and his secretary had abandoned me. Day after day of hatred, fury and powerlessness had followed. Every night, every single breath had been marked out in seconds by the remorseless clock of humiliation, injured honour and frustration. Perhaps it was no accident that I was tormented by that nasty tertian fever from which I had not suffered for years. It had consoled me little that, about a month before, a notary had come to Villa Spada in search of Atto: he said that the Abbot had instructed him to draw up an act of endowment but had failed to turn up to the appointment at which he was to sign it. Now I had the confirmation: Melani had not premeditated breaking his promise; simply, the instinct to flee had *in extremis* got the better of him.

Cloridia was sorry for me; despite her anger and humiliation as a mother at being denied her daughters' dowry, she was soon able even to make light of it all. She said that Melani had just been doing his job as a spy and a traitor.

Obviously, I had never set my hand to the memoir for which the Abbot had paid me. He was not really interested in it. I had thought thus to keep the money as partial compensation for the dowry he had failed to make over to my little ones. On 27th September, however, I did take up my pen, impelled by an event the gravity of which put my selfish suffering in the shade. I began to keep a little diary, which I am setting out below.

27th September 1700

The sad day is upon us: Innocent XII has passed away.

On the last day of August he had suffered an alarming relapse, so much so that the Consistory planned for the next day had to be postponed. On 4th September (as I had gradually come to learn from the broadsheets which the Major-Domo read out to the servants) his health had improved, and, with that, hopes had revived for his recovery. Three days later, however, his state again worsened, this time seriously. Yet his constitution was so strong that the illness lasted even longer. On the night of the 23rd and the 24th he was administered the Eucharist. On the 28th, he ordered that he was to be brought to the room where Pope Innocent XI, whom he had so revered, had breathed his last.

The physician Luca Corsi, no whit less capable than his illustrious predecessor Malpighi, had done all in his power. Human assistance was, however, no longer of any avail. Spiritual support was provided by a Capuchin friar to whom the Pope made his general confession.

"*Ingredimur via universae carnis*", "we are taking the way of all flesh," said he, moving to tears those who accompanied him in his extreme travail.

Yesterday night, his sufferings were aggravated by sharp pains in one side; however, it proved possible to restore him with a few sips of broth. But at four in the morning, he gave up the ghost.

The body will be brought from the Quirinale to Saint Peter's in a plain wooden coffin chosen by the Pope in person. He leaves behind him an exemplary reputation as father of the poor, a disinterested administrator of the Church's estates and a pious and just priest.

Now the betting is truly open for the election of the next Pope. Prognostications for this or that cardinal can be voiced aloud without any fear of offending the honour of the Holy Father and his poor sick body.

This should have been Abbot Melani's finest hour: at long last exploiting his network of acquaintances, making friends among those attending the conclave, getting wind of indiscretions, proposing strategies, propagating false rumours to demoralise the other side. . .

None of that is to be. No clever interpreter of political manoeuvring, no magus of Vatican alchemy will be by my side. I shall observe the conclave from the outside, wide-eyed and with my soul in a state of suspense, like all the other members of the public.

8th October

Tomorrow, the cardinals go into conclave. The factions are on a war footing, all Rome is holding its breath. The city is full of gazettes and broadsheets setting out the composition of the parties that will be entering the lists. Satires, dramas and sonnets flourish, lampoons abound.

Plays are circulated quite without shame or fear of God, lambasting the whole Sacred College, while according special attention to Cardinal Ottoboni and his particular tendencies: in *La Babilonia*, he is given the role of the chambermaid Nina; in *L'Osteria*, he becomes Petrina; in *Babilonia Crescente*, Madam Fulvia, in *Babilonia trasformata*, a certain Venetian Angeletta. Everyone kills themselves laughing.

The other day, I came upon a sonnet in which poor Pope Innocent the Twelfth (*"Duodecimo"*) becomes Innocent Duodenum. Out of modesty, I shall not reproduce it here.

Besides all the jokes, serious information also circulates. The imperial and Spanish cardinals number eleven, at least on paper. The French are in equal numbers. The party of the Cardinal Zealots is the most numerous, numbering nineteen. Some of these (Moriggia, Carlo Barberini, Colloredo) I have seen at Villa Spada. The group of the Virile are ten, and include the Chamberlain Spinola di San Cesareo; likewise the Drifters. The Ottoboniani and Altieristi (called after the family names of the popes who raised them to the purple) are twelve. These include my master, Cardinal Spada, together with Albani, Mariscotti and, obviously, Ottoboni. Then come the other popes' appointments, the Odescalchini, the Pignatellisti and the Barberini. . .

According to the gazettes, the divisions cut across all party lines, and so are infinite. Some see rivalries and alliances according to age groups, gifts, aspirations, caprices, even tastes: there are the bitter cardinals, in other words, those known for their ill humour (Panciatici, Buonvisi, Acciaioli, Marescotti), the good-natured and easy going (Moriggia, Radolovich, Barberini, Spinola di Santa Cecilia), the middling ones (Carpegna, Noris, Durazzo, Dal Verme) and lastly, the unripe ones, who are less than seventy years of age and therefore too young to be elected (Spada, Albani, Orsini, Spinola di San Cesareo, Mellini and Rubini).

Negroni is seventy-one years old but has made it clear that he is not willing to be elected; he will vote for whoever merits the appointment, so he swore, and against the undeserving. The latter, of this everyone is convinced, are the overwhelming majority.

Even upright souls will, however, find the way difficult. No favours will be granted, even to those who have all their affairs in good order. Carlo Barberini, for instance, is about the right age, but has to contend with the hatred of the Romans for his relatives (which has lasted for the best part of eighty years), as well as the hostility of Spinola di

San Cesareo and, above all, his own stupidity. Accaioli is opposed by Tuscany and France. Abroad, Marescotti is hated only by France, but in Rome also by Bichi (the feeling being entirely mutual). Durazzo is envied for the fact that he is related to the Queen of Spain. Moriggia is too close to Tuscany, Radolovich to Spain. Carpegna is not in good odour with any of the crowned heads of Europe, Colloredo is detested by the French and despised by Ottoboni. Costaguti is notoriously incompetent. Noris suits no one because he is a friar. For whatever reason, Panciatici is favoured by no one.

Many foreigners will not come, being taken up with urgent business of their own (these are said to include the Austrian Kollonitz, the Frenchmen Sousa and Bonsi and the Spaniard Portocarrero). But the struggle will be very hard indeed, so much so that the eminences may wish to opt for a more rapid solution in order to avoid bloodshed. Some say that white smoke may emerge within a fortnight or so, perhaps even less.

18th November

Nothing of the kind. A month and a half has passed since the beginning of the conclave, yet there's not so much as the shadow of a new Pontiff. The Sacred College of Cardinals seems in fact quite indifferent to the election of the new Pope. We have in fact seen nothing but fruitless manoeuvres whereby candidates have been ruined and burnt out. Everything is blocked by France, Spain and the Empire, in a crossfire of vetoes which implacably bars the way to candidates who do not meet with their approval. The independence and prestige of the Church are obviously in pieces, but the cardinals care nothing for that.

Throughout October, things have gone on like this, with a superabundance of verbiage, while first this candidate, then that, is cast into the fray, like so many manikins cast in the fire: Noris, Moriggia, Spinola di Santa Cecilia, Barbarigo, Durazzo, Medici. All proposed, some even joining the fray on their own initiative, all rejected.

The one serious candidature has perhaps been that of Marescotti, who started out with twenty guaranteed votes, but met with French hostility, which makes him ineligible. Colloredo was proposed: in reality, he is absolutely *persona non grata* to France, and can therefore get nowhere. Everyone was so sure that Colloredo could not make it that they voted for him *en masse* and he came within a hair's breadth of election, thus causing some half dozen heart attacks in the Sacred College.

Despite the meagre progress, all manner of things have taken place within the sacred walls of the conclave: endless arguments, envy, hatred among the eminences. More than once, the masters of ceremonies have had to silence the brawling by ordering "*Ad cellas, Domini*" and forcing the cardinals back to their little cells. There has been no lack of unseemly rows among those attending the conclave who have as usual been caught out listening at one another's doorways. There was even a fire that started, perhaps a case of arson: to repair the damage, an architect and four master masons had to be called in urgently.

The atmosphere is, however, not warlike but mean and nasty. The struggle is informed, not by some lust for triumph, but envy. Rather than competing, what counts is to cripple one's adversary: the winning horse is still not there. It is as though everyone were waiting for something.

The more we go on, the more world-weary and lethargic the mood of the eminences. One morning, Marescotti, the one who was supposed to hold all the best cards, had a nasty fall when putting on his drawers and hurt his head. On hearing the news, the other eminences roared with laughter.

On 31st October, a letter came from the Nuncio to Spain, addressed to Innocent XII. The Nuncio did not know that he had died. Again, there was loud laughter among the eminences.

Monsignor Paolo Borghese who, in his capacity as Governor of the Conclave, is supposed to maintain order and decorum within the Sacred College, makes up for the weakness of his brains with the power of his purse, providing endless banquets within the secluded walls of the College. The dining tables are ornamented with sumptuous displays of flowers and fruit, which are renewed every three days.

In Rome, meanwhile, bread is growing scarce and becoming dearer by the day. The merchants are making money out of the hunger and sufferings of the people, who are exhausted and embittered. The Cardinal Chamberlain Spinola di San Cesareo is suspected of taking part in this speculation and trafficking. After seeing him plotting with Spada and Albani, I do not find it hard to believe this gossip.

In town, Prince Vaini is sowing panic by writing bad cheques, starting brawls and mocking the cardinals assembled in conclave who, in the interregnum between popes, are supposed to govern the city jointly but lack the courage to arrest a troublemaking prince or to do anything about the food shortages and public disorder. After seeing how Prince Vaini did just as he pleased at the Villa Spada, the home of the Secretary of State, nothing could ever surprise me.

Everywhere, we are confronted with an endless series of commotions, assaults and assassinations. As always happens whenever the seat of power is empty, Rome lies under a dark cloud of violence and oppression. This is a time of pessimism, bilious humour and ill will.

As though that were not enough, worrying news keeps reaching us about the health of the King of Spain. On 24th October, Cardinal Borgia, head of the Spanish faction, was supposed to arrive at the conclave from Spain and a cell had already been arranged for him alongside those of the other cardinals. Instead, he let it be known that he would not be coming. It seems that the King's illness has become too serious; from what one hears, on the 27th he received the sacraments and the physicians have now abandoned all hope of saving him.

20th November

The news reached us yesterday. King Charles of Spain has died. It happened on 1st November.

The tidings soon made their way around the conclave. During the night an express courier had arrived from France for their cardinals, then another for Cardinal Medici, sent by his brother, the Grand Duke of Tuscany, followed by a third despatch sent by the French Ambassador to Cardinal d'Estrées.

It seems that their eminences have at long last been shaken by something of an earth tremor. The succession to the Spanish throne is open. The whole world awaits the choice of a wise new pontiff who will be able to mediate between the powers and avoid a long, bloody war.

Now they say that we shall have a new pope tomorrow. The factions have woken up and set to work looking for an agreed candidate. In town, the most disparate prognostications are being voiced: Marescotti's name is mentioned among others, and even Barberini's.

Now, I too am beginning to see more clearly. That was why there had been all that temporising in the conclave, all those candidates unceremoniously dumped, all that time-wasting, banqueting, joking and misplaced mirth. . .

Here then was the event for which the Sacred College had been waiting: that Charles of Spain should die, so that the situation would become truly grave and urgent (as if the election of a pope were not grave and urgent enough).

There it was: an *emergency*, that was what they needed. If grave and unpopular decisions need to be taken, the circumstances must first become critical, such that no one can any longer say, "One moment, we cannot do this." Atto was right: difficult decisions are taken in states of emergency. And where they do not exist, they must be created, or at least awaited.

But what, I wonder, do their eminences and the powers that influence the Sacred College intend to do? I find myself thinking back to the teachings which Atto imparted to me in an obscure Roman underground passage some seventeen years ago, when he said to me: in affairs of state, what counts is not what you think, but how. No one knows everything, not even the King. And, when you do not know, you must learn to suppose, and to suppose truths which at first sight may appear to be utterly absurd: you will then learn without fail that it is all dramatically true.

So now I understand: they mean to elect a pope who in normal circumstances could never be elected. For example, one in poor health (like Spinola di Santa Cecilia), or unpopular with this or that power (of whom there are so many). But who?

23rd November

The single most unlikely turn of events: Albani.

They have elected Albani. Forty votes out of sixty-eight.

Everyone said he was not *papabile*, that he was too young: only just fifty-one years old. Even Cardinal Spada, who is four years older, was not on the list of those eligible. Of course, Albani, as is well known, has plenty of relatives: everyone is sure that he will shower them in gold at the Church's expense. But still, they have elected him.

Until a few days ago, he was not even a priest. He took Holy Orders in great haste and said mass for the first time on 6th October, and on the 9th, he joined the conclave. Not being a priest, he was not even a bishop: but the Pope is also Bishop of Rome. Albani will therefore receive his episcopal investiture after the election, from a cardinal's hands. This has not happened for 108 years.

Well-informed commentators say that Albani was perfectly aware of being a contender, nor was it by chance that at the first count he received six votes which at the time went completely unnoticed. Hardly had the news of the Catholic King's death arrived than Altierani, Ottobonisti, Odescalchini, Pignatellisti and Barberini all sang his name in unison. The French pretended they wanted a deferment, but it was quite clear that they had in mind no one but him.

I am certain of it: this was all pre-arranged. Albani was the Pope *in pectore* who was already trying on the tiara in the wings while awaiting the death of the King of Spain. The French had his name canvassed by their friends in other factions (whom, it is said, Louis XIV has, since time immemorial been corrupting with rivers of gold). Meanwhile, Albani, thanks to his public arguments with Atto at Villa Spada, had rid himself of his Francophile reputation, so that the others imagined that they were electing an independent pope; instead of which they have chosen a most faithful ally of the Most Christian King. The game became clear only at the very end, when the French cardinals took everyone by surprise by voting for him *en masse*.

This was no election, but a comedy. Even the pretexts which Albani devised when they told him that he was about to become pope seem somehow improbable. He said he was assailed by qualms of conscience; that perhaps he would be unable to accept, and that he did not feel up to the task. The other day, he even became unwell and took to his bed, apparently throwing up, with traces of bile in his vomit. Yesterday, he got up again but, amidst tears, said that he would be unable to accept. One can see from a mile off that this is all put on, everyone says so. As an old lion of politics, he wants to be begged to be pope, to pass himself off as a modest man and thus to silence his critics. He knows perfectly well that everywhere they are already carving portrait busts of him in pontifical garb, and on the façades of churches and public buildings, his family arms are already appearing. At Saint Peter's, the stage for the ceremony of investiture has already been set up; the arms of the Albani have already been carved on the chair on which the new pope will be borne into the basilica.

At this juncture, in order to put an end to the hypocritical refusal, Albani has consulted four theologians who have patiently illustrated for him the *ratio precipua* that obliges him to accept the tiara, and today the election has been made public.

25th November

At six in the evening, a courier arrived at the Spanish Embassy with the second great tidings.

A few hours after the death of the Catholic King of Spain, his will was opened and read: as successor to the Spanish throne, it designated Philip of Anjou, the second son of the French Dauphin and grandson of the Most Christian King. The news was kept secret until the 10th, when Louis XIV at Versailles officially accepted the will. It seems he exclaimed with satisfaction: "*Il n'y a plus de Pyrénées!*" It is true, the Pyrenees no longer bar the way to Madrid: the whole Spanish monarchy will now pass into French hands.

The Spanish Ambassador, the Duke of Uzeda, immediately brought the news to the Pope, even going so far as to wake him up. The Pontiff was so delighted that he awarded Uzeda's Maestro di Cappella a benefice as canon at Valladolid.

But knots do not dissolve, they get caught up in the teeth of the comb. It is already being bruited abroad that the Empire does not accept the verdict and is threatening to send its armies to Italy, in order to take over the Spanish possessions in the peninsula. France cannot stand by without reacting. The fuse of war has been lit.

I alone in the city see the concealed and unsavoury links between the facts. The bargain was clear: Louis XIV had promised Albani the papacy. As a *quid pro quo*, he wanted his grandson on the Spanish throne.

Atto, Buvat and Maria had provided the signature for a forged will. However, in the months leading up to his death, Charles had asked Innocent XII to mediate, and from his request it was quite clear that he had no intention of designating a Frenchman as his heir. It was therefore necessary to send him an answer which did not give away the conspiracy which was taking shape; one that, on the contrary, played into the conspirators' hands. Spada, Spinola and Albani had seen to this. They had prepared a suitable answer in which – instead of responding to the request for mediation – Charles II was advised to appoint outright as his successor a grandson of the Most Christian King. This way, when the false will was opened in Spain, no one would be surprised that Charles should have chosen a Frenchman: even the Pope had recommended him so to do. . . The two forgeries, the opinion and the will, were in fact so designed as to corroborate one another. Once the opinion had been drawn up, the three cardinals had experienced no difficulty in assuming the authority of the Pontiff and had obtained the task of replying to the Spanish Sovereign's request.

Counterfeiting the missive from the Pope was all too simple: he in fact never signed letters or wrote in person to princes and sovereigns. These, he dictated to a secretary and then had sealed by a cardinal. It is no accident that Albani, now that he has become Pope, should have put an end to this custom. He has already proclaimed that, in order to be both humble and expeditious, he will personally draft and sign all the most important documents. . .

And where do I stand in all this? By following Atto, I had become a pawn in these very games. Without being a cardinal, I too had made the new Pope.

But above all, this had been the work of Abbot Melani. Thanks to his rows with Albani during the festivities at Villa Spada, Atto had succeeded in cancelling out the only shadow over that Cardinal's person: his reputation as a Francophile.

That explained why, when I asked Atto how he dared scandalise the company with his shameless speeches, he had not answered me. The fact is that he had to appear in the guise of a fanatical Francophile, while Albani, by quarrelling with him, was meant to gain himself the reputation of a man above all factions. So, it had worked out. And from that play-acting, there had emerged the new Holy Father.

Thus, Atto had pulled off his wager. As he had announced at the outset, he had succeeded in leaving his decisive mark on the destiny of the papacy. What was more, he had succeeded in doing so before the conclave even began.

It was no accident that Albani should have chosen to be pope under the name Clement XI: was not Clement IX the Pope whose election Atto boasted he had arranged thirty years previously?

Abbot Melani had not then lied to me. He had also come to Rome for the election of the new pontiff. What he had told me at the outset had seemed to me a pack of lies, but now turned out to be true. Yet, no one in his place could have simultaneously manipulated both the Spanish succession and the conclave, navigating between the King of France, Maria Mancini and the thousand dangers which we had faced together. He, this shrivelled old man, had accomplished just that.

March 1702

✠

Maria Mancini was right: it had all been pointless.

As I pen these lines, Italy has for the past year been the scene of a horrible war which will soon spread everywhere. The astrologers have announced that the conjunction of Mars and Jupiter this month presages many battles and calamities.

Last spring, the Empire invaded the north-west, advancing on the Grand Duchy of Milan. In July, the French led by Catinat, a mediocre general, were defeated at Carpi and had to abandon their positions between the Adige and the Mincio. The Austrians then crossed the Po and seized the fortress of Mirandola. They were not even stopped by the entry into the war of Piedmont and the French squadrons of the Maréchal de Villeroy, who was taken prisoner at Verona. Events were not turned around until the arrival of Vendôme. He fielded eighty thousand fresh and well-equipped troops, regained Modena and saved Mantua and Milan, while the Austrian forces were tired and their reserves used up. At this point, it is possible that by opening up a passage through the passes of Tyrol, the French may advance on Bavaria and join up with their army of the Rhine to move against Vienna and strike a mortal blow at the Empire.

Not even this, however, can bring the war to an end. France is on the point of being attacked by England and Holland, who cannot wait to see her humbled: the Most Christian King has deceived them. He had signed with them a treaty for the partition of the immense Spanish monarchy; then, instead, using Charles II's will, he grabbed everything for himself, reneging on his agreements. Thus, the conflict will soon spread to every corner of the continent.

Curiously, the hero of this war has Italian blood in his veins. He is Prince Eugene of Savoy, the son of the Duke of Savoy and a woman whom by now I know well from Atto's account: Olimpia Mancini, Maria's terrible sister.

Prince Eugene should have become a Frenchman, but when he was still very young, Louis XIV neglected and humiliated him, causing him to leave his kingdom. He placed himself at the Emperor's service and has now become the greatest general of all time. At France's expense. Ah, Silvio, Silvio. . .

The Connestabilessa thus proves to have really been the woman of destiny: Eugene, her nephew, dominates the conflict which will decide the fate of the world. Her evil sister Olimpia has thus at last found an outlet for her malignity: her son is the military genius who sows terror wherever he turns.

As at every decisive turning point in history, prophecies are coming true. Maria Mancini's father had read in her horoscope that she would be the cause of tumults, rebellions and even a war. He had seen rightly: if the young King had married her and not the Spanish Infanta, he could not have laid claim to the succession of Charles II. And this war would never have taken place.

For two years, I tormented myself with the thought of the plot in which I had perhaps been the precious, decisive pawn. A year ago, I at last made up my mind and wrote an account of these events. I even had a frontispiece printed, with a wealth of decorations, and placed it at the beginning of these pages. I shall send the whole lot to Abbot Melani, seeing that he paid me for it, and shall at the same time claim my daughters' dowries. Now that they are twelve and eight years of age, I still have a good deal of time before it will be too late to find a good husband for them.

Will he answer me? At times I am overcome by floods of rancour against that champion of intrigue and mendacity. Then the scapular of the Madonna of the Carmel comes into my hands, with the three little pearls which he kept for seventeen years in memory of me and returned to me in Ugonio's lair. And then I say to myself that I should perhaps recall Abbot Melani only with feelings of affection.

I fear that there will be no more time for making claims. Atto Melani, Counsellor to the Most Christian King and Abbot of Beaubec, is (or would today be) seventy-six. I look around and see that few, very few men of his age are still on their feet, still healthy and vigilant; or even so much as alive. The dangerous life he has lived can only have left its mark on his weary bones. It remains only for me to hope.

❧

Now, the present worries me even more than the future. Maria did well to warn her Louis that the forged will would resolve nothing.

Now that the cannon are firing, I too am all too well aware that all those intrigues, all those efforts to resolve the Spanish succession by deceit, while avoiding war, were in vain. Philip of Anjou mounted the Spanish throne, as the Sun King wished, but France was dragged into a conflict with the other powers from which the whole world may never recover. "A great fratricidal struggle, a new Peloponnese war," the Connestabilessa had prophesied.

In those July days at Villa Spada, I had believed I was making myself useful to my little daughters. Instead, I had aided and abetted a plot which was driving Europe to destruction. Was that the reward for all that effort on my part, for climbing the cupola of Saint Peter's in the dark?

Two days ago, I went to look for the answer in the place which in the past had furnished me with more answers than I had found anywhere: the Vessel. I needed solitude, and at the same time, I needed someone to talk to. Cloridia was out assisting with a childbirth. Melani and Buvat were in Paris – the Devil take them. I wondered whether the curious individual might still, however, be where I had left him. Two years had passed, but there are times when nothing is impossible.

❧

King Solomon said: "In much wisdom is much grief: and he that increaseth knowledge increaseth sorrow."

As though not a day had passed, I found him in his usual place, perched on the cornice of the Vessel and – need I say it? – playing the *folia* on the violin.

He had at once greeted me with the usual quotation from the Bible, as though he had read in my eyes what it was that I sought. How could I fault him for that? To the Vessel, one came only as a seeker.

"And he also said that in wisdom, and in knowledge, is vanity and vexation of spirit," the Dutchman added.

It was true, so true. Now that I knew, I suffered. As when I met Abbot Melani nineteen years ago and my young boy's illusions fell one after the other under the hammer blows of reality.

"That is precisely what folly exists for," the violinist added, speaking loud and clear to make himself heard as he pressed on the bow, his face melting into a broad smile. "Folly gladdens the heart and, as

Hildegarde of Bingen preached so well, converts the *tristitia seculae* into *coeleste gaudium* or, in other words, it transforms pain for the world into the joy of heaven!"

After two years, I was once again hearing the *folia*. The notes played arpeggiato drew Albicastro's words and his very limbs after them, remoulding them to the proud accents of the dance. In counterpoint with his words, those concepts became unfamiliar, ineffable music.

For a few minutes, he seemed intent only on playing, and I decided to move on a little further. Once again, I entered the park of the Vessel, walking quietly; my thoughts, however, were soon racing, fluttering to the burning rhythm of the *folia*.

Illuminated by the resonant lightning flashes of that music, the events I had lived through took on a thousand facets, ogling me and letting me run after them, then suddenly letting their commotion fall silent, so that sometimes I would think, "There, I have them," only for them to start swirling in some quite different guise. When at last they'd foiled my green certitudes, they seemed to suggest to me new ways of knowledge.

Outside me were the thousand worlds of the *folia*. Within me, in my thoughts, there were, however, two worlds. In one of these, Atto and Maria were squalid spies in the service of the King of France, who in their letters, in order to trouble the waters, pretended to weave an amorous intrigue. In the other world, however, Abbot Melani was the faithful, gallant messenger of love between the Connestabilessa and the Most Christian King, taking advantage of politics to court as they had done forty years before, still using the same pseudonyms, Silvio and Dorinda, as in their readings from the time when they were living out their love.

Which of the two worlds was real, and which illusory? Had I seen only masks, or men and women of flesh and blood?

While the music filled all the space around me, I sharpened thought's scalpel. What had Atto said to me on the day when he took flight? "If the King of France's separation from Maria Mancini were now to bring Bourbon blood to the throne of Spain, the two would not have been separated in vain."

Then I understood. Those two worlds, the world of the spies and that of the lovers, were not mutually exclusive. They co-existed and even fed one another.

Maria and Louis had been separated because of Spain. Forty years later, they were still writing to one another, and still because of Spain. Their passion had had to give way to reasons of state, with which it was nevertheless firmly interwoven. Maria spied for Louis, but out of love. The secret code was *The Faithful Shepherd*, once their favourite reading. And Atto acted as go-between, then as now.

If Maria had not loved Louis, perhaps she would not even have obeyed his orders. This was clear from her letters. "I understand the point of view shared by Lidio and yourself, but I repeat my own opinion: it is all pointless." She would never have wished to bring the forged signature of Charles II to Madrid; a useless piece of deceit, she thought, and one that would turn against its author.

Like Croesus, King of Lydia, before him, who wanted to hear Solon tell him that he was the happiest of men, the Most Christian King wanted to demonstrate to the Connestabilessa that she would by means of that false signature be bringing him the crown of Spain on a silver platter. Then he would be the most powerful of kings and thus the happiest of mortals. Atto had announced it to Maria: "What you will receive when we meet will convince you . . . You know what value he sets upon your judgement."

But she, like Solon, had shaken her head. Had she not written it clearly? "What today may seem good will tomorrow turn out to be a disaster. For oftentimes God gives men a gleam of happiness, and then plunges them into ruin."

She did not believe that false will could, by fulfilling the Most Christian King's lust for power, make for his happiness as a man. But for the sake of her old love, she had given in: "I shall come. I shall do as Lidio desires. So we shall meet at the Villa Spada. This I promise you." Louis expected of her a double obedience, to love and to the state.

So, said I to myself, what the Abbot had delivered had been far more than a mere token of love. That sheet of paper bearing the words *yo el Rey* had changed the world's history.

Yet Atto had entrusted it to me, a humble peasant and servant to the Spada household. He had not handed it in person to Maria. Why?

So as not to dirty his hands and to deliver through an ignorant messenger that false signature which burned hotter than a thousand bonfires; that, I had thought two years earlier, in the full spate of my anger. Yet, the Abbot had accompanied me to the very door of the convent: an imprudent move for one supposed to have premeditated everything.

No, the law of the two co-existing worlds, that of feelings and of vile politics, applied also to Atto. At the last moment – this I realised only now – his heart had given way. He had lacked the courage to stand before the woman whom he had loved for thirty years without ever having seen her. He had not dared to appear to her with his shoulders weighed down by too many winters; nor, perhaps, to behold her as she now was. Were not Atto's eyes perhaps the very eyes of the Most Christian King? If Maria did not wish to show herself to the King, then perhaps it was as well that Melani should not see her either. He would not have wished to betray her or to lie to Louis. Sooner or later, the day would have come when the Sovereign would have put the inevitable question: "Tell me, is she still beautiful?"

I, who had seen her, could have told the Abbot that perhaps she had never been more beautiful, that never would I forget her, the white luminosity of her face and hands, the ardour of her great chestnut eyes when they met mine, the scarlet ribbons skilfully woven into her curly tresses.

But that had not been possible. Atto had gone.

Meanwhile, the *folia* continued inexorably, and my cogitations with it. Atto had sealed the fateful letter to Maria negligently, too great a lapse – this, I realised now only with the calming of my anger – for it not to have been deliberate. He had not had the strength to keep lying to me to the bitter end; he had wanted to confess all the deceit to me, but after his own fashion. This was followed, quite inevitably, by his precipitous flight. He himself could not stand the truth.

And Maria's letters? Was it an accident that I should have found them in Atto's chambers and secretly read them? Oh no, with Atto, nothing was left to chance. What would those words *yo el Rey* have meant to me if I had not read Atto and Maria's letters? Little or nothing, ignorant as I had been at the outset of the succession to the throne of Spain and the will of Charles II.

This could mean only one thing. He knew that I had read the letters. Indeed, he had wanted me to read his correspondence with the Connestabilessa. And I had fallen into the trap.

How ingenuous I had been. And how clever I had thought myself when I found those letters among the Abbot's dirty linen. Atto had put them there deliberately, certain that I would soon remember how he and I, seventeen years before, had found the answer to our investigations in a pair of dirty under-drawers. To use me effectively as an informer and then to be able to make use of my help, he needed me to be well informed about the question of the Spanish succession. He who does not know is like one who cannot see, and I was there to notice and report back. Yet Atto could not instruct me openly: I would have put too many questions to him which he could not answer. So he had come up with that trick. And when he had not wanted me to read his letters (the last of which truly did contain too many inconvenient truths) he had concealed them elsewhere, in his wig.

He had not, however, expected me to overcome that obstacle. In the end, I had, after all, succeeded in reading them, thus coming very close to the truth: I had learned that Atto had lied to me about the three cardinals. But then the poetic supplications to Maria, who still had not arrived at Villa Spada, had confused my mind.

Yet, even as he wrote those lines of love, the Abbot knew full well that she would never be attending the festivities! And the fact of having penned those heartfelt verses was not caused by surprise at her delays but by the pain of knowing her to be so near, so very near, yet out of reach because of the very mission that had brought them both to Villa Spada. The two worlds continued to co-exist side by side.

I would have preferred not to discover any of these things, I thought to myself in the now declining late afternoon light. If the Abbot had not given in to tardy and pointless scruples of conscience in regard to me (after having put my life in peril time and time again!) he would not have felt impelled to flee and, as he had promised me, we should have gone together to the notary for the donation of my little daughters' dowries.

I wanted to go and flush him out him in Paris, the renegade. In an involuntary gesture, my fist hit out in the void in search of Atto's jaw.

"You'd like to avenge yourself, young man, is that not so?" asked Albicastro, reappearing before me as he modulated a *staccato* variant on his *folia* on the violin.

"I should like to live in peace."

"So what's preventing you? Do as young Telemachus did."

"Again that Telemachus," I burst out. "You and Abbot Melani. . ."

"If you live like Telemachus, whose name literally means 'far-away fighter', you'll live in peace," chanted the Dutchman, matching his syllables to the rhythm of his music.

"'Tis a clever man who can understand you. . ." I murmured in response to the lucubrations of that bizarre individual.

"Telemachus pulled on the bowstring, but his father Ulysses, in disguise, gestured that he should desist and stopped his hand," Albicastro recounted, passing on to a new variation on the theme of the *folia*. "And then Telemachus said to the suitors: 'It may be that I am too young, and have as yet no trust in my hands to defend me from such a one as does violence without a cause. But come now, ye who are mightier men than I, essay the bow and let us make an end of the contest!' Do you know what that means? Young Telemachus could perfectly well have drawn his father's bow. But vengeance was not his to take. Thus, you too, arm yourself with patience and let the Lord do as He will. Look, my son," he continued in gentler tones, "this world of ours, which has gone on since Homer's day and perhaps even long before that, is the world of folly, of the 'far-away fight': the Last Day has not yet come, that in which, amidst laughter and jesting, Ulysses' fatal bow will be drawn. But let us not ask ourselves how far off that day may be," he warned, and then recited:

> *Jerusalem fell to the ground,*
> *For whom our Lord had so long waited;*
> *And Niniveh likewise was fated:*
> *When Jonah warned, they quit their debt*
> *And sought no longer term to get;*
> *But later still they lapsed again –*
> *No Jonah came to warn them then.*
> *Thus everything has term and measure*
> *And goes its way at God's own pleasure.*

Once again, I found myself listening, two years later, to the rhymes of that poem, *The Ship of Fools*. The verses seemed to fit every one of the experiences I had lived through, from the Vessel to the *cerretani*.

"Sooner or later, I shall read that book by your well-beloved Brant," I reflected aloud.

"While we await the coming of the time," Albicastro went on, quite unperturbed, "let us live and love! And may the threats of the suitors be worth less than a ha'penny's worth for us. Go back home, my son, embrace your family, and leave off all those thoughts. The folly of he who loves, said Plato, is the most blessed of all."

I wondered whether Albicastro, with all those obscure sayings of his, did not perhaps belong to some obscure heretical sect. One true thing he had, however, said: I should bury the past and return home. Avoiding any further comment, I bowed and began to walk away.

"Adieu, my son; we shall not meet again," he replied, for the first time at the Vessel beginning a piece other than the *folia*.

He surprised me, and I came to a stop; the music was tormented and nervous, evoking a sense of some imminent menace. With sharp, repeated bowing, Albicastro was wresting from his instrument all the tragedy which these things can sometimes unleash, transcending their laughable dimensions, that little wooden carcass with its four gut strings.

"Will you be returning home?" I asked him.

"I am off to the wars. I am going to enrol in the Dutch army," he replied, drawing near, while the rhythmic hammering of that hard and almost obsessional motif spoke of cannonades, drums, forced marches through the mud.

"And what then of your far-away fighting?" I asked after a moment's surprise.

"I name you my successor," said he solemnly, breaking off from his playing and touching my shoulder with his bow in a gesture of investiture. "Besides. . ." he laughed before turning his back on me and walking towards the gate, "you earn good money in the armies of Holland!"

I gave up trying to understand whether or how much he was jesting. He moved off with his violin on his shoulder, then began yet another piece of music: a melancholy adagio, an utterly pure vocal line on which the Flying Dutchman's bow improvised trills and turns, appoggiaturas and mordents, delicate *florilèges* of a melody which, better than any earthly leave-taking (for music is not something merely human) bid farewell at the same time, to me, to the Vessel, to peace, and to times past.

ॐ⳩

And now I too could be on my way. I made a last tour of the gardens of the Vessel. Once again, the wind rose, uncovering the fiery face of the sun.

The weather had suddenly become almost spring-like, and it felt as though someone had turned back the clock's hands by a couple of hours. I was moving towards the entrance, when my attention was caught by a rustling of clothes and trills of light laughter.

It was then that I saw her. Behind a thick hedge, as when first we had caught sight of her: a delicate screen which enabled one to see without being seen, to know without knowing.

This time they were old; not mature, old. Wrinkled faces, hoarse voices, hooded eyelids. Nonetheless, they seemed as gay as when Atto and I had beheld them from the first-floor windows, at the age of twenty. They walked side by side, bent but smiling, commenting on some bagatelle; she gave him her arm.

I held my breath. I wanted to draw closer, to understand whether I had really seen what I thought I had. I looked for a break in the hedge, tried to make my way around it, changed my mind again, turned back and looked once more.

Too late. If they had been there, they were now elsewhere.

I did not await their return. I knew from experience that there would be no such returning.

I thought one last time of Albicastro. He was leaving that abandoned villa, which in reality was so overflowing with life, to throw himself into the world's turmoil, now nothing but wars and destruction. I remembered what he had told me two years before: just like the Sileni of Alcibiades, the clumsy statuettes which conceal divine images within, what seems death, is living, and correspondingly, what seems life is death.

Leaving the Vessel, I realised that the sky had again taken a turn for the worse: the light had suddenly become opaque and crepuscular.

I felt the skin on my arms grow rough with disquiet. I knew, however, that in that place, time could become a vortex and turn back on itself. So why be surprised if the wind and the leaves, the clouds and the sun accompanied the dance?

ॐ

"What has happened to you? I've been looking for you for hours!"

I was as pale as a shroud. Worried and surprised, Cloridia took me in her loving arms. She had come to meet me on the way home.

Without drawing breath, I explained to her all that I had just seen; she smiled.

"Your Abbot would speak of fantasies, of hallucinating exhalations or even of some trick, and perhaps he'd start quoting from one of those little treatises on physics that are so fashionable now."

"And what do you think?" I asked, thinking of the trick with the camphor in Ugonio's lair, which had made me believe I was dead.

"I think that you've seen, or imagined, what would have happened if the King of France and Maria Mancini had not been separated; they'd have grown old side by side."

"So, once again, I've witnessed in the Vessel the good things that might have happened and never did," said I. "But why did I never see what bad things might happen?"

"I could put it like this. First: this villa provides a refuge only for what should *rightly* have happened but which did not take place because of. . . let's call it a 'distortion' of history, a deviation from the natural order of things."

"And the second reason?" I asked, seeing that Cloridia had interrupted her train of thought.

"I could, I repeat, I *could* use big words and explain to you that the good, all that's right and good, really does exist – just that. It issues from God the Creator, so it exists, in the highest sense of the term. And it continues to exist even when, in the arena of things terrestrial, it must give way to overwhelming malign forces. This is because the good is pure and incorruptible affirmation and it is not possible for it not to exist. Thus it is never annihilated. And you may be sure that, in other times and under other guises, it will reappear."

"And evil?"

"You know perfectly well that I detest philosophy. But, here too, I could quote Saint Augustine of Hippo: Evil is negation. Unlike the good, it does not exist in itself, but only as the destruction of what is right and good. Therefore, when evil that's planned is defeated by the good, it goes nowhere, but disappears utterly. In other words, even its deceitful appearance disappears, the empty husk which misled men. That is why you will never find a place like the Vessel which provides a receptacle for bad intentions or evil plans left unrealised."

I looked at her in some perplexity: she was talking as though all this were the most natural thing in the world. We covered the rest of the way home in silence.

"For you women, everything's so obvious!" I sighed, when we reached the yard of our farm and I removed the shoes given me by

Atto, exchanging them for my peasant's clogs. "You'd not be surprised if you saw a donkey fly."

"Perhaps that's because, as you men say, we've less brains than you," said my wife, taking off her coat and removing the blue ribbon from her hair.

"No, I meant that you are always so much wiser than us."

"It was no accident that a woman, not a man, crushed the serpent's head with her bare foot," added Cloridia. "Mind you, I only said that I *could* tell you all these things. . ."

"So, what are you telling me then?"

"I'm telling you that you've simply had a hallucination. A product of your imagination. Good for a novel, I'd say."

Dear Alessio,

Now that you will have reached the end of my two friends' text, kindly permit me a brief leavetaking.

This time, I needed undertake no research to verify the authenticity of the events narrated: along with the typescript, I received a disc containing all the pieces of music mentioned therein and an appendix of documentary proofs. This is just as well: from the place I am in, I should certainly have been in no position to conduct any such investigation, let alone to trace a recording of Albicastro's fascinating but unknown *folia*, or even an aria from *The Faithful Shepherd*.

To you, I leave the pleasure of checking on whether the content of what you have just read is true. The task is far less demanding than you might fear. Besides, the unknown performers of the music on the disc will keep you good company.

As you will read in the pages that follow, Rita and Francesco commissioned two graphologists to examine the signature on the will of Charles II of Spain. The result is unequivocal: it is a forgery.

Enough of that, I shall disclose nothing else to you. Rather, you will still be expecting an answer to another question: why did I send this to you? Simply because in Rome, so close to the Holy Father, it will surely be of more use than here, in the hands of a poor bishop reduced to the humble role of a parish priest in far-off Tomi. But do not waste your time whisking your fine soutane through the inner corridors and the back rooms of power: that would lead nowhere. Permit me here to remind you of that warning by Ovid, the Latin poet who is my companion in misfortune, as quoted by Atto Melani:

"Thy lot is mortal, but thy wishes fly / Beyond the province of mortality."

I am confident that your person will in the end bring good fortune to my two friends. "How could that be?" you will no doubt be asking yourself sarcastically, but also – this I know – with some disquiet.

The answer is in the mind of God, *quem nullum latet secretum.*

Documentary Proofs

✠

The signature of Charles II of Spain

If it is true that Charles II's signature was forged, the question arises: what would have happened if the fraud had not been perpetrated?

There would have been no War of the Spanish Succession; or perhaps the alliances involved in the conflict would have been different, as would its outcome. Perhaps the Spanish Empire would have been peacefully subdivided among the various powers, as provided for in the partition treaty. France, by avoiding a tremendous conflict, would have maintained its position of predominance on the continent, and perhaps even the revolutionary events of 1789 would have taken on another character, or would have taken place at a later date, or been less violent. Europe would probably, at the end of military operations, have assumed a very different form. Perhaps the whole course of subsequent history would have been radically different. And today, there would not be a Bourbon on the Spanish throne.

How does one establish whether a signature is false? That's obvious. One calls in a graphologist; or rather, two.

There are authentic signatures of Charles II in the archives of most of the great cities of Europe, where the diplomatic correspondence of the kings of Spain with their ambassadors and with other sovereigns is kept. Here are five signatures of Charles II, penned at various times during his short life:

1677   1679   1687

1689   1700

And here is the signature on his will, kept in Spain in the General Archives of Simancas:

Even an untrained eye can see that this firm, sure, agile signature cannot be that of a chronic invalid like Charles II who, in the last months of his life, was almost constantly bedridden and worn out by illness (the will is supposed to have been signed less than a month before his death). The other signatures are uncertain, irregular and sometimes shaky. The closer he drew to death, the more tremulous they become. Incredibly, the last of all, that of the will, when Charles was a hair's breadth from the end, was penned with the grace and insouciance of a boy.

But laymen can be wrong. Therefore, two expert graphologists were called in, both frequently consulted by the courts: one comes from the neighbourhood of Verona, the other from Naples. Both were, obviously, kept in the dark about each other's identity.

The first response came from the north. Dr Marina Tonini wrote:

> . . . *comparison between the signature in question (X), dated 3 October 1700, and that dated April 1700 must inevitably give rise to serious doubts as to the authenticity of the signature to the will. It will, moreover, be observed that, in the signature dated April 1700, the "l" is totally absent from the word "el" in "yo el Rey". This phenomenon is, moreover, entirely consistent with the seriously disturbed grapho-motricity which appears in the text of A5. At this point, one may legitimately wonder whether the subject was capable of performing a simultaneously gentle and flexible movement, as contained in the signature to the will.*
>
> *Therefore, on the basis of the foregoing observations, and within the limits arising from the availability only of photostat copies, it is legitimate to conclude that in all probability the signature to the will was not written by the hand that penned the authentic signatures.*

The expression "in all probability" shows that Dr Tonini had to leave a technical margin of uncertainty, as is often the practice among graphologists, because she did not have the original of any of the signatures to hand, but only photographs and photocopies. This obstacle was, moreover, impossible to circumvent, since the letters from which they were taken were in Spain and Austria.

Something else was needed, and this came with the other expert's report, that of the Neapolitan lawyer and judicial graphologist, Andrea Faiello. Here, luck played a part: from the days of his university studies, Faiello had been familiar with the affair of the Spanish succession, as well as being familiar with his city's historical archives. Consequently, there was a marked advance in the case, in relation to the already meticulous examination performed by Dr Tonini. Faiello went in person to the Naples State Archives in order directly to view other signatures of Charles II on original documents. This enabled him to evaluate the whole matter more comprehensively. And here is the result:

In the signature to the will, according to Faiello's expert report,

. . . all signs of "writing in bed" *are completely absent. These should include frequent superpositions, tremors, jostling, revisions and, in general, signs of growing tiredness in the hand [. . .] (a tiredness which should be all the more evident given the state of health of Charles II at the time when the signature is supposed to have been made. . .).*

Instead, the writing "flows" (graphic sign: "flowing writing", *meaning the kind of writing which runs confidently to the right, with a tendency for the graphic trait to move horizontally rather than vertically, regardless of the haste or calm of the movement itself or of the care or carelessness with which the letters are written – forward-moving tendency: impetuosity, dynamic feelings and willpower).*

Moreover, one notes the presence of the graphic sign: "agile writing" *associated with writing in which the letters or parts of letters are not aligned on the real or imaginary base line but jump up or down [. . .]. By comparison with the writing which is of certain authenticity, there is an obvious deformation in the "slot" (the space between the "staff" – the descending trait, and the hair stroke – ascending trait) between the first development of the final "paraph"* [meaning: the seal] *of the signature and the corresponding elements in the comparative writings. The slot in question is unquestionably narrower than those, which remain constant, of the signatures left by Charles at various times in his life and with the development of the various complex pathologies which debilitated him to the point of causing his death. This paraph is also different as regards the angles of the staffs and hair strokes.*

The overall trait appears, moreover, to be substantially free from blots, alterations, smudges, thickening, hesitations and retouching of the line. Both the endings of the letters and the beginnings are traced with a fluidity of execution unquestionably attributable to a physical state different from that of the Sovereign and to a practiced hand producing letters by means of the same morphological processes.

CONCLUSIONS

The undersigned, in a calm state of mind and with all scrupulousness, concludes as follows:

The person who penned the signature at the foot of the last will and testament dated 3 October 1700 presents none of the characteristics of the autographs authentically signed by Charles II Habsburg;

The signature in question is therefore spurious.

So it is true. Charles II's will, in which he named Philip of Anjou, the grandson of Louis XIV, as his heir, was never signed by Charles himself. Perhaps he signed another will, which was subsequently destroyed, leaving the throne to an Austrian Habsburg. But that is mere speculation. Only one fact is certain: the House of Bourbon came illegitimately to the Spanish throne and its present occupant sits there on the basis of a forged will. It might be argued that Francisco Franco, after the Second World War, organised the return to the throne of King Juan Carlos de Bourbon. But Franco only chose a direct descendant of Philip V, a Bourbon, still enjoying the consequences of that false signature.

The two experts' reports were deposited at a notary's practice:

Dr Stefan Prayer
Notariat Dr Wiedermann und Dr Prayer
Vivenotgasse 1/7
A-1120 Vienna (Austria)
Tel. +43-1-813 13 56
Fax +43-1-813 13 56 23

Anyone may consult these two experts' reports, either by going in person or by asking to be sent an authenticated photocopy at their own expense. Thus, one can, so to speak, literally touch with one's hand this particular flagrant deception – one among the many that have muddied human affairs.

The authentic signatures analysed come from:

1677: Vienna, Haus- Hof- und Staatsarchiv, Spanien, Hofkorrespondenz
    7 (Fasz.10), c. 1
1679: *ibid.*, c. 12
1687: Pfandl, L., *Karl II – Das Ende der spanischen Machtstellung in
    Europa*, Munich 1940, p. 176
1689: Vienna, Haus- Hof- und Staatsarchiv, Spanien, Diplomatische
    Korrespondenz 59, c. 503
1700: Pfandl, *op. cit.*, p. 448

Dr Faiello also examined personally the following original signatures of Charles II kept in the Naples Historical Archives:

Archivio "Giudice Carracciolo di Villa"; settore Pergamene, busta n.
    134
Archivio "Sanseverino di Bisognano"; settore Pergamene, busta n. 29
Archivio "Giudice di Cellamare"; settore Pergamene, busta n. 94,
    doc. n. 15

The will of Charles II is deposited in Spain in the General Archives of Simancas, Estado K, busta 1684, n. 12.

An opinion or a mediation?

Nothing but a clear and orderly description of the facts could clarify the conspiracy whereby the three most powerful cardinals of the moment (the Secretary for Breves, Cardinal Albani; the Secretary of State, Cardinal Fabrizio Spada; and the Chamberlain, Cardinal Spinola) bypassed the authority of the aged Pope Innocent XII and sent the King of Spain the advice to name a French heir. This was a necessary precondition for the falsification in Spain of Charles's will, since the latter wanted to be succeeded by a Habsburg. The two spurious documents, the false papal opinion and the false will of Charles II, were designed to corroborate one another. A perfect crime, and everyone was taken in. Until now.

❧

It all began in the spring of 1700, when it was first rumoured that Charles II had drawn up a will in favour of a member of the House of Habsburg: the Archduke of Austria, the fifteen-year-old son of Emperor Leopold I.

On 27th March of that year, the Papal Nuncio to Madrid wrote to Rome: "It is probable that the King will choose as his successor a prince of his own blood, one from the House of Austria, and not a Frenchman." It seems, then, that Charles still had it in mind to appoint a member of the House of Habsburg (Landau, M., *Wien, Rom und Neapel. Zur Geschichte des Kampfes zwischen Papsttum und Kaisertum.* Leipzig 1884, p. 455, no. 1).

As Maria tells in her letters to Atto (cf. Klopp, O., *Der Fall des Hauses Stuart,* VIII, Vienna 1879, p. 496 *et seq.*), at this point, Charles II asked his cousin Leopold I to send his younger son, the Archduke of Austria, from Vienna to Madrid. He even had a naval squadron made ready in the port of Cadiz, to go and collect the Archduke. It was clear that Charles would make him his heir. However, the Most Christian King intervened; as soon as he learned the news, through his ambassador, he sent a message to Charles II to inform him that he would consider such a decision as a formal breaking of the peace. He at once had a fleet far more powerful than the Spanish one made ready at Toulon, to intercept and bombard the ship bringing the Archduke of Austria to Spain. Leopold did not dare make his son run such risks. Charles II then suggested that the Archduke should be sent to the Spanish territories in Italy. But Leopold I hesitated: after years of fighting against the Turks in the east, the Empire was unwilling to bleed its subjects in its defence. This, the King of France knew. Louis had, moreover, understood that the time had come to strike the decisive blow; in order to scare the Spaniards even more, he made public the secret pact for dividing their kingdom into which he had entered two years previously with Holland and England. Charles II rushed back to Madrid from the Escorial in dismay. The court was in a state of emergency: the Council of State was afraid of France and was ready to accommodate a grandson of the Most Christian King as heir, rather than risk a French invasion.

On Sunday 6th June, the Spanish Council of State decided to ask Louis XIV to name a grandson to be heir to the kingdom (Landau, *ibid.*) On 13th June, Charles II asked the Pope for help (cf. Galland, "Die Papstwahl des Jahres 1700 in Zusammenhang mit den damaligen kirchlichen und politischen Verhältnissen", in *Historisches Jahrbuch der Görres-Gesellschaft*, III (1882), p. 226, and Pfandl, L., *Karl II... op cit.*, p. 442). At the same time, Charles II wrote to his cousin, the Emperor Leopold, in Vienna, informing him that he had asked the Pope for a mediation and attaching a copy of the letter sent to the Pontiff.

At the conference of ministers called in Vienna to discuss the matter, the purpose of the request was described as follows: "Concerning the letter from the King of Spain, he writes that he has referred to the Pope for mediation." (The original says *remissio ad mediationem*: cf. protocol of the conference of the Imperial Council of 6th July 1700, Vienna, Haus-, Hof- und Staatsarchiv, *Geheime Conferenzprotokolle*, Conferentia vom 6 Juli 1700. Cf. also Gaedeke, A., *Die Politik Österreichs in der spanischen Erbfolgefrage*, Leipzig 1877, II, pp. 188–89).

The letter containing the request for mediation was materially present at this conference of the Imperial Council on 6th July, and was annexed to the minutes; however, it disappeared at the end of the nineteenth century: Klopp sought it in vain in the State Archives of Vienna where it was supposed to be (O. Klopp, *Der Fall... op cit.*, VIII, p. 504 no. 1).

That was not all. In Rome, on 24th July, after a long wait, Lamberg was at long last granted an audience with the Pope. On the matter of the Spanish succession, the Holy Father cut the interview short, saying, according to Lamberg, that: "Since he cannot have dealings with the Prince of Orange, [in other words, the Protestant English King William III] nor could he interpose his mediation (cf. Lamberg, L. v., *Relazione istorica umiliata alla maestà dell'augustissimo imperatore Leopoldo I*, Vienna, Nationalbibliothek, p. 30). Lamberg then reminded the Pope that the English and Dutch entered into the question only indirectly. The principal problem was in fact France. The Pope replied: "This is a wretched business. But what can we do? *We are denied the dignity which is due to the Vicar of Christ and there is no care for us.*"

What is the Pope referring to here? In all probability, to the men closest to him: first of all, Spada, his Secretary of State, then the Secretary for Breves, Albani, and the Chamberlain, Spinola di San Cesareo; those best placed to undermine his authority and manoeuvre on their own behalf. By then, however, the falsified opinion had already left for Spain.

When it did, however, reach Madrid, the Pope's opinion did not change Charles II's mind. According to the protocols of the conferences of ministers in Vienna on 23rd and 24th August 1700 (Vienna, Haus-, Hof- und Staatsarchiv, *Geheime Conferenzprotokolle* of 23rd and 24th August. Cf. also Redlich, O.,

Geschichte Österreichs, Gotha 1921, VI, p. 503), Charles is reported to have sent a message via the imperial envoy to Madrid, Ludwig Harrach, restating his unaltered intention to keep the Spanish monarchy entirely in the hands of the House of Habsburg. On 10th September, Charles is reported to have gone on to express to the Council of State his disapproval of the pressures which the Council itself was exercising on him to appoint a French prince. Charles II was very sick, almost handicapped, but among his few clear ideas were doubtless those with which he had been brought up: to leave his kingdom to another Habsburg because, as he himself put it, "only a Habsburg is worthy of a Habsburg".

Nor was that the end of the matter. Charles also wrote to his ambassador in Vienna, Duke Moles (Ottieri, F.M., *Istoria delle guerre avvenute in Europa per la successione alla Monarchia delle Spagne*, Rome 1728, I, p. 391), ordering him to assure the Emperor that his heir would be a Habsburg.

It was quite clear to everyone that the Spanish King, although weak and ill, would never have signed a will in favour of France. There was only one solution: such a will had, of course, to be signed; but by someone else. That is what happened.

Speed record

Even the manner in which the Papal opinion was drawn up is noteworthy.

On 3rd July, the Spanish Ambassador, the Duke of Uzeda, was received in audience by Innocent XII. The fact is surprising, since Uzeda had only just been received the day before. He brought with him a signed letter from the King of Spain dated 13th June, which had just been delivered to him by urgent courier: it was a request from the Spanish monarch to the Pope.

Marshal Tessé (de Fralay, R., *Mémoires*, Paris 1806, I, p. 178) reports what Uzeda told him about that audience in 1708: initially, the Pope made difficulties; he had refused to express an opinion on so delicate a matter and yielded to Uzeda's pressing requests only after the latter had submitted to him the views of jurists and theologians (Landau, p. 452 *et seq*.) By that time, Uzeda had already gone over to the French side, but was still pretending to be a friend of the Empire, and of Lamberg, as the latter was to discover too late (cf *Relazione*, p. 8). To convince the Pope to write a reply to the King of Spain, Uzeda enlisted the help of the three men closest to the Pontiff: Secretary of State Spada, Secretary for Breves Albani and Chamberlain Spinola di San Cesareo (Landau p. 453, quoting Tessé).

On 12th July, the old Pope gave in. Lamberg (*Relazione, ibid.*) was to note later that, on that day, Uzeda "was lacking in the principal respect and [. . .] contravened the faith which *sanctissimum in humani pectoris bonum est*". On 14th July, the Pontiff officially appointed the three cardinals as members of the congregation responsible for drafting an opinion (*ibid.*, p. 23).

On 16th July, the Pope's reply was dispatched to Charles II (Voltaire, *Le Siècle de Louis XIV*, Lione 1791, II, p. 180).

Thus, it took the three cardinals only two days, from 14th to 16th July, to decide the Spanish succession. It would have been reasonable to expect that, faced with so burning an issue, the three cardinals should have held meetings among themselves and, at the very least, consulted jurists, historians, experts in dynastic law, and so on. It would have been reasonable to expect that the process of hearing, weighing up and drafting conclusions, should take a few days, not to say a week or two. As it was, Albani, Spada and Spinola wrapped the whole thing up in barely forty-eight hours: "The opinion, issued following lengthy and serious consultations, [sic!] was accepted by the Pope and his reply was dictated by Cardinal Albani to a scribe sworn to secrecy and sent to Madrid by urgent courier." (Galland, p. 226, as cited by Ottieri and Polidori, P., *Vita Clementis XI*, Urbino 1727, p. 40).

The opinion of the Holy See on the fate of the world was drawn up in no time. An old, sick Pope, who was to die not long afterwards, and one of the least efficient bureaucracies in Europe had, incredibly, beaten all speed records. Does that seem strange? The fact remains that historians have believed the tale to this day.

Only rare, timid, voices have dared advance the suspicion that the Pope's opinion was misappropriated. Among these exceptions, the Spanish historian Dominguez Ortiz writes: "The original of the Pope's reply is unknown and there is a suspicion that the opinion (favourable to the French succession) issued by the three cardinals may have been falsified." (Dominguez Ortiz, A., "Regalismo y relaciones Iglesia-Estado en en siglo XVII", in *Historia de la Iglesia en la España de los siglos XVII y XVIII*, volume IV of the *Historia de la Iglesia en la España*, Madrid 1979, pp. 88–89; cit. in Menéndez Pidal, R., *Historia de España*, Madrid 1994, XVIII, p. 155).

In any case, there was no difficulty in manipulating or counterfeiting the Pope's reply: Innocent XII did not sign documents personally. It is interesting to note that Albani, his successor, behaved very differently, once elected Pope under the name Clement XI: "The number of documents drafted or corrected by Clement XI [. . .] is surprisingly high. Few popes have written as much and therefore no other Pope's autographs have been preserved in such large numbers." (Pastor, L. v., *Geschichte der Päpste*, Freiburg 1930, XV, p. 10). Perhaps Albani feared that some over-zealous cardinal might interfere with his writings, as he had done with those of his predecessor.

Disappearance of the proofs

Obviously, it would have been easy to demonstrate clearly, once and for all, that Charles requested a mediation and not an opinion, if Charles's request and the Pope's reply had come down to us. Instead, despite the importance of those missives, not so much as a line remains. It was, however, corroborated at the time that there existed at least three copies of Charles's request and two of Innocent XII's reply: all have completely vanished. The coincidence must inevitably cast a heavy veil of suspicion over the whole affair.

Here is the list of disappearances:

The original request sent by Charles II and the copy of the reply given by Innocent XII both disappeared from the secret archives of the Vatican in Rome, yet should, according to the Vatican archivists, have been in their place (the disappearance had been noticed in the nineteenth century: cf. Galland, p. 228, no. 5).

In the General Archives of Simancas in Spain, both the copy of the missive from Charles II and the original of the reply given by Innocent XII are missing (in 1882, the director of the Spanish archive had reported their disappearance: cf. Galland, *ibid.*)

As has already been mentioned, the copy of Charles II's letter sent by Charles in person to the Emperor Leopold I is missing from the Vienna State Archives. (This too was known to be missing in the mid-nineteenth century: cf. Galland, *ibid.*, verified in person. Klopp, too, could find no trace of it: cf. *Der Fall. . .* cit., VIII, p. 504, no. 1).

Lastly, there is no longer any trace in the archives of the Ministry of Foreign Affairs in Paris of the two apocryphal versions of the letters found and published by C. Hippeau (*Avénement des Bourbons au trone d'Espagne*, Paris 1875, II, pp. 229–30 and 233–34). Both of them soon disappeared and no historian apart from Hippeau can claim to have seen them.

There is practically no European capital from which there has not been some strange disappearance.

A brief word about the two apocryphal letters republished by Hippeau: in 1702, there circulated in Italy in a leaflet the presumed letter from Charles II, together with the reply from Innocent XII, according to which the Pope advised Charles to name a French heir. Lamberg (Klopp, *ibid.*) went to see Albani when he had already become Pope Clement XI and asked him to explain these, seeing that he had personally headed the famous congregation for the Spanish succession.

Albani told him that in those letters ". . . there is some small truth, but much that is false. . . and suffice to say that in truth neither the request by Charles II nor the reply by Innocent XII were precisely as stated in the leaflet."

The Pope then authorised Lamberg to print and publish his words (Klopp, *ibid.*; Galland, p. 229, no. 5).

Despite the Pope's public disclaimer, the two apocryphal letters were (perhaps for want of anything better) taken for valid by a number of eighteenth-century historians. Among other things, these documents gave the date of dispatch of the opinion as 6th July, and not 16th. In the centuries that followed, this gave rise to a long series of errors in the chronological reconstruction of the facts, the effects of which can be felt in many history manuals.

Pope Albani and Atto Melani

The newly elected Pope Albani wasted no time in expressing his gratitude to Atto. Barely two months after his election to the pontificate, he instructed Cardinal Paolucci, Secretary of State, to write to Monsignor Gualtieri, the Papal Nuncio in France, a letter full of appreciation for Melani, with the promise that he would, at the earliest opportunity, return the favours which the latter had rendered him (Florence, Biblioteca Marucelliana, Manoscritti Melani, 3, c. 280):

Our Lord is well informed of the advantageous reputation which Signor Abbot Melani enjoys at this Court and of the good use to which he puts this in such a way as duly to contribute to the service of this Holy See and of its Ministers and, having at various times received certain testimonials thereof from the latter [. . .], not only does His Holiness gratefully remember these things, but he deigns to show himself most willing to reward the good works of the said Signor Abbot with acts of his paternal benevolence on such occasions as may prove favourable to the interests of the latter's household here.

In the State Archives of Florence (Fondo Mediceo del Principato, filza 4807) many other testimonials are to be found to the unceasing attention with which, in the months preceding his departure for Villa Spada, Abbot Melani followed the health of the dying Pope and the movements of the various cardinals with a view to the forthcoming conclave. On 4th and 8th January, he wrote to Gondi, Secretary to the Grand Duke of Tuscany, that Louis XIV had ordered all the French cardinals to leave for Rome on about 20th January so as to be present at the conclave. Then, on 25th of the same month, he reports that many cardinals did not leave for Rome, having received the news that the Pope's health was "constantly going from good to better"; other French cardinals had, however, set out before receipt of these tidings.

Atto had, moreover, been perfectly aware for months that the old Pope had effectively been stripped of his power by various cardinals among his collaborators, despite the fact that, in his letter to the Connestabilessa, he candidly denied such rumours. On 1st February 1700, he wrote to Gondi:

However much the Cardinals at the Palace may strive to conceal the truth, we are informed that his spirit [that of Innocent XII] varies greatly and that the distribution of responsibilities to various prelates has been arranged by themselves, although people believe that His Holiness is still able to work.

OF COURSE, THE REST IS ALSO TRUE. . .

Maria and Louis

Atto Melani really was a bosom friend of Maria Mancini, as well as an admirer of her famous sisters. One of these, Ortensia, in her memoirs (*Mémoires d'Hortense et de Marie Mancini*, ed. Doscot, Mercure de France, Paris 1965, p. 33) recounts that "an Italian eunuch, a musician of Monsieur le Cardinal, a man of great wit" paid court to "both my sisters and me". She adds that ". . . the eunuch, her [i.e. Maria Mancini's] confidant, who fell out of favour owing to his absence and to the death of Monsieur le Cardinal, undertook to make himself indispensable to me; [. . .] This man had kept rather free access to the King from the days when he was my sister's confidant [i.e. Maria again]" (*cit.* in Weaver, R.L., "Materiali per le biografie dei fratelli Melani", in *Rivista italiana di Musicologia*, XII (1977), p. 252 *et seq.*)

Maria's letters to Atto, in which the Connestabilessa also addresses the Sun King, using the pseudonyms "Silvio" and "Lidio", really do exist. They were discovered by the authors in Paris, together with the reports which Maria sent Atto from Spain on the imminence of the War of the Spanish Succession. These reports provide a detailed picture of Maria's activities as a source of information. Her French contact was always Atto, who reported to Louis's ministers, presenting, explaining and commenting on his friend's reports (Maria's letters and Atto's related writings are in C.P. Rome Suppl.10 – Lettres de l'abbé Melani, in ms. pp. 120, 185, 187, 206, 222, 259, 281, 282, 285).

While carrying out this dangerous work, Maria seems to have kept Louis's image clearly before her eyes: as when she writes to Atto from Toledo on 9th August 1701 (ms. p. 285 et seq.), confessing to him, when observing Philip V: "I feel so tender when I see him, remembering his grandfather when he was his age".

Hitherto, no one knew of this forty-year long correspondence between Atto Melani and Maria Mancini, even less of the coded allusions to Louis XIV contained therein. Because of this, among the numerous and well-documented biographies of Maria Mancini (from Perey, L., [pseudonym of Luce Herpin], *Une princesse romaine au XVIIe siècle*, Paris 1896, to Dulong, C., *Marie Mancini*, Paris 1980), none has until now touched upon her real, decisive role in the King's life.

Unknown until today, and discovered by the authors in the Biblioteca Marucelliana in Florence (Manoscritti Melani 9, pp. 157–58r) is the farewell letter which Maria wrote to the Sovereign and which Atto delivered to him secretly, as told by the Abbot himself on Evening the Fourth. In reality, Atto did far more than take a look at that letter: before handing it to his king, he copied it carefully. And this is most fortunate, as it is the only surviving love letter between Maria Mancini and Louis XIV. The letter, originally written in French, copied and kept amongst Atto's personal correspondence, and prudently omitting date, sender and recipient, is simply and allusively entitled "Lettre tendre", or tender letter, and the identity of Maria Teresa, Infanta of Spain, the King's future wife, is concealed under the pseudonym Eleonor:

I take my leave of you, Sire, and I write to you from the same palace where we both still are, and from which we are both about to depart. The ways we shall be taking are very different: you are about to bring joy and love to the hearts of all your subjects in France; you are about to pledge your faith to a Queen, upon whom you will then bestow yourself. Ah, Sire! Could you ever have imagined that I should witness so sad a spectacle? By giving Eleonor your hand, you inflict the final blow against my life. Shall I live, my God? And see you on another's arm? You will perhaps say to me, Sire, that I myself counselled you to enter into this fatal marriage. Ah, Sire, you do not know that I always do pitilessly whatever my honour demands of me. But I have not suffered any the less for this. I can tell you that I give you back your freedom, your country, your peoples, and, cruellest of all, that I give you a Spouse. I had not claimed such an honour: perhaps I would have wished that it be destined to no one. I have indulged no illusions about this, but my fancies have nonetheless been extravagant. I have desired that you should be a plain gentleman. Had that been the case, I would have done more for you than you have done for me, in the plight in which I now find myself. What an idea, alas! It still pleases me at this very moment, while in the rest of my thoughts I can find nothing but horror and desperation. If when your wedding ceremony takes place I am still living, it will be only to spend the rest of my days in an austere place. Awful iron spikes, erect and terrible, will stand between you and me. My tears, my sobs, cause my hand to tremble. My imagination clouds over, I can write no longer. I know not what I say. Adieu, my Lord, the little life that remains to me will be sustained only by memories. O charming memories! What will you make of me, what shall I make of you? I am losing my reason. Adieu, my Lord, for the last time.

Innumerable clues suggest that, even in the last years of his life, the Sun King still thought, and thought intensely, of his first love. A few examples will suffice to illustrate this. One day, he instructed Philidor, one of the court musicians, to draw up an inventory of all the works performed during his reign. The two often spoke together of this: Philidor admitted that he had, however, been unable to note down Pan's tale in the *Ballet des Plaisirs*. The Sun King then sang the verses at once from memory. "He still remembers an air to which he had danced almost sixty years before and which he had probably whistled for an entire season, as was his wont, when accompanying his dear Maria on their walks on the terrace of the Tuileries or, even further away, towards the Renard gardens" (Combescot, P., *Les petites Mazarines*, Paris 1999, p. 402).

In 1702, a self-styled Capuchin father was arrested and taken to the Bastille, suspected of espionage. His gaoler, Lieutenant d'Argenson, found on him letters and a mass of locks of hair from his former mistresses, including ladies from the cream of society. Among these, Maria's name came to light. Blinded by the adventurer's ambiguous charm, she had, indeed, had a relationship with him and had even gone so far as to present him to the new King of Spain, Philip V.

Word of this reached the Sun King himself. Now, observe that the moment he heard that his former beloved had been among the Capuchin's conquests, he ordered that his interrogation should be taken to the limit. Maria, who was at that time in Avignon, learned of what had happened with disquiet; this might lead to her being accused of spying against France. But above all, she tried with trepidation to discover whether he too, the King, had learned of her liaison with the shady adventurer. Even in the face of far more pressing issues of espionage and trouble with the law, what preoccupied both her and the King was anxiety about what favours she might have accorded others and what he might have learned of this.

In 1705, after over forty years, Maria returned to Paris. Through the Duc d'Harcourt, she received from the King an invitation to visit Versailles and an offer of economic assistance. She turned both down. She was too proud to give in or to show her former beloved the mark of time on her own face. They did not meet, nor would they ever do so again.

Maria wanted to be buried in the place where she found death. So it was: she died on 8th May 1715 in Pisa, struck down by a sudden indisposition. In accordance with her will, the epitaph on her tombstone was *pulvis et cinis*, dust and ashes. The plaque is still visible today near to the high altar of the church of the Holy Sepulchre.

It took a month for the news to reach Rome, where her children were, and thence to spread throughout Europe, where it came to the ears of Paris and the Sun King. It may be a coincidence, but when Louis XIV heard the news, he fell ill. A few days later, the King left Versailles and moved to his residence at Marly. At Whitsuntide, the tidings changed: the surgeon Mareschal advised Madame de Maintenon that the Sovereign too was moving inexorably to his death. His spouse became agitated and silenced him. But Louis's condition worsened visibly until in August none could continue to deny the evidence: it was gangrene. He died on 1st September.

If Abbot Melani had not died the year before, at a great age, he might perhaps have observed with feeling: "Louis and Maria could not live alongside one another but they departed together."

The Faithful Shepherd, which Louis and Maria read together and from which the verses cited in their letters are drawn, was one of the greatest literary successes of the past few centuries. From the moment of its first performance at the court of Ferrara in 1598, it enjoyed an unusually wide throughout Europe right down to the eighteenth century.

At the court of France, there were several tapestries with scenes taken from Guarini's poem, including those of François de la Planche, otherwise known as van der Plancken, mentioned by Atto in the book, and those of his son Raphäel (cf. "L'objet d'art", May 2001, article on the exhibition of tapestries "Délices et Tourments" at the Galerie Blondeel-Deroyan in Paris). Even the words of thanks which Maria addressed to Fouquet in the gardens of the Vessel are authentic. The letter containing these words referred to by Atto Melani is kept in Paris (Bibliothèque Nationale, ms. Baluze 150, c. 237; cf. also Dulong, C., *op. cit.* p. 101).

The description of Maria Mancini, as she appears in her first apparation at the Vessel, is also authentic (cf. the description of her by an anonymous contemporary in the concluding letter contained in *Memorie della S.P.M.M. Colonna, connestabilessa del regno di Napoli*, Cologne 1678). Likewise, all the episodes and anecdotes concerning the Sun King's mistresses are true (cf. the innumerable writers of memoirs of the period and the exceedingly well-documented book by Simone Bertière, *Les Femmes du Roi-Soleil*, Paris 1998).

All Maria's accounts of Charles II and the Spanish court are historically documented (cf. Pfandl, L., *Karl II – Das Ende der spanischen Machtstellung*, Munich 1940).

Solon's prediction, which Maria Mancini cites in her letters to Atto ("For oftentimes God gives men a gleam of happiness, and then plunges them into ruin.") was to come true: between 1711 and 1712, almost all the descendants of the Most Christian King died. The Grand Dauphin, father of the Dauphin and son of His Most Christian Majesty, died in 1711. The following year it was the turn of Marie-Adelaide of Burgundy, His Majesty's granddaughter, the mother of two children, the last heirs to the throne. Marie-Adelaide died of smallpox aged just twenty-six on 12th February 1712. Her husband the Dauphin, devastated by the bereavement, fell ill in his turn and died six days later. Their two children followed: first, little Louis, a fine boy of five, died, drained by blood-letting, on 5th March. His younger brother fell ill too, but survived. He was only two years old, had not yet been weaned, and was only just beginning to talk.

Destiny then took its revenge on the man himself. The Most Christian King trembled: he was old and could not bear the thought of dying without an heir. So he turned to the King of Spain, the former Duke of Anjou who had come to the Spanish throne as Philip V. He remained, of course, Louis' grandson; indeed he owed him his crown. But Philip refused, openly disdaining the possibility of succeeding his grandfather, preferring to remain in Madrid and reign over his new country.

Worn down by mourning, sequestered in disconsolate silence, by a strange retribution of history he found himself in the same predicament as Charles II of Spain twelve years earlier: at the head of the most powerful kingdom in Europe, but without heirs. It was certainly not his little barely two-year-old great-grandson, vulnerable to any number of diseases, who could be counted on to continue the lineage and maintain the kingdom.

Louis was to prove fortunate, albeit posthumously: the child survived and succeeded him on the throne as Louis XV. But today, his dynasty is extinct (and the dynastic claimants to the throne are members of the Orleans line). The Bourbon dynasty in Spain, descended from Philip V, is, however, as fecund and prolific as ever (Juan Carlos has several brothers and children).

So, Capitor's last prophecy also came true: by means of the forged will of Charles II, Louis XIV had taken the crown of Spain from its legitimate heir. He did not foresee that, by means of that same will, the crown of Spain would rob France of its heirs.

On 29 July 1714, one of Abbot Melani's great fears came true: Louis XIV promulgated an edict opening up the succession to his bastard children. From that moment on, as Atto put it, it was no longer necessary to be a queen's son to become king: anyone, literally anyone, could do so. So that every citizen might well ask: why not me? The answer to this question was one day to be settled by the guillotine.

Atto and Maria

Abbot Melani really was in love with Maria Mancini, even as an old man, and so he was to remain to the day of his death. He stayed in close correspondence with her, yet was never to see her again. The pair sent each other frequent and precious gifts (like the Bezoar stone and the shell from the Indies in silver and gold) and Maria stayed several times as a guest at Atto's properties in Pistoia. She even went to visit his relatives.

The relationship, which was hitherto unknown, was discovered by the authors at the Biblioteca Marucelliana in Florence, to which the Ministry for Cultural Assets and Activities recently bestowed the nine volumes of Atto Melani's correspondence, acquired by the Italian state through an antique dealer. Maria Mancini's biographers had not previously known where she had spent the last years of her life: Atto's letters throw light on this too, showing that the Connestabilessa spent long periods at Atto's palazzo in Pistoia and, in summer, at his country residence.

This love, which lasted an entire lifetime, is evidenced by many letters from Atto: first, to his brother Jacopo and then to the latter's son Luigi, the heir to and continuer of the Melani line.

Even in the last letter which the old castrato wrote to his relatives on 27th November 1713, just a month before dying, his unrequited love for Maria still caused him to sigh (Bibl. Marucelliana, Manoscritti Melani, 3, pp. 423–24):

> *When I read your letter of the 4th of this month, I felt I must be dreaming, hearing that the Signora Connestabilessa is still at Pistoia.*

"I felt I must be dreaming. . .": moving and unexpected words on the lips of an old man of nearly ninety at the very end of his life. Maria made him dream to the very end. Then he was seized by the fear that his beloved might suffer from boredom during her stay in his palace at Pistoia:

> *"[. . .] I don't know what amusement you could have provided her with, unless she allowed visits by those ladies* [those of the Melani household] *to play a game of* hombre.

Maria had for years wandered throughout Italy, especially in Tuscany, often staying at Atto's home, while he was kept in France by the Sun King, who repeatedly rejected the old Abbot's requests to return a while to Pistoia. Atto could no longer bear the torment and was assailed by an overpowering desire to see his Connestabilessa again. He therefore decided, although he was already at the end of his strength, to journey to Versailles at the end of the winter, to go and beg the King in person:

> *Pray God that I may go to Versailles next April because I absolutely want to take my leave of the King in order to come to you, and intend to request two years' leave of absence.*

But destiny proved to be against him. Atto did not survive the winter. He died in his house in Paris on 4th January 1714.

Two years earlier, in a letter dated 27th June 1712 (Bibl. Marucelliana, Manoscritti Melani, 3, pp. 407-8) we find Maria at Atto's house, on the farm of Castel Nuovo in the Pistoia countryside. Here too, the octogenarian Abbot cannot conceal the excitement this news causes him and announces that he is sending a rich dressing gown as a gift for his friend:

> *I am most moved to hear that the Signora Connestabilessa has deigned to return to Pistoia, and I do hope that, during the great heat which I understand you have been having there, you will have enjoyed much of the good air at Castel Nuovo. The heat in these parts is so excessive that it has passed 33 degrees on the thermometer. . . At the earliest possible opportunity, I shall be sending the Signora Connestabilessa a dressing gown of ordinary taffeta, which was delivered to me by Madame la Duchesse de Nevers and is of her invention, so that she may make use of it if she likes this fashion.*

The Connestabilessa must by now have been at home with Atto's nephews: in a letter dated 3rd May 1712, the Grand Duke of Tuscany Cosimo III writes to Melani that she even went to see the Abbot's new-born great-nephew (Archivio di Stato di Firenze, Mediceo del Principato, filza 4813a):

> *I can tell you that the Signora Connestabilessa, who is in this city* [i.e. Florence] *heaped praises on your fine house and the villa you have in Pistoia, but far more so on the splendid little nephew whom God has bestowed on Your Worship, telling me that he looked like the little Child Jesus of Lucca.*

In the same correspondence (Bibl. Marucelliana, Manoscritti Melani, 3, pp. respectively 148–49; 156–57; 192–93), there also appear the Bezoar stone, useful against poison, and the little gold and silver seashell pill-box: Maria's two gifts which Atto has with him at Villa Spada:

Paris, 27th December 1694
Madama Colonna has sent me a very beautiful oriental Bezoar stone, as I had requested, to guard against the distempers with spotted fevers which have been prevalent around here during recent months.

Paris, 14th February 1695
Madama Colonna has sent me a stone which was given to the Queen Mother and is almost as big as a hen's egg. It is priceless, being a real oriental stone, and all the Nuncios returning from Spain try to obtain these, since they are highly regarded in cases of malignant fevers, as they provoke sweating, and are against poisons. This stone is to be found in the body of an animal, and I have been promised a paper on its properties.

Paris, 14th January 1696
[. . .] citron pastilles. Marchese Salviati gave me some of these in the past few days to put in a little gold and silver sea-shell which comes from the Indies, beautiful, as gorgeous as can be, and which was sent to me by Madama Colonna.

They were never to meet again, although in the end they seemed like a harmonious old couple. A fine walking stick of great value and cost, Atto writes proudly on 11th February 1697, was given him "by Madama Colonna, who paid eighty francs for it". He trusted her as he trusted no one else: when Maria recommended him medicinal remedies, the Abbot believed her so strongly as even to contradict his own nephews (7th December 1711).

Capitor, the portrait with the parrot, Virgilio Spada

The Bastard did in fact visit Paris in March 1659, bringing the madwoman Capitor in his retinue. It is also true that, immediately after this visit, Mazarin drastically changed his attitude towards Louis and Maria and did all in his power to separate them; no one has ever understood why.

The little song which Atto sings before Mazarin with Capitor is called "Passacalli della vita", by an anonymous author, published in *Canzonette spirituali e morali*, Milan, 1677.

The *Still Life with a Globe and a Parrot* by the Flemish painter Pieter Boel, which was among Capitor's gifts, is in Vienna at the Gemäldegalerie der Akademie für bildende Künste (inv. nr.757). Boel had only recently been living in Paris when Capitor's visit took place, and it is not surprising that he should have been able to paint the presents intended for Mazarin. The description in the book of the two marine deities depicted on the charger and of their strangely overlapping legs which do not seem to belong either to the one torso or the other, is completely faithful to the picture (visible on the Internet at the site: http://www.ruhr-uni-bochum.de/pressemitteilungen-2002/jpg00046.jpg).

The other depiction of Capitor's gifts (commissioned by the Bastard, according to Atto's tale) is a painting by Jan Davidszoon de Heem, formerly in the Koetser Collection and to be found today in the Kunsthaus at Zurich. It is interesting to note that this second painting contains the celestial globe (the counterpart of the terrestrial one given to Mazarin) and the goblet with a stem in the form of a centaur, but not the most important subject: the golden charger is half covered with a drapery, so that one can only see the team of sea horses drawing the chariot of Neptune and Amphitrite, while the two deities, the finest and most interesting part of the dish, are hidden. Might the intention perhaps have been to hide the secret of the Tetràchion?

The characters

The personal relations between Elpidio Benedetti and Abbot Melani are clearly established. Benedetti did in fact go to France in order to visit Vaux-le-Vicomte, the château of Nicolas Fouquet (cf. Di Castro Moscati, D., "L'abate Elpidio Benedetti", in *Antologia di Belle Arti*, new series, nos. 33–34, 1988, pp. 78–95), as affirmed by Atto in the book. In his will, Benedetti did leave the Abbot "four large oval-shaped pictures of marine scenes, in their frames carved from walnut and gold, and two other roundels, one of Galatea and the other of Europa, in their gilded frames, as well as a small picture of an idealised coronation of the present King of France when he was a boy, designed by Romanelli, like the other two above, together with a *studioletto* [a kind of bureau] in semi-precious stones [. . .], begging him to accept these as small mementos expressing my appreciation of the many favours which he did me during my long stay in Paris". (Archivio di Stato di Roma, Trenta Notai Capitolini, uff. 30, notaio Thomas Octavianus, vol. 305, c.479v).

Benedetti must in fact have had ties with all the Melani family, seeing that Atto's other brothers were beneficiaries of his will. To Filippo, he left "two little perspectives by the late Salvucci, in arabesque-decorated black and gold frames". To Alessandro Melani went objects which suggest convivial relations: besides "four little heads of cherubs, rather well made", there is also a precious set of utensils to keep wine cold, as well as "glasses and cups for chocolate".

Atto and Buvat, too, really were friends and collaborators. In his memoirs, Buvat confirms that Atto tried to convince his superiors to raise his meagre salary. The attempt, as we learn from Buvat's plaintive handwritten annotations, unfortunately came to nothing ("Mémoire-Journal de Jean Buvat", in *Revue des bibliothèques*, October–December 1900, pp. 235–36).

The Bibliothèque Nationale in Paris also has (mss. Fr. n.a. 11220–11222) a collection of *Nouvelles à la main* from 1700 to 1721: notices on domestic and foreign policy collected by Atto (but also by others, seeing that he died in 1714) and largely copied, as the catalogue of the library informs us, by the hand of Jean Buvat.

Finally, Jean Buvat is among the protagonists of Dumas Père's novel *Le Chevalier d'Harmental*.

Sfasciamonti, too, was a flesh-and-blood character. The eighteenth-century Roman diarist Francesco Valesio (*Diario di Roma*, Milan 1977, II (1702–1703), pp. 272–73) notes the presence of the catchpoll a couple of years after the events in the book, while engaged in an action worthy of him: the seizing of a prostitute's clothes. The operation was not successful: Sfasciamonti and another sergeant were put to flight by a guard of Count Lamberg, who enjoyed the right of immunity (and consequently, the right to refuse police entry) in the place where the seizure was to be effected. Atto's little pistol must have hit some nerve in the old guardian of the law, for according to Valesio, Sfasciamonti walked with a limp.

The reform of the pontifical police proposed by a certain Monsignor Retti, as whispered by the two prelates spied on by the narrator, first when chocolate was served and later during the game of blind-man's-buff, was in fact considered at the time of Innocent XI (cf. G. Pisano, "I 'birri' a Roma nel '600 ed un progetto di riforma del loro ordinamento sotto il pontificato d'Innocenzo XI", in *Roma – Rivista di studi e di vita romana*, X (1932), pp. 543–56).

Like so many other wise reforms, it was never implemented.

Il Chiavarino, whose baptismal name was Giuseppe Perti, was also an historical figure (cf. Valesio, I, 434). His brief and eventful life ended at 2 p.m. on the 8th July 1701: found guilty of thefts and homicides, he was hanged at the Ponte Sant'Angelo. In the face of death, he acted piously: in his last moments, he repented and did an act of contrition. Mounting the scaffold, he begged the people around him to say a *Salve Regina* for his soul. He was twenty-two years old.

True (both in the physical and moral sense of the word) were persons like Corelli, Nicola Zabaglia and Lamberg. (The latter's fervent and ingenuous nature emerges clearly from his already-mentioned *Relazione*, as from his manuscript reflections concerning the Roman Curia preserved in Vienna at the Haus-, Hof- und Staatsarchiv, Botschaft Rom-Vatikan I, Nachlass Gallas; cf. also Rill, G., *Die Staatsräson der Kurie im Urteil eines Neustoizisten (1706)*, in Mitteilungen des Österreichischen Staatsarchivs, XIV (1961), pp. 317 et seq.)

Arcangelo Corelli published his *folia* in Opus V, in the very year 1700.

The Flying Dutchman of the Vessel, Giovanni Enrico Albicastro, must have had a special love for Italy, seeing that he chose to be known by an

Italian pseudonym (in reality, he was called Johann Heinrich von Weissenberg). His bizarre status as a violinist, composer and soldier, although closely studied by Professor Rudolf Rasch of the University of Utrecht (whom the authors thank for the information which he supplied them), remains largely wrapped in mystery. He lived between about 1660 and 1730. Of Bavarian origin (which may explain his excellent knowledge of Sebastian Brant), it is known only that he arrived in Leiden as an adolescent and fought in the War of the Spanish Succession, as he himself announces at the end of the book. He left many compositions (trio sonatas for strings, violin sonatas, concertos and cantatas) which have only in the past few decades received the attention they deserve.

The Ship of Fools by Sebastian Brant is perhaps the German book that has enjoyed the greatest success over the centuries. Published in Basel in 1494 on the occasion of the Carnival, it is illustrated with woodcuts by Albrecht Dürer.

The staff of Villa Spada (Don Paschatio, Don Tibaldutio, stewards, horsemen, scullions, etc.) may all be found, complete with names and surnames, among the family papers kept in the fondo Spada-Veralli of the Rome State Archives.

Atto tells that Cardinal Spada was always at pains to avoid making enemies. This psychological detail is not untrue. It is borne out by many letters addressed to his relatives and kept in the fondo Spada-Veralli of the Rome State Archives.

Atto's arm, the women of Auxerre and the secrets of the conclave

When Atto says that he hurt his arm eleven years earlier, in Paris in 1689, it is quite true. In the Florence State Archives (Mediceo del Principato, filza 4802) there is, among other things, a letter from Atto to Gondi, secretary to Prince Cosimo III de' Medici, written on 12th September 1689:

Although my quarantine will come to an end in six days' time, I am still troubled by my arm and my shoulder, and without the continual visits I have received, I should have died of melancholy and desperation, because if it were not for this accident, I should have gone to Rome with the Duc de Scionnes. However, God's Will be done, and if no other disasters befall me in this my Climacteric year, I shall have every reason to give thanks to His Divine Majesty because, by all rights I should have died in that ditch.

That the arm in question was the right one may be deduced from the fact that the previous letters are not in Atto's hand: a sign that the accident prevented him from taking up his pen (Abbot Melani was not left-handed) and compelled him to have recourse to a scribe.

The episode on the court's passing through Auxerre, as told by Atto on

Day the Sixth, is also true. It is to be found in a letter from Melani to Gondi, again in the Florence State Archives (Mediceo del Principato, filza 4802), dated 5th July 1683:

> *The Court cannot wait to get back to Versailles, having suffered considerably during this voyage: Monsieur de Louvois suffered greatly from stomach ache, but after three bleedings he was better. It is said that the King has lost much weight and that all the ladies have been spoiled by the sun. They say that, when they were passing through Auxerre, where the women are rather good-looking, all the people came to look at the Royal Persons and at the Ladies who were in the carriage with the Queen and, when the latter put their heads out of their carriage to see the people in the streets and at the windows, the people of Auxerre began to say* 'à qu'elle son laide, et qu'elle son laide' [sic!]*: whereupon the King laughed long and loud and went on talking about it for the rest of that day.*

The treatise which Atto wrote for the Sun King, and which was stolen by the *cerretani*, really does exist. The authors found the manuscript in a Parisian archive and intend soon to have it published. The title is *Mémoires secrets contenant les evénements plus notables des quatre derniers conclaves, avec plusieurs remarques sur la cour de Rome*. It is an enjoyable manual, rich in anecdotes and notes on the court of Rome, on the art of influencing the election of popes by more or less licit means, with a view to obtaining the success of the candidate most favourable to France and the Most Christian King.

The meetings between Albani, Spada and Spinola really did take place at the Villa del Torre, today the Villa Abamalek, the residence of the Russian Ambassador (cf. Valesio's Roman diary, I, 26).

Cerretani, pilgrims, midwives

The records of the interrogations of the two *cerretani* by Sfasciamonti, using less than orthodox means, are both real. The two researchers who had the good fortune to see them had them published. (For Il Roscio's statement, cf. Massoni, A., "Gli accattoni in Londra nel secolo XIX e in Roma nel secolo XVI", in *La Rassegna italiana*, Roma 1882, p. 20 et seq.; for both statements, that of Il Roscio and Geronimo, cf. Löpelmann, M., "Il dilettevole esamine de' Guidoni, Furfanti o Calchi, altramente detti Guitti, nelle carceri di Ponte Sisto di Roma nel 1598. Con la cognitione della lingua furbesca o zerga comune a tutti loro. Ein Beitrag zur Kenntnis der italienischen Gaunersprache im 16. Jahrhundert", in *Romanische Forschungen*, XXXIV (1913), pp. 653–64).

The first statement, according to Massoni, was in the Secret Archives of the Vatican where, however, it is impossible to locate, since the author failed to provide the archive references. According to Löpelmann, a copy of both is to be found in the Royal Library at Berlin under the reference *ital. fol. 17. fo. 646r-659v.* (This was no doubt the case until the city was flattened by Allied bombardment in 1945).

Thieves' cant – known in Italian as *furbesco* or *lingua zerga* and in English as gibberish or Saint Giles' Greek – not only existed, but has a long tradition in all European languages. Even the elementary Roman "tre-ese" obtained by alternating "tre" with other syllables (translated using the intercalated syllable "tee" in English, as in the word "teeyooteelie" which the narrator hears before falling into the manure) is still commonly spoken at the great market of Porta Portese in Rome by vendors who want to communicate with one another without being understood by their customers. The anonymous glossary consulted by Buvat is *Modo nuovo d'intendere la lingua zerga*, Ferrara 1545.

The final speech of the Maggiorengo General of the *cerretani* was written down and is today to be found in the Biblioteca Ambrosiana in Milan (manuscript A 13 inf. attributed to Jacopo Bonfadio).

Right down to this day, the origins of the *cerretani* and their links with the ecclesiastical authorities have remained enveloped in a curious fog of mystery. As Don Tibaldutio reveals to the narrator, at the end of the fourteenth century, the *cerretani* had a regular permit to beg for alms in the city of Cerreto, on behalf of the hospitals of the Order of the Blessed Anthony. This permit from the Church authorities tends to confirm their active tolerance *ab origine* for the *cerretano* movement.

If the information were true, it should be possible to find a trace of it in the charter of the city of Cerreto, which was drawn up in 1380. Unfortunately, this has been lost. There does exist a sixteenth-century copy of it, but, as Don Tibaldutio mentioned, the part concerning begging for alms was torn out by hands unknown: one can still go to the communal archives of Cerreto to see this for oneself.

All the traditions, ceremonies, customs and vices of the *cerretani* and other groups of mendicants, as cited in the book, are authentic down to the smallest details (cf. *inter alia* the essay by P. Camporesi which can never be praised enough, *Il libro dei vagabondi*, Turin 1973). For the Company of Saint Elizabeth cf. Ribton-Turner, C.J., *A History of Vagrants and Vagrancy, and Beggars and Begging*, [repr.] Montclair, New Jersey 1972.

The tricks with camphor used by Ugonio and the *corpisantari* to scare whoever ventured into their lair, like the theory of the corpuscles which Atto uses to explain the apparitions at the Vessel, are to be found in De Vallemont, M.L.L., *La phisique occulte*, Paris 1693, mentioned by Melani. The authors confess that they did not, however, have the courage personally to verify whether the experiments with camphor really do work.

All the accounts of the Jubilee are entirely true, including the cases of pilgrims abducted and forced to labour in the country. The same goes for Don Tibaldutio's disquisitions on the validity of the Jubilee indulgence (cf. for example Zaccaria, F.A., *Dell'Anno Santo. Trattato storico, cerimoniale e polemico*, Rome 1824).

In her discourses on obstetrics and paediatrics, Cloridia demonstrates a profound knowledge of the famous treatise *La commare* by Scipione Mercuri (Venice 1676), in which is to be found, *inter alia*, the legend of King Gerion of Spain, with his three heads. The cases of monsters like the Tetràchion, prodigies and deformities are all authentic and are to be found in Aldrovandi, U., *Monstrorum historia cum paralipomenis historiae omnium animalium*, Bologna 1642 and Paré, A., *Deux livres de chirurgie* (book II, *Des monstres tant terrestres que marins avec leur portraits*), Paris 1573.

The mystery of the Vessel

By now, the reader will not even need to ask whether the Vessel really existed. The ruins of Villa Benedetti (as its founder called it) erected by Elpidio Benedetti from 1663 onwards, are still visible on the Janiculum Hill, not far from Porta San Pancrazio. The entire description of the villa and its gardens during the visits of Atto and his friend, including the walls covered with maxims and the distorting mirrors in the penthouse where Atto and his friend see (or imagine they see) the Tetràchion, faithfully follows historical testimony, starting with the book of descriptions of the Vessel and the detailed list of the sayings which Benedetti had published anonymously under cover of a pseudonym (*Villa Benedetta descritta da Matteo Mayer*, published in Rome by Mascardi, 1677; second edition with a few small additions by P. Erico, Augusta 1694). All other details concerning the Vessel and Benedetti can be examined in the extremely well-documented study by Carla Benocci, *Villa Il Vascello*, Rome 2003.

Benedetti really did leave the villa, as Atto tells, to Philippe Jules Mancini, Duc de Nevers, Maria's brother and nephew to Mazarin. However, the latter never lived there; indeed he never even saw it as he was never to return to Rome. It is not known whether there were tenants in the villa or whether it was uninhabited in 1700. The relevant parish records (*Stati delle anime*) for those years, those of Sant'Angelo alle Fornaci, have disappeared.

In the history of the building (cf. A. Chiarle's interview with Carla Benocci, "Villa del Vascello", in *Hiram* 3/2002), the existence was noted of "anomalies" and "disconcerting details", including the ship's form dear to Christian symbolism, which, in Benedetti's creation has its prow pointing towards the Vatican. Moreover, the superabundance of symbolic references to the French court "does not ring true, almost as though it were a cover for an innovative and profoundly ethical world-view". The distorting mirrors in the penthouse "are a disquieting element, designed to elicit wonder, but also to suggest that tangible reality is really something deceptive, concealing a very different reality".

The sayings and maxims so avidly read by Atto and his younger friend come from texts of various origins. Among these, one is particularly important: *Il Principe Buono, ovvero le obbligazioni del Principato* (Rome 1661), the Italian version of a work by Armand de Bourbon, Prince de Conti, translated and published in Rome by Benedetti himself. This stresses the religious basis of all the Prince's actions and the need for him to observe all the Christian theological and cardinal virtues: an innovative vision, even radically so, but never straying from the guiding principles of Christian morality.

The Vessel was, then, a complex of extraordinary originality, a bulwark expressing profound moral precepts. This was, moreover, the impression which the villa made on many visitors to Rome throughout the eighteenth century, and it was mentioned in the tourist guides of the time as a pure jewel, on a par with the most sumptuous patrician dwellings.

But all things come to an end. In June 1849, during the troubles of the Roman Republic, Giuseppe Garibaldi and his troops were quartered at the Vessel, opposite the Casino Corsini ai Quattro Venti, the base of the French militia which had come to besiege Rome and restore it to the Pope. In the Villa Benedetti, all the great names of the Italian Risorgimento were to be found: Bixio, Mazzini, Saffi and Armellini, to mention only a few, as well as Garibaldi himself. Many died, not without the religious comforts of Friar Ugo Bassi. These included the 23-year-old Goffredo Mameli, author of the national anthem of the future united Italy, who died in the arms of the famous and most patriotic Princess of Belgioioso. The cannonades went on for twenty-seven days and the whole area of the Janiculum Hill was devastated, including the Villa del Torre and Villa Spada. The worst damage was, of course, suffered by the two villas which had the ill-fortune to have been chosen as headquarters: the Vessel was almost completely destroyed.

The ruins looked quite remarkable in the immediate aftermath of the bombardments. The ground floor was still standing, including the semicircular projection from the building and the imposing east wing, which survived up to the second floor. The heights on which Benedetti's villa stood out so majestically now displayed sharp, towering ruins, visible for miles around. From every corner of the hill shone the coloured remains of frescos and wall decorations. The ruins became one of the favourite subjects of the landscape painters of the time.

Once the French had driven off the Italian Risorgimentali and returned Rome to the Pope, they made an estimate of the damage: they acknowledged that the soldiers' raiding and plundering had destroyed what survived the cannonades. The total cost of reconstruction was reckoned at twenty thousand scudi, of which the French themselves properly agreed to shoulder two-thirds as being their due. Then, for mysterious reasons, no one did anything. Although various owners succeeded one another, the policy remained the same and the villa was kept as a simple vineyard.

Once Rome had been reintegrated into Italy in 1870, the Vessel was celebrated as the "place of heroes". In 1876, King Victor Emmanuel II conferred on General Giacomo Medici – his first aide-de-camp during the clashes of 1849 – the title of Marchese del Vascello (Marquis of the Vessel). The year after, the general bought the property but did not rebuild a thing; on the contrary, it seems he had what remained of the first and second floors demolished.

In 1897, King Humbert and Queen Margherita came to visit. The Vessel was celebrated as one of the shrines of the Risorgimento, but nothing was done to restore it.

This is even stranger, bearing in mind that, as Benocci points out in her book, the cultural debate on reconstruction had for several decades been an international one and many had contributed to it: from the English critic, essayist and art historian John Ruskin to the architects Eugène Viollet-Le-Duc and Camillo Boito.

That was not all. Just opposite the Vessel, the former French headquarters – the Casino Corsini ai Quattro Venti – were thoroughly restored in 1857–1859. A splendid villa, but far inferior to Benedetti's creations, both in terms of intrinsic value and originality.

In 1897 Medici extended the park of the Vessel by acquiring an adjoining property and even had new service buildings constructed. The money was clearly available, but it was not spent on the seventeenth-century building, which was abandoned and even demolished piecemeal. Was this not the "place of heroes" which had had the honour of housing Garibaldi and Mazzini in person? The soldier and patriot Medici (who had gone so far as to place the ruins of the Vessel on his own coat of arms) really did not seem to give much thought to all that.

Today, of all the great edifice only part of the ground floor walls has survived, from which an apartment for rent has been built. The owners are the Marchesi Pallavicini Medici del Vascello, the descendants of General Medici.

There must be other explanations for the deliberate and prolonged neglect of the Vessel (despite the fact that it had frescoes of immense value like the *Aurora* of Pietro da Cortona). "It seems to be a *damnatio memoriae*," says Signora Benocci. A condemnation to oblivion: now, why should that be? Perhaps because the disquieting fame of the Vessel was as a "place of heterodoxy in the seventeenth century and of Garibaldi's revolutionaries in the nineteenth", and, as the scholar puts it, "even two centuries later, it still frightened people".

Is the Vessel an esoteric place? One wonders whether the theatre of Atto and his friend's adventures might not really be the ideal place for spectres of the past and for images of what might have been and never was. . .

The people who live there might know something about that, but the ground-floor apartment has not been let for some time. Its last occupant, a well-known executive, is dead. It seems to be the Vessel's destiny to remain uninhabited.

The garden has been divided in two. One part still adjoins the ruins. The other, including the original entrance to the villa, belongs to the nineteenth-century house built by General Medici after the destruction of the Vessel. Today it it the seat (is this a coincidence?) of a well-known organisation with a rather complicated name and which is certainly not ignorant of matters esoteric: the Masonic Lodge of the Grand Orient of Italy – Palazzo Giustiniani – at no. 8 Via san Pancrazio, whom the writers thank for having kindly guided them around the villa and shown them the same view over the Vatican as could once be enjoyed from the Vessel.

Villa Spada

Villa Spada still exists. It too was wrecked during the fighting in 1849, but was subsequently restored. Today, it is the Chancellery of the Irish Embassy to the Holy See (Via G. Medici no. 1). With exquisite kindness, the Ambassador's wife, Mrs Fiamma Davenport, personally guided the writers around the villa and its park for a whole afternoon. The latter is, unfortunately, far smaller today, owing to the unregulated carving up of land which, in the thoughtless sixties, seventies and eighties (and still today, in some countries) has razed to the ground throughout Europe much of what had miraculously survived the bombardments of the Second World War.

Nor has anything been invented in the description of Palazzo Spada in Piazza Capodiferro and its interior (in particular, Borromini's famous perspective gallery and the Room of the Catoptric Meridian). Cardinal Fabrizio Spada really did have restoration work done during the wedding. Today the palace is the headquarters of the Council of State and part of it may be visited.

Virgilio Spada's collection of curios is still kept at the Biblioteca Vallicelliana in Rome, hard by the Oratory of the Philippine Fathers. Unfortunately, it was sacked by Napoleonic troops in the nineteenth century: of the original collection, only a very small part, of little value, has remained. What was there originally, we do not know. The inventories disappeared when it was looted.

The nuptials of Clemente Spada and Maria Pulcheria Rocci were in fact celebrated on 9th July 1700. The description of the ephemeral decor and the floral embellishments at Villa Spada, the menus of the banquets, the scenes featuring the wedding, Don Tibaldutio's sermon, everything down to Tranquillo Romaùli (grandfather and namesake of the Master Florist of Villa Spada): every detail may be found in many treatises and diaries of the time. One example is: Posterla, F., *Memorie istoriche del presente anno di Giubileo MDCC*, Rome 1700–1701.

The diaries and documents of the period confirm the gossip, hearsay and polemics which animated the dinners and picnics at Villa Spada. The cardinals, nobles and ambassadors really were there; their friendships and enmities were as described, as were their physical appearances, their idiosyncrasies, even their little tics. Atto, for example, is not indulging in empty name-dropping when he says he is a friend of Cardinal Delfino, of Cardinal Buonvisi and of the Venetian Ambassador Erizzo.

Delfino was Atto's diligent correspondent and a precious source of information for him: in a private Roman collection, there is a cache of letters sent for long years by Cardinal Delfino to Abbot Melani. In Paris, there are traces of the relations between Atto and Delfino in the Archives of the Ministry of Foreign Affairs, Correspondance politique, Rome, suppl.10 – Lettres de l'abbé Melani, c.70 sgg. (letter sent by Delfino from Rome on 3rd April 1700, in which he tells of his manoeuvres in relation to Cardinal Ottoboni in favour of France, with a view to the conclave).

Similarly, Atto wrote weekly for forty years to Gerolamo Buonvisi and his nephew Francesco, both cardinals; while the favours which Atto, at Erizzo's request, rendered the Venetian Republic in France, earned him the title of Patrician of Venice, as he himself was to recall.

The games and pastimes organised for the festivities at Villa Spada are to be found in many manuals of the period, as are the fragments of conversation on the use of hounds, on birds' eggs and on falconry. Here is one example, to cover them all: the artifices and hunting entertainments described by the Bolognese Giuseppe Maria Mitelli (*La caccia giocosa*, Bologna 1684).

The farce by Epifanio Gizzi *Amore premio della costanza*, performed before the guests at Villa Spada, was printed in Rome in 1699.

The Sacred Ball

These days, the ascent to the top of Saint Peter's could not, for better or worse, take place as in the book. In the final stretch, a metal staircase has been added which takes one over the huge steps in the last part of the cavity between the two walls of the cupola, which were somewhat uncomfortable for those not adept at rock-climbing. Since the 1950s, moreover, access to the Ball has been sealed off: only the *sampietrini* can get in. This is no great loss for common mortals: in recent times, only high-ranking members of the aristocracy had been allowed to visit the Ball.

One can console oneself by going on foot (forget about the lift, it is well worth the trouble) to the terrace just underneath it: the panorama remains as breathtaking as ever. One can enter the Ball in one's imagination thanks to an article by Rodolfo de Mattei ("Ascesa alla 'palla'", in *Ecclesia*, no. 3, March

1957, pp. 130–35), which lists the illustrious visitors of the past (including Goethe and Chateaubriand), as well as providing certain details of its construction.

Just ask one of the *sampietrini* and you can still have a description of the great bronze sphere and its four slits at the level of a man's eyes, one for each cardinal point, through which the first rays of dawn enter. The *sampietrini* do in fact still go up to the Ball; indeed they go far higher. Harnessed with ropes and hooks, and risking their lives, they first climb the sphere and then the great cross set above it, in order from time to time to replace a small iron rod, the true culmination of the whole basilica: the lightning conductor.

PIECES OF MUSIC PERFORMED IN *SECRETUM*

✠

On a ... to ... Serene ...
... Hampton Court.

Nor ... nor loud ... wade
... mourn, when ye ... shall ... Fateress
The ... Chaucers ... live no ...
... ... muse in ... ... sung
... lonely Bowers, ... shall ...
... chearfull ... Her ... ... appear.

Imperial Eagle on her R[oy]ally shall ...
... hands now fierce Bavarians fell
... ... by ... Pencil ...
... ... him ... conquests brought
... ...
... ...
... ...
... ...